The 2nd Random Tangent Anthology

Also From Chris Hollywood

The Random Tangent Anthology
My Body Is A Battlefield
The Encyclopedia Antiversia
The Nexus Of The Universe

By Chris Hollywood

Different Perspective Studios

This is a work of fiction. Names, characters, places and incidents are the products of the author's deranged imagination, are used fictitiously and are not to be construed as real. Any resemblance to actual events, locales, organizations, or persons, living or dead, is entirely coincidental, or purposely constructed by the author to confuse, mock, or scare readers.

Copyright © 2016 by Chris Hollywood
Edited by Chris Hollywood
Book Design by Chris Hollywood
Artist Photo by Sarah Mills of SMile Photography

All rights reserved. No part of this book may be used or reproduced in any manner whatsoever without written permission, except in the case of brief quotations embodied in critical articles and reviews.

First Edition

ISBN 978-1-365-48961-7

Contents

1	The Watch	11
2	A Special Place In Hell	65
3	The Importance Of Being Constantly Surprised	103
4	Jaywatch	163
5	How To Be Monolithic	237
6	Frank And The King	283
7	Good For Business	351
8	Correctile Dysfunction	429
9	Murderproof	507
10	Things That Separate Us From The Monkeys	589

For you people. You know who you are.

The Watch

Random Tangent

*I*t had been six months since Mongrel Stevens' mother had been beaten to death. It had been five months since her killer had been sentenced to prison. And it had been four months since Mongrel realized, with no small amount of loathing, that he'd have to visit her murderer sooner or later, if only to ease his conscience. The deed had been done by a boy, or rather a young man with the mind of a child, named Biscuits, whom Mongrel was looking after at the time. He couldn't help feel some responsibility for what happened, yet he couldn't just forgive the boy either. So confronting him face to face might help bring some resolution. Maybe then he could move on with his life to bigger tragedies. Also, it had been one week to the day that he'd stubbed his toe really *bad*. He walked around with a limp for four days. There was no blood but it totally felt broken. It wasn't, and eventually got better. But that's not really relevant to this story. Anyway...

The Watch

How do you pick up the pieces of an old life? How can you return to the way things once were? How can things go back to normal after so much weird had happened?

Mongrel Stevens stood at the bus stop pondering this to himself. A decrepit old lady sat next to him in her wheelchair, gawking steadfastly at him, desperately trying to figure out what he was trying to figure out. Mongrel tried not to notice her, but it was obvious that his trying not to notice her was being noticed. He wanted his mind to amble about, but it wasn't getting far. What the hell did she want anyway?

Dunttstown really did not need a bus service, which was probably why it had one. The bus made sixteen stops in each direction, back and forth, up and down the main street, a hundred times a day. Periodically the bus driver would venture further out of town just to shake things up a bit and keep passengers on their toes. Occasionally these out-of-town excursions would take them close to Dunttstown Penitentiary, which was Mongrel's destination that day, and explained why he was waiting for the bus to begin with.

Ordinarily Mongrel avoided the bus like an alcoholic avoids sobriety. He had a license, and could drive, but found that driving was pointless if you happened to live in Dunttstown. He walked everywhere he needed to go, usually proclaiming that he was allergic to the bus. But when need arose for him to prove this he abandoned the guise, since it would have required a trip to the hospital. So now he pretended to be allergic to the hospital; too many bad memories caused him severe head trauma and the odd spell of cardiac arrest.

Mongrel looked at his watch; it read 8:08[*]. The interesting thing about his watch was that it always read 8:08. This was not because it was broken but because it wasn't a real watch; it was a hand-drawn representation of a watch. After numerous times when he'd actually needed a watch, and the even more numerous times when he'd failed to obtain one, Mongrel had decided to simply

---

[*] The reason Mongrel chose the time 8:08 was because, so far as he figured, that particular time could pass for *any* time of the day. Morning, evening, afternoon, night, dusk, dawn, they were all covered. And no matter what was going on, or what he was doing he could always tell the time since it read the same forwards or backwards, or even upside-down.

Random Tangent

draw one on his wrist instead and save himself at least some of the trouble. Although this was by no means an accurate way to keep track of the time, there were several benefits to using an ink watch. For starters, it was much cheaper than a real one, required no maintenance (except for perhaps reapplying the ink every now and then), and was exceedingly difficult to break or lose (unless you happened to get your arm chopped off or broken – although neither of these events actually stopped the watch from functioning).

The current time – whether it was actually 8:08 or not – did not indicate that the bus was late. Or early. These terms implied that the bus was on a schedule, when in fact it wasn't. Since the route the bus took was just one really long road, most of the time it was never out of sight. Thusly it didn't need a schedule; just a pair of binoculars.

"Most people wonder why I take the bus," the old woman said without warning. "I guess they have a right to wonder. I mean, I do have these wheels."

Mongrel groaned. He tended to do that a lot, especially when he was in a foul mood, like today. Here are some other things Mongrel tended to do: get involved with people/situations against his will, put his foot in his mouth, make enemies, avoid fish, get assaulted, and remain alive despite the world's proclivity for murder. The list would go on but there are only so many hours in a day, or words on a page.

And since you're getting caught up on all things Mongrel Stevens, here's some more, probably useless, information: he was of average height, weight, age, race, gender and intelligence, among other things. So all in all, nothing special.

Yet, here he was, being spoken to by this woman as if he was the only other person on the planet. He hadn't said anything, or given any indication that he was even remotely interested in communicating with her. He hadn't provoked her into a conversation against her will. He hadn't even looked at her. In fact, he'd gone out of his way to mind his own business, and had tried to mentally block her out. But no! She wouldn't have any of that, now would she? The old bag just *had* to open her mouth.

"I'm not one of those people who are wondering," he said without looking at her.

The Watch

She ignored him and kept talking. "But I *can* walk, I tell you. I just prefer not to. They don't call me Mrs. Walker for nothing."

Now she'd gone and done it, she'd roused his interest, but just barely; enough to cause him to risk a small amount of chitchat with her, and then curse himself later for doing so. He sighed, stepped back to give a cyclist room to pass by, and turned to face the woman. "Why, then, do they call you Mrs. Walker?"

She smiled toothlessly up at him. "Cause it's my name, sweetie."

Mongrel sighed contemptuously. "Well then can I call you Mrs. Shutup?"

Her answer was drowned out by the sound of an oncoming bus.

The Dunttstown bus was far from being a normal, good old-fashioned bus like you'd find in most cities. In fact it wasn't even close to being in the same vicinity as weird. For starters, it was a painfully bright shade of chrome. The entire surface of the bus was polished to a brilliant shine that would blind anyone curious enough to venture into its path (even the windows were two-way reflective glass). The seating was made up of two rows of steel folding chairs bolted to the floor (which was a vast improvement over the old interior, which could be likened to a series of stalls like you'd find in a barn). The bus also had a periscope.

Nancy Yumpta, the bus driver, was ex-navy, and for most of her years on the Force she was the captain of a submarine. Since leaving the military she found she wasn't comfortable in any moving vehicle without a periscope, and so insisted they install one on her bus, thereby making it more seaworthy. The mayor at the time, the epically lazy Troy Talbot, was too apathetic to argue over the sheer ridiculousness of her demands, and gave in immediately. He then went on vacation, which was a trip to his backyard; anywhere further away would have required too much effort on his part.

One foggy September night nearly a year ago Nancy had ventured out of town and down a lonely dirt road for a lark. The wiper motor had blown, and she'd gone through a nasty bunch of muddy potholes that rendered the windshield useless. Had she not

Random Tangent

had the periscope then she and her three passengers would have been stuck for hours, or at least until someone went outside to clean off the windshield. When she returned to the bus terminal she threw a victory party for herself to rub it in the faces of her colleagues, and most agreed that she was less crazy than they'd first assumed, but not by much.

The bus ground to a squealing halt in front of the two pedestrians, and the door opened. They looked up at the bus driver. The bus driver looked down at them. This went on for some time before she asked, "Well?"

Mongrel didn't need to be asked twice. He climbed aboard and began fishing change out of his pocket. "Uh, how much is it?"

Nancy preferred, if she had the option, not to directly communicate with her passengers. She found that it interfered with her work; bus driving was a serious business. She tapped the sign on the metal box in front of her. The sign read $2.00. Mongrel deposited, without counting, what he assumed to be the correct amount of change, and then turned back to Mrs. Walker, who was still standing, or sitting, on the sidewalk.

Since the inception of the Dunttstown bus service a few years ago, the bus itself had never been properly handicapped-accessible. All six of Dunttstown's handicapped citizens had begun a formal protest, but the complaints fell on deaf ears, or rather no ears, as the mayor had, at the time, not been seen for weeks. Eventually the campaign for a better bus was abandoned.

"Will you help me up?" Mrs. Walker asked.

"That would involve me getting out of this chair," the bus driver said before Mongrel could even conclude that the old woman wasn't talking to him, "which ain't gonna happen. Also, I don't want to touch you."

Mrs. Walker looked visibly upset over this remark, but kept it to herself. She'd lived to be this old by not picking arguments with the wrong people.

"You want up?" Mongrel asked her. She nodded enthusiastically at him. "Well then get up! Getting up is an up, and you told me you could do that. So what's stopping you?"

"Come on, old woman," Nancy said, "I ain't got all day."

The Watch

This time Mrs. Walker wasn't able to hold back her tongue. "I'm not old, I'm big-aged!" But that was all she had to say. Being as old as she was, talking too much left her breathless, and she couldn't stay angry for long. Her emotions tended to fail her almost as often as her bladder. She looked down solemnly at her wheelchair and tried to think of a way out of the situation. Sure she could still walk, but it came at a cost, like crippling pain, exhaustion, and the loosening of her bowels. She was stubborn enough to attempt it every other week, but now was not a good time. The reason she was bravely venturing out of her nursing home was to purchase some adult diapers at the local five-and-dime, as she was currently without.

"Go around!" the bus driver suddenly yelled, waving her arm out the window at a car behind them. She then leaned around Mongrel and looked down at the old woman. "Last chance. Get going or get dying."

Mrs. Walker looked around nervously, still unable to determine the wisest course of action. "Uh..." she finally said.

"Fine, stay here and rot, you old bag," the bus driver said, and closed the door. She then careened the bus back onto the road and down the street.

Mongrel took a seat directly behind the driver so he could watch the road, a habit he couldn't break. He took a good long look at the other passengers. An old man sat across from him reading a week-old newspaper. He appeared to be decaying to the point where parts of him were falling off. A girl who looked much too young to be riding the bus by herself sat a few seats behind him. Lastly there were two women sitting at the back, one of whom reminded him of one of the beasts from the Ofishal Evlis Fan Club Of Dunttsville, a group of women dedicated to the King of Rock and Roll. The Club apparently also required its members to have a large sexual appetite and no concept of grammar. Mongrel didn't recognize the other woman sitting next to her. Not wanting to catch the attention of either of them, he promptly turned around to face the road.

"There's a whole sidewalk for you to enjoy!" the driver shouted out her window as she passed a cyclist. He appeared to be the same man who'd passed Mongrel earlier at the bus stop.

Random Tangent

Mongrel looked out at the bicyclist as they passed him. "He doesn't really seem to be hogging the road.

"I have no patience for bikers," she replied, and he could feel her sneer as she said the words. "People just don't know how to drive around here. Look at this guy in front of me. *Look at him!* If he were going any slower he'd be going backwards! He's doing the *speed limit!*"

Mongrel looked at the car in front of them, and indeed it was doing what appeared to be a legal velocity.

"The speed limit!" she said again, as if it was heresy. "And look now, he's slowing down! She blew the horn a couple of times and leaned her head out the window. "What the fuck are you slowing down for?"

Mongrel looked back at the little girl sitting a few seats behind him. She seemed oblivious to the raucous going on at the front of the bus. He turned back around to watch the drama. "I think he's trying to catch that red light."

Sure enough, they both came to a stop at the next red light. There were only two of them in Dunttstown; one at each end of Bloor St., which ran the entire length of Dunttstown. They figuratively marked the town's boundaries. Only a few buildings and houses lay beyond the corner, and then the open country.

And somewhere beyond lay Duntt Pen.

"Do you think you'll be stopping by the prison?" Mongrel asked.

She grunted and spat on the floor. "If you want."

"We knew it was you!"

Mongrel turned to see not one, but two Ofishal Evlis Fan Club Of Dunttsville t-shirts in front of him. Looking up, he saw the two women. One had a goofy grin and shoulder length auburn hair thrown into the world's most disheveled ponytail. This was Lily, who had a double-digit IQ (and neither was a large number). The other woman had longer, darker and more unruly hair. She had blue eyes, red lips, and what looked like a gold tooth. Up close, she gave Mongrel the distinct impression that he had no idea who she was.

"You recognize us, do you?" the unknown woman asked to his blank stare.

The Watch

"I recognize *her*," Mongrel said, pointing to Lily and recalling the day he'd met all the girls. Well, most of them.

"My Twix™ bars melted together," Lily pouted, holding the chocolate bar out to show him. "Now it's a twik."

"Yeah, how could you forget that?" the other woman said, rolling her eyes. "I guess you don't remember me – I didn't stick around to chitchat anyway – I went after that Elvis impersonator. Never caught him though. You know where he is?"

Mongrel shook his head quickly, and then his whole body shook as the bus lurched. The two girls crashed into his lap.

The bus was now in the other lane – which was thankfully devoid of oncoming traffic – passing the slow car in front of it. As they drew up next to the car, Nancy opened the doors and gave the driver of the car the middle finger, and then threw a brick at him, creating a dent in the driver-side door. She then closed the bus doors and drove off ahead.

"Drive-by brickings are getting worse and worse around here," said the older man who seemed to be falling apart. He shook his head in disgust, then his newspaper in more disgust before going back to reading it.

Mongrel looked down at the women, whose faces were buried in his lap, and whose own face was a twisted wreck of horror. If memory served him correctly – and it usually did when past trauma was involved – the women of the Elvis fan club were not to be trusted with, well, sexual matters, and this could be misconstrued as one.

After prying themselves away from him, Lily continued munching on her twik bar, but the other woman noticed Mongrel's expression and laughed. "Don't worry, we're not like Wendy," she said. "Besides, she called dibs on you anyway."

Mongrel's twisted look of horror gave way to a look of confusion. "What?" Wendy was one of the other founders of the Ofishal Evlis Fan Club Of Dunttsville, and if you went by sheer weight, made up nearly ninety-five percent of the club's members. He'd had a hit-on-and-run incident with the vile woman and barely escaped without being raped. His mind, being the instrument of torture that it was, kept him up some nights wondering how such a thing would have been possible; one would have to launch an expedition to discover the woman's erogenous zones but it would probably never be heard from again, possibly getting lost in her surrounding foliage. He shuddered.

"Oh yeah, she told us all about you, you sly dog. Putting the moves on our Wendy." She nudged Lily, but the only reaction she got from her was more noisy chewing on her twik bar.

"*Me*? Putting the moves on *her*?" Mongrel couldn't believe what he was hearing. "That's not what happened! I – I don't even have any moves!"

"It's a shame too," she continued, ignoring him and walking her fingers up his chest, "cause I'm a far better catch." She winked at him.

Even though this still-nameless woman was indeed far more attractive than the moon-sized behemoth who'd apparently claimed him – if only for her gift of being one-fiftieth her size and not requiring a wide-angle lens to view properly – now was not the time to flirt. He needed something to change the subject.

"Detour?" the bus driver suddenly shouted. "I don't think so!" She threw the bus down a dirt road opposite the detour route, causing everything on the bus that wasn't chained down to be flung around like a tether ball.

Mongrel had been vaguely keeping track of where the bus was going to make sure he didn't miss his stop. They'd ventured passed the outskirts of Dunttstown only a minute ago, and already they seemed to be in trouble. He wasn't sure where this dirt road they were now traveling down went, but he saw something that might be important.

"Uh, that sign back there said NO EXIT," he said to the bus driver.

"It just means no *paved* exit," Nancy replied. "We'll be fine."

The two women lay in a crumpled pile of arms and legs in front of Mongrel, dizzy from their spill to the floor. "I bit my tongue," Lily said. "Does anyone have a band-aid?" She then went off in search of her twik bar, which had also made a journey to the floor, but on a much different trajectory.

The other woman got to her feet and took a seat beside Mongrel, and held on to the nearest pole for dear life in case any

The Watch

further unforeseen bus-driving insanity arose. "Anyway," she extended her hand, "I'm Tracy Gormet, and that's Lillian Lily."

Mongrel shook her hand. "Lily *and* Lily?"

"No, her first name is Lillian and her last name is Lily. Her parents aren't much brighter than her. We just call her Lily, cause one is enough."

"No argument here."

They bounced and swayed all over the twisty, bumpy road, causing Lily to bounce and sway all over the bus like a drunken harlot. She finally found her missing twik bar, and stumbled back to them, proudly displaying her prize. She then continued to devour it, despite the dirt and crud now coating it.

Suddenly they were almost sideways as the bus flung itself down into a ditch and began to cross acres of farmland. Plumes of dust were vomited from the back of the bus as Nancy drove the hell out of it. Wildflowers were destroyed. Stalks of corn were eaten alive by metal and rubber. Various livestock lazily wandered out of the way of the oncoming bus, completely unconcerned[*]. With all the shaking and rattling Mongrel wondered how the whole bus held together. After a few more minutes of this chaos the bus swung sideways again, and then they were back on the open road.

"That was fun!" Lily shouted. "Let's do it again!"

Nancy gave her a wild sneer through the rearview mirror and said, "We'll have to if we want to get around that detour again."

"So," Tracy said, shuffling over until she was practically sitting on Mongrel's lap, "where are you heading?"

"Actually, I'm getting off at the next stop."

"Oh." This seemed to put a damper on her mood. "That's too bad. We could've been getting off together!" She laughed at this. Even Lily laughed at this, which surprised Mongrel. Then he too started laughing. The girls of the Evlis Fan Club were too much, but they had spunk.

But then Mongrel began thinking to himself, maybe it was him. First the behemoth, Wendy, had fallen under his spell – a spell he didn't recall casting and wished hadn't – and now Tracy. One by

---

[*] This kind of thing happened at least a couple times a week, and by now they were indifferent towards it.

one they were all coming on to him. Was he more of a chick-magnet than he realized? Was he, in fact, a stud?

"Duntt Pen," Nancy shouted, slowing the bus down.

Mongrel smiled at Tracy. "Looks like this is my stop."

She smiled back. "I used to come out here with the girls from time to time. Used to have a thing for inmates. Prison uniforms are so...sexy. Orange is my favourite colour, did you know that?"

"I didn't," he said, getting up. He was about to look out the window to see just what the prison looked like when someone slapped his ass, so he instead looked down at the girls. Lily had finished her twik bar and displayed it through her smiling teeth at him, and waved goodbye. Tracy wouldn't make eye contact but it was obvious that she was trying not to smile.

Brimming with confidence, he strutted the few feet to the front of the bus, gyrating his rear end as wildly as he could without losing his balance. Once at the front he turned back to the girls, smiled and winked. Tracy held up a pinky and thumb to her head and mouthed the words 'call me.' Not knowing what else to do, he winked at her again.

The most accurate way to describe what happened next was this: Mongrel approached the open door and as he began to exit the bus he reached up to grab the thin, flimsy door jam, and in a grand display of strength hoisted himself up a few measly, yet important inches in a valiant attempt to nonchalantly swing out the door in what he assumed would be a 'cool' manouever, and in an even grander display of profound failure lost grip of the door jam in mid-swing, fell mostly outside the bus, with his head crashing painfully onto the bottom step. There he remained for a few miserable minutes as the bus driver let the doors close repeatedly on his head before reluctantly getting up out of her seat and using her foot to give that head a nice, good shove off the step and onto the ground.

Nancy then casually sat back in her seat, closed the door, and continued on her normal route which ventured halfway to Duntt River, and then proceeded back to Dunttstown, and repeated as often as the day and quantity of passengers would allow.

There was a time in the not-too-distant past of the surrounding area when the idea of a bus – or any person, for that matter – traveling to Duntt River was an idea that one could be damned to Hell for having, for Duntt River is known by another name: Donut Lake, so called by the heathen swine who live in the nameless town on the island that sits in its middle. From an aerial view Duntt River, with the nameless island directly in its center, looks exactly like a donut, but the name does not, however, do the landmark justice. The beastfolk of the island call it a lake when it is actually a river flowing in a circle (the legends that explain this phenomenon are both curious and imaginative, but otherwise completely ludicrous; no official scientific explanation has ever been offered). It is because of this slight misconception of the inhuman dogs of Donut Lake, and the fact that they refuse to name the town or island within the River, that they are deemed the spawn of the Devil and are enemies of the good folks of Dunttstown. An uneasy truce exists between the people Dunttstown and the islanders, which succinctly boiled down to everyone avoiding the hell out of each other. A bus entering their domain would not be dissimilar to the Four Horsemen of the Apocalypse stopping by for a cup of tea and then raining down fire and lightning and rotten pumpkins and other such things.

    Then came old man Cleopard, who dwelled somewhere between the two towns. Cleopard was a farmer, an inventor, an anarchist, and an idiot. He grew rich selling his Nustard sandwich spread, gained notoriety for occasionally parking his tractor *inside* downtown stores, and was once famously quoted for saying, "If it weren't for the lack of sleep and sanity, I'd be more sane and well rested." After having his license forcibly revoked on account of his many parking violations, Cleopard went to work getting the bus to stop by his farm, since he still needed access to Dunttstown. Unfortunately his farm happened to be situated halfway to Duntt River, the last place in the world anyone not from Donut Lake wished to go. Initially the town simply denied his request, but then he began protesting: physically assaulting the buses, stalking the bus driver, strategically positioning detour signs, goat floggings, creating gigantic pot holes, and the occasional public attempt to make contact with the dead. Eventually the mayor, Troy Talbot, came into his office long enough to sign a new deal for the bus to travel as far East as old man Cleopard's farm, but no further.

Random Tangent

Approximately halfway between Dunttstown and the Cleopard Farm Mongrel lay on the ground in front of Duntt Pen, overcome with pain, nausea, and unconsciousness. Vultures circled around for a little while after, but soon realized that there were other, healthier things to peck at.

Some time later Mongrel awoke with a scream. He then quickly covered his mouth with his hands and some bird shit to stop the scream from escaping and waking up the dead[*]. A look came across his face as he realized that birds had relieved themselves on his hands and that he now had those hands on that same face. He took a minute to vomit and then wipe his hands off on some nearby rocks, before readying himself for his next challenge.

The next challenge was figuring out how long he'd been unconscious. He looked at his watch, which read a reliable 8:08. This was roughly the same time he had gotten off the bus, so he figured he'd only passed out for a brief moment. Day was still light, he hadn't been torn to shreds by vultures, and the bird shit in his hands was still relatively wet, suggesting that indeed time had not aged much since he'd last been conscious. Having that straightened out, he stood to face Duntt Pen.

Duntt Pen stood before Mongrel. He assumed so, at least. The prison was doing a remarkable job of imitating a vast field of grass. Under normal circumstances Mongrel would not have believed his eyes, as they routinely failed him. But these were not normal circumstances, and this was not a normal prison. The vast field Duntt Pen was posing as was surrounded by a large wire fence that stretched endlessly in either direction.

Mongrel looked to his left and to his right, looking along the fence for some sort of door. What he found was a small sign which read: WELCOME TO DUNTT PEN. PLEASE DISTURB THE FENCE.

He thought this over. If everything television had taught him was correct, the fence was undoubtedly electrified. The sign was

---

[*] Not an uncommon occurrence in these cursed lands. The dead occasionally woke up and shuffled about, looking for a bite to eat, or the latest celebrity gossip, or where the hell they'd put the remote, or what have you. They were more of an annoyance than anything.

The Watch

likewise undoubtedly put up by some juvenile guards to persuade him to voluntarily, yet unknowingly, subject himself to a rousing game of shock-the-monkey. And of course there had to be, completely without doubt, a camera trained on him to capture forever the insidious practical joke and, again without the tiniest shred of doubt, end up posted some internet website for the entire world to see. Everyone in Dunttstown would see it. Everywhere he went he would carry the stigma of that prank, and people would laugh and point fingers and through potatoes at him. He would hang his head in shame and never live it down. His life would be ruined. If he were lucky he wouldn't survive the electrocution.

But there was nothing for it. He swallowed hard, held up a hand, and approached the fence the way a tree approached a chainsaw.

He was about to knock on the fence when a muffled, voracious, hacking cough came from behind him. The cough came mid-word, which was presumably, "Hey!" and trailed off into an uneasy wheezing.

Mongrel was too surprised to be surprised over this, if that made any sense, and calmly turned around to confront the cougher.

The medals were not the first things Mongrel noticed, even though there was a staggering amount of them – and I do mean completely and utterly staggering. It was truly an awe-inspiring collection. If the cougher hadn't been wearing a tie, Mongrel wouldn't have even known there was a uniform underneath them. They covered every inch of whatever the man was wearing, and gave the impression that he was wearing nothing *but* the medals. There could have been one for every member of the army on the uniform. But Mongrel didn't notice them right away. He also failed to immediately notice the man himself, let alone his small empire of medals.

For what it was worth, the man was slightly shorter than Mongrel, rounded in the middle, and gave the impression of immense authority. He was dressed in a navy commander's uniform (completely adorned with medals for every conceivable honour), and wore an impressively noble-looking commander's hat that was also completely adorned with medals and was about eighteen sizes too big for his head (probably to accommodate more medals). He had an exceptionally bushy, graying moustache that covered his entire mouth and half his nose. The other half of his nose was covered by large motorcycle cop sunglasses. The stub of a cigar stuck out from somewhere in the middle of the moustache, giving the impression that the moustache itself was smoking the cigar. So from top to bottom we have oversized hat, oversized sunglasses, oversized and smoking moustache, and we'll round things off with a sharp but otherwise uninteresting chin.

But again, we can file all of this into the things-Mongrel-did-not-notice-first category.

The first thing that Mongrel actually took notice of was Duntt Pen itself. It stood in all its grand, bland glory behind the smoking commander, opposite the fence on the other side of the road.

Mongrel skipped several beats and went straight for the most pertinent question, "Okay commander, so what's the fence for?" He pointed a thumb at the fence in question in case there were any other fences that, on top of numerous other things, he'd failed to immediately notice.

The commander coughed again before attempting to speak, getting that part out of the way. "I'm Chief of Police, not commander." The moustache tended to do most of the talking, causing the cigar to bob to and fro with the commotion.

"Sure, okay," Mongrel waved off, "and I'm Mongrel Stevens. But what's with the fence?" He again thumbed behind him, and this time actually turned to visually confirm that it was still there, and was still, in fact, a fence.

The Chief coughed again. "It's a decoy."

"A decoy for what?" Mongrel asked, actually interested.

"Look, this a prison," the Chief's moustache said. "Prison's tend get broken into, so having a decoy cuts down on that. It's not rocket science."

"Don't you mean broken out of?"

"Huh?" the Chief put a hand to his ear.

"Broken out of," Mongrel repeated. "People tend to break out of prison, don't they?"

The Watch

"No, no...well yes, that's true. But for the times that someone tries to bust in here break a friend out that decoy's a lifesaver. Or life-ender, I s'pose. It's electrified, see."

Mongrel nodded but still couldn't wrap his head around the decoy prison concept, and had to look at the fence once again before he asked, "Are you saying that people actually look at that fence and really believe there's a prison behind it? Even though there's a completely real and obvious prison on the other side of the road?"

The Chief walked across the street and put a hand on Mongrel's shoulder. "You don't seem to be getting this, but doesn't surprise me cause you don't seem too bright. Not a lot of crackers up there, huh? Well picture this," he spun Mongrel around to face the fence, "you're coming here to break out a buddy, you see the fence, read the sign – you did read the sign right?"

Mongrel looked at the Chief and nodded.

"Great! So you read the sign and what you do?" Mongrel didn't answer right away so the Chief shook him a little. "C'mon, what do you do?"

"...Touch the fence?" Mongrel offered.

"Bingo! You touch the fence. Then BAM! You're dead. And lemme ask you question: were you about to touch the fence 'fore I stopped you?"

Mongrel thought for a moment, "Well..."

"Aha!" the Chief shouted in Mongrel's ear. "You see? Almost got you! So it works."

"I wasn't gonna touch it," Mongrel was quick to defend. "I was...skeptical."

"But least you were thinking about touching it. That's what counts. That's all I want, just touch the fence."

"Then why'd you stop me?"

"Figured you wasn't trying bust someone out of here. No one who arrives by bus and lays on the ground for three hours is smart enough plan anything that conniving."

"Three hours?" Mongrel looked at his watch; it still read 8:08.

Random Tangent

"Didn't fit the type, so I figured come out and save your ass. You can return the favour some time. Actually when I heard you scream thought I was too late. What'd you scream for anyway?"

Mongrel didn't know how to answer that question and keep his dignity at the same time. "Uh...I...uh..."

This prompted the Chief to ask, "Was you screaming, wasn't it?"

"Uh, no. Not me at all."

The Chief scratched his left eyebrow and said, "Must be them damn hill banshees then. So what brings you here? Get kicked off the bus?"

"Something like that," Mongrel grumbled under his breath. "What are hill banshees?"

The Chief ignored the question, put his arm around Mongrel's shoulder and began walking him towards the gates of the real Duntt Pen. "Well let's get you inside and cleaned up; smell like bird shit."

"It was a really dirty bus."

"Mmm," the Chief nodded as they passed the gates and entered the prison grounds. The gates silently closed behind them. Mongrel observed two guard towers on either side, one of which, he assumed, housed the gate controls. However, both lookout points at the top of the towers remained curiously empty, and he didn't see any security cameras, which made him wonder how whoever operated the controls knew they were inside.

The grounds themselves were impeccably neat, which surprised Mongrel. Despite the fact that most of it was dirt, there wasn't a speck of dirt around. Small tufts of grass sprung up here and there, mostly just to give the otherwise barren landscape some character and a dash of colour. The fields across the street made far better romping grounds, but this was by far the neatest piece of earth Mongrel had ever seen. He might even consider eating off of it, except for the fact that it *was* dirt.

It is no mere coincidence that Mongrel thought this, because the grounds were kept so meticulously clean so that prisoners could, in fact, eat off of it. Punishments at Duntt Pen leaned more toward the 'unusual' and less toward the 'cruel' types. Sometimes, actually, they were downright absurd, as in the case of *dirt for desert*. *Dirt*

The Watch

for desert was reserved for prisoners who complained constantly about the quality, quantity, and/or the recognisability of the food. Prisoners who also began food fights, stole food, tampered with food, or were refluxophiles[*] were also given *dirt for desert*. Basically, the punishment involved having all utensil privileges (which included glasses and plates), revoked for a week or more. All meals during that time would be thrown onto, consumed from, and occasionally stomped into, the ground. This was an especially loathsome punishment when some kind of soup was being served.

The Chief stopped suddenly, removed his arm from around Mongrel, and quietly surveyed the area. After a long minute he spoke. "Used to get protesters out here, you know?"

Mongrel didn't know this, but figured not saying anything was just the same as saying so.

"They mostly women who in fell love with the prisoners. Lonely bunch they are. Had a gang once. All of 'em wore same shirts; had Elvis on 'em or something."

Mongrel listened on, still saying nothing. But he couldn't help notice that the Chief spoke peculiarly. It wasn't an accent, but he couldn't put his finger on it. It was almost as if whatever sentences he was putting together in his brain were missing some of the words.

"Mostly protested the death penalty," the Chief continued. "All 'em had big signs: 'Down With Death,' 'Kill With Kindness,' 'We Love Elvis.' Them sorts."

"We have the death penalty here?" Mongrel asked, finally beginning to hold up his end of the conversation.

"Well not exactly. I mean, we might cut 'em up some. A little pain never hurt nobody, I always say. Kill 'em with kindness, huh?" The Chief shook his head. "Why kill 'em with kindness when you can kill 'em with an axe? It's less expensive, and quicker. I mean, they can't survive their head and body being more than three feet apart, ain't our problem."

"Nah," Mongrel agreed. "If they can't be bothered to keep their own blood in their bodies, it's not your fault."

---

[*] Refluxophiles are people who willingly engage in and actually enjoy vomiting. No bullshit. Look it up.

Random Tangent

The Chief looked at Mongrel and smiled. Then he slapped Mongrel violently on the back. "That's right! You're right. I like you Stevens. Might not have lot of crackers in your box, but you're all right." He silently extended his hand to Mongrel.

Mongrel looked at the hand, then took it, but was too busy trying to figure out what the cracker reference meant to do anything else with it. After a brief minute he realized that the Chief didn't want to just hold hands and properly shook it. "Mongrel Stevens," he said, almost apologetically.

The Chief remained silent.

"And you are…officer…commander…?"

"You can just call me Chief," said the Chief. He broke the handshake and began walking towards the prison once more. Mongrel followed.

Duntt Pen was similar to Dunttstown in the fact that it was oddly shaped and proportioned. An aerial view of the complex would present a very distinctive image: the game of TIC-TAC-TOE. One might get the impression while wandering its halls that the only colour of paint that existed at the time of its construction was gray. Indeed every square inch of floor, wall, and ceiling real estate was the same sickening shade, but this was to confuse inmates. If anyone ever attempted to escape they could easily get disorientated and lost amongst the labyrinth of identical corridors.

"So what brings you to Duntt Pen?" the Chief asked. You a tourist?"

"Uh, no," Mongrel said. "I'm here to visit a…well, he's not really a friend…"

"He a tourist?"

Mongrel looked at him. "No, he's not a tourist. He was just in my care for a little while."

They'd reached the front doors, and the Chief opened the door for Mongrel. "What's he in for?"

Mongrel stepped inside. "Well, he's in, thank you, he's in here because he killed my mother, bu-"

"Sorry to hear that."

"Thank you, but the official record mentioned something about bad grammar…?"

The Watch

The Chief stroked his chin and let his cigar stump bobble up and down for a minute. "Oh yeah! The bean guy! What's his name? Cookies? Crackers?"

"Biscuits."

"Yeah that's it! Biscuits. Howdy Gettz!"

A tall officer strolled briskly towards them, tipped his hat and continued out the door.

"So what's this whole grammar thing anyway?" Mongrel asked.

"Well far as I know when he was up on the stand he apparently babbled lots of nonsense, horrible spelling, terrible grammar. Hey Pekker!"

"COP." Pekker waved politely before disappearing down a hallway.

"Cop?" Mongrel asked, and then sarcastically answered his own question, "Pretty original nickname there."

"It's short for Chief Of Police," the Chief said.

"Ah," Mongrel wheezed out, mentally retracting his statement.

"We need to work on your cracker index, son."

Mongrel smiled tersely, still not getting the whole cracker thing.

"So yeah," the Chief continued, "with his linguistics education so poor, really had no choice in throwing him in here. You came to see him, that right?"

"He's in prison because of his *spelling*?" Mongrel was shocked

"More his grammar, but that too."

"But he *killed* my mother! Doesn't that count for anything?" Mongrel tried to keep his fuming to a minimum.

"They really didn't get far enough into trial to decide who killed who, or why, far as I recall. No. No, he's in here cause of that. The grammar thing. And you wanna see him, right?"

"Bad grammar is just cause to be locked up now?" Mongrel inquired as politely as he could.

"Not necessarily. But in this case, yes. Yes it was. I understand where you're coming from, but you really had to be there understand how bad this boy's gram-"

Random Tangent

"I *was* there!"

"You were? You heard everything came out of his mouth and you're arguing with the sentence? You really don't have a lot of cheese on your cracker, do you?"

"I'm arguing the fact that he's *not* in here because he killed my mother. What the hell is wrong with the judicial system? And my cheese and crackers are just fine, thank you."

The Chief shuffled around for a moment, noticeably upset. He removed his sunglasses and looked Mongrel in the eye. "There ain't nothing wrong with the system. The young man was tried and sentenced based on fact he wasn't grammatically competent enough to stand trial. In here he's undergoing intense training on everything from the alphabet to Wheel Of Fortune. When we're convinced he can solve a crossword puzzle on his own, he'll be good to go."

Mongrel waited for a minute to see if the Chief would continue. He didn't. "Good to go…where? Home? Free? Back to trial? Bermuda? What?"

"Well, we'll cross that bridge when get to it. Now you're here to visit him?"

"Cross that bridge…" Mongrel shook his head. He had to stop the rage building inside him before he blacked out and did some murdering of his own. Forcing his thoughts to drift to soothing things like butterflies, waterfalls, and Twinkies, he tried to calm himself down.

A familiar voice entered Mongrel's ear at that moment. "Are ya daft? I don't even owns a bleedin' car! Who's the boss 'round 'ere? Lemme speak to him."

Mongrel looked into the next room and saw Captain Pete arguing with an officer behind a desk. "Captain Pete?" he called.

Both men looked at Mongrel, then the officer turned around and began scanning the Most Wanted pictures on the wall beside him. Captain Pete's demeanor turned even more sour than it already was, as seeing Mongrel was never a good omen for him. He cursed for a solid minute before turning back to the officer and saying, "Why don't ya lock up that there fella?" He pointed sharply at Mongrel. "Does more harm'n'good he does. A real menace I tells ya."

The Watch

The officer didn't listen, but instead shouted some orders to some other cops, and soon a dozen men were all over Captain Pete, kicking, punching, and using their billy clubs for all they were worth. They beat on him until he was ripe with unconsciousness, and then drug him away somewhere.

"Hmm..." the Chief said to himself, "Have to see what that was about later." He then slapped Mongrel on the back. "So, wanna see the boy?"

Mongrel nodded. "Yes, I came here to see him. Will that guy be okay?"

The Chief's cigar wandered around in his moustache for a minute before he asked, "What time you got?" He nodded his head towards Mongrel's wrist.

Mongrel looked at his wrist and answered, "Eight-o-eight."

More cigar bobbling. "That AM or PM?"

"Uh, either one."

This last thought required a clearing of the throat. "All right, I suppose could fix something up. Usually visiting hours don't start till eleven, but since you're here can't make you just sit around all day. Switchblade!"

Mongrel's eyes went wide. Now *there* was a name he recognized. It was a name that belonged to a dear friend. A friend that nothing tragic had yet happened to. A friend he hadn't seen in a long time. A friend who was nearly as close to sane as he was.

He zipped around as quickly as he could, with a huge idiot grin on his face, but found he was not facing the officer he was expecting. It was a woman, and he gawked at her.

What should have been a loafing man in sunglasses and a long brown coat turned out to be a mid-thirties woman in a police uniform. Her eyes were blue, Mongrel noted, recalling that he didn't know what colour officer Switchblade's eyes were because of the sunglasses. She had dirty blonde hair down to her shoulders, which also failed to remind Mongrel of his old friend, who had cop-short black, but graying hair, usually kept under a fedora. She could not have been further from the image Mongrel's mind conjured.

"Yes, Chief?" she asked.

"Switchblade," the Chief continued, "take Stevens here to visit Biscuits."

Random Tangent

The woman looked at the Chief questioningly, then at Mongrel even more questioningly, and finally glanced back to the Chief. "You sure? You do realize what time it is, don't you?"

"I'm well aware the time, Switchblade. This man's got some important business. See to it, will you?"

This is where Mongrel might have interjected that his business wasn't really all that important, only he was still focused on the new officer Switchblade, and wasn't listening.

"And speaking of business, I got some my own." The Chief then turned and walked away, eventually wandering down some corridor out of sight.

The new officer Switchblade sighed and shrugged. "Whatever." She turned her attention to Mongrel, shrugged again and said, "Follow me."

She turned and walked down a different corridor. Mongrel ambled slowly behind her, still trying to wrap his head around the woman. His wife? Was it his sister? Were they even related? What if they were the same person?

Mongrel's thought process ground to a halt.

Sex-change? Could it be? Could officer Switchblade have undergone such an operation? But why? As gross as it sounded, it was certainly possible. It had been a nearly a month since they'd seen each other; that kind of surgery could be done in that time frame – although not in Dunttstown because the hospital staff had been on strike for months. Mongrel didn't want to think about it.

They entered a small room with a metal table situated in its center, and two matching chairs placed on either side. A large metal door stood on the other side of the room. This was clearly the place where visitations occurred. But Mongrel wasn't ready to see Biscuits just yet; he had to get the vision of officer Switchblade as a woman out of his mind. Otherwise it would haunt him every other Sunday, which would make his life miserable because he really enjoyed Sundays.

"Excuse me," he said, "may I ask you a question?"

She stopped and turned around to face him, and shrugged.

"Uh, okay then," Mongrel took a moment to prepare himself for the worst. "Are you related to the other officer Switchblade?"

The Watch

She didn't answer immediately, which Mongrel took as a bad sign. Finally, she shrugged and asked, "The other one? Do you mean my husband? Harold?"

"*Harold?*"

"My husband's name is Harold." This didn't help Mongrel, so she gave some mental prodding. "Taller guy, always sarcastic? Loves the Indiana Jones movies?" Mongrel's blank stare remained. "Has an unnatural fear of mashed potatoes? Can't skip? Not that he doesn't know how – he actually can't."

Mongrel figured he might try to communicating in a way familiar to the woman, so he shrugged. But he did so in a way that suggested that he had no idea what she was talking about.

"Never takes off his sunglasses? Rides a scooter called Molly?"

"That's him!" Mongrel cried. "That's my officer Switchblade!"

"No," she corrected him, "that's *my* officer Switchblade."

"Yeah, well, okay...wait..." Mongrel paused; something important had just occurred to him. Something his mind wouldn't just let slide by and go uncontested. It wasn't that he was so relieved by the fact that the officer Switchblade he knew and loved was still a man and that he could keep on loving him in the same way – cause the other way wasn't very appealing to him, even if that did sound gay. It also wasn't that his love for officer Switchblade should have been unconditional, whether he was male or female. It also had nothing to do with the fact that Mongrel was standing in front of another member of the Switchblade family, and that, not only was there so much he didn't know about his friend, but there was so much he didn't know about the world in general. The thought that needed to be sorted out before anything else was: Molly. "He calls his moped Molly?"

"Scooter, moped, same thing." She shrugged. When she saw that this failed to help Mongrel get over the whole Molly thing, she shrugged yet again and offered, "Yeah, Molly. I don't know why he calls her Molly, but he does." She shrugged once more and this seemed to satisfy him.

Mrs. Switchblade was a habitual shrugger. She shrugged at everything; hello, goodbye, stop or I'll shoot. She shrugged if

Random Tangent

someone asked her to pass the salt; she shrugged when Harold asked her to marry him; she shrugged at her father's funeral. She shrugged while Nero fiddled, she shrugged at Waterloo. She shrugged for Jack the Ripper, and now, Mongrel Stevens, this shrug is for you.

"I suppose it doesn't really matter." Mongrel sighed and looked up and the unbelievably uninteresting ceiling. Blotches of what he hoped were pizza sauce were splattered here and there. "I've got to learn to just let things slide. I mean, he saved my life once, so it shouldn't matter what he does. He ever tell you that?"

She shrugged. "He saves lots of people's lives."

Mongrel thought hard, trying to think of something that she might have heard about him, hoping that officer Switchblade had mentioned him to her. Little did he know, he wasn't important enough to even be murdered – not by any random act of kindness – so it was a futile pursuit. "He once tracked me all the way to Cuba?"

She squinted at him. "That was *you*? Took my man away from me for a whole week? Left me all alone during the worst case of turrets I ever had?" Apparently it was not a futile pursuit.

"Tourist?"

"*Turrets*," she corrected. "I have a rare form of Turrets Syndrome. It comes and goes. I'm on medication, and it helps, but I still get outbursts. That's why I work at a prison; the random horrific language helps me fit right in."

"Oh." This time Mongrel shrugged; it was catching. "Then yeah, that was me."

She looked him up and down, but more quickly down than up; vertigo was not a feeling she handled well. Then she shrugged for the umpteenth time that day. "It's all right, I ain't mad at you. He enjoyed Cuba anyway; they gave him nice badge, so he was real happy. He mentioned you, but I don't remember the name."

Mongrel stuck out his hand. "Mongrel Stevens."

She shrugged and shook it. "Abegale Switchblade."

"So, his name is Harold?" Mongrel asked. "I didn't know that."

The Watch

"Well, *I* still call him Harold. A few years back he legally changed his name to Officer. Course, that was my suggestion. He's a strange man, but I love him."

"You know, come to think of it, he did mention that he was married. He also said that you were cheating on him a guy called Almighty Frank. Is that true?"

Abegale thought for a moment, which required some shrugged, naturally. "Frank Estabara?"

"I only know him as Almighty Frank. Or Mr. Sir."

"Yes, Mr. Sir, that's him."

Mongrel's jaw hit the floor. He was stunned. "What? Why would you do that? Officer Switchblade seems like a nice enough guy to me."

She got close to him and spoke quietly. "Well just between you and me," she looked around carefully, ensuring that it was in fact just the two of them, "Frank may be a midget, but not below the waist, if you know what I mean." She nudged him. "He's my mighty Frankenstein."

Mongrel went pale. "I really did not need to know that!"

More shrugging. "Shouldn't have asked then."

"I didn't ask for *that*! You didn't have to tell either, you know. Frankly," Mongrel paused to reflect on his vocabulary choice, "it's none of my business, and I'd have been happier if you'd told me so."

"Fine," she shrugged. "It's none of your business. Any happier?"

"Not really," he grumbled.

"Besides, he doesn't mind. He's more married to his work than me. We got into a fight over it one time, and that's when I told him to change his name to Officer. I didn't think he'd really do it, but…" she trailed off into a series of shrugs.

Mongrel knew deep down inside that this had gone way past none-of-his-business and was now venturing into the kind of territory that resulted in restraining orders. "Well I'm sure that's all good and well and fine, so long as he's all right with it. Guess you'd better bring out the boy and let me have a look at him."

Abegale looked at Mongrel and then at the table in the middle of the room. Ordinarily this *was* the room where visitations took place, but that was during ordinary visiting hours. These were special circumstances, as instructed by the Chief. "Oh he ain't coming out here – you're going in there." She thumbed over her shoulder to the door behind her.

The room grew quiet. Mongrel grew nervous.

"In there?" he finally asked. He looked around her at the door. "With all the...prisoners?"

Abegale shrugged, of course.

The air grew stale. Abegale grew impatient.

"Is it safe?"

Again, Abegale shrugged.

Time grew long. But finally Mongrel grew a pair.

"...Sure. Why not?" He nodded. "Let's do it."

"Great!" Abegale whirled around and positioned herself in front of the door. Carefully, she took a set of keys out of her back pocket, selected a shiny gold one, and proceeded to unlock the door. She then swung it open with an overly dramatic creak, and ushered Mongrel in.

Although Mongrel's pair were unseasonably large, his feet felt glued to the floor. He forcibly dragged them to the door, and paused to catch his breath. He was about to enter prison.

Prison.

The electric chair. Fires. Riots. Knifings. Gang-raping. Beatings. Tossing salads. Shooting and killing. Hooting and hollering. Solitary confinement. Gambling with cigarettes. Bribing guards. Cellmates. Pressing licence plates. Getting the top bunk. Three square meals a day. Parole. Senseless madness. Mad senselessness.

Abegale gave him a vicious jab that pushed him into...another hallway. This one was noticeably smaller than the rest, and was bereft of every colour except grey, much like the rest of the building. It was every bit as drab and lifeless as Mongrel had imagined a prison hallway would be.

A clang and locking sound interrupted Mongrel's trance-like stare, and what little appreciation he had of the hallway abated. Abegale joined him and they marched to the end of the hall, where another large metal door stood. Carefully selecting another shiny

The Watch

gold key, Abegale unlocked it. Then door swung wide, silently, and Mongrel stepped out onto the prison floor.

The words CELLBLOCK D were painted on the floor in dull blue letters. Two stories the held forty cells that held eighty prisoners. Murders, rapists, child molesters, taxi drivers; the worst people imaginable.

Mongrel coughed, and it echoed. It was quiet. Too quiet. Brutally quiet. In fact, it was peaceful. Rampantly peaceful. The odd chaotic tranquility of the place made Mongrel want to scream. He verged on panic…only there was nothing to panic over, which made him want to panic all the more. The slightest bit of hostility would have cheered him up to no end. This bothered him.

Abegale strode passed him. Mongrel followed her slowly, trying to keep his nervousness unnoticeable, lest the rapists sense his fear. He looked high and low. One by one, prisoners began lining up in their cells. They stared at him with interest – too much interest from some of them, and those were the ones to worry about. Most troubling, they all remained silent. Mongrel shuddered.

They came to a stop outside cell D17. Mongrel had to he provoked via tap on the shoulder to relinquish his attention from the inmates and project it into the cell.

As soon as he did this a childlike scream exploded from the cell and a maniac charged at him, ran straight into the cell bars, and knocked himself flat on the floor. This flagrant display of lunacy startled Mongrel to such a degree that he launched himself backwards in fright, and likewise landed flat on the floor, almost in unison with the maniac in the cell.

Several sounds invaded Mongrel's ears while he rolled on the concrete floor, trying to regain his bearings. First came an eruption of laughter from what must have been the entire cellblock, followed by what he eventually realized what Abegale beating her nightstick on the bars of some cell to quiet the unruly gang. Once the laughter subsided he heard the quiet moans of the lunatic inside the cell. Mongrel sat up to observe the prisoner in his natural habitat.

The prisoner did the same, taking a good long look at his visitor, and then screamed again. "Mon!"

Random Tangent

Biscuits nearly leaped to his feet, and would have run straight into the cell bars again had it not been for Abegale's swift thinking. She quickly unlocked the cell door and threw it open, just as Biscuits ran through it, and instead crashed into Mongrel on the floor. More laughter ensued.

"Mon! I missed you so much! You come to see me! You like me!"

"I'll leave you two alone for a bit," Abegale said before leaving them alone for a bit. She walked back to the door they'd come through, and left through it.

Mongrel heaved Biscuits off himself and stood up, trying to regain both composure and dignity, but not gathering much of either. "It's less that I like you and more that I keep doing the honourable thing."

"So..." Biscuits threw some thoughts around his head. "...you don't like me?"

"No."

"Oh." Biscuits stared at the ground, more thought-tennis going on in his head. "But I made you a gift." He pointed behind him in the cell.

Mongrel rolled his eyes and wandered over to the cell check it out. Who could say no to a gift, after all? He wasn't sure what the boy's idea of a gift was, nor what sort of gift could be obtained while in prison, but he tried to be optimistic.

Biscuits ran ahead of him like a child running to open gifts on Christmas morning, and began rummaging through his belongings. Mongrel stopped at the cell door, not really wanting to step foot inside. He glanced around the small, cramped area. It appeared that Biscuits had the whole little place to himself, although there were two beds[*]. A tiny window at the top of the cell let in small traces of light and air. A small toilet hid itself in the corner but did little to hide the small sausage inside it, nor unpleasant experience of using it. A tiny desk held a tiny pencil, tiny notepad, and some tiny books. Small wonder why the tiny space made the biggest of men a little crazy.

---

[*] It would be more correct to say that there were two half-beds, since put together they might make a complete set of one single-sized mattress. They were that infinitesimal.

The Watch

"Here!" Biscuits announced triumphantly. He slammed down a uniform – a prison uniform – on the desk, which was so small he nearly missed it. The uniform was the most revolting shade of orange ever conceived by deranged human minds, and had the name MONGREL stitched across the back. "For you!" the boy said with an obscenely wide smile.

Mongrel looked at the uniform, not knowing what to think. Why the hell would Biscuits get him a prison uniform? Or was it a jersey? It had his name on it. Did he expect him to wear it?

"I made it for you!" Biscuits said after Mongrel's silence had gone on long enough.

"Is that a uniform?"

Biscuits nodded furiously.

"Why does it have my name on it? Are you guys all on a team?"

"All unaforms have names on them."

Mongrel sighed. "I just said *uni*forms. With an *I*, not an *A*. Did you not see that? Can you not...never mind. Why did you get me a uniform?"

"I made it for you."

"*Made* it for me did you? Sure you did. Just like you made your bed over there?" Mongrel nodded to the beds, both of which were unkempt. What, was the boy sleeping in both of them? "The only thing you make here is licence plates."

"We make lots of stuff here!" Biscuits retorted. "We make desks, and paintings, and, and not a lot of people die eether!"

"Well whatever. Why did you make it for me?"

"So you'd look like me and fit in."

"Seriously?" Mongrel could barely contain his disgust, his disapproval, and...what else...how about dismay; that's alliterative. "There's no way I'm putting that on."

The boy sulked. "Please?"

"*No!* Why would I want to dress like a prisoner? Then I'd look like I belong here. Is that what you want? You think they'll mistake me for you cellmate and keep me here? Are you a moron?"

Biscuits looked sheepishly to the ground. "Yes."

Mongrel said nothing. At least the boy agreed with him. But something suddenly didn't agree with Mongrel: Biscuits *agreed* with him. Had prison really beaten him down into a subservient creature? But wait, there's more – did they just have an entire intelligible conversation?

"Hold on a second," Mongrel said, "are you using contractions?"

Biscuits, still looking at the floor sheepishly, began fretting. "Yes."

"Wait, hold on another second. Do you even know what a contraction is?"

"Yes."

Mongrel calculated a quick test in his head. "Keep holding on now, okay, what did you do to my mother that put you in here?"

Biscuits looked up and thought. "I smash – *smashed* – her face in with hammer!"

Mongrel's eyes grew wide; he was astonished. "Yes! That's right! That's exactly what you did." He mentally took a step back. It had only been a couple months but Biscuits had been making huge improvements in his life. He could hold his own in a conversation, his grammar had grown immensely better, and he'd even cut back on the fretting. Prison was really turning his life around. The system worked. "How do you know this?"

Biscuits shrugged. "Cause I did it?"

"Okay, not what I meant." Mongrel ran his hands over his face. "How do you know all these new things?

I giant smile appeared on Biscuits' face. "The Derf teach me!"

Mongrel's eyes grew so wide they hurt. "*Derf?*"

The boy nodded enthusiastically.

"Derf is here? Derf is *alive?*"

Biscuits' face suggested it was made of rubber as it stretched his smile to ghastly proportions. Mongrel had to look away in disgust. His eyes found the unflushed toilet, which he deemed far less repugnant.

"Come," the boy chirped, tearing out of the cell and down the cellblock, "I show you!"

More out of curiosity than anything, Mongrel followed. But had he known what was to follow he might have thought twice, for as soon as he left the cell the cat-calling began. The once eerily

The Watch

quiet inmates, no longer in the presence of an officer, were now a frothing bunch of madmen.

"K'Mere boy, Ima cut you up and down and eat your liver with some fava beans!"

"Take it off you sexy thang!"

"Puppies!"

"Dead man walkin'! Lemme outta here and I'll murder ya so hard you'll die from it!"

"I want your watch man! Gimme your watch!"

Mongrel, with each step moving him closer to Biscuits and the door he stood beside, stopped walking. He looked down at his wrist, at the fake watch drawn on it, which still read 8:08. This was a good thing because if the time had been anything else there would have been cause for alarm. At the moment the only cause for alarm was the fact that someone wanted his watch. No, that someone thought it really *was* a watch. And wanted it. Mongrel subconsciously covered his watch with his hand and hurried through the door.

Biscuits followed behind him, letting the door slam shut. They were in another lame grey hallway.

"You just go wherever you want?" Mongrel asked as Biscuits led him down a series of corridors, occasionally passing a uniformed guard (and one not-so-uniformed guard). "Nobody stops you?"

"There all my freinds," the boy replied. "They trust me. Long as I don't let the other guy come with me, they let me go wherever I want."

"What other guy?"

"Here," Biscuits said, pointing to a door. Mongrel tried to peek in though the small glass window but the boy shoved open the door and frolicked inside. Mongrel followed.

The room was not of exceptional size; perhaps the shape and dimensions of a small bedroom. No windows adorned its walls, but the rank odour of literature and rotting minds had settled in the room like a stubborn old man who refused to leave. A small, ancient television set sat haphazardly on a rickety old table, surrounded by grade school textbooks. Bookshelves lined one of the walls. Books, pamphlets, VHS tapes, and other paraphernalia lined the bookshelves. Juvenile graffiti lined most of them. A chalkboard stood in the corner

In the opposite corner sat a drab and rusty robot. It being as gray as everything else around there, Mongrel almost missed it. The main body of the unit was about the size of a washing machine, including a window in the front, through which could be seen circuit boards and wiring and what looked like a human brain. Two clunky tank treads held up the body, although they failed to make it appear even slightly mobile, and scrawny, useless-looking arms hung from each side. What would be considered the head of the ensemble of mechanical scrap was nothing more than a small LCD monitor. It displayed an animated face that looked to have been drawn by cross-eyed four-year old with a broken hand. The entire contraption was alien and creepy.

Biscuits sauntered over to the machine and hugged it, showing a degree of affection Mongrel never knew the boy had. After a moment he realized that he remained alone in the room, and turned back to find Mongrel still standing in the doorway as if waiting to be invited in like a vampire. A curious and confused expression on his face.

"What is that, a homemade WALL-E?"

"This is Derf," Biscuits said.

Mongrel stared at the machine, not quite understanding.

"*DERFtron*," the machine suddenly corrected. "I am your Dynamic Educational Reading Friend." The voice was robotic, monotone, and definitely creepy. Mongrel was happy it looked rusted to the spot, feeling like he had the mobility advantage, should it decide to rise up against mankind.

"This is Derf?" he asked.

"*DERFtron!*" the machine repeated, actually sounding annoyed.

"That's not Derf; it's just a weird machine."

"I am not weird. I am DERFtron."

"It's Derf," Biscuits insisted. "You member Derf don't you?"

"Derf was human, don't *you* remember?"

A few red lights on the machine went off but were ignored, as was its voice. "It's DERFtron, guys, come on."

The Watch

"He members you," the boy said.

This made Mongrel pause. "What do you mean?"

"He talks about you sometime."

"Sometime*s*," Derftron said. "And no I don't. And also: all capitals in Derf, please."

Mongrel looked at the machine, and the machine's monitor swivelled slightly to face Mongrel. The stared at each other. "What?" DERFtron finally asked.

"How does you know me?"

"It's Derf!" Biscuits said again, beginning to get exasperated.

"It's DERF-frickin-tron!" DERFtron exclaimed. "Seriously! How is only one of you getting this?"

The room was suddenly silent after this outburst. Biscuits and Mongrel looked at DERFtron, who for the moment lost its computerized voice and sounded almost human. The face on the monitor looked sheepish, and it turned away, pretending to be interested in something else.

"It can't be..." Mongrel whispered. The voice sounded remarkably like his old friend Derf (whose name was actually Fred, but he's dyslexic, so...). But how was it possible? Where had Derf been all this time, and what had happened to him? And most importantly, why wasn't he dead?

It was almost a year ago that Mongrel, Biscuits, and Derf were last all together in the same place: the Brats'R'Us adoption agency[*], the last of a franchise designed to get lonely kids into the hands of desperate parents, ex-parents, wannabe parents, or pedophiles. The idea was that one of them would remain there, but things did not go according to plan.

We needn't go into the details, but the entire building collapsed and Derf was found with a piece of steel running through his head in an almost comical fashion. Not wanting to just leave him there, Mongrel dragged him along afterwards, whether taking him home, or to a hospital, or just for a walk, no one can say for

---

[*] Online auctions are the new standard; not only do they present the challenge of pseudo-gambling over human lives, but the agencies can turn a nice profit as well.

sure. It eventually dawned on him that getting your brain pieced was the kind of activity that could kill a man, and that maybe he was just dragging around a corpse. Not the kind of thing a normal person tended to do. Thusly was Derf abandoned, left to rot on the sidewalk.

The steel beam lodged in his skull, interestingly enough, saved his life during these critical few days. The seagulls that inhabit Dunttstown are not your average kind of seagulls (then again, Dunttstown is not your average kind of town, so the seagulls are more or less a product of their environment). Normal seagulls make due with eating anything remotely similar to food to keep themselves fed and healthy. Well, fed, at least. Dunttstown, however, does not keep a well-stocked supply of edible garbage, and so its resident seagulls are forced to adhere to a far less strict dietary regimen. Their source of food was essentially anything small enough to swallow whole. Nuts and bolts, pebbles, small pieces of concrete, legos, loose change, you get the idea. Anything remotely warm and swishy, like road kill or vomit, was a treat for them, and any trace amount of actual food was hoarded and fought viciously over.[*]

The seagulls wasted no time picking Derf apart over the course of his last couple days. But since birds are not endowed with teeth, and are instead equipped with a comparatively useless beak, it was a slow process. They were able to remove a substantial amount of his skin and were digging into his internal organs, when help arrived.

Bosley was not your ordinary mad scientist. For starters, he wasn't even mad, although it was quite difficult to ascertain this. And indeed it's only after you understand the logic behind his actions that you can believe that, damn, he *has* to be sane. His logic was essentially this: he believed that he might have, in fact, already lost his mind. Any real mad scientist would believe, completely and indubitably, that they were sane, whereas only a sane person would consider the possibility that they weren't.

The irony behind this is that Bosley hadn't lost his mind, but had actually accumulated several more. Some people do literally

---

[*] The seagulls of Dunttstown traveled in gangs and routinely killed each other over food.

The Watch

lose their minds; Bosley had managed to find them. He currently had four, and it is for this reason that he was excessively brilliant.

The reason it was so difficult to believe he wasn't mad was that instead of putting his great minds to work curing cancer or inventing time travel, he had spent the previous year developing, testing, and confirming a theory that disproved the existence of goats.

Bosley had been accidentally travelling through Dunttstown (read: lost) when he spotted Derf, or what was left of him, amongst a pile of seagulls. What was left of Derf was pretty much just what was left of his brain. The seagulls couldn't get to the rich, juicy brain bits because of the large chunk of steel in the way, and therefore stuck to devouring the rest of him. His leftover brain matter was still functioning, and Bosley decided to keep it to play with. I mean, who would throw away most of a perfectly good brain, especially considering how hard they were to obtain, even on the black market?

So Bosley took Derf back to his lab, far away from prying eyes and governmental authority, and began a new project. Most of Derf's body was a write-off, but the brain was still useful, so Bosley used it to power a new supercomputer he'd recently constructed. He then programmed Derf with all manner of neat software and information: martial arts, directions for flying any aircraft built after 1958, how to make balloon animals, the collective works of Edgar Allen Poe, 1001 tasteless boob jokes, his secret recipe for awesome chilli sauce, access codes and passwords for every major financial institution in North America, etc.

However, what Bosley wasn't able to do, despite his sincerest efforts, was bring Derf back to a conscious existence. Maybe Derf's brain was too far gone, or maybe Bosley just lacked the genius, but for whatever reason, it didn't work. Derf, all his thoughts and dreams and memories, was gone forever.

Considering the project a failure, Bosley donated Derf to the Dunttstown Penitentiary (where hopefully some residents might find some comfort in knowing just what had happened to him), to assist in rehabilitating convicts. There he became DERFtron (Dynamic Educational Reading Friend), and Biscuits' new best friend.

"Derf is my best friend," Biscuits said.

Mongrel looked deep into DERFtron's monitor. "Derf, are you in there? Are you still alive?"

"It's *DERFtron*," DERFtron said sternly. "DERF. Tron. I'm not telling you again."

It should be noted that using the name Derf was now a misnomer, as Derf was now *DERFtron*. No longer amongst the technically living, Derf was now amongst a heaping pile of metal and machinery. Since the last time Mongrel had seen his friend, Derf had undergone an existential modification where his fragile, flesh-and-blood body was eschewed in favour of a more durable, robotic chassis.

"Do you remember me?" Mongrel prodded. "Mongrel Stevens."

"Uh…" DERFtron seemed at a loss for words. "My databanks of information contain minimal source files on the name Mongrel Stevens, but-"

"Can he see me?" Mongrel asked Biscuits, who shrugged. "I don't see any eyes to go with that brain."

"DERFtron was not programmed with facial recognition software and as suc-"

"You know what?" Mongrel interrupted again. "This is pointless. He's just a stupid machine now."

"Hey!" DERFtron and Biscuits said simultaneously, taking umbrage.

"What? It's just an ugly, shabby computer now; it has no feelings."

DERFtron suddenly did a remarkable impression of sighing, head shaking, and a rolling of the eyes. Then it muttered, "I remember you, asshole."

Mongrel's eyebrows shot up and he took a step back. Gone was the droning, synthesized voice, replaced with Derf's own. And on the monitor, where there was once a pixelated, violently disturbing image of a face, well, there still was a pixelated, violently disturbing image of a face, only now it looked more like the real Derf. And the real Derf was alive, was in the machine, and was pissed about it.

The Watch

"Oh yeah. I tried to forgive that you had me pushed out a hospital window. I tried to forget that you got me shot. I tried to move on after you left me for dead. But you just keep showing up."

"I, I," Mongrel stammered, not knowing what to say.

"And then that mad scientist found me. Saved my life, sure, but he turned me into this thing!" DERFtron's animated face looked down over his no-longer flesh and blood body in despair. However, since he didn't have a neck, or eyes or anything like that, it was a simulated experience, and the others were not involved. "Who knows what that maniac *really* wanted to do with me? I played dumb until he thought I was useless and got rid of me. So now I'm here. Life is great, eh?"

Mongrel remained silent. He hadn't been directly responsible for any of Derf's tragedy, but certainly contributed to his problems with careless actions and a flippant attitude. Derf's predicament was at least partially his fault, and he began to bloat with guilt.

Biscuits beamed at Mongrel. "See? He members you!"

"*Remembers*, buddy. DERFtron said to him.

"Look," Mongrel finally said, "I'm really sorry about everything Derf. Really. I've been a terrible friend."

"It's *DERFtron*...you know what? Fuck it. Derf is fine. Whatever."

"Sorry," Mongrel said again. "You've had a shit life, and it's my fault isn't it?"

"Oh I ain't a man anymore. Can't you tell?"

"You *aren't* a man anymore," Biscuits corrected DERFtron.

DERFtron sneered at the boy. "Shut up."

"Is there any way I can make it all up to you?" Mongrel silently prayed that Derf didn't ask for a new body. How would he make *that* miracle happen? He knew Dunttstown had its own black market somewhere, but he didn-

Suddenly a ringing sound began echoing through the halls.

"Dinner!" Biscuits cried, and ran out of the room.

Mongrel looked at his watch; it read 8:08? A little late for dinner, he thought. Or early. Perhaps this place was a lot like a hospital, where everything was three hours ahead of time. He made for the door.

Random Tangent

"Wait!" DERFtron cried. "There is something you can do for me. You can get me out of here!"

"How you figure I'm gonna to that?" Mongrel asked, looking back at him.

"How *do* you figure...sorry, force of habit. It's your fault I'm in here, so you need to fix that."

"How is that my fault? I didn't put you here!"

"Hey! I almost died because of you. You owe me!"

Mongrel stood in the doorway for a moment, not knowing what to do. "Look," he finally said, "I'll think of something, okay? I don't know wha-"

Biscuits had come racing back and grabbed Mongrel's arm, and yanked him down the hall. "I said dinner! You not hungry?"

Mongrel was too busy trying not to trip over his feet to respond. As he was pulled through a maze of hallways and corridors, he fought the wave of dizziness and nausea, and tried to keep his sense of direction intact. This eventually proved too great a challenge for his meagre mind to handle.

After what seemed like a sufficient amount of time to guarantee that Mongrel would never be able to navigate back to the outside world on his own, they came to a stop in a large room. The sound of a hundred angry men invaded his ears. The smell of a dozen badly prepared food items invaded his noise. And one rather large inmate invaded his space.

"Hey boy, told you I wanted me that watch."

It probably would have been better for Mongrel to get his bearings straightened out after the ordeal his mind had just been through, but he decided to postpone that arrangement and deal with the immediate threat. He got to his knees, and then, with great determination, crawled to his feet.

The inmate who'd wanted his watch, presumably, stood in front of him. The man was a bit taller than him, reeked of B.O., had the same prison haircut as everyone else, and had one eyeball that was smaller than the other, crammed into the upper corner of his eye socket. The man was baring his teeth, but Mongrel wasn't sure if that was because he was angry, happy, or physically incapable of closing his mouth enough to cover them.

"You hear me, boy?" the inmate asked.

The Watch

Other convicts were beginning to take notice of the brewing conflict. Mongrel swallowed and looked around the room at them, hoping someone would intervene and save him. He really didn't want to lose his watch.

Then he noticed the guards patrolling the area, and felt more at ease. Surely they wouldn't let any harm come to him, since he was a guest at the prison. That assumption made, Mongrel felt invincible.

Naturally, we all know this is going to end badly for him.

He looked at his watch and smiled. "Oh, you mean *this* watch?"

"Yeah, that watch," the inmate said. "You got another one?"

Another piped in, "And I want yer shoes."

Mongrel rubbed his watch with his hand. "Well, this isn't the kind of watch you can have."

The thug looked taken aback. "What, is it one of them look but don't touch watches?"

"Yeah." Mongrel smiled again. "That's exactly it."

The thug spat on the floor. "I don't like them kind of watches."

"Well then you won't want this one then."

"So turn it into the touchin' kind!"

The gang began laughing heartily at this, but Mongrel failed to see what was so funny. "Sorry, "he said, "if I could do magic tricks, the first thing I'd do is stick your head up your ass."

This caused most of the laughter to die because shit just got real. More people began to take interest, putting down their utensils - although others became fervently disinterested, and tried to mind their own business, eager to distance themselves from what was to come. Biscuits whimpered and ran off somewhere to hide.

The convict cracked his neck audibly. "That so?" he asked.

Mongrel yawned and looked at his watch, then nodded with obvious disinterest. "It's so."

"Seems like we have a funny man!" the convict proclaimed. Other assorted inmates shouted threats and insults at Mongrel in response to this allegation. "And funny man thinks he can perform magic tricks!" More sporadic verbal abuse.

Random Tangent

"Uh, actually," Mongrel started, "I said that I *couldn't* perform magi-"

"Tell me something, funny man," the inmate continued, "can you pull rabbits out of a hat?" Mongrel was about to answer the question but the inmate didn't let him. "Well how about pulling my foot outta your ass?"

Howling laughter erupted in the dining hall again. Mongrel joined them, even though he didn't really think the joke was that funny. "Ha!" he shouted. "Ha and ha! That's funny. You're a clever guy." Mongrel reached out and put his hand on the inmate, having the audacity to actually lean on him. "But you know what's even funnier? Your face." He then thought, meh, he could do better. "And your mother. And whatever you did to get put in here. I bet that's funny too." Mongrel didn't look the inmate in the eye as he said this, but instead casually looked at his fingernails, pretending to inspect them, and trying – and failing – to whistle. So while no visual communication took place, there was a sort of touchy-feely kind of sharing; the thug communicated his rage via the intense heat his body began to generate, which Mongrel could feel through the prisoner's clothing.

Slightly alarmed by this, Mongrel decided to take a step back and give this visual communication thing a try instead. But when he did this all he got was more of the touchy-feely stuff, which took the form of a fist to the face.

The pain, oh the pain! Mongrel's marbles swam. It felt liked someone had punched him in the face. He couldn't remember the last time that had happened, but whether or not that was because the punch itself had scrambled some neurons integral to remembering that very incident, or because he just had a terrible memory, he couldn't say.

He fell backwards and landed on the hard, concrete floor. He heard Biscuits scream, and lots of laughter, but no one yelling stop, or whistles, or gunfire of any kind. Where were those guards, on coffee break? He decided to sit up and have a look around, but saw only a steel lunch tray coming in his direction.

Mongrel woke up so hard it hurt. Or, perhaps he just hurt in general. It was dark, but aside from all the pain it was difficult to

The Watch

determine anything else about his surroundings. To get a few more bearings on the situation, he decided to sit up.

The last time he'd sat up had proven to be a bad move. The steel lunch tray being swung at him would have found its target one way or the other, but it was the sitting up that had done him in. The force of the collision caused his head to bounce back towards the concrete floor, where they met once again, and exchanged consciousnesses. Naturally, floors don't have a conscious, so this swap was a one-sided affair.

On second thought, maybe it was good that Mongrel had passed out, since what followed was a four-on-one physical assault of ghastly proportions. Thankfully, before they'd gotten to the raping the guards returned from their coffee break and broke up the shenanigans. Pity too, since Mongrel had passed out and wouldn't have put up a fight. The guards dragged Mongrel and Biscuits back to the cell, where they could spend the rest of lunch alone and without food.

The other inmates had been punished with a rousing game of *brickballs*. This wonderfully torturous game has its victims hurling bricks at each other with the intention of damaging the testicles. Once you began peeing blood, you were excused from the game. This would go on until only one man was still peeing any shade of yellow. He would be excused with this dignity and balls still intact.

The second time Mongrel sat up in the cell with Biscuits turned out to be another bad idea. Pain swelled here and there, exploded around this other part, and this area right over here – I'm not even sure what it is since it's been so badly slaughtered – but this part is just a symphony of anguish. The tune of a thousand aches echoed through his head, and it took him a minute to hear Biscuits asking him if he was all right.

"I feel like I've been mugged by a train," Mongrel said, poking and prodding around his body, trying to find a spot that didn't hurt. "What happened?"

"They beat you up. Why do you do that?"

Mongrel tried to look at his watch to gather the time, but was too dizzy to make out the numbers. "Do what? Get beaten up?"

Random Tangent

"Talk like that to them. There big bad men. You shouldn't make them mad." Biscuits' eyes were wide with the gravity of this revelation, but Mongrel couldn't see them.

"Well *excuse* me, but I thought the guards would step in and stop them, but…"

"They did. Them and the puppy guy."

"…they all disappeared at the worst possible time. The hell is wrong with them? And where am I?" He'd tried looking around but hadn't had much success. With the trauma that he'd been through he expected to be in some infirmary, but it looked like he was in a prison cell for some reason. No matter where he was in this godforsaken place it all looked the same.

"Back in my cell," Biscuits said.

After a moment to let this sink in, Mongrel asked, "*Why?*"

Biscuits shrugged.

Mongrel rolled off the bed in an attempt to make for the door. This proved a difficult venture, given the obscene amount of pain his body was still enduring. When he finally struggled his way all five feet to the cell door, it wouldn't open. He looked to Biscuits, who shrugged again, and decided the boy had been spending too much time with Abegale Switchblade. He spit a small puddle of blood on the floor and said, "I'm never coming to visit you again."

Biscuits looked shamefully to the floor. "Sorry."

Clearing his throat, which felt like coughing up fire, Mongrel hollered for the guard. He had to holler four more times before someone finally showed up. The guard who eventually answered the call was a little dumpy fellow with scraggly brown hair and coke-bottle glasses. He shone a flashlight into the cell and rubbed his chin at them.

"Can I go?" Mongrel asked him.

The guard looked at each of them in turned for a good solid moment before repeating the question back. "Go?"

Mongrel looked at him, and then back at Biscuits. If this helped the guard communicate with outsiders then it wasn't working for Mongrel. "Yeah. He ain't coming with me, don't worry." He thumbed over his shoulder at Biscuits, who again looked shamefully to the floor.

The Watch

The guard repeated the same complicated ritual of eyeing them both. He then asked the same question, but this time added a "Where?" at the end and complimented it with some sneering.

"I don't know," Mongrel sneered back at him. "Maybe to a hospital?" He tried looking himself up and down, hoping the guard would do the same and realize that, good lord, what happened to you? But when Mongrel lowered his head, he almost fainted do to the lack of blood in it (most of it had leaked out through every orifice in his body, including a few that hadn't been there before). He took his time raising his head back up, and found that the guard hadn't bothered to give him so much as a cursory glance. "Or perhaps I'll just go home and have a nap."

This time the man did eye Mongrel up and down and managed to ignore Biscuits for once. "You'll be fine," he said. "Just try to stop bleeding. Now lie down and be quiet for the night." He turned and began walking away. "And try not to swallow your tongue."

"Wait! You gotta let me out! I want to go home!"

"You are home, jackass!"

"I don't *live* here! I'm not a prisoner!" Mongrel yelled so hard he thought he felt his internal organs coming up.

After a moment, the guard wandered back into view. "What's this?"

Mongrel took good look at the guard's nametag: Cliff. He was going to going to have a word with Cliff's supervisor about his demeanour. "I'm a guest," he huffed, exhausted from the yelling. "Look, just go talk to Switchblade."

"Which one?" Cliff asked.

"Doesn't matter."

"Well they've both gone home for the night," Cliff said jovially. This seemed to amuse him.

Mongrel was going to run his fingers through his hair in frustration, but thought the better of it, just in case his hair fell out in his hands. "What about the Chief?"

Cliff sighed. "Look, what I see here are two prisoners, one in uniform, one not – and you're lucky I'm letting that slide – and two beds. Now I don't care if you go to sleep or not..." he eyed something on the desk, "...Mongrel, but you will shut up, or I'll put you to sleep myself."

The uniform. Mongrel turned to look at the disgusting orange uniform, the so-called gift Biscuits had given him, still sitting on the tiny desk. *The fucking uniform.* He then glared at Biscuits again and mouthed the words, "I will kill you." Biscuits couldn't read lips, but knew this did not bode well for him.

"That ain't mine," Mongrel stated, matter-o-factly. He could feel Biscuits' dismay behind him. Of course he didn't want the damn uniform, and he didn't care if it hurt Biscuits' feelings. The boy just did not understand how stupid a gift it was.

"Oh? It's not?"

"Nope. Seriously, totally honestly, sir, I really don't belong here. I'm just visiting." Mongrel put his hands up, as if surrendering. "Seriously!"

Biscuits nodded enthusiastically, although this in no way helped with the situation. In fact, it actually worked against Mongrel. Most of the guards in the facility knew all too well that Biscuits hadn't received enough proper education to allow him to follow any conversation through to a satisfactory conclusion. The boy could barely perform menial tasks such as tying shoelaces, combing his hair all in the same direction, telling the time correctly (even in digital), or even which side was left-hand or right. The Chief of Police was fond of saying 'if brains were dynamite he wouldn't have enough to blow his nose.'

Cliff eyed Biscuits some more and then looked at Mongrel, now certain he couldn't trust either one of them. No man who was befriending Biscuits was innocent, so far as he was concerned. "All right, what's your name then, if it's not Mongrel?"

Mongrel swallowed. "Uh...Nathan."

Cliff waited a minute before asking, "You got a last name too?"

Mongrel thought for a second, trying to come up with a name that wouldn't be associated with any prisoner. A name that didn't exist would be best. He then slowly sounded out, "Sypawecq."

The guard let the name roll around in his mouth before taking out a notepad and pen. "You mind spelling that out for me?"

The Watch

"Sure," Mongrel replied, although that meant spelling it out for himself at the same time. "S as in...see, Y as in you, P as in...pneumonia, A as in are, W as in why, E as in eye, C as in cue, and Q as in..." he thought desperately for a minute, not able to think of a word that began with Q. His brain seemed to fail him when he needed it the most. Finally he spat out, "Queue."

"The guard scribbled it all down, trying to make sense of it all. "Is that native?"

"Yeah," Mongrel said. "Mikawashi, actually."

"Hmm," he said. "Well I'll be back in a bit then." He turned and walked down the hall to the offices.

Mongrel exhaled loudly and slowly shrank to the floor. If he'd been more cognizant he might have noticed, in the cramped little cell where everything seemed too small, there wasn't even much floor to sink to. He was about to begin cursing out Biscuits, but figured he should instead use what remained to his energy to crawl to the nearest bed. So he passed on that idea, struggled to the bed, and passed out as soon as his head hit what passed for a pillow in Duntt Pen.

A clang rang in Mongrel's ears and he crashed to the concrete. Aches and pains, bruises and sprains, throbbed as he rose to his feet. He looked down at the little half-bed, and then at the floor. It was only a short distance between the two, but it might as well have been a mile for all the agony the fall had caused him. He then looked up at Biscuits, who still slept peacefully in the bed above his.

Cliff stood by the cell door, flashlight in one hand, nightstick in the other, ready to play another sonata on the bars should the need arise.

Mongrel looked at his watch, wondering how long he'd been asleep. It was dark in the cell block; probably after bedtime. But with the help of Cliff's flashlight he was able to see his watch; it read the same time as always. "Damn," he said, "time crawls in here. No wonder prisoners go crazy." Thankfully he wouldn't be staying any longer here in this dungeon. He grabbed Biscuits by the hair and yanked him off his bunk. "Wake up! This is important. It's time to say goodbye."

Random Tangent

When Biscuits was done rubbing his head, they limped over to the door together. Mongrel smiled as well as his fractured face would allow, taking as much pride as he could in what he would call a victory. *Terribly sorry for the mix up, Mr. Steve...er, Sipa...Sypew...whatever your name is. You're free to go. Here take the keys to my Mercedes. Keep it, as compensation for your trouble.*

As they looked out at Cliff through the bars, Mongrel couldn't help but wonder to himself whether or not Cliff actually owned a Mercedes, or if any of the guards did. Maybe the Chief, perhaps.

After a minute wandered by without any chit-chat Mongrel thought that maybe Cliff was waiting for him to start the conversation. "So? Am I good to go?"

Cliff looked as if he was deep in thought. "I'm sorry, what?"

A shiver of irritation flashed down Mongrel's spine, making him clench his teeth. It was deathly quiet on the cellblock; there was no way Cliff hadn't heard him. Was he deliberately being obtuse? No wonder prisoners began riots. "Me go home now?" he spat out in frustration. "Sleep in own bed? Shit in own toilet?"

"Oh," Cliff said, as if the question surprised him. "No. I'm afraid not."

This answer surprised Mongrel. "Why not?"

"Cause you're not on the list," the guard said. "Nice try though."

"Not on the list? But – but doesn't that mean that I don't belong here? I'm *not* on the list!"

"Yeah, and that means you *do* belong here."

"But how can I belong here if I'm not on the list?" Mongrel cried. "Everyone's on the list right? If all the prisoners are on the list, and I'm *not* on the list, the-"

"No, not the prisoner list: the *guest* list."

"How can...wait, what? *Guest list?*"

Cliff sighed. "Yeah, the guest list, you jackass. All the guests have to sign the guest list, get a time stamp...whatever, doesn't matter. It don't apply to you."

A crazed look appeared in Mongrel's eyes. "I was never told to sign a guest list!"

The Watch

"That's cause you ain't no guest!" the guard shouted, having gotten tired of the whole charade a while ago. "Now pipe down and get back to knitting, or whatever you're doing."

Mongrel, still enraged, looked over his shoulder and saw a ball of yarn sitting on the desk. What the hell was Biscuits doing with yarn? "I *am* a guest!" he screamed. "Cliff, buddy, you gotta help me out! That prisoner list, you got one, right?"

The guard sighed. "Look, if you *really* aren't a prisoner, then where's the other guy?"

"What other guy?"

"Two inmates to a cell, you know how this works." Cliff looked around the cell with mock interest. "I see two of you here, so if you're *not* supposed to be here, then where's the guy who *is* supposed to be here?"

Mongrel shrugged. "I don't know – he's *your* prisoner."

"No, *you're* our prisoner. Now quit pretending you ain't."

"Oh come on!" Mongrel whined. "What's it gonna take for you to believe me?"

"Look, I'm done with this little game," Cliff said, and began to walk away.

"No wait, Cliff! Come back. I'm not Nathan! My name is Mongrel Stevens. *Stevens!* I got ID!"

"Shut up man!" someone hollered. "Tryin' to sleep over here!"

Cliff wandered back, muttering, "This better be good."

Oh it'll be damn good, Mongrel thought. He reached for his wallet, but squeaked out a cry full of surprise and anguish when he found it missing. Apparently the fight back in the cafeteria wasn't just a beat down; it was a mugging.

"Uh...I..." Mongrel struggled.

Cliff sneered some more and shook his head, then walked away again without saying a word.

"Cliff!" Mongrel yelled, but didn't know what to follow that up with.

From out of view Cliff hollered back, "Give it up, man. It's over!"

"*Cliff!*"

Random Tangent

There was a dull metallic clang as the door closed, and he was gone. He limped back over to his bed and sat down. Now he finally had something to panic over. Looking around room, he could feel the walls closing in on him on the outside, and anger boiling up on the inside. His eyes settled on the ball of yarn. Orange yarn. Had Biscuits actually knitted him the uniform? Was that what he was doing with the yarn? The boy *had* said he'd made it for him. He meant he'd personally made it for him, all by himself. A small pool of guilt welled up inside his head, fighting for space amongst the disorientation, rage, and pain. The uniform was just supposed to be a gift. A stupid gift, but a gift nonetheless.

"It's cold in here!" a voice down a few cells down cried out. "Can someone turn the heat on?"

As if in response to this question, a rather loud fart echoed throughout the cellblock, spurring a few giggles.

"Oh God!" the voice cried. "Turn it off! Turn it off!" More laughter erupted.

But Mongrel didn't find it funny. He didn't want to laugh. He didn't want to be here. He wasn't *supposed* to be here. He glared at Biscuits, who stood in the corner of the cell, next to the toilet, looking sorrier than ever. Mongrel tried to feel bad for him, but it wasn't working. He knew that all of this was just a perplexing series of coincidences that would get worked out eventually, but the anger inside him was winning over. Mongrel was seeing red. And stars. He was still seeing stars.

Suddenly Biscuits pulled down his pants and sat on the toilet.

Mongrel lay down on the bed and turned over to face the wall, disgusted. Well, that was it. He couldn't kick the boy's ass while he was taking a dump – that would be like hitting a man with glasses, or beating up a retarded kid. Actually, it *would* be beating up a retarded kid. It just wasn't cool.

He tried to drift off to sleep, figuring that there was no way he could be angry and snap at any moment if he were unconscious. There would be no trek back to his house tonight with a stranger he'd just met. No journey home. No new friend. Just the dark, the quiet, and the stench of a fresh turd.

The Watch

The End

Well, Mongrel's really in a pickle now, eh? He shouldn't worry, though. There's a general rule that states: left to themselves, things tend to go from bad to worse. In Mongrel's life the opposite was true; if he left things alone, his problems usually worked themselves out. Too bad he always had to interfere and muck things up. He needed to learn to *not* mind his own business. The chief of police spent a lot of time that day in the bathroom, which was the business he was speaking of, and was going on a two-week holiday starting the next morning. Abegale Switchblade also had the next couple days off, so everyone who knew Mongrel was a visitor wouldn't be there the next morning. Should be interesting. Biscuits spent the night having the most epic bowel movement of his life (there was a bug or something going around the prison). His missing cellmate quietly followed Abegale out of the cellblock after Mongrel had shown up, then quietly disappeared, and quietly managed to never come back. Mrs. Walker was so ashamed with her inability to get out of her wheelchair – even though she *could* walk – that she felt like killing herself. She was going to wheel herself out in front of a passing car, but couldn't find any that she liked. Tracy and Lily spent a few more hours on the bus for the joys of driving through farmland – and by joys I mean the kind similar to those you'd find riding a washing machine. The bus driver, Nancy, sitting in her comfy bus-diver seat with the heavy duty suspension, didn't enjoy the ride as much. Pity too, because the woman badly needed an outlet for all her pent up rage that didn't involve vehicular manslaughter. The old man who was falling apart on the bus turned out to be old man Cleopard. He'd been the person who'd started drive-by-bricking years ago, and was pleased to see it finally catching on. Now, of course, he pursued different, and heavier leisure time activities: kidnapping, extortion, and receipt forging. The inmate who wanted Mongrel's watch went on to win the game of *brickballs*, spent the night in the infirmary for brick-related injuries, and had his sentence reduced the next day for, ironically, good behaviour. DERFtron kinda just…you know, sat there all

Random Tangent

night, and didn't do anything. His life really sucks. I mean, *really*. Cliff really couldn't be running errands and looking up names and lists all night because he had other pressing matters, like the execution via lethal injection of another inmate named Captain Pete. The poor guy was just coming in to dispute some parking tickets – a case he thought he could win because he didn't even own a car – but in a case of mistaken identity, was thought to be a wanted serial rapist who'd been evading police for years. The perpetrator himself, Captain Peter Alphonse Moor, the Third, is still at large.

I would like to thank my friend Will Smith (*not* the celebrity, although one in his own right) for his inspiration for this story. Will has and heavily relies on a non-existent watch which he uses for everything from the time, the date, the weather, sports scores, whatever he needs. It predicts the future, recalls the past, and occasionally predicts the past and recalls the future. It gives him directions, offers dating advice, and sometimes even does the laundry. It's the most important piece of clothing he doesn't own.

Random Tangent

A Special Place In Hell

Random Tangent

A Special Place In Hell

Mongrel woke with a start. His heart raced. His head spun. He'd just had the worst dream. In it, he'd gone to visit Biscuits in prison, and met a bunch of crazy people, such as officer Switchblade's wife, Derf, who was still alive – and now a machine, and a possible new love interest in Tracey Gourmet. He'd also gotten the hell beaten out of him (or into him, considering the unholy agony his body was left in), by some convicts, and through a complex series of events managed to end up an inmate himself. And all he got was a lousy prison t-shirt.

But it was just a dream.

"Ya up, boy?"

Mongrel turned his head to see Captain Pete, alive for the time being. Something was wrong with this picture, but he wasn't sure what it was.

"'Bout time. Couldna wake ya meself or I woulda. Had a bad dream did ya? Well it's gonna seem like a good one time I gets through with yas. Come on, let's go."

Random Tangent

"Uh..." Mongrel began. It seemed like a good way to start a sentence, but he was at a loss as to where to go from there. Why would Captain Pete want Mongrel to come with him? Something was definitely wrong with this picture. Normally the good captain wanted to get away from him, what with all the dying Mongrel caused – inadvertently of course. Last time he'd been hit by a bus. It wasn't Mongrel's fault, but if he hadn't been there...

"Where are we going?" he asked.

"Ha!" Captain Pete spouted. "You'll see. You'll see."

But Mongrel couldn't see. No light shone through his bedroom window, suggesting it must still be dark out. But where was his nightlight? And what had happened to the glow of the LCD clock by his bed? It glowed so bright that Mongrel had to turn it away from him at night so he could sleep. Maybe the power was out; that would explain the clock, the nightlight, and the extra layer of dark outside. But something in the back of his mind was screaming at him. Some piece of logic he was mentally reaching out for that wasn't there.

"Wait," Mongrel said. "Why do you want me to come with you? Aren't you afraid of dying?"

"Bah!" the captain muttered

"But you're always complaining about that."

"I said bah!"

Mongrel thought for a minute. "There was the meteorite, the bus, and the aliens...the mafia..." He counted his fingers as he recalled each death. "You spontaneously combusted once, remember? That one wasn't my fault. Well none of them were really my fau-"

"I saids bah and I means bah! Now are ya coming or not?"

"Not until you tell me where we're going." Mongrel crossed his arms and sat resolute. Then he tried to swing his legs over the side of his bed. Yes, *tried*. It proved a futile endeavor because at the moment, he wasn't sitting on a bed.

In fact, he wasn't sitting on anything.

But he *was* sitting, and that was what mattered. Mongrel looked around for a moment, particularly in the direction of his bed. Just icky blackness was there. He reached down and felt nothing. Indeed, something seriously wrong was going on with this picture.

A Special Place In Hell

Captain Pete arred a few times. "I's gonna show ya a coupla things, boy. Things ya wish not to see. Things that'll haunt ya the rest o' yer life, which, if I had me own way, wouldna be very long."

"Well that's a relief," Mongrel sighed, deciding not to worry about the lack of his bed, light, and perhaps his mind. Things would sort themselves out. For all he knew this was just another dream. Maybe that's why the picture was all wrong; it wasn't a picture at all.

This comment seemed to annoy the captain. He scrunched up his face in his most disapproving grimace. "Why?"

"Cause for a moment I thought I was dead."

"Ah," Captain Pete nodded. "No. Not yet. Not yet."

Mongrel looked around. "This doesn't even look much like Heaven anyway. At least, not what I thought it would look like."

"Oh y'ain't goin' to Heaven anyway, boy," Captain Pete smirked, "I's sure of that. There be a special place in Hell for ya, mark me words. Anywhat, after all the misery ya caused me, tis payback time now."

"But why?"

"Cause of the misery, didna ya hear?"

Obviously this wasn't a good enough answer for Mongrel. He sat on the nothingness, refusing to do anything unless Captain Pete obliged him.

Shaking his head, Captain Pete spat onto the nothingness. "Yer bein' very difficult 'bout this. There'll be payback for that too, you'll see." He adjusted his belt. "'Member the time I's in the hospital gettin' me appendix out? Well 'parently I didna survive the operation. Tis what the papers said anyhow."

Mongrel nodded. "Rings a bell."

"Well I did survive, till ya comes along, bringing that there Death fella with ya. Drags me off into the void he does. And I told ya I's gonna be back. Tells ya I did. And here I be, ready to return the favour."

"So...you're gonna kill me?" Mongrel asked, swallowing hard. That better not be what was wrong with the picture.

Captain Pete snorted. "If I could. Nay. I's gotta do that whole Christmas Story thing, ya know? Showing ya yer past, present'n'future and whatnot?"

Random Tangent

"Oh." Mongrel looked around, still seeing nothing but lots of nothing, getting a sense of deja-vu. He felt like he was in the place between places. He tried clapping his hands, but the dark didn't turn off. He shrugged. "Don't you have to be an angel for that?"

"What d'ya mean?" Captain Pete looked down at his body. Mongrel looked down at the captain's body as well, and it was around this time that he noticed Captain Pete was ethereal-like, ghostly white, and floating in mid air ten feet from him. So *that's* what was wrong with the picture: Captain Pete was still dead today.

"...Oh," Mongrel said, shrugging. "Nevermind. I didn't...well, I mean, I just woke up, so I'm a little...yeah, groggy, still." He shrugged again. "You're still dead." Somewhere in the back of his mind he figured he should be at least slightly frightened because a ghost was in his presence. But the other parts scrounging around his mind didn't seem to be paying attention. This was ever Mongrel's curse; his brain had trouble communicating with itself.

Captain Pete snorted again. "Well that makes ya the captain of obvious then."

"And you're the captain of Pete." Mongrel giggled like a school girl, until he saw that Captain Pete did not share his amusement. "Come on, that was funny."

"So what does funny boy wanna do first? Past, present, future, or other?

"Other?"

"Ha! Trick question, boy! Y'ain't gots no choice. Ima show you what I wants to. What d'you think 'bout that?"

Mongrel was still in the process of waking up. Some days took longer than others. He found that generally the more sleep he got the longer it took to get it out of his system. And the less sleep he got the less sane he felt. Life was all about balance, after all. Quite frankly he was just happy to wake up and find that he wasn't in prison, and that it had all been a bad dream. Of course now it appeared that he wasn't safe at home in his bed either. But still, he was out of prison, so it was an improvement. And now Captain Pete actually wanted to spend time with him. He was already dead, so Mongrel couldn't do any damage. This was practically a dream come true.

A Special Place In Hell

He smiled at this thought.

This annoyed Captain Pete. "Ya won't be smilin' much longer, boy." He began pacing back and forth in mid air, his pegs touching nothing. This was, as far as he was concerned, a much easier method of walking. His pegs took some measure of balance, and were always finding holes that he was sure hadn't been there before. He might've been better off without them, but the other option was a wheelchair, and no pirate, in his opinion, should ever end up in a wheelchair. He'd rather be dead.

So far so good.

"Ya know," the pirate captain grinned, "I knows what ya fears."

An image appeared between the two of them, blurry at first, but slowly coming into focus. It was Shamus Bond.

Eyes grew wide. Pulse quickened. Heart raced. Mongrel tried to back away from the image, but there wasn't anything to grab onto that could help him push distance into the way. Damn the nothingness!

Captain Pete laughed evilly.

Shamus was sitting, perhaps at a table – the image did not include his surroundings – with a handful of playing cards. He was wearing a white suit, still disgustingly neat, and a red tie. His hair was parted on the wrong side from what Mongrel remembered, but then again, he was trying not to.

"Bond. Shamus Bond," Captain Pete said. "He ain't done with ya yet, boy. He knows where ya live, and he's plannin' revenge."

Mongrel said nothing. He was too afraid to.

"He sees ya when you're sleepin'. He knows when you're awake. He knows when you've be bad or go-"

"That's Santa Claus," Mongrel cut him off.

"Bah!"

The image of Shamus began to grow larger and larger until it surrounded them. They were now inside the picture. No, as Mongrel looked around, he found they were inside the anti-agent's home. Shamus was indeed sitting at a table, with three other men, playing cards. The room itself, much like its owner, was meticulously neat. Nothing seemed to be out of place; colours coordinated beautifully, pictures on the wall were, well, picture perfect. Even the drapes billowed in the breeze in an organized fashion. It made Mongrel sick – with fear.

"Are we actually here?"

"No. Not really." Captain Pete spat on what was apparently not the real floor. "We's just vistin'. Sorta like lookin' through the lookin' glass sorta thing."

Mongrel was almost relieved. "So none of this is real?"

Captain Pete scrunched up his face again, this time in thought. "Well it's...kinda...not 'xactly one of them para-hoxes, but...uh, I means this is really happenin' right now, but we ain't really here."

"I know, you said that."

"Look, boy, just shut yer yap and watch."

Suddenly the room grew blurry, and sounds began to filter in, muffled at first, but they slowly gained clarity. Voices mumbled, the wind whispered, orchestral music played, snacks were crunched.

"So I left her such a good tip."

The words were clear, and now the visuals matched them. The four men were sitting around the table playing poker in Shamus' flat. Wine and crumpets were being served. They were all dressed well and spoke with those appallingly gentlemanlike English accents that made Mongrel feel like a clumsy, ill-mannered idiot.

"I mean, a really good tip. You should have been there, I tipped the shit out of her!" the one continued. Mongrel got the distinct impression that the man wasn't into women. *"I almost feel bad for the poor girl."*

"Well I do feel sorry for her," said another one. *"Please pass the crumpets."*

The man passed the other man a basket. *"Why's that?"*

"Because she probably thought you were making a pass at her." He grabbed the basket and spent a good deal of time selecting one of the pastries. He then grabbed a napkin and folded in across his lap, but didn't begin to eat it.

"I think anyone can tell Martin's a flaming homosexual," Shamus said, *"it's practically written on his forehead."* Playing the

A Special Place In Hell

dealer for this hand, he drew another card from the deck and laid it down next to three others; a queen of hearts, seven of diamonds, and four of hearts. The new card was a ten of spades. *"Ten of spades. Raise twenty."* He threw some chips into a pile in the center of the table.

The forth man, who hadn't spoken yet, got up from the table and wandered over to the record player. He was the only one with graying hair, and looked quite a bit older than the rest. *"Oh, I love this part,"* he said, turning the volume up a few degrees.

"Yeah. If it was a bloke I'd have left him my card instead, or a note saying his tip is in my trousers!" Martin laughed ferociously.

"Call," the other one said, also tossing in some chips. *"Will, don't turn the music up too loud or whats-her-name upstairs will go off her trolley."*

"Nonsense!" Shamus said. *"You leave that just the way it is, and if Mrs. Bakker has anything to say about it I'll shove a pineapple up her backside. And are you calling or what, William?"*

"Fold." William said.

"Well I'm calling," Martin said after taking a big gulp of wine.

"You brought me here to watch them play cards?" Mongrel asked.

"Just keep watchin'."

Shamus, drew another card and laid in on the table; it was a nine of hearts. *"Oh, interesting,"* he said. *"Check. Anyway, what do you lads think?"*

"Of what?" Martin asked.

"Of the plan," the unnamed man said. He then addressed Shamus, *"You'll need a local."*

"Oh right," Martin giggled, *"the one that got away. Got plenty of those myself."*

"I'm always up for revenge," William said, returning to his seat. *"Count me in."*

"Aren't you retired?" the unnamed man asked, finally beginning to eat his crumpet. He pondered his hand for a moment before throwing a few chips into the pile on the table. *"Raise thirty."*

Random Tangent

William farted audibly. *"Pardon me. I prefer to call it freelance work."*

"Seriously, Will?" Martin said, putting a hand over his nose.

"I do have a local," Shamus said, seeming not to mind the gaseous intrusion. *"He's lived there for years, knows more about the area than anyone. Seems a bit bonkers, but a jolly good chap for what we need."*

Martin threw his cards in, folding his hand. *"I suppose you can count me in, if for nothing other than the trip,"* he said, speaking through his hand. *"I haven't been out of the country in months now, since corporate's got me on a desk. Oh, God, Will! That's rancid! But I don't know if I can handle the torture stuff. Kinda gives me the willies. Can't we just ransom him?"*

Shamus took a sip of his tea. *"No point."*

"I've looked into that," William agreed, nodding. *"I ran a background check. He's got no living relatives, hardly any friends. Local law enforcement consists of a handful of idiot cops and a strange mayor who speaks no English. I don't think he'll even be missed."*

"What about the cop that got you?" Martin asked, looking at Shamus. *"Guess you were the idiot on that one."* This brought a round of laughter from everyone but Shamus.

"Oh enough, honestly." Shamus said, perturbed. *"If you recall I got him back. I sent him to some Godforsaken country in South America. Besides, I think they were both in cahoots together."*

"Are they talking about me?" Mongrel asked, horrified.

As if hearing the question, Shamus looked directly at him. Mongrel held his breath and tried to faint. Then he heard something; a knocking sound.

"Blast! That better not be Bakker!" Shamus threw his cards down and removed himself from the table, and left the room.

Mongrel and Captain Pete followed Shamus as he strolled down an impeccably neat hallway to the front door of his apartment. After lifting the latch, he pulled the door open wide to reveal a small dumpy lady in an ugly green dress. She carried no cane, but looked like she badly needed one.

"What?" Shamus asked, annoyed.

A Special Place In Hell

"Could you possibly keep it down up here?" she asked.

He appeared to consider the question, then answered, *"Why...yes, I do believe I could. Although it isn't a very appealing suggestion."*

"Well it's very appealing to me!" she exclaimed. *"I'm trying to have a nap."*

"Oh!" he said, as if this had caught him completely by surprise. *"I see. But then again, I don't really care about your problems now, do I?"* He didn't wait for a reply; instead he quietly closed the door in her face.

No sooner had he done this than the banging on the door began again. Shamus huffed and heaved the door open again. *"Back so soon?"*

"Please," she begged him, *"I'm trying to sleep."*

"You'll get plenty of that soon enough."

"I'm just a poor old lady, and I need my rest."

"How do you even manage to hear anything anyway? You certainly don't seem to be listening to me."

"I am always so tired, and I don't sleep well with my back."

"Look, look," Shamus shushed her. *"I completely understand what you're trying to say and I wish there was something I could do to help, I really do. But what you need to understand is fuck off!"* He then slammed the door in her face and shouted. *"And if you keep bothering me I'll have the police notified and charge you with verbal assault!"*

Dusting off his hands, as if he'd gotten them dirty, Shamus walked back into his dining room where he and the others were playing cards. Martin and the still unnamed man quickly darted back to their seats.

"Sorry about the interruption. Now where were we?"

"You were about to call me," unnamed man said.

Shamus sat down at his seat and took another look at his cards. *"How much?"*

"Forty."

"Forty!" Shamus exclaimed, causing Martin to snicker. After a moment's hesitation, the anti-agent grabbed a stack of chips and threw them in. He then laid down his cards, face up on the table. *"Trip nines,"* he said triumphantly.

Random Tangent

The other man revealed his hand and smiled smugly. *"King high flush."*

Shamus looked at the cards in shock. *"Blast! Why'd you tell me to call?"*

It was of course a rhetorical question, but William answered it. *"Because he looked at your hand."*

"What?" Shamus asked. *"Colin!"*

Colin shrugged. Martin snickered some more.

Running his hand down his face in an effort to relieve stress and regain composure, Shamus counted backwards from ten to one. Once finished, and relaxed, he spoke. *"Anyway, are we all in this?"*

"Depends when we're doing it," Colin said. *"I'll be in Moscow the weekend of the tenth."*

"Whoops! "Captain Pete said "Canna show ya no more."

The scene paused, and then faded to black. Once again they were enveloped by a thick nothingness that for some reason reminded Mongrel of the scent of cottage cheese.

"Wait, bring that back!" Mongrel said. "What do they say? When are they gonna…you know?"

The captain smiled snidely and shrugged. "Sorry. Show's over."

"But what happens after this? Like, they're gonna come for me, right? When?"

"Don't know," the captain shrugged again. "Well actually I does know, but I's not tellin'."

"But this is my *life* we're talking about!"

Captain Pete's smiled faded and disappeared, and he glared Mongrel in the eye. "Well why don't we talk 'bout me own life then? Eh? Oh, 'tis right, I don't gots one. Care to comment?"

Mongrel stared begrudgingly at where the ground should have been but wasn't. This didn't unnerve him. Having spent time in the place between places, space, and McDonald's, not having a floor to stand on was more of an inconvenience rather than a cause for alarm. In fact it was oddly freeing. "Wasn't my fault," he muttered to himself.

"What?" Captain Pete raised a hand to his ear.

"I said those weren't my fault!"

A Special Place In Hell

"Oh, I s'pose the gods just be yankin' me chain then?" he spouted, throwing his pirate hands in the air and pacing around the nothingness. "Pickin' on ol' Cap'n Pete are they? Well nows me turn to be pickin' on you, boy. Revenge, see?"

Mongrel fumed quietly to himself and said nothing.

Captain Pete snorted and began to hobble away. "Come on, let's go. Off to the next one."

Although it couldn't be stated with any amount of certainty, considering their lack of physical surroundings, as Mongrel followed the ghost of Captain Pete, he felt like they really were walking somewhere. The only evidence he had of this was the growing sound of thunder. No, not thunder, but a rumbling of some sort. A strange cantankerous humming rising in pitch and depth. He grew worried.

Suddenly Mongrel was face to face with himself.

"Gah!" he shouted, jumping back in surprise, slipping, and falling. Actually, considering the nothingness they were surrounded by you couldn't really say he fell; he just failed to keep standing. Captain Pete pointed and laughed at him.

Somehow another *him* had joined them in whatever void they were in. It wasn't like looking in a mirror; this version of himself must have been a good ten or fifteen years younger, but he recognized his own face, especially the look of terror on it. Staring up at himself, who was staring down at him, upside-down, Mongrel couldn't fathom what was going on. "How...?"

"What's that?" Captain Pete asked after a minute to regain control. This took a minute because he found the predicament alarmingly hilarious.

"How can this be the present?"

The old pirate felt this last question didn't add to the hilarity at all, seeing as how it threw semantics into the mix and confused him something terrible. "Huh?"

"Well you said we're doing the Christmas Story thing. So the first one with...him," he thumbed over his shoulder, as if giving a general direction in nowhere would somehow indicate Shamus or even a particular moment in time, "would be the past. So this should be the present, right?"

Random Tangent

Captain Pete stumbled and stuttered with the best incoherence Mongrel had ever heard in trying to answer the question. His mind wandered into the outskirts of logic, but then decided to go around the long way.

Mongrel didn't have time to waste standing around himself. "How can this be the present?" he repeated, trying to help the pirate. "Shouldn't it be showing me here? Right here, right now? Or maybe back at home in my bed? This me looks like I'm a teenager. This looks more like the past to me. So, like, what the hell?"

The captain rolled his eyes around his head in confusion. "Well...look, I's never really meant to do nothin' in no particular order, so neverminds all that."

"Well then was Shamus my future? My past? Like, what? When does that happen?"

"Hey, who's running the show 'ere? You or me?"

It was obviously a rhetorical question, but before Mongrel could not answer he was interrupted by a southern drawl.

"Forgive me. The generator takes time to get going in the morning. Just like myself."

The nothingness gave way and soon the three of them – two Mongrels and a Pete – were all hanging around at the top of a large cavern, one of them literally. The large cavern was maybe three or four stories high and sparse save for a large rock off to one side, directly under them – or more specifically, the Mongrel that was hanging upside-down. This Mongrel, it was now apparent, had a rope tied to his ankles and secured through a pulley to a switch far below.

"Where am I?" Mongrel asked, meaning his other self. "Hell?"

This set Captain Pete roaring with laughter again. Eventually he managed to squeak out, "Not yet, not yet!"

"Well it's just that I know this place. I've been here before."

"So ya been to Hell before? Wouldna surprise me."

Mongrel, tired of being the butt of every joke, glared in exasperation at the old pirate. "You know, you're not helping."

"Helpin'? You think I's here to *help*? Ha!" The old pirate began laughing some more.

A Special Place In Hell

Shaking his head, giving up on the argument, Mongrel returned his attention to the floor of the cave as two men entered the cavern.

One of them was Bossa Nova.

Chills flew up and down Mongrel's spine. This wasn't fair; first Shamus, and now *him*. All the people who were trying to kill him were being paraded in front of him like a, a…parade. Mongrel was almost angry at the absurdity of it all. But this was everyone, right? There wasn't anyone else trying to gun him down, was there? He tried to think, but couldn't concentrate, which only left him believing that there *had* to be someone else since he couldn't conclude otherwise. This made him woozy with fear and exhaustion. Instead of his heart racing it slowed down. His head swam. He broke into a cold sweat and grew pale. He began to look deathly ill.

This pleased Captain Pete immensely, and he giggled like a spoiled school girl. "It ain't over yet, boy. Nay! We's just gettin' started!"

"Wait, that's the local, isn't it?" Mongrel asked. "Shamus was talking about Bossa Nova, wasn't he? Oh shit, oh shit, oh shit…" This was almost too much for his meager mind to handle, and he wondered if he could faint into the blissful ignorance of unconsciousness.

"Ah, here we are." Bossa Nova said, drawing Mongrel's attention below.

The two men stopped beside the large rock. Bossa Nova, the infamous one-man mafia of Dunttstown, with whom Mongrel had had many unfortunate confrontations, was dressed, as usual, entirely in white. He wasn't wearing glasses like he had been when they'd first met, suggesting that this setting was indeed several years prior to that fateful day, or at the very least an alternate reality. Mongrel didn't recognize the man who was with Bossa Nova, but the man apparently knew who he was, as, surveying his surroundings, he took great notice of him, hanging upside down from the roof of the cave, and he looked horrified.

"Nova, what is the meaning of this?" He gestured toward the hanging figure of Mongrel, in case his outrage could be misconstrued. Some people, after all, really hate rocks, or caves in

Random Tangent

general. Or perhaps it could even have been a philosophical question; what is this rock, this earth? Why am I here? Where am I? Who am I?

"Who is that guy?" Mongrel asked Captain Pete, knowing he shouldn't expect an answer. "I mean, I'd be upset to see me like this too, but that guy seems to know me. Do I know him. I mean, does the me here know him?" He poked his other self in the side.

"Just hush up'n'watch! Ya talks too much."

"This here is Peaches the rock," Bossa Nova said, gesturing broadly to the boulder before them. *"New to the family. Can't wait to try her out."*

"I don't care about the damn rock!" the man cried angrily. *"What are you doing with my son?"*

This is where Mongrel might have said something like, 'Huh?' or 'What did he say?' but he was too busy being dumbfounded.

"Now take it easy Mr. Stevens. I warned you this might happen."

"What warning did you ever give me that even remotely suggested you'd kidnap and torture my son?"

"...Dad..." Mongrel said, awed. He tried to wander down from the top of the cavern to take a closer look but found it difficult to move spatially without the convenience of any support, like, say, a floor. He struggled hopelessly, looking like he was trying to hold in a bowel movement. Captain Pete found this endlessly hilarious.

Bossa Nova began pacing circles around Mongrel's father. *"Well if you recall I did send you a postcard..."*

Mr. Stevens looked down to the ground, thinking. Finally he said, *"Oh yeah, that."*

"Now I gave you enough time to come up with my money, but I'm not getting any younger. So I've come to collect."

"You let my son go or I'm not discussing anything with you."

"What's that now?"

"Dad," moaned the Mongrel that was hanging upside down, startling both Mongrel and Captain Pete. *"Help me."*

Mongrel's father seethed. *"Get. Him. Down."*

A Special Place In Hell

Bossa Nova walked over to the switch that secured Mongrel's rope. *"Oh I could do just that, Mr. Stevens, I really could."* He put his hand on the lever. *"I could let him go. Drop him right down here if you like."*

Mongrel struggled above. *"No! No don't! I like it up here, actually. Now that I think about it."*

"Wait!" Mongrel's dad jumped, holding up his arms the way people did when they wanted a brief respite, as if it actually granted them that. *"Leave him up there,"* he said, defeated. *"Let's talk."*

Releasing his hold on the lever, Bossa Nova strolled back over. *"Glad you feel that way. Good to have you finally come around."* He slapped him on the back.

"Look, Nova, my store has just started to turn a profit. I just need a little more time."

"My dad has a store?" Mongrel looked to Captain Pete. "Where is it? Is it still in town? What's it called?"

"Don't rightly recall the name if I 'member correctly. But tisn't there no more. It be POISE'N'US now."

"I believe we're passed all that now." As Bossa Nova said this he gave one of those 'you know what I mean' looks.

But Mongrel's father didn't understand. *"What do you mean 'passed that?' What do you want from me?"*

A cocky smile grew on the face of the drawling southerner. *"Only everything."*

"Everything? Like, everything I own?"

Bossa Nova's circular pacing began again. *"Remember, if you will, back when we forged that agreement?"*

Mr. Stevens didn't nod or agree or gave any indication that he did, but the way he hung his head suggested that it was all coming back to him.

"In return for my backing," Bossa Nova continued, *"you were supposed to give me your first born son, and half of your second. The top half, if I recall correctly."*

"What?" both Mongrels cried in unison.

"So really, what I have up there hanging around for my amusement is rightfully mine. Wouldn't you agree Mr. Stevens?"

"You can't own a human," Mr. Stevens muttered angrily.

Random Tangent

Bossa Nova squared him a look. *"And you shouldn't cut deals with crocodiles."*

Still looking solemnly to the ground, Mongrel's dad remained silent.

"And where, pray tell, is the rest of my reparations? Hmm?" The large southern-accented man continued to walk around Mongrel's troubled father, stroking his goatee, like a predator encroaching upon its prey. *"Now I could quite manage to seize the rest of, shall we say, your assets, on my own, much like I did with your first up yonder. But I'm a man of principle!"* Nova slammed a fist into his other, open hand. *"And pride, and honour."* He hammered his fist with each conviction. *"And mercy."*

Finally the two men locked eyes, and exchanged more than just glances. Not a word was spoken between the two, but they were communicating. Mongrel, the one *not* upside down, was on the edge of his feet, daring not to so much as breathe as the two men battered their wills against one another.

"I would have accepted monetary remuneration instead of flesh and blood, you understand. I gave you a chance, Mr. Stevens. I gave you time. But you simply refused to cooperate. So I had no choice but to attain retribution by taking from you not just what I wanted, but what was owed. Now, sweet merciful man that I am, I'm kindly making you another offer" He paused to let this sink in. *"What would you give to save your children?"*

Mongrel's dad was the first to break eye contact, looking away to the floor again. *"Everything,"* he said, not a question but a summation.

Bossa Nova nodded. *"Everything. Everything you own. I'd let you keep the store, of course, and your family. That is, after all, the very reason we're here."*

"Dad," moaned the upside-down Mongrel again.

"Hold on son, I'm thinking."

"What?" Mongrel cried, this time with more desperation in his voice. *"You serious?"*

His dad shot a look up at him. *"Well look, this isn't an easy decision for me. I have a lot of stuff. Expensive stuff. Rare stuff."*

"Dad! I'm your son!"

A Special Place In Hell

"I know, I know, but I've got a rare Guatemalan stone painting. You can't just walk into Wal-Mart and buy one of those – there's like, two in the world!"

"But I'm your son!" Mongrel bellowed from the roof of the cave.

"Yeah, I'm your son!" Mongrel agreed with himself. "And you only got one of me!"

"That's exactly my point," his dad retorted, *"I've got two of you. Certainly I can spare one."*

"Dad! What the hell? Seriously!"

"Two of me?" Mongrel whispered to himself. "I've got a brother?"

A minute passed, during which the tension was so thick you could almost see it. A dread silence hung in the air, egging the tension on like gravity urging a mudslide.

Finally Mongrel's paterfamilias shot apologetic eyes to his son and slowly shook his head. He turned his gaze to the big man in white and sighed. *"No. I'm sorry, but I'm gonna have to pass on this one."*

This was the last thing the floating Mongrel heard before fainting. Remembering to breathe had taken a backseat to all the action and drama that was unfolding below.

Bossa Nova was surprised. This was not at all how he thought things were going to turn out. He really wanted that stone painting.

"Are you shitting me?" screamed the Mongrel who was still conscious. *"I'm your fucking son!"* Mongrel's father looked back up at his son. *"Try to look at this from my point of view. Would you save me if I were in your shoes?"*

"Hell no!"

"See, that's what I thought. I'm glad you understand."

"Faintin' in the middle o' me show? The nerve I tells ya!" Captain Pete was furiously trying to poke Mongrel awake. Unfortunately, being a ghost, he was not endowed with a physical presence and couldn't actually maul the consciousness back into him like he wanted. "Wake up, boy!" he screamed. His pegs kept smoothly sailing through Mongrel's head unimpeded, and while he found this humourous, it did nothing to satiate his hunger for violence and retribution upon the boy. "Can't keep breathin' long enough to say alive? Makes no sense! Wake up!"

"GahhhhholyshitwhatthehellisgoingonwhereamI!"
Mongrel had just snapped out of the worst dream ever.
Ever.
In it, he was being haunted by a ghost that was subjecting him to the most horrifying alternate realities imaginable. And what was worse, they were supposed to be true, actual events that had, or would unfold at some point. But when, and which ones? He tried to shake the inanity out of his head, and stood up. Well, he didn't really stand up; he just reoriented himself into a standing position.
Wait a minute…
…it was still really dark.
"Well?" someone screamed angrily.
"Gah!" Mongrel jumped and turned around in one move, coming face to face with the ghost of Captain Pete and the reality that it wasn't a dream.
The old pirate stood there, arms crossed, tapping his peg on the nothingness, which made no sound. He was not amused. "I's gettin' bleedin' tired of havin' to wait 'round for ya to wake up!"
"S-sorry," was all Mongrel could manage to say. He tried to get his racing heart under control while still trying to come to terms with his predicament, He wasn't doing well with either.
Captain Pete pointed a stubby finger at him. "You do that one more time and I's gonna leave ya here. Got it?"
"Got it," Mongrel muttered.
The pirate straightened himself up and adjusted his belt. Having gotten that bit of threatening out of his system he felt he could calmly continue with his carnival of horrors, so long as everyone stayed awake and didn't pester him with stupid questions.
Mongrel, of course, had a stupid question. "So, uh, I blacked out back there and I'm just trying to put this all together, but did my dad say I had a brother?"
"Don't know," the captain sighed. "Wasn't listenin.'"

A Special Place In Hell

"My dad is dead. So if he was alive in that little...movie, or whatever, then that was the past. It already happened. So why don't I remember any of it?"

"Don't know that neither."

"And if I have a brother, why don't I know about that either?"

"I don't bleedin' know!" Captain Pete said, getting agitated. "Look, can we forget about this'n'move on?" He began floating away, leaving with or without Mongrel. "You're goin' to love the next one," he hollered.

Mongrel begrudgingly followed behind, doubting quite severely what the captain had said. In fact, he felt that the last dream he'd had – the one where he was in prison fighting for his life, with Biscuits, of all people – was less traumatic than this. But he knew he wasn't going to get anywhere worrying about why he couldn't remember his past. And he figured there would be more disturbing questions waiting for him before this ordeal was over. Best not to tax his brain too much.

After a moment of wandering in the nothingness with his ghostly tour guide he heard another voice, also strangely familiar, except that this was female.

"Honey?" the voice called. *"I have something to tell you."*

Going through the list of all the women he knew, Mongrel couldn't quite put his finger on it. It wasn't his mother; that was obvious. She was dead anyway, although that probably meant nothing here. There was the new bus driver, Nancy something. No wait – that was a dream. She most likely didn't even exist. What about the girls from the Elvis fan club? It could have been one of them, but it was hard to be sure. Beby? It *did* sound like her voice, but she would never call him 'honey.'

Sunlight drifted into the blackness, but did nothing to brighten it up. It just hovered there like an oncoming car with a headlight out. Mongrel held up a hand to shield his eyes as they continued towards it.

"What is it sweetheart?"

Mongrel knew that voice; it was *his*.

Suddenly they were in the light. And they were in his backyard. And it was early in the afternoon. And he was in trouble.

Random Tangent

Beby was stalking over to him. Although she didn't appear angry and ready to pounce on him for reasons that defy logic and would puzzle philosophers, Mongrel knew what she was capable of, and what was surely on her mind: violence. She looked similar to what he remembered, except maybe her hair was longer. And perhaps she'd put on a couple more pounds - but *just* a couple! Maybe only one, even. She still looks great! Fantastic! He didn't mean it! Please don't hurt him!

Mongrel would've ducked and ran if it weren't for one other small thing he noticed: her boobs were now enormous! What had happened? Breast enlargment surgury? A growth spurt? Had she suddenly began eating her vegetables? Was she stuffing her bra? He ogled them openly, vaguely aware that she couldn't see him and he could stare all he wanted. It was wonderful.

Captain Pete noticed Mongrel's enjoyment and it irritated him. But there was nothing he could do.

Beby reached Mongrel and sat down next to him on the grass. *"So... I'm late."*

The look that crossed Mongrel's eyes suggested a lot; confusion, hunger, and perhaps that he'd like to run naked, backwards, through a field of corn. His mouth, however, said nothing. He just looked at his watch – holy crap! He actually had a watch! An *actual* watch! And Beby had huge boobs and wasn't trying to kill him? Maybe this reality wasn't that bad.

"Haven't, uh...haven't we..." Mongrel stuttered.

"I'm pregnant!" she cried, interrupting his attempt to string enough words together to form a sentence.

Mongrel instinctively tried to spit-take, but since he hadn't been drinking or eating, he ended up dry heaving for a moment. He collapsed on the grass next to the others. The idiot Mongrel of this reality did the same, standing up first before dropping to his knees. *Pregnant?* Him and Beby? Beby and him? Them? *Both* of them? Together? That would mean they had...but that doesn't...what the? Who? Huh? What?

"Whatsa matter?" Captain Pete snickered. "Too much for ya?"

"I can't have a kid," he replied after a minute to remember what words sounded like. "I'm not ready."

A Special Place In Hell

"Well maybe he is." The captain pointed at the other Mongrel.

"I can't have a kid," the other Mongrel said, looking deeply into the ground. *"The world isn't ready."*

"See?" Mongrel looked up a Captain Pete. "Even *I* knew that." Apparently this Mongrel wasn't that stupid after all. He and Beby were a couple in this reality? Maybe it wasn't that bad.

Mongrel slowly lifted his head up to Beby. He was smiling. *"Guess they've got nine months to figure something out."*

She smiled back, and they hugged. It was touching until she said, *"Four."*

Mongrel let her go. *"Huh?"*

Still smiling, and still looking at him, she stood up, and ran her hands along her stomach. *"I'm five months along."*

"So...you're five months late?"

She nodded.

He stood up to look her directly in the eyes. *"And you couldn't have mentioned this when you weren't as late? I mean, if this was a conference or something and you were five months late you'd be five months out of a job. How long have you known?"*

"I knew something was wrong," Mongrel said. "I just knew it."

Just as Beby was about to answer, Biscuits ran up to them, shouting, *"Daddy!"*

Mongrel didn't say anything about this. He'd mentally only got so far as thinking that Biscuits had just called him *daddy* when his brain paused. It was similar to how your computer might take a while to download a large file; his head was taking a minute to adjust to the new information.

Mongrel groaned, irritated. *"What? Can't you see I'm busy?"*

"But ther–"

"Sorry!" Mongrel raised a hand to shush the boy. *"Your mother and I are having a conversation, and it's very important.. You'll have to wait your turn."*

Biscuits looked down grumpily and kicked the grass. *"Fine. What's so important?"*

Random Tangent

Captain Pete waved a hand in front of Mongrel's face, but got no reaction. He continued staring off into space as his brain compiled.

"Your mother is pregnant."

The boy looked at Beby, and then back at the man who was apparently his father. It was obvious that this didn't mean anything to him. *"Is it...um, contajus?"*

"No. It means you're gonna have a little brother or sister," Beby said, ruffling his hair. The boy apparently liked the sound of this. Either that or he really liked having his hair ruffled. Then he glanced at Captain Pete and his look turned sour.

Beby removed her hand from the boy's head and placed it along Mongrel's face, cupping his left cheek. *"I'm sorry. I just didn't know how to tell you."*

He grabbed her hand. *"But I've always wanted kids!"*

"No I haven't!" Mongrel said, taking part in the experience once again.

"Why do you think I adopted Biscuits?"

"Oh shit, he wasn't joking," Mongrel said, looking nauseous. "My brain didn't make that part up. Why, me, why?" He tried to throttle his other self. Biscuits jumped away a few feet when he did this.

Captain Pete laughed at Mongrel's attempts to handle the situation. "Ya don't want kids?"

Mongrel gave up trying to choke himself and looked at Biscuits, who appeared to be trying not to make eye contact. Then he focused on the old pirate. "It's not that. I just don't think I could handle a kid. Look how I am with you, and you're a grown man!"

"S'a good point."

"Whoever gave me a kid should be charged with assault, cause that's child abuse."

Biscuits was tugging on Mongrel's shirt sleeve, desperately trying to get his attention. When this failed to illicit a suitable reaction he began whimpering like a dog.

"What is it?" Mongrel asked, annoyed.

"There's peeple watching us." The boy pointed at Captain Pete, then at Mongrel. *"Gosts."*

A Special Place In Hell

The home that Mongrel now occupied formerly belonged to his deceased mother and was close to the middle of nowhere. The nearest neighbour was more than a day's hike to the north. If a plane were to crash near Mongrel's house and no one was home, any survivors would die before they could be rescued, unless they resorted to cannibalism (which, given the quality of airline food, is more of an eventuality anyway).

"What? Where?" The other Mongrel looked down to where Biscuits was pointing, staring straight at himself. It sent chills down Mongrel's spine.

"You can see ghosts, Biz?" Beby asked.

The scene paused. "Okay..." Captain Pete said, beginning to hobble back into the darkness. "...time to get goin.'" He seemed a little perturbed.

Mongrel followed him. "Can he actually see us?"

"Don't know."

"But we're not really here, are we? I mean, you said this was the past, or present or whatever. This is just a, a image, right? None of this is really happening, is it?"

"Course it's happenin'!"

"It is? But how can he see me if I'm already there? I can't be there in two places!"

"Look," Captain Pete suddenly stopped and turned to face him, "I don't know what's wrong with that boy. I's just as willied as you. Nobody never mentioned nothin' 'bout that in the manual."

"What manual?"

"Nevermind!" the old pirate shouted, beginning to hobbling away again.

Mongrel ran a hand over his face. "Oh man, I could totally go for a nervous breakdown right now." After two dreams in which the most...no, wait, *one* dream in which the most horrible things had happened to him, and then one reality. Or at least it was *supposed* to be reality. Well, some parts of it obviously couldn't be real, but...you see, this was why Mongrel needed that breakdown; sanity isn't all it's cracked up to be. Fewer brain cells could've handled this. Sometimes less is more.

"Anyway, it's over, right?" Mongrel asked, running to catch up. The interesting thing about the void that surrounded them was

Random Tangent

that there was no direction, time, space, or anything that could be said to give spatial construct. The nothingness encompassed everything and it encompassed nothing, which makes total sense, and no sense at all.[*] Mongrel didn't actually physically move anywhere; he just repositioned himself closer to Captain Pete.

"Over?" Captain Pete didn't seem to understand.

"I mean, we're finished. I can go home now, can't I?"

"What? No. Not yet, boy." The captain seemed amused by this.

Mongrel's eyes bugged out of his head. "Not *yet*? But we did them all, past, present and future. What more is there?"

"Ya forgot *other*."

"*Other?*" Mongrel asked. "I thought you were joking about that."

Captain Pete laughed, seeming to be back in a good mood. He kept hobbling and said nothing, and Mongrel knew better by now not to try to extract any information out of him. He followed along quietly, wary of what was to come. What the hell did *other* mean anyway? And what was with all the walking? It's not like they were actually moving spatially.

After a moment noise began to filter in, as did light. Noises tuned themselves into words and phrases. Shapes coalesced into people and...fruit? Mongrel found himself standing in a market, indoors, surrounded by fruits and vegetables. People went out of their way to ignore him – as they should since he wasn't really there. Actually, where was he?

"Where am I?" he asked.

The old pirate hobbled his way over from the potatoes. "I don't bleedin' know! Look around! We're in a grocery store or somethin'. D'you think you can just get pineapples anywhere? Try gettin' one at me barn store! You won't leave happy!"

"No," Mongrel said, "I mean, where is the me that's supposed to be here? Or is there a me that's in this one?"

Captain Pete didn't answer right away, but looked around discretely.

---

[*] Which makes even less sense.

A Special Place In Hell

"So what are you saying?" a voice boomed somewhere ahead of them. *"You want a piece of me?"*

"Ah," the pirate pointed, "there ya be."

Mongrel turned to see himself over near the baked goods, looking a little older than he knew himself to be. His hair wasn't quite graying but laugh lines and crows feet and fanny cracks[*] were beginning to appear. His other self was facing a man he'd never met before. *"No, as a matter of fact, I don't. But I will take a piece of your mom –* that's *how I swing."*

The man smirked, apparently happy with the retort instead of angry. *"That's it old man. That's the monster. Show me what you got."*

Mongrel turned to walk away. *"You won't find what you want in me. I'm retired."*

"Retired? From what?" Mongrel looked at Captain Pete. "And did he just call me *old*? Who is that guy?"

The captain sighed with a retched slur. "There ya go again! Why d'you always think I knows everythin'? I don't know everyone you do, ya know!"

"I'm not here for training old man!" the man continued. *"I don't need training. Hell, I trained Yoda! I'm here to beat you!"*

"What did he say about Yoda?" Mongrel asked, drawing closer to his other self.

At that point the other Mongrel stopped, and turned his head slightly. *"What did you say about jedi master Yoda?"*

Other folks began taking notice of the argument, but tried to go about their business.

"I was Yoda's master," the man said smugly. *"We battled all the time, you know, as part of training. And he was fine when I started teaching him., but I guess one too many blows to the head...that's why he talks funny."* He began laughing sadistically.

Mongrel turned to glare down the stranger. *"No one makes fun of jedi master Yoda."*

Mongrel had never seen himself this way; he looked...evil.

"So you want a piece of me now or what?"

---

[*] A fanny crack is when your forehead wrinkles arch together in the middle, appearing like a butt crack.

Random Tangent

"*That and a piece of every one of these cakes.*" Mongrel spread his arms wide, drawing attention to the abundance of pastries. "*I like to blend them together to make new cakes. But I always let my pet hamster try it first. If she likes it then I'll eat it.*"

The man spat on the floor. "*You get a piece of me and that piece will kick your ass from the inside out. But that's not it, cause after that it'll absorb into your blood stream – but it won't become a part of you, no; you'll become a part of me. See, that piece will infect you, and slowly, you'll change into me. That's how I make my clones.*"

Mongrel yawned. "*Tough guy, huh? My yawns are so powerful they've been known to bring satellites in from orbit.*"

"*Oh yeah? My lungs are so strong that if I sneeze against the wind I can make the seasons change early.*"

"*Yeah I guess that's pretty good.*" Mongrel shrugged. "*But I can tie my shoes with my feet.*"

"*I'm a world-class kickboxer.*" The man danced a little jig, showing the dexterity of his lower appendages. "*Probably the best in the world. I can actually kick your ass without using my feet.*"

Mongrel rubbed his chin furtively. "*I don't know... I mean, if you don't even use your feet, it can't really be kickboxing, can it? Maybe you're not doing it right. Me on the other hand, I once kicked a retarded kid so hard he gained a hundred IQ points. I think he went on to win a Nobel prize or something.*"

"Oh this is *so* cool!" Mongrel said, nearly boiling over with excitement. "I've always wanted to watch one of these! And I get to see myself in action? Awesome!"

"*Trust me, I know how to use my feet. I can kick you in places you never knew you had, like the back of the face. I can even kick your ass over the phone. Of course, I never need to use a phone. I can yell so loud that wherever the person I want to talk to is can hear me. I usually refrain from doing this, however, because the power of my voice can level city blocks, kill animals, and cause thousands to go deaf.*"

"*Well I can shove a fart back into an ass!*" Mongrel was more proud of this feat than he dared to let on. "*Can you do that?*"

The man spit on the floor again, bothered by this because he could not. "*No. But when I fart you'll get third-degree burns. And*

A Special Place In Hell

that's even if I don't light my fart on fire. I don't do that anymore. I did that once in the Sahara Forest. I'm sure you know it's a desert now."

"I do," Mongrel nodded. *"I can rip out a man's hair from the inside-out."*

"I once beat a man to death with his own corpse."

"You're quite violent, aren't you?" Mongrel asked the man.

He nodded enthusiastically. *"Makes me happy. I can arm wrestle myself!"* he shouted like a small, proud child. Then he proceeded to do so.

"I'm not allowed to burp in public anymore without at least a two hour warning, you know, because of all the property damage and hearing loss." Mongrel was ashamed to admit this but he'd never admit it.

"You're not so tough," the man said. Mongrel wasn't sure whether this was to himself, whom he'd just beaten in arm wrestling, or to him. *"I wipe my ass with steel wool and floss with barbed wire."*

"I am too tough!" Mongrel retorted. *"Tougher than you. I survived my own abortion!"*

"Yeah! That's it!" Mongrel cried, cheering himself on.

"Well I was born ten months premature!"

Mongrel laughed. *"And I bet you had your beard when you were born too?"*

"That's right!" he grabbed his beard and yanked it up over his head. *"And I trim this baby daily with a chainsaw!"* He paused and seemed to reflect on this. *"Looks like I could use a shave too. My five o'clock shadow appears at noon."*

"I iron my shirts while I'm still wearing them." Mongrel then looked down at the shirt he was wearing. *"Well, not this one."*

"Ironing your shirt is good, but it won't help you in a race."

The way Mongrel's face produced the expression of confusion was enough to make some of the other shoppers sick.

"Drag coefficient," the man explained, although this failed to help. *"See, when I run, I use a special, streamlined suit. Of course, I don't really need it. Even without it I'm so fast I can run around the world and high-five myself."*

Random Tangent

Mongrel looked worried. "Come on, me, I can do better than that."

"Well look, you seem like a pretty tough guy, but you got nothing on me. And if I can't beat you with my awe-inspiring strength, I'll beat you with my mental superiority. I know everything, man. I know the end of pi; it's three. Wait, now you know. I mean... it's four. Yeah."

By this time other folks had begun together around to watch the two men argue. Some were even placing bets.

"You are not *superior to me,"* the stranger said. *"I can make lemonade out of orange juice – and it's way better!"*

"I build nuclear reactors out of wood and give them to the Chinese."

"Do they work?" he seemed genuinely interested.

"Of course they work!"

"Then you should give one to me, not the damn Chinese. I hate the Chinese!" the man shuddered, suggesting that he found them more repugnant than detestable. *"They won't let me in. That's why they got that wall."*

"I hate spoons," Mongrel admitted. "Can't use 'em. Not even with soup. Man, soup is a bitch!" He shook his head, thinking about soup and how much he loathed it.

"Aliens exist, you know. The only reason they haven't invaded is because they're waiting for me to die. They don't like me. I don't know why. I'm a pretty nice guy, aren't I?"

Mongrel thought this over. "Well, aside from the violent tendencies, yeah, I guess so. And I know that aliens exist; I was up on the mothership once. They worship fries."

"Some people have belly button rings and they were different ones every day. I wear different belly buttons every day." The man lifted up his shirt to reveal his choice for today. Some people applauded.

Mongrel looked around at all the people who had stopped shopping and were now watching the fight. "I've never gotten an applause," he said, somewhat dejected.

Captain Pete mimicked patting him on the back. "Cause y'ain't that good."

"Am too," Mongrel muttered under his breath.

A Special Place In Hell

"*You see this scar?*" the man pointed to an area just under his right nipple, which was unusually shiny. "*Surgery. I had this nipple implanted after my old one rotted and fell off – it's true what they say about eating your vegetables. I had it chrome plated before they attached it.*"

Mongrel inspected the scar. "*Cool. But check this out: I'm the only one who's allowed to talk about Fight Club.*"

"Yes! Fight Club!" Mongrel shouted. "I love that movie. Don't you?" he asked Captain Pete, who said nothing because he'd never seen it.

"*Meh,*" the man shrugged, "*I didn't care for that movie. Too violent. And I know that's oxymoronic cause I like violence, but I like oxymorons even more. Here's one: I can make fire using ice cubes.*"

"*Speaking of fire, there's a special place in Hell reserved just for me. Level fourteen, I think. I know Hell is only supposed to go down to level nine, but, well, they're giving me fourteen. That's what I was told anyway.*"

"Arr!" Captain Pete arred. "Tis true."

"*Why fourteen?*" asked the man.

"*I don't know, but I'm gonna ask when I get there.*"

The man nodded, accepting this answer. "*I intend to live forever. I'm eating the hearts of babies to help.*"

"Ew!" Mongrel cried. "*Gross. I hate babies. Taste like…gah! I wouldn't want to live forever, and I don't plan to. But I do plan to speak at my eulogy.*"

"*I can lift myself up over my head.*"

Someone in the throng of shoppers who'd stopped to watch the fight shouted, "*Kick his ass, Hank!*"

Mongrel yawned again. "*I can dig half a hole.*"

"*You're yawning an awful lot. You tired, or am I boring you?*"

"*No, no. I mean, yes, you're boring me, but I'm not tired.*" He yawned some more. "*I have to be put in a coma each night to sleep, otherwise my snoring wakes me up.*"

"*I can't sleep. I actually can't. Tried everything. Sleeping pills do nothing. Tranquilizers make me blink more, but that's it.*"

"*I blink a lot, and I can blink so fast I can put out fires.*"

Random Tangent

"My parents used to rip me in half so I would learn how to heal from it," said the man, whose name was apparently Hank. "Now I've built up an immunity."

"My parents locked me in a box with wild chipmunks as a punishment."

"I think I've used that one before, although it's true," Mongrel said. "Dammit, he's beating me. I'm better than this!"

"I lost my virginity before my parents did," Hank said.

"Until a botched surgery a few years back I could swallow a rubic's cube whole and shit it out solved. I sued over it, and I think that's one of the reasons the hospital is on strike."

"I'm a mountain tamer."

Mongrel dug a pinky finger into his right ear and wiggled it around. "What? A mountain lion tamer?"

"No, a mountain tamer. I hunt down and catch wild mountains. Then I tame them so they're easier to climb."

"Damn, this guy is good," Mongrel said, shaking his head. Captain Pete nodded in agreement.

The other Mongrel was also impressed. "What a useful public service. My uncle was castrated when the cat that was sleeping in his lap had a nightmare."

Hank's eyes narrowed. Mongrel's eyes widened; he knew that look. "He's not..."

"I'm just a figment of your imagination. I don't even exist!"

A hush descended upon the crowd. Dust seemed to drift in from parts unknown. Both Mongrels were speechless. Hank stood there, impressively smug with himself.

"That's my line!" Mongrel finally shouted. "He can't! He just...he can't..."

Captain Pete began laughing.

The crowd that had gathered began chanting, "Hank! Hank! Hank!"

The Mongrel on deck tried to compose himself. "When...when I switched companies to save m-money on car insurance, I saved all of it." He looked around sheepishly. "I don't...I don't pay anything now."

Hank closed in on him. "Before I showed him the light, James Bond drank his martinis stirred."

A Special Place In Hell

"I hear voices!" Mongrel cried, backing away from Hank. *"They talk to me, but they're long-distance, and I have to pay for the collect calls."*

"I can read lips with my eyes closed. I can speak Braille. I can talk to mimes."

"No," Mongrel whispered, tears welling in his eyes. He didn't want to watch, but couldn't look away. "No, this can't be happening."

Captain Pete rolled on the floor, he was laughing so hard.

It was obvious that the Mongrel in this universe was shaken to his core. He didn't really know what to do; this had never happened before. Fighting to speak over Hank and the crowd, he tried his best. *"I...I-I can skip backwards."*

Hank continued stalking closer and closer to Mongrel. *"I can build snowmen in the summer, and I can build trees – that's right,* build *'em! I can conjure the sun at night, or the dark in the morning. I eat lunch for breakfast!"*

Still backing away into the produce aisles, trying to put some distance between Hank and himself, Mongrel fought for the words. *"I...I..."* Then he tripped over an onion that was laying on the floor, and crashed into a basket full of them. They tumbled all over him and rolled away in every direction. When the mayhem had finally diminished, Mongrel looked up at Hank, who was looming over him, with an odd smirk on his face.

"And I can kick you ass in a bullshit fight," he said.

The crowd went wild.

Mongrel's jaw hit the floor, and his eyes widened so much they hurt. This...just couldn't be. It *couldn't!* He'd never lost before. He could see tears welling up in his double's eyes, and feel them stinging his own. His heart went out to himself.

Captain Pete meanwhile was laughing himself into a coma. He'd never seen anything so funny. The look on not just one of Mongrel's faces, but two! Failure in stereo. Priceless. This had been worth all the effort.

"I hate onions," Mongrel muttered, picking himself up off the floor.

Hank turned to him and offered a helping hand, smiling broadly, but Mongrel swatted it away, thinking that getting up himself somehow left him with more dignity. He had trouble enough as it was not breaking down and balling like a baby. Drawing himself to his feet, he looked around at all the faces that had witnessed his defeat. They all seemed somewhat pleased – whether with Hank's victory or with Mongrel's loss – he couldn't say.

Still smiling, Hank said something to his defeated rival, but Mongrel had stopping paying attention to the scene, unable to focus on anything other than his own defeat. It was probably something to do with Mongrel putting up a good fight and being the best he'd ever fought and that even though he won he was still the world's biggest ass, he surmised.

"This didn't actually happen, did it?" He turned to look at Captain Pete, who was still busy laughing so hard he could barely breathe. But he was a ghost after all, so it shouldn't have concerned him anyway. Rolling in mid air, kicking his little pegged pirate legs, tears streaming down his face, struggling to catch his breath, the old pirate just couldn't contain himself.

"Hey," Mongrel grumbled, "it's not *that* funny."

The Mongrel in the scene said something about this not being the end of something, and that he hadn't seen the last of someone, and then the scene stopped. The darkness slowly enveloped them once again. Captain Pete continued laughing uncontrollably.

"Okay, okay! That's enough!" Mongrel cried, annoyed beyond even his most forgiving standards. "You've had your fun. Now can I just go home?"

But the good captain was laughing too hard to hear him. Slowly, however, the laughing turned into an uneasy hacking. Then the hacking gave way to some rough coughing, which proceeded to transform into choking. Captain Pete tried to grab his throat, but not being composed of flesh and blood or anything pertaining to a physical presence, he couldn't.

Mongrel watched, alarmed, but didn't know if he should do anything, like help. In his defense, what could he have done to help a ghost anyway?

Soon Captain Pete, having given up on trying to grab his neck, began grabbing fitfully at the nothingness, which, obviously

A Special Place In Hell

and appropriately, given its name, did nothing. After a moment of this, his arms slowly slackened to his sides, and the coughing, hacking, wheezing noises grew fainter. Then they faded away altogether, and the blackness became severely quiet.

"Pete?" Mongrel asked when he couldn't stand the silence any longer.

The captain remained quiet. Deadly quietly.

He walked over to the body of his former friend-turned-torturer; he looked dead. "Hey." He tried to nudge him with his foot, but ended up putting his foot through the captain's head, literally. This didn't seem to affect the old pirate; he remained lifeless (well, even more so), staring up at the nothingness.

"This is *not* my fault," Mongrel said. "I didn't...I mean I tried to..." he stopped, realizing that he was now talking to himself.

The scene had faded away and he was all alone. Looking around, and only knowing he was doing so because he could feel the muscles in his neck moving, he tried to find some indication of what his course of action should be. But he found nothing. He stood there, not knowing what to do.

"Crap! Now how am I supposed to get home?"

The End

What Mongrel has yet to fully comprehend is that nearly everything Captain Pete had shown him was real. Captain Pete was really a ghost, and he was shown four mostly true glimpses of his past, present, and future. What *is* up for debate is just which was which, and whether or not the good captain had gotten them in proper order. Shamus Bond would indeed make another attempt on Mongrel's life sooner or later, but one of his crew will not be going along. Mongrel's father, Pharquard, had once had a business contract with the famed one-man mafia Bossa Nova, but the details, at least for the time being, are sketchy at best. Beby could possibly be the love of Mongrel's life, but it will take a miracle for her to realize this. Biscuits had been practically adopted by Mongrel once before, and while it's unlikely that it will happen again, he is the

Random Tangent

only person (other than his former slave master, Almighty Frank) the boy knows, and in order for him to be released from Duntt Pen he'll need a place to stay. Hank, if that is his real name, remains anonymous. Oh, and Captain Pete laughed himself into a coma, and Death was not pleased with him at all. So it pulled the figurative plug, complaining that the old pirate had been a lousy ghost.

The Importance Of Being Constantly Surprised

The Importance Of Being Constantly Surprised

Mongrel Stevens' life was not making much sense. In fact, his life had not been making much sense for quite some time. Just look at some of the things that have recently happened to him: he'd adopted a slave – a youngish boy[*] named Biscuits – who'd killed his mother over some cookies. So the lad was sentenced to a few years in prison, not over her death, however, but because of his illiteracy. Then when Mongrel came to visit the murderous dog, a complex series of misunderstandings led him to become the boy's new cellmate. If that wasn't enough, Mongrel had an insanely improbable pet known as a mon, kept in contact with the Grim Reaper himself, and had a former friend named Captain Pete who kept dying around him, yet seemed perfectly healthy upon their next meeting, and completely aware of the circumstances – and not too happy about them.

Oh, and let's not forget all the people trying to kill him. The head of the Dunttstown mafia, Bossa Nova, a British anti-agent named Shamus Bond, and...well that's about it. Still, two professional killers out for your blood would be enough to make you question your life's choices. Sometimes Mongrel figured he'd

---

[*] Biscuits was actually in his late teens, but due to his lack of upbringing, had the mind of a child. Thusly everyone treated him as such.

be better off spending the entire day in bed, refusing to interact with the outside world on any level.

Today would have been a great day for that, but unfortunately fate had other plans. He woke up screaming, much like he often did, and sat bolt upright in bed. He'd just woken from the worst nightmare ever – which was within the second-worst nightmare ever, like a dream within a dream. Then he stopped screaming because it hurt. Sitting up also hurt. He grabbed his head, but grabbing hurt too, both his hand and head.

Everything hurt!

"Shut up!" someone yelled.

"Mon? You okay," someone far closer asked.

Wondering what he'd done in his sleep to cause his body to be in so much pain, Mongrel jerked his head around, trying to see who was talking. It was still dark, so he couldn't see much. A quick scan around his bed revealed nothing, but someone was in his house. *In his freaking room!* Was he being robbed?

A clang echoed through his room, followed by footsteps. Someone else was coming.

Suddenly a shadow jumped in front of him, and he shot back in fright, hitting a wall that must have been only inches away from him. Searing pain shot up and down his spine. He tried to cry out in pain, but bit his tongue instead.

"You okay?" the voice asked again, so close now that Mongrel could touch it. So he did, thrashing his legs all over the shadow that contained the voice and hurting himself even more in the process.

"Ow! Ow, ow, ow!" the voice cried. A *familiar* voice, now that Mongrel thought about it. "Mon, its me! Stop!"

The footsteps stopped in front of Mongrel's bed. Then a bright light was in his face.

"You two pipe down in here or I'll throw you in the hole!"

"No, no," the shadow cried. "We be good!"

Mongrel held a hand up to shield his eyes, wondering whose voice it was. Then the light moved away from his face and over to the shadow, giving his eyes a chance to adjust to the illumination. They slowly focused, and he saw the flashlight. Then he followed the stream of light and saw…Biscuits.

The Importance Of Being Constantly Surprised

He wasn't at home at all.

Worse – far worse – he was in prison.

It wasn't just a bad dream – it was real. This didn't surprise him, although it probably should have. Given the road his life was on it made sense somehow. There was probably an important lesson in all of this, but for the life of him he just didn't care to learn it. He began to wonder, which was worse; being in the living nightmare of a dream world, or being in the living nightmare that was prison? At least in the dream world his head didn't hurt.

"Don't make me come back here," said the man with the flashlight. The light then shot away and footsteps moved back in the direction from which they came. A minute later another clang belted throughout the cellblock.

Still pressed up against the wall, and still in a frightening amount of pain, Mongrel felt like crying. He remembered *not* being in prison. He remembered being in his comfy bed. He remembered…Captain Pete.

His *actual* dream began floating back to him. Then he remembered Shamus Bond, and some other British people. And he remembered…his dad! He saw his dad! And…Bossa Nova? Yes, he saw Bossa Nova too. He also remembered someone named Hank. Bits and pieces were flying all over his mind, trying to come back to him but not knowing where to land. His head swam, and he felt woozy from the trauma, half mental and half physical.

Wait a second – if his dream was actually real, then was the dream within the dream real too? Oh man…

Biscuits hopped over to him, wary of the threat of more leg trashing. "You okay?"

Slinking back down into his bed and blanket, he muttered, "No," and turned to face the wall, eager to fall back to sleep and get away from this world – but hopefully not into a dream like the last one.

Indeed, Mongrel's life was not making much sense. Although when you think about it, is it really so hard to believe? After all, how much sense does something need to make to be sensible? And how little sense is required to be considered senseless? It's generally a matter of opinion. Or sanity. There's a saying that suggests truth is stranger than fiction, which is a load of

Random Tangent

rubbish if you put enough thought into it. Simply imagine the strangest true thing you can think of, and then picture it inside-out, covered in bionic mushrooms, and on fire at the bottom of the ocean, where it's being eaten by anorexic, constipated flying purple gerbils. I rest my case.

Morning came too soon. Last night's nightmare tricked Mongrel's brain into thinking he hadn't gotten any sleep at all. If he had to rise, he certainly wasn't going to shine.

When the bell echoed through the halls he tried to ignore it. When all the cell doors opened with a deafening clang, he tried to ignore that too. He also ignored Biscuits when he hoped off the top bunk, scrambled to arrange and tidy the cell, and attempted to get him up. He ignored the clamour of inmates rising and doing the same as his cellmate, and he ignored the guards inspecting their work. He even ignored the footsteps as they approached his cell, the authoritative cough, and the yelling to get up. What he couldn't ignore was the wallop on the head to get him to pay attention.

"Get the fuck up you maggot!"

Mongrel rolled off his slab of concrete and out of his paper-like suggestion of a blanket, holding his head, trying to suck it up and be a man. Like a newborn yak, he staggered to his feet, not making a peep, and nervously tried to look the guard in the eye.

The guard, however, made eye contact difficult; he was a big guy. He towered over Mongrel and most of the other prisoners by nearly a foot. His eyes were the colour of anger. Veins bulged out of his neck. His hair was sparse and matted, and looked very uncomfortable on his head, almost like it wanted to jump off. His nametag read McCulloch, and he was far scarier than any of the inmates Mongrel had met so far. Here's why:

McCulloch smashed his club over Mongrel's head again. This wasn't for the hell of it, or to please him in any way; it was simply because he could.

"Why aren't you in your uniform?"

Mongrel lay in a crumpled pile of flesh and bones on the floor. With the air of a drunkard he began searching for the way back to his feet. He was not successful.

The Importance Of Being Constantly Surprised

Biscuits meanwhile was valiantly blending into the surroundings and not drawing any attention to himself.

"I asked you a question, maggot!" He bent down and threw Mongrel into a standing position, only to swat him down again to the floor.

"Cause it's not mine?" Mongrel wheezed out. Birds and stars and…goldfish…circled his head. So much for sleeping in, he thought.

Suddenly the floor fell away from him, and he was face-to-face, upside-down, with the guard again, who was holding him up by his belt and growling.

When James McCulloch was just a little guy he was still pretty big. Other kids at school were too afraid of him to want to be friends. Teachers were too afraid of him to give him bad grades, even when he'd earned them. His parents were there for him, but only physically. When he was in his early teens they'd both hit each other in a bizarre head-on collision, and while they survived, both ended up comatose. At the Dunttstown Al-Mustah Hospital[*] they were both declared 'medically fit for sustained periods of limited activity' and sent home for James to look after. James eventually grew into a violent young man and wound up with a job as a prison guard, which most felt was the perfect career choice for him.

"I suppose I could put it on though," Mongrel ventured before the oaf could say anything, "if it would make you happy."

McCulloch frowned. Or was that a smile? Mongrel was delicately placed back on the floor, where he tried to stay for a few minutes until a boot, rammed into his stomach, encouraged him to

---

[*] Named after Ichabod Al-Mustah, a scientist who had donated five-thousand dollars – by far the largest settlement[**] the hospital had ever received – after they cured his asparagus toe, a condition similar to athlete's foot in most respects, and is considered to be its twice-removed, retarded cousin. Ichabod had gone in for a routine visit to remove the warts on his buttocks, and inadvertently had other ailments treated, namely his asparagus toe, which he was researching. It took Ichabod another two years to develop the infection again.

[**] Because of his treatment, Ichabod incurred a setback in his research, and tried to sue the hospital. The judge who oversaw the case decided it was a stupid waste of time and reversed the charges, forcing Ichabod to pay the hospital instead. In order to save face, the settlement was disguised as a donation.

get moving. Then he woozily got changed into the uniform Biscuits had made for him.

As he did this, McCulloch surveyed the cell and, satisfied, patted Biscuits on his head, then left to inspect the next cell.

Once he'd left, Biscuits darted over to Mongrel. "You gotta be carful here," he said. "Just do what I say, okay? You gotta change; its rong."

Mongrel looked down to see that he'd put his uniform on backwards, and desperately wanted to pass his beating along to the boy – after all, it was partly his fault that he was in there – but figured now wasn't the best time. He began fixing his attire. "I shouldn't even be here."

"I know." Biscuits tried to help Mongrel dress, but was shoved away. "I don't know where Jay went."

"Who's Jay?"

"The guy whos supozed to be here."

The sounds of random shouts and beatings wandered over to them. Mongrel purposely didn't look to see what was going on, lest the guard come back and to give him some more permanent bruises for not minding his own business.

"Well we need to tell someone. If I stay here much longer my head will cave in from the beatings." Mongrel thought for a moment. "I just need to talk to the Chief. Can you get me to him?"

"I'll try."

"Alright maggots, line up!"

The sounds of a thousand footsteps and shuffling bodies resonated throughout the cellblock. Biscuits rushed out of the cell to join the rest of the inmates, who were all lined up along a blue line running the length of the hallway. Worried that his next beating could be the straw that breaks the camel's back and leave him permanently colorblind, Mongrel quickly finished getting dressed and joined them, squeezing in between the boy and an older Mexican named Solvo. Actually, Mongrel couldn't say he was Mexican, he just *appeared* that way. His new year's resolution that year had been to stop judging people by their appearances, since many judged him that way (most believing him to be as stupid as he looked, if not more so); this Solvo could've just had a great tan.

"Move out!"

The Importance Of Being Constantly Surprised

As one unit, with the exception of Mongrel, who tried as best he could to pretend he knew what he was doing, everyone turned to their right, and began marching towards a door at the end of the hall. Biscuits followed a little too closely behind Mongrel for his liking. He knew it was probably just how prisons were, with everyone crammed in small place after small place, but he wasn't used to having his personal space being molested. He tried to ignore it, focusing on the back of Solvo's head and trying to keep his distance (but not looking like he was trying to keep his distance). He tried to march casually, but he was still sore from the previous day's assault, and limped and hobbled his way across the floor. When passing through the door, he realized it was the same one Biscuits had taken him through when they'd gone to visit DERFtron. Turning his head back towards Biscuits as he marched, he asked, "Where are we going?"

Solvo answered him instead in what sounded like a deep Mexican accent. "Breakfast."

Mongrel looked at his watch, needing confirmation of the time. Then a thought occurred to him: maybe his watch was the reason for his troubles in the first place. Had he been relying on someone else for the time he might have been forced to wait until regular visiting hours to see Biscuits. This mess could have been avoided.

On the other hand, the Chief didn't have to let Mongrel in to see him, or at least could've gotten him to sign that stupid guest list. Abegale didn't have to leave him alone inside the cellblock, letting him run amuck with the boy. And Biscuits sure as hell didn't have to knit him this ridiculous uniform. No, there were far more people to blame for his problems than himself. Rarely, he figured, were any of his misfortunes his own fault.

"I'm not that hungry," he lied. Having not eaten much of anything for nearly a day, Mongrel could probably be talked into eating anything. Even rotting pig vomit wasn't out of the question, so raging was his hunger.

Looking back over his shoulder at him, Solvo gave him a surprised look. "But today is leftover day!" Biscuits seemed to perk up at this announcement.

Random Tangent

"What's leftover day?" Mongrel asked, staring at Solvo's thin mustache, and silently berating himself for *still* judging him to be a Mexican.

"They put all the leftover food from the past week's meals into a big pot and cook it, and make new meals from it. It's *so* good!"

"Oh…boy!" Mongrel quipped, not able to find the words to properly express his disgust. "So does that mean some of the food is, like, a week old?"

Neither man answered his question. Solvo because he was pondering the ramifications of seven-day-old food; Biscuits because he had no idea how long a week was.

Mongrel didn't need a response to know that he wouldn't be partaking in the Dunttstown Penitentiary breakfast experience. "Well now I'm *really* not hungry."

After marching down a myriad of corners and corridors they entered the food court, where meals were prepared and eaten. The air smelled, naturally, of rotting pig vomit, which Mongrel supposed was breakfast. Just what were they feeding these inmates anyway?

Deciding that he'd rather starve than eat rotting pig vomit, Mongrel quickly pulled Biscuits aside. "If I stay here much longer my stomach is gonna get the better of me and I might start eating that." He was referring to the stench of breakfast. "Do you know where the Chief's office is?"

The boy nodded.

"You need to take me there, like, now."

Biscuits clearly didn't like this idea. "But its left over day. Let's do it after."

"No, now. I'll bring you lots of leftovers when I get out of here."

"And cookies?"

"What?"

"You bring me cookies too?"

Growing up as a slave in Almighty Frank's dungeon had left the boy alarmingly ill-prepared for life in the real world. His experience with food was primarily leftovers from Frank's illustrious meals; the rare dish of what he called 'unused food' was

The Importance Of Being Constantly Surprised

something to behold and celebrate, and usually obtained through thievery, or on the odd occasion when his master was exceptionally pleased with him. Once on the outside the boy had developed a penchant, then an obsession, with sweets, mainly cookies. It was this obsession that led him to brutally murder Mongrel's mother with a hammer.

In prison, however, the boy found routine, guidance, education, and stability. He found it quite similar to his life as a slave, only he was given more freedom, better clothing, and his food actually came on a plate. To say the least, he was thriving in Duntt Pen. He was gaining an education and making friends. He was avoiding all the worst things of prison life, such as the shankings and rapings[*]; in fact he was rather well liked by most of the inmates and guards – particularly McCulloch, who'd taken a severe liking to the boy, treating him almost like a son.

"Okay, fine," Mongrel agreed. "I'll bring you whatever you want. Just get me out of here."

The boy smiled liked he'd just won the lottery. He grabbed Mongrel's hand and led him around the various tables and groups of inmates sitting down to eat, over to the far side of the room and out into another hallway.

"So you really know your way around this place?" Mongrel asked.

"Yep," Biscuits nodded.

If Mongrel had truly believed in the boy's navigational skills he would have made one more request: avoid any guards. As a result, they rounded a single corner and ran into McCulloch.

"Good morning," he said.

Mongrel and Biscuits stopped in their tracks. They didn't say anything, but looked guilty.

McCulloch didn't say anything else; he just eyed them suspiciously, expectantly, like he was waiting for them to make a move. His eyes dared them to.

Finally, Mongrel thought he'd say something. "Uh, I don't know how good it is, but I'll agree with you on the morning part."

---

[*] The prisoners all agreed not to rape the boy, figuring that it would be akin to beating up a retarded kid. Naturally there were some inmates that enjoyed this particular pastime, and protested this special treatment.

Random Tangent

The guard smiled, but it came out more like a sneer. "Funny. And where are you two heading on this plain ol' regular morning?"

"Gotta see the Cheef," Biscuits spouted.

"Oh, not before breakfast!" This sounded like the worst idea in the history of ideas to McCulloch. "It's leftover day!"

This did not have to be explained to Biscuits, as he was already sold on the idea. Mongrel, on the other hand, was not for sale. "We're not that hungry," he said.

The guard didn't seem amused by this. He'd taken an immediate disliking to Mongrel and wanted to throw his weight around and break in the new guy. His sneer skewed straight into a scowl. "Look, newbie, you must have arrived yesterday on my day off, so someone forgot to brief you proper. See, around here, you do as I say, or I'll do as I please to your face." He hunkered down, getting face to face with Mongrel. "Now I've been going easy on you so far, but that'll change quick, fast, and in a hurry if you don't march in there and *eat*."

He screamed the last word so loud Mongrel thought he'd lost a layer of skin, and his ears rang for a few minutes afterward. Unable to hear himself, he was pretty sure he said, "I'm not a prisoner. I was visiting Biscuits and got stuck here. The Chief will understand. That's why I need to see him."

McCulloch put his hand to his chin and seemed to ponder this. "That so?"

Still not able to hear properly, Mongrel had to rely on his near-crap ability to read lips, and thought the guard was calling him a 'fatso.' He looked down at his belly and could almost feel his stomach beginning to digest itself. Leftovers almost sounded appetizing. But getting out of prison was more important than eating, and he could celebrate his freedom with a sandwich.

The guard too looked down at Mongrel's uniform. "Then where'd you get your little pj's there?"

"What?"

"You almost had me there Stevens. Now go get breakfast."

His hearing beginning to return, Mongrel couldn't believe what he thought he'd heard. "No, it's true! Take me to the Chief! You'll see."

The Importance Of Being Constantly Surprised

"Might surprise you to know then that the Chief left for vacation earlier this morning." He chuckled as he revealed this juicy bit of information.

Mongrel was indeed surprised. He looked to the floor as his brain quietly talked amongst itself about what to do. "Ah!" he finally said. "What about officer Switchblade?"

"Switchblade? That freak o' nature? He don't come in here. He runs the cop shop. Now you go to *break*fast or I'll break something else for ya."

Freak of nature? Mongrel thought. But he said, "Not *that* Switchblade. I meant Abegale."

"Oh, she's got the next few days off I believe."

Now Mongrel's surprise was reaching epic proportions. How long was a 'few days'? How long would it be before someone could straighten this all out? How long was he going to have to fend for himself? He hadn't even been in prison a whole day, and look at the shape he was in. His body couldn't wait that long; he'd leave Duntt Penn in a body bag. He looked to Biscuits, who said nothing and appeared to have no idea how bad this turn of events was. "So…um…what do we do then?" he asked.

McCulloch hunched down so he could get face to face with Mongrel again, and then got in his face. "You're gonna go eat leftovers like good little girls. And if you have any problems with leftovers, it'll be Dirt For Desert for the rest of the week. I'm in charge of every waking moment of your life from now on. You are *my playthings*. So you might want to start doing what I say before I decide start playing mean with my toys." Satisfied he'd done just the right amount of threatening, he straightened back up and crossed his arms, mustering all the menace he could and throwing it into a glare.

Feeling as though a hole was being burned through his skull, Mongrel turned and skulked back into the lunch room with Biscuits, although now he *really* wasn't hungry.

That was it. He was trapped here. Not for long, sure, but for long enough. If what he'd experienced of prison life in only a few hours was any indication, he wouldn't *survive* a few days. It was like a death sentence. He looked down at his ugly orange uniform; he didn't want to die in that colour.

Random Tangent

Wallowing in his own self-pity, Mongrel aimlessly followed Biscuits through the lines and smells before he realized it he was sitting at a table with a tray of food in front of him, although the only reason he could call it food was because someone asked him if he was going to eat it.

"Huh?" Mongrel asked, finally coming around. He'd been staring into space, lost in his own miserable thoughts for some time. A Mexican accent broke his lack of concentration.

"You going to eat that?" It was Solvo, sitting across from him. Biscuits had sat him down at a table that his friends were sitting at.

"Are you Mexican?" Mongrel blurted out, deciding to get to the bottom of things.

Solvo shook his head and simply said, "No."

"Oh." He didn't press for more, figuring if he wasn't at the bottom, then halfway down was good enough. Mongrel looked at his tray, inspecting the three amorphous blobs quivering on it. One was a dark shade of green that he instinctively though was pure mold. Another appeared to be shredded meat in a thick sauce. The third looked moderately less repulsive. If he had to guess, he figured it was a variety of vegetables ground up and slopped into a bowl. Keeping it, he slid the mold mound and meat jell-o across to Solvo, who eagerly accepted them.

"So you got something against Mexicans?" he asked.

"What? No."

"Well you asked if I were Mexican before giving this to me. What if I were Mexican? Would you still have given it to me?"

Mongrel shrugged and said, "Got nothing against Mexicans. Just curious. You still could've had my food. Waste not want not."

Solvo chewed some green mould for a bit, pondering this. "Well actually I guess you could call me Mexican if you want," Solvo finally confessed. "It's where I'm from. Or at least my parents. It's in my blood, right? But I've never been there."

Mongrel nodded but wasn't listening, instead focusing on what remained on his tray. He studied the vegetable pudding, trying to figure out what it really was, what vegetables may be involved. Finally deciding there was only one way to find out, he picked up a

The Importance Of Being Constantly Surprised

dull (in every sense of the word) fork and scooped up a small amount. Bringing it gingerly to his face, he sniffed it. When suicide didn't spring to mind as being preferable to ingesting it, he put it in his mouth.

Regretting it immediately, he reluctantly swallowed. Then Mongrel put his fork back down, knowing he was done eating. Perhaps that small amount of food would last him a while. Didn't most reptiles eat once a month or something? He just had to think like a snake.

Sitting to his right, Biscuits was giving the impression that he was starving, gobbling down his food like he thought someone might take it from him, which was likely his motivation. Between mouthfuls he spouted, "Try this," and tapped Mongrel's cup. "It's good."

Mongrel reached for it, but didn't believe what the boy had said. It was filled with a cloudy fluid that smelled...not bad. He shrugged, and drank a small portion. After a moment to assess the flavour, he decided it was good. *Really* good. He drank some more. Damn, it was delicious! He could only describe it as every fruit flavour mixed together to create some super juice – which, giving the day's theme, was probably exactly what it was.

He wanted to gorge himself on it, but knew that would end the goodness too soon, and Mongrel didn't like the prospect of seconds in this place. Now he knew why leftover day was so adored. He began to relax and savour his tasty beverage, and somehow things didn't seem so bad in there. He settled down with his cup and tried to be deaf and apathetic, but it did not come easily to him.

"...You haven't heard about the meltdown in Shchevret? Whole place went nuclear a month ago..."

"...And frankly, I don't think I'm being raped enough..."

"...Oh yeah, hookers are expensive these days. I usually split one with someone..."

"...And that's what I told him – it's a hobby. It ain't murder, it's recreational homicide..."

"...Puppies!"

Obviously he wasn't able to tune everything out.

Random Tangent

Then the bell rang. Inmates began to gather up, signaling what Mongrel assumed was the end of breakfast. He quickly downed the rest of his delicious juice and hopped to his feet to follow Biscuits and the others.

"So what's next?" he asked with newfound enthusiasm. "Probably better learn the routine if I'm gonna be here for a while."

"Cleaning," Solvo told him as they wandered back to the front of the cafeteria to return their trays. "We go back to the cell block and clean the place. Mail usually comes then too."

Mongrel nodded, somewhat interested. "Mail huh? And we can write people too?"

"Course," Solvo stated, matter-o-factly. "They encourage it. Keeps our minds on the outside world, so we don't forget. Get institutionalized."

They lined up as instructed by the guards and headed out, single file, marching back to their cells the same way they'd come. "Institutionalized?" Mongrel asked, but thinking more about this letter writing business. He could write someone, eh? Maybe send for help. But who would he write? And how long would it take to get there?

"Some people are in here for the long haul," Solvo said. "They forget what it's like out there in the real world if they're here long enough. Stop wanting out. Stop trying to get better, atoning for their sins and whatnot."

Mongrel walked behind him, half listening, half focused on his letter. He could write his lady, Beby, maybe. As irrational and short-tempered as she was, she was perhaps the sanest person he knew.

He stopped in his tracks. She was the *sanest* person he knew. Captain Pete, Big John Charlie Marbles, Almighty Frank, the Blind Cracka brothers, Officer Switchblade, Freddie Farcus, Emmanuel Cheeseburg, Elvis and the women from his fan club...was that the scope of his life and his connections in it? Everyone else he knew was either dead or wishing he was. Mongrel was surprised how lonely he suddenly fe–

"Keep moving, asshole," Someone said, shoving him from behind.

The Importance Of Being Constantly Surprised

Not turning around to see who it was, Mongrel made up his mind to contact her. It was a long shot, but what did he have to lose? He wasn't just going sit on his bruised ass and wait for help to arrive; he would be proactive.

"You give someone pieces of the outside and it brings 'em memories," Solvo was still going on. "That's why the Prison Sweethearts Program is so big; get us all women that we'll want to meet on the outside. Gives us motivation to get rehabilitated and get out."

"So you guys all got girlfriends?" Mongrel asked as they filed into their cell block.

Solvo shrugged. "Some of us do. Biscuits does."

Mongrel's eyes widened in disbelief. "*He's* got a girlfriend?" This practically came as a slap in the face to him. He'd been single for a long time, longer than he'd care to think about. But why? He was average looking, a pretty nice guy, and mentally competent – doubly so if compared to the rest of the bachelors in Dunttstown. He was by far a better specimen of a man than Biscuits was, wasn't he?

Or…maybe not. Loneliness crept into him. The female population by and large seemed to ignore him, and the scant few who didn't, like the ladies of the Evlis Fan Club, he desperately wished would. Dunttstown didn't exactly have a prime allotment of women (or men for that matter), but it did have Beby. For all her anger management issues and bizarre mood swings, she was irresistible when she wanted to be. But getting together with her would take a miracle.

And that was it. There were no other women in his life, and no one seemed the least bit interested in the joy (or misery) of his company. Maybe he should write someone else other than Beby? Branch out a bit? If Biscuits could pick up chicks, then why not him? Besides, he would never in his life be more of a badass than now, as a prisoner. And girls liked bad boys, didn't they? Couldn't hurt to try anyway.

"Halt!" someone shouted, and everyone came to a stop. Two of the guards, McCulloch and one Mongrel wasn't familiar with, did some sort of count, before relieving everyone their cleaning duties.

Random Tangent

Wandering into the cell behind Biscuits, Mongrel took survey of the area, of life behind bars. The cramped space left little room to breathe, and the rigid routine little room for individuality. How could one be themselves within such confines? They all dressed the same, shared the same space, ate the same food, etc. There was no room for anything else. Every waking moment controlled by someone else. An entire life squeezed into a cage, into its most basic functions. He couldn't imagine being forced to live there for years on end. "How do you do it?" he asked the boy.

Biscuits looked up at him, half-smiling, unsure if Mongrel was talking to him or himself.

"How do you live here? Mongrel asked again. "Like this?"

The boy's smile disappeared and he turned away. "You woodn't understand."

Mongrel sat down on one of the beds. "Why do you say that?"

Without turning to look at him, Biscuits grabbed a broom and began sweeping. "I know what everybody thinks of me." Before Mongrel could ask, the boy continued. "I'm not as stupid like everybody thinks. I know when you look at me and how the way you talk to me."

"What are you talking about?"

Biscuits didn't answer, and for a moment, remained silent. Then asked, "Do you know how old I am?"

Mongrel didn't, and said so.

Finally turning to look at him, Biscuits had tears in his eyes. "Neether do I. But you think I'm a children, cause that's how you treat me – like a children."

"Child," Mongrel corrected.

"You see? You still doing it! That's how everybody treats me." His voice grew louder, angrier. "Is that what I am to you?"

"W-what? No!"

"The life I had before...well, its not much diffrent then here. I grew up like a slave. A *slave*. I don't know my mom or dad, or how I got to be a slave. Locked up every nite in a cage, beaten all the time, fiteing for food. My life was hell. Then I meet you, and things got a little better, but you treated me like a children too."

The Importance Of Being Constantly Surprised

Biscuits then corrected himself, "Child. I don't want to be one anymore."

"Okay...so what do you want to be?" Mongrel asked.

The boy shrugged. "Just normal. I know I'm not normal. I didn't go to skool or have a normal life like everybody else, okay, so I don't know how to act or talk or anything. But that don't mean I'm a child. I just want to be treated like normal." Tears streaked down his cheeks.

Mongrel didn't know what to say, other than a meek, "Sorry." He was taken aback by this shocking revelation. He didn't know Biscuits carried around that much pain inside. Was he *that* bad to the boy?

What if Mongrel wasn't the saint he thought he was? He'd just learned yesterday that he was responsible for Derf now being a robot, and also hating his life. And what about Captain Pete? As much as Mongrel didn't want to admit, he had something to do with his habitual dying. Was it any wonder people were trying to kill him? Maybe he belonged here in prison. Maybe that was karma.

"Now I'm here," Biscuits continued, "and I like it. It mite not seem good to you, but this place is the best to me. I got friends, and I got food every day, and I'm learning from Derf. That's all I want."

Mongrel still didn't know what to say, but settled for, "Well I'm glad for you."

Anger no longer dwelled in the boy's eyes, but the pain was still there. "I'm glad I killed you mom. It was the best thing I ever did."

These were words Mongrel hadn't been ready to hear. When they passed into his ear canal, they slipped right by his eardrums like a thief sneaking passed a sleeping guard. The anger that had drained away from Biscuits found a new host in him. He stood up. "What did you say?"

"There a problem here?"

They both turned to see a guard standing in the cell's doorway.

"No," Biscuits quickly answered, wiping his face with his shirt sleeve.

Random Tangent

The guard studied them for a moment before letting the matter go. "Letter, kid," he said, tossing an envelope at Biscuits.

The boy fumbled for it, and ended up having to pick it up off the floor. He carefully held it close enough to his face to suggest he needed glasses. Suddenly he cried, "Sasha! Sasha!" and tore the letter open.

"Sasha?" Mongrel asked.

"Girlfriend," the guard explained.

"Ah," Mongrel sighed, the loneliness seeping back in and the anger returning to homelessness. He fancied that Biscuits' girlfriend was a dumpy little thing, covered in hairy warts and…no, that wasn't right. That wasn't fair to the boy. He was being petty. He was being a lousy friend. He was surprised at himself and how miserable it felt to be Mongrel Stevens.

"No mail for you," the guard said to him, "but you got a visitor."

This upset Mongrel. *Of course* he didn't have any mail; he'd been there for less than a day, and it takes longer than that for a letter to go through the post office. And besides, no one on the outside knew he was here. Unless the guard thought he was Biscuits' other cellmate, Ray, or whatever his name…wait, what?

"What?"

"Someone is here to see you," the guard spelled out for him. "Now go on. Ain't got all day."

Mongrel got up, giving Biscuits one last look as he left the cell. The boy seemed to have forgotten all about the confrontation as soon as his letter arrived. He was so excited with it that he didn't even notice Mongrel leave.

Looking around at the rest of the cell block, Mongrel tried to be happy for Biscuits, but jealousy kept rising to the top. All around him other inmates were getting mail, some supposedly from women on the outside. Others were busy cleaning with brooms and mops. One guy near the end of the room seemed to be dancing. Spinning around without a care, he strayed too close to a puddle of mop water, and slipped and crashed painfully to the hard concrete. No one else seemed to notice.

"You going or what?" The guard was pointing towards a door at the far end of the cell block.

The Importance Of Being Constantly Surprised

Two things went through Mongrel's mind: the first was that the guard had no idea who Mongrel was. This was probably because Mongrel wasn't actually a prisoner, and so the guard was not familiar with him, didn't know why he was in prison, or whether or not he was trustworthy, or sneaky, or anything. What if he tried to escape? What if he tried to murder someone? What if he took a huge dump in the hallway and wiped it all over the place? To just let him wander about the compound by himself was just gross job negligence.

The second thing that went through his mind he voiced out loud. "I don't know where to go."

The guard sighed. "Haven't you had a visitor before?" This must have been a rhetorical question, since he brushed passed Mongrel and led the way, not waiting for an answer.

Mongrel felt a pang of fury bend its way around his body. *Of course* he hadn't had a visitor before. He *was* a visitor. Were all the guards this stupid? It's no wonder all the prisoners were so hostile; even Mongrel felt like snapping and throttling the next person to cross him. He tried to conceal his rage as he followed the guard.

After a journey that Mongrel was certain he could not have made on his own, even with precise directions and a GPS, they arrived at what was apparently the visitation room. The guard ushered Mongrel inside, but didn't follow.

"You can find your way back?" the guard asked.

A quizzical look appeared on Mongrel's face as he tried to mentally retrace his steps to the cellblock. After a few seconds of this he felt like he was getting carsick. "No," he finally said.

The guard looked at him for a moment, not sure whether he believed what he'd heard. Then a smile broke ground on his face and he slapped Mongrel on the back. "Funny guy." With that, he left, presumably heading back to the cellblock to continue delivering mail.

Mongrel shook his head. Just what kind of prison was this anyway? How did it function like this? The more he thought about it the more he felt that this would be an awful place to have to live. It wouldn't even be nice to visit.

Random Tangent

He glanced around the visitation room; it certainly looked like the right place. He was on one side of a large room that was divided down the middle by a series of booths. The nearest one was occupied by someone named Shoon, who was talking to whom Mongrel assumed was his mother. Walking over to the fourth stall, Mongrel took a seat and waited.

It had been only four months since Biscuits had been incarcerated. All of Mongrel's friends and family – well, not his family, which began and ended with his mother – knew the boy was in prison, but no one knew that Mongrel was going to visit him. It had been a spur of the moment thing, even though he'd been meaning to do it for a while. He just woke up one morning and decided that today would be the day he crossed it off his list of things to do. Only the folks he'd met on the bus yesterday knew of his whereabouts.

So who was coming to visit him?

Maybe they weren't. Maybe they were here to see Biscuit's other cellmate, Ray or something. Well they were in for a surprise.

That was it! This visitor would know Mongrel wasn't Ray, that he wasn't even a prisoner at all, and finally this mess would be settled. It was perfect! He'd be out of there in no time!

Mongrel sat at the edge of his seat, eager to see the door open on the other side of the room. After what seemed like an eternity, someone finally entered, and it was not who he was expecting.

It was Beby.

For a moment Mongrel's heart stopped, and he actually felt like a prisoner. He'd been locked up for less than a day, but it felt like forever since he's last laid eyes on a women. He could hear the whistle stirring in his lungs, taste the cat-call on his lips, feel the urge in his loins[*]. Even Shoon seemed to shut up for the time being to ogle the women.

Beby locked eyes with Mongrel, stomped over to the stall in front of where he sat, fumed and flew into her chair. She didn't seem surprised to see him, but she could go off at any second.

---

[*] His loins were the real prisoners, held captive in his trousers for far too long and for a crime long forgotten.

The Importance Of Being Constantly Surprised

Mongrel watched her, mouth agape, like a dear caught in the headlights of a car. Then what started as awe of her presence gradually turned to dread over her sudden appearance here. How did she know he was in prison? He was the only person who knew he was here – so who told her? He certainly hadn't been gone long enough to be declared missing, had he? How long had be slept for?

Slowly another realization dawned on him. Maybe she hadn't know he was here. Maybe she didn't come to see him. What if she was really there to see Ray, or whatever Biscuits' former cellmate's name was. Was she dating him? Was she his prison sweetheart? It made more sense than her just randomly showing up out of the blue.

Speaking of colours, Beby was seeing red. She erupted like Mount Vesuvius, screaming at what must have been the top of her lungs. Accusations and threats and who knows what else spilled from her mouth, and as Mongrel watched, trying again to use his inability to read lips, he realized that the room was soundproof.

After a minute of silently screaming, a guard came over and said something to Beby. She looked more annoyed than was humanly possible, and channeled that frustration through the window. Slowly, deliberately, she picked up the phone that hung on the wall, and waited for Mongrel to do the same.

Instinct told him to run, to hide, that no good could come of this. But he sat there staring at her, frozen. The grave look that grew on her face suggested that the longer it took him to pick up the phone, the worse it would be for him. He knew he shouldn't keep her waiting, but found it difficult to grab the phone. His brain knew he was in trouble, and out of self-preservation was doing its best to prevent him from picking up the receiver. But he had to know why she was there. So out of sheer morbid curiosity, he eventually he got his body under control and managed to pick up the phone on his side of the glass.

What happened next surprised Mongrel. She said, "Hey sweetie."

For some reason this reminded Mongrel of a time when Beby wasn't annoyed with every little thing he did. His mind wandered, trying to recall such a time, although he knew there never was one. But strangely, something *was* coming back to him.

Random Tangent

He remembered the two of them together, outside. Biscuits was there too. And they were all...happy? Yes, they were. He couldn't be certain of much, except that it never happened. Was it a dream?

Suddenly she slammed her hand on the glass. "Hey!" screamed into the earpiece. The twofold sensory overload grabbed his attention like someone grabbing his throat, and he snapped back to reality. "Just what the hell do you think you're doing in here?"

"Uh...I, I'm just visiting," Mongrel stammered.

This answer did not please her, and the verbal assault began. She said a number of things amid a series of shrieks and screams that made his ears ring. Things suggesting that he didn't belong there, or was stupid for being there anyhow. Who was looking after his place, or places? Who was paying the bills, watering the plants, feeding the animals? He couldn't just shirk his responsibilities like this. She wailed about the weather, she cried about her hair, and Mongrel was almost, but not completely sure that she used the word pomegranate in there somewhere. He was sure he'd go deaf if he didn't do something to calm her down.

"Quiet!" he said, and interestingly, she stopped talking. This might not seem like irony, since he demanded silence and got it, but with Beby, telling her to shut up usually garnered the opposite reaction. She sat in the chair on the other side of the glass and waited for him to say something. Sighing inwardly, he desperately wanted the silence to persist, but knew the only way to achieve that was to keep talking. "So...what brings you here? Dating a prisoner?"

This rendered her speechless, or at least rendered it to continue for a moment. "You think that's funny?" she asked when that moment was up.

"Well I do seem to be quite the comedian around here."

She looked him over. "You *seem* to be beaten within an inch of your life."

Mongrel looked himself over too. His natural flesh tone had given way to the colour of bruises. Dried blood remained in streaks and blotches on his skin. His eyes were not only blackened, but slightly burnt. Only his prison uniform looked fine. He shrugged, which hurt, but he tried not to show it. "Meh. Just allergies."

The Importance Of Being Constantly Surprised

"I think…I think you're still bleeding, over…" she pointed at him but he paid no attention.

"Just ignore it and it'll go away. That's what Mom always said." He paused to reflect. "So you're dating Ray?"

This time she wasn't so quiet. "Who the hell is Ray? And who I date is none of your business! Unless it's you, then it's your business."

"So…" Mongrel was at a loss, "you're not dating a prisoner? Then why *are* you here?"

"Dating a prisoner?" she snorted. "You're the only one I'd even *consider* in this dump."

Mongrel's heart skipped a beat.

Just then another inmate entered the room and sat down at a booth, waiting for his visitor. At the same time, Shoon and his visitor departed.

"So what'd you do to wind up in prison?" she asked. "You don't belong here. Did the mayor have something to do with this?"

Mongrel answered her question with one of his own. "Did you say you'd date me?"

"Ugghh!" she bellowed over the phone in frustration. "I finally meet a decent guy and he gets thrown in prison! And you're not even taking this seriously!"

"Sorry." Mongrel took a deep breath. "I'm not actually a pri-"

"You know what, I don't care!" She got up, but still held the phone. "Just find out where the conjugal visit rooms are; I ain't letting you turn all gay in here, so we're gonna fuck like rabbits. See you next week." She tossed the phone on the desk, not bothering to put it back on its cradle, and hurriedly left the room.

The whole conjugal visit remark notwithstanding – his brain was too overloaded to compute that piece of information (it'll catch up with him later) – he was speechless for a moment. What had just happened? He pounded on the glass and shouted into the receiver "Wait! Beby come back! You gotta tell them I don't belong here! You gotta tell them about the mix up! Come back! You gotta help me!"

Random Tangent

The inmate sitting two booths over glanced down at him suspiciously, then returned his attention to the door on the other side of the room, waiting for his visitor.

Presently, that visitor arrived. It was Captain Pete.

The prisoner waved. Pete smiled. Mongrel gawked.

"Pete!" Mongrel banged on the glass again. "Come here! Help me!"

Captain Pete's looked at him, and his initial reaction was that he'd seen a ghost. Then a smile slowly began to creep back onto his face, followed by laughter out of his mouth. Some words followed this, but Mongrel couldn't hear any of them.

"Stevens!"

Mongrel turned to see a guard beckoning from the doorway.

"Time's up. Let's go."

But Mongrel stayed put, watching Captain Pete laugh.

The inmate waiting for Captain Pete, whose name, according to the back of his uniform, was Brecklyn, had no idea what was going on. "What's going on? Why's he laughing?" he demanded.

"Stevens!" the guard repeated.

Mongrel tried to gesture for Captain Pete to pick up the receiver on his side, but the guard had grown tired of waiting, and came in to fetch him.

"Wait! He's here to see me!" Mongrel held onto the phone for dear life as the guard tried to drag him away. "He's my visitor!"

"No he ain't," Brecklyn said. "He's mine."

Finally losing grip on the receiver, which dropped to the floor, Mongrel struggled to free himself. "I gotta talk to him!"

The guard, having grown weary of this game, walloped Mongrel on the head, which, due to the high level of physical exhaustion he was under, knocked him unconscious.

Captain Pete laughed ever harder.

"Mon? Mon wake up!"

Mongrel stirred, and slowly opened his eyes to sunlight. "What happened?"

"We don't know." It was Solvo who answered. "We just found you laying here. Think one of the guards brought you out."

The Importance Of Being Constantly Surprised

Sitting up off the ground, Mongrel took notice of his surroundings. They appeared to be outside. He sat a few feet away from the door he was presumably thrown out of. All around him prisoners loafed about, chatting, exercising, molesting, sometimes all at the same time. Some were lifting weights, while others were playing games like basketball or hacky-sack. A couple guys by the far fence were playing grab-ass. A hundred unintelligible conversations hung in the air, which felt like rain. Clouds were slowly moving in from the east.

Mongrel crawled over to the door, sat against it and buried his face in his hands. Beby was his one chance to get out of there, and he'd blown it. "What am I going to do?"

Biscuits sat down beside him; Solvo remained standing. "This'll get sorted out soon," he said. "Just gotta hang in there."

"Yeah," Biscuits agreed, slapping Mongrel's shoulder.

"Don't touch me," Mongrel said gripping his shoulder in pain. "I don't think I can hang in here much longer. I'm the new guy, and new guys don't last long. I'll be lucky to survive the day, let alone a week."

"Hey," Solvo said, pointing at an inmate about fifty yards away, "that guy's been watching you since you got out here. Think he's got a thing for you."

Mongrel looked across at him, and they made eye contact. "That guy who looks like Mr. Clean?"

"Yeah, that's him."

"Well whatever thing he's got, he can keep it."

"Hey, just trying to take your mind off your misery," Solvo said. "That's how we get by here."

"What, raping each other?" Mongrel asked.

"No, no. Well, sometimes."

Solvo was generally raped much less than other inmates. He'd noticed a sharp decline in his rapings ever since Biscuits had arrived, but couldn't figure out the connection. As it turned out, many prisoners assumed Solvo and the boy were a couple, and most didn't approve of it, considering the general consensus that Biscuits was practically a child. Many conspired to alert McCulloch about it, knowing he liked the boy almost like a son, but no one had any proof it was actually going on (due to the fact that it wasn't). Everyone was waiting to catch them red-handed.

"I don't want to hear about it," Mongrel said, thinking that would end the discussion.

"What's raping?" Biscuits asked, almost as if to spite Mongrel.

"It's when someone forces themselves upon you sexually," Solvo answered. This didn't seem to register with the boy. "Didn't DERFtron teach you about this?"

Biscuits shook his head.

"Don't," Mongrel said. "Please don't."

"No birds and bees shit, eh? Why I gotta do everything?" He then proceeded to tell the boy the ins and outs of sexual molestation. What Biscuits learned in those few educational minutes horrified him to no end, and he was rendered incoherent by the mental atrocities.

Mongrel waved a hand in front Biscuit's face but gained no reaction. "Why'd you have to tell him that? Now look at him; you put him in a coma. I need him to get out of here." The gravity of what he'd just said hit him like a truck. He *needed* the boy. As much as he didn't like it, he didn't know the first thing about prison life, and Biscuits was like a juvenile tour guide. Would he even have lasted a day without him? He seemed to be making friends with Solvo as well, and while he made for more intelligent conversations, Solvo wasn't allowed to roam freely around the prison like Biscuits, and Mongrel needed that advantage. McCulloch also liked the boy, and wouldn't let anything happen to him, so Mongrel knew if he stuck by Biscuits he had a better chance of surviving. "Now what am I gonna do? You trying to get me killed?"

"Well it's practically a pastime in here," Solvo said, sitting down beside them. "We all do it from time to time. Better he learn from me than the hard way." He chuckled at the double-entendre. "Besides, someone's gotta break in the new guys."

With this remark Mongrel jerked away from Solvo, who just chuckled more.

"Relax," he said. "I'm not gonna rape you. Not with that attitude at least."

The Importance Of Being Constantly Surprised

Suddenly a shadow fell on them. "Looks like my boy Pete's got a beef with you."

Mongrel looked up to see Brecklyn, the inmate Captain Pete was visiting. Brecklyn was a pretty big guy, at least looking up at him from the ground. He was bald and had a goatee, and reminded Mongrel of some actor whose name escaped him.

"Seems like you keep getting in the way of his continued existence."

"His what?" Mongrel asked.

"I think he means you tried to kill him," Solvo whispered.

"Oh. Well I don't *try* to kill him," Mongrel whispered back. "I succeed."

"You killed someone?" Solvo seemed surprised. "I didn't peg you for that. Don't seem like the killing type."

"Well I didn't really kill him; it was an accident. Several accidents."

"What do you mean? You made it look like an accident? It took a few tries?"

"Hey!" Brecklyn yelled, "I's talking to you."

Mongrel, feigning annoyance, returned his attention to the big man and rolled his hand as if to say, 'fine, go on, if you must.'

"Says he don't know why you here, but he wants me to make your stay is as unpleasant as possible." He cracked his knuckles.

"Well, you're certainly doing just that," Mongrel said nervously. "I feel miserable just being around you."

Brecklyn raised his eyebrows in mock surprise. "Say what?"

Knowing he'd only made things worse by saying that, Mongrel tried to explain. "Uh, what I mean to say is that just the sight of you is making me sick." He cringed again, and could almost feel the pain that was about to be inflicted upon him.

"Boy, I'm gonna snap my foot off in yo ass!"

Mongrel needed to get out of there before his mouth got him into more trouble. "Yes, very sick here. I do believe I'm falling ill. Watch it – I could puke all over you! Solvo would you take me to the…uh…"

"Infirmary?" Solvo suggested.

Mongrel snapped his fingers. "That's it!" He made to get up.

Random Tangent

"Sit down!" Brecklyn snapped at him. "You ain't going nowhere."

Mongrel snapped his fingers again. "Worth a shot."

Brecklyn began pacing in circles. "I'ma torture you for weeks man. You gonna wish you was dead, but I won't let you die, see. I mean, I'll kill you eventually, probably burn you up alive. But then I'ma make, like, a pot or somethin' out of yo ashes, and then smash the pot all up." He smiled and nodded gravely, as if all that was worst thing he possibly do. But he wasn't finished. "But I ain't done yet. See, then I'll melt the pot down, you know, the broken pot pieces, and mix you into some horse food and feed you to my dog– I feed him horse food cause he a real big dog, you know what I'm sayin'? Then he gonna turn you to shit, and shit yo ass out, and sometimes he eats his own shit – yeah it's gross, I know – but there's a good chance you gonna get eaten, and then shit out again. Gonna be rough, man." He then spat on the ground.

All Mongrel had to say to this was, "You have a dog? In prison?"

"I gots lots of bitches in this house," Brecklyn smirked, and held a hand up to high-five someone. He then noticed no one else was there to hear his witty remark, and lowered his hand. "And you gonna be the next one. Gonna make you my new bitch."

Mongrel swallowed. "Bitch, as in..."

Brecklyn nodded and licked his lips in a vomit-inducing manner. "Aw yeah, that's right. Once you been beat real good it be easy. See at first you gonna resist, right? Try and fight me off. But after weeks of me layin' into you like you owe me money, shit, you be beggin me for some love and tenderness."

Mongrel held up a hand, like he was in school and had a question. "So how does all this raping go on all the time? Don't the guards find out? Don't they do something about it?"

"No," Solvo replied. "Some of them are even in on it."

"Of course they are," Mongrel muttered, shaking his head. "I don't suppose there's any way I can talk you out of this?" he asked Brecklyn, wishing he had a wallet full of hundred-dollar bills, or a gun, even a rape whistle – something.

"No way; this is for Pete," Brecklyn said. "I'd do anything for him. He's like a father to me."

The Importance Of Being Constantly Surprised

"Well hold on a minute. Do you just do whatever he says? Do you *believe* everything he says? He told you I keep killing him – well he's still alive! You just saw him. We both did. Does that make any sense to you?"

Brecklyn looked down, thinking.

"How could I have killed him if he's still alive? He's an old pirate, he's crazy, and he doesn't know what he's talking about. And you'd be crazy if you listened to him."

"Boy, you do not call me crazy. That's one thing you just don't do."

"Yeah, don't call him crazy," Solvo agreed. "That's mean."

"Sorry," Mongrel said.

"Now Pete ain't never steered me wrong," Brecklyn said. "Ain't never lied to me neither. Now maybe you're right or maybe he's right, but the way I see it, long as I don't kill you, ain't nothing can't be fixed. Better safe than sorry, know what I mean?" He moved in on Mongrel.

As much as Mongrel hated to admit it, he could understand the logic behind the man's actions. He closed his eyes and tensed up, preparing for the assault, hoping he'd be knocked out as quickly as the last time.

"This is for Captain Pete!" Brecklyn proclaimed.

"Captain Pete?" someone else suddenly screamed.

In a matter of seconds a blurred, hulking man appeared, grabbed Brecklyn, and lifted him off the ground. In the air, Brecklyn had both his arms wrapped around his waist, twice, and then broken in no less than four places each. He was then sat gently on the ground and patted on the head like a dog.

"Not again!" Brecklyn choked out before passing out from the pain.

"Charlie?" Mongrel asked, finally opening his eyes to view his savior.

Big John Charlie Marbles beamed down at Mongrel. "Found you strange puppy man!"

Despite that fact that Mongrel fancied himself a cat person, he laughed. "Boy am I glad to see you! What ar-"

Random Tangent

Before Mongrel could finish, Charlie reached down, grabbed Mongrel, and jerked him into a tackle-hug[*]. "Charlie missed you so much!"

Mongrel tried to say thanks, but couldn't gain enough oxygen for the vocal manoeuvre. Big John set him back down beside Solvo and patted his head like he did Brecklyn, but thankfully Mongrel wasn't in as much pain as he was.

"So what are you doing here?" Mongrel asked him. "Don't tell me it had something to do with puppies."

"Puppies…" Charlie mentally wandered off, and rolled his head back in thought. "One time I gave puppy bath in the washing machine. He was white so I used lots of bleach. But he came out all wrinkly, so I had to iron him."

Solvo answered for him. "He's actually a volunteer."

"Volunteer?"

"It's like how some mental hospitals have people that aren't really committed there. You know? They just stay cause they want to?"

"So he can leave any time he wants?" Mongrel looked at Big John, amazed and bewildered. "So why does he stay?"

"Guess he likes it here," Solvo replied. "Guards don't mind him. They even tolerate Big John."

"Huh?"

"You know, when Charlie gets angry."

Mongrel thought for a second, thinking back to his previous encounters with the puppy lover. "So when Charlie gets angry he turns into Big John? Like the Hulk?"

"I always thought of it as a Dr. Jekyll – Mr. Hyde sort of thing, but yeah."

Charlie, still in his own world of puppy bliss, remained ignorant of their conversation. "Puppies…" he murmured, drooling softly.

"But what about when he gets angry?" Mongrel asked pointedly. "He kinda, like, tends to rip people in half and stuff."

"I think the guards like it. Keeps everyone in line, you know?"

---

[*] Henceforth known as *tuggle*.

The Importance Of Being Constantly Surprised

"Anyway," Mongrel paused, "Weren't we talking about something else before?"

"Rape?"

"No, not rape!" Mongrel groaned. "What is it with you and rape?"

Solvo shrugged. "I don't know. I haven't been raped in a while. Just lonely I guess."

Mongrel looked at the man, trying to feel disgusted, but finding some sympathy as well. He wished it made him sick, but it didn't. "Can we just talk about something else?"

"Okay...how did your visit go?"

Suddenly Mongrel's eyes widened, his heartbeat raced, and his head hurt. "Conjugal visit?"

Recalling his brief encounter with the feisty redhead, Mongrel's brain caught him up to speed on passed events and dropped a bombshell on him. A *conjugal* visit? But that would mean Beby wanted to....to... A conjugal *visit?* This went way beyond a mere date. *A* conjugal visit? Could he even be naked in front of someone? He'd had some bad experiences in the past. *Conjugal? Visit? A?* It didn't make any sense. He knew there had to be some other explanation but he couldn't find one. This was all too much for him. He stood up and sat back down, shaking his head and muttering.

"You okay?" Solvo asked him.

"She...she wants to have sex. With *me*."

Now Solvo was as confused as Mongrel. "That's good isn't it?"

"No," Mongrel shook his head, but didn't offer an explanation.

"Why not? You gay?"

"No. I'm not gay. It's just that, I mean, we haven't really even dated. I didn't even think she liked me like that."

Solvo put his hand on Mongrel's shoulder. "There's nothing wrong if you're gay."

"I'm *not* gay. Look, you don't know her like I do – something's wrong. With anyone else that would be a good thing. Well not *anyone*, but...you know. Trust me, as good as it sounds, it can't be good."

Random Tangent

"Hey, new guy!"

They looked to see the Mr. Clean look-alike heading their way, and he looked quite upset about something. The man was completely bald, unlike most of the prisoners, and had a remarkable set of brilliantly white teeth.

"Are you new here?" Mongrel asked Solvo.

"Been here three years."

Mongrel grumbled. "Guess he means me then." He turned his attention to the look-alike. "What?"

The look-alike finished stomping his way over and cracked his neck. "Don't like new guys."

This remark annoyed Mongrel since as far as he was concerned he wasn't a new guy, and trampled his already downtrodden spirits into the ground. By now his foul mood was so embedded into his soul that an exorcism would be needed to remove it. "And just what are you going to do about it?"

"Well," the look-alike had to think for a moment. "We beat 'em up a little, and rape 'em. Mostly rape I guess."

"See?" whispered Solvo.

Mongrel shook his head, annoyed. "Why does everyone want to rape me?"

"You are a pretty good-looking guy," Solvo answered.

After a brief minute of trying to look at his own face, Mongrel gave up. Although even without any aid he knew what he looked like. What he felt like was a different matter. All the abuse he'd sustained in prison had added a healthy dose of cuts and bruises and discoloured skin to his complexion, but he could probably still pick himself out of a police lineup. "No I'm not," he finally replied. "And certainly not now – I probably look like a walking corpse."

"Well…" Solvo thought out loud, "you are the new guy. Fresh meat."

Mongrel nodded, but not to anyone in particular. "Yeah. Uncharted territory."

"The new prison slut."

Turning to face Solvo with a look of utter disgust on his face – which was hard to discern through all the wounds and sores – Mongrel said, "Don't ever call me that."

The Importance Of Being Constantly Surprised

"So," the Mr. Clean look-alike interjected. "Shall we get started?" He took a step towards them.

"Whoa!" Mongrel cried in alarm, trying to scoot away but getting nowhere. "Now? Here? In broad daylight?" He looked up at the clouds ganging up in the sky, chasing the sun away like a kid being forced to take the long way home from school to avoid bullies. "Or at least the slim daylight."

"Um," Solvo started, raising his hand, "are you including me in this? You said 'we' so do you mean the three of us or just you two?"

"I'm afraid this deal is just for the new guy."

Solvo was obviously disappointed with the news. He hung his head and dismally muttered, "Okay."

"The amount of light doesn't matter to me," he continued, talking to Mongrel. "So do you have a favourite position?"

"You know I'd honestly rather get beaten within an inch of my life again instead of…this," Mongrel said, pausing to reflect how true this was. He'd had so many fists and boots slammed into his body, and ungodly amounts of violence unleashed upon his face, that he'd begun to build a tolerance towards it. "I don't suppose you could beat me more and rape me less?" Mongrel asked.

The look-alike chuckled at this and his entire demeanor changed. "Well I do have some packages, so we can discuss your options."

"Options?" Mongrel had no idea what he was talking about.

"Well, if you're *really* opposed to rape, then your best option is what I call the Switchup. It's a lite plan, which is good for beginners. It's got both rapings and beatings, and they alternate, so you'd get raped one day, beaten the next, and then raped the day after, and so on. Now what makes this great for new guys is that the rapings and beatings only happen once a day, and we can work out a schedule that works for you."

"We?"

"Me and my business partner, Ockley," he tried to gesture out into the field somewhere, but apparently couldn't find him. "Well he's out there somewhere. We run GOBARS: Guirmo and Ockley Beating And Raping Services. "I'm Guirmo." He proffered his hand, and Mongrel reluctantly shook it; he didn't want to be rude.

"Actually," Guirmo continued, "Ockley came up with another package you might be interested in, called the Puerto Rican Weekend, which is basically like a cell phone plan – you get no rapings during the week, but it's unlimited during the weekends. And don't ask me why Puerto Rican; I don't know. Neither of us is Puerto Rican. But it's got a nice ring to it, you know?"

Mongrel was bewildered. Rape was a business? "Uh, I don't suppose you have, like, a brochure or something I could look at?"

Guirmo nodded. "Got one back in the cell. Til then though, this one's on the house." He reached down, and before Mongrel knew it one of his shoes was off.

"Hey," Mongrel said, "get away from me." He began thrashing around.

Guirmo struggled with Mongrel, trying to calm him down. "Relax buddy. This is just business. Trust me; you'll thank me when it's over."

"*Thank you?*" Mongrel was incredulous. "Like hell I will!"

"No, seriously," Guirmo continued, managing to get Mongrel's pants undone, "you don't want none of these other guys doing it. Breaking you in. They're animals."

Mongrel fought as if his life depended on it, which it nearly did. "*You're* the animal!"

At that moment a figure entered the scene. It was short and round. So round was it, in fact, that it could have rolled along. But it personally decided to evolve feet because it felt more sophisticated with them. It had no eyes, but could sense where it was going. It had a multitude of inexplicable senses, like the sense that a light bulb is going to burn out, or the phone was about to ring. It knows how to scare a tree, it can hear mimes, and it always knows where Waldo is. And it could tell the contents of any can of soup just by listening to it. It was also stark raving red, and had a voracious appetite.

"Mon!" Mongrel cried. "Help me! He's trying to rape me!"

"Mon," said the mon, which meant, 'Sorry, I'm just here for the cameo. You're on your own.' Then it left.

The Importance Of Being Constantly Surprised

"I'm good at this, I'm telling you," Guirmo told Mongrel, continuing to remove his clothes.

Suddenly Big John loomed over them all. "Leave puppy man alone," he said, lifting Guirmo off the ground by his hair[*]. After inspecting the inmate for a moment, Big John proceeded to rip him in two down the middle, and then set both halves down.

Mongrel pulled his pants up and looked at the mess before him. "You see?" he said to Solvo. "That's what Big John does. Ripped him right in half. Most people are probably in here for doing less than that."

Solvo just shook his head. "He'll be fine. Just needs a few stitches. But he was right you know, about being good. Especially with his hands. The man's an artist."

"What the hell?" Mongrel was trying to tie his pants up, but there was a problem. "How'd he untie my pants? There's no drawstring!"

"I told you he was good. Rape is an art to him. My first night here I shared a cell with him. I smuggled some stuff in here up my butt, and the next morning he had them. Didn't even wake me up." He shook his head. "Unbelievable."

Settling for wrapping his pants around his waist, Mongrel looked again at Guirmo. "Well, that's got to be the best pick pocket job in the world, but it's still gross. Can we talk about something else?"

"Okay, what?"

"Puppies?" Charlie suggested. "One time I built a time machine out of a DeLorean, and used puppy to test it. It was a success."

This didn't sit right with Mongrel. "And the puppy was fine? It lived?"

"No," Charlie said, "Later some Libyans came and blowed everything up with rockets, including puppy. Stupid Libyans."

"That's more like it. So tell me Charlie, you can leave prison whenever you want?"

Charlie nodded.

---

[*] It is said that in times of great stress, people are capable of great, even impossible feats of strength. This is how Big John was able to lift Mr. Clean by his hair, despite the fact that he had a fashionably clean-shaven head.

Random Tangent

"Like right now?"

More nodding.

Mongrel stood and began walking back and forth. "So then, if we switch clothes…and I pretend I'm you…"

"Won't work," Solvo interrupted. "Simpson's did it."

"Huh?"

"Simpson. He used to be a couple cells down from us. He snuck out a while back in Charlie's clothes. Now the guards look for that."

A voice abruptly cut through the air. It sounded to Mongrel like McCulloch. "All right, line 'em up boys. Play time's over; time to get to work."

Biscuits was still comatose, but he was slowly coming back to reality. Mongrel had to help him to his feet. "You guys work here?"

Solvo draped one of the boy's arms over his shoulders and Mongrel did the same on the other side, and they carried him towards the far side of the field where the other inmates were gathering. "Of course. Prison ain't all fun and games you know."

"Oh? I hadn't noticed." Mongrel said sarcastically. "So what do you do?"

"I'm a relabeller."

"…Right," Mongrel said after a minute. "And what is that?"

"I change expiration dates on food and other things." When this explanation resulted in an incredulous look from Mongrel, Solvo felt compelled to elaborate. "All the food you buy has to have an expiration dates. It's the law or something. But most things don't expire when they say they do, and some things don't go bad at all. Like water; it doesn't go bad. Or honey."

"I make puppies!" Charlie said excitedly, and was ignored.

"I've always wondered about the expiration date on water," Mongrel said. "Never made sense to me. What happens when it expires? Does it separate into H's and O's?"

"Exactly. And stores won't stock stuff that's expired. So what I do is change the expiration date on stuff. They give me a crate of water, and I change the date on in for two years later. Then it can go back to stores and be sold and no one knows any different. Saves a ton of money and it's less wasteful too."

The Importance Of Being Constantly Surprised

"Is that legal?"

"Beats me. Unethical maybe, least for some things. Gotta be careful though; it has to look authentic. And you need to get the date just right, or it looks suspicious. You can't put a box of crackers out there with a shelf life of three years – people won't believe that."

The men approached rest of the inmates and joined in the line just as rain started to fall. The guards were casually doing a head count, clearly in no hurry to allow anyone inside. Solvo mentioned to someone about the two inmates Big John had manhandled, and a couple guards went over to inspect the damage.

"Glad the rain held out," Solvo said. "Hate working when I'm soaked."

Mongrel wasn't sure if he was talking to him or someone else, but asked, "You work outside?"

"Hmm? No, but we have to go right to work now, not back to our cells to change clothes. Sometimes it rains all day, and outside time is on a schedule. We go out rain or shine. And depending on what you're relabeling it can be a real bitch when you're all wet."

"The guards don't care?"

"Only that the work gets done."

"Figures. What does Biscuits do?"

"He knits clothes."

"Ah. Should've guessed that." Mongrel looked down at his uniform. "Seems pretty good at it."

"Don't believe that crap about kids in other countries making clothes and stuff in forced labour camps. I mean, sure, lots of stuff probably comes from there, but lots also comes from prisons. More than people know."

Biscuits stirred at the sound of his name, and made a few unintelligible attempts at speaking.

"What's wrong with him?" a guard asked suddenly, pausing his head count.

Doing his best to answer, Biscuits mumbled incoherently. Mongrel just smiled nervously.

The guard eyed the three of them suspiciously. "Does he need to go to the infirmary?"

Random Tangent

Mongrel's eyes glazed over, and somewhere in the back of his mind a light came on, shedding some much needed light in those dark crevasses where some good old-fashioned thinking could take place. Calculations were performed. Performances were calculated. Theories were assessed. A tiny imaginary monkey clapped its hands in encouragement. Then a voice somewhere in his head said, 'yes, it can be done.'

"Yes," Mongrel told the guard, "it can be done."

The guard eyed them for a moment before waving them along. "Whatever. Go on then. But if I don't see you at work in twenty, it's Mower Mouth for all three of you." He then looked up into the sky as a gentle rain began to fall. "Perfect time too."

Mongrel nodded. "Won't be a problem." He waited for the guard to get out of hearing range before asking Solvo what Mower Mouth was.

"Gotta cut the grass with your teeth," he replied. "Usually naked."

"Yummy. Okay, Charlie I need your help."

"With...what?" Biscuits asked, "I can help."

Grumbling, Mongrel adjusted his grip on the boy. "No. You just play dead, or be asleep or something. Solvo, let Charlie help me with this. I got a plan."

Charlie was happy to oblige, but tried to do too much, hoisting both Biscuits and Mongrel onto his shoulders. Biscuits did his best to remain as limp as his body would allow, and Mongrel fought his way down to his feet.

"No! No, put him down," he demanded, gathering attention from his fellow inmates. "You gotta do as I say."

Charlie shrugged, launching the boy to the ground, face first. Biscuits moaned into the dirt, which was fast becoming mud. The other prisoners watched intently, amazed to see Charlie following instructions, trying to learn Mongrel's secret. Charlie's destructible, nearly invincible nature would certainly be useful in the right hands, if it could be controlled.

Mongrel closed his eyes and took a deep breath, trying to remain calm. "Just pick him up and help me carry him, like me and Solvo were doing."

The Importance Of Being Constantly Surprised

"Move out!" a guard bellowed, signaling that the head count was successful. The crowd of inmates reluctantly drew their attention away from the spectacle that was going on and started marching inside, out of the rain.

Doing as Mongrel instructed, Big John lifted Biscuits out of the mud and stood him up straight, where they could both grab him. Then they began carrying him towards the door. The boy tried not to squirm or fidget, but his marbles had been scrambled during the face plant, and he'd lost control of some motor functions. If anyone were to ask, Biscuits would say he felt lucky to have his friends there to take him to the infirmary, which was ironic since his friends were the ones responsible for his predicament. Also, they weren't going to the infirmary.

"What do you want me to do?" Solvo asked, walking behind them.

"Nothing," Mongrel said. "I mean, just go to work, be happy, get raped and whatnot. If my plan works, I'll be gone, and never coming back!"

"Oh," Solvo sounded disappointed. "Well, good luck then."

They entered the door to the compound; everyone stomped the mud off their boots. Mongrel quickly turned his entourage down a side hallway, leaving the rest to continue on their way. Solvo gave him a wave and a disheartened look. They'd probably never see each other again.

"Thanks for helping me out around here," Mongrel said to him, waving back. "And thanks for not raping me."

"Some day, my friend," Solvo replied, his voice fading as he marched down the hall. "Some day."

Mongrel stopped waving, a pit of unease forming in his stomach. He felt dirty somehow. He waited for the long line of prisoners to march away, waited for the noise to settle, waited for the right time to move.

When he did finally glanced into the hallway again to check that the coast was clear, McCulloch was waiting for them. "Lost?" he asked.

Mongrel swallowed hard. "Uh, no. Um, we're just taken Biscuits to the…uh…" Blast, why could he never remember the name of that place? "Um, he's hurt, see?" He tried to hold Biscuits higher but only managed to do exactly nothing.

For his part, Biscuits moaned.

McCulloch did his best not to show how much the boy's suffering bothered him. He sniffed loudly. "And you need his help?" He pointed at Big John but kept his eyes fixed on Mongrel.

Big John nodded fiercely, shaking Biscuits like a rag doll, and said, "One time, I tied puppy to some fireworks. He was gonna be the first puppy in space – but the fireworks just exploded. But don't worry; I will try again."

This gained no reaction from the guard, except for a wild sneer. "Seems to me there's something wrong with this picture, wouldn't you say?"

On the contrary, Mongrel would not have said that. In fact, he didn't see anything wrong with two guys taking someone to the prison hospital. Honestly, were they supposed to just leave the boy out there in the pouring rain like an animal? What kind of place was this if *that* was expected behaviour? Wasn't everyone supposed to try to get along and become better people or something? Of course, Mongrel didn't say any of this, but he did manage to open his mouth and let in hang there provocatively, so at least he did something.

McCulloch leaned down close and said, "Infirmary's that way," and pointed behind Mongrel.

"Oh," Mongrel coughed, relieved. "I-I knew that." They turned around and began to hobble away.

"I'll be there to check up on you in a bit," the guard hollered after them.

After they'd turned a couple corners Mongrel motioned for Big John to put Biscuits down. They leaned him up against the corridor wall.

Once he was sure they were alone, Mongrel whispered sharply, "Biscuits! Wake up!"

The boy wearily came around. "Wh…where are we?"

"I was hoping you could tell me. We need to get to Derf. Can you take us there?"

Biscuits slowly looked down the hallway, and then up it, and then carefully rose to his feet. "Yeah. This way."

The Importance Of Being Constantly Surprised

They began moving, when Mongrel added, "And please, avoid any guards this time."

The three men entered the small room, making sure it was empty, and that no one followed them. DERFtron stood in the corner, like he always did.

"Would you mind calling be Derf?" DERFtron asked. "Like, seriously."

Mongrel didn't answer DERFtron, but instead turned to Biscuits. "Okay, good. Now I need one more thing from you – my clothes."

The boy looked at Mongrel's orange prison uniform, confused.

"Not these. The clothes I had on when I came to visit you. They should be back in the cell on my bed." He groaned inwardly, not wanting to think of anything here as his. He did not have a bed, or a cell. What he did have was an escape plan.

"Oh, okay." Biscuits nodded and took off out the door.

Mongrel turned back to DERFtron and sized him up. He crossed his arms in thought, running over the plan in his head, determining whether or not it would succeed. Either way, he figured, he had to try. And if he got caught, what would they do? He was already in prison. Maybe they'd throw him in the hole, or solitary confinement, or whatever. That didn't sound so bad. He would certainly survive there for a week, avoiding all the rape and abuse, until this mess got sorted out. If his plan failed, if that was the worst case scenario, then he had nothing to lose. It would be stupid *not* to try. This boosted his confidence. It could only get better from here on out.

"I see you're still alive," DERFtron said sarcastically. "What's the goon for? And it's *Derf*, not DERFtron. Please?"

"Charlie's here to help," Mongrel answered only one of his questions.

"With what? There are no puppies in here. Not that he'd be of any help to *them*."

"Carry you," Mongrel said as he closed the door to give them more privacy. He walked over to DERFtron. "I figured you'd be pretty heavy and I can't do it myself."

Random Tangent

DERFtron flashed a confused face on his monitor. "Fine, call me DERFtron, whatever, I don't care." He sighed and then asked, "Why are you carrying me?"

"Because we're all breaking out."

"Oh *finally!* Can't wait to get out of here and get my body back and become *Derf* again and not this DERFtron bullshit." He straightened up and gave his tank treads a brief run, making sure they still functioned. "But you don't have to carry me."

Stepping back, with a look of surprised anger on his face, Mongrel was speechless. All he could do was hold his arms in the direction of DERFtron's treads and grunt questioningly.

"What?" DERFtron asked.

The look of surprised anger ventured up the machine's facial monitor. "Those work? All this time?"

"Yeah. So?"

The fury built up inside Mongrel. "You asshole!"

"*What?*"

"All this time I've been feeling guilty cause of you!"

"Guilty *because* of you," DERFtron corrected.

"*Shut up!* Those things work, and you can move. This whole time you could've walked right out this door. You could've left any time you liked."

"No, I can't f-"

"But instead you make *me* feel guilty, feel responsible that you're here. I've been having the worst time of my life! Trying to avoid getting beaten up, and raped. Anyone ever try to rape you?"

Mongrel paused, as if waiting for a reply, so DERFtron tried to speak. "I ca-"

"I've had terrible nightmares!" Mongrel interrupted again. "And I've been worrying about how to get you out. How to get *myself* out! You don't need my help at all!"

"I can't fit through the damn door!" DERFtron screamed.

This revelation shut Mongrel up. "Oh," was all he could say.

"Don't you think I've tried that?"

Mongrel just shrugged, and looked dismally at the door. So now what? That was his plan; Charlie would help carry him through the door and outside, pretending to be repairmen. But if the door wasn't an option… "How'd they even get you in here?"

The Importance Of Being Constantly Surprised

"So you thought these didn't work?" DERFtron asked, referring to his treads. "You think I'm impotent? I ain't impotent! *Everything works!* Probably better than yours!"

"...Shit." Mongrel was at a loss. He scratched his head. "If we can't use the door, then what are we gonna do?"

"Make new door?" Charlie suggested, and then handily created a huge hole in the wall opposite the door.

Jumping back to avoid the debris flying everywhere, Mongrel cringed at not only the damage, but the noise as well. It wouldn't be long before every guard in the penitentiary knew what was going on.

"That'll work," DERFtron said.

"Charlie! What the hell?" Mongrel walked over to inspect the damage. While the hole in the wall was big enough for DERFtron to fit through, what delightfully surprised him was that the hole didn't lead to another room in the building; it led outside. It wasn't going to be the most subtle escape, but at least it was going in the right direction.

Charlie just smiled proudly.

"Is this why you brought him?" DERFtron asked, rolling over to see for himself. "Not bad. Oh, it's raining. That sucks."

Mongrel, remained silent, listening for any alarms or raised voices that could mean trouble. You don't just level a prison wall without attracting attention.

After a moment footsteps approached the door. Then someone knocked. Mongrel held a finger to his mouth for everyone to remain silent, and for a moment, all was still. Big John refrained from talking about puppies. DERFtron ceased computing. Even the rumble stopped piling. Then the door opened.

Biscuits poked his head around the door. "You okay? What happen?"

Mongrel almost fainted. He couldn't take this kind of pressure. "Get in here!" he whispered furiously and motioned with his hand.

Unsure of whether Mongrel was angry at him or not, Biscuits tepidly entered the wrecked room. "I brawt your clothes."

"Thanks," Mongrel said, and quickly ripped them out of the boy's hands and began undressing. "Charlie, you go out into the hallway – you're on door patrol now. Make sure nobody comes in here."

Charlie saluted in perfect military fashion, and left the room, closing the door behind him.

Figuring that should buy them some time, Mongrel continued getting dressed. "You can't go out in the rain, can you, Derf?"

"Affirmative."

"Okay then, looks like we need a getaway car." Mongrel finished putting his shoes on and looked outside, trying to locate something suitable.

DERFtron crawled over beside Mongrel. "I'd probably fit into a van better."

Biscuits remained where he was, putting two and two together. Finally, he shouted, "No!" and ran over and hugged DERFtron. "You can't go!"

Mongrel shook his head over this, partially because he was amazed to find the boy could still surprise him, and partially because it was one more freaking thing in the way of his escape.

"You my best friend," he boy sobbed.

The monitor that was DERFtron's face displayed a mixture of frustration and regret in stunning 720p resolution. One of his mechanical arms reached up and around Biscuits, mimicking a hug. "You *are* my best friend," he said. "And I always will be. Just because I'm leaving doesn't mean I'm not your friend anymore."

Biscuits continued sobbing. "But you're my only friend in the world!"

"That can't be true," DERFtron said. "You really think there's no one that cares about you? What about Mongrel?"

Knowing that his recent behaviour towards the boy hadn't exactly been nurturing or supportive, Mongrel could understand why the boy would be reluctant to consider him a friend. But still, could you blame Mongrel for his attitude? He was trapped in prison with the person who killed his mother. He'd taken things rather well, as far as he was concerned. If anything, Biscuits should be happy Mongrel hadn't killed him.

"What about Solvo?" Mongrel suggested. "You guys seem to get along alright. Or Charlie?"

The Importance Of Being Constantly Surprised

Biscuits pulled away from DERFtron to look at Mongrel. Tears streaked his face. Snot flowed over his mouth and chin. He nodded, then turned back to the machine. "But who will teach me?"

"Teach you?" DERFtron exclaimed. "Why? What makes you think you still need me? Look at you! You're reading and talking at nearly a fifth grade level! I don't think there's much more you can learn from me. You are *so* smart!"

"Really?" Mongrel and Biscuits both asked.

"Absolutely! Why, you impress me on a nearly daily basis, although that's probably because I have such little expectations of you."

Biscuits smiled, despite the insult, and hugged DERFtron again. "Where will you go? Take me with you!"

DERFtron sighed and hugged the boy back. "You can't come with me; you need to stay here. I have to go back to that crazy mad scientist who made me like this. I'm gonna make him fix me. But don't worry – I'll come back."

The boy finally released his grip and backed away, still happy, yet somehow sad. "Okay. I'll miss you!"

"I'm going out to find a van," Mongrel said, eager to get the show on the road. "Biscuits, I might need your help – you know this place better than I do." He hopped over the debris and out into the rain.

"I'll miss you too," Derf said. "Hey, you called me Derf!" Of course DERFtron was mistaken. "No I heard it, don't deny it." Tragically, DERFtron's fuses began to start frying with all his calculating mistakes. He grumbled angrily and said, "Fine. Whatever. It appears I am mistaken." He then glared at Biscuits. "What are you still doing here? Get out!"

Biscuits tried following Mongrel over the rubble, but wasn't as sure-footed. Of course, with the rain blowing in and making the bits of concrete and plaster and whatnot slippery, it was only natural for the boy to stumble and fall into the muck a couple times. But after a short journey that was painful to watch, he stood, a muddy mess, next to Mongrel.

"You know your way around out here?" Mongrel asked, surveying the land.

Biscuits nodded. "Yes."

Random Tangent

"And you know where all the security cameras are?"

The boy nodded again.

"And you know wher-"

"There's a van!" Biscuits shouted, and tore off to the nearby, and completely visible, parking lot.

Mongrel was both surprised and unnerved that he hadn't seen this with his own eyes. Was his vision going? Maybe he was so nervous about breaking out of prison that he wasn't focusing. Or it could be that…you know what? Time was being wasted; he'd worry about it later.

He was about to follow Biscuits over, when the boy stopped and turned around. Without explanation, he ran back, scrambled over the debris and back into the building. Irritated but undeterred, Mongrel continued on his way to the van.

At first resentful of the rain, Mongrel soon came to appreciate that it had drawn everyone inside. As he drew close to the panel van he didn't see any guards patrolling the prison grounds. He also noticed that the van did not belong to the Dunttstown Penitentiary, but rather to Guy Lady Technicians. His previous plan to act like a repairman might have worked after all. Hoping this meant that the prison was undergoing so me sort of security overhaul or anything that meant the cameras weren't working, his spirits were buoyed.

He looked in the back window, but couldn't see much due to the dark tinted glass. Then he tried the door handle, but it was locked. His optimism was further dampened when the side door also refused to open.

When he found that the front passenger door also proved locked, he cursed and slammed his head against the window – and heard glass shatter. But he didn't do it. Ignoring the slight pain he felt in his head, Mongrel backed away from the van and looked around. Over by the hole in the wall DERFtron looked out, waiting patiently. The air was still. The prison seemed to be ignoring him. Shrugging, he wandered around the front of the van to the driver's side and was about to try the door handle when the glass blew out at him.

Screaming and falling backwards to avoid getting glass in his face, Mongrel tripped over a headstone.

The Importance Of Being Constantly Surprised

The van door opened and Biscuits jumped out. "Mon? You okay?" He ran over to help Mongrel up.

"You? The hell? I thought you went back inside?"

"I needed this." Biscuits held up Mongrel's prison uniform.

Mongrel looked at the uniform incredulously. "Why?"

"To brake glass. Had too get in the van."

Getting to his feet, Mongrel studied the van, impressed with the boy's ingenuity. Then another fact became apparent. "Um, how did you get in?"

"With this." Biscuits waved the uniform in Mongrel's face.

"No, I mean...well look, you just used that to bust out the front window, right?"

The boy nodded.

"From inside?"

The boy nodded again.

"So how did you get inside in the first place?"

"With this!" Biscuits repeated more forcefully.

Mongrel realized he wasn't going to get anywhere and gave up, and climbed into the van to investigate. His first stop was the ignition, which was empty. Downtrodden but not beaten, he pressed on, searching for the keys. He found papers, binders, a ridiculous amount of cell phones, all neatly organized, but no keys. He was about to make his way to the back when he saw the left rear door was hanging open, with the window smashed in. That would explain the glass he heard shattering.

"Did you do that?" Mongrel asked Biscuits, getting out of the van and pointing to the back.

Biscuits rolled his eyes, nodded, and shook the uniform in his face again.

"Why?" Mongrel asked, and then held up his hand to stop the boy from answering. "Why did you break the rear window to get in, and then break the front window to get out?"

Instead of rolling his eyes this time Biscuits rolled them all over in thought. He looked at the back of the van, followed by the front, and then the sky, and then the ground. This seemed to be a tough question for the boy.

"You know what? Forget it. Looks like we're not getting far anyway; I don't think we'll find the keys."

Random Tangent

"Don't need them," Biscuits said, and climbed into the van.

Mongrel watched as Biscuits ripped apart the dashboard under the steering wheel and exposed a bundle of wires. He separated a few and severed them with his teeth, and then twisted some of the strands together, causing the van's engine to roar to life.

"Holy shit!" Mongrel cried, dumbfounded. "I thought that was only a movie thing! How'd you learn how to do that?"

Biscuits climbed back out of the van and smiled hideously wide. "Solvo tawt me."

Still not believing his luck, and knowing it couldn't last much longer, Mongrel got behind the wheel. "You need to work on you silent *ghs*, but this is awesome! Come on, get in."

The boy ran around to the passenger side, excited to feel useful. He smashed in the window, reached inside to unlock the door, and let himself in.

Mongrel sighed. "I could have just…whatever." Shifting the van into reverse, he backed it across the grass and over to the hole in the wall, getting as close as he could. He then got out and went to help DERFtron.

"Finally!" DERFtron said as Mongrel clambered over the remains of the wall, Biscuits in tow. "I could feel myself beginning to rust!"

"Yeah, well, I couldn't find a colour I liked," Mongrel replied sarcastically, holding the van's rear doors open. Fortunately the rubble from the wall provided a sufficient ramp for DERFtron to climb into the back.

"Gee, break enough glass in here?" DERFtron grumbled. "Good thing I have treads, you maniacs!"

Once DERFtron was inside and comfortable, Biscuits climbed in and hugged him again. "I'll miss you, and right you every day. I mean *write* you every day."

DERFtron hugged the boy back. "Uh, okay, if you say so. I'll miss you too. Watch your feet."

Biscuits then hopped out of the van and hugged Mongrel, who was at a loss for words over the boy's affection. Didn't prison usually turn people hostile?

"Why don't you come?" he asked.

The Importance Of Being Constantly Surprised

Biscuits looked up at Mongrel, and appeared to think about this. "Really?" he finally asked, his eyes tearing up again. He looked to DERFtron, who up until then had the word *No!* flashing on his monitor in big red letters, and was making cutting motions across what would be his neck.

"It's up to you," DERFtron said, although he obviously thought it was a bad idea.

This prompted a further commitment to thinking on the boy's part. After deliberating for a few minutes, he shook his head. "No, I stay here."

"Good," DERFtron said, reaching out with his mechanical arms to close the rear doors.

"You want to stay here?" Mongrel asked. "In prison?"

Biscuits shrugged. "I like it here."

Mongrel raised his eyebrows, but wasn't surprised. While being incarcerated would not exactly have been a nice vacation for him, what with the beatings and raping and such, it was a wholly different story for the boy. Within these walls the boy had found a life he'd never had, a life Mongrel had taken for granted, and who was he to take that away from him?

What did alarm him was the realization that he'd miss the boy. Despite all he'd been through the last couple days, he knew it wasn't completely Biscuits' fault. If anything, Biscuits had been a good friend, and who couldn't use more of those?

"We going or what?" DERFtron called from inside the van. "Christmas is getting closer!"

"Okay," Mongrel said, ruffling Biscuits' hair, "You stay here. I mean, you gotta do your time anyway, right? And I wouldn't want to get caught harbouring an escaped fugitive."

Biscuits nodded. "I no."

"*Know!*" DERFtron called from inside the van.

They hugged again, and Mongrel's eyeballs began sweating. "I'll come visit you again. But don't make me anything else!" he joked.

"You bring me cookies!" the boy said excitedly.

"Oh yeah." Mongrel had completely forgotten. "I remember, and I will." He closed the van's rear doors and began to make his way carefully over the remains of the wall to the driver's door.

"Mon?" Biscuits called after him. Mongrel turned to look back at the boy. "I'm sorry I killed your mom."

This turned Mongrel's mood a little sour. "Would you stop bringing that up? It's a memory I haven't repressed yet!"

"Sorry."

Mongrel hopped in and closed the door. Fussing with his seatbelt, he muttered about how he couldn't wait to get away from the place.

"Let's get out of here!" DERFtron said.

Mongrel started the van and began driving around the side of the building, looking for the road that led back to Dunttstown. "So you didn't want him coming?" he asked DERFtron.

"Well, don't get me wrong, he's a sweet kid, but he drives me insane!"

"Yeah I know," Mongrel chuckled. "I probably would've regretted it if he came anyway."

After they rounded another corner the road came into view, and Mongrel sped up to get to it. This is where things took a turn for the worse, as one of the van's tires blew, and the whole vehicle swayed violently to the side. Mongrel tried to regain control but overcorrected and they began lurched the other way. Out the front window Mongrel could see the electrified fence phasing into view as they slid out of control. Then he saw the bus stop sign, and what appeared to be Captain Pete hobbling madly out of the way. There was a loud thud, followed by a *yelp*, and the van went into the ditch and rolled over onto its side and ground to a halt.

"You okay?" Mongrel asked once the world had stopped spinning.

"I'm a machine," DERFtron said proudly, "of course I'm fine. What happened? Don't you know how to drive?"

Mongrel shook his head, which he ironically felt would help him gain some bearings. "I must've hit something." He touched his aching forehead and felt and small patch of blood. Other than that he figured he was fine.

"You fucked up the van!"

"It's not my fault!" Mongrel cried. "I couldn't control it!"

"Can't you even crash properly?"

"You want to drive?"

The Importance Of Being Constantly Surprised

"Well not now! Look at the mess you've made!"

"I told you something hit me!"

"No, *you* hit something."

"I'll hit you!"

"Bring it on, human!" DERFtron manoeuvered himself into a standing position.

Mongrel fumbled for his seatbelt and released it, falling against the door. Lying in a pile of cell phones and glass, the fight died in him. He looked across to the passenger side, which was now facing the sky. He knew his luck would run out sooner or later, but he hoped to have gotten a little farther away from the penitentiary. Misery settled on him like bird shit; he knew his getaway had tragically come to an end. But knowing he couldn't just sit there and wait for rescue, he began climbing up.

DERFtron saw what Mongrel was doing and followed his lead. He slowly turned himself around and tried to prop open the back door. The side that was closest to the ground was easy, and even formed a small ramp. The top-facing door on the other hand, was problematic. Gravity refused to let it stay open on its own, and DERFtron's mechanical arms had limited movement, so he couldn't hold it open as he rolled out. Instead he had to let it hang, his head-monitor brushing it open as he exited, which resulted in a long scratch down his screen. He winced but didn't go further outside. "You're gonna have to go get another van. I can't be out in the rain." Then he saw something made him regret saying that. "Oh…shit."

"Well I guess I could try," Mongrel said, poking his head out the passenger window. "I'll have to get Biscuits again." He pulled himself up and out, careful to avoid any shards of glass, and looked around. He was facing the electrified fence opposite the prison. The rain was bringing up a fog in the field it enclosed. And lying in a crumpled heap next to it was the bloodied, smoking carcass of Captain Pete.

Mongrel jumped down off the van and into the ditch, and crashed and rolled into the mud a few yards from the good captain. Wincing as he got to his sore feet, he made his way solemnly over to Captain Pete's body. He stopped after only a few feet, unable to look any closer. A deep pit of despair welled up within him. Once again Captain Pete was dead, and this time it really was his fault. But he knew he couldn't stand there forever, and walked around to the back of the van – and stopped dead in his tracks.

McCulloch stood there, arms crossed, yet holding an umbrella, looking quite unpleased. "Told you I'd come check on you," he said. "Mind telling me what you're doing?"

"Um…" Mongrel began slowly. He glanced back at the van, and at Derf, who looked defeated, and then turned back to the guard. "I didn't do it."

McCulloch surveyed the wrecked van behind Mongrel, at DERFtron hiding inside, and at Captain Pete's carcass. "What exactly is it that you didn't do?"

Mongrel threw his thumb over his shoulder and made a circular motion with it. "Any of…of that."

"It was like this when we got here," DERFtron said, trying to help.

"Well I think you did do it," McCulloch said, and then spat on the ground. "Wasn't all your fault though; one of my guys shot out your tires."

Mongrel shot a glance at Derf. "Told you!"

"Yeah," McCulloch nodded. "Guy's gonna be pissed though. You really did a number on his car."

"Me?"

"You drive like a maniac."

"Ha!" DERFtron exclaimed. "Told *you*."

Mongrel stuttered and sputtered. "But I…I…" he hung his head. "I guess you got some weird punishment for prisoners that try to escape, huh?"

"Mmm-hmm," McCulloch said. "We used to have a demolition derby for the inmates. They'd all get to work on their own cars. Keeps 'em occupied, and they liked it."

"That doesn't sound so bad."

"Well, we gave motorcycles to escapers. Handcuffed 'em to the handlebars."

"Oh." Mongrel tried not to imagine the horror. "And you still do that?"

The Importance Of Being Constantly Surprised

"Not anymore. Budget won't allow for it. Now we'd just tie you to the bumper of a cop car and drag you around the yard real fast. Donuts are fun."

Mongrel shuddered, unable to keep the images out of his head this time. "Don't suppose it would do any good to try to convince you I'm not a prisoner?"

McCulloch nodded again. "Yeah, I know."

Jerking his head up so fast it hurt, Mongrel couldn't believe what he'd heard. "What did you say?"

"I went and checked the files. Seems you ain't incarcerated like the rest of these assholes."

"So you believed me?" Mongrel was dumbfounded again. The last few hours and been like a roller coaster for him, and he wasn't sure he could last much longer without his heart failing him out of shock.

"Well, it was more your attitude than anything. Everything that happened didn't make sense with you. Everywhere you went, and everything you did, it was like you didn't know what to do or where to go. You always acted surprised every time something happened, like it was all new to you."

"It *was* all new to me."

"You didn't act like a prisoner, is all I'm saying," is all McCulloch was saying. "Most of 'em act defeated, and even if they don't like it they accept the fact that they belong here. But not you. Plus, I saw how you were with the boy, and what you did for him. I appreciate that."

Now Mongrel was confused. Just what *had* he done for the boy?

"He looks up to you, you know," McCulloch continued. "Anyway, sorry for roughing you up in there. Just business, you know. You'd be surprised how many people try to pull the same stunt."

"Probably."

"As for him," he said, pointing at DERFtron, "I don't know what you're doing with him, but how about I just don't ask? As a way of apologizing and hoping you don't sue the prison."

Mongrel thought about this. It hadn't occurred to him, but he pretty much had a great case against them, which could result in

Random Tangent

big bucks. And he certainly could use some extra cash. Maybe he'd look into it when he got back.

"We've already lost a ton of money. Even have to recycle the food sometimes to make ends meet. If we lost any more money we'd have to close down and release all the prisoners."

"Well shit," Mongrel said. "Guess I can't sue you then."

McCulloch nodded. "That's good. So you just take DERFtron and get out of here. I know Biscuits will miss him, but maybe I can take his place, teach the kid. Things could work out okay."

"Oh yeah, you'll do fine," Mongrel said, slapping McCulloch on his back, which he didn't seem to like. Knowing he should get out of there before the guard got angry and changed his mind, Mongrel made to leave, but stopped and asked, "Can I have your umbrella?"

Grumbling and looking up at the clouds, McCulloch handed over his umbrella. "Sure. Guess you'll be walking, since the bus won't be here for hours."

"Thanks."

"You take care. I gotta go call an ambulance for that guy before he dies." McCulloch began walking back towards the prison.

"Who? Captain Pete?" Mongrel asked. "He's dead."

McCulloch stopped and turned around. "That his name, Pete? Rings a bell?"

"Yeah, I...uh...kinda know him. We...used to go to high school together." For some reason Mongrel felt it best not to be completely honest about their relationship.

Glancing over at the body, McColloch sneered a little, confused. "Why's he look much older than you?"

"Well he was a teacher, see." Mongrel could feel his stack of lies wobbling like a Jenga tower. "That's how we were there. Together. At the same time."

"You sure he's dead?"

"Mongrel nodded. "Oh yeah. Trust me."

"All the same, I can't just leave him out here." McColloch turned and marched back to the prison.

And that was it. Just like that, Mongrel was free. It almost seemed too good to be true. Everything he'd been through – the

158

The Importance Of Being Constantly Surprised

beatings, the near rape, the boy – it was all over. He could go back to his life now. Even though it had only been a day, it felt like he'd been in Dunttstown Penitentiary a lifetime. And he knew he told Biscuits he'd come back to visit, but it would be a while.

"Well?" DERFtron called. "Are we going or what?"

Mongrel came over, a look of confused joy on his face. "Looks like the coast is clear. We're free! And I got you an umbrella." He held it over DERFtron's head as he exited the van.

"Oh *great*, an umbrella." DERFtron looked at it dismally. "Does that mean we're walking?"

"Well, you'll be rolling," Mongrel joked.

DERFtron wasn't amused. "Can't you just go get another van?"

"I don't know how to hotwire cars."

"Well I do."

Mongrel thought for a moment. "I don't remember seeing any more vans back there."

DERFtron shook his monitor. "Worst. Breakout. Ever. Hold that over me, I don't want to get wet."

"So what's our next move?" Mongrel asked, adjusting the angle of the umbrella.

"You gotta get me back to Bosley, that mad scientist."

"Bosley? That name sounds familiar. Well I gotta get home first. I need a good night's sleep. Had a terrible dream last night. I could also use a trip to a decent hospital." He then laughed to himself.

"What?"

"Well it's…it's just that I haven't walked home with anyone in so long. It's been, like, three stories."

"Huh?"

"Never mind. Where is this Bosley guy anyway?"

"Bolivia."

Mongrel looked at DERFtron, not liking the sound of that. "I'll have to pack a lunch."

They began moving out, heading eastward back to town. The walk would take them about an hour, then maybe they could catch a ride the rest of the way home. With Mongrel holding the umbrella over DERFtron and not himself he'd be soaked, and would need a…well, whatever the opposite of a shower was, he'd need one of those. He'd probably need a shower too, come to think of it. And definitely something to eat; he could almost feel his stomach digesting itself.

"Hey," DERFtron said, breaking the silence, "thanks for doing this."

"Well, sorry for leaving you for dead."

"Don't sweat it. I'd have done the same to you."

The rain continued pouring down, but Mongrel was already as drenched as he could be, so it didn't bother him. He couldn't wait to sleep in his own bed again. Eat his own food. Life his own life. Just…relax. Then he'd be off on another adventure.

But this adventure was finally over.

Content with that in mind, he walked home, next to DERFtron, feeling good for the first time in what seemed like days. Perhaps it wasn't so bad being him, he thought, which came as no surprise at all.

"Wait a second," Mongrel said suddenly. "What about my conjugal visit?"

The End.

But you knew this was coming. Mongrel finally walked in his front door, drenched, exhausted and with feet covered in blisters, thinking it didn't take Frodo this long to get the damn ring to Mordor. Perhaps it was time to buy his own car and prevent any more of these long walks home. Derftron, excited to have a plan to get his own body back, failed to realize that while it's not hard to put a brain in a machine and make it work – at least not if you're a mad scientist – doing it the other way around presents its own problems. For example, where are you going to find a spare body? McCulloch grew closer to Biscuits as a result of DERFtron leaving the prison, and decided to adopt the boy when his sentence was over. He also looked into Biscuits' *real* and missing cellmate, Jayson Miles, who by then had to be miles away from Duntt Pen. Let the manhunt begin. Big John violently guarded the door like

The Importance Of Being Constantly Surprised

Mongrel told him to – for two solid weeks. He eventually had to be lured away with, what else, a puppy. They threw it in a cage and Big John followed, where it caught the poor animal and hugged it so tightly that its brain squeezed out though its nose. Beby spent a lot of time preparing mentally for her conjugal visit with Mongrel, and when she came in the next week, and he wasn't there, oh man, she was *not* pleased. Biscuits became heavily involved with his outside girlfriend, Sasha, and they were planning on their own conjugal visit soon. The boy is in for a surprise. Impressed with Guirmo's business savvy and, uh, handling skills, Solvo figured he'd try his own hand at the rape industry. His tactics were unconventional, with a focus on romance and seduction, involving victims that were more willing to participate. He was also able to convince Biscuits to join him in this venture, which opened up a niche market only they were privy too. Even some of the guards became customers. All of this, along with their monthly rape sales, put them on top of the rape industry. When Guirmo recovered from being ripped in half he was shocked to find his business partner, Ockley, had let GOBARS slip into decline. Going freelance, be launched his new Perpendicular Plaid plan, but failed to attract new clients, even when offering group discounts. Brecklyn, whose arms were horrifically broken, again, learned how to become a contortionist and used that special ability to escape from prison. He soon took up a career in protective services. Captain Pete was savagely mowed down and killed in traffic while waiting for the bus outside of Dunttstown Penitentiary. He decided when he came back to life that his pegged legs were doing him more harm than good. Something had to be done about them…

Jaywatch

Jaywatch

The stranger stood upon a precipice overlooking Dunttstown. The precipice needn't be exceptionally tall to achieve this view, since Dunttstown wasn't terribly large; it was meandering, off-balance, and perhaps even suspicious, but it wasn't large.

It was nighttime, and all was silent. But if you listened closely, you could hear the town snoring. It didn't light up like most places at night; with the exception of a handful of street lamps, Dunttstown was dark. Even the shadows had shadows.

The stranger knew this town well, having been born there. The rain having stopped, he folded up his umbrella, which he'd fashioned out of a stick, a few lengths of wire from an old fence, and a dead bird, and then flicked on his radio.

"...ure this is the right place?" came in a faint whisper.

"119 Chickenweed Lane. That's what the map says. Square in the middle of nowhere." This voice was in the foreground, closer to the mic.

"There aren't any other houses on this road. How do we know this is the right place?"

Random Tangent

"Because there aren't any other houses on this road! This has to be the place. Anyway, we cut the power, boss. Heading around back now. Looks like no one's home. No car in the driveway. Damn, back door's locked too. Bollocks. I wanted to be quiet about this."

"B AND E THEN." A new voice, more dominating.

"Yeah, I guess we'll have to."

'And actually this isn't really the middle of nowhere. Katrina's Rock is in the middle of nowhere.'

"Is that the rock with 'Timmy' written on it?"

'Yeah.'

"WOULD YOU GENTS STOP BLATHERING AND GET ON WITH IT?"

"So why is it called Katrina's Rock?"

'Don't know. Never loo-'

The stranger hit scan on his radio; it was a boring conversation anyway. He was looking for something else.

"... ILES, AN ESCAPED CONVICT FROM DUNTTSTOWN PENITENTIARY. LOCAL AUTHORITIES BELIEVE HIM TO BE HEADING FOR DUNTTSTOWN. STAY TUNED TO JAYWATCH FOR MORE INFORMATION."

Now that was more like it. The stranger smiled.

Mongrel awoke to the sound of breaking glass. He groggily sat up in bed and rubbed his eyes. He looked around his room, trying to expedite the return of his lucidity, but it was dark, and he couldn't see anything.

A chill went down his spine. Where was the glow of his alarm clock? Where was his fluffy pillow? Where was...where was Biscuits?

"Bastard fish," he muttered. He was still in prison. He *had* to be. His escape, his walk home, his wonderful shower; it was just another stupid dream. Of course, it also meant his near-rape never happened, so there was that.

Just what the hell was going on with his brain? He was having so many dreams within dreams he was starting to lose count of them, lose track of reality. Was it all the head-bashing, or was he actually in the Matrix? He'd suffered through more assaults in the past few days than the average person received in a lifetime. He needed to see a shrink or something about it, if Duntt Penn. had a shrink. Or at least maybe he could just dream about seeing a shrink. Would that work?

Then a door creaked open, which Mongrel took as great news. Prison doors don't creak; they clang, if he recalled correctly. Not only that, but this particular creak was one he recognized. The only door he knew that creaked was his back door, which meant he really was at home after all!

The hinges on the back door of his house emitted a strange high-pitch squeal that Mongrel hoped for the sake of the sanity of the planet couldn't be duplicated elsewhere. It was so poignant and jarring that his ears refused to accept it as sound and completely ignored it. So he couldn't actually hear the door, but he could feel it. His brain sensed the sound waves like a disturbance in the Force, and didn't know how to handle it. Because of this it would come up with random, bizarre methods of dealing with the problem. Sometimes he would lose bowel control, other times he would go temporarily blind. Occasionally he would simply lose consciousness. This time his hair began falling out of this head.

Mongrel was so excited about this that he leapt out of bed, slipped on his pillow, which was on the floor for some reason, and crashed to the floor. Tufts of hair drifted lazily around him. He rubbed his head dizzily, thinking two things; first, that explained where his pillow went; and second, why was his back door opening?

"Derf?" he called out meekly. He then cleared his throat and called again, louder, but each time yielded no response. Concerned, he staggered to his feet and snuck over to the bedroom door. Opening it silently, he poked his head out and glanced around. Moonlight streamed through the windows, causing shadows to fall on everything, making the house look alien.

"I can see you!"

The sound startled him, but Mongrel quickly recognized the slightly mechanical voice of DERFtron, his friend trapped in a robot, downstairs in the combination living-room-kitchen. It was obvious that DERFtron couldn't see him, since he was upstairs, but just who *could* DERFtron see? Mongrel crept to the stairs as quietly as he could.

Since his mother's passing, Mongrel had slowly begun moving into her old home. No money was owed to the bank on it, and with him apparently being the sole living member of the family, it was completely his. It was unfortunate that the place was next to the middle of nowhere, which was a steep ride from Dunttstown, where his apartment was. He'd committed himself to shopping for a car in the future.

While he liked his little apartment because it was cheap and had a great location, he couldn't say no to free rent, and the extra space would certainly be useful. The only reason he still kept the apartment was for the bathroom. The walls of the facilities at his mother's place were adorned with pictures of the family, and he felt like they were watching him whenever he tried to use the toilet. It was an uncomfortable feeling he couldn't shake. He knew the simple solution, but he hadn't yet been able to move any of his mother's belongings yet; it still felt too soon.

"What the hell is that thing?" a voice cried.

"Cool, it's a robot! This guy has a robot?"

Inching down the stairs, Mongrel tried to get a look at the burglars, but all he saw were two beams of light focused on DERFtron.

"Where do you even get a robot?" one of the men asked.

"Probably built it."

"What is he, a mad scientist or something?"

"Now, now, you don't got to be a mad scientist to go 'round building robots; just got to have the right amount of knowhow. And mad scientists do more than build robots you know? Some of 'em do good work too."

"Geez! This a touchy subject for you?"

"Well me granddad was a mad scientist. Lots of folks talked ill of 'im, but he was just misunderstood. Kept saying once he got his tree formula right they'd change their tune. See, he was trying to grow trees inside out, that way the wood's on the outside, 'stead of the bark. And without the bark there's no limit to 'ow wide it'd grow. Trees would be nice and fat, and you could just slice off the amount of wood you need, 'stead of choppin' it down. And it'd grow back if you after a few years. End all this deforestation nonsense."

"If you don't mind," DERFtron said, tired of waiting, "you're breaking into private property. I have already alerted the poli-"

"Ew! A rat!" one of the men suddenly shouted, jumping onto the couch.

Jaywatch

Since his father's tragic farming accident years prior, Mongrel's mother had stopped clearing the house of wild animals, preferring their company to the empty silence. Of all the local fauna that came and went, only the rats decided to remain permanently. They eventually became family pets, each being given a name, bed, etc. Unfortunately, Hershule wasn't the best cook, and had a voracious appetite for fresh meat. Soon the livestock became deadstock, and then the pets began appearing on the menu. Now, only one remained: a fat ugly one named Bartimus.

"I'll get it," the other man said, and began stomping on the floor.

"No!" Mongrel shouted. He made to rush in and save the day, but tripped and fell down the remaining stairs. In the commotion Bartimus fled the scene.

As Mongrel rubbed his knee, wheezing in the corner of the bottom step of the staircase, a flashlight wandered its way over to shine in his face. It lingered there for a moment before someone said, "Is this him? Looks like he's home after all."

DERFtron came over to not lend any assistance, merely saying, "You have rats? Why didn't you tell me you had rats? I hate rats."

The other flashlight hopped off the couch and came over to join in on blinding Mongrel. "That's him alright. Much uglier in person, isn't he?"

Mongrel was not about to lay there and be facially criticized. "Hey, I'm handsome until proven ugly by a jury of my peers. Now would someone mind telling me what the hell is going on? And get those lights out of my face."

"You see?" one said, moving the flashlight away. "Told you we shouldn't have cut the power. This would've been easier if we could see better."

"And *that's* why you were no good at this," the other retorted. "This way we get to use flashlights, which means we get to see what we want to see, and no one else does. And without the flashlight…" the beam shot away, "he can now see us."

With the light no longer in his eyes, Mongrel could now see the two men, albeit breathed in shadows. They were dressed fastidiously posh, almost alarmingly so. In fact, something about their attire made Mongrel ill at ease, as did their British accents, which for some reason only became apparent with the light out of his eyes.

"Maybe you just need a robotic body like mine," DERFtron said. "I've got night vision, x-ray vision, thermal vision, sonar, radar, infrar-"

One of the men flicked a switch on DERFtron's back, shutting him off. "Wish my wife had one of these."

"You can turn him off?" Mongrel asked, astonished.

"Of course, it's a machine isn't it? Any machine can be turned off." The man stuck out his hand to Mongrel. "Anyway, I'm William, and this here is Martin," he jerked his head behind him towards the other man. "We'll be your kidnappers this evening."

Mongrel got to his feet and shook each man's hand, unnerved by their manners more than anything. "Um…why, may I ask, are you doing this?"

"Can't say no more," William said.

"This is covert," Martin said excitedly.

William nodded in agreement. "Now I know it's night and all, but we still can't have you knowing where we're taking you. Rules is rules is rules. So we need to blindfold you. Martin, grab a cushion; that'll work."

Martin wandered around for a bit, searching with his flashlight, occasionally banging his shin or knee into something and politely cursing.

Something slowly came to Mongrel's attention as Martin's search progressed. It wasn't that these men reminded Mongrel of one of his mortal enemies and that they could be connected, and he could be in grave danger. It also wasn't the fact that, despite all the strange and awful things that had happened to him, he'd never been kidnapped before. So, you know, cheers to new experiences. What crossed his mind was simply this; there were no cushions.

"We don't have any cushions," he said.

Among the multitude of his mother's eccentricities was a fear of couch cushions. Mongrel wasn't sure what the technical term for it was, but he himself suffered from ichthyophobia; the fear of fish. He presumed most of his irrational character flaws had come from his mother, including his penchant for shiny things and, try as he might, his inability to avoid getting into arguments with mimes. He'd also lately been finding himself talking to inanimate objects, which reminded him of how his mother often talked to her shoes. Or maybe it was her feet she was talking to, but the shoes were just in the way. Perhaps the shoes affected her feet's hearing?

"You don't have any cushions?" Martin asked, flabbergasted. "What kind of home has no cushions?"

Mongrel shrugged in response, but in the dim light it probably went unnoticed.

Martin shook his head. "These yanks really are a poor breed."

"Canadian," Mongrel muttered, although in the dim light it probably went unheard.

"Well if we can't blindfold you then we'll just have to put you out for a bit," William said. "Can't let you see where we're going."

"You could just grab a rag or a scarf or something," Mongrel suggested, not wanting to be knocked out. As far as he was concerned he seemed to spend more time being unconscious than actually sleeping, and he worried that one more bump on the head could put him to sleep permanently.

William shook his head. "'Fraid not. They can slip off or come lose. In my experience they just don't work. Need to cover the whole head."

"What, do you do this for a living or something?" Mongrel intended for this to be a joke, and even managed to chuckle a little to support this. But neither man shared his jubilance, and in fact looked quite severely at him, not at all impressed with his attempt at humour. "I got pillowcases in my bedroom," he said meekly.

William snapped his fingers and pointed up the stairs, and Martin, like a dog, went to fetch them.

"Um, I don't suppose there's any way I could talk you out of this, is there?" Mongrel asked.

"Oh come on," William slapped him on the back. "Now don't be like that. There's naught at all to worry about. Nothing but a little routine kidnapping, is all."

"You mean you guys aren't gonna kill me?"

Random Tangent

"Well..." Willaim didn't seem to know what to say, "not us, personally. But okay, yeah, you might want to worry about that. But do try to keep it to yourself; I want to enjoy this."

Mongrel turned his face up in what meant to be incredulity, but came across more like a sneer. "You enjoy this?"

"It's been a coon's age since I done any field work," William explained.

Turning at the sound of feet shuffling down carpeted stairs, Mongrel only managed to see a blur of shadows as a pillowcase came down over his head. "Um, what exactly is it that you do?"

"Sorry mate, can't tell you no more."

"Or he'd have to kill you," Martin explained, and then snickered more than a fair amount for what wasn't a very funny pun.

"I'm gonna be killed anyway aren't I?" Mongrel asked, not really wanting to know the answer.

"What makes you say that?" Martin asked, still giggling. "We work for the British government. Lots of hush hush stuff, so we can't say for sure."

"Martin!" William snapped.

"What? You're retired, so it's not like I'm blowing your cover or anything. Besides, he'll be dead soon, so who's he going to tell?" He snapped his fingers. "*Bugger!* It was supposed to be a surprise."

"I keep telling you: your big mouth always gets you into trouble."

Mongrel let the two men argue as he mulled over some thoughts. Didn't Shamus Bond work for the British government? The Majesty's secret society or something? Could he be behind all this? But wouldn't Shamus come for him directly? Didn't he work alone? He did during their last encounter. Isn't that a rule or something? Didn't James Bond work alone? If only he'd seen more James Bond movies...

"You never listen to me!" William shouted.

"Well maybe if you stopped telling me what to do all the time I'd start listening."

"Guys!" Mongrel shouted. He couldn't see them with the pillow case over his face, but he could tell by their silence that they were both looking at him. "If you two can't get along, then I don't want to be kidnapped by you. Come back some other time or send someone else. Now if you'll excuse me, I'm very tired." He turned and tried to walk up the stairs, but tripped on the first step and smashed his head into the sixth, breaking his nose and knocking him unconscious.

"Wish they all could be this easy-peasy," William said.

"A county-wide search for missing Dunttstown Penitentiary inmate Jayson Miles is now underway. He is reportedly six feet tall, two-hundred pounds, has cropped black hair and a dark complexion, and also has transparent eyelids. If anyone has any information on his whereabouts please cal-"

The stranger turned off his radio; he was trying to keep a low profile. He wasn't trying to avoid anyone in particular – he was trying to avoid *everyone*. And it wasn't because he didn't want to interact with anyone – it was simple a matter of doing what was right. Most people wouldn't want him around, and those who didn't mind his presence simply didn't know who he was, which would change if he engaged them.

Much as he'd like to avoid it, he was going to have to venture into town for supplies. If he timed everything right, he could get everything he needed without drawing attention to himself. Once he had all the materials he needed, he could create everything he needed from scratch – his building skills were nearly limitless[*].

Unfortunately he had no money, and was going to have to find an alternative approach to acquiring his supplies.

All the more reason to go unnoticed.

It took Mongrel a minute to remember that his head was concealed in a pillowcase, which was why he couldn't see anything. It took him another minute to realize that it was blood he tasted, and that his nose must have been broken, hence the throbbing pain. More minutes were used up figuring out that he was outside, and on

---

[*] He once constructed a working nuclear reactor out of a refrigerator, a box of crayons, a jar of soy sauce, and three chickens.

Random Tangent

pavement, and that sound he'd just heard was tires screeching to a halt.

Interestingly, he'd been knocked unconscious earlier by a blow to the skull, and now he'd been jolted awake by another from the hard landing after he'd been flung out of the back of a van. Not being securely tied to anything, his kidnappers assumed he'd be a good little hostage and be still and quiet for the duration of the trip. What was not taken into account was the fact that Dunttstown is quite dark at night, and driving on the opposite side of the road does not come naturally after years of the contrary.

A car door opened and closed, followed quickly by another one.

"I'm telling you I closed the door properly."

It sounded like Martin, who Mongrel thought sounded a little gay.

"Well what do you expect from these cheap American vehicles?" William. "Hopefully the poor chap is still alive. But maybe I should drive?"

"Gladly!" Martin agreed. "They're all backwards over here, driving on the wrong side of the road and putting tomatoes on their chips. Animals."

"Well I put ketchup on my chips so maybe I can figure out the whole driving thing."

"I can drive," Mongrel muttered as they grew close.

"There, you see?" Martin asked. "He's alive and well."

"What'd he say?"

"I said I can drive," Mongrel repeated, "and I'm not that well. Did one of you hit me? I think my nose is broke." He rolled around on the ground for a moment, trying to get to his feet. His hands were useless for this procedure since they were tied behind his back, and thusly made the maneuver unmanageable.

He was fortunately picked up off the ground a little more roughly than he'd have preferred, and tossed back into the van far more roughly than he'd have preferred. As far as preferences went anyhow, he'd much rather be back in his home, sleeping on a giant pile of money next to the woman of his dreams. And spaghetti. He could really go for a big plate of spaghetti right now.

"Sorry mate," William said, "but you don't know where we're going, now do you?" This was obviously a rhetorical question, as he didn't wait for an answer, closing the van door behind him.

The van had been stolen from the parking lot beside a cell phone store, and despite the advertising on the side, was barren of guys, ladies, and anything remotely technical. The van was comprised of two front seats, and a rather vacant cargo area in the back, where Mongrel did most of his wallowing. After a brief stint of this, he got to knees and shuffled over to the front of the van and listened to the radio as the other two were getting in.

"...from Dunttstown Pennitentiary a little over twenty hours ago. Jayson Miles was seven years into his life sentence for the rape, torture, and murder of a local farmer. The body of the farmer was neve-"

"If you told me where to go I could drive there," Mongrel said. "I mean, you're planning on killing me anyway, right? So it's not like I can give away your secret hideout."

William clicked off the radio. "What?"

"Secret hideout?" Martin asked. "I like the sound of that. Can we get one?"

"We don't have a secret hideout," William said, somewhat annoyed. "It's just a little shack to the East, just past the prison I believe."

"So much for giving away too much information," Martin chastised.

"Well it's not like he's a threat. Like he said, he's going to be dead soon anyway."

Mongrel's heart sunk further into the abyss in his chest. Even though he'd brought it up, the talk of his death wasn't something he could be cheerful about for long. "Don't you at least want a ransom? I gotta be worth something."

"Nah. From what I heard we're gonna torture you, you know, muck you around for a bit, and then off you."

The words 'muck' and 'off' wandered around Mongrel's head, not sounding nice. "So I'm gonna be mucked off? But that's not how this is supposed to go. If you're kidnapping me then I'm entitled to a ransom. Or *you* are, I mean."

Random Tangent

"I never heard anything about a ransom," Martin said.

"Nope. Nothing," William agreed.

"Well have you been kidnapped before? Cause I think I know what I'm doing. If you're just gonna kill me then why the bag over my face? Why the secret hideout? Why do this all at night? Why even bother to wake me in the first place? Just break into my house and shoot me!"

Martin looked at his companion. "He's got a point."

"For the last time, there is no secret hideout," William said, patting Mongrel on the shoulder. "Now look here, mate, orders is orders is orders. We're to bring you back to the ranch and have a little fun. More for us than for you of course."

"Ranch?"

"Wait a minute," Martin said, "what do you mean you've done this before?"

"I didn't say that," Mongrel said. "Now, what ranch? Where are we going?"

"Yes you did. You said you knew what you was doing."

William concurred. "You did say that."

Mongrel sighed. "I just…it's just that…okay, fine. I *did* say that. I've kidnapped before. Happy?"

The two men were quiet for a minute. "What else you done?"

Shaking his head, Mongrel couldn't believe this was happening to him. What a day? Or a night? It was only…

"Uh, what time is it?"

"Quarter to four," Martin replied.

It wasn't even four in the morning, and this day was already turning out to be no better than the last – and he was in prison the day before. Actually, this one would be worse, considering that he wasn't supposed to live to the end of it. Maybe he'd have been better off in prison.

"Oh, you know, the usual," Mongrel said, "raping and pillaging, kidnapping and whatnot. Even did time in Duntt Penn."

"You don't say!" William said, seemingly impressed.

Martin looked wide-eyed at him, but Mongrel couldn't see this. "You were in there? Like as a prisoner?"

Jaywatch

Mongrel considered several responses, most with less deceit than he'd exhibited so far. But they were long and drawn out and would require a good bit of exposition to convey properly, which he wasn't in the mood to give. He instead settled for a quick, "Yep."

"What's it like in there?" Martin asked, genuinely interested. He generally had no problems whatsoever meeting gentlemen, since they were practically everywhere. The problem was trying to find men of a particular persuasion. Martin did nothing to hide the fact that he was gay. In fact, he displayed it proudly, and once even tried to become a professional. This was a problem because, while anyone, including the blind, deaf, and dead, could see he was gay, he hadn't a clue as to anyone else's sexual orientation. His 'gaydar' was broken, as it were. As such, meeting like-minded individuals often required some embarrassing trial and error.

Prison, on the other hand, would eliminate most of these situations. It was almost expected of you to enjoy[*] the company of other men.

"How're we doing?" William suddenly asked. "I mean, as a bit of professional critiquing."

At that moment the radio came alive. *"What's taking you two so long? Where are you?"*

William grabbed the CB, "Sorry. Had to stop, uh, Martin got carsick."

Martin glared at him, and William shrugged in apology.

"Fucking fairy. Well stop lollygagging and get a move on. This old codger is driving me mad!"

"Well, looks like play time's over." The two men settled back into their seats. "Try to relax. Maybe even have a nice nap while you're back there."

"Yeah, right," Mongrel muttered. "Consider the taking the scenic route, if you will."

"'Fraid not. We're late enough as it is." William started the van and punched the gas hard enough for Mongrel to lose his balance and fall to the back, where he landed on the rear doors hard enough to crash through them, and landed on the pavement hard

---

[*] Of course, the level of enjoyment might vary from inmate to inmate. But participation was still mandatory.

enough to be knocked unconscious once again. Looks like he was going to get that nap after all.

The van screeched to a halt, then reversed quickly to where Mongrel was laying, nearly running him over.

"As if this isn't hard enough as it is," Martin said as he exited the van.

William joined him, annoyed. "Next time we get something with a bloody boot!"

Together they picked Mongrel up and tossed him back into the van.

Figuring he'd leave Dunttstown before he drew too much attention to himself, the stranger headed East. He normally wouldn't have gone in this direction, since it ventured near the prison, but he had unfinished business to take care of. An old mentor of his needed to be seen.

A long time ago, back when the world was younger and made sense more often than not, he'd met the old man. He was old even then, but in a non-specific way. Old like the sky, like a mountain, like stone; it was impossible to tell his age simply by studying him. But you could almost feel it. Like heat waves radiating off flames, or the smell of a fart that's all but dissipated, you could sense it in his presence. It was an oldness that was as much a part of him as his skin and bones.

He was ancient, but had been ancient for a long time. Because of this the stranger knew he'd still be alive.

And crazy.

Much like age only accumulates over the years, so too did insanity, and the old man had enough to spare. It was as if he collected it, bred it. The level of his insanity would have embarrassed any psychopath, caused psychiatrists to give up practicing, and caused you to question your faith in reality. And there still would have been enough left over to convert all the world's Christians to scientology.

The stranger had unfinished business with the crazy old bastard, and he was coming for his resolution. Using the supplies he'd acquired in town, he'd constructed what he called a *kartcycle* (half motorcycle, half go-kart) out of a couple washing machines, a handful of coat hangers, a milk crate, and some toast. It wasn't one of his finest works, but it would get the job done.

It was only a matter of time now.

Mongrel awoke to the feeling of being dragged across the ground on his face. He wanted to keep his consciousness to himself but found it difficult when his head started banging off steps as the journey ventured up stairs. He heard a door creak open, and mellow old-timey music invaded his ears.

"Finally!" someone shouted. "D'you know what time it is?" This someone might have had a British accent like the others, but until Mongrel could see the person it would remain a mystery.

"Sorry," a voice that sounded like William said. "This guy was a bit of a handful. And that bloody van is a piece of work, I tell you."

"Rubbish." Definitely Martin; his voice had a certain…charm. "Are you gonna give us a hand or what?"

After a minute of grumbling, and some scraping of chair legs, Mongrel was dragged around for a bit, down another flight of stairs and into what could have been a walk-in freezer, such was the temperature. He was then hastily thrown into a chair, but not tied to it. The pillowcase remained over his head.

Hobbled footsteps then came down the stairs to join the men. "Sorry about the mess down here," a creaky old voice said. "Just some old projects I never got around to completing. You get used to it." The sound of a fart suddenly emitted into the basement. "You'll get used to that too."

The men made some disgruntled noises. One began coughing.

"Oh…a, hmm…I think one wasn't quite ready," the old voice said apologetically. "Rushed to market, as it were."

"That's disgusting!" said someone who sounded like William.

"This him?" the old voice asked.

"Yep," William said, his voice strained. "This is the poor bastard."

The hobbled footsteps approached and stopped in front of Mongrel. "Would you look at the size of the face on him? Just don't get faces like that anymore. Back in my day people were all faces, maybe with some arms and legs poking 'round the side. Made it easier to tell us all apart. That's why crime was less too."

A sigh echoed around the room. "That ain't his face, the other man said."

Suddenly the pillowcase was whipped off Mongrel's head so fast he was almost burnt. "Ah!" he cried, and looked around at the faces, somewhat embarrassed by his reaction.

"Hmm," the old man said, "Well I suppose that's a little more like it. Too bad. Looks kinda funny."

The old man was dressed in a blue housecoat – similar to Mongrel's – and pink slippers. His skin was shriveled around his face and sunk in so far that his eyes appeared to be bulging out. What little hair that remained on top of his head was a scraggly mess, and he had a bit of a beard going on at the bottom. It didn't look like much was holding him together, as if for some reason he'd far outlived his lifespan. One small accident and his body would collapse upon itself. The other men were dressed alike, as if they were part of a band; neat suits and matching ties, and shoes so shiny they could blind you in the right light. Clean-shaven with hair parted decidedly on the left, they reminded Mongrel of hit men. His mind was producing an epic sonnet of apprehension.

Remaining silent, Mongrel cursed himself for being shy in front of people he was just meeting. He wished his face was still covered. William and Martin stared back at him, seemingly proud of...something. The new, or rather old guy appeared to be studying him, probably making sure he was in fact the right person. The old man was...wait a minute...

"I know you," Mongrel said, looking not at the old man but at his breath floating in front of him, although he managed to raise a hand and point at him

Despite this, the old man still asked, "Who?"

"*You.*" Mongrel threw some gusto into his pointing, giving the man one hell of a singling out. "I saw you on the bus just the other day."

The old man began laughing and slowly turned himself in a circle, propelled by a series of farts.

Jaywatch

"Oh God!" Martin gagged, and covered the lower half of his face with his left arm. William waved a hand back and forth in front of his face and proceeded to shuffle away from the other men, distancing himself from the stench.

Only the unnamed forth man seemed immune to the noxious emissions. Yet he was all but unperturbed. "I've been dealing with this all night. There's not a fresh bit of air in the house, and I don't think dry cleaning will do anything to remove the fumes from my shirt." He looked down at his shirt. "Pity; it was one of my favourites."

"At least he'd trying to help warm the place up," William muttered.

When the old man faced Mongrel again he stopped farting and vigorously shook his hand. "Cleopard's the name. And yes, that was me, spying on you on the bus."

"Spying?"

"Doing some…ah," he turned to the others, "what do you call it?"

"Reconnaissance," William answered.

"Yes, *reconnaissance*." Cleopard seemed to think back, recalling memories from when he was only old instead of ancient. "Didn't have this reconnaissance thing back in my day, no. We just went in blind. Made it up as we went along. That's what real men did. And we nev-"

"Oh put a sock in it," the still unnamed fourth man said. He then shoved Cleopard out of the way and took his turn shaking Mongrel's hand. "The old man's out of what's left of his mind, and that ain't much. I'm Colin."

Once all the introductions were complete, pieces began settling in Mongrel's mind. It would take a moment for them to all come together, so he decided to fill the awkward silence.

"You guys seem awfully polite."

"Well this can often be a gruesome business," Colin said. "My old man used to say 'you can get more with a kind word and a gun than you can with just a kind word alone.' I know what he meant, but there's no harm in being nice to people. Even people you mean to kill."

Random Tangent

"Uh, yeah," Mongrel agreed nervously. "About that, why are you going to kill me?"

"Just a job," Colin replied.

This reply seemed to upset Cleopard, who shook his head and began mumbling to himself.

"What?" Martin asked.

"No, don't ask," Colin was quick to say, but it wasn't quick enough.

"Jobs!" Cleopard said loudly. "Call this a job? Back in my day we had jobs. Had three by the time I was five. Didn't have school back then, you was just put to work when you could walk. Some of 'em had to crawl, the slow-learners."

"See, that's what happens," Colin said. "This is what I've had to put up with all night."

Martin shrugged. "Sorry."

William tried to guide the conversation back to answering Mongrel's question. "Look, it's just business. Most of us here are involved in what you might call shady dealings. We do things that aren't exactly legal, strictly speaking."

"But it's legal when we do it," Martin chimed in.

Mongrel looked back and forth between the two men. Was that it? That was their explanation? There had to be more to it.

"It's complicated," Colin said, realizing that there was probably no explanation Mongrel would find acceptable.

As if to segue their conversation into another topic, the floorboards above their heads began creaking under the stress of footsteps. The conversation halted, and everyone held their breaths, with the exception of Cleopard, who was muttering about people not having lungs back in his time.

"When I was a kid we'd have to pump our arms in and out all the time to force air into our bodies."

Suddenly the footsteps stopped, and for a ponderous moment time stood still. Then the sound of a muffled cough, followed by a polite clearing of the throat – *British* polite – wafted down to the basement. It was obvious to Mongrel that the person above them was also of British origin, and a shiver flew down his spine. He did not want to be there when that person came downstairs to join them.

Jaywatch

The footsteps then began moving again, much quicker now, heading for the basement door. All eyes darted towards the stairs as the door opened, and someone began to descend.

It was Shamus Bond.

"Having a party without me?" he asked.

"'Bout time you got back," Colin said. "Between you and these misfits gone," he gestured towards William and Martin, "I've had to put up with this coon by myself. If I was getting' paid for this gig I'd demand double!"

"Where were you anyway?" Martin asked.

"Just surveying the area," Shamus said, still surveying the area. "I saw you return and came back. Some problems?"

"No, no problems," William shrugged. "Learn anything useful in your sightseeing?"

Shamus raised an eyebrow at him, then lowered it again. "Oh yes, quite a lot actually. There's a cliff to the West, a lake to the North, and the barn outside is filled with a ghastly amount of spiders."

"That's a river," Cleopard said. "Duntt River. Not a lake."

"Same difference, "Shamus said. "Water's water. Now you said you had no problems with the lad?"

"None whatsoever," Martin confirmed.

"I see, I see." Shamus looked around the basement briefly, and began pacing. After a moment, he stopped and looked up. "Found the place all right? Directions were adequate?"

"Oh quite."

A nodding of the head from Shamus, then he returned to his pacing. This time without stopping or looking up he asked, "And he was home?"

"He was indeed. Bit of a mess he was too."

Shamus frowned in a way that suggested this news pleased him. But there was something else that was not. "And you *did* bring him here? Yes?"

Everyone nodded at the same time.

"Good, good. Then where, pray tell, is he?"

This brought about some confusion amongst the room full of men. They all looked at each other, until one of them, William, finally said, "Well, take a look for yourself."

Random Tangent

"I *have* been looking for myself. I've searched this whole bloody house. He isn't here. Did you happen to kill him and burry the body and return with an apparition?"

The confused look didn't leave William's face. He gestured with his arm toward the chair in the middle of the room.

Shamus' eyes, which were glaring at William, briefly flicked over to the chair, and then returned to William to glare some more. He gave no other reaction.

"Uh, Will…" Martin started.

William suddenly realized that something must be horribly wrong, and turned to look for himself

The chair was empty.[*]

The stranger stood upon a precipice, again, wondering how it was he kept finding them. He was certain there weren't this many precipices in the area before he'd been incarcerated. What had happened to the world?

Looking down upon the quaint little house, many memories came flooding back to him. He'd grown up around the area. Well, off and on; a little here, a little there. A man isn't made all at once, they say. He recalled being taught by the old man the ways the world worked, the ways it didn't, and most importantly, the ways it wasn't supposed to, but did.

Many people will tell you that it's the little things that matter most, yet it's these little things that people tend to overlook. The stranger exploited this ignorance, manipulating the world around him like a Rubik's Cube. The laws of metaphysics, the structure of time, the very nature of reality, these were child's play to him. He was the old man's best pupil. Probably his only one, actually; no one else could tolerate his perpetual gas. It wasn't the stench, but never-ending supply. The old man was constantly farting. The wind stayed broken around the Cleopard home.

Movement on the periphery caught his attention; someone was approaching the house. He pulled out a pair of homemade binoculars he'd made out of pack of cigarettes, a few rubber bands, and a stick of gum, to get a closer look. The man was tall, languid,

---

[*] I *told* you Mongrel didn't want to be there when Shamus got there. Don't look so surprised.

impeccably dressed. Catching a scent only he could smell, the stranger could tell the man was British.

The man entered Cleopard's house. Not bothering to knock, he must have had business there. The stranger decided to bide his time and see how this played out.

Putting his binoculars away, he began to hunt his way down toward the house. It could be called a farm house; a large barn sat amongst acres of fields, a well sat a few meters in between the two structures, and several tractors in various stages of decay lay scattered about. But the land itself was never used for agricultural purposes, with the exception of whatever the old man did to create his Nustard sandwich spread. Try as he might, the stranger just couldn't figure out the secret recipe. Talented as he was, the old man was his better. Cleopard still harboured secrets, but did he still have lessons to teach?

The stranger was there to prove that he was no longer the student.

Rain began falling as he picked his way among the tractor wreckage, and he wished he'd brought his umbrella with him. He felt something in the wind just then, and came to a stop. Crouching down, he pulled out his binoculars and looked toward the house. Someone was crawling out of the basement window.

While the British people and the old one argued amongst themselves, Mongrel sat in his chair and watched them, all the while shivering at the chills using his spine like a freeway. It suddenly occurred to him that he should leave. Just get up and go.

"Bu-"

Just get up and go. *Now.*

As quiet as he could, he eased out of his chair and around to its back, and then inched his way over to the wall. It was dark over there. Mongrel never really liked the dark, but tolerated it, much in the way one must tolerate an inlaw's horrific body odor when giving an obligatory hug after not seeing each other for years, especially when the reason for the disparity is because they simply *can't* tolerate the horrific body odor. Darkness in an unknown place bothered Mongrel even more; he knew he couldn't stay long.

Random Tangent

Finding the wall, and then finding his way along it, Mongrel was careful to manoeuver his way around the junk Cleopard was collecting; balloon animals, musty blankets, jars of something called 'nustard.'

Nustard.

The word hung in Mongrel's mind with the weight of a minivan. He circled around the box to get a better look, when something bright invaded his eyes. After a minute to focus he looked up at the light and saw the moon. More importantly, he saw a window.

Reaching up to it, he nudged it, and it quietly slid open. He looked back over his shoulder at the four men, all of them looking up the stairs at whoever was approaching. Mongrel had a sick feeling he knew who it was. Grabbing a jar of nustard, he stood on a nearby box and helped himself out the window.

"Idiot…" Shamus muttered, pinching the bridge of his nose.

"Hey," William said, "are you calling us idiots?"

Shamus looked at each of them in turn before replying. "No, Will, I'm calling myself an idiot because I keep forgetting how stupid you can be sometimes."

This remark seemed to relieve Martin and confuse Colin, but William wasn't amused. "So you *are* calling us idiots?"

"Yes! You're all a bunch of raving idiots! Where is he? Where is Mongrel Stevens?"

They all looked around in exasperation, suddenly feeling as foolish as the anti-agent made them out to be. The basement, although large and well stocked, held more shadows than its size and layout suggested. There was a myriad of places to hide.

"Looks like he went out the window," old man Cleopard suddenly said. Without moving an inch, he was unaccountably eating out of a jar of nustard. How he'd gotten one from across the room was a mystery. Licking his fingers off and farting, he continued. "Took one of my jars too. You gonna go get him? I want my nustard back."

"Looks like someone knows what they're doing," Shamus said to his men. He turned and was about to head back up the stairs, only Cleopard stood in the way, blocking the exit. He didn't appear to be doing this for any reason; he simply stood there, casually eating his nustard.

Shamus glared at him. Cleopard looked back, oblivious to what was going on. Finally Shamus asked, "Could I interest you in moving out of my way?"

Cleopard looked to the floor, and then to his left, followed by his right. Satisfied that he'd observed his surroundings enough, he looked back at Shamus. "Why? What's in it for me?"

"Exercise," the anti-agent said, shoving the old man to the side and bounding up the stairs. The others followed.

The basement door opened into a quaint little kitchen. Creaky cupboards lined the walls. A rickety table sat in the center, covered in topographical maps, a couple cups of old coffee, and a bowl of what Cleopard had earlier described as *goatmeal*. The back door of the house stood a few feet to their right, next to a refrigerator that seemed like it was trying to escape. It shook and rattled and shimmied all over the floor as far as its power cord would allow.

"Careful with that thing," Martin said, pointing to the appliance. "It's possessed or something. I swear it tried to bite me earlier."

The old man came up behind them and wandered over to the table to resume eating his goatmeal, first dumping a large amount of nustard into it. "Murphy's been a good fridge to me all these long years," he said.

They all looked at him.

"Did he just call the fridge *Murphy?*" William asked.

Cleopard spread some mustard and cut some cheese, but otherwise didn't respond.

Ignoring everyone, Shamus asked, "Do you all have flashlights?"

"We got a couple in the van," Martin said.

"Right. Get them."

"I'm not going near that thing!" Martin slowly began backing away from the refrigerator. "It's out to get me."

"Murphy's a good boy," Cleopard said. "He don't bite."

Random Tangent

"Then just go out the front!" Shamus said, annoyed. He knew the more time they wasted, the further away Mongrel could be getting.

Martin saluted and left the room.

Adjusting his suit and posture, Shamus then addressed Cleopard. "Old man, do you have a flashlight I may borrow?"

"Back in my day we didn't have flashlights. If we wanted to see something we just waited 'til the sun came up. Sometimes had to wait all night. Built patience."

"Oh never mind." Shamus made for the back door when suddenly the refrigerator jumped at him, striking him hard in his left knee and sending him crashing into a nearby shelf. Shamus made an attempt to grab the shelf for support but his weight was too much, and the shelf collapsed on top of him. He fell to the floor, pots and pans bouncing off his head and shoulders.

"Down Murphy," Cleopard said with a complete lack of interest.

"Bloody hell!" Shamus exclaimed. "That thing really *is* possessed." He shakily got himself to his feet, brushing off the debris. "Looks like we're all going out the front."

He limped his way out of the kitchen. The others followed him through the dining-room and into a hallway that led to the front door. Upon their arrival they found Martin standing in the doorway, looking outside.

"It's raining," Martin said before anyone could ask him what he was doing.

Everyone gathered around the entrance and peered out into the night. It was indeed raining; not hard, but enough to soak through your clothing if you stood out in it for more than a few minutes.

"And?" Shamus asked.

Martin looked down at his suit and brushed it down even though there wasn't a speck of dust on it. "This is my favourite suit."

Cleopard pushed passed them on walked out onto the front step. Holding his hand out to feel the drops of rain, he frowned and farted again. "Back in my day rain was wetter. Just don't get rain like you use-"

Jaywatch

"Oh just get out!" Shamus yelled, shoving them out into the rain.

Mongrel rolled onto the wet grass outside the basement window, exhausted from the effort. He felt very much out of shape. Maybe it was the fear running through his veins that made his limbs feel like lead. Maybe it was the idea that he *had no idea* what he was going to do. Run? Hide? He shook his head in the grass, annoyed at how futile his options seemed. The rain felt nice, anyway. He got to his feet and found himself face-to-face with a stranger. His heart jumped in his stomach, and he dropped the jar of nustard. But he didn't scream. He knew he opened his mouth to scream, but nothing came out. This confused him. He tried screaming again, but his body refused to cooperate.

The stranger shook his head and held a finger to his lips to indicate *shut up*. Suddenly his hands were all over Mongrel, patting here, searching there, as if he were a cop. What alarmed Mongrel was that while this was going on the stranger's face never left his. The stare never left his eyes.

"You dropped this," the stranger finally said, placing the jar of nustard in Mongrel's hands. "Be careful with it. Causes terrible gas."

Mongrel jerked his head down to look at the ground. The jar had to have been a good three feet away from his hand. "How did you reach that?" he asked, looking back up at the stranger, who had now backed away to a more comfortable distance, affording a brief study.

The stranger was a mystery wrapped in a riddle shrouded in a conundrum. You could learn nothing about him by just looking; he required further study, yet a proper assessment glanced off him like light off a mirror. He was a man – that much was certain – of average height and build...maybe a bit chunkier, but with the loose-fitting clothing it was hard to tell. He had dark skin; not black, but...well, maybe it was a tan? You know what? It was night, and impossible to know for sure. He wasn't bald, but didn't really have any hair. It was somewhere in the middle, like stubble of indeterminate colour all over his head. His voice sounded deep and light at the same time; soft-spoken yet aggressive. And the aggression seemed to emanate from everywhere, like it poured out of his pores. He was violent just standing there. A bomb ready to go off. But it was held in check by something. He was dangerous and tame at the same time. Like Chuck Norris mixed with younger, angrier Chuck Norris. Like a bull; capable of creating chaos out of thin air, but calm and serene under normal circumstances. He was a man made of opposites that cancelled each other out. Mongrel pictured himself trying to describe the stranger to the police – should he live to have the chance - and looking like he'd lost his mind.

"Don't worry about it," the stranger replied, tilting his head back, enjoying the feeling of rain on his face. "Who are you and what are you doing here?"

Thunder rumbled in the distance and a flash of lightning momentarily lit up the sky, giving the stranger a menacing appearance. Mongrel swallowed, wary about disclosing too much information about himself in the presence of people wanting him dead. Often, every little bit counts, but there was something to be said for leaving a few bits unaccounted for. "I don't even know where here is."

The stranger glared at him, unsatisfied with the lack of answers. He studied Mongrel momentarily and said, "I remember you."

In a night already full of alarming moments, this statement did nothing to ease Mongrel's nerves. He was sure he'd never met the man before in his life, or in a passed life, if such things existed. "No you don't," he said, trying to throw the stranger off.

And it worked; the stranger was indeed thrown off, but only briefly. It was a rare occurrence and he was therefore impressed. He smiled. "Yes I do; from the prison."

Now Mongrel was thrown off. "You're a guard?"

"I'm a prisoner. *Was* a prisoner."

This prompted Mongrel to scan the horizon around him, trying not to seem bothered by this knowledge. It was a defense mechanism that only managed to click in every now and then. "And you escaped?" Then a few lines of thought joined together in a cohesive line of reasoning. "Holy shit! You're the one on the radio! The guy they're talking about! Jaywatch!"

Jaywatch

The stranger's smile widened, a sense of pride growing in him. "Got a nice ring to it, eh?"

Now aware that he was dealing with yet another murderer, Mongrel began fretting. "Um, if you're going to kill me I think it's only fair to warn you that they've called dibs."

"Who?"

As if in response to the question, a loud crash came from inside the house, and muffled, angry voices began shouting. The stranger momentarily forgot about Mongrel and focused his attention on the house just as it grew quiet again. "What's going on in there?"

Mongrel looked up at one of the windows, dearly hoping someone was hurt in the commotion. "They're just trying to kill me," he said, still trying to seem nonchalant.

"Well they're not doing a very good job. If I wanted you dead you'd have been dead yesterday."

This didn't seem to be the kind of thing a friend might say, and hearing it didn't help Mongrel relax in the slightest. In the interest of easing the tension, he felt it would be best to learn what the stranger's intentions with him were, if he had any at all. "So does that mean you don't want me dead? And why yesterday? Weren't you in prison yesterday?"

Still staring up at the house, the stranger ignored him. "Why are they trying to kill you?"

"Oh I don't know," Mongrel threw his hands in the air, "maybe it's a hobby."

"Ah. Recreational homicide. Popular in prison too."

Mongrel nodded in agreement. "So, uh...you're not with them?"

The stranger scanned the house, not just with his eyes, but with his other senses as well. He could feel the presence of five men. He could taste anger in the air. He could smell the farts. The old man was inside.

From a very young age he knew he was not like other children. Things were just clearer to him than they were to other kids – even other adults. His brain seemed to not only detect things other people couldn't, but it interpreted the information in unusual ways. He'd honed these skills over the years, and by comparison, folks who had extrasensory perception seemed merely above-average next to him. By the age of ten he could count the stars in the sky by smell alone. By twelve be was able to hear the different sides of a coin. Fifteen brought him the ability to actually taste fear. It was these talents, this potential that the old man had seen in him. He took the kid under his wing and taught him how to develop these gifts. Now, he could feel colours, smell numbers, and hear mimes. He could, like the television commercials suggested, actually taste the rainbow. He could levitate for short periods of time, correctly guess your age to the month by the taste of your right knee (the left one tastes differently, apparently), and he was *Batman*.

Well, not really.

"No," he said.

"Cool, cool." Mongrel looked toward the horizon again. Considering that the stranger hadn't answered his question about whether or not murder was in his future, he figured he'd do what he could to avoid it, just in case. "Well, Mr. uh, murderer, I best be off. Got some running and hiding to do. Some death to be avoiding." He began to shuffle away.

"The name's Jayson Miles, but you can call me Miles. And I ain't gonna kill ya. If anything I should be thanking you."

Out of curiosity, Mongrel stayed put. "Why?"

Miles looked at him, studied him. "You really don't remember me?"

Mongrel shook his head.

"I was Biscuits' cellmate. When you came to visit him I was able to sneak out. I'm a free man because of you."

The pieces of a puzzle he didn't even know he was trying to solve began to fit together for Mongrel. "You? You're the one everyone was talking about? Biscuits *did* mention you, I think, but I didn't know what he was talking about. And everyone else thought I *was* you!"

"They thought you were me?"

"They kept me locked up there for weeks!"

"I only broke out two days ago."

"Could you not have left a note or something?"

Miles chuckled. "Sorry. It was kind of a spur of the moment thing. How long was it before they realized their mistake?"

"Realized their mistake? Ha! They didn't. *I* had to break out too."

"Really?" Miles was now more impressed. "How?"

Before Mongrel could answer raised voices came from around the front of the house.

"Well I'd love to stay and chat, but you know, maniacs are heading this way."

"I'll handle them," Miles said. "Go hide in the barn."

"Really?" Mongrel wasn't sure what to think about this. Someone else fighting his battles? He generally ran away from fights – unless they were bullshit fights; the other kind tended to leave him, well, for dead, and he was tired of having impending death hanging over his head. "Thanks, I guess. There are four of them, you know?"

"Five."

Mongrel shrugged. "Okay, fine, five. But one's an old man. Wait, how'd you know there were five?"

The convict looked at him. "I'm just concerned with the old man. He's the most dangerous of all of them."

"Okay…" This didn't sound right to Mongrel, and it didn't remotely answer his question. How long had Miles been in prison? The old man might have been dangerous at one point, but that point was years ago. Besides, there was British anti-agent amongst them, so to say the old man was the most dangerous was a ludicrous suggestion. "If you say so."

"You don't know him like I do. Now get to the barn. If you need me, just whistle."

"But I-"

"I'll be able to hear you. Trust me."

"I can't whistle."

Miles looked at Mongrel like he was crazy. "Just put your lips together and blow."

Mongrel looked to the ground and shook his head. "Why does everyone always say that? What, do you expect me to just learn on the spot? Look buddy, I said I *can't* whistle, not that I didn't know how to. I'm, like, defective or something."

Random Tangent

Frowning, Miles dug into his coat pocket and pulled out a tiny flute. "Just play something on this then. I'll come."

Living in Dunttstown can be very trying at times. Bizarre things happened, people weren't normal, even time occasionally didn't seem to age properly. It was as if the area was exempt from reality. Simply trying to survive from day to day was a mind-boggling endeavor. Mongrel had never quite gotten used to the inanity, and he could barely go a day without something confusing him. Today was no different. "You carry around a flute with you all the time?"

"No, I just made it a minute ago."

"Oh you *made* it did you. I thought it grew that way." Mongrel sighed. "I'm sorry. I don't mean to be so irritable. It's raining, I'm cold, people are trying to kill me-"

"So you've said."

"...And I'm not even sure if I have to buy more milk. I think it expires today. Or tomorrow. What time is it – I mean day?"

"You should just go."

Mongrel took the flute. "Whatever. Hope you can dodge bullets." He shook his head and gave Miles a sympathetic look, then began trudging towards the barn, making squishy sounds in the long, wet grass with each step.

"I don't have to," Miles whispered to himself, smiling. He turned and headed around the side of the house.

Martin closed the van door and headed back to the porch where the others were standing, holding up two flashlights. "These are all we got."

Shamus swiped one of them from Martin's hands when he was close enough, and flicked it on. "Right. You and Will go check out the barn. In this rain he'll surely be looking for somewhere dry to hide." He handed the flashlight to Colin. "Colin, you patrol the area around here. I'm going back up the hill to get a bird's eye view. He won't get away."

"What about me?" Cleopard farted and asked.

"You stay in the house, old man," Shamus said. "Think we could all use a bit of *fresh air*."

"Yeah," Will snickered.

"What about you?" Colin asked. "Don't you need a flashlight?"

"No. I can see fine; I'm an Agent." He sighed. "I'm sorry. I don't mean to boast. I know none of you made the cut, as it were, and I've had the training*..." he trailed off, afraid he might be alienating his crew. "But look, you're all here because I believe you're the best at what you do. And I'm sorry if I've been a bit of a crank. This Stevens fellow...he seems to bring out the worst in me I suppose. When this is over I'll treat you all to a vacation!"

Everyone seemed to like the sound of that. Even Cleopard farted his approval.

"Ah, no. Not you, old man. I never want to see you again after tonight."

Cleopard didn't say a word, but hung his head and dismally broke wind.

"Can the misses come? William asked.

"Sorry, gents only. Right then – break!"

Martin and William began making their way towards the large barn. Shamus headed East, straight for the large cliff that would give him an excellent view of the landscape. If Mongrel hadn't found himself a place to hide and was trying to make a run for it, Shamus would spot him.

Colin took a moment to study his flashlight before giving it a sweep around in a wide circle. He decided he'd go check out the various tractors and farming equipment first, shining the light on the ground several paces in front of him to lead the way.

He hadn't taken more than a few steps before stopping. The beam from his flashlight had caught something – shoes. He slowly panned the light upwards over a pair of pants and a shirt, to a face that was peering intently at him.

"Who are you?" Colin asked.

The stranger smiled maliciously. "None of your business."

Colin opened his mouth to call for the others but barely had a chance for the words to fail to come out. In a flash, the stranger

---

* Anti-agents undergo rigorous and relentless training on all matter of skills and subjects, including, but not limited to: wilderness survival, computer-hacking, weapons-training, hand-to-hand combat, gourmet cooking, finger-painting, extreme-etiquette, and how to use your cape as a floatation device.

swung his arms in a large arc and clapped his hands together, seeming to catch every drop of rain and sending a torrent of water at the Irishman. The ensuing flood hit Colin's face and eyes with such force it stung, soaked him from head to toe, and very nearly drowned him (since his mouth had been open). Stumbling backwards, Colin slipped on the wet grass, lost his balance and fell to the ground. The stranger, as quick as a bolt of lightning, was there to lend assistance, allowing his boot to break Colin's fall. Although it was so quick it could have been mistaken for a boot to the head. In either case, Colin wasn't getting up; the fall had taken a lot out of him – his consciousness, for example.

Standing over him, feeling the man's conscious floating aimlessly around, the stranger was content with how the events had unfolded. He remained silent, motionless, sensing outward if anything had changed. Had anyone heard or seen them? Had the authorities learned of his whereabouts? Was the convenience store in Dunttstown still open? He found himself wanting some chips at that moment.

Satisfied his exploits hadn't attracted any unwanted attention, he inhaled deeply, catching the scent of his next target. Grabbing Colin by the ankle, the stranger dragged him around the side of the house and toward the well.

As Mongrel approached the barn he looked it over, sizing it up. It was more enormous than he'd previously thought. It had seemed like an ordinary barn, but the closer he got to it, the more he discovered he had further to walk; its size had given the impression that it was closer than it really was. The dark of night didn't help either. Something about the barn bothered Mongrel; not its size, but…it was menacing somehow. He got the feeling he shouldn't be going in there, that nothing good would come of it. Then he figured he was being foolish. He'd be better off inside than out in the rain. The nervousness he felt was no doubt the result of an arduous night – a night that seemed far from over.

Putting the flute in his housecoat pocket, he politely knocked on the barn door, but didn't know why. He scanned the door, looking for a handle or something to pull it open with. Finding none, he settled for pushing the door instead. When this too didn't suffice, he tried knocking again, and sighed violently when this still failed him.

"Why don't you try the door?" a polite British voice asked.

Mongrel almost screamed in alarm, but for some reason still couldn't. Was he coming down with laryngitis or something? He turned to see two of Shamus' men heading his way, or at least assumed it was them; a flashlight was shining in his face, and he could only hear their voices. "You scared the crap out of me," he said. "And this is the door, isn't it?"

"You know," one of them said as he opened the *real* door a dozen feet to Mongrel's right, "I've never liked that turn of phrase."

"What?" the other man replied. He sounded like Martin. "'Scared the crap out of me'?"

"Yeah."

"I know what you mean; it's vulgar."

"It's not meant to be taken literally," Mongrel said in defense.

"Well that's just the thing. At some point it was taken literally. Someone had to be the first bloke to mess his trousers after a good scare, right?"

"I don't want to think about that," Martin said. "Turns me right queer."

This sounded strange to Mongrel. "Aren't you already queer? Martin, isn't it?"

The flashlight lowered. "Aww, he remembers my name!"

"Well your voice is kinda..." Mongrel didn't want to say 'gay' but wasn't sure how to put it, "...memorable?"

"He means you sound like a nancy boy," the other man said. Mongrel assumed it was William.

Martin seemed horrified by this. "What? He does not!"

"Sure he does," William said. "Don't you?"

"Uh..." Mongrel didn't really want to agree, but he didn't want to lie either. Really, he just wanted the night to be over with.

"See, he agrees."

"I meant *sick* queer," Martin protested.

"Don't know what you're so upset over. You *are* a nancy boy."

This didn't seem to pacify Martin. He grumbled to himself.

Random Tangent

"Look, if I say I don't think you sound queer will you say you never saw me?" Mongrel asked, trying not to get hopeful about the proposition.

William shook his head. "Don't think so, mate."

"Yeah," Mongrel hung his head, "rules is rules and all."

Martin began patting his pockets. "Think I forgot the radio." He tried to shout out but was having a difficult time of it.

"That's right," William said, walking over and putting an arm on Mongrel's shoulder. "That's right. I appreciate you understanding. Most folks just don't seem to get it."

Suddenly Mongrel threw his jar of nustard at Martin, who was still failing at yelling to alert the others, clonking him on his head. Then he shoved William as hard as he could into Martin, who fell clumsily to the ground. Mongrel didn't wait to see what happened to William; he quickly darted inside the barn and closed the door behind him. He felt along the wall beside the door and found a bar, which swung down and locked the door.

This motivated him, but he felt a fool nonetheless. Had he found the actual door in time he could have been able to duck inside without being caught. He tried to blame old man Cleopard for the barn being built wrong, but deep down he knew it was is his own fault. His best friend – or make that *ex*-best friend – Captain Pete owned a barn store, so he should have learned a thing or two about barns in all the years they'd known each other. At least he thought Captain Pete still owned the barn store. It had been a while since they'd talked, since their falling out, since his habitual dying.

Shaking the thoughts from his head, Mongrel turned and was about to venture further into the barn, except that it was so dark inside he couldn't see anything. He heard the men cursing politely outside, and knew he couldn't just hang around, so, arms out in front of him, he blindly stumbled his way deeper into the barn.

After not more than a few feet he came to a ladder, and decided to climb up. No sooner had he reached the top, the barn door swung open – apparently that bar hadn't locked the door after all – and moonlight spilled inside, chasing away some of the darkness and replacing it with shadows. The two men cautiously stepped inside, one swinging the flashlight in a long, slow arc, left to right.

Jaywatch

"He can't hide forever," he heard William say.

"This place gives me the willies," Martin said in response.

Mongrel hid behind a wooden pillar as a beam of light passed by. He pulled the flute out of his pocket, unsure of what to do. They were right - he couldn't hide here forever; they'd eventually find him. He could try to find another exit, although he had enough trouble finding the first one, so locating a second one seemed an impossible challenge, especially in the dark. That's assuming there even was another exit. Maybe he could lure them away from the first one and then sneak back out? Martin and William weren't the brightest pair, but Mongrel knew them limits of his own intelligence and didn't like his odds. He brought the flute to his mouth, knowing it was only a matter of time before they found him. What did he have to lose?

Time. He had time to lose. Miles said he'd hear the flute, but Mongrel found that doubtful with whatever distance lay between them and with him lacking any flute-playing ability. But there were two men below who would definitely hear him, find him, torture him, stick him in a box with wild chipmunks – unspeakable horrors. Better not to play the flute and spend the time devise...wait, what was that? Mongrel felt something crawling along his fingers. He pulled the flute away from his face to have a closer look, and in the dim light could just make out that it was a spider. A big, ugly spider.

Startled, he dropped the flute and shook his hand furiously. The spider finally dropped to the floor, and he began madly stomping around all over the place, kicking up piles of hay. In his fervour he wandered into some large cobwebs crossing a couple pillars that were precariously close from the edge of the flooring. If Mongrel had bothered to learn about barns back when he and Captain Pete were still friends, he would know that he was in a hayloft. To ensure that hay stayed dry, it was stored as high as possible off the ground, on a second storey if available, much like in this particular barn. These haylofts usually had a hatch in the floor through which the hay was dropped, or no railing or wall on one side so that the hay could just be pushed off to fall to the grou-"

"Would you shut up?" Mongrel cried as he danced around fitfully, getting dangerously close to thin air. In his struggle to free himself he managed only to get tangled in more and more of the blasted things. He screamed in panic – at least as much as his laryngitis would allow.

"I think I hear him up there," Martin said. He shone the light upwards just in time to see Mongrel, wildly flailing his arms, fall off the second tier, bounce off a stack of hay and land directly on him. His flashlight went flying further into the barn, finding a spot from where it could cast nice, spooky shadows.

William, at first jumping back to avoid the collision, wandered back over without any sense of urgency. "You all right, mate? That looked pretty nasty."

Both men lay sprawled on the hay covered ground, moaning quietly. Martin didn't seem to be in any condition to move. Mongrel was no longer worried about being covered in cobwebs; instead he was worried about the state of this manhood. Holding himself gingerly between his legs, he wearily got to his feet.

"You all right?" William asked again.

Mongrel looked at him. Why did he care? "Probably not. Why do you care? You want me dead anyway."

William rolled his eyes and crossed his arms. "Well that may be true, but I can still show a bit of sympathy. Besides, we got to keep you alive until the end, so you can enjoy it." He thought about his choice of words, and added, "So to speak."

"You people are so polite it sickens me."

"Now, now, ain't nothing wrong with being polite. Manners is manners."

"Nope. Sick." Mongrel fell to his knees and threw up whatever he hadn't had for breakfast that morning. "See? Told you."

Helping Mongrel back to his feet and trying to brush off some of the cobwebs, William asked about Martin, who still hadn't moved much. "What do you make of him? I think you broke him when he broke your fall."

Tepidly clutching his testicles again, Mongrel winced. "That's not all he broke." He looked down at Martin. "I'm sure he'll be fine. Just needs a few hours of not trying to kill me."

"Now hold on, we ain't the ones trying to kill you. And between you and me, he's a bit squeamish."

Now he wanted to get technical? "Right. You're just the...the, uh..." he couldn't think of the word, "human thieves."

"You mean *kidnappers*?"

Mongrel stopped rubbing his crotch and began rubbing his head. He really needed a vacation. "Yeah, whatever. Um, would you mind grabbing the flashlight? I need to see if I'm bleeding. Can't see anything in the dim light."

"I think you're all right, but maybe just to be on the safe side. Watch your step." William gently grabbed Mongrel's arm and ushered him around the small pile of vomit over to a hay stack, and sat him down. "Now don't you go anywhere. I'll be right back." He wandered off to the far corner of the barn, following the decreasing, twisting shadows spawned by the beam from the flashlight.

Feeling smarter than normal, Mongrel allowed a smile to spread on his face before quietly sneaking back to the barn door. He stepped outside, feeling the cool rain on his skin again, and peeked back to see if his escape had been noticed. It hadn't.

Deciding not to close the door and instead leaving it the way he found it, he ran back toward the farmhouse. Actually, limped is a more appropriate description, but the slight hill allowed him to pick up more speed than he otherwise would have been able to. He passed a rusty tractor on his left, followed by the well on his right, and was only a few meters from the house when something bad happened.

Not more than ten minutes earlier, after Mongrel had chucked the jar of nustard at him, Martin dizzily got to his feet and regained his balance and composure. Cursing quietly to himself, he stumbled over to where the jar had landed, picked it up, and pitched as far as he could. The nustard landed close to Cleopard's house, where Mongrel tripped on it, stumbled and fell. The momentum he'd built up running carried on, causing him to slide on the wet grass and crash through the glass of one of the basement windows.

The good news was that he landed on a pile of boxes that seemed to have been filled with soft blankets and sweaters and such. The bad news was that a wobbly shelf decided to lose its balance and tip over on him, spilling all manner of sharp, heavy, exciting objects everywhere.

Random Tangent

Mongrel, dimly aware of the basement light turning on and of footsteps coming down the stairs, began slowly digging his way out of the wreckage, all too aware that even more damage had been caused to his nether regions, and tried to calculate all the horrible things that had befallen him since he'd been crudely woken in the middle of the night. He'd fallen out of bed, been knocked unconscious twice, was attacked and molested by spiders and covered in cobwebs, had been part of a human car crash, had his head beaten around more than he'd care to imagine, and he was sure his nose had been broken. He also could almost feel his swimmers floating upset down, and assumed the odds of him ever becoming a father were unlikely at best.

Perhaps dying would've been the easy way out? Was all this fighting worth it? If he lived, then of course it was. But if after everything that had happened he still ended up dying he was going to be really upset.

The sound of wind breaking drew Mongrel's attention to the bottom of the stairs, where old man Cleopard was standing.

"You okay?" he asked.

Mongrel glanced down at his swollen groin. "I feel like my nuts have been strapped to a boulder that's rolling down a mountain."

Cleopard came over to inspect Mongrel, sniffing here, poking there, farting all the while.

"Ow!" Mongrel shied away. "Stop it."

"Uncanny," the old man said. "You're like the son I almost had."

"Almost? Don't you mean the son you *never* had?"

"No. I almost had you. In a manner of speaking."

Throwing his hands up in exasperation, Mongrel was nearly at his wits end with the old man – and hadn't even been in his company for five minutes. "*What* manner of speaking?"

Picking up one of the remaining jars of nustard that hadn't been broken, Cleopard mumbled to himself. "Such a waste."

"How am I even remotely *almost* your son?" Mongrel rephrased his question.

"This nustard that I make, know what's in it?"

Jaywatch

Mongrel grumbled to himself. It had been a strange night, filled with strange people who were making him think strange thoughts. If he was going to die he at least wanted to leave the world with everything taken care of and no unfinished business. Didn't you stay on Earth as a ghost if you died with unfinished business? He'd heard that somewhere. Unfortunately, if he wanted to learn something about his past he was going to have to go through Cleopard to get it.

He shook his head and cursed his dismal luck. "What's in it?" he asked with a sneer that would sink a thousand ships.

The old man opened the jar and stuck his finger in the nustard. "Mostly just spicy mustard and nougat." He brought the finger to his mouth and licked it clean. "But also a dash of lightning."

"So, you catch lightning in a bottle, so to speak?"

"So to speak," Cleopard repeated. "Did you know you can create life with electricity?"

Mongrel shook his head, wary that he may have opened Pandora's Box in talking with the old man; many said he was a lunatic.

The lunatic nodded. "Ever heard of Crosse's Acari?" He didn't wait for an answer. "Crosse was a friend of mine way back in the day. Bit of a weirdo if you ask me, but a nice guy. Smart too; did lots of experiments." He paused to pass gas. "One experiment of his, he was trying to make glass crystals or something, and was using electricity on some chemicals and poof, created life."

"Sure," Mongrel said, not believing a word. "And what does that have to do with me?"

"These tiny little bugs just came from out of nowhere," Cleopard continued, ignoring Mongrel. "Really freaked everyone out. The church called him evil and he gave up science and became a hermit or gypsy or something. But I looked into his work – he didn't patent it or anything. In fact he kept saying it was all just an accident, that he didn't know what he was doing. Weirdo. Anyway, I tried to do the same thing he did and poof, created you."

Mongrel crossed his arms and raised his eyebrows, but said nothing, waiting for the ludicrous story to proceed.

Random Tangent

"Not just like that though, and I wasn't doing it completely on purpose. I began producing my nustard back in...oh...uh...well, you know. And it wasn't going as well as I'd liked; couldn't get the spices just right. Tried many things, but nothing worked. Then one day I was eating some on the porch and got struck by lightning, and from then on it tasted so much better."

"Wait," Mongrel felt he had to join in on the conversation, "you were struck by lighting? And lived?"

Cleopard nodded. "Yeah, why?"

"And didn't go to the hospital or get looked at or anything?"

"It's just a bit of lightning," Cleopard replied, shrugging. "Back in my day people got struck by lightning all the time. Happened six, seven times a day if it was storming out bad enough."

Mongrel shook his head, regretting his interjection. "Whatever. Forget it. Just get on with your story; I have maniacs after me and really don't have time to chat."

"So now what I do," Cleopard continued without missing a beat, "is cook all the nustard in my bathtub. I got a car battery sitting on the toilet and some jumper cables, and I just fry the nustard a little bit, and poof!"

Mongrel waited a minute before asking, "Poof what? Then what?"

"Well that's it. That's how I make my nustard."

"You took the time to explain all that to me, but what, if *anything*, does it actually got to do with me?"

"Oh that's how you were created, son." Cleopard crossed the remaining distance between them and patted him on the shoulder."

"Don't touch me," Mongrel said, flinching away.

"One of the jars spawned life, just like in Crosse's experiments. I let it ripen in the tub for a few years and it slowly turned into an infant. Course wouldn't you know it I accidentally sold that jar." He chuckled to himself. "I tell you, if I weren't for my hands I wouldn't have fingers!"

"Please tell me you don't shower in the same tub," Mongrel said, not really wanting to know the answer. "And what did you say about your hands?"

"Oh I don't shower at all. In fact I don't really use anything in that room. Now I bet you're wondering how I knew it was you, right? I mean, you sure have changed since I sold you. Probably wouldn't even fit in a jar now."

Unsure of why he was wasting his time – valuable time that could be spent remaining alive – talking to the old man, Mongrel tried to recall what his mother had once told him about his father. Something about coming home with him in a jar, and his father spreading him on toast. Naturally, it made no sense, but that was par for the course for his entire life.

But could it be true? His mother was more than her fair share of nuts, and old man Cleopard was giving her a run for her money, but what Mongrel couldn't wrap his head around was how both their stories seemed to line up. Could it all be merely a coincidence? While unlikely, it was just as implausible that they'd gotten together to craft this ludicrous story. What would be the point, anyway? One last great prank on him? There had to be another explanation. Maybe crazy was like a disease and everyone shared the same symptoms.

"What about the toilet?" he asked, trying desperately to ignore as much as he could of what the old man was saying. "You must use that?"

Cleopard farted and said, "I just use the well out in the field."

Mongrel groaned. He needed to disengage from the old man and continue running for his life. Looking at his non-existent watch, he gasped. "Wow, look at the time, I really should be on my way."

"Aw, do you have to go?"

"Yeah, it's passed my bedtime. And, you know, murderers are running lose and whatnot. Can't be too careful. Besides, I think I left my house broken into, and I should go check on it. Make sure it's still there."

"Could I offer you a piece of me?" Cleopard asked, a strange gleam in his eye?

"What?" Something clicked in Mongrel's mind, and he got a sense of déjà vu. "Are you coming on to me?"

"Do you want a piece of me?" Cleopard repeated. "If you stay, that is."

Random Tangent

"No thanks, I don't swing that way." Something else clicked in Mongrel's mind.

The old man chuckled some more. "After all you've been through tonight you must be at least a little upset. Don't you want some revenge?"

More things clicked in Mongrel's mind, and the sense of déjà vu was getting worse. It felt like he'd said those words before – like he'd had this conversation before. But that was impossible, since he hadn't met the old man until that night.

Actually, that wasn't true; he'd seen Cleopard on the bus on the ride to Dunttstown Penitentiary. Was there more he couldn't remember? What else was he missing?

"Come on, show me what you've got!"

Mongrel glared at the old man, things clicking so fast he couldn't keep up with them. Somehow, he knew what to say next. "No one makes fun of jedi master Yoda."

This confused Cleopard. This might not sound like a big deal, since his level of sanity bordered on non-existent, but it was. People called him crazy but the truth was his mind was free, and although it flew the coup more often than it stuck around, he was lucid enough to be aware of everything going on around him. He had a very special relationship with reality. If he couldn't fathom something one way, he'd fathom it another. If something didn't make sense this way or that, he'd understand it backwards. One way or another, he found a method of comprehension. So to actually confuse him to the point that he couldn't find a venue of logic was quite a feat.

"You're right," Mongrel said, taking a step back and glancing around the basement, "it has been a long night. But I've had longer. Once I was awake for nearly two weeks; kept counting sheep. I was in the millions or something, and thought I *was* a sheep by the time I finally succumbed to sleep. They found me naked in a field of grass with some old hillbillies trying to rape me. Of course, it turned out I was asleep the whole time and just thought I couldn't sleep. For two whole weeks! The sheep thing still happened though. Really was in that field for two weeks. And can you believe I was still tired when I finally woke up?"

Cleopard fidgeted. "Er, um, the men that were trying to make sweet, sweet love to the sheep, er, you...did they, uh, ever find out who they were?"

Disturbed by the wording of the question, Mongrel quickly answered before his brain had enough time to think about it. "I guess not."

"Oh good, good. Or bad, I mean," the old man seemed relieved. He shook his head. "Sex with sheep, eh? Unfortunately, back in my day we didn't have sheep; we had pet rocks. Now I'm not talking about the kind they sold in stores; the kind we had were for adults only. And they were almost as good as sheep, if you know what I mean."

Mongrel knew what Cleopard meant, but wished he didn't. How, he wondered to himself, could there not have been sheep back in his day? Sheep had been around for thousands of years, haven't they? Just how long ago was Cleopard's day? This is probably what he should've asked, but what slipped out instead was, "How do you have sex with a rock?"

"Oh it's quite simple. What you do i-"

Throwing his hands over his ears, Mongrel shouted, "Puppies don't go to band camp!"

Once again Cleopard was taken aback. "What?"

More things were coming back to Mongrel from his past. But when exactly were they coming from, and why? More importantly, however, was the feeling he got that nothing good would come from it. What could it all mean?

"Um," he thought quickly, "what I meant to say was...I had a puppy once, and I sent it to band camp...where it could learn to play instruments with other pets, you know? But it, like, ate the other puppies and got kicked out." He knew it wasn't very good and winced as he said it. He couldn't focus. So many other things were fighting for attention in his mind.

"Dog lover," Cleopard muttered. "You people make me sick."

"At least I'm not a sheep lover."

"That sheep was asking for it!" Cleopard shouted, on the verge of anger. But he calmed himself down and added, almost as if correcting himself, "Shep."

Random Tangent

Mongrel was shocked that the old man could be tricked into confessing such atrocities so easily. What was slightly more troubling is that Cleopard wasn't the slightest bit embarrassed by the admission. But worst of all was his last remark. Giving a quizzical expression and waiting were not enough to goad the old man into explaining what he'd just said, so Mongrel gave up and asked. "Shep?"

"Oh, sorry. I believe the singular form of sheep should be 'shep'."

Trying to both nod and shake his head at the same time, Mongrel made himself dizzy. He looked at the floor to steady himself and said, "Right. Of course. I depluralize and repluralize words all the time. Geeses, teethbrush, audient."

"Linguistics is crazy, isn't it?" Cleopard asked.

"Utter batshit," Mongrel agreed.

There was a moment of silence as both men stared at each other with a bit of mutual respect. Naturally it couldn't go on forever, and after a minute Cleopard coughed expectantly.

"Oh, right," Mongrel said. "Let's see...um, I once ate a full twelve course meal made entirely out of playdoh." He laugh quietly to himself. "Man, I filled my toilet with some wacky colours that week!"

"Ooh, pretty," Cleopard's mind wandered as he considered trying playdoh for himself; the well could do with a bit of colour. When he came back to reality he said, "The TV show Sixty Minutes did a half-hour broadcast about my left testicle a number of years back. I've never seen it myself but I'm told it was quite informative."

"Why the left one?" Mongrel asked.

"Well, the right one couldn't be found. It used to go out on benders on the weekends, and one weekend it just never came back."

"I'm so sorry."

"Oh it's all right. Almost a relief actually. It got violent when it drank, so..." he trailed off, lost in memories. "We were gonna stage an intervention..."

"I feel your pain. I had a brother once. But one day I told him to get lost, and no one ever saw him again."

Jaywatch

Brother.

The word stuck out like a fat guy at ballet practice. He had a brother. Or did have one, at least. He didn't understand it, since he had no memories of him, but somehow he just knew. Somehow he'd always known. Well, he'd known for the passed two stories, at least.

Suddenly it all came flowing back to him, like visions from a dream. Captain Pete, *A Christmas Carol*, adopting Biscuits, being in a relationship with Beby, his dad, Bossa Nova, Shamus Bond...

Wait a minute...if Shamus was now after Mongrel then it *couldn't* have been just a dream. Everything was real, or would be soon enough.

But there was more. There was...Hank.

He remembered losing a bullshit fight to someone named Hank. He lost a game he'd never been bested at. And he knew it was going to happen – it had to be true. Captain Pete had shown him a handful of visions; the one involving Shamus and his crew hunting him down had come true, so it stood to reason that the others would too. Like it or not, he wouldn't remain undefeated for long.

He looked up at the old man, the fight gone out of him. What was the point of going on now? It was over. Everything was over. He might as well pack in all in and just let Shamus kill him and get it over with.

"Back in my day kids went missing all the time," Cleopard was saying. "Usually ended up in JELLO vats or Chinese food or something. Helped control the population too. Things are just too out of control these days; we need to start eating children again."

Mongrel was quiet for a minute, unable to muster the energy for a response. Finally he just shrugged and made for the stairs, grumbling dismally to himself.

"What's this? Where are you going? Giving up are you?"

Turning to look back at the old man, Mongrel didn't know what to say. Should he apologize? Should he keep fighting, even though it was futile? Well, perhaps one final shot. "I'm just a figment of your imagination. I don't even exist."

"Nothing exists," Cleopard stated. "Everything's in my head."

Random Tangent

"Yeah, that's what I thought." Mongrel resumed his journey to the stairs.

Cleopard spat on the floor. "You know, back in my day kids had more respect for their elders. They'd take 'em for walks and check their back hair for lice. Give them treats sometimes, if they were good."

Sighing wretchedly, Mongrel shot a glare at the old man. "Let me ask you something: if the old days were so bloody great then why do you old people bitch about them so much?"

"Excuse me?" Cleopard asked, shocked by such insolence. "Back in my day things were better."

"Oh yeah, *much* better. Did you have to walk uphill both to school and home?"

"Sometimes twice a day," Cleopard nodded, almost proud. "Gave you good moral fiber and sometimes hemorrhoids."

This angered Mongrel. "You know, just because these days we have global warming, and terrorism, and Ben Stiller, it doesn't mean it's all that bad."

"And Nintendo."

"What? What's wrong with Nintendo?"

Now it was Cleopard's turn to grumble. "Never did beat the original Mario Bros."

"And what did you have back in your day?" Mongrel asked, ignoring the comment since it caused him painful memories as well[*]. "Stonehenge?"

Before Cleopard responded he shuffled a few feet to his left and smiled broadly. If Mongrel didn't know any better he'd have sworn the old man was posing for a picture. A flash even seemed to flicker across the basement walls to support his suspicions. "What was that?" he asked.

"Now you show some respect!" Cleopard yelled, snapping out of his pose and resuming the confrontation with Mongrel. "Stonehenge had the best puppet show you've ever seen!"

"I've never seen a puppet show before," Mongrel said quietly, suddenly aware of how empty and meaningless his life was.

"Well you just go and see it, and you'll see it's the best."

---

[*] He too had never beaten the original Super Mario Bros.

"Wouldn't it also be the worst, since it'll be the only one I've ever seen?"

Cleopard was silent for a minute while he pondered the logistics of this. Finally he said, "No, it'd still be the best."

"Whatever. I'm not going to Stonehenge; place gives me the creeps. You know, aliens and whatnot."

"Back in my day we didn't have aliens, we ha-"

"Yes you did!" Mongrel cried, exasperated. "Aliens didn't just start existing recently. That's like saying there weren't any people either back in your day."

"Well," Cleopard's eyes flitted around the room, "what if there weren't?"

"Think about that you idiot. That means you didn't exist either. How can it be *your* day if you weren't even in it?"

"I...uh..." Cleopard scratched his head in confusion.

This was all futile, thought Mongrel. He knew he couldn't stay on top forever, but he didn't think he'd be taken down so soon, and not like *this*; to an old man who couldn't even keep a straight argument. He still felt like he was on his A game; that his wit was so sharp you could slice someone's throat with it; that even though his head had taken more beatings than a piñata, he could still handle a crazy old man.

"Okay, that may be true, but back in my day we di-"

"You know what?" Mongrel asked, showing that his rudeness knew no bounds as he interrupted the old man again. "It's not exactly *your* day, okay? You don't own it. And look around you; you're still alive. This day you claim as yours is still happening. If you live 'til tomorrow you can claim that today, right now, was your day too. In the future you can look back at today...wait." Something else clicked in Mongrel's head. "What did I just say?"

"You said 'what did I just say?'"

"No, before that."

"Depends on how far back you mean." Cleopard adjusted his pants. "You've been talking a lot lately."

The future.

In that weird dream that wasn't really a dream Captain Pete had shown him, amongst other horrific things, the future. And it was possible that this Hank person was from the future. No, he *had* to be in the future. Hadn't Hank called him an old man in the vision? That fight wasn't in his past, or he'd remember it, and it obviously couldn't be the present, so it had to be the future. Not only that, but just because he'd lost that fight in the future, it didn't mean he had to lose this one. As far as he knew, he remained undefeated until then.

There was hope.

Mongrel put his game face back on. "Talk too much, do I?" He cracked his knuckles, and then his femurs. "I can talk at around seven-hundred words per minute. It's so fast that only chipmunks and hummingbirds can understand me." He paused to think about this. "Except that they can't understand me, you know, cause they're chipmunks and hummingbirds. But if they could…you know…?"

"Oh I know what you mean," Cleopard lied. "I can hear mimes. Can hear everything they say."

"Don't they just act? I mean, they don't actually say anything."

"Nope, and I can hear them!"

"Okay…how that's working out for you?"

"Oh they're fantastically boring!" Cleopard said, farting excitedly.

"You know what *I* find boring? Your stupid 'back in the day' stories. And yo-yos; those are boring too."

"Oh I have this great yo-yo trick. What I do is I pul-"

"Boring!"

Cleopard sneered and wiped the drool from his mouth. "Back in my day folks didn't get bored. When there was nothing to do you took your own life."

Mongrel rolled his eyes at yet another 'back in the day' story, but had to admit there were times when he'd considered suicide purely for the entertainment value. "Seems like back in your day you people had lots of ways of thinning out the herd. Personally I think we could use more of that these days."

"You talking about herds of sheep?" Cleopard asked, beginning to drool again. "Cause I definitely agree; we need more sheep!"

"No, I meant..." Mongrel paused to let a shudder roll through his body, "...I meant keeping the population down."

"Ah, that. Help control the human population. Have your kids spayed or neutered."

"Isn't that something Bob Barker used to say?"

"Who's Bob Barker?"

"You know, from The Price Is Right? Well not anymore; someone else hosts the show now. But, uh, back in your day he hosted it." Crap, now he was saying 'back in the day.' He had to get away from the old man before more things began rubbing off on him. "It's a game show."

Cleopard stroked his chin thoughtfully. "Oh yeah, I remember now. I was on that show a long time ago. Shook his hand. I won my way on stage by bidding one dollar on a pair of pig antlers."

"Pigs don't have antlers."

"I know, right? Anyway I made it to the showdown at the end of the show, but I overbid by a few million dollars and went home with nothing. Absolutely nothing."

"What about the pig antlers?"

"I thought you said pigs didn't have antlers?"

"I did. I mean they don't." Mongrel wanted to rip his hair out, but since it had started falling out earlier that morning he assumed it didn't need the help. He screamed silently to himself. After a minute to calm down, he pressed on. "We used to have them for Thanksgiving, pigs. Mom would actually make a turkey out of pigs. She also once tried to make carrots out of potatoes, but that went horribly awry. 9-1-1 blocked our number after that."

"We didn't have peas back in my day; just had small pebbles we painted green. Couldn't chew 'em; had to swallow them whole. Couldn't digest 'em either; they just passed right through you. Which brings me to my next point – you people don't recycle your food nowadays."

Mongrel shuddered again. "Yeah, well, there's a reason for that, and it's because you're insane. You were insane back in your day, you're insane now, and if we're all unlucky you'll be insane for many years to come. And I grow weary of your insanity. Let me tell you how things were back in *my* day." He cracked his femur

Random Tangent

again, thinking he should probably go see a chiropractor. "Back in my day brothers could share a pair of eyes; none of that 'everyone gets a pair' crap. And when you woke up in the morning your toilet wasn't always there – you just took your chances. Back in my day people would try to rob you with fish."

"Rob your fish?"

"No, rob you *with* fish. No knife or gun or anything; that's too easy. You had to have balls to pull a fish on someone."

"Back in my day boys weren't born with both their testicles; they were surgically attached later. But you had to earn them!" Cleopard smashed one fist into his other hand. "Had to beat up and old woman or climb a really ugly tree. That was part of becoming a man."

Curious about this, Mongrel asked, "What exactly makes a tree ugly? The wrong colour?"

"Oh trust me; you'll know an ugly tree when you see one."

"You know what I see? I see an old man who doesn't know when he's beat." A smile spread on Mongrel's face. "Cause I also see the future, and I win this fight."

"Oh..." Cleopard said, sounding hurt. "Well, why didn't you say so earlier? Could've saved some time." He shrugged and scuffed his shoes on the floor.

"Sorry. It's been a long night. My brain is a little scrambled; hard to remember things."

Cleopard walked over and put his hand on Mongrel's shoulder. "Oh I know all about scrambled eggs. Did I ever tell you how I saved money on car insurance back in my day? I sent in a porcupine with every payment. My broker, he loved porcupines, but he never could catch 'em. Don't know what he did with 'em either."

Mongrel removed the old man's hand from his shoulder. "Give it up, Cleopard; it's over. I won. And what did I tell you about touching me?"

"Oh, right." Cleopard smiled tersely and farted apologetically. "Well let's get you upstairs for a victory meal. You must be famished! I'll make you some of my goatmeal."

"What the hell is *goatmeal*?" Mongrel asked. "And why can't I yell?"

"That'd be the hill banshees. Now you're gonna love my goatmeal; I use real goat in it."

Suddenly acutely uninterested in goatmeal, Mongrel followed Cleopard up the stairs. "Hill banshees? I think I've heard of them before."

The two men entered the kitchen part of the house, although calling this room a kitchen could be considered somewhat of a misnomer as Cleopard did not use the room for all his kitchen-type activities. He cooked using his stove, sure, but only because it happened to be there. He prepared his nustard in his bathtub. He gutted his fish in what he called his 'fish closet,' and he washed his dishes with a garden hose on the front lawn. The kitchen was just another room in a house full of rooms to the old man.

For Mongrel, who was seeing the room for the first time, it appeared very much like your average kitchen. A hallway wandered off to the left side of the room; a table occupied it's center; a counter began behind it, ran right along the wall to a corner, continued down the adjacent wall passed a sink that appeared to be a seldom-used, and ending at a fridge that was trembling with fear, or excitement, or was perhaps just suffering the effects of a localized earthquake. Next to the shuddering fridge to Mongrel's right was the back door. He eyed it hungrily. The pain and swelling between his legs had lessened to a dull throb; maybe he could make a run for it.

Cleopard sat himself down at the table opposite the basement door, leaving the hill banshee remark unexplained and not bothering to get Mongrel the goatmeal he'd promised. He stared up at Mongrel for a moment, then farted.

"What are they?" Mongrel asked, walking over to look out the window over the sink, careful to avoid the fridge, which seemed to growl at him.

"What are what?"

"The hill banshees."

"Oh, them. Just some spirits got lost in the hills. They don't like anyone screaming. Soon as you leave the road they silence you. Want to be the only ones screaming. If you listen closely on a quiet night you can hear them. Sounds like the wind, mostly. But sometimes you can hear their voices, shrill and pleading, like chocolate pudding."

Mongrel had no idea what the old man was talking about, but found himself wanting pudding. He remained silent, letting Cleopard continue.

"Course, you shouldn't listen to 'em anyway. Legend has it that they'll hypnotize you and make you follow 'em, and get you lost too. End up just as lost as they are." He shook his head solemnly. "Lost so many gophers that way. Have you noticed? All the gophers are gone?"

"Uh..." Mongrel said, more to himself than in reply. Not only had he not noticed the lack of wildlife, but also, who gave a shit about gophers? "Well, it's really dark out. So how'd the spirits get lost anyway? And where's my damn goatmeal?" All the running and hiding for his life had left him hungry.

A sigh came from somewhere behind Mongrel, accompanied by the word, "Finally."

Mongrel turned to see Shamus Bond standing by the entrance to the hallway. His eyes goggled. His nerves tightened. His heart sank, and then stopped altogether. For the entire night, Shamus had been an illusion, merely his imagination, perhaps; the worst case scenario. Mongrel hadn't heard his voice; no one had mentioned his name. It was entirely possible that the anti-agent had nothing to do with any of this, and Mongrel had clung to that hope like snot clings to one's finger.

But now the hope was gone. The illusion became clear. Reality set in. Shamus Bond was there, in the flesh – or rather in a damp but otherwise repulsively decorous suit. His usually meticulously groomed hair was slightly matted from the rain. His shoes, normally buffed beyond what is normally acceptable in society, now shone with an almost demonic brilliance, also courtesy of the rain. In fact, all that was missing was a well-timed bolt of lightning and some thunder to make this a scene straight out of a bad horror movie. Except this wasn't a movie; it was very real.

"Don't know much about them myself," Cleopard said, seemingly unaware of Shamus' presence. He paused to fart before continuing, "They were lost long before I came along."

Jaywatch

"You won't believe the night I've had," Shamus said, eyes locked on Mongrel. "Worth it, though, now. But horrendous all the same."

"Well I hope it's been as bad as mine," Mongrel said. He knew should have run out the back door earlier when he'd had the chance. It took all his willpower to keep his knees from shaking and his bladder from emptying. "Or worse. Yeah, hopefully worse, you know, if it has to be one or the other."

Shamus reached into his pocket, causing Mongrel to flinch. "Oh grow up," he said, pulling out a two-way radio. Putting it to his mouth, he spoke into it, "Got him cornered in the house." Then to Mongrel, "I wasn't going for my gun – but rest assured, I do have it. A gun would be too quick; I want this to last all night." He smiled evilly.

"Look, uh, I'm sorry for all the trouble I've caused, but I won't cause anymore. Promise." Mongrel began inching toward the back door. "I'll just be moseying along now."

Beginning to circle around the table to cut Mongrel off, Shamus shook his head. "Oh I think you should stay. It won't be any trouble at all."

"No, no, I really should be going," Mongrel said, circling the table in the opposite direction, keeping it between him and Shamus. Cleopard still sat at the table, farting occasionally but not seeming to pay much attention to either of them. "I – I think I left my house on fire. I should go check on it."

"I wouldn't worry about it; you won't be needing it anymore. Things are about to get interesting around here; I wouldn't want you to miss anything. Besides, weren't you about to have some goatmeal, whatever the devil that is?"

"I'm not hungry," Mongrel lied, wishing he still had that flute, although he didn't know what good it would do. "I'm also not available to be killed at the moment, so you're going to have to try again another day."

Shamus raised an eyebrow at him. "I'm sorry?"

"Well it's not like you called me up ahead of time to arrange this, did you?" Mongrel stated rather than asked. "You didn't make an appointment. And if I let you kill me without an appointment, well, it wouldn't be fair to the other people who want me dead."

"My dear fellow," Shamus said, deciding to ignore Mongrel's comments, "do you have any idea how much grief you've caused me?"

"I'm sure you deserved it."

Gritting his teeth and scowling, Shamus spoke into his radio again, "Guys, house, now." He then politely put the radio back into his inside suit pocket and adjusted his posture before resuming his stalking around the table. "You still don't get it, do you? This is a job. I was paid to kill you. *Paid.* I'm not doing this for my amusement."

"So you're not enjoying this at all?"

Shamus paused before answering. "Okay, fine, I am. But tell me, what's wrong with enjoying one's profession?"

"You're a murderer!"

"It's a *business*, and I happen to be quite good at it. In fact, I had a perfect record until you came along."

Mongrel was about to apologize, but stopped himself. "I'm sure you'll get over it."

"Well my client won't. I actually had to give a refund for the first time in my life. Do you have any idea how embarrassing that is?"

"What do you mean a refund? Your government gives refunds?"

Shamus was silent again, and stopped stalking Mongrel around the table. "Ah, hmm. Very well then. All that talk about working for the Queen...well...that was some time ago." He looked to the floor, appearing to be ashamed. He then rubbed one shoe on the pant leg of the other, buffing the already brilliant shine further. "The anti-agents were disbanded several years ago I'm afraid. I'm freelance now."

"So you're your own boss now? Good for you," Mongrel said, not really caring.

"Thank you."

"So wait, if you gave a refund doesn't that mean the job is done? I mean, like, the contract is nullified, or whatever?"

"Well...technically yes."

"So why are you still trying to kill me?"

Jaywatch

"Because..." Shamus stopped himself from saying 'for shits and giggles' but otherwise didn't have a legitimate answer. "Because you're our one-thousandth customer and you've won the grand prize."

Even though both men were standing still, Mongrel still managed to stumble upon hearing this. "You serious?"

Shamus rolled his eyes. "In all the years I've been doing this I've completed every mission, finished every assignment, and gotten a medal for every conceivable accolade. I've even shaken the Queen's hand!"

"Really?"

"Er, well...not personally. She's far too lovely and pure to be touched by my sinful hands, so someone very prestigious was appointed to shake her hand in my honour."

"Right..." Mongrel said sarcastically.

Gritting his teeth again at the insolence, Shamus pressed on. "But all that changed after you came along. You somehow slipped through my fingers, and tarnished my reputation. You ruined my good name, and thus became my nemesis. You were the only case I hadn't solved. The only debt I hadn't paid, the onl-"

"Yeah, yeah," Mongrel interrupted, "the one that got away."

"Yes, the one that got away." The interruption served to fuel the anti-agent's fury. "Killing you was one of my tasks and I failed. I failed the Queen, and by extension all of Britain. I was chosen by the Queen to become an anti-agent, to serve her royal highness, and by extension all of Britain. And I will perform every duty, every task required of me, to honour her, and by extension all of Britain."

"The Queen chose you? What makes you so special?"

"Well, the Queen didn't choose me herself, personally; she's far too lovely and busy for such menial tasks. But someone very prestigious was appointed by her to choose me. And you remaining alive is like a slap to the face of the person chosen to appoint me to serve the Queen. You are vicariously slapping *my Queen*! And I *cannot* allow that!"

"Dude," Mongrel said, taking a step back from Shamus's outrage, "you know I'm gonna die eventually, right?"

"Yes, but there's no good reason for my Queen to see Heaven before you do."

Random Tangent

"How about because she's old as hell?"

Before Shamus could blow his top Cleopard suddenly joined the conversation. "We didn't have Heaven back in my day," he said, looking over a jar of nustard, which he didn't have moments ago. How he obtained it was a mystery since he couldn't possibly have gotten it without either of them noticing. He opened the jar and began pouring it into his goatmeal. "Or Hell. When you died you just went and stood in a long, long line. Stretched on forever. Course, it moved pretty quick so it seemed like you were getting somewhere."

"And just what are you saying?" Shamus asked, his anger forgotten for a moment. "That you've died? Back in your day? Otherwise how would you know anything about Heaven and Hell?"

"Well death wasn't as permanent back in my day."

"Oh, I see," Shamus said, unconvinced. "So you died and came back to life? How efficient of you. And this kind of thing happened all the time back in *your* day?"

Cleopard chewed his goatmeal at Shamus and farted, but otherwise didn't answer.

"What was at the end of the line?" Mongrel asked.

Shamus pinched the bridge of his nose in exasperation, having a hard time keeping himself together. "Tell me, old man, when...when exactly was your day, exactly?"

"Oh let's see now..." Cleopard tilted his head back to look at the ceiling and think, "it was ought-sixty-twelve I believe. Good year, as I recall."

That about did it for Shamus; his last nerve had been stepped on. "You know, I've had about all I can take of you, old man. You don't even *try* to make the slightest bit of sense. You live in the middle of nowhere in this hellhole of a land, you have a refrigerator that is either rabid or possessed by demons..."

"Actually the middle of Nowhere is West-"

"Shut up! You keep eating this disgusting nustard, and, and goatmeal – both of which smell like they came out of a toilet. And this goatmeal stuff cannot possibly have any goats in it since there's not a bloody goat in sight. And I honestly don't know what you're still doing alive, since you could be the great-great- grandfather of Father Time!" He leant down close to Cleopard then. "And let me please give you some advice: for the love of Her Majesty, *stop fucking farting!*" Straightening back up, he violently pulled his two-way radio out of his pocket and screamed into it: "Where the bloody hell is everybody?"

Something strange happened when Shamus spoke into his radio this time: it echoed.

After his voice bounced all over the kitchen everyone glanced around to see where the echo was coming from. It didn't take them long to locate another radio situated in the center of the floor not three feet from the table. It had not been there moments ago. They all looked at the radio, and then at one another, confused.

Cleopard got up from the table and picked it up. Turning to Shamus, he asked, "You drop this?"

Shamus waved his radio – which was still in his hand – in the old man's face. "I think not. It must be from one of my men. But where did it come from? How did it get-"

"It's mine."

Suddenly Jayson Miles was standing in the room among them. Just like the radio, he'd appeared in the blink of an eye, without warning or logic; one minute they were alone, and the next he was there. Shamus jumped so high with fright that his head nearly hit the ceiling. Mongrel tried to scream but, well, you know – hill banshees. Cleopard calmly sat himself back down at the table and took another bite of goatmeal before spitting it out in shock.

"Holy mother of...I thought you were dead!" he said.

Miles stared down the old man, preventing a sinister smile from sneaking onto his face. Untold hours of waiting, plotting, had led to this moment. Years spent in prison, biding his time, as the clock perpetually ticked off the minutes leading up to this final showdown. The time had finally come. "No. Just in prison, no thanks to you."

"Oh," Cleopard said. "Well, you're welcome."

"No, I said *no* thanks to you."

Cleopard tilted his head sideways like a confused dog. "Hmm...well, you're welcome all the same."

The old man hadn't changed a bit, thought Miles.

Mongrel couldn't believe his eyes. The ex-con had returned, and had perhaps even taken care of the rest of the thugs. Now only

Random Tangent

Cleopard and Shamus remained, and although the anti-agent was well-trained, Mongrel had to acknowledge that at least now it was two-on-two; a fair fight, depending on your definition of 'fair.' Hope began to race through his veins.

Having calmed himself down and convinced his heart rate to lower itself to a more efficient tempo, Shamus decided to insert himself into the conversation. "Excuse me, who are you?"

"Don't you know who this is?" Cleopard asked him, astonished.

Shamus looked at the other two men in turn, his expression now also resembling a confused dog, but without the tilted head. And if that dog could talk it would say 'really?' He cleared his throat before asking, "If I knew who he was, then why, pray tell, would I ask who he was?"

"This is Jayson Miles," Cleopard said, farting. "My son."

"No I'm not," Jayson corrected.

"No, he's not," Cleopard admitted. "But he recently came back from the dead."

"No, I haven't."

Cleopard frowned. "No, that's not right either. But he could if he wanted to."

Miles seemed to ponder this, eventually shrugging in a noncommittal way.

"Ah yes, the chap from the radio." Shamus said, studying the man. "So tell me, is coming back from the dead common knowledge around these parts?" He looked at Mongrel. "What about you?"

"Actually, yeah, I know ho-"

"Shamus threw up his hands in defeat. "It's just not possible! Is it? Are you all serious?"

Everyone nodded

"So I'm the only one who, who...if I die, it's permanent?" He looked to the floor and said, more to himself, "Why the devil weren't we taught that in training? Perhaps it's something new?" He looked up at them; Mongrel he wanted dead, and the old man, well, Shamus wanted nothing more to do with him. But the convict...yes, he could be of some value. "Tell me, Mr. Miles, what other skills do you have?"

"Oh he can do anything!" Cleopard answered for him. "Or build anything! He's a whiz with technology. I mean I may be pretty good with making things myself – I did create life after all – but I've got nothing on him." He turned over the radio in his hand. "Jayson, how did you make this radio?"

Keeping his eyes on the old man, but speaking to everyone but him, Miles said, "I created it using an old radio and a couple batteries."

Cleopard continued to study the radio. "Amazing! I never would have thought of that."

"So, wait," Shamus said, "that radio is yours? You didn't get it from one of my men?"

Miles shook his head. "It's mine."

"Ah. Very good then. I was beginning to worry something ill might have befallen them. Perhaps you'd bested them in a scrap or something, and that's how you'd obtained it." Shamus frowned. "That still doesn't explain why they aren't answering. Anyway, I'm terribly sorry, my name is Bond. Shamus Bond." He walked over and offered his hand.

For the first time since spontaneously appearing in the room, Miles took his eyes off the old man. He turned to face the anti-agent and shook his hand. "You can call me Miles. And I did best your men in a scrap. Wasn't much of a scrap though."

Shamus jerked his hand back. "What?"

Mongrel allowed himself a small, quiet cheer after hearing this news. He wanted to jump for joy and sing out his glee, but didn't bother, figuring the hill banshees would render him mute. He settled for enjoying the rattled look on Shamus' face, although somewhere in the back of his mind he knew he should probably be trying to sneak away while everyone was distracted. It had worked once before that evening.

"You know why I'm here," Miles said, returning his attention to the old man.

Cleopard slurped up the last of his goatmeal and farted. "You missed me?"

Miles grit his teeth. "You left me in prison. Can't let that slide."

Random Tangent

Shamus took a step closer to the two men. "I'm sorry, did you just say you took out my best men?"

"I slipped," Miles said in mock exasperation. Then to Cleopard, "You could've gotten me out whenever you wanted. Hell, you could've prevented my conviction if you'd shown up at the trial."

Cleopard shrugged and opened another jar of nustard. "I was busy." He then dumped half the jar of nustard into another bowl of goatmeal, which seemed to be materializing out of thin air.

"What do you mean?" Shamus asked. "Your trigger finger slipped?" The radio had mentioned Jayson Miles was a murderer, but honestly, the convict had been free for only a matter of hours and he'd already picked up where he left off? The man was a brute; a barbarian even! Shamus would have to teach him some manners.

Sighing in a most disgruntled fashion, Miles turned to face Shamus. "They're not dead, okay? Don't worry about them. Now if you don't mind, I'm in the middle of something." He quickly turned back to Cleopard. "If you'd have shown your face everyone would've known I hadn't murdered you."

"They also said you raped and tortured me!" Cleopard said, sounding impressed.

"Yes I know. I was at my own trial."

"If they're alive then what exactly did you do to them," Shamus asked, trying to get to the bottom of things.

Miles cracked his neck and faced Shamus once more. "Alright, if you do mind then how about you mind your own business?"

Mongrel could see the anger welling inside the Brit, and was loving every minute of it. He himself would not have dared to speak to Shamus like that, and while he was enjoying the show, he knew trouble was brewing. Things were only going to get worse. And he still couldn't shake the feeling that he should leave. Seriously.

"So did you even care?" Miles asked the old man. "I was gone for years, and you didn't even try to prove my innocence!"

"I don't know what you're so upset about," Cleopard replied. "You could've broken out whenever you wanted."

Shamus watched the two men bicker back and forth, unable to comprehend what was going on. On one hand, his men were apparently still alive. But on the other, he'd never been so disrespected in all his life. What was with these Westerners? They were backwards, tactless ingrates, and he'd had enough of their imbecility. Tonight, all that ended.

He took another step over and tapped Miles on the shoulder. "Excuse me."

"There's such a thing as having respect for the law, you know?" Miles stated, rather than asked. "I may completely molest the laws of nature, physics, and occasionally gravity, but I do draw the line. Besides, I kept waiting for you to do the right thing, to show up and prove I didn't kill you, but I-"

"And rape and torture me."

"Yes, that too, but you never showed. Being in prison was legitimate, and if I broke out that would be too. I'd be a fugitive, at least for a little while. And it would all go on my permanent record. Wouldn't be able to get a decent job or leave the country. They say you're fully pardoned by these things still follow you around, fuck up your li-"

"Excuse me!" Shamus said again, louder and with more forceful shoulder tapping.

Miles glared at Shamus. "I'm sorry, what was your name again?"

Shamus' eyes widened. Forgotten his name? *Sacrilege!* "My name is Shamus Bond. Anti-agent XYZ of Her Majesty's Secre-"

"Shamus," Miles cut him off, "are you a fucking child?"

Sputtering was the only way the anti-agent could communicate at that moment, such was his incredulity.

"The *adults* here are trying to have an argument. Now run along and go play or something. You're British aren't you? Why don't you act like one and stop being so rude."

Shamus gasped. Mongrel snickered. Cleopard farted.

"I-I'm the one being rude?" Shamus asked, quite beside himself with rage.

"Yes."

Still reeling, Shamus couldn't wrap his head around this insolence. He was British, for crying out loud! *British!* You were supposed to be polite to the British. It was a law or something, wasn't it? And not only that, he was an anti-agent! Or used to be,

Random Tangent

anyway. He'd traveled all over the world, wrecking havoc, creating disasters, maiming and murdering with the best of them. Wait, he *was* the best of them! And he did it all with a stiff upper lip and unwavering manners. He'd done such a good job as to warrant an audience with the Queen herself. The *Queen!*

"*The Queen!*" Shamus shouted.

Everyone looked at him, and he looked back, somewhat shocked and appalled by his outburst. Trying to calm himself down and remain civil, he continued. "I'll have you know that I have had an audience with the Queen herself."

Miles was unimpressed. "So? Who gives a shit about the Queen?"

And that was it. Cleopard stopped farting. Mongrel held his breath[*]. The crickets outside stopped chirping. Even Murphy, the refrigerator, stopped violently shaking. Shamus saw fleeting images of red and death and whatnot, tried to scream – but the hill banshees forbade it – and jumped on Miles.

After struggling for a moment, Shamus finally got his hands around the convict's neck, and began pulling him to the floor. Dragging him across the room, the anti-agent tried choke the life out of Miles, who still seemed unimpressed.

In fact, Miles seemed more annoyed than anything. Then he just…stepped out of Shamus' grip. In an instant he was back at the table and talking to Cleopard. "Well I'm back now, and you're gonna pay for everything."

Cleopard seemed unperturbed about this, but Shamus was extremely perturbed. He looked around the room, startled. "What the hell?" he asked, bewildered. One minute he had Miles in his clutches, and the next he was wrestling an apparition. Had he hallucinated the whole thing?

Mongrel had witnessed the entire scene but he still couldn't believe it. Miles had simply *walked out* of a headlock as if it was a minor inconvenience.

Getting up off the floor, Shamus did his best to pretend none of that had happened. He then charged at Miles, at the last minute

---

[*] Considering that the old man had momentarily stopped breaking wind, this would have been the best time for Mongrel to take in all the fresh air he could. Common sense, however, was a rare trait in his lineage.

raising his right leg to kick him as hard as he could in the back – and missed. Shamus stopped, again confused. He was now standing directly in front of the ex-con, so how could he have missed? He surely couldn't have gone through him. Gritting his teeth in anger, he turned and took a swing at Miles' head. Then another, and another, each time hitting nothing but air. What made this extraordinary is that Miles wasn't ducking or dodging the blows, but was actually standing still.

"What's wrong with you?" Shamus asked, infuriated. "Are you physically incapable of being assaulted?"

Miles sighed and shoved the anti-agent out of the way. "Isn't there someone else you can go annoy?"

Mongrel ceased enjoying Shamus' frustration at this point since he knew the answer to that question. Yes, there was someone else Shamus could bother – him. Why was he just standing around watching when he could be getting away?

"I'll deal with him in a minute," Shamus replied. Exasperated well passed his breaking point, Shamus drew his gun and held it point blank at Miles' temple. "Right now you must die." He pulled the trigger.

Jayson Miles did not duck. Nor did he jump to the side. He did not twitch, jerk, shudder, tremble or otherwise give any indication a gun was fired at him. Instead, he ignored the shot, got down close to Cleopard and whispered to him, "This has been a long time coming."

With that he threw a fist at Cleopard with such ferocity that the old man and the chair he was sitting in flew back and crashed into the kitchen counter. The chair splintered and shattered, but contrary to what you might expect, the old man remained in one piece. He ricocheted off the counter, slid across the floor a few feet, and without pausing, walked back and sat himself down in another chair at the table. As if nothing had yet happened, he looked up at Miles and said, "All right, fine. Let's get this over with."

"Just remember this," Miles said, ignoring the old man's ignorance. "Next time I won't go so easy on you."

Shamus stood, mouth agape, just staring wide eyed. Not only had he witnessed the ancient Cleopard shrug off a blow that would have broken a normal man's back, but he also saw Miles

Random Tangent

take a bullet to the skull and…what? Deflect it? Absorb it? There's no way he could have dodged it, but what had actually happened?

He opened his mouth and shut it a few times, but this did little to assuage his disbelief. He looked at his gun, turning it over in his hand a couple times. It seemed fine. He shot a hole in the ceiling at random, making everyone[*] else in the room jump, and it seemed to work just fine. The only thing he could do, he finally realized, is try again. "Let's try this again," he said, raising his gun to Miles' head and pulling the trigger, this time twice.

Miles hung his head, which was smoking slightly, and shook it. Without saying a word, he turned to face the anti-agent and wagged a finger in his face.

Shamus looked at the finger, and then into Miles' eyes. The look of bewilderment was becoming a permanent feature of his face.

After a good amount of finger-wagging, Miles moved his hand to Shamus' ear and snapped his fingers; a simple gesture that was so much more than it appeared to be. The anti-agent's eyes instantly grew bloodshot and bulged out of his head. His nose began bleeding. He dropped his gun and both his hands shot up to his ears, and he began crying softly. After a moment he slowly dropped to his hands and knees and began to crawl his way out of the room.

Mongrel didn't know what Shamus had heard, but he himself heard the chandelier ring, the house groan, and the chorus of a thousand crickets from miles around chirp in response. He also thought he heard Murphy whimper and was sure he felt his hair tighten on his scalp. The English language had yet to invent a word audacious enough to convey the level of shock Mongrel was experiencing, so let's say he was *uberstunned*. He didn't know what had just happened, but he was sure most of it had been epic. "Holy shit!" he said quietly. "What did you do?"

Miles shrugged as if it wasn't a big deal. "All I did was snap my fingers at the same frequency as the signals his ear drum relays to his temporal lobe, which caused a synaptic overload and sent his nervous system into shock."

---

[*] By everyone I mean just Mongrel.

Jaywatch

Not quite understanding what Miles had told him, Mongrel nodded his head in a way to suggest exactly that. "Epic," he said, mostly to himself.

"He'll be lucky if he ever hears out of that ear again."

"Didn't have ears back in my day," Cleopard said, getting up from the table to stand with them. "Didn't need to go 'round hearing everything for no reason. And things were quieter back then too. Not so much noise. Nowada-"

"You have ears," Miles interrupted.

"Did you get them later?" Mongrel asked. "Surgically?"

"Grew 'em," Cleopard replied, as if it should be obvious.

"Listen old man," Miles took a colourful object out of his pocket, "you've had a long night. Go play with this for a while." He tossed a Rubik's Cube at him.

Cleopard caught the cube and studied it, and slowly his eyes grew wide. For as long as he could remember (which actually wasn't that long, considering he'd lived far longer than most), the Rubik's Cube had haunted him. The colours, the patterns, the infinite possibilities. Twist, turn, rotate – it didn't matter; Cleopard would spend days on end without food, without sleep, diligently toiling away at the device, trying to solve it. But he would get nowhere. He'd tried bargaining with it, and reasoning with it (as much as he could, given his capacity for reasoning), even bribing it. Once he even took it apart and ate it piece by piece in an attempt to absorb its power. As sane as he wasn't, the method of madness required to solve the puzzle eluded him. It was his arch nemesis.

"We didn't have toys like this in my day!" he screamed, fumbling the cube around in his hands as if it was too hot to hold. "When we wanted to have fun we just spun around 'til we got dizzy. Some kids couldn't take the centripetal force and that's how retards were invented." He then bolted out the back door, leaving the screen door banging open in the breeze.

Mongrel walked over to close the door and, despite multiple warnings, was attacked, raped, and murdered by Murphy...so to speak. Failing to scream, Mongrel collapsed through the door and fell down the steps, landing on the damp grass.

Miles came after him, stopping first to place his hand on the refrigerator. "Easy girl," he said, calming the machine down almost instantly. Satisfied that the fridge wouldn't be a danger to anyone anymore, he stepped out into the crisp night air helped Mongrel to his feet – or rather, foot. "You okay?"

"Well," Mongrel groaned, "if that's the worst thing that happens to me tonight then I'll be just fine." He inspected his sore ankle, rubbing it tenderly where Murphy had bit him. "Gonna be a bitch of a walk home though."

"Hmm…" Miles looked around, his eyes slowly drifting to the precipice where his kartcycle was parked. "I got a ride. It's won't fit two people but if you give me a few minutes I can fix it."

Together they walked to the edge of Cleopard's property and made their way up the hill. Cleopard himself was nowhere in sight. Shamus likewise had disappeared. Mongrel limped next to Miles, his arm draped over the convict's shoulder. Despite the modest amount of pain he felt surprisingly good about everything. Considering how bad things had begun that night, and how much worse they could have gotten, it was no wonder; he was lucky simply to be alive. There was only one thing left that was bothering him.

"I gotta ask a question: how do you know Murphy is a girl?"

Miles grunted questioningly.

"Well you said 'easy girl' earlier. Cleopard calls it Murphy, and Murphy is a guy's name. So why did you call it a girl?"

"Are you really wondering about the sex of a fridge?"

Mongrel wondered instead about his own sanity for a minute. "Okay, good point. So why does Cleopard call his fridge Murphy?"

"Because he's crazy."

"Ah. And you're not crazy, right?"

Miles laughed. "No."

"Okay, good." Mongrel smiled, then frowned. "Sorry I lost your flute."

Grunting questioningly again, Miles asked, "What flute?"

"The one you gave me earlier? You know, to call you if things got bad?"

"Oh right, that flute. Don't worry about it. It was just something I whipped up on the spot. I can make another."

"You can make flutes? They teach you that in prison?"

Jaywatch

"I figured it out myself," Miles said, shrugging like it was no big deal. "I made that one out of three car tires, and old VCR, some string, and a handful of dimes."

"What?"

"It wasn't anything special. Like I said, I can make another one. I'm just glad it came in handy."

Mongrel stopped limping, not because they'd reached Miles' kartcycle, but because he was confused. "What do you mean? I didn't use it?"

"Yeah, but I heard you *try* to use it."

Now Mongrel was quite baffled. "You heard me, what, *not* use it?"

"My hearing is good, what can I say?"

After all the things he'd seen Miles do, Mongrel knew he shouldn't have been surprised by this, and tried not to be. He attempted to change the subject. "So what are you going to do now? I mean, you're still a wanted criminal, right?"

Miles shook his head. "I took care of that. See, the cops think I killed the old man, so all I needed to do was show that he's still alive to prove my innocence. So I made a camera out of a candle, a pair of sunglasses, a couple slices of watermelon, and a box of crackers, took a pic of him and sent it to the cops. I even sent them a text; said, 'told you so, from Miles'."

"You think that'll work?"

"It better, or I'll have to resort to plan B."

"What's that?"

"Kill them all and leave no witnesses."

The two continued to talk and laugh as Miles prepared the kartcycle for the journey home. They were fast becoming the best of pals.

And this would have been the end of the story if a van hadn't come careening up the hill towards them.

"Oh yeah," Mongrel said, watching the vehicle approached with deadly speed, "I guess we could've just taken the van. Forgot about it." He shrugged.

"No biggie," Miles said, pushing Mongrel out of the way just as the van was about to run them down. He then lunged the other way, barely avoiding being hit himself, and managed to catch the sideview mirror of the vehicle and delicately fling himself into the thankfully-open passenger-side window.

Shamus looked over as Miles plopped roughly onto the seat beside him, and then back out the front window. He swore the man had just been in front of him. In fact, he'd have bet money that he had run the asshole over. But then, with complete disregard for physics, he was right next to him. It was the bullet-to-the-head incident all over again. "The hell?" he asked as they drove off the cliff.

Momentarily distracted by the fact that he was now driving across open air, Shamus let his foot off the gas. He also mentally took note that he was not a cartoon character – although there were many times he certainly felt like one. Maybe if this freelance contract killer career didn't pan out he could look into becoming a toon; he had the experience, after all. But until that happened he wouldn't be able to screech the van to a halt and reverse back to the ledge, much like in the cartoons of old, and narrowly avoid catastrophe. Of course, being a bad guy, he wouldn't have been afforded this skill anyway because only the good guys can defy physics to their benefit, but Shamus was probably too busy to realize this.

Turning to Miles, he asked, "Really? What do you thi-" and was cut off when the convict stuck a foot in his mouth, or at least tried to. Shamus recoiled and tried to speak again but found himself on the receiving end of a barrage of fists, boots, and the occasional map book – an assault that was going quite well until the van hit the water. The driver-side airbag immediately deployed and startled the consciousness right out of Shamus for a moment. There being no passenger-side airbag, Miles crashed into the windshield, cracking it.

After a moment to wearily orient himself, Miles found a trickle of blood running down his forehead. He shook off his dizziness and took stock of his surroundings. The vehicle had begun to drift downstream – or perhaps upstream; with Duntt River it was impossible to know – and cold water had begun spilling into the cab. Shamus was still unconscious next to him.

He pulled himself from the sinking van, fighting his way out the window against the incoming current, and swam to shore, leaving Shamus to fend for himself. Miles wasn't a murderer and didn't feel right about the situation, but felt, in the long run, he was doing a good deed in letting the anti-agent wash out with the tide, so to speak. Besides, had he saved Shamus from the wreckage he might have tried to kill him again, which wouldn't end well for anyone (least of all himself).

Miles took a minute to catch his breath and watched the van float down the river and disappear into the night. Then he scaled the cliff, figuring it would be faster than taking the long way around. When he reached the top he found his half-finished kartcycle, which Shamus had luckily missed with the van, but couldn't find Mongrel anywhere. He tried to call out, but the hill banshees made that endeavor impossible. Then horror struck him; for all his otherworldly talents he sometimes forgot his own strength, and when he'd pushed Mongrel out of the van's path earlier he'd actually pushed him right off the cliff.

Mongrel had fallen down into Duntt River and he never came out.

At least, not in this story.

The End

This story would have gone on forever if I hadn't ended it, seriously. I thought a cliffhanger might be nice for a change. Mongrel didn't die; that would be silly. But he hit his head on the water pretty hard and knocked himself out for a bit. Thankfully he was washed ashore downriver before truly horrific things continued happening to him. Miles decided to go look for Chuck Norris. He'd heard much about the famed martial artist/actor/laxative[*] recently and wanted to match wits with him. Shamus, able to use his cape as a floatation device and breathing apparatus (it pays to get yourself good quality cape), escaped his underwater tomb. Foregoing his idea of becoming a cartoon, he went back to the drawing board on his plans for revenge against Mongrel. He also added another name

---

[*] Chuck Norris has beaten the shit out of so many people in his life that most medical journals now classify him as a laxative.

Random Tangent

to his list of scores to settle: Murphy the refrigerator. Murphy didn't do anything other than continue to act like a fridge. Cleopard threw the Rubik's Cube into the well and was intent on sealing it shut, but then found the body of Colin. Taking Colin for dead, despite his later protests that he wasn't, the old man began using him to create new Diet Nustard; the great taste of Nustard, but with only one calorie! Upon hearing Mongrel failing to play his flute, Miles had come running and kicked both William's and Martin's faces in the ass, and then tied their legs together. They eventually crawled their way painfully to the nearest airport and left the country for good. DERFtron spent the night turned off. However, only the machine part of him turned off; his brain remained active, and since he couldn't otherwise move anything, it was like being completely paralized. Such fun! Oh, and somewhere, somehow, Captain Pete died. Again.

How To Be Monolithic

Frank And The King

The sun shown down in that annoying way that fills your vision with red, even though your eyes are closed and you're trying to rest. Seagulls squawked their annoying squawk and circled maliciously overhead. And Mongrel lay in that annoying angle he always laid in when we're beginning a story with him laying on a beach. Waves of water gently lapped around his ankles. He groggily sat up, rubbing his eyes, half expecting to see a mon, a monkey, or an Elvis. But after a quick glance around, he found himself alone.

Blurry visions of the night before flashed though his mind: the convict and his miraculous skills, the old man and his rabid refrigerator, Shamus and his thirst for blood. He hadn't dared to hope he'd see the light of another day, yet here he was.

Wait...*where* was he?

Standing up and letting his dizziness subside, Mongrel scanned his surroundings. He was on another beautiful beach – somehow he only seemed to find them whilst unconscious – but with no discerning landmarks he was at a loss as to where. The river before him wasn't too wide, and he could see across the other side, but nothing seemed familiar. He wasn't even sure which side of the river he was on; Dunttstown or…he shuddered, not wanting to think about it. He turned to venture inland, deciding not to swim across and risking death in the toxic waters. Although for all he knew he was heading in the wrong direction, he hoped for the best. Besides, he'd been brought up to always side with the least immediate form of death.

A sparse assortment of trees awaited him, swaying silently as he trudged by. He gingerly stepped through the brush, somewhat dismayed that he was without footwear. However, it also meant that he wasn't tramping around in sodden shoes and socks, and considering he still felt lucky to be alive, he might as well continue to look on the bright side.

After a few minutes of trekking he came to a clearing with a distressed-looking log cabin in the middle, which hopefully meant his playful romp in the woods was at an end. Although, somewhere in the back of his mind he knew, especially in these parts – wherever these parts happened to be – that civility was not synonymous with civilization. A dilapidated barn sat off to the side of the field, looking utterly abandoned. Ugly patio furniture was set up near the door, next to some ugly gardening equipment. Mongrel didn't see a garden at first glance but assumed it too was ugly. In fact the entire area was so unpleasing to the eye that the only decent thing one could to would be to set fire to it, which could only be an improvement. Bracing himself for the muddled mess that was human interaction, he approached the cottage and politely knocked on the aesthetically-challenged door.

Moments later the inner door swung open and an older, portly man in a bathrobe stood staring at Mongrel. He seemed genuinely surprised. "Don't get much visitors out in these parts. What can I do for you, son?"

Mongrel had planned on his first question to be concerning 'these parts,' but said, "Uh, I was lost in the woods back there…" he looked behind him and pointed in the direction from whence he came, "and I-"

"Who is it, Mabel?" came a voice from further inside the domicile.

"Just a lad, came from the woods."

Suddenly an older woman came into view. "From the woods? Is he a tree person?" She lowered her glasses and squinted long and hard at Mongrel. "What's your name?" Then back up at the man beside her, "Does he understand us?"

"Course he understands us! How'd I know he's from the woods if he couldn't speak English?"

"My name is Mongrel Stevens," Mongrel said.

"Well maybe you saw him coming from the woods," the woman said, putting her selective hearing to good use.

"Oh yes," the man said, rolling his eyes, "I've just been sitting around watching the door all morning."

"Well, tree people have a very distinctive look," she continued. "And quite an odour I should say as well." She looked at Mongrel again and began sniffing.

"I'm not a tree person," Mongrel said, leaning away. "I'm just lost. I need to fin-"

"Lost?" she exclaimed, opening the door and grabbing Mongrel, pulling him into a ferocious hug. "Oh my goodness! You poor dear. Come inside, you must be famished!" She released him and rushed back into the cottage.

Mongrel stared after her, flabbergasted, and then at the man, who was holding the door open for him.

"Come on, we don't bite. Not anymore anyway." He chuckled to himself.

Mongrel *was* hungry, so he marched inside, hoping the comment was made in jest.

The interior was humbly decorated with antique furniture and a variety of animal pelts. Mongrel glanced about but didn't see any rifles or hunting regalia and chose to assume the furs were fake and hadn't been violently ripped off of wild animals. Besides, it settled his nerves to believe he wouldn't be seeing any guns.

He was led into a kitchen more modern than the exterior of the cottage suggested. A large window let in a stream of warm sunlight, which shone directly onto a large table in the middle of the room. He was invited to sit down, and moments later the woman placed a spoon and a bowl of yellowish goop in front of him.

"What is this, goatmeal?" Mongrel asked.

Random Tangent

"What's goatmeal?" she asked, sitting down adjacent to him.

Mongrel studied the goop, and gingerly poked it with a spoon. "Nothing," he said. "Probably just remembered it from a bad dream last night." Taking a deep breath, he lifted a small spoonful to his mouth, smelled it, and then tasted it.

It wasn't half-bad. He took another, larger bite.

"It's banana pudding," the woman offered. "Do…do tree people like banana pudding?"

"Of course he likes it," said Mabel, who was standing by the sink with his arms crossed, "he's eating it isn't he?"

Indeed Mongrel *was* eating it. His hunger seemed inexhaustible. Apparently nearly being murdered left one with a ravenous appetite.

"Well bananas grow on trees," the woman argued. "Maybe it's kind of like cannibalism to him?"

Mongrel, with a mouthful of pudding, spouted his dismissal of the notion, but neither of the couple understood. He swallowed his pudding and tried again. "I *do not* come from the trees. I don't even know what that means. I'm not a tree hugger – I mean I like them and all but…you know."

They both looked at him gravely, as if he'd just confessed to killing their dog or something. It made Mongrel feel very uneasy. Had he said something wrong? Was it better to have been a tree hugger?

"Um…very good pudding," he said, trying to change the subject. This garnered no response from the couple, save from them exchanging solemn glances with each other, as if they were coming to terms with euthanizing the family dog. Why did his mind keep going back to dead dogs? Had he dreamt of Charlie Marbles last night?

"Um, I love trees, actually," Mongrel said. "Really love them. Like, a lot! I'm a tree guy all right. That's me. Me with a tree, heh. Why, I'd marry one if I could." This did nothing to change the expression on their faces. If anything it made things worse. Mongrel gave up and asked, "You're not going to eat me are you?"

"What?" the woman cried. "We'd never! Mabel, tell him!"

"We only tried that once," Mabel said. "But it was just a curiosity."

"We are *not* cannibals," the woman said, getting up to stand beside her husband. "Why would you say such a terrible thing?"

"I don't know!" Mongrel said defensively. "You're the one that brought up cannibals earlier. Sorry."

"We have bananas and bread and lots of other food," Mabel said, gesturing around. "No need to eat people anymore."

Mongrel looked at the two of them. "I'm sorry. I guess it's just this cabin in the middle of the woods. Kinda creepy. A lot of scary movies take place in cabins. With woods. And have people in them."

"Middle of the woods?" the woman asked.

"We're just on the outside of town, son," Mabel corrected.

"Oh." Mongrel didn't know what to say. Then something struck him. "Wait, did you say you tried eating people once?"

Mabel threw his arms up towards Mongrel, as if to stop him. "Okay, okay…look, I think we got off on the wrong foot here. My name is Mabel, and this is my lovely wife, Mabel." She waved, and he put his arm around her. "We're just two humble old folks who just like to live peacefully by ourselves. We don't bother no one."

"We're certainly not cannibals," the woman said.

Mongrel nodded at her, but didn't mean it. "I'm Mongrel. Mongrel Stevens." He proffered his hand and they each shook it in turn.

"Perhaps I could offer you a lift into town?" the male Mabel asked.

"And it was more than once," the woman said, "but the first one was an accident."

"Yes," Mongrel said. "Town sounds good. I'd really like to leave. Right now."

Mabel sighed and uncrossed his arms. "I'll just go put on some proper clothes." He left the kitchen and disappeared down a hallway, leaving Mongrel alone with his wife.

Smiling tersely at her, Mongrel took another mouthful of the pudding, nearly finished it now. "So," he said after swallowing, "you gonna have any pudding?"

Random Tangent

Hunger glowed in her eyes and he immediately regretted asking. "Oh I'm quite tired of eating pudding. I had all my teeth taken out a few weeks back and got dentures now. Still getting used to them. Ate so much pudding..." she laughed and shrugged. "You get cravings for other things you know?" She eyed him hungrily again.

"I...I should imagine," he stammered, hoping Mabel wouldn't take long.

"Blood pudding, now, tha-"

"You know," Mongrel said, louder than he meant to, "that's a lovely, uh...garden! Yes, a lovely garden you have out front. I'm gonna go have a look at it." He wasn't going to stay in the kitchen with the crazy woman a moment longer. Standing quickly, he made his way to what he figured was the front of the house – assuming that he'd come in the back – hoping to find a door somewhere. He wasn't even sure they had a garden (although he had witnessed the existence of several gardening implements), but it was the first thing he thought of as an excuse to get outside.

"Garden?" she asked, getting up and following him. "That bed of weeds? Well maybe that looks nice to a tree person, but to us people it's really nothing special."

Mongrel thankfully found the front door and opened it. A fresh breeze blew onto his face, and the scent of freedom wafted through the air. He relished it. Then the tree person remark hit him and he grit his teeth. Why couldn't these people just accept that he was a regular, normal human being? Not wood, but flesh and meat and...

A thought occurred to him.

"You know..." he turned around, shocked to find her standing a foot from his face. "As a tree person, I can't imagine I would taste very good at all."

She looked taken aback. "No?"

"Naw! All the wood in here," he pointed to his arms, "you'd get splinters in your teeth. Bad for digestion too."

Mabel nodded slowly and seemed disappointed. "Yes. I guess you'd be right. Wait, so you *are* a tree person?"

"Uh...yeah. I am."

Clasping her hands together excitedly, she whispered to him, "I knew it. It's the smell."

Mongrel looked down at his body; he didn't notice anything. "Really?"

"Bet you'd make pretty good firewood too." She winked at him.

Realizing his gamble hadn't quite paid off, Mongrel turned to the open doorway again. Seems his life was in danger whether he was a human or a tree. He looked outside to see a large oak tree in the middle of the yard, and the road a few meters passed it. An older truck sat in the driveway, which was lined with a tall white fence; it looked to him like one of those kind of trucks that shouldn't be running but nothing seemed to kill it, and provoked older folks into saying things like 'they don't make 'em like that anymore.'

"I don't think I'd burn well," he said. "Not being ninety percent water and all."

"I thought it was people that were mostly water."

He shrugged. "Well, you know what they say. I'm just gonna go wait for your husband by th-"

A hand suddenly clamped down on his shoulder. "Where do you think you're going?"

It was Mabel, the husband. Terror shot up Mongrel's spine like lightning. He was so close to escaping, but now was going to be eaten by these ravenous cannibals. Or chopped up and used for firewood. He couldn't decide which was worse.

"You think I'm gonna let you walk all the way into town? With you being half tree? Don't deny it, I heard what you said. Now come on." He gave Mongrel a gentle shove out the door.

Mongrel raised his eyebrows in surprise but otherwise did what he was told. They both stepped onto the front steps and descended them, making their way to the old truck. Not knowing what to think, Mongrel decided to just let things play out before he could figure out his next move. He couldn't assume the danger was over – for all he knew it was just beginning. He needed to keep his guard up.

Random Tangent

"Oh, Mabel?" the husband called to his wife. "Do you need anything from town?"

Mabel poked her head out the front door. "Maybe you could bring home another barn? The old one's gotten itself all covered in spider webs again. Just a little one though."

"We told that barn over and over to stop allowing spiders inside," Mabel said to Mongrel, hopping into the truck. "Mabel's terrified of them. But if it won't listen then we've just got to throw it out and get a new one."

Mongrel was about to open the door and hop into the truck next to the man, but had reservations. Maybe this was his chance to run for it? Maybe getting into the vehicle would turn out to be a mistake? Maybe soon he'd look back dismally at this moment as the worst decision of his life?

But what if they weren't going to kill him after all?

"How far is it into town?" he asked.

"Well it's quite a hike," Mabel answered.

Sighing and knowing he'd regret it somehow, Mongrel climbed into the cab, deciding to take the risk.

The engine turned over a few times, whining like an old goat, but after a minute it roared to life. "This old girl never let's me down," Mabel said, patting the dashboard. "They don't make 'em like this anymore."

"So why do you and your wife have the same name?" Mongrel asked. The question had been on his mind for a while.

Mabel shrugged. "That's what we were named by our parents."

"Doesn't it get confusing?"

"No. We know who each other is. She calls me and I know who I am. And I don't mistake her for any other Mabel. Nothing confusing about it."

"I mean don't other people confuse you."

"Well we mostly keep to ourselves. People seem happy to keep it that way too."

"That got anything to do with you eating them?"

A smirk grew on Mabel's face. "Now we were just pulling your leg there, son. Having a laugh. Don't get visitors much, like I said, so we make the most of it."

Mongrel felt relieved but still kept his guard. The last thing a cannibal would admit to was *being* a cannibal. "Well that's a relief."

"Hell son, if we were gonna eat you why would I be taking you into town?"

"I don't know," Mongrel replied. "Keep me on my toes? Maybe you want to give me a sporting chance? Thrill of the hunt? So where are we going anyway?"

"Into town, don't you remember?" He put the truck in gear and backed out the driveway.

"No, I mean what's the name of the town? I don't know where we…"

They'd hardly gotten onto the road when the town came into view. Their cottage was the last on their side of the road, separated from the rest of the town by a wall of close, bushy trees and the large fence. They weren't more than fifty feet from the next house.

"…are. We're *this* close to town?" Mongrel asked. "We could've walked."

"What do you mean 'this close to town'? We're the last ones, all the way out here!" Mabel shook his head. "I'm trying to do you a favour, son; that's a long way to walk for a tree, even a person who's only half-tree like yourself."

Beginning to regret admitting he was a tree person, Mongrel was about to come clean about it. "Well I appreciate everything you're doing; the ride, the not eating me and all, but you should know something."

"That sure was funny! You should've seen your face." Mabel pulled the truck over, parking it in front of a convenience store. They were still within sight of the cottage, or at least the wall of bushes in front of it. They had been driving for less than a minute. "Here we are."

"Where are we, exactly?"

Mabel helped himself out of the truck, and Mongrel did likewise. "This is Jack's Convenience store." Mongrel was about to say that's not what he meant, but didn't get the chance. "Now I know what you're gonna say; the sign still says 'Gerry's Convenience' 'cause Jack didn't want to confuse anyone. He won it

Random Tangent

in a poker game from Gerry about a year back, and he thought it might hurt business if he changed the name too soon. Jack isn't as well-known as Gerry was. People can be fickle, you know?"

"Morning Mabel," a passing stranger said, stopping to shake hands.

Mabel nodded. "Morning, Gerald."

Gerald didn't look as old as Mabel; his hair was only beginning to gray. But he was dressed as neat, with his shirt tucked in and shiny leather shoes that reminded Mongrel of Shamus Bond. He also wore a fedora hat. "Haven't seen you in ages! How's the misses? Still making those amazing meat pies?"

"Not as much as she used to," Mabel laughed. "She's still getting used to her new chompers." He bit his teeth together a couple times. "But in time, you know?"

"Dentures eh? When did she get those?"

"Oh…they came in the mail about a month ago. They're *Chevaliers*."

"Chevaliers, eh? Fancy stuff." Gerald seemed impressed. He then turned his attention to Mongrel. "And who's this young man? Finally found your long-lost son?" He nudged Mabel in the ribs.

"No, no! This here is Mongrel Stevens. He's a tree person."

"A tree person?" Gerald asked before Mongrel could argue. "Now is that the kind that was raised by tress? Or do you just fornicate with them?" "

A disgusted look came across Mongrel's face. "*Fornicate* with them?"

"Ah, good choice. Not as good as sheep, but to each their own. That's why they call them 'woody's' eh?" he nudged his elbow into Mabel's ribs again. "Well I best be off. Give Mabel my best. Good to meet you too, Mr. Stevens, and good luck with the trees. Hope you don't get any splinters." He shook Mongrel's hand before continuing his jaunt down the sidewalk.

"Gerald's an old friend," Mabel explained as they began walking. "Don't see him much anymore, not since we moved out of town. But I come in every now and then. Mabel mostly stays at home; she likes to keep to herself. We both do, but we need to come in sometimes for things. She only comes if she has to."

How To Be Monolithic

"Look," Mongrel said sternly. "I'm not from the woods, okay? I'm really just a normal guy who got lost. I just woke up next to the river and don't know where I am. So could you at least tell me so I know which way to go home?"

"What do you mean, son? You're *not* a tree person?"

"No. I was just, um, pulling your leg – like you did with me, pretending to be a cannibal."

"But what about what you said to Mabel?"

"I was just...I mean, she seemed so excited by me being a tree person, and I didn't want to take that away from her. Like you said, you don't get visitors much, and I was just trying to make the most of it."

"Oh." Mabel seemed genuinely disappointed. "Well okay, I guess that's fine. And I think you must mean the lake. It's a lake; not a river."

Something about this notion struck Mongrel as odd, frightful even, but rather than dwell on it he continued trying to get to the bottom of things. "Sure, whatever. So if I wanted to get to Dunttstown, which direction would I swim?"

"Oh you'd definitely want to use a boat. Don't go swimming in the lake – it's haunted[*]."

"What? Haunted? How can a lake be haunted?"

"Well I'm sure I don't know, son," Mabel shuffled around nervously, appearing to be uncomfortable talking about it. "It's a strange place though, let me tell you. Folks who go swimming mostly don't come back. Some people think it's not even a lake at all, but a river."

---

[*] Since anyone who goes swimming in the lake is never seen again, the demonic, moronic people that live on the island believe it to be haunted. But it has nothing to do with spirits and everything to do with pollution, although where all the pollution comes from is a mystery. It fact, it's the only body of water you can actually get a sun tan from swimming in, even at night. On the Dunttstown side of the river – and it *is* a river – the honourable, decent folks know it's the rampant pollution killing anyone dumb enough to stick so much as a toe in the water, and not spirits. The hope was that if left unchecked for too long the water might become so toxic it would start to dissolve the island, or maybe even become sentient and eat it. But until that day, signs were posted, forbidding entering the water.

Random Tangent

"Ri...riv," Mongrel's mouth went dry. "Did you say...?"

"Can you imagine that? A river going 'round the island? Why, it makes no sense at all."

"I...island?" Mongrel's blood went cold. His spine turned as stiff as a board. In fact, he felt very much like the tree he'd been imitating. "It does," he whispered, more to himself.

"It does?"

"I mean it is...is...Donut Lake." He turned away from Mabel, not wanting to show the fear in his eyes, and looked around. All the stories he'd heard growing up came fleeting back to him. The crazed islanders, worshiping the moon, putting training wheels on their bicycles. Teaching their children to question authority and hit things with sticks, and actually *walking* them to school. Practicing voodoo and studying homeopathy. These people actually went to bed when the sun went down. He stood there reeling, actually wishing he were back on Old Man Cleopard's farm, face-to-face with Shamus.

"You okay, son?" Mabel said, snapping his fingers in Mongrel's face.

Coming back to the present, Mongrel stared into the old man's eyes, the fear still there. "I..." was all he could manage.

"You look like you've seen a ghost." He looked around for a minute before finally seeing something useful. "Here now, come with me, son. I think you need to sit down."

"I...think I could use a stiff drink," Mongrel finally said.

"Well I know just the place. Come on." He draped Mongrel's arm over his shoulder and together they hobbled down the sidewalk. Mongrel didn't need the assistance walking; his feet were fine. His brain, on the other hand, had been impounded. He didn't recall most of the journey, but when they turned into a small shop he was able to read the sign 'The Café.'

The shop appeared to be a small pub, full of tables and chairs, and a scattered assortment of patrons. Mabel sat Mongrel down at a table near the door, and just as he was about to take a seat himself someone hailed him, and he excused himself, mentioning that he'd not seen this fellow since he was last in town (which happened to be only a couple days ago), and they had much catching up to do.

Mongrel gradually came to terms with his surroundings, and began to think of a way to get himself back to the relative safety of Dunttstown, when he saw Loafmeat at the bar, wiping the counter.

Loafmeat was an old friend who ran the only bar in Dunttstown: *El Éfac*. He was a large, brooding man who was never without a hat, and had facial hair that could only be described as epic. He seemed, Mongrel always thought, that he wouldn't be out of place on a pirate ship, pillaging and plundering with the best of them. But what on Earth was he doing here, bartending for these detestable swine? He went over to the bar at the back of the restaurant to find out.

"Hey," he said, approaching the bar. Two other men at the bar turned to look at him but went back to their beers and conversation when it became clear he wasn't talking to them.

"What can I get for you, sir?" Loafmeat asked him after convincing himself that the counter was clean enough.

Mongrel spread his arms wide as if to say 'it's me.' But when that didn't work, he actually said it. "It's me."

Loafmeat studied him for a moment, his eyes becoming thin slits with his scrutiny. He then shook his head and said, "Afraid I'm not familiar with that one."

"No, it's *me*," Mongrel said again, lowering his arms.

"Don't know you neither."

Sighing, Mongrel took a seat at the bar. "What, you don't remember me? We've been friends for years." Then something struck Mongrel. "Wait, is it these people?" He looked around suspiciously. "What have they done to you? Can you even talk about it? Just wink if you can't."

"Sir, I have no idea what you're talking about. But I can get you something to drink if you'd like. May I recommend a fine home brew of a local talent? Grows his own barley and it's rather good ale if I say so myself. Don't recall his name, but he comes from off the island." He picked up a glass and began to polish it. "Or if you're not feeling so adventurous, perhaps a little pick-me-up?" He gestured to one of the many bottles of liquor behind him. "You look like you could use one, if you don't mind me saying."

Random Tangent

Mongrel looked at him, stunned. This was not like his friend at all. Maybe it had something to do with the local beer? If it was local then it couldn't be trusted.

"Come on Loafmeat, you really don't remember me? Mongrel Stevens? From Duntts...ah...off the island?" He couldn't risk anyone overhearing his conversation, and decided he'd better leave things a little vague.

The bartender looked at him, somewhat confused. "Close," he said with a chuckle, "but the name's Meatloaf. Like the singer, I'm sure you know."

"He's a hack," one of the men at the bar said.

Meatloaf chuckled some more. "You'll have to excuse Mr. Shabby there. He's our town know-it-all. And make no mistake he knows quite a lot."

"I know it *all*," Shabby said, hopping off his stool and coming over. "And just who are you? And where are you from?" Shabby asked, tapping a pointed finger on Mongrel's chest. He acted like he was trying to pick a fight, but appeared too drunk to be able to start one.

"Uh..." Mongrel tried to think quick, "If you know everything, then you should already know where I'm from." He hoped the tactic would work. Shabby sneered at him but said nothing.

"He's not from around here," Mabel said, coming to what he thought was the rescue. Apparently his meeting with his old friend had been adjourned. "Dunttstown, I believe he said."

"No I didn't," Mongrel said quickly.

Mabel looked at him for a minute. "Yes you did. You told me y-"

"Nope. Just wanted to get there; I'm *not* from there. I'm really from the woods." Mongrel said loudly, attracting more attention than he would have liked. He pointed his thumb over his shoulder as he looked at all the faces gawking at him strangely. "Yep. I'm a tree person...whatever that is."

"What's a tree person?" someone asked.

"You mean you live in the trees?" Meatloaf asked. "Like, in little tree houses? Like Tarzan?"

"Does he have sex with trees?" asked a man at the bar.

"Naw!" yelled someone else Mongrel couldn't see. "He's a tree hugger. He goes out and finds them trees with X's marked on 'em – you know, the ones slated for an axe-kicking." He laughed at his pun. "Chains himself to the trees so's they don't get cut down."

The throng of men murmured theories amongst themselves while Mabel tried to make himself heard over them, asking why Mongrel kept changing his story. Was he a tree person or wasn't he? This went on for a few minutes until, like a flock of birds, they all turned to Shabby, the man who claimed to know everything, awaiting the supposedly real answer. Shabby stood with his arms crossed, staring at Mongrel and pretending to blow smoke in his face.

"Now this is a non-smoking bar, Mr. Shabby," Meatloaf warned. "You mind yourself."

"He's made of wood," Shabby finally announced. He rapped his knuckles on Mongrel's forehead, making him wince. "Go on, try it for yourselves."

A roar of hushed voices filled the room, discussing this news, but no one was trying to tap Mongrel's head, as Shabby suggested they should, and Mongrel was thankful of that.

"And a killer!" Shabby shouted, pointing a finger at Mongrel again and silencing everyone.

"I'm not a killer," Mongrel protested.

"Not yet maybe, but soon you'll be a stone-cold killer. Or should I say *wood*-cold killer." He glanced around at the assembled men. "That's right. Trees are nature's killing machines. Man's oldest and deadliest enemy. Always traveling in gangs, they stand there, like silent monoliths. Never know when they're gonna catch fire or fall on you, crushing your skull like a watermelon." He smacked one fist into the palm of his other hand for effect. "I, for one, don't trust 'em. It's not a matter of if, but *when* they attack. You can't turn your backs on them for one second."

The group remained silent, contemplating this. Mongrel was dumbfounded by the accusation.

"Does that seem right to anyone?" Meatloaf asked. "I don't know…"

Random Tangent

Mongrel turned to him, even more bewildered. The man, the Loafmeat he knew, *always* knew right from wrong. Or at least felt it. It had something to do with his morals, which were out of whack or something; he couldn't remember. The point is; Loafmeat was the measure of right and wrong. But this man who stood before him, actually *asking* whether something was right or wrong, was *not* Loafmeat. He couldn't be, even though the likeness was striking.

"You're…you're not Loafmeat," Mongrel cried at him.

"No," the man said. "Thought we'd been through that."

"Oh yeah." Mongrel hung his head.

"Would you mind if I ask you a question, Mr. Tree, sir?" he asked.

Mongrel nodded, "Sure. What?"

"Well, as a tree…and being plant life in general – and I mean no offense in any way – but…well, does it offend you to see folks drinkin' beer? 'Cause of the barley and all?"

Other people seemed to agree with the question. Some were even concerned, going as far as to hide their glasses from Mongrel's sight.

"Um…no."

A wave of relief washed over the crowd. Some smiled and even appeared to toast him. Mongrel appeared to be the center of attention in the bar, which was not a good sign – especially here. He needed to fly under the radar. There was no telling what these people would do to him if they learned where he was from; they were utterly bonkers. Mongrel looked around at them, cajoling and having a good time. It was if they actually enjoyed the company of one another

And for the time being they weren't paying any attention to him.

He quickly made for the front of the bar, and exited into the warm sunlight. He paused, soaking in the rays, unsure of what to do now. He glanced up and down the street; it was devoid of traffic for the moment, so he walked across to what appeared to be a park, if they had such things on the island. It was quiet out here, at least compared to the bar, and he could think without being interrupted, or accused of having homicidal tendencies. He sat down on a bench, once sure that it wasn't going to spring a trap, and buried his face in his hands.

How had it come to this? The island. The last place in the world he'd ever want to be. Actually, maybe he shouldn't think that way. Only a few days ago he was in prison, and thought *that* was the last place he'd ever want to be. He didn't want to make that mistake twice. "There are certainly worse places to be," he said, more to karma than to himself. Nodding inwardly, hoping he hadn't jinxed himself, he casually looked around.

A mother pushing a stroller with another child in tow were wandering towards a large water fountain. Were they planning on throwing money into it, wasting it? Or perhaps she was going to drown her babies? They got to the fountain and sat down. The little girl behaved, minded her manners. They spoke quietly about something – Mongrel was too far away to overhear – and didn't seem to notice or care that they shared the park with other people, such as the old men playing a game of chess behind them. Both had been locked in a stalemate for so long they could have been dead and no one would have noticed. To his left, the sound of laughter invaded his ears. He turned to see two children tossing a Frisbee back and forth. Neither appeared to be very good, and only rarely was the plastic disc caught by a hand; usually it was retrieved from the ground. And yet, the kids weren't shouting obscenities or trying to kill each other. In fact they acted as if the whole thing was normal, as if they were *expected* not to catch it and *still* have fun. It boggled Mongrel's mind.

A young couple behind Mongrel sat on a blanket, having a picnic, talking about raising a family. These monsters wanted to raise more monsters? *This* was the world they wanted to raise children in? He shook his head in disgust, and wondered if he shouldn't be nodding it instead if he wanted to fit in, such was the backwards nature of these people. Meatloaf, Loafmeat's evil twin, even had his name backwards. He didn't have a sense of right or wrong at all. His beard probably wasn't even carnivorous. And Mr. Shabby didn't lose his temper the way he always had in the past, and actually had an answer for Mongrel – it wasn't right, but everyone else believed him. The whole town was completely backwards. They fixed their cars and kept them running instead of leaving them to sit and rust and become the lawn furniture they were supposed to be. They helped their neighbors and gave to the poor and needy. They didn't have a body bin at the hospital, and actually expected everyone who walked in with a problem to be fully conscious and aware of it – and even then the doctors held true to the old axiom of treating the worst-off patients first. He wouldn't be surprised to find a Captain Pete on this island who didn't die every time they met.

Now that was an intriguing concept.

This place, this island, was like Bizzaro World from Superman comics: everything was backwards. Backwards Shabby, backwards Loafmeat, who ran *The Café*[*], which, now that Mongrel thought about it, was backwards and English for *El Éfac* (which is French because the language is backwards), the bar Loafmeat ran. There was probably also a Blind Cracka who wasn't blind, and an Almighty Frank who wasn't perpetually drunk.

And a Captain Pete who never died.

In this backwards, evil land, maybe there was some good to be found.

"There you are."

Mabel sat down on the bench next to him. Mongrel wasn't startled like he would've been in Dunttstown when someone snuck up on him, and that was disconcerting.

"Wondered where you'd gotten off to. Didn't even see you leave."

"Well I, uh…needed to get some sun. Too dark in there."

"Uh huh," Mable nodded. "Spoken like a true tree. Why do you keep on switching your story? You told me you weren't a tree. The Shabby says you are. Care to tell me the truth?"

Mongrel answered his question with one of his own. "Didn't you have to get a barn or something?"

"Now hold on a minute, son. What's with you flip-flopping your story? Are you a tree person or ain't you?"

---

[*] While The Café was a non-smoking establishment, Él Efac only had a non-smoking section. Patrons were advised to keep their smoke on their side of the room, and those who failed to do so were asked to leave.

"Uh…" Mongrel didn't really know what to say. "I don't really like to tell people, you know. Seen enough alien movies to know what the government would do if they found a new species. I don't want to be locked up and experimented on. So I just try to act human."

"Well you're safe here. We're good people, most of us, and we'll keep your secret. And you're doing a good job pretending to be one of us."

Mongrel shrugged. "It's in my genes I guess. My mom was human, my dad was a spruce. I think. I never really knew him growing up. He was never around. I just have a few pictures. Every now and then I think I see him when I'm hiking through the woods but…anyway, is there a barn store around here?"

"Yep. It's just up the road a piece."

"Is it run by an old pirate?"

Mabel seemed to think for a minute. "Well I don't know if he has another job but I've never seen him pirating, or whatever it is pirates do. He's a short fella though, and has wooden legs like a pirate."

Hope blossomed in Mongrel's bosom, and a smile broke out on his face. "I should like to meet him."

The drive over took longer than necessary. Mabel insisted on walking back to his truck –actually passing 'Yon Captain Pete's Other Barn Store' – to get a closer parking spot, all for the sake of not having to walk farther than they had to. Mongrel wished he hadn't decided to continue the charade of being a tree person since it might have saved them the trouble. But now they stood in front of the store. The sign read CLOSED, though it obviously wasn't. This was promising; Dunttstown's Captain Pete never turned his sign over either.

Mongrel knew this could possibly be disastrous, that it could end in tragedy, but he had to know for sure. As much as he wanted to ignore it, or wish it were all just a series of inexplicable coincidences, he couldn't deny that something strange, something otherworldly, something…stupid, was going on between him and Captain Pete. Something was just plain wrong in the world. There

Random Tangent

was no logical reason for Captain Pete to be the physical embodiment of Kenny from South Park, to keep dying, to keep being tortured.

But maybe right here, on the island, was the answer to their problem. Perhaps the way to break the cycle lay in the very store in front of him. He mentally prepared himself for what could happen, good or ill.

"Are we going in or what?" Mabel asked suddenly.

"Uh...yeah," Mongrel muttered, snapping out of his thoughts. He gestured for Mabel to lead the way.

Mabel opened the door and Mongrel followed him inside. The air smelled of wood, hay, and curiously enough, coconut, putting Mongrel at ease for some reason. He was also pleased to see a few customers loafing about, which was an unusual sight; back in Dunttstown he had never once seen a customer in Captain Pete's store.

After wandering around the aisles of barns and barn accessories for a couple minutes, they finally came across the captain, stacking a huge pile of barns by himself. His height certainly made it a challenge.

"There he is," Mabel said, walking over. "Excuse me, Mr. Pete?"

"It's Captain," the captain muttered to himself and turning towards them. "*Captain.* Now wha-"

Captain Pete froze, immediately spotting Mongrel, and jerked back. The stack of barns wobbled violently but didn't topple.

"I'd like you to mee-" is all Mabel got out.

"Yous gotta be kiddin' me!" Captain Pete blurted out, his shock rapidly turning to anger. "Ya comes here? To the *island*? The one bloody place I knew ya wouldna come? But ya hunts me down anyway?"

"Now hold on," Mongrel said. "I didna – I mean didn't – hunt you down. I didn't even know you were here."

"Yes you did," Mabel said. "I told you he was here."

Captain Pete glanced quickly at the old man, but wanted to keep his eyes trained on his supposedly-accidental murderer. He nodded his head at Mabel. "See? Even he gets it. Ya acts like tis all just a big mistake, like ya has nothin' to do with me dyin'. But I knows better."

"What's he talking about?" Mabel asked.

"It *is* just a mistake," Mongrel said. "But here, maybe I've found the answer, the solution."

"Forget it!" Captain Pete slowly backed away a few feet. "I's not listenin' to ya no more. Nothin' good ever comes from it."

"No, this island is backwards from Dun…" Mongrel looked at Mabel, whose face was a train wreck of confusion, "…from where we're from. People are backwards, and things are backwards, and maybe this is backwards too." He gestured between the two of them.

Captain Pete stopped backing away and squinted at Mongrel, as if trying to see through him.

"Here on this island things are different," Mongrel continued. "Whatever this thing is between us could be different too. What if you don't die here? Back home you die, but here you live, because it's backwards. You see what I'm saying?"

The old pirate was silent for a while, mulling this over. "Backwards, eh?" he finally said. "You mean you dies 'stead of me?"

Mongrel's blood went cold again. He hadn't thought of that. "I, uh…I hadn't thought of that." He swallowed hard. "That's not really what I meant. I-"

"Now that ya mentions it, I's noticed a bunch o' strange things 'round 'ere." The captain took a few steps toward Mongrel.

"Would someone please tell me what's going on?" Mabel asked.

Was it a mistake coming here? Mongrel wondered, taking a step back. He wasn't sure what to do. Should he run? Should he be afraid for his life? Would Captain Pete actually try to kill him?

"Look rounds ya boy, there be people here," Captain Pete gestured all around him, still advancing towards Mongrel. "Customers, ya calls 'em, right? 'Tis new to me. Strange. And folks is nice'n'good to each other. Ain't that the daftest thing?"

"Yeah, really weird," Mongrel agreed. The captain had a peculiar look in his eyes that Mongrel had seen before. It was a crazed, verge-of-madness look. Any minute now he might start frothing at the mouth. Mongrel was deeply disturbed. Not by all this, but just in general.

Picking up a shovel, the good crazed captain continued walking and talking. "I knows all the bleedin' stories 'bout the island - and I now know theys all true - but I comes here anyhow, thinkin' maybe I's be safe froms ya. That ya wouldna cross the river, cause it'd be suicide. But ya made it, curse me luck. How *did*s ya gets here, boy?"

Mongrel shrugged, honestly not knowing. He scanned his surroundings, looking for something he might use to defend himself, in case Captain Pete attacked him.

"Bah! Don't matter. Ya brings me a gift!" He smiled, displaying an assortment of crooked teeth with a shiny gold one amongst them. "And I plans to use it. Come 'ere."

Mongrel turned and ran.

"Stop him!" Captain Pete shouted. "He's thievin'!"

Dodging people and merchandise, Mongrel ran down the aisles, heading for the door. It was busier in the store than he remembered, which was good for the captain, but bad for him. Everyone gawked at him; some ducked out of his way. His getaway seemed to be going well until turned a corner and crashed into an older woman, and they both toppled to the floor, taking out a mountain of paint cans.

"Sorry! Sorry. Ow! So sorry," Mongrel mumbled, trying to get to his feet in the wreckage.

"Get off me!" the woman cried. "Help! Rape!"

Captain Pete rounded the aisle, smiling now that he had Mongrel in his sights again. "I'dn't noticed that things be backwards here 'tils ya mentioned it. But yous right. Maybe 'tis your turn to die." He laughed gruffly and swung his shovel.

By now all the commotion had gathered the attention of the entire store. People had stopped browsing and began making their way over to see what was going on. Mongrel had to fight his way through a small crowd to get away from the mad captain.

Yon Captain Pete's Other Barn Store hadn't looked so large from the outside, but now that he was trying to leave, Mongrel couldn't find the exit. He'd followed the rays of light to some windows and was wandering along them, but so far had found nothing. Has he missed the door, overlooking it in his panic? He felt like someone in a horror movie, trying to get the key in a lock but it just wasn't going in. Maybe those movies were closer to reality than he thought. The answer had to be right in front of him but he just couldn't see it.

"But what if yous wrong?"

Turning, Mongrel found Captain Pete slowly hobbling towards him. He wasn't alone now; a couple men flanked him, one on either side. Neither looked particularly menacing, but the growing army the captain was amassing was alarming.

"What if this place ain't backwards; just...different?" Captain Pete continued. "Maybe I still dies when ya comes 'round, and ya goes on livin'. Maybe I's should run'n'hide."

Darting down another aisle, Mongrel tried to keep some distance between them. When he got to the end of the aisle he looked left and right, unsure of which way to go. Where was the exit? He came across a box full of three-foot long metal poles. He grabbed one for each hand, just in case, and felt somewhat less anxious. "Maybe you *should* run," he hollered back.

"And run wheres?"

Mongrel jumped and spun around, finding the captain only a few yards away.

"There's nowheres you won't find me. Ya *always* finds me. Every bleedin' time. All me life I's been runnin' and hidin' froms ya. Well not *alls* me life, but ya knows what I means. Anyhow, the runnin' stops here." He slammed his shovel on the floor.

Customers began appearing again, wondering what the commotion was all about. There were more customers than Mongrel remembered seeing before. Were they coming in to watch the fight? He glanced around at them quickly, then back to Captain Pete. "I don't want any trouble," he said, then turned to bolt again.

He was stopped by a couple large men – the same two who'd been flanking Captain Pete moments ago. One of them said, "Well you brought the trouble when you began shoplifting."

"We don't take kindly to shoplifters around here," the other said.

"I wasn't shoplifting," Mongrel nearly pleaded.

"Oh really? Then what are these?"

Mongrel looked at the metal poles in his hands. "I don't know – metal poles? And I wasn't stealing them. In fact I just picked them up just now."

"Don't let 'im get away." Captain Pete said. "He's a bleedin' liar. Always was'n'always will be."

"I'm not a liar," Mongrel said. "I've never lied to you."

Captain Pete spat on the floor. "Oh really? I s'pose yous gonna say ya never killed mes neither?"

"Well, not actually. Like, not with my bare hands. I haven't."

"Well I still ends up dead." He took a step towards Mongrel, hefting his shovel. "But now 'tis your turn, boy."

"Um, let's not do anything hasty," Mongrel said, swallowing hard.

"Hasty?" Captain Pete asked, nearly shocked. "Ya thinks this just came to me? 'Tis been a long time comin', it has. Many nights I's laid awake'n'dreamin' o' ways to gets me revenge. But I canna do nothin'. Every bleedin' time ya gets near me I's dead 'fore I knows it. But not this time."

Mongrel turned to run again but was blocked by the two men.

"We don't like folks who run away from their problems," one said.

"Well you won't be seeing me again after this. Promise. Excuse me." He tried to push through but the men wouldn't budge.

"We don't like folks who disappear around here."

"Give me a chance," Mongrel said, trying to squeeze between the men. "Maybe you'll like me."

"He ain't from 'round here," Captain Pete said. "He don't know how things'r'done."

Murmuring swept through the crowd, and Mongrel could feel the heat of embarrassment spreading on his face. He could feel all the eyes on him. How was he going to get out of this jam? He wished he hadn't come. He wished he'd never gotten that stupid idea.

"I-I'm from the woods. I'm a tree person," he said.

How To Be Monolithic

Captain Pete roared with laughter. "Ya gotta be bloody kiddin' me! Ya ain'ts no tree person. Ya ain'ts even from the island."

Thoughts began to run through Mongrel's head. He knew his old friend was going to blow everything and reveal that Mongrel was from Dunttstown. Then the shit would hit the fan. What would these people do to him? Have him tore limb from limb? Gang–rape him? Teach him an alternate, terrifying version of the alphabet? Lock him in a dungeon and feed him gruel for decades? He wondered what he could do to stop Captain Pete. He wondered if he could make a run for it. He wondered what gruel tasted like. He wondered why something strange wasn't happening and causing Captain Pete an untimely death.

"It's true, he's a tree person," Mabel said from somewhere in the crowd.

Mongrel scanned the sea of faces but couldn't find him. "Woods are woods," Mabel continued. "What difference does it make where they are?"

"Cause he ain't from no woods…"

It seemed to happen in slow motion. Mongrel's grip adjusted on the metal rod in his right hand, and before he knew it, the rod was in the air, launched at the captain's head. He didn't even realize he'd thrown it, and for a second he thought it came from behind him. It was almost as if he was in a movie and it turned out he was a secret spy with some slick moves, only he had been brainwashed and didn't remember anything. He was Mongrel Bourne.

But this was no movie, and Mongrel was no secret agent. The rod he launched flew short and landed on the floor, bounced and rolled, and smacked against the old pirate's shins. The crowd nonetheless was stunned, and Captain Pete was a little perturbed.

Still in slow motion, and still feeling like he was in a movie, Mongrel spun around, the other rod raised, and smacked one of the men behind him on the side of his head. The man grabbed his ear and moaned, and lurched to the side, nearly falling over. The path now partially clear, Mongrel barged through with little trouble, and ran, his life actually depending on it.

Random Tangent

"Stop him!" Captain Pete yelled.

The crowd did little to aid the captain this time, since Mongrel now carried a weapon and had proven he wasn't afraid to use it. The metal rod whipped back and forth as Mongrel made his way around the store, trying to find a place to hide. It banged against the odd display or barn accessory, sometimes spilling merchandise onto the floor. He felt good about this, thinking it might slow down any pursuers. But the rod would also whip against his leg occasionally, causing him to wince and wonder if he should toss it aside. He didn't; having a weapon brought him comfort, and had already gotten him out of a bind. It was his new best friend. His brother in arms. His father, mother.

Secret lover.

"Shut up," Mongrel muttered.

As he made his way to the back of the store, he came upon the pile of barns Captain Pete had been stacking earlier. Perhaps he could hide in one of them? He couldn't keep running around the store forever, but he couldn't find the way out. It was like a secret lair or something; only those who knew it well knew where the exit was. What he needed was a place to hide and plan his next move. So he ducked inside the barn, hoping no one saw him. If he was lucky – which he usually wasn't – people would give up looking and assume he'd fled the building.

The barn floor hadn't been outfitted with any hay[*], causing the place to look a little alien to Mongrel. It was nothing like the barn he'd been in the previous night; for example there were no spiders, which was a blessing. On the down side, it wasn't as dark inside as he was hoping for, making hiding more difficult. But there was no turning back now; a mob would be waiting for him. Captain Pete had the entire town on his side. How long had he lived on the island for to have so many friends? Was it because Mongrel was an outsider? Is that why they call turned on him so easily? But how did they know he wasn't from there? Was it because no one recognized him, or because the captain had said so? Was it as simple as his word against Captain Pete's?

---

[*] Hay is sold separately in a variety of colours and flavours to match any décor and/or palette. This week only try the new strawconut (a mix of strawberry and coconut) hay bails – buy 2 bails get 1 free!

How To Be Monolithic

He found a ladder to the hayloft and although knowing he'd regret it later, tossed aside his weapon so he could climb it to the second floor. He then crept over to a window to check if he'd been seen entering the barn, but he noticed that it was a very short jump to the roof, where he could climb to the next barn up. Throwing caution to the wind, he perched his legs on the window ledge, and after balancing himself, jumped. He landed roughly but didn't slip, and there was enough friction to crawl up the side. Making his way up to the highest point of the roof, he found, to his luck, the door of the barn on top was open, and he climbed inside. The barn was a little tipsy, but seemed stable.

After a minute to catch his breath, Mongrel turned to see what was happening outside. From that height he could see the entire store. Some people had gathered below, and were milling around. Others were still wandering around the store. No one appeared to have noticed him. Perhaps he could lay low here for a while. Perhaps he'd be safe.

"Ya things ya be safe here?"

Mongrel jumped and landed facing the opposite direction. Captain Pete was standing a few feet away. He still had his shovel, and didn't appear the least bit out of breath like Mongrel was.

"How'd you get up here?" Mongrel asked, panting.

"What, ya thinks I don't know how to climb me own barns? Been sellin' these bleedin' things for years. Stacked these meself." He stomped on the floor a few times, causing a shudder to roll though the structure.

"Please don't do that," Mongrel said. "Not sure how stab-"

"Oh you don't like when I does this?" Captain Pete stomped some more, causing the whole barn to shake. Mongrel grabbed a pillar and held onto it, and waited for the tremors to subside. The old pirate laughed. "Tis a bit new to me, havin' ya scared o' me. I likes it."

"Look," Mongrel said, still holding onto the pillar, now using it as a shield, "it doesn't have to be like this. You don't have to kill me."

Captain Pete looked hurt. "Kills ya? Ya thinks I's gonna kill ya?"

Random Tangent

Mongrel peaked his head out from behind the pillar, hopeful. "You mean you're not going to kill me?"

"Well, yeah, I s'pose I's gonna kill ya." He laughed some more.

Nodding, Mongrel withdrew behind the pillar again. "Yeah, I figured. But you don't have to. I'm not gonna kill you here."

"No?"

"No. I mean, it's not like I've really killed you before, technically, but I know it's weird what's going on. I know you die, and it has something to do with me. I can't explain it; it makes no sense, but whatever. It happens. But here I think you're safe. You haven't died yet, right?"

Captain Pete didn't answer, but seemed to think about this.

"Usually you'd be dead by now, right? But you're not, and you won't. So you don't have to kill me. If I ever get off this island I swear I'll never come back. You can stay here and you'll never see me again. It'll all be over."

"I don't knows," the captain still seemed to be deep in thought. "Still kinda likes me way better. I spects never to see ya's again – ya gots that part right. But I's gonna do it me own way'n'kill ya real good. Who knows, maybe you'll even live throughs it like I does."

Mongrel let his eyes wander to the floor, thinking about this. What if Captain Pete was right? What if he did live? Wake up in his bed or something the next morning completely fine, albeit mentally scared with a perfect memory of what happened. He didn't like it. Why couldn't something bad happen to the captain at that moment? What was it going to take for history to repeat itself? Were things really, truly backwards on the island? Was Captain Pete immune to dying as long as he was here?

Captain Pete took a step towards Mongrel, bringing his shovel up. "Been a while since I's done battle. D'ya wants a weapon? Seems only fair. What happened to yer threaded rod? Canna kill ya unarmed."

"My what?"

"You knows, that metal pole you threws at me. Thought yous had another one. Throws like a girl you does, by the way."

"Oh that," Mongrel shrugged, "I uh, must have lost it. But I'll take a weapon if you're offering."

"Well I s'pose I can let it slide this once," Captain Pete laughed. "Next time though, I'll gets ya a good'n'proper weapon. Now is you gonna come 'ere, or is ya gonna make me chase ya?"

"Actually…" Mongrel ran. Not too far behind where the captain stood was a ladder that led to a hayloft above. Mongrel circled the long way around, and when he came back to it, jumped and caught the fourth rung up. He climbed as fast as he could, but in seconds was blindsided by the swing of a shovel. Crashing to the floor and causing the whole structure to shake violently, Mongrel heard laughter again. He rolled over to see Captain Pete standing over him with the shovel raised in the air, and rolled quickly out of the way as it slammed down to the floor, dodging it by mere inches.

"Captain," Mongrel wheezed, the wind knocked out of him from the fall, "please don't kill me. It won't change the past." He dodged another shovel blow. "It won't make us even."

"Oh we's be even all right."

"No. I never tried to kill you. They were all accidents." Mongrel rolled to his feet, dodging another swing of the shovel and still wishing another accident would befall the old pirate. "I don't want you to die. I never did. I never actually tried to kill you. It just…happened. But this, what you're doing here, is murder."

The captain stopped swinging his shovel, letting him talk.

Mongrel backed away towards the open bay door, staying out of swinging range. "Well, attempted murder, at least. And once you start down the dark path, forever will it dominate your destiny. Consume you it will, as it did Obi-Wan's apprentice."

"What?"

"I mean you're not a murderer, Captain Pete. All you want is for the dying to stop, right? You don't *really* want to kill me."

"Are ya daft, boy?" the captain asked. "I's not a killer? I's a bloody pirate. Used to kill five, six families a day. Usually 'fore lunch."

"Oh," Mongrel said dismally. He should've figured that. "Even the children?"

Random Tangent

"Aye. And the way their wee necks snap..." his eyes got misty, reflecting. "Tisn't all fun'n'games being a pirate, boy. Tis a kill or be-killed world. At least you I *does* want to kill." He came at Mongrel.

Suddenly the entire barn lurched, and Mongrel had to stop himself from sliding through the door and falling, if not to his death, than to certain injury. The two men were putting too much weight on that side of the barn, causing it to tilt. Captain Pete stumbled back to the other side, making the structure lean the other way. It rocked back and forth with every move they made to stop it from rocking back and forth. Rather than discourage their efforts this only made them fight harder to keep their feet. Captain Pete had to toss his shovel aside so he could use both arms to steady himself. Eventually things grew stable again. But the damage had been done; any sort of movement made the barn wobble dramatically.

Mongrel and Captain Pete stood immobile, staring each other down. This went on for several minutes; neither one saying a word. The tension was palpable. The rabble of people wandering around the store wafted through the barn. Surely they'd heard all the commotion and seen the stack of barns trembling. It was pretty obvious they all knew what was going on. It was the last thing Mongrel wanted, the world watching him die. Well, maybe that was the second-last thing he wanted; *dying* was the last thing he wanted.

They stood their ground, neither moving for fear of toppling the barn/jenga tower. Mongrel noticed again the scent of coconut, but this time it did little to settle his nerves. He glanced out the door, seeing people in the aisles below. Were they looking for them or just shopping? Oh look, there was a door to the backroom. Where was *that* when he needed to escape earlier?

Captain Pete was on the other side of the barn, feeling like he couldn't have been further away from his nemesis. He wished he still had his shovel; he could at least have thrown it at Mongrel. Anything would've been better than just standing around.

"So," Mongrel finally broke the silence, "what do we do?"

"You should run'n'take a flyin' leap out that door'n'land on yer head! Be much 'preciated."

How To Be Monolithic

Mongrel glanced out the door again, mulling over the suggestion, hoping there might be something soft to land on. But he saw nothing he'd be willing to risk his life with. "Yeah, I think not. But let's assume I don't kill myself, accidental or otherwise, what's your big plan: to kill me in broad daylight? In front of dozens of witnesses? I'm sure that'll be great for business. How do you even have business here on the island?"

"What d'you mean?"

"Well, I already guessed you'd left town to avoid me. Figured that part out myself. But why here, on the island? With these people? You know some of them are cannibals?"

"Bah," Captain Pete said again, waving a hand dismissively, "hogwash."

"No it's true. I ran into a couple today."

"And lives to tell the tale I see. Life's *real* fair."

A sudden realization swept over Mongrel. "They don't know, do they? That you're from Dunttstown? You haven't told them. 'Course, why would you?"

Captain Pete's eyes narrowed. "Why would I?"

"Yeah. I mean, who knows what they'd do, right? You'd know better than me; you've been here longer. Make you eat your own liver or something. Turn you inside out from your asshole. Ooh, maybe make you watch TV soap operas." He shuddered.

After raising an eyebrow at these suggestions, a grin appeared on the captain's face. The grin grew, teeth bared themselves, and laughter came rushing out. Captain Pete, to Mongrel's utter confusion, stomped a peg on the floor until he realized that wasn't safe, but held his gut and continued to laugh. There wasn't much he could do in his current predicament with the barn, but there were still ways to torment his foe. He pulled out what appeared to be a walkie-talkie.

"What's that," Mongrel asked.

Captain Pete chuckled more in response. He held the device to his mouth, pressed a button, and said, "Attention customers of Captain Pete's Barn Store. We be closing in fifteen minutes, so kindly get yer stuff and pays me for it. If the shoppin' day seems to 'ave come to'n'end too fast for ya's, then comes back tomorrow for more great deals'n'savin's. Don't forgets to check out the strawconut bails. The sweet scent o' fresh, ripe strawberries matched with the soft undertones o' 'xotic coconut tis sure ta brings a pleasant 'roma to yer barn. Tis on special all week, two fer one. Oh'n'by the ways, ya'll know that there fella I been chasin' 'round me store? Like I's said 'fore, he ain't from 'rounds here..."

Time suddenly seemed to slow down for Mongrel. Not only did sheer horror engulf him, but he got to experience an eternity of it. His heart, however, sped up rapidly. Go figure. A million thoughts ran through his head in an instant. The faint murmur of people below faded away – although that might be because everyone had stopped talking and was listening to Captain Pete's announcement. There was nothing Mongrel could do to stop the truth from getting out. Captain Pete was only a dozen or more feet from him, but it felt like a million miles. Mongrel was helpless.

"...Tis true. Tis true. He be not from the island..."

The twisted, evil glare from Captain Pete honed in on Mongrel, taking in every pained expression, every nuance of terror. It was like soaking up rays of glorious sunshine. It was divine.

Would they stampede the barn like a mob, with torches and pitchforks? Would they burn him at the stake? Would they offer him a last meal (the thought of steak made him hungry)? Would they make him hold hands and say grace? Would they make him watch Ben Stiller movies until his eyes literally bled and rotted out of his head? Mongrel had no idea what the islanders would do to him, and worse, no idea how to stop them.

"...He be from a little town East 'o 'here..."

But he suddenly knew how to stop Captain Pete.

Mongrel looked over his right shoulder, where the bay door stood wide open. Both his doom and his freedom lay beyond, and any movement towards either would bring the barn down.

Perfect.

He ran and threw himself into the corner of the barn to the right of the door. The whole structure shook, and began to lean to the direction Mongrel had pushed it. It then slanted sideways, tossing him along the broad side, and began sliding down the roof of the barn below it. As it slid it rotated in the direction of the fall, the bay door coming around to give a view of the floor it was about to impact.

Captain Pete tried to brace himself for the worst, but was suddenly flung out the open door as the barn crashed to a stop. He landed on his back on the cold tile floor with a sickening thud.

Mongrel rode out the collision in the safety of his corner. He got bounced around a bit, but nothing more than a few cuts and bruises. If anything it had been somewhat fun, like a violent carnival ride. He crawled over and peered out the bay door, which he found was only a few feet from the ground – and where Captain Pete laid sprawled on the floor. His shovel had also managed to flee the barn, landing nearby.

Upon jumping down to the floor, Mongrel wandered around for a moment, studying the barn. Why hadn't it fallen completely to the floor? He eventually found it's roof crushed against a pillar, and it was balanced between it and the barn beneath it. For some reason Mongrel thought this was cool. He went back to Captain Pete, whose eyes were still open, staring up into the barn he'd just fallen out of. He looked dead. He thought about checking for a pulse, but Mongrel didn't want to touch his body – if only because he didn't want to leave any fingerprints. Speaking of evidence, he surely didn't want to get caught next to a dead body. There'd be questions. And a case could be made that he'd done this to the captain.

Then again, accidents happen, right? He looked around at the mess – which no one could prove he'd made – and was confident he could escape any blame. In fact, if he escaped completely by leaving the scene of the crime he could claim to not have even been there when it happened. He'd better skedaddle, lest anyone see him.

Mongrel took one last look at the old pirate, feeling a twinge of guilt. He *had* done this to him. He toppled the barn, he sent his old friend falling to his death, he climbed the barn to hide. Hell, it was his idea to come here in the first place. The guilt swelled in him, filling his stomach like lead. It was all his fault. Once again, he was responsible for Captain Pete's death.

No. He shook his head, he didn't want this. It wasn't murder. Captain Pete was going to blow his cover, and who knew what those people would to do him? It was self-defense. He came to see the old pirate to make amends, to see if things were different on the island. It looked like he was wrong after all.

Then Captain Pete coughed. Mongrel jerked backwards in fright, tripping over the shovel. He crawled back over, somewhat relieved that the old pirate was still alive, and yet the fear crept back in through the backdoor of his mind. He could still talk. He could still reveal Mongrel's secret.

Gurgles poured from Captain Pete's mouth, along with a trail of blood. He seemed to be trying to talk. Mongrel leaned in closer to hear. Then:

"Here!"

Mongrel jumped back again as Captain Pete started screaming.

"The bastards over 'ere! He's tryin' to kill me! He's from Duntts-"

Suddenly Captain Pete caught a shovel between his teeth, silencing him. Mongrel followed the shaft of the shovel and found hands holding it.

His hands

Captain Pete had been nearly decapitated when the head of a shovel flew through the air and imbedded itself in his jaw. And Mongrel was holding it. He watched in horror as blood pooled on the floor. This time the captain really was dead, he had no doubt. And this time it really was his fault.

He heard voices. They sounded far away, but that was probably due to his tunnel hearing.* He knew they were much closer, and at any minute would stumble upon the tragic scene. Mongrel got to his feet, almost needing assistance. He couldn't come to terms with this.

Murder.

"Hey!"

Mongrel turned to see a woman rounding a corner. She put her hands to her face, shocked at what she was seeing. He turned

---

* Similar to tunnel vision in most respects, where one can only see what is going on directly in front of him. Tunnel hearing blocks out all but the most important sounds.

and fled, making for the back room that he'd seen earlier from inside the barn.

He crashed through the door, and stopped, looking for where to go next. An emergency exit sign showed him the way, and within seconds he was out of Yon Captain Pete's Other Barn Store, running down the middle of the road. But the further he ran the more the impact of his actions caught up with him. Tears welled in his eyes.

He was a murderer now. He couldn't excuse or explain away his actions. It wasn't an accident this time, or a force of nature, or anything else. It was him. Captain Pete was dead because he'd killed him.

Mongrel kept running. He ran until his legs hurt and his lungs burned. Then he ran more. A psychologist might suggest he was running from himself, and who he was becoming. Or that he was running from what he'd done. But that's just silly. People pay shrinks to reveal this garbage? The world is crap, isn't it?

So no; Mongrel was running because he wanted – needed – to get off this godforsaken island. It was backwards, right? And maybe it wasn't just backwards, but made visitors backwards too? When Captain Pete lived in Dunttstown he never once tried to kill Mongrel. And if Mongrel were back in Dunttstown he'd never have even thought to kill Captain Pete. It was the island. It was these people. It *had* to be. He was turning into an animal. He was developing a taste for blood. Maybe that's what happened to Captain Pete. He had lived here too long and turned into one of them.

Well not Mongrel. He ran until he saw trees, and ran passed them. He passed tree after tree until he was amongst them. He ran until he couldn't hear the sounds of the town any more, and finally stopped. He looked around briefly, making sure he was alone, that no one had followed him, before collapsing to the ground. Heaving sobs wracked his body. He howled his mental torment while trying to suck in much-needed air, causing his chest to convulse in spasms. He cried until his eyes hurt. He cried over the loss of innocence. He cried like he'd spilled his milk. He cried himself to sleep.

Random Tangent

When Mongrel woke, dusk was descending upon the world. He could feel dried tears and snot clinging to his face, pulling his skin taught when he yawned. Standing and scratching his ass, he looked around, momentarily forgetting where he was. But once the grogginess of sleep wore off it all came back.

He glanced around at the trees, thankful for the solitude. It was peaceful here. The trees didn't judge him. They didn't care what he'd done, or where he was from. He didn't have to hide from them. The whole day he'd been trying to convince the islanders that he was a tree, or at least part-tree. Maybe he should give it a try? He stood still and spread out his arms, and tried to clear his mind of all thoughts.

Yes, a tree. A silent monolith.

Perhaps this is where he belonged; amongst the trees, where he couldn't hurt anyone. He wasn't sure how long he stood there, but he was enjoying the silence – which lasted until he farted. Due to the lack of a breeze, the smell enveloped him, and he felt it was time to move on. Besides, he was a doing a lousy imitation of a tree – except for the homicide; he'd nailed that part. He had become a wood-cold killer, just like Scabby Shabby had said. Mankind's oldest enemy. Nature's killing machines. Trees couldn't be trusted, he'd proclaimed. Mongrel didn't want to pretend to be a tree anymore. He didn't want to be on the island anymore.

Mongrel marched. He wasn't entirely sure which way to go, but he hoped his chosen direction wouldn't lead him back into town. On the other hand, if he found the river what was he going to do? He surely couldn't swim across; that would be suicide. Could he build a raft? He had done it before when he escaped Mon Isle, so it was possible. Actually that wasn't true; the only reason he'd gotten off the island is because the mon had been there to assist him by regurgitating a raft. This time he didn't have a mon, or time to build a raft. By now a lynch mob would be scouring the area for him. Wanted posters with his face on them would be getting hung on every light post and telephone pole. How they'd gotten a picture of him he couldn't say. Any minute now he expected to hear a helicopter flying overhead. The manhunt was on. He was out of time and out of options.

After a little wandering Mongrel came, thankfully, to Duntt river. The water was gently, leisurely strolling by. The setting sun was to his right, still above the horizon and giving off an orange glow, making the water look somewhat like lava, not that Mongrel needed any more reasons not to swim in it. Unfortunately he didn't have much of a choice. Home, salvation, and donuts lay it wait on the other side of the river, so it was either swim across or head back. Bracing himself for the worst, he dipped a toe in the water. It didn't burn, or turn black, like he thought it might. In fact the water felt nice. He sunk in his whole foot, followed by the other, and stood there, enjoying the cool sensation. He used to enjoy swimming; he hadn't done so in a long time since Duntt River was the only body of water within a half hour's drive, and it was off limits. Dunttstown did have a municipal pool, but it was frequented by seniors citizens who wore swimwear indecent for their gender, or size. Or species. Many of them also had cleanliness issues, and seemed to use the pool as a place to bathe. After the pool had been desecrated by their use, you couldn't see the bottom, it smelled terrible, and often caused hair loss. It has also been credited with more than a few infant deaths, but these claims have all gone unsubstantiated. The only reason the seniors were still allowed to swim there was because most of them continued to donate funds to keep it open.

A noise from behind startled him and stirred his fears, and Mongrel quickly turned around to find…nothing. Sounding like twigs crunching underfoot, it might just have been some animal out and about in search of food, shelter, or sex. But it also could be someone searching for him. Mongrel couldn't afford to take that chance.

Returning his attention to the water, Mongrel said a quick prayer and waded in, thinking 'you only live once.' Unless you're a cat, of course. Or Captain Pete. Once the water was nearly to his waist he dove in, and swam, trying his best not to ingest any water, lest he wish to neuter himself from the inside out. He kept his eyes closed, peeking every so often to see how close he was to the other side.

Random Tangent

Nearly half way across he paused, hearing the sound of an engine. He opened his eyes to have a quick look, and saw a boat approaching.

Islanders.

The sun being in his eyes, Mongrel couldn't make out any details, but it reminded him of the boat from the movie Jaws, and he dearly hoped there weren't any man-eating sharks, amongst the other, unknown horrors in the river. Knowing he was too far from the shore to swim for it before the boat would be upon him, Mongrel took a deep breath and ducked under the water, the only way he could hide from the approaching lunatics who were undoubtedly hunting him. It was quiet under beneath the surface, but he could hear the warbled echoing of the boat's engine nearing, getting louder. He didn't know how long he could stay down there, but hoped he could last just long enough for the boat to pass him by. He opened his eyes a crack, enough to see a large shadow looming nearer, and realized that the boat's speed wasn't fast enough for him to wait it out, and actually seemed to be slowing down. He was going to have to come up for air. Then his eyes began to sting and he closed them, and he suddenly, desperately wanted his head above water. Risk being caught or risk being dead.

He broke the surface as daintily as possible, keeping as much of himself hidden as he could, and risked a peak. He boat was only a few feet away. And it had the word POLICE written on its side.

"Mongrel?"

Mongrel saw Officer Switchblade's head poking over the side of the boat, and was so relieved that he peed[*].

"What the *hell* are you doing?" his friend asked.

"I...uh, just...trying to..."

Before Mongrel could form a coherent answer, Officer Switchblade had jabbed a pole in the water at Mongrel, who grabbed it, and was dragged onto the boat. "Thanks," he said after catching his breath.

Nodding in a 'don't mention it' kind of way, Officer Switchblade shook his head. "Swimming in the river? The hell,

---

[*] Mongrel relieved himself in the river because he was so relieved. Get it?

man? Didn't you read the signs[**]? Don't you know what's in there? It ain't water."

"I had no choice," Mongrel said. "I had to get off the island."

"You were on the island?" This amazed the officer to no end. "How'd you survive? How'd you get on there in the first place?"

"I don't know; I woke up there. I think I fell into the river last night from up on a cliff and just washed ashore the next morning."

"You mean you've been in the water twice? And lived?" This seemed a nearly impossible feat, and Officer Switchblade's amazement could not have been higher. "You should see a doctor."

"All the doctors are on strike still, aren't they?"

"Oh yeah. Well I wouldn't have any kids for a while anyway. Maybe ever. They'd probably come out with two heads or something."

Mongrel thought about this. "That'd be kind of cool."

Now Officer Switchblade was thinking about it. "Yeah, actually I wouldn't mind seeing that. Okay, have kids then."

"I'll get right on that," Mongrel said, rolling his eyes. "But after what I've been through last night I think my kids will be born brain dead or something."

"Rough night?"

"Oh yeah! Almost died more than once. Shamus Bond came after me again."

"Wait, you were there?" Officer Switchblade's amazement was reaching unhealthy, even dangerous levels, considering the twinge of anger seeping in. "What happened? I heard something was going on, that Bond was in the area with a gang of thugs or something. Love to get my hands on him again, ever since he tricked me…"

"Well he kidnapped me and tried to kill me. But the Jaywatch guy saved me. What's his name? Jayson something?"

[**] The signs do not read NO SWIMMING or SWIM AT OWN RISK or anything like that; they simply read GOODBYE.

Random Tangent

With his amazement now at death-defying amount, Officer Switchblade spun around in a circle, hand to his forehead in the fashion folks used when they proclaimed they were about to faint. He needed to relax a little before his heart gave out. "Holy shit! Jayson Miles!" he cried, not heeding the warning. "The escaped convict? He was there too? The murderer saved your life?"

"He's not a murderer. Old Man Cleopard is still alive."

Officer Switchblade's amazement grew ever higher, making him dizzy with vertigo and risking serious head trauma or brain damage or something if he didn't calm down. "Are you kidding me? He was old when I was a kid! He's gotta be four-hundred years old by now!"

"I think he's starting to fall apart. Jaywatch – I mean Jayson came to fight him, for revenge or someth-"

He stopped, since the officer had fainted, collapsing to the floor. The level of shock wracking his mind wasn't sustainable for his merely-human brain. Mongrel found a small metal bucket in the cabin and used it to fetch some water over the side of the boat, and threw it into his friend's face.

Sputtering back to consciousness, Officer Switchblade took a moment to regain his faculties before asking, "Fight him over what?"

"I think you should calm down," Mongrel told him, shaking his head. "You're way too excited. It's not good for you."

"Aw come on. I'm a cop; I need to know this stuff."

Mongrel sat back down on the floor next to him. "Fine. Jayson was charged with killing Cleopard, right? But Cleopard wasn't dead, and he never did anything to show it. He never turned himself in, or whatever, and let Jayson get convicted and go to prison for years. Sad, really. So Jayson finally broke out and wanted revenge."

"Yeah, that makes sense." Officer Switchblade got to his feet, only then realizing he was soaking wet. "What the?" He looked at the bucket, then at Mongrel. "You didn't…"

"What?"

"Aw man! Not the river water!" He began to remove his clothing as fast as he could. "Why'd you do that for?"

Mongrel shrugged. "You were out cold."

How To Be Monolithic

"So? I'd have come around."

"What if you didn't?"

"Then I'm dead, right?" Once he was naked[*], the officer packed all his clothes tightly into the bucket. "Peacefully too. Now I might die a slow, agonizing death. Did I swallow any? Maybe I should make myself vomit just in case."

"You'll be fine," Mongrel said, trying to ignore anything below his friend's waist. "I was just swimming in it and I'm fine. Even got a tan."

"Yeah, and it's practically night." Officer Switchblade looked Mongrel over and said, "You're peeling already."

Mongrel glanced at his arms and shrugged again. "Still, I've got a nice, healthy glow."

"You've got a nice, healthy rot. If you die from swimming in the river, I'll arrest you." He put the bucket down at the far end of the boat. "You wanna toss your clothes in here too?"

"Pass. I'd rather be wet than naked. And what if someone saw us? Naked? That'd start rumours."

"Better rumours than death."

"Look, I finally got everyone to forget about that one night and I want to keep it that way. If I'm gonna die from the river it's gonna happen whether I ditch my clothes or not – it's too late for me there – but I'd rather not also have rumours chasing me to my grave."

"Suit yourself." The officer darted back into the cabin, and after a minute came back out, still naked, holding a book of matches. He lit one and dropped it in the bucket, and the clothes caught fire, even though they were wet.

"Do you have any other clothes you could put on?" Mongrel asked, tired of avoiding looking at his friend.

"This is what you were swimming in," Officer Switchblade said, ignoring the request. "You'd never have made it to the other side. I saved your life, you know."

---

[*] Except for his sunglasses. Due to a bizarre accident that I have yet to come up with a creative explanation for, Officer Switchblade's sunglasses are permanently attached to his face.

Random Tangent

"Okay, fine. I'm sorry for swimming in the freaking river, and thanks for saving my life. Now will you please go put some clothes on?"

"I'm just saying there are more pleasant ways of committing suicide. And I don't have a change of clothes."

Mongrel grumbled and protested. "I wasn't committing suicide! I just had to get off the island. If anything I was trying to save my life, not end it."

Officer Switchblade chuckled. "So what were they like, the barbarians? You met some, right?"

"Oh they were weird. They used manners and stuff. They chit-chat, and obey gravity. They hold in their gas in public."

"Heh...weirdos." Switchblade went into the cabin and started up the boat again. "You know on their birthdays they set their cake on fire just to blow out the flames?"

"Why?" Mongrel asked. "What purpose does that serve?"

"No idea. Makes no sense."

Mongrel was quite for a moment. "I think some of them eat people."

"Wouldn't surprise me. Hope that island eats *them* soon. Hey, what about their metric time? Did you figure it out?"

"Never thought to ask about that." Mongrel shook his head. "Damn. Probably won't get another chance. Hope I don't, anyway."

Together they walked, or rather sailed home and continued to be awesome buddies.

"Wait," Mongrel said, "we can't sail home."

"Why not?" asked Officer Switchblade. "Cause this isn't a sailboat?"

"No, becau...well yeah, that too. But because I live in the middle of nowhere. The place is practically a desert. No water."

"Ah. Well let's just go to my place then."

Mongrel seemed alright with that. "You live on the river?"

Officer Switchblade said, "Nope," and left it at that. The boat sputtered away into the sunset, causing waves of flammable water to ripple behind them. Little did the two men realize that should they light the river on fire, it would consume the island and its inhabitants. Then gone would be the scum of Donut Lake. Gone would be all the baffling idiosyncrasies. And gone would be all the wicked, sinful acts of inhuman depravity.

But evil was allowed to live that day my friends, and this small act of mercy could one day lead to the damnation of all.

The End

Mongrel went back to Officer Switchblade's place where they had a nice long chat over some mint tea. Mongrel caught his friend up on his incident at the prison and meeting his wife, and Switchblade recounted the time he spend his summer as a midget. He was known as Officer Pocketknife back then, and was reportedly younger. Captain Pete was given a royal burial, and every one of the disgusting island natives was there to bid him an emotional farewell. Perverts. The Mabels never got the barn since Captain Pete had passed. They'd never seen such a travesty in all their lives. Mabel was so distraught that he turned into an alcoholic, while his wife began eating flesh again. She meant to only start with squirrels and other rodents, but the fur didn't agree with her, and she began hunting hitchhikers, prized amongst the homicidal for their generally smooth skin and ability to go overlooked by the police when searching for missing persons. She also had to do most of the driving since her husband was now a drunk, which aided her with her hobby. Meatloaf began asking around about this Loafmeat person, deciding eventually to track the man down. Gerald was so amazed by meeting a real-life tree person that he decided to become one himself. Scabby Shabby took a few men from the bar out to the woods with the intention of burning down the whole forest. They were never seen or heard from again. Rumour has it that the trees attacked and raped them to death, then consumed their bodies.

Frank And The King

It annoyed Mongrel that it was such a beautiful day in Dunttstown.

The temperature was exactly perfect. You could wear whatever you felt comfortable in and not be too cold or too hot. You didn't have to run to the shade or worry that your skin was going to melt off if you didn't have on enough sunscreen. Likewise, you didn't have to bring a sweater with you for when the sun got obscured by some passing clouds. You wouldn't work up a sweat just checking the mailbox, or feel too chilly if you were near a body of water. And the wind blew just enough to compliment the heat and feel refreshing.

It all got on Mongrel's nerves.

Children were in school and many people were at work. Traffic wasn't congested. You didn't have to wait in line for your morning coffee. The mail was right on time. Even your loan shark wouldn't be too hard pressed to give you just one more day to come up with the money, because what's one more day, right? It's too lovely out to be worried about money. But you'd better have it by tomorrow, seriously. Or else.

Random Tangent

And it infuriated Mongrel.

There were new shows on TV later that day to look forward to. The fruit in Mongrel's kitchen was still fresh, and the milk hadn't yet passed its expiration date. The dishes and laundry had been done.

It was, quite simply, a perfect day.

And it drove Mongrel insane because he wasn't going to get to enjoy it. He'd agreed the day before that if he wasn't busy, he'd try to take DERFtron back to his mad scientist owner. And try to be busy he did. He accomplished all his chores with a devotion he hadn't shown since swearing off bisexuality[*]. He even found petty, trivial things to keep him occupied, such as doing all the laundry in the house, whether it needed to be done or not. And during the whole hour he'd spent doing the single dish in his sink, ensuring that it was spotless to a degree that the Queen herself would think twice before using it for fear of damaging its magnificent complexion, he didn't manage to think of a single other thing to excuse himself out of the deal.

"Are we going or not?"

DERFtron found Mongrel sitting on the front porch, watching the grass grow, waiting for his favourite part.

"You know, I've noticed a trend," Mongrel said. "Ever since this started, things have gotten worse and worse for me."

"Mon," said the mon, meaning, 'it's about damn time I showed up.'

"First, it was just goofy shit, like landing on Mon Isle, or exploding on a plane, or getting abducted by aliens. But now I'm getting thrown in prison, people are trying to kill me. I get stuck on the demon island, and for all I know I could be rotting from the inside. I'm probably sterile..."

"Mon," the mon agreed. But it also meant, 'I mean, how long has it been? Four stories? Five?'

---

[*] Mongrel had been with a man once, and whether or not that man just wasn't the one for him or he realized that, *oh my God*, men are disgusting, it was as unpleasant an experience as Mongrel had in his life. He'd honestly rather eat a bag of rotten onions every day for the rest of his life than give it another try.

Frank And The King

"Yeah, things are *real* bad for you," DERFtron said. "You got your own place here. All I got is left that's actually mine is a brain."

Mongrel didn't glance up at the ranch, which formerly belonged to his mother, bless her hamstrings, but could feel the place looming over him. Her passing several months earlier meant the house belonged to him, although he didn't quite feel that way himself. He could almost still feel her presence, which may or may not have something to do with many of her belongings still hanging around.

"And now I'm supposed to somehow get to Bolivia," Mongrel continued, "which is waste-deep in cannibals and poisonous trees, and mosquitoes as big as your fist."

"They're not really that big. And it's *waist-deep*, not waste-deep."

Mongrel glared at the machine. "Don't. Just…don't." He ran a hand through his hair and sighed. "And what is he even doing in Bolivia in the first place? Why not somewhere closer, like on this freaking continent?"

"I'm not sure," DERFtron said. "But it's got something to do with the FBI I think. He's trying to stay off the grid."

"Engh," Mongrel grumbled dismissively, pinching the bridge of his nose, trying to stay the migraine that was beginning to form. He knew it wasn't going to be a pleasant trip. Nothing was simple anymore. His life was getting worse, day by day.

Suddenly the wind blew a voice into Mongrel's face, which sounded like it belonged to his deceased mother. He stood and glanced around, not entirely sure it wasn't his imagination.

"What is it?" DERFtron asked. "I don't sense anything."

DERFtron, being part computer, was equipped with every kind of sensory input available at the time of his creation by the scientist Bosley; night vision, infra-red, tactile feedback, x-ray, sonar, echolocation, and virtually everything on the electromagnetic spectrum, to name but a few.

"Mon," said the mon, which meant it could take them to Bolivia if they asked really nice. And that the voice kinda sounded like his mom.

Random Tangent

"Really?" Mongrel asked, forgetting the wind. "That would really help."

"What did he say?" DERFtron asked.

"He said he'd help get us to Bosley."

DERFtron looked at the mon. "How? And how do you get all that from one word? How do you even understand that thing?"

"Could you do that for us?" Mongrel asked the mon. "We need to see this guy, Bosley. He's a mad scientist or something. Can you get us to Bolivia?"

"Mon, said the mon, meaning, 'Look around. I already did.'

Mongrel looked around and saw...Bolivia. Of course, he couldn't be certain of it since he'd never been there before and didn't know what to expect, but he had no doubt that he wasn't in Dunttstown anymore. It was much hotter – quite different from the perfect weather back home. Large, wild-looking trees surrounded them, as did a handful of smallish men clad in very little clothing. They each had a long spear, taller than they were, and wore faces comprised of shock and anger.

"How...did..."

Don't be too harsh on Mongrel; it was a confusing situation. How was he supposed to figure out that the mon had ingested him, and then regurgitated him in Bolivia, but *before* they'd actually left his home. Therefore, since he still hadn't left home yet, he had no memory of the journey he hadn't yet taken. Time would catch up with him in a few minutes, but you can probably understand how disorientating it would be.

"Wait," Mongrel said. "Hold on for a second. How can this supposed journey not have happened yet if we're already here? How can I still be at home right now? I can't be in two places at once."

Mongrel Stevens was one of a small minority of people who still didn't get how his life worked. He should know better than to question the logic or plausibility of the events that unfold around him, especially when the mon was around.

One of the smallish, nearly-naked men approached them, holding his spear at the ready. He poked Mongrel gently with it.

"Hey, stop it," Mongrel said, shoving the spear aside. Then to the mon, "What about Derf?"

Frank And The King

"Mon," the mon sighed, which meant, 'he's here too. Would you *pay attention?*'

"What the hell?" someone asked.

Mongrel turned to his right and saw DERFtron standing there.

The smallish tribesman didn't know what to think about Mongrel's blasé behaviour, but wasn't pleased. It growled at him and said something in its native tongue.

"So...I was inside you?" DERFtron asked the mon.

"Mon," the mon confirmed.

"What was it like?"

"Mon," said the mon, which meant, 'none of your business.'

The smallish, nearly-naked man shouted something at them, or perhaps at one of the other smallish, nearly-naked men. He waved his spear around menacingly. Soon some of the others began shouting, appearing to have a loud argument, but over what Mongrel couldn't tell.

"Can you speak their language?" Mongrel asked DERFtron.

"Of course; Bosley programmed me with virtually every language on the planet. He wouldn't leave out the native language."

"So Bosley is a native like these guys?" Mongrel gestured around them at the tribesmen slowly creeping closer on all sides.

"No, no, he's a white guy like you and me." DERFtron paused to reminisce about his flesh and blood body as a few of the tribesmen jumped on him and began trying to jab their spears into his undercarriage. "Well, like I *was*. I meant the local language of the area, not *his* language."

"Ah, well that's good. I can't exactly communicate with him otherwise." One of the larger of the smallish tribesmen tackled him to the ground. "Do you think you could ask them to stop this nonsense?"

DERFtron began speaking to them, and after a minute they all climbed off and stood staring at him, looking puzzled and alarmed. That was when the yelling started. DERFtron yelled at them in his strange robotic voice, and they yelled at him, and sometimes each other, occasionally waving their spears around. This went on for a few minutes before Mongrel got up off the ground and butted in.

Random Tangent

"Mind if I ask how things are going?"

"I think they want us to follow them."

"Why not?" Mongrel shrugged. "It's not like we know where we're going anyway."

"Mon," said the mon, asking, 'is everyone just gonna keep ignoring me?'

Soon the large group, led by a few of the tribesmen, followed by Mongrel, the mon, and DERFtron, with more of the tribesmen bringing up the rear, were marching through the dense jungle. A few of the natives flanked the trio on each side, just in case they decided to make a run for it.

After twenty minutes or so they came to a large open area dotted with small fires and many huts made a canvas-like material. A small, twisting brook flowed between the huts, bisecting the village. It was almost quaint, accept that there was more dirt than grass underfoot here, due to the higher traffic of tribesmen. And everywhere you looked, people were all nearly naked; men, women, children, the elderly. Mongrel did his best not to stare.

They were brought into the largest of the huts, and presented to a tall tribesman. He wore an elaborate headdress of feathers that looked to have taken an entire flock of ostriches to create. At least a dozen necklaces of beads of green and blue and pink hung from his neck, some coming as far down as his knees. Although he wasn't a plump man, he appeared to have bosoms, and his belly button stuck out unnaturally far. It looked like a second nose on his stomach. Mongrel assumed he was their leader.

"This must the Chief," DERFtron said.

"I gathered," Mongrel replied.

One of the tribesmen ran over to the Chief and quickly bowed low to the ground. The Chief then sat down on an ornate wooden chair and the two men chatted for a bit. After their discussion the Chief stood and circled the trio, speaking briefly with a few of his subordinates.

"They're deciding what to do with us," DERFtron said after a minute.

"What to *do* with us?" Mongrel was a little upset. "How about let us go? We haven't done anything wrong. Maybe they could take us to Bosley, if they know where he is. And get these

Frank And The King

bloody spears out of our faces!" He shoved away the spear of a tribesman who'd gotten a little too close with it. He yelled something and scampered off.

"I did!" DERFtron said. "I think..."

"You *think*? You said you can speak their language!"

The Chief silenced them all by smacking one of his subordinates on his ass with a loud, cracking slap. The subordinate cried out in shock and pain, and rubbed his delicate posterior. More talking commenced as the prisoners waited in silence for their fates to be decided. After a while, the Chief smacked his *oblibip*[*] on his ass again, apparently concluding this pseudo trial.

Mongrel and DERFtron were marched outside and over to a circular area at the far side of the village. A large fire burned in its center, and several stumps were erected on one side, which was presumably where the Chief stood to address the public. The outsiders were led to the other side of the fire pit where a number of stakes were planted in the ground, and were bound to two of them, their arms wrapped behind their backs; DERFtron's a little haphazardly since his arms were limited in their movement. The mon was ignored completely and left to wander about the village at its leisure.

"So what's going on here?" Mongrel whispered to DERFtron.

"Well, I told them everything you said, and explained that we mean them no harm."

"I see. Seems like you did a great job," Mongrel said sarcastically. "So this must be their way of welcoming us into the tribe then."

"This would be their way of killing us."

Mongrel nodded quietly, trying not to get mad. "And why are they trying to kill us?"

"I don't know."

---

[*] An *oblibip* is the ceremonial ass of the Chief. Similar to a judge's gavel, an oblibip is used to call order to a courtroom, or to decree orders. They are also used to tally scores in tribe games, announce the time of day at predetermined intervals, and as a method of applause – all, of course, with the slapping of the ass. *Oblibips* must have a high tolerance for pain, and have a firm, but resonant buttocks.

Random Tangent

"How do you *not* know? I thought you could understand them."

People from all over began to gather around. Human sacrifices weren't widely practised in the tribe; usually reserved for special occasions such as their day of deity warship, and *fmuvmuv*, which was basically just an ass slapping competition. An impromptu filleting of human flesh certainly attracted a lot of attention.

"There are a lot of subtleties in their language, okay?" DERFtron snapped defensively. "It's not that easy to sort though it all. For all I know it's not even the right language."

Sighing inwardly, Mongrel could feel his grip on his calm demeanour slipping. "What do you mean?"

"I mean maybe they're not Mojo"

This meant nothing to Mongrel, and he felt like a moron having to keep asking questions. He wished DERFtron would simply explain things completely. Was that part of him being a computer? Only performing what it was asked to? "What's Mojo?" he asked.

"Their tribe. There's, like, dozens of different tribes around here. Maybe I got the wrong one. They all look alike, you know."

Now Mongrel's temper was bucking like a bronco and he was having difficulty hanging on to it. "Considering we're about to die, that's a hell of a fucking mistake to make. Now *fix it*!"

The Chief gave a voracious slap of his *oblibip's* ass, silencing the murmuring crowd and drawing all attention to him. The *oblibip* grunted through clenched teeth but otherwise didn't complain about his duties. It was, after all, a prestigious position in the tribe, garnering much envy from his peers.

Once everyone had shut up and taken their seats on the ground the Chief began a long diatribe about...well, I don't speak Mojo, or whatever their language is, but it appeared that many insinuations and accusations were made about the outsiders, with much finger pointing accompanying them. Often the crowd would cheer or jeer these proclamations. Mongrel and DERFtron could do nothing but listen and wait for their sentences to befall them.

The most important item to be discussed amongst the villagers was how to dispose of the unwanted guests. Should they be stoned, burned at the stake, or mooned to death[*]. Seeing as how the tribe had an unnatural affection for derrieres, it was only natural that mooning won by a landslide vote.

Several of the tribe's most upstanding members were chosen and paraded in front of Mongrel and DERFtron. They briefly honoured the victims, placing gifts of clay vases and shiny stones at their feet, and lengths of beads around their heads, then various articles of clothing were discarded and the mooning commenced. Of course, the removed clothing consisted merely of a bunch of leaves, as standard tribal wear didn't leave much to the imagination.

Mongrel and DERFtron looked at the asses before them, and then to each other. "Well, I guess this is better than them killing us," Mongrel said.

"What if this is just the opening act? Maybe we're like dinner and a show."

"You mean they're going to eat us after?" The thought hadn't occurred to Mongrel; he was still mulling over his imminent death. He looked back at the row of asses and said, "I rather don't like the sound of that. And I must say, having bitten my tongue one too many times, I don't think they'd like me."

"They already don't like you."

"I meant how I'd taste, dumbass."

"Hey, compared to you I'm a smartass, and that's way better. Plus, they're not going to eat me, so I'm definitely coming out on top here."

"Why aren't they gonna eat you? What did you *really* tell them?" Thoughts of betrayal floated around Mongrel's head, and he could feel his anger begin to rise again. "You *can* understand them, can't you? What did you say about me?"

DERFtron stared at Mongrel for a moment before shaking his robotic head, which wasn't much more than an elaborate LCD display. "How about because I'm made of metal?"

Mongrel skimmed his eyes dismally up and down DERFtron's mechanical body. "Oh yeah."

"Dude, you should calm down before you give yourself a heart attack and ruin their...well, whatever they're doing."

---

[*] This usually ended up being death due to dehydration; having an allergic reaction to staring at asses is a rare condition for one to be afflicted with.

Random Tangent

"Maybe that's the idea, to die before they can kill me. Not give them the satisfaction. And quite frankly, considering the predicament we're because of you I think I've managed to keep my cool pretty well."

Trying to sputter, which came out like a buzzing noise, DERFtron asked, "What do you mean 'because of me?'"

"Well if you could just talk to them in their own bloody language maybe they wouldn't be trying to kill us. In fact, if you hadn't just *had* to come see Bosley in the first place we wouldn't be here at all. How do you even know he *can* fix you?"

"I *don't* know, but he's the first person I'd go to, which is why we're here. And it's not my fault we're in this mess – your mon could've dropped us off anywhere but this is the spot he picked."

Mongrel was about to retort to this, but suddenly they were both silenced. At the mention of the mon, memory of being inside it came flooding back to them. Time, after apparently taking a detour down a long, dark country road, had finally caught up with them, and they stared off into space for a few minutes, reliving the experience. It was an almost instantaneous journey, like going in and coming out the other side, as if the mon was just a door, but the dramatic change in gravity and spatial orientation did a number on the mind. It was like a suffering a concussion without the physical harm.

"Wow," Mongrel said, being the first to come around. He looked at the ground, and then slowly glanced up at the row of asses, some now with their cheeks pulled apart to enhance the viewing pleasure, which brought him back to the present.

"I think I would like to delete that file from my memory," DERFtron said quietly.

"How does Blind Cracka do it? No wonder he's crazy."

"Who?"

"What were we talking about?" Mongrel tried to scratch his head, wanting to supplement his question with supportive body language.

"The mon, I think."

"Oh yeah. It's not Mon's fault you can't speak to these guys."

Frank And The King

DERFtron got defensive over this. "It's not that I *can't* speak to them, it's that I don't know which language to use."

"Well try them all."

"That could take forever! Do you know how many languages there are? And where is your mon anyway? Just ran off and left us to die? Well, you at least."

"Mon," said the mon, meaning, 'right here.'

Always the curious tourist, the mon had been wandered around the village, taking in the sights. It grabbed itself a hat made of feathers and beads to help it blend in a little, but soon everyone left, rendering the hat useless. But it kept the hat anyway. I mean, why not? The village wasn't very large, and before long the mon grew bored of digging through personal belongings and came looking for its pet.

"Mon," the mon said again, which meant, 'can't I leave your two alone for a minute without you getting into trouble? And what's with the mooning?'

Mongrel breathed a sigh of relief. "There he is."

"This is your fault," DERFtron said to the mon.

"It is not," Mongrel argued. Then to the mon, "Derf can't speak their language."

"Can too!"

"Then do it!"

"I *did*!"

"Didn't work. You failed, you big failure."

"Mon," the mon sighed. *Kids.* Looks like it would have to do everything.

The mon strolled over to the *oblibip* and ate it. The amassed crowd, already quiet and enjoying the ceremony, was shocked further into silence. Even the mooners momentarily lost focus and a few brown eyes blinked, losing the staring contest.

"Mon," said the mon, which meant, 'Oh so *now* everyone's paying attention to the reality-defiling walking ball with a stomach the size of infinity.'

The Chief was horrified. He jumped up and was about to attack the mon, when his subordinate was regurgitated at his feet.

Random Tangent

The *oblibip* stared at the ground and off into space at the same time, coated lightly in slobber, reliving the same experience Mongrel and DERFtron had just gone through.

The Chief put a hand on his shoulder and mumbled a few things, probably asking if he was okay.

"I am fine," the *oblibip* said. When the Chief looked at him strangely, he restated, "I am fine. I...*oh*..." he put his hands over his mouth, dumbfounded by the words coming out of his mouth. When he tried again he was speaking in his native tongue, and he got into what sounded like a heated debate with the Chief.

"Hey!" Mongrel shouted. "Now that you can understand us, can you tell your Chief to let us go?"

The *oblibip* glared at them. "What evil is this you have done to me?" he shouted. "Why can I now understand you?"

"We're not evil," DERFtron said. "Just let us go, and you'll never see us again. Or at least just let me go. I'm a robot so you can't really hurt me anyway."

"Hey!" Mongrel cried. "This is the last time I help you!"

"Oh relax, I'm just kidding."

The Chief then began demanding things from his *oblibip*, and soon a heated debate broke out. Only the natives knew what they were arguing over, but things were eventually settled and the *oblibip* came over to confront the outsiders. Mongrel was now able to get a good look at the man. He was dark-skinned like everyone else, but had white paint on various parts of his body. He wore silver bracelets on his right wrist and left ankle, and a larger one around his neck. The white paint formed a line down the middle of his face, bisecting it, and also covered his lips. More white in the form of dots lead from his hands up his arms to his chest, ending with his nipples. Wait, did he even have nipples?

"Why are you here?" the *oblibip* asked them. "You should not be here."

"Trust me," Mongrel said, "We do *not* want to be here. So please just let us go. And take these asses away, seriously. Like, what the hell?"

The *oblibip* glanced at the asses but quickly looked away, as he was not worthy enough to gaze upon them. "These are the finest asses in our tribe. It is a most honourable death. You are very lucky."

"Yeah," Mongrel muttered sarcastically, "we're *so* lucky that you're trying to kill us. Praise Garblejamba. Why are you trying to kill us anyway? What did we do?"

"It is not what you did, it is what you did not do." He approached Mongrel and grabbed at his pants. "What is this thing?"

"These *things* are pants," Mongrel snapped. "Or thing. Whatever. You guys don't wear pants, I know. But is that a crime around here?"

"You are concealing your most important possession. Yes, that is forbidden."

Mongrel thought for a moment. "So if I dress like you guys you'll let me go?"

The *oblibip* seemed to think about this, then walked back to the Chief and had a brief discussion with him. The Chief apparently relented to this idea, and tribal clothing was brought before Mongrel.

"I was just kidding," Mongrel said as he was untied from the stake. They forcibly removed his clothing, reminding him of almost being raped in prison, and threw them in the fire. Now naked, he did his best to cover up. The people of the tribe seemed to be enjoying the show.

"Nice ass," the *oblibip* said, nearly drooling. "You should be very proud."

"Thanks," Mongrel grumbled. "Now please get me something to wear. I'm not going to walk around naked." The *oblibip* gestured to the tribal wear, and Mongrel picked it up, holding it as if it were roadkill. "I can't wear this. Models in Playboy wear more than this and they're nude."

"You said you would wear it."

"I didn't *say* I'd wear it. I *asked* if that's what you wanted."

"Yes, we want this. Do you *want* death by mooning?"

The Chief then bellowed something and the *oblibip* shouted something back. "The Chief says you have one minute or he will personally moon you himself."

With a groan that would have scared Superman, Mongrel began dressing. The article of clothing wasn't much more than a gstring with leaves wrapped around it like a miniskirt. It didn't quite reach the bottom of his butt cheeks, and if he were to bend over, he was sure to give the tribe's elderly heart attacks.

DERFtron whistled at him as he was loosed from the stake. "You dirty slut!"

"Shut up. You're gonna have to wear one too."

"I'm pretty sure they don't have one in my size."

"Well then why are you being freed with me? Why were they even trying to kill you – you don't even have an ass to hide?"

"Beats me," DERFtron replied, having given up trying to understand the natives.

The *oblibip* ran over to the Chief so his ass could be slapped approvingly. Various tribe members also began slapping each others asses in applause. Mongrel felt obligated to take a bow, much to the horror of DERFtron, who was standing behind him.

Soon the crowd began to disperse, returning to their normal lives, some disappointed with the lack of human flesh for dinner. The mooners also seemed displeased with the outcome, that the Chief had decreed the guests were no longer to be harmed since they were now honouring the dress code.

"Mon," said the mon, coming over to admire Mongrel's attire, and saying, "Nudity does *not* look good on you."

"I don't have much of a choice." Mongrel tried to dig the wedgie out of his ass. "It's either this or die."

"I don't know..." DERFtron said. "If it's between staring at their asses or your junk..."

"Hey, don't call my...thing...junk. I never understood why people called it that anyway. Junk is something you'd want to throw away."

"I *would* throw that away." DERFtron then looked down at his mechanical body and muttered, "Actually, I miss my penis."

"So how do you like it?" The *oblibip* asked, referring to Mongrel's revealing outfit. Having sorted things out with the Chief, he was free for the rest of the afternoon.

Mongrel glared at him. "I hate it, O...bli, bleep. Whatever your name is. Bleep? Sounds like a swear word. What is your real name anyway?"

Frank And The King

"My name, in your language, if you spelled it, would contain only punctuation, like the asterisk and exclaiming point."

Mongrel thought for a moment. "So your name *is* a swear word?"

The *oblibip* shrugged. "I guess so."

"Well then, since you guys love asses so much, how about I call you 'Assface?'"

"Oh yes!" Assface said. "That is a most great name!"

"Seriously?" Mongrel asked. "I was being sarcastic."

"Yes, I like it very much. Thank you! I shall be Assface the shaman!"

"Shaman?" Mongrel's brain brought some very important thoughts to his attention. It wasn't too long ago that he'd had a terrible nightmare involving Captain Pete that played out like a carnival of horrors. But what he thought was just a dream was turning real; the series of events the captain had showed him were starting to come true. Mongrel needed to know which event would be next so he could prepare for it, or better yet avoid it altogether.

"Tell me," Mongrel said, "what does a shaman do, exactly?"

Assface smiled broadly. "A great many things. I am a great healer and can cure the greatest of ailments. I can communicate with the great entities of the spirit world and seek their guidance. I can interpret dreams with great accuracy. And I am a pretty great cook too if I do say so mys-"

"Great," Mongrel said, cutting him off. Frankly Assface was beginning to grate on his nerves. Talk about having a big head. Assface was an apt name for him. "I have a dream for you to interpret. Probably several. You got a crystal ball or something?"

"Let us go back to my place," Assface said, taking Mongrel's arm in his and grinning.

"Do you have to do this now?" DERFtron asked. "We're free to go, so let's *go*." He was eager to leave the ass fetishists behind before they tried to play dress up with him too.

"This is important," Mongrel said as they began walking arm in arm with Assface. "I need to know which parts of my dream are gonna come true. Captain Pete said one of the visions was a fake. Well he said 'past, present, future, and other' but I need to know which one the 'other' is."

Random Tangent

"Other doesn't mean fake, you know."

This stopped Mongrel's thoughts dead in their tracks. Or rather his thought it its track. DERFtron was right; this 'other' could still come true. Now he had yet another problem to deal with. Was there no end to this madness?

"And the one in the past," the robot continued, "didn't you already go through that one? Don't you remember it happening?"

"No..." Mongrel said after thinking about it.

"Then how can one be in the past if you haven't experienced it yet? Unless you have a shitty memory."

"Look, I don't know," Mongrel said. "All I know is that one of the visions came true, so I need to find out about the others. Maybe I have nothing to worry about, but until I know for sure I'm gonna worry about it."

"Fine, fine."

The stroll to Assface's hut didn't take long. The village was a dwarf (in size, not content), certainly one of the easiest to take if a rival tribe invaded. Luckily, their rampant fixation with posteriors kept any would-be-enemies away, similar to how someone looking for a hostage would not immediately head for a mental asylum. It's just not cool to pick on the retarded.

They approached a circular hut and Assface drew aside along brown curtain acting as a door, and Mongrel and DERFtron entered.

"Mon," said the mon, meaning that it had already perused inside and was going to wander the wilderness for a while, looking for a snack. It would be back when they needed it, which they surely would. And watch out for the shit bucket.

It was dim inside the hut. A small fire in the center was reduced to a few glowing embers. A couple small candles cast flickering shadows across all manner of strange and exotic things. Various animal skulls hung from the ceiling on strips of sinew. Sacks of cloths, beads and feathers lined one end of a long fur mat that Mongrel assumed was a bed. A metal pot – that would have been put in a corner if the hut had one – emitted a putrid aroma, and was surrounded by a collection of clay pot.

"I must apologize," Assface said, releasing Mongrel's arm and grabbing a clay pot. "If I was expecting company I would arranged my home to be more suitable for guests." From the pot he fished out some powder and tossed it on the fire, causing it to flame to life.

"You could've swept some of the dirt up a little," DERFtron said, for which Mongrel elbowed him in the side for, and then held his arm in pain.

"The whole floor is dirt," Mongrel said, rubbing his elbow.

"I'm just saying," DERFtron said defensively. "*They* choose to live like this, not me."

Assface arranged mats for them to sit on and set a board on the floor. The board was black with intricate symbols etched in white. He then grabbed a handful of pebbles and whispered something to them before giving them to Mongrel. He instructed Mongrel to hold them and think of the questions he needed answers to, and then rub them on his ass.

"What?"

"Hold some pebbles in each hand and rub my ass with them." Assface bent over in front of Mongrel and raised his leaf skirt slightly, although the gesture was more to give Mongrel a good view than to help; his skirt was short enough on its own.

"Do I have to?" Mongrel asked, looking anywhere but in front of him.

"Hey, you wanted to do this," DERFtron mocked. "It's *important*."

Mongrel grumbled and begrudgingly did as he was told. He closed his eyes and reached for the ass, and ground the pebbles into it.

Assface seemed to enjoy it a little too much. "Yes...mmm...do not be shy, get right in there."

After a few seconds Mongrel jerked his hands away. "Okay we're done with that."

"Are you sure?" Assface asked, turning around. He seemed disappointed. "Then when you feel the stones are ready, drop them on the board."

Holding them a moment longer, Mongrel closed his eyes again and thought of Mr. T, and tossed the pebbles down. He opened his eyes to see Assface studying the pebbles intently. This went on for several minutes until Mongrel finally asked, "Well? What do you see?"

Assface groaned and shook his head. "All I see are a bunch of pebbles."

"What's that supposed to mean?"

"I think it means he's not a very good shaman," DERFtron said.

Mongrel elbowed him again and regretted it as more pain shot through his arm.

"It is true," Assface whimpered. "I see nothing. I am a failure." He hung his head in shame.

"Should I have rubbed your ass more?" Mongrel asked.

Looking up and smiling, Assface agreed. "Yes, we could try that."

"No, no," DERFtron interjected. "You're a failure and we're wasting our time here."

Returning his head to its low-hung, shameful state, the native sighed. "You are right. I am no shaman. I tried my best to learn everything from my father, but he died just after I was born."

"So basically you learned nothing?"

Assface shrugged and nodded.

"Told you we should have split earlier," DERFtron said.

Mongrel sighed. This was his one chance to learn what was in store for him, to fight the future, to prevent Captain Pete's predictions from coming true. What was he going to do now, call one of those dial-a-psychics advertized on television? As if.

"I am sorry, Assface cried, his eyes tearing up. "I thought that I could do it, that maybe the gods would see that our love was pure and grant me the gifts to help you."

"Does the rest of the tribe know you're a fake? That you can't...wait, what?" Mongrel wasn't sure he'd heard that last part right.

"I was a fool to think you could love me," Assface continued. "With an ass like yours you could have anyone you pleased."

DERFtron looked at Mongrel's ass. *"Really?"*

Mongrel needed a moment to let this all sink in. The shock of the revelation boggled his mind, and his usual reaction to...actually, he had no normal reaction to this situation. It had never come up before. Hence, he needed to leave immediately. "Yes, that was very foolish of you. Now if you don't mind, we need to be going."

"*Finally!*" DERFtron said, heading outside. "We're off to see Bosley!"

Assface grabbed Mongrel's hand as he was about to follow his friend outside. "Please do not tell anyone about this."

"That you're gay?"

"No, about my failure as a shaman. That I just make it all up. Everyone believes in me. I will help you find your friend Bosley, anything you want, just please keep it a secret."

"Wait, you know Bosley?"

"He knows Bosley?" DERFtron cried from outside.

"Can you take us to him?" Mongrel asked.

Assface was reluctant to agree. "It is dangerous to go so far from the village."

Mongrel sighed again, knowing he'd regret this. "I'll let you rub my ass if you take us. Assface's lit up like he'd won the lottery. "But *just* for a second."

"Oh yes! Yes of course." They joined DERFtron outside the hut. "This will be like a date!"

"This is *not* a date!" Mongrel said sternly as they set out.

A building stood in the distance, a few hundred feet away. White, two-stories high, few windows, creepy shadows; it looked like the kind of place a one would go to for a fine afternoon of murder. You could smell the stench of malevolence. Assface refused to go any closer, not because the place screamed death but because he considered Bosley, and indeed all post-modern humans disturbing, with their fancy haircuts, hygiene, and worst of all, pants. But he assured them that this was where the man should be.

"What do you mean *should* be?" Mongrel asked. "Is this where he lives or not?"

Assface shrugged. "Sometimes he is here and sometimes he is not."

Mongrel ran a hand over his face. If he had come all this way for nothing... If he experienced the mind-bending journey

Random Tangent

inside the mon, narrowly escaped being mooned to death, and was forced to run around in the wild practically naked[*], giving all the meat-eating carnivores a good look at what could be for dinner, just to find Bosley on holiday, he was going to beat someone.

He looked at Assface malevolently.

"Is it time to rub yo-"

"No! It's not..." Mongrel sighed and rubbed his face again. He was going to have to get it over with sooner or later. And since this was as far as Assface was willing to go, his journey was over. It was time to reward him. "Okay, fine."

The jubilation expressed by the native could only properly be expressed using made up words, and even then it wouldn't suitably be conveyed. Assface knelt down eye-level with Mongrel's posterior and slowly reached out to caress it. He stroked it lovingly, his eyes glazing over, drool beginning to seep from the corner of his mouth. This began with one hand, rubbing one cheek, and was soon joined by the other to cover more skin and, ahem, double his pleasure. Then the groping began. What started as a light massage that was somewhat enjoyable grew steadily in pressure.

"Okay," Mongrel said, beginning to feel like a prostitute. "That's enough."

But Assface refused to relinquish his prize. Restrained fondling soon gave way to desperate, wanton seizing of Mongrel's assets. His fingers dug in deep, his eyes grew wild.

Mongrel tried to pull away but the grip on his ass was too strong. "What the hell? Let go!"

Suddenly Assface released Mongrel, his eyes wide with shock. Mongrel, holding his rear, scampered a few feet away and turned to look at him assailant. He didn't say anything, but the expression on his face demanded an explanation. Assface too scampered away, crab-walking backwards on his hands and feet. Everyone just stared at each other for a long, uncomfortable moment.

"...*Dude*..." DERFtron said.

---

[*] Actually, he had to admit that the thong wasn't as uncomfortable as it looked, although he wouldn't want to look at himself in the mirror. And it was oddly flattering that everyone thought he had a great ass.

Frank And The King

"I...I am sorry," Assface whimpered. Grovelling on his knees, he shuffled a little closer. "I did not mean to...to...I am sorry. Your ass is just so, so...beautiful. I had t-"

"I think you should go," Mongrel said. "Thank you for helping us."

Assface shambled closer to Mongrel and his delicious ass, dragging his knees on the dry, crusty grass. "Please! Come back to my village; with your ass you could be king!"

This was an interesting proposition for Mongrel. A king, eh? He could certainly get used to that kind of lifestyle. Living in a lavish home, everyone doing his bidding, being waited on hand and foot by beautiful woman – he sure wouldn't get that in Dunttstown. Back home there were old people, homeless people, people not right in the head. Drunk people, stupid people, and a few who wanted him dead. Here he could start over and make a new life for himself.

Then again, what kind of life would that be? While he'd eventually grow accustomed to the attire, there was no way he'd ever get used to life without indoor plumbing. He couldn't crap in a hole for the rest of his life. And what was he going to wipe his ass with, leaves? That would surely lead to getting poison ivy all over his crotch. No thank you.

"You're not actually considering that are you?" DERFtron asked after Mongrel remained silent for too long. "You can't live here, in the wild, with no TV."

"He's right," Mongrel said. "Sorry."

"TV? What is that?" Assface was confused but determined. "I will get you TV. Lots of TV. All the TV you can eat!"

But Mongrel and DERFtron had already turned and were walking away.

"The juiciest, most succulent TV you ever tasted. You will see!" Assface cried behind them. He then put his head between his knees and cried in the other definition of the word, as the most exquisite ass he'd ever seen walked out of his life forever. Never again would he look upon such perfection, and it saddened him deeply. He would return to his tribe a changed man, but not for the better.

Random Tangent

"I really don't see what's so great about your ass," DERFtron said as they marched across the field towards the sinister-looking building. "My ass was just as good, if not better than yours. Back when I had an ass."

"Hey, the man knows quality," Mongrel said. "My ass *is* fantastic."

"Pfft," DERFtron scoffed. "I've actually had people stop me on the street to take pictures of my ass. My human ass, I mean."

"I'll have you know that I almost won the Miss America pageant solely because of my ass."

"Almost won? What happened, they find out you were from Canada?"

"No, they found out I was a man."

"Huh," DERFtron said. "Wonder how they found that out."

"Shut up," Mongrel muttered.

"What? It's not like you have any proof."

They stopped talking, having reached the building. Silence seemed appropriate given the disturbing sight of the structure; it was like a sleeping dragon and they were afraid of waking it. While the dragon-building looked positively evil from afar up close it simply looked deserted. Sitting alone at the end of a long dirt road that stretched to the horizon, the building looked out of place in the wilderness. The few sporadic windows probably didn't let in much light, and Mongrel didn't want to venture inside a dimly lit abandoned sweat shop. The countless horror movies he'd seen over the years suggested this place was anything *but* abandoned. But they'd come too far to chicken out now. The clock was ticking; if they were going in, they certainly weren't going to wait until nightfall.

Together they walked around the building until they came across a door. It's brown paint was peeling badly but it looked solid. A large bay door was located a few meters further along the wall, also in need of a fresh paint job.

"This better be the right place," Mongrel said, about to knock on the door. "Assface better not have lied to us."

DERFtron agreed. "We've come too far for this to all be for nothing."

Mongrel knocked, and they waited.

Frank And The King

After a stretch of time long enough to suggest no one was home, the sound of many locks being unbolted could be heard through the door. Then after another minute a rope ladder hit Mongrel on the head.

"Ow," Mongrel cried, brought to his knees. He rubbed his head and got back to his feet, then looked up. A head was peeking out from a window high above the door. "What was that for?"

The head then disappeared. Mongrel, frustrated but not seeing any other choice, began climbing the ladder.

"What am I supposed to do? DERFtron asked.

"I don't know," Mongrel replied from halfway up. "Check the door. Sounds unlocked to me." DERFtron was about to do just that, when it suddenly opened.

A man stood in doorway. "I wasn't expecting *you*," he said, coming out to and glancing around as if he hadn't seen the outside world in a while. He wore trousers with flip-flops, a blue polo shirt and, appropriately enough, a white lab coat. He was a dashing man, with a superb set of teeth and a mighty fine, albeit severely sunburnt chin. His hair was a mess, looking like it was trying to fly off his head. One might think he'd recently been electrocuted. His eyes were somewhat crazed, but intelligence lurked inside; someone was running the show.

"Just who were you expecting?" DERFtron asked.

"Are you Bosley?" Mongrel asked, climbing back down.

The man waited until Mongrel was back on the ground before looking at him questioningly. "Do you know the King?"

Mongrel was about to answer 'yes' after he thought of his friend Elvis, the Elvis impersonator. Then he was about to say 'no' when it occurred to him that the man might be thinking of the *real* Elvis Presley. But perhaps he didn't mean the king of rock and roll, but some other king. He thought of the Chief of the Mojo tribe and about Assface's proclamation of him being a king. Then his mind went further; King Arthur, King Kong, the Lion King, the various kings of England... Maybe this was a trick question? "The king of what?" he finally asked.

"Good enough for me," the man said, and ushered Mongrel and DERFtron inside. What awaited them was a large room full of computers, gadgets, and bookshelves lined with books, binders and

Random Tangent

an odd assortment of knickknacks. Bits of junk were strung everywhere; leftovers of hundreds of projects of unbridled ambition. A couple open doors led to other parts of the building.

The man closed the door behind them and began fastening the dozens of locks. "You don't strike me as a tribesman. Your English is really good."

"I know," Mongrel said, "it's their dress code. It was either wear this or die, basically. Think I made the right choice. So are you Bosley?"

The man held out his hand for Mongrel. "I am indeed Bosley, but you can call me Bosley."

"Oh thank God!" DERFtron said.

Mongrel shook his hand. "We came a long way to see you. So is Bosley a first name or last?"

"Don't really know." Bosley smiled tersely and didn't seem to want to divulge any further, but he did. "That's all that was written on my birth certificate. My parents died before I was born."

"Not your fault man. No shame in it," Mongrel tried to empathise. "I never really knew my family either. Both my parents and grandparents were only childs. I come from a long line of dead ends."

"The only family I have now is the one in my head."

Mongrel raised his an eyebrow. "You're not schizophrenic are you?"

"No, no, nothing like that," Bosley replied. "I do have narcolepsy though, and I sleepwalk a lot. So my life might be a little like that movie *Fight Club*. I wake up and find I've moved things around or did some more experiments." He shrugged. "Keeps life interesting."

"So you just fall asleep randomly throughout the day and get beaten up?"

"Well I do find the occasional bruise that I can't explain, but I'm not actually getting into fights like in the movie."

"Why don't you set up a camera to record what you do?"

"Meh," Bosley dismissed, "wouldn't have time to watch it anyway. Got too many projects on the go."

"What about hallucinations? Do you see people?" Mongrel gestured to DERFtron and himself. "We don't count."

Bosley chuckled. "As far as I know everyone I see and talk to are real."

Mongrel nodded but wasn't convinced. "So this family in your head..."

"The family I mentioned are just the extra minds I found. Lost minds. Not exactly a traditional family; we can't communicate with each other or anything. They're basically good for extra processing power. It's like quantum thinking, you know?"

Eyebrows raised again, Mongrel asked. "You sure you're not out of your mind? Cause we can come back later."

"No we can't," DERFtron quipped. "I came for my body. I want it back."

"Your body?" Bosley seemed confused. "You mean you *know* you're inside a machine? You're *conscious?*"

"Yeah," DERFtron said, a hint of caution in his otherwise computerized voice. "So?"

"Don't you know what this means?" Bosley cried.

A look of confused anger would have been written all over DERFtron's face, but with the limited animations available to him to display on his LCD screen, it was not apparent. So instead he displayed the words CONFUSED ANGER on his screen to Bosley, which only delighted him more.

"It worked!" he proclaimed. "It actually worked. I guess it took a little while, but you actually achieved consciousness."

"Are you calling me slow?" DERFtron asked, irritated. "Cause I am *not* slow. I could think circles around you. I've always been conscious - I just hid it from you because you're crazy. Now give me back the rest of me!"

"Well hold on now," Bosley started, holding his hands up, "it's not tha-"

Suddenly his wristwatch began beeping. He hung his mouth open in shock and ran over to the corner of the room, where he grabbed what looked like a motorcycle helmet, and began strapping it on. "I've found a way to predict when my body is abo-" He managed to get the helmet buckled on tight and was halfway back to them when he crashed to the floor like someone had shot him. The helmet bounced off the concrete floor and he slid a couple feet before coming to a rest. He lay deathly still.

Random Tangent

Mongrel and DERFtron looked at each other. "At least he wearing that helmet," Mongrel said.

"That would certainly explain the bruises. So now what?"

"I guess we just wait for him to wake up." Mongrel glanced around the room, figuring he'd need to find something to pass the time. He walked over to a chalkboard where some diagrams had been written. Many notes accompanied them, but Bosley's handwriting left something to the imagination; legibility for example.

"I think he's waking up," DERFtron said.

Bosley's body was indeed rousing. First his feet began shaking, and the motion travelled up his legs and seemed to spread through his body. Soon it looked like he was having a seizure. DERFtron was about to ask if Bosley had epilepsy, and Mongrel was about to say he didn't know, when the body grew still again. After a minute, he slowly staggered to his feet.

"He might just be sleepwalking," Mongrel said, returning to DERFtron's side.

The sleepwalker turned his neck to one side, cracking it loudly. Then he yawned and farted loudly, letting loose a burst of air from both directions. If he wasn't careful he was sure to wake himself up with all the noise. Following this he scratched his tummy and performed a series of stretches, all while making chewing motions with his jaws. Once done with his afternoon wake-up routine, he stared directly at DERFtron.

"He's looking at me," DERFtron whispered. "It's creepy. His eyes are open – why are his eyes open?"

"Well?" Bosley suddenly said in a peculiar British accent. His eyes swept up and down DERFton's body once, and his arm gestured towards Mongrel. "Care to introduce me?"

"Now he's talking to me. Did he mention anything about sleep*talking*? Why is he talking to me? Do I play along?" DERFtron whispered to Mongrel.

"I don't know. Why are you whispering?"

"Well he's asleep, right? I don't want to wake him up."

"Oh, good idea," Mongrel whispered back.

"I'm not asleep, and I can hear you," Bosley said, crossing his arms. "Now again, who is he? Friend? Prisoner?"

Frank And The King

"Crap, you woke him up," DERFtron said. "You're not supposed to wake a sleepwalker. Now he's gonna have a heart attack and die."

"He's not gonna die."

"If he does, and I don't get my body back, I'm gonna kill you."

"If you don't start answering my questions I'm going to start shitting my pants," Bosley cried, and this declaration, more than anything, got their attention. They both shut up, not wanting any bowel movements to intrude upon the conversation. Bosley glanced back and forth between them, eventually tossing his hands in the air as if to say, 'well?'

"Uh, I'm a friend," Mongrel answered cautiously. "Don't you remember us? You just invited us in."

"*This one* I remember," he said, pointing to DERFtron.

"Aren't I the popular one," DERFtron muttered.

"And as far as you're concerned," he pointed at Mongrel, "since when did the locals start speaking English?"

"I'm *not* from the tribe," Mongrel said, exasperated. "I don't even look like them – I'm white!"

"Well excuse me for living!" the man said. "I thought you were albino." Bosley rubbed his hands together expectantly and turned to DERFtron. "So what have you found out?"

"What?" DERFtron asked. "Look, I just came for my body. Are you still sleeping?"

Bosley slapped himself on his forehead and began taking off his helmet. "I'm sorry." He turned to Mongrel. "I apologize. It's the Wernicke-Korsakoff Syndrome – makes my memory go bananas."

"I thought you had narcolepsy?" Mongrel asked. "Or do you have that syndrome thingy too?"

"Narcolepsy? Did I say that?" he scoffed. "No, just the memory issues. I'm working on a cure. But don't worry Derf old pal, I haven't forgotten you. I'll have you back in a body in a no time."

"You will? Awesome! I thought it was going to be a problem."

Random Tangent

"No, not a problem at all. Why, did that idiot Bosley say it could be a problem? Listen, I'm twice the scientist he is, and three times as mad. It'll be a piece of cake."

"Huh?" Mongrel asked.

"What?" DERFtron concurred.

"I know brain transplants can be a little taxing, and you might be slow to process things or remember things, but the technology just isn't there yet. Not in its entirety at least. But I found a solution that I think you'll find most agreeable."

Mongrel and DERFtron once again exchanged looks of confusion. Mongrel took the lead in asking, "Who...who are you, then?"

"Ah!" The man they thought was Bosley ran over to an old stereo cabinet and fished a cassette out of a box, After reading the label he gave an 'Aha!' and popped it in the stereo. After an uncomfortable minute, an up-tempo beat began playing, and he began to sing:

> I'm not sure if you've heard this song yet
> My memory is kinda hazy
> I'm don't know how long ago we met
> But you probably think I'm crazy
>
> I'll show you all I'm not insane
> Not once you get to know me
> And soon the world will know my name
> And acknowledge my royalty

Mongrel's jaw dropped open. "Is he serious? We're doing a musical number?"

"Did he just call me slow? Again?" DERFtron asked.

> Allow me to introduce myself
> I'm the King, it's got a nice ring
> It's no use crying for help
> Cause no one will be coming
>
> Now why should you two make a fuss

Frank And The King

Over this supervillain?
I'm dripping with pure awesomeness
And really good at killin'

For too long I've bided my time
Keeping myself to the shadows
But look out cause I'm in my prime
Time to tell the world Hello!

Allow me to introduce myself
I'm the King, it's kinda my thing
It's no use calling for help
You'll have to do my bidding

I've got balls made of shiny brass
All the girls want to date me
And even when I kick your ass
You'll find it hard to hate me

I come off as a little weird
But I'm such a terrific guy
With a voice like silk and a epic beard
I'm a...hey!

    Bosley stopped singing, hitting STOP on the stereo. He ran his hands over his clean-shaven chin. "What happened to my beard?"

    "Oh thank God that's over," Mongrel muttered. "Can we never do that again?"

    "You never had a beard," DERFtron answered.

    "Oh yes I did," the King stomped over and got in DERFtron's display. "I had a grand beard. Took me hours to grow! Hundreds of hours!"

    "So you're not Bosley?" Mongrel asked.

    The King glared at him, obviously displeased. "Do I look like Bosley to you?"

    Mongrel let his eyes roam up and down the King's body. "Is that a trick question?"

Random Tangent

"That man is crazy!" the King fumed. "Crazy I tell you! I'm a mad scientist, and *I* can admit it. Bosley is just plain crazy – he practically admits it himself. And he got rid of goats!"

"Oh yeah, I heard about that."

"He preheats his toaster, hangs the toilet paper on the wrong side, and talks to himself all the time."

"Well, taking to yourself doesn't make you crazy; maybe lonely."

"He talks to inanimate objects too."

"Well, do they talk back to him?"

"Hell the devil should I know?"

Mongrel had a difficult time answering this. "Because...I mean...how do you *not* know?"

The King grabbed Mongrel and jerked him to within an inch of his face. "You do not want to give me attitude, boy. Not after what happened to my beard."

"What happened to your beard?" Mongrel squeaked out.

"I don't know!" the King yelled. "That's what I'm saying. I'm having a bad day and you do not want to make it any worse." He let Mongrel go. "Me and that maniac aren't attached at the hip. I don't know what goes on in his head."

"How do you know," Mongrel asked timidly, afraid to anger the man, "that he's not going on in *your* head?"

"What?"

"I mean maybe he's just a figment of your imagination. Happens all the time."

"Yeah," DERFtron chimed in. "Nothing to be ashamed of. Doesn't mean you're losing it."

"There's pills you could take for that."

The King looked back and forth at them, as if *they* were the crazy ones. "What's wrong with you guys? Haven't you heard the news? First he disproved goats, and now he's found a way to make wood rust. How could he possibly be made up? Who'd be behind it?"

Mongrel and DERFtron looked at each other; neither had an answer for that.

"Tell me my nemesis is all in my head?" The King shook his head. "You're just intent on making my day worse, aren't you?

Cause I tell you, if Bosley was a fake all this time, it would make my life much more difficult."

"Why?"

"Because he's not real. Think about it; you can't kill someone that's not real. I'd rather have a mortal enemy than an immortal one."

Mongrel had to concede that point; it made a strange kind of sense.

"You!" the King announced, rushing over to DERFtron and putting his arm around him. "*You* know Bosley is real."

"I do?"

"Of course you do. I sent you into his lair for reconnaissance. What have you found out?"

"Uh..." DERFtron looked to Mongrel, who shrugged. "...um..."

"Come on, you must have learned something!"

DERFtron began backing away, trying to distance himself from the conversation. "So, wait, you said you sent me to Bosley? So does that mean you made me?"

"Yes," the King said as if it was obvious. "And I can unmake you too. Now tell me!"

"Okay, okay," DERFtron tried to think. "Um...okay, he's very close to us. Right this very now." He then nodded as if this was a big deal, that the King should be impressed with this intel.

But the King was not impressed. "I know that! I know where he is you idiot. I wouldn't have sent you to him if I didn't even know where he was."

"Well why don't you go kill him then?" Mongrel asked. "If you know where he is, then just stop on by for a cup of tea. And when you ask him for some sugar and he says he's all out, then you kill him. It'd be completely justifiable."

"But what if he *has* sugar?"

Mongrel frowned. "Uh, well..."

"You know what? It doesn't matter. I'm not going over there – the place is booby-trapped."

"It is?" Mongrel and DERFtron asked in unison. Then they both began nervously glancing around the room.

Random Tangent

"Bosley may be a lunatic, but he's a brilliant lunatic. So come now Derf, tell me something new. Something juicy."

Wanting to keep backing away, but afraid of booby-traps, DERFtron again tried to come up with something on the spot. "Um...his parents died before he was born."

"I know that too!" the King roared. He advanced on DERFtron with his hands out as if he was planning to strangle him, which is just silly because you can't strangle a robot.

"He has a voracious fear of peanuts!" DERFtron squealed as the King closed in on him.

"He does?" the King relented, resisting his urge to maim.

"...Yeah, sure. Why not?"

"Is he allergic to them?"

"Uh...I'm gonna go with no?"

This upset the King, and he was on the move again. "Then what use is that to me? How does that help my plans?"

"I don't even know what your plans are," DERFtron whimpered, cringing and raising his arms in defence.

Once again the King stopped. "Oh, that's right. Would you like to know?"

DERFtron peeked out from behind his arms. "If it'll stop you from hurting me."

"Oh don't be silly," the King said, walking over to a white board, "I wouldn't hurt you." He picked up a dry-erase marker and was about to begin drawing when he stopped and turned to them, a strange look in his eyes. "Wait a minute. You're on his side aren't you?"

"What? No!"

"He's somehow figured out my plan and reprogrammed you to work for him. Is that it? You're a counter-operative now?"

DERFtron looked at the King for a moment, appearing to be considering the question, before repeating, "No!"

The King put the marker back down and clasped his hands together. He appeared calm, but a violent storm was brewing beneath his demeanour. "You almost had me fooled. Trick me into revealing my grand scheme just so you can run back to Bosley and ruin everything."

Frank And The King

"You honestly have no idea what you're talking about," DERFtron said, shaking his monitor. "You *are* Bosley, you dumbass!"

The King's face became a train wreck of confusion. Obviously the accusation made no sense, but if he recalled correctly, which was often a challenge, he did suffer from Wernicke-Korsakoff Syndrome. It made him forget things. Had he forgotten who he was? Was it at least *possible*?

No. No it wasn't. It was just another trick. "You must really think I'm stupid to fall for that," he said.

"Maybe not stupid, but crazy."

"Yeah, we totally think you're crazy," Mongrel agreed.

"Crazy?" the King blurted out, as if the mere suggestion was ludicrous. "Is it crazy to want to kill your arch nemesis in front of his own family with a bunch of spider monkeys with little hatchets?"

"Well, maybe," Mongrel said, "if you take into account that he has no family."

"Ha! Is that what he told you?" The King wrung his hands together sadistically. "Well I managed to get a sample of his DNA and traced his lineage. He has a great uncle living in Canada. So tell me I'm crazy now!"

So Bosley *did* have family. He might still be an only child, but he wasn't alone in the world. And he didn't even know. Somehow, Mongrel had to tell him. Unless the King really was crazy.

"We're from Canada," Mongrel pointed to DERFtron and himself. "How do you know one of us isn't his uncle?"

"Don't be crazy," the King dismissed. "Neither of you are old enough."

"Oh so *I'm* the crazy one now?" Mongrel retorted, getting defensive. "I'm so *not crazy* that I have a psychologist come to my house once a week to personally check me out for himself."

The King tried to stroke his beard, but frowned angrily upon finding it still missing. "I could really use that sort of service myself. And how are your results?"

"He always writes down the same thing: TBD. I think it means Total Badass Disorder. I hope they never find a cure."

Random Tangent

"It probably means Totally Brain Dead. Why don't you let me test you to find out for sure?"

"Nah, that's okay. I know I'm not crazy. I mean, does a guy who taught myself how to skydive by throwing myself out of an airplane and figuring it out on the way down sound crazy?"

"No more than someone who whittled a crown out of cheese and wore it for a year. Much, much cheaper than a crown made of gold my friend."

"What did you do with the crown after?"

"I ate it, of course," the King said as if was the most natural thing in the world.

"Ah."

"What are you doing?" DERFtron whispered furiously at Mongrel, meaning his banter with the mad scientist.

"Don't worry, I got this." He returned his attention to the King. "I once spent an entire week tracking down a chicken to help it cross the road. And when I finally got him there, you know what happened? Nothing. No enlightenment, no spiritual revelation, it didn't even save me money on my car insurance. Nothing at all. And if that didn't drive me crazy then I must be crazy-proof."

"Or you're already crazy," the King countered. "I once ate a hockey puck to see if it had cream filling. I mean, a puck looks just like a Ding Dong^{TM}, you know those Hostess cakes?"

"You're right! They do!" The news came as a shock to Mongrel, and it took him a minute to recover. "I never noticed that before. There's so much more to food than we'll ever know. Whenever I order pizza, I order two. I make a big show of mulling over them and comparing them before selecting which one to eat. Then I throw the other one out. See, I want my pizza to feel special. If that's crazy, I don't know what isn't."

"But what about the other pizza?" the King asked. "The one you don't eat. Aren't you worried that it'll feel dejected?"

"Well I'm not eating that pizza, so it gets to live. It's win-win."

"Yeah, okay. That makes total sense to me."

DERFtron gawked at the King as much as his GUI would allow. "Dude, where did you get your sense? Cause you should take it back for a refund."

Frank And The King

The King ignored DERFtron and said, "I plan on launching a campaign to show everyone that aliens are trying to take over the world. But the reason we don't know about it is because they live inside us – not all of us; just people with outie belly buttons. That's their giveaway. That's where they live. So in order to kill the aliens, you have to gut yourself with a butcher's knife."

"But if you did that the suicide rate would triple overnight!"

"Well, the world is overpopulated..."

"Oh, I didn't mean it was a bad thing. You'll save people by killing them!" Mongrel began applauding. "It's brilliant!"

The King curtsied. "Oh it's nothing really."

"No it's something all right. The most I ever do for humanity is try not fart in an elevator."

"Don't short change yourself," the King pointed at Mongrel. "That is a valuable public service. I can't tell you how many times I've wanted to kill people like that. But I *can* tell you how many times I did."

"How many?" Mongrel and DERFtron asked in unison, and because DERFtron asked, the King didn't answer, since he was still ignoring him for no apparent reason.

"I used to kill birds," Mongrel said after a minute. "Usually just the seagulls that gathered around you in the parking lot when you were trying to eat your burger, you know?"

"Yes I know the ones. Pesky buggers. I used to throw rocks at them but soon they started eating the rocks. I swear they'll eat anything."

"Rocks?" Mongrel scoffed. "I use grenades. Sure, you might be able to kill a couple birds with a stone, but you can kill a whole shitload of them with a well-timed explosive."

"I like the way your mind thinks."

"Really?" Mongrel blushed. "I'm usually ashamed to walk around with it. My brain doesn't always think all the way to the top, if you know what I mean. I'm not crazy, but sometimes..." he paused for a moment to think. "Why is that people can be *in*sane but *out* of their minds? They both mean the same thing, right? Am I the only one who's noticed that? Does that make me crazy that I noticed that?"

Random Tangent

"That's an interesting observation. I'll have to look into it when I have the time. Speaking of time, I once spent a day in a temporal time loop – but not one of the good ones. I had to eat the same plate of spaghetti countless times. Now I can't eat spaghetti anymore, and used to love spaghetti." He shook his head and kicked a nearby bookshelf, causing several large books and some glass jars to topple to the floor, shattering. As he was still doing to DERFtron, he ignored them.

A horrified expression engulfed Mongrel's face. "That's awful! I make a mean spaghetti, and it would kill me if I couldn't enjoy it anymore. Seriously, I think I would literally have a heart attack and die if a doctor told me I couldn't eat spaghetti anymore. I have several people wanting me dead; they would kill me to get that kind of information." His horrified expression returned and he then quickly put his hands over his mouth. "Oh shit! Please don't tell anyone about this! I would die if word got out, I would just die!"

"There there now," the King placated, "your secret is safe with me. No one is going to kill you with spaghetti, unless it's me, and I promise not to without a good reason."

Mongrel was relieved for a few seconds until his brain processed the entire comment. "Uh...what exactly would be a good reason?"

The King shrugged. "Could be anything, really. I don't always need a reason to kill. I went to a Star Trek convention last year and spent the entire time discretely strangling anyone wearing a red shirt, and then hiding the bodies. I killed as many as I could, but I – I'm only one man." He seemed genuinely regretful of his shortcomings. "I keep thinking back and seeing things I missed. I could've done better, I could've gotten more." He shook his head dismissively and wiped tears from his eyes. "Anyway...over the next few days it was all over the news and everyone made such a big deal over it. I can't imagine why – it's just Star Trek."

"I think I remember hearing about that," DERFtron said, still trying to insert himself into the conversation and getting angrier with each failed attempt.

"That is perhaps the most sane thing I've ever heard from someone trying to convince me he wasn't crazy," Mongrel said ponderously.

Frank And The King

Smiling broadly at the compliment, the King said, "I'll do better next year, you'll see."

"I don't think I could kill anyone." Mongrel thought back to his last encounter with Captain Pete. "Well, not on purpose at least. I want to, believe me, and not just my enemies. Lots of people who could use a bit of 'deathening' up."

"Oh it's not that hard. You just have to remember that the law is a man-made concept. We're all animals at heart. Animals have no laws...well, except for the law of the jungle, maybe."

"It's not the law – I know that's faulty. I guess it's the principal, you know? The sanctity of life and whatnot. My conscience wouldn't let me kill anyone."

"Oh pish posh now. A conscience is a waste of mental resources. Killing one another is in our blood, our genes. Our very existence is built upon it; survival of the fittest, right? It's only natural for you to rip out someone's heart and stomp on it while they watch to ensure that your lineage lives on and theirs doesn't. And to deny that urge is to entrap yourself in a life devoid of purpose, a refusal of your basic human instincts. This is why people are depressed. This is why men cheat on their wives. This is why war, no matter how much we try to stop it, always rages on somewhere in the world. If you take away anything – electricity, food, the police, even gas for our cars – society simply collapses. People turn on one another, every man for himself, martial law – the way nature intended. Because chaos is the natural order of things. You take away civilization and killing become easy, even necessary."

Mongrel looked at him. "You are perhaps the most sane crazy person I know."

"You should join me. There is much I could teach you. Much we could learn from each other." The King then got a strange look in his eyes. "I'm in need of another brain; my last one had a faulty loyalty gene." He glanced at DERFtron briefly before remembering that he was ignoring him. "I could use a brain like yours." He approached Mongrel with his arms stretched out like a zombie.

The booby traps forgotten, Mongrel began backing away. His mind was screaming *zombie!* at him. "No, wait, you don't want my brain. Turns out I'm crazy after all. I'm so crazy that sometimes I run around naked outside my house with my arms stretched out like an airplane, but really I'm thinking I'm a goldfish. But with wings. Crazy, huh?"

The King stopped pretending to be a zombie. "Not *too* crazy. I once tried to genetically engineer flying goldfish – cause what kid wouldn't want one of those as a pet? I'd be rich!"

"What if it flies away?" DERFtron asked, but his question fell on deaf ears, and the words CONFUSED ANGER appeared on his display again. No one noticed.

"I would totally want one of those," Mongrel said, more to himself. "I could also really use a poltergeist in my house – as a guard. Don't get me wrong, guard dogs are great and all, but I think a guard poltergeist would be so much better. Way scarier too. Who would break into a haunted house?"

"That's...brilliant!" the King decreed. "Are you sure you're crazy? Many highly intelligent people are crazy."

"Oh no, I'm crazy. Crazy like a fox." Mongrel knocked on his head and made a funny face. "See? Nothing. And believe me, I'm not that smart, especially when it comes to math. That's how I lost my last job."

"You were fired for poor math skills?"

Mongrel shifted his hands as if weighing options. "Well not exactly. The building caught on fire. Burned right to the ground. Yeah, *that's* how bad I am at math."

"I suppose we all have our moments when our brains fail us..."

"Not me," DERFtron tried to interrupt, but failed since ignorance was running around loose in the warehouse. He wasn't going to put up with it for much longer.

"...but that doesn't necessarily mean you're crazy. You don't happen to...oh I don't know, rip your hair out and save it, do you?"

"Actually..." Mongrel smiled tersely, "sometimes I even make little hair puppets out of them and sell them to neighbourhood kids. They're quite popular."

"Ah, I see. That's too bad." The King was disheartened. "It's hard to find a decent brain these days. Pretty much have to run

Frank And The King

into them by accident. That's how I found him," he thumbed over his shoulder to DERFtron.

"What?" DERFtron asked.

"Found him just lying on the ground, birds having their way with him. Not sexually of course, but...with the eating. Looked like someone just threw him away – now *that* was crazy."

Mongrel giggled. "That was me!"

The King's jaw dropped. "No way!"

"Way!"

DERFtron shook his monitor. They were talking about him like he wasn't even in the room.

"You're bullshitting me!"

"I'm trying to. Told you I was crazy. My dad used to say I didn't have enough O's in my Cheerios. I never knew what he meant until years later when I bought a box."

"Oh don't get me started on cereal," the King rolled his eyes. "Stopped eating that crap myself ever since my Rice Krispies^{TM} started mouthing off to me. You should have heard the tripe they were saying. Threw more than one bowl of cereal across the room, I can tell you that. Sometimes I'd just stick 'em in the microwave and set it to infinity." He shook his head, reminiscing.

"Your microwave has an infinity setting?" DERFtron asked, and then waved his arms, trying to get noticed. He knew it wouldn't work but thought he would give it one last try. This was the last straw.

"Your food talks to you?" Mongrel asked. "That's the kind of hallucinations that get you put in mental hospitals."

"Good thing there are none around here then, am I right?" the King held up his hand for a high five, but when it became apparent that he wasn't going to get one, he lowered his arm and said, "I haven't lost my mind. In fact, it's firmly chained up inside my head so it can't get away. What do you think of that?"

"Yeah, that's nice." Mongrel held up a foot. The King raised his hand again, apparently anticipating a high five. "No, down," Mongrel chastised, "put it down." The King did as he was told, dejected. "Now how many toes am I holding up on my foot?"

"Feet? Those are feet? I thought they were really long legs. Where are your toes?"

Random Tangent

Mongrel put his foot down, his suspicions confirmed. "I hate to be the bearer of bad news, but you're no longer amongst the sane."

"What? No, that can't be."

"Sorry." Mongrel shrugged.

The King began pacing back and forth. "I play Sudoku, I eat my vegetables – well not broccoli, but no one would blame me for that. *Yuck!* I get regular haircuts..." a realization came over the King and he stopped pacing. "It's the beard isn't it? I lost my mind when I lost my beard."

"You never had a beard. You probably hallucinated it."

"I do not hallucinate!" the King yelled.

"Oh really?" Mongrel asked. He'd been waiting for this moment. "I'm just a figment of your imagination. I don't even exist."

The King's breathing stopped and his heart raced. His eyes widened and his mouth opened. He began uttering words, but perhaps they too were hallucinations; his lips moved but no sound was coming out. He moved closer to Mongrel with his arms out again like a zombie, only this time his intentions were simply to touch Mongrel, to see if he was real. But he stopped, not wanting to confirm the truth. Instead he turned to DERFtron. "Derf? You're real, aren't you?"

DERFtron glared at the King. "Are you talking to me? Are you saying you can hear me now? I thought I was dead to you."

"Bu you're really here, right?"

"Actually, I'm pretty sure I'm not, considering how much you're ignoring me. I might as well be on another planet."

This was the final clincher for the King. He really had lost it. A faraway look spread across his face and he slumped to his knees. "So it's true," he whispered. "I am crazy. Just like you."

Mongrel came over and was about to put a hand on his shoulder but restrained himself at the last moment, not wanting to spoil the King's illusion. "It's okay. It's quite a lot of fun being crazy."

The King suddenly got up and spun around to face Mongrel, anger in his eyes. "And what would you know of it? You're not even real."

Frank And The King

"True," Mongrel agreed. "I'm just trying to help. I *am* your own thoughts speaking to you, or something."

"Well just shut up. Shut up and go away."

"Yes, perhaps that might be for the best." Mongrel made for the door.

"Hey, we can't leave," DERFtron said, moving over to block Mongrel's exit. "I don't have my body back yet."

"Crap," Mongrel muttered.

"Go!" the King shouted behind them, his rage building. "Both of you!"

"Ah, we kinda can't, we came here beca-"

"Fine!" the King cut them off. "If you won't leave, I'll force you out." He picked up a shard of glass from a broken vase that had tumbled from the bookshelf earlier, and ran at them, screaming.

Mongrel screamed too and ran for the door. He tried to open it but a dozen locks held it firmly shut. He wouldn't be escaping that way. He ducked as the King buried the shard of glass in the door, and scooted off to the side. "I'm in your head! *I'm in your head!*" he shouted. Shouldn't you be stabbing yourself?"

The King busied himself trying to free his weapon. "It'd be much more satisfying to stab you." He then looked at DERFtron and said. "You're next."

"Please," DERFtron dismissed, not at all concerned. "Like you could pay attention to me long enough to do *anything*."

Running through an open door and down a dark hallway, Mongrel realized he needed something to defend himself with. He entered a room to his right and felt along the wall for a light switch, wondering why Bosley bothered living in a warehouse with few windows. Finding a switch, he flicked it on and found himself in a kitchen. It was rather tiny; a small table stood against the wall to his right, a fridge and microwave stand occupied the wall behind it. Across the entire adjacent wall was a counter with rows of cupboards both above and below it, and bisecting the counter was a sink full of dirty dishes.

Mongrel began pulling open drawers, looking for something he could use. He was fully aware of the grime and food-encrusted knives in the sink, but he wanted something cleaner.

"There really isn't anywhere to hide."

Random Tangent

Mongrel spun around to see the King standing in the doorway, his shard of glass glistening in the light. He could hear DERFtron coming down the hallway behind him, mumbling something. He reached behind him into the last drawer he was rummaging through, grabbed something and yanked it out, hoping it was something menacing. It was a spoon. He swallowed and said, "I'm just your imagination playing with you. If you kill your imagination you'll destroy your mind!"

"My mind?" the King cried. "I've already lost that! He came at Mongrel again with the glass raised above his head.

Not knowing what else to do, Mongrel threw the spoon at the King, catching him in the eye. The King gasped and reached up to hold his face, nearly poking out his other eye with the shard. A small trickle of blood emerged as the glass scraped across his forehead; he didn't seem to notice. Sensing his chance, Mongrel charged and tackled his enemy to the floor.

"Having fun?" DERFtron asked, peeking into the room.

"You could certainly help me out here."

"Oh *now* you want my help? You seemed just fine earlier."

Mongrel staggered to his feet. "He wasn't trying to kill me earlier."

"Well maybe you should try ignoring him too. Maybe he'll go away. If you don't give him the satisfaction of killing you, he'll just get bored and go away."

"I'm *trying* to not give him the satisfaction, now move!" He shoved his way passed the robot and out into the hallway again. Behind him the King was gathering himself to his feet, and would resume his pursuit any second now.

Down the hall, Mongrel looked frantically for a place to hide, a weapon, something useful. The next door he tried opened into a large washroom with more than enough stalls for one man, and also no way out should he try to barricade himself inside. Further down he came across what appeared to be a vault. A metal door, cold to the touch, stood out in stark contrast to the pale walls. He didn't even bother trying it, knowing trapping himself inside would be a death sentence.

At the end of the hall stood a spiral staircase, and having no other options, Mongrel took it. The top opened up to another

Frank And The King

hallway heading back to the way he'd come. A row of doors lined the wall to his right. He tried them all, hoping to locate the room with the rope ladder, but of the two doors that weren't locked he only found a few beds; no escape and no decent place to hide. Perhaps, he thought, maybe hiding wasn't going to solve the matter. He could try to wait out the King's memory, figuring that sooner or later he'd forget all about Mongrel, but DERFtron was still out there, and that might keep the madman's memory jogged.

"You can run but you can't hide!" the King's voice called from the stairwell.

"I thought you were going to kill me with spaghetti!" Mongrel hollered back.

"I'm all out."

"Well I can come back!" He rounded a corner at the end of the hall and found a hole in the floor with a pole running through it down to the floor below. Confused at first, Mongrel soon understood that the building used to be a fire station. Sensing approaching murder, he grabbed the poll and jumped down. With the King busy searching for him on the second floor, Mongrel might have a chance to get some of those locks undone, and could escape.

But this is not what happened. Mongrel's instincts were correct when he sensed the King nearby, but it wasn't from behind him; it was from below. As he slid down the pole, he heard a beeping sound like Bosley's watch had made earlier, and then hit what felt like a speed bump. It jostled him a bit, and he jumped the last few feet, thinking the floor was closer. Tumbling to the ground with all the grace of a brick, Mongrel scrambled in alarm over to the door, unconcerned with any damage he'd caused, and began fiddling with the locking mechanisms.

"Uh, hey!" DERFtron asked behind him.

"We gotta get out of here, Derf. Not much time."

"Are you ever gonna stop ignoring me?"

"Derf *please*! Unless you know how to pick locks the-"

"Watch out!"

Out of instinct, Mongrel ducked and shot to his left, rolling on the floor. He quickly came to his feet and prepared for his next move, feeling like a ninja. But nothing happened. His eyes scanned

Random Tangent

the room, eventually finding the King's body lying at the bottom of the pole. He wasn't moving.

"Had to get your attention somehow," DERFtron said.

Realizing his cat-like reflexes hadn't saved his like, the feeling of a ninja faded in Mongrel. "What did you do?"

"Me? You're the one who landed on him; I didn't do anything. I think he's dead."

"I didn't kill him. Just knocked him out."

"Well according to my scanners..." DERFtron bent over the King's head, where a large welt was forming. "...Yep, no brain activity. He's a goner."

"What? Not again. He *can't* be dead."

"Again?"

"Never mind. Long story."

DERFtron tried to cross his arms, but found his body incapable of the manoeuvre. "Well you were the one that just *had* to wake him up. I told you he was gonna have a heart attack."

"If he was gonna have a heart attack he would've one earlier. They happen instantly."

"Well maybe *he's* the slow one." DERFtron looked down at the body of the King. "Call me slow? Sayin' I ain't got no brain? I'm *all brain* motherfucker!" He tried to flash some gang sings but with his mechanical arms all that did was make him appear mentally challenged. "Hey, fuck you!" This outburst caused one of his arms to fall off. He watched it clang to the floor and said, "Okay, okay. Sorry. We cool."

"You've come a long way from your days as a grammar Nazi," Mongrel said, shaking his head.

"Aw shit!" DERFtron suddenly cried in alarm. "Who's gonna put me back in my body now? Why did you have to kill him?"

"Sorry! He was chasing me around and trying to stab me! And you didn't do anything to help!" Mongrel hung his head. "Why does everyone try to kill me?"

"Well you do tend to bring out the homicidal tendencies in people."

Mongrel was about to elbow DERFtron again but this time managed to stop himself. "Look, why don't we at least go find your

Frank And The King

body. Maybe we'll figure something out. The King said he was gonna put you back in it, so it has to be around here somewhere." He started opening cupboards and digging around.

"You know what?" DERFtron said after a minute. "Don't worry about it. Won't do any good."

"Why not?"

"Don't you remember? My brain was all that was left of me when Bosley found it – or the King – whoever found it. There's nothing left of my body to go back to."

"So you're saying we came all this way for nothing? And you're telling me this *now*?" Mongrel tried not to get angry. "You couldn't have figured this out earlier? I think being a robot has made you a little forgetful of how fragile we are. I was almost murdered to death by a mad scientist, practically raped by a man obsessed with my ass, and only a couple hours ago the last thing I was supposed to see on Earth was some asshole's asshole! And the day's not even over yet! We could've stayed home; it was *such* a nice day out today!"

"Murdered to death?"

"Okay, okay, calm down," Mongrel muttered to himself. "You're still alive. This is just the way your life is. No need to give yourself a heart attack – that's just what he'd like, isn't it? Well it's not gonna happen."

"Okay, so maybe I didn't think it through. But in my defence, he probably could've done *something* to help; he's supposed to be a genius after all."

Mongrel snapped his head at DERFtron. "Yeah, and he's also a psychopath. You've met him before, hadn't you noticed?"

DERFtron had not noticed Bosley's maniacal side before. In fact he didn't know there were other sides, other *minds*, of his personality. But he did begin to wonder why Bosley hadn't added his mind to the rest. Why was he made into a robot instead?

"It's because you're a dumbass that can't think ahead," Mongrel spouted dismally.

"What? How did...?"

"Sorry; I wasn't supposed to read that. I'm just irritated. Death's been looming over my head the last few stories, and..." Mongrel sighed and pinched the bridge of his nose. "Forget I said that. I meant to say I've been having a bad life. That's all." Then an idea came to him. "Wait, you said he had other minds, right?"

"No, I nev-"

"You *thought* it. Whatever. But where are the other bodies?"

"You lost me."

"Bosley has other minds, right? What about the bodies that came with them? They gotta be around here somewhere. Maybe you could use one of them?" Mongrel began searching around the room.

This didn't sit well with DERFtron. Being implanted in someone else's body? It had a creepy science fiction vibe to it. "But what if I don't like that body? What if it's ugly, or fat? What if it's a girl?"

"You want to spend the rest of your life as a robot?"

"Fine, fine. I'll try to keep an open mind." DERFtron moved around the room, sorting piles of junk. "But even if we find a nice body, who's gonna put my brain inside it?"

"Maybe we can find another mad scientist?"

"Oh yeah, sure, cause they're a dime a dozen. Might as well just place a personal ad in the papers: Man seeking man for exciting medical experiment. Must be friendly, preferably a mad scientist, totally not homicidal, and enjoy long walks on the beach."

"And puppies."

"What?"

"I don't want to work with someone who doesn't like puppies."

"Who doesn't like puppies?"

"Trust me, we'll find the one asshole in the world who hates puppies. And the only people in the world that hate puppies are homicidal maniacs."

"Ah okay, I see what you...what the...?" DERFtron exclaimed.

"What?" Mongrel ran over to see what his friend had found. Beneath a few stacks of plywood another machine like DERFtron had been unearthed. They weren't exactly identical; the newer, or rather older model appeared more rusted, had a smaller monitor for a head, but its mobility treads looked wider. Through the small window in the front, reminiscent of a front-load washing machine, the brain that powered it could be seen.

"Wow!" Mongrel cried, slapping DERFtron on the back of his body. "Another you! And look, another brain inside – told you! There has to be another body around here to go with that brain." Assuming it was also built like his friend, Mongrel reached around back of the machine and found a familiar switch, and flipped it. They waited quietly as the machine booted, watching lines of code scroll up the monitor.

"This is like some weird version of the twilight zone," DERFtron said, breaking his silence. Mongrel agreed but didn't reply.

Soon the lines of code disappeared and a digital face appeared in the monitor, which was now shown to have a lower resolution than DERFtron's own. A camera atop the monitor swivelled back and forth between its two new friends. "I am Shabbytron. I know all."

"Shabby?" Mongrel was confused. "We just had a Shabby in the last story."

"What's a Shabby?" DERFtron asked, but got no answer.

"I have been programmed with knowledge running the entire expanse of human history. There is nothing I do not know, so don't even think about trying to trick me."

"Is that right?" DERFtron asked, taking offence to this. "Look at you with your tiny little head. I bet I know ten times the stuff you do."

"Impossible," Shabbytron said. "I know everything. *Everything*, you got that, asshole?"

"Asshole? That's probably the only thing you got that's bigger than mine."

"Okay, *that* didn't sound gay," Mongrel said. "What is this, some kind of sibling rivalry?"

"The only thing you *have* that's bigger than mine," Shabbytron corrected.

"Hey, don't do that to me you little shit!" DERFtron yelled, smacking the other robot. "*I'm* the one who does that. It's what my name stands for. I know correct grammar and pronunciation of every word in every language ever created in the history of mankind! And I'm including Pig Latin, Leetspeak, Ebonics, Klingon – I can watch Return of the Jedi and don't even need subtitles!"

"I know a bitch when I see one," Shabbytron replied. "And I'm looking at one right now."

"I know how to knock you the fuck out!" DERFtron ran his body into Shabbytron, his remaining arm swinging wildly. Shabbytron's arms moved slightly, as if to defend itself, but their mobility was not as advanced as DERFtron's.

Mongrel wormed his way between them, trying not to get sliced by flying metal. "Okay, break it up you two."

"What the hell is this guy's problem?" DERFtron demanded

"Don't worry; I know how to deal with him." Mongrel looked the machine straight in the lens and asked, "Why do people walk *into* the street but *onto* the road?"

Shabbytron glanced back and forth between them, not answering right away. "Before I answer your question," it finally said, "I would like you to think for a minute – if that's not asking too much of you – about my unfathomable intelligence and the vast amount of knowledge I possess. More information is up here," it pointed a mechanical hand at its monitor, "than a person of your intelligence could possibly understand. There is *so much* in here that it would simply be a waste of my time and intellect to try to find this trivial, pointless piece of data, this needle in the proverbial haystack that is my enormously large mind. It's like searching through volumes upon volumes of encyclopaedias for a single entry. It's a waste of processing power. It would be far easier for me to tell you that I don't know the answer than to actually take the time to answer your stupid question – time that could be better spent solving quantum mechanics equations and unravelling the mysteries of the universe. So, having said all that, and even though I *do*, in fact, know the answer, I don't know the answer."

Mongrel laughed and patted Shabby-Mon on its monitor. "Yeah, yeah. Awesome. Never fails." He turned and walked away, back to his search for a body.

It delighted DERFtron to see his rival humiliated so, and he laughed a strange robotic laugh. "Who's the bitch now?" he shouted, following Mongrel.

Frank And The King

Continuing on their self-guided tour of the converted fire hall, they found mountains of construction material and computer parts, a few mannequins, a room full of various jars and containers filled with all manner of liquids and chemicals, and a curiously large amount of kiwi fruit, but no body.

"Are you hungry?" Mongrel asked after a while, heading back to the kitchen.

"Gee, I might be if I had a stomach."

"Right." He began rummaging through the cupboards looking for something to eat, aside from kiwis. "What do you do for nutrition then? You can't just run on electricity – your brain must need *something*." He pulled out a TV dinner from the refrigerator freezer and supposed it would have to do. He put it in the microwave and turned it on.

"I don't really know," DERFtron replied after thinking about it for a minute. "I haven't eaten anything in months and I don't seem to be dead, so I must be doing something right."

"Wish all diets were that easy. You know, all in all, I think this trip was a success. Aside from nearly being raped and murdered and not finding your body, I mean."

"Yeah, *major* success," DERFtron agreed sarcastically. "We made friends with a foreign nation, put down a psychopath, and made history by being the first humans inside a mon. Where did you find that thing anyway?"

"They come from Mon Isle. It's a little island off...well, you won't find it. And we weren't the first inside Mon."

"Who was?"

Mongrel checked to see how much time was left on the microwave. "I'm not sure, but the first person I met was Blind Cracka."

"Ah, so that explains what you said before. I was wondering what a blind cracker was. Why is he blind? And a cracker?"

"Long story. And come to think of it he wasn't the first either. I know another guy, Fred Farcas – yeah another Fred; you're not even the first Fred – he was swallowed by Mon the early nineteen-hundreds I think."

"Holy! How old is your mon?"

"Beats me."

Random Tangent

"How many people has your mon eaten? He got any dead bodies in there?"

The microwave beeped its final beep and Mongrel opened the door. "That's actually a good idea. Mon could have anything inside it." He grabbed the TV dinner and screamed.

"What?" DERFtron cried.

Mongrel yanked his hands out of the microwave, the TV dinner stuck to his fingers. "It's cold! Fucking cold! Nuclear winter cold!" He threw his hands around until the plastic tray of food finally flung off, carrying bits of flesh, hitting the wall and shattering into pieces. Mongrel stopped screaming and looked at his hands. The tips were a raw pink and the skin was gone. He wasn't bleeding; his fingers were frozen.

"It's a micro-chiller, not a microwave."

They both looked at the doorway, where stood the King, and screamed again.

"Zombie!" Mongrel shouted, grabbing a handful of spoons out of the utensil drawer he'd left open earlier and throwing them at the mad scientist, and then cursing from the pain this caused in his fingers.

"Hey, stop!" the King cried, ducking. "I'm not a zombie!"

"What are you then?" DERFtron asked.

"I'm a Frank! What are you?"

Mongrel and DERFtron looked at each other. Was this another personality or a trick? "I'm Mongrel, and this is Derf," Mongrel answered, wary of this new development.

"Derf?" Frank looked confused. "Oh right, he made two of you. I thought you were the other one," he thumbed behind him, "the shabby one. I didn't think he could move."

"That moron?" This upset DERFtron. "You thought I was that hunk of junk?"

"Yep," Frank replied, and that was the end of that as far as he was concerned. "So what are you guys doing here? And what's with that?" He gestured to the ensemble Mongrel was barely wearing. "You don't look like one of them. Or talk like them."

Mongrel pulled out a chair and sat down at the table. "Just trying to fit in. And speaking of fitting in, how many personalities does Bosley have fitted into his head?"

Frank And The King

"Four, as far as I know. Himself, me, the King, and the other guy."

"What other guy?"

Frank joined Mongrel at the small table while DERFtron remained where he was. "He's in a coma, so I don't know his name or anything. He's just Coma Guy to me."

"Oh!" DERFtron shouted. "That's when you were brain dead earlier, right?"

Frank shrugged. "Probably."

"We thought you were dead."

"So let me get this straight," Mongrel said, "the King is Bosley's arch nemesis, and he's all in his head?"

Frank shrugged. "Pretty much."

"Huh. Some people have imaginary friends – he has imaginary enemies."

"Hold on a second; we're not made up. Bosley isn't schizophrenic. We're all real people."

"What do you mean?"

"Okay, you know how some people lose their minds? Bosley figured out a way to find them."

"I thought that was just a figure of speech," Mongrel said.

"Apparently not."

"So you're all real people trapped inside one body, and your own real bodies are out there somewhere?"

"I hope so," Frank said. "I hope I have a body waiting for me."

"Do you happen to know where you left yours?" DERFtron asked. "I need a replacement."

"Sorry dude, no can do. But if I did know I wouldn't tell you – it's *mine*. I'm sure you can find your own."

"I'm trying to."

This was all too weird for Mongrel. It was the kind of nutty adventure you'd see in a movie or read in a book. He glared at you, the reader momentarily before asking Frank, "How do you know all this and they don't?"

"I just pay attention. As smart as those two are, they're idiots. The first thing a truly smart person realizes is that he doesn't know everything; but *they* think they got it all figured out. Bosley thinks its narcolepsy and the King thinks it's that memory syndrome. And since they think they know what the problem is, it never crosses their minds that there could be another explanation."

"So why don't you tell them?" Mongrel asked. "Leave a note or something?"

This is where Frank would have done a spit-take if he'd had anything been in his mouth. "Are you kidding me? Coming between a mad scientist and a raving psychopath? One is try to teach rocks[*] the alphabet and the other does human experiments for fun! No thank you. I'm staying out of it. Quite frankly I'm already in the line of fire and they don't even know I exist."

"I can see his point," DERFtron said.

"But if they knew what was really going on they might stop fighting and get everything sorted out. You might get your body back."

"If I tell them everything they'll only try to kill each other – and me in the process. And honestly I've given up on ever getting my body back. By now some high school kids have dissected the hell out of it, or some drunken hobos have fornicated with it. Not sure I'd want to go back to *that*."

"So there aren't any bodies laying around this dump at all?" DERFtron asked forlornly.

Frank looked at DERFtron. "I didn't say that." He got up without saying another word and left the kitchen. They followed him down the hall to a locked door. He fished around in his pocket and produced a key ring with a dozen keys on it. After a few minutes of trying a couple he finally found the right key and unlocked the door. He pulled it open and gestured for them to walk inside.

"You go first," Mongrel said, recalling the day's events and withholding his trust. For all he knew he was still dealing with the King and this was a clever trap. But Frank complied and walked inside.

A burst of cold, steamy air erupted in his wake, and Mongrel understood it was a walk-in freezer. Holding a body in

---

[*] Bosley firmly believed that limestone is the most intelligent of all rocks, and that rocks were once sentient and the dominant life forms on Earth. Perhaps one day their kind shall return in all their glory.

there would certainly make sense. He and DERFtron followed Frank in, curious and intrigued. The room wasn't large, but the fog of frost limited visibility, giving the impression that the walls could have been further away. Metal racks lined the walls, stocked with boxes and bins of all shapes and sizes. A few canisters of various gasses occupied one corner; large brown sacks of who knows what were in another. Slabs of beef hung from the ceiling.

"Why does Bosley keep his freezer locked?" DERFtron asked.

Frank closed the door behind them and said, "It's locked in case one of the bodies comes back to life as a zombie."

Mongrel looked at Frank and said, very seriously, "You can't come back to life as a zombie. Zombies aren't alive. And why did you close the door? You didn't just lock us in here did you?"

"Don't worry, we're not locked in. But we gotta keep the cold in or it wastes too much power. This whole place runs on solar energy."

"All right." Mongrel looked around. "Where are all the bodies?"

"There's only one body in here, and he's an ugly bastard."

"He?" DERFtron asked. "Good. At least it's a guy."

"What? You don't want your own boobs to play with?" Mongrel chuckled as he searched through the fog. Finally he saw a small crumpled body laying in the corner amongst the pile of sacks. He moved closer to see the face, which was encrusted with a layer of ice. Then Mongrel's mouth flopped open in horror.

It was Captain Pete.

"I guess having boobs would be...interesting," DERFtron said, having carefully thought the matter through. "You know, if I had to look on the bright side."

"You can't have this body," Mongrel said, rubbing his hands together for warmth but coming across like he was scheming.

"Why not?"

"Because it would complicate my life in ways you can't imagine."

"With all your breathing fogging up the air I can't see anything." DERFtron joined Mongrel in the corner.

Random Tangent

"You used to be among the breathing, so quit your bitching."

"And with any luck, and this dude's body, I'll be breathing again in no time." DERFtron finally got close enough to get a good look at the body in question and his heart sank, or whatever counterpart a heart would have in his chassis. "Whoa, he *is* ugly. And short. And he's got no legs? How am I supposed to walk in this thing?"

"I don't know," Frank replied. "But this guy did. Probably just takes some practice."

"I'm not sure I want this body."

"You're right. You don't want this body, trust me," Mongrel said in his most assuring tone, hoping his friend would listen.

"I don't see what the problem is," Frank said. "You're not gonna get your own body back, so whatever you get will take some getting used to. This one will just take a little more adjusting."

"Yeah..." DERFtron said, beginning to relent.

"But Derf you can do better," Mongrel pleaded. "Wait for something better to come along."

DERFtron glanced up and down the body of the dead Captain Pete. "Maybe I can look at this as a starter body. A fixer-upper. When I outgrow it, which shouldn't take long given its size, then I can move on to something better."

Mongrel simply could not allow this. "I can't allow this! I know this guy, and his body sucks. It's unreliable. Prone to breaking down. Seizures, tumours, anal leakage, you name it. Can't even stay alive for a whole story. Derf, you really need to consider all your options."

"What options?" Frank asked. "He can't just go to the store and pick out another body. It's not like he has any choice; it's this guy or be a robot."

"He has an extremely tiny penis!" Mongrel shouted.

They both looked at him funny, and Frank asked, "You've seen this guy naked?"

"I...uh..." Mongrel bit his lip, "...I've heard, like, rumours and stuff."

"Maybe I do have other options, DERFtron said, more to himself. "What if I could just go out and bag my own body? I could

338

Frank And The King

wander back to the Mojo tribe after dark..." he trailed off, plotting homicide.

"That's the spirit!" Mongrel shouted, relieved. One thing he did not need in his life was another Captain Pete – seeing as how he'd managed to convince the other one to become homicidal. Nothing good could come of it. He briskly rubbed himself, trying to get the blood flowing better, and looked down at the body of the dead captain, unable to comprehend the horror of a friend being trapped inside it. If DERFtron chose that body, would it change anything? Would there be two Captain Petes? Would he be able to tell them apart? He didn't know, and didn't want to know. He needed to stop something like this from ever happening. He had the sudden urge to grab a hammer and smash Captain Pete into hundreds of pieces. But not just to keep DERFtron from using it; he couldn't explain why but looking down at his former friend, this *Petecicle*, made him angry, and he wanted to hit him, to maim and beat him. To destroy his body as he did their friendship long ago.

"No I don't," Mongrel said, but deep down he wanted to hurt the captain. As much harm as he had inadvertently caused the old pirate, he himself was also in pain. Not only had he killed Captain Pete repeatedly, but he had suffered mental trauma with each inflicted death. The psychological scarring cut him to the bone, and he couldn't help but feel bitter and resentful.

"I don't feel that way," Mongrel lied. "You caused all this to happen to Captain Pete, not me."

"Dude, let it go," DERFtron wisely interjected.

"As long as you let go of this body."

"Fine, fine. It's ugly anyway. Let's get out of here; I think my joints are rusting."

Frank shrugged and grabbed a frozen pizza. "You guys were hungry, right? We actually *do* have a microwave." He was about to try the door but noticed there was no handle.

"What's wrong?" Mongrel asked. "Open the door. It's freezing in here. You see what I'm wearing, right?"

"Uh, the handle..." Frank said quietly, contemplatively.

"Just use your key."

"The key only works from the outside."

Random Tangent

"So...?" Mongrel was trying to be optimistic. "You said we weren't locked in, right?"

"We're locked in," Frank muttered.

"Ah. I see." Mongrel began pacing. "And what was it I said earlier about being locked in here?"

Frank sighed. "Yeah, yeah, spare me the lecture."

"Hey, you have no idea what I've been through today – I've almost been killed twice! And now I'm trapped in here wearing next to nothing. I'll freeze to death in five minutes!"

"I don't know what happened. The handle has always been there."

"Well do you know how to fix it?"

"No." Frank thought for a minute. "How did you fix yours? I mean, avoid being killed?"

Mongrel stopped pacing. "Mon helped the first time."

"What's a mon?"

"Mon," said the mon, walking in from the fog.

"Mon!" Mongrel cried, "Where have you been?"

This of course was a silly question. Where *hadn't* the mon been? It had wandered the jungle and ate exotic fruits and animals; it roamed the prairies and ate wild alpacas whole; it swam in the river and ate strange fish; it climbed the tallest mountains but didn't stay because there wasn't much to eat. It travelled to other planets and other dimensions, met interesting life forms and consumed them. It traversed into the light, and out the other side; it strolled into hell and dined with demons. It visited the afterlife, the before life, and everything in between. But it always came back to the now, when it was needed. Besides, the now was always the most interesting place to be.

"Mon," the mon replied, meaning, 'So what do you need now?'

"What do I want?" Mongrel asked, "Hmm...tough question. Peace on Earth, a cure for cancer, a bajillion dollars, a way out of here..."

"An awesome new body," DERFtron added

Frank watched them all and asked, "Is he like Santa Claus?"

"Mon," the mon sighed, and regurgitated the fire hall kitchen.

Frank And The King

They all looked around; Mongrel with relief, Frank with confusion, DERFtron with apathy. Frank decided to ignore everything that had just happened, choosing instead to believe he wasn't actually conscious right now, that this was a dream, or a trick of the mind or something. He silently went to the corner of the room and unboxed the pizza. A microwave had been mounted to the wall directly above the oven, but Frank ignored it and placed the pizza in the oven and turned on the heat.

"I thought you were going to microwave that?" Mongrel asked.

"You ever have microwaved pizza? It's shit."

"So what is this micro-chiller?" DERFtron asked.

"It's kinda like the opposite of a microwave. It uses vacuum energy or something to suck the heat out of whatever you put in it. Make a warm can of pop ice cold in about half a minute."

Ignoring their conversation, Mongrel was about to pat his mon on its head, but there was a hat in the way. "What's with the hat?"

The mon had pilfered the hat earlier in the Mojo village and hat since been wearing it around. No one else had seemed to notice it. "Mon," it said, meaning, 'I happen to like it, thank you very much. Helps me blend in with the natives – something you might want to *stop* doing. Seriously. Ick.'

"Yeah about the natives; thanks Mon. That's twice today you've saved my life. I hope I can return the favour some day. Not that I ever want to see your life in danger."

"Mon, said the mon, which meant, 'No biggie.'

All conversations were suddenly halted when a beeping sound intruded upon them. Mongrel looked at the microwave, thinking that the pizza was done awfully quick, even though he'd seen it go in the oven.

"That's me," Frank said, taking a seat at the table. "Bosley programmed the watch to go off whenever a mind shift was about to happen. Something to do with heart rates or body temperatures or something. So brace yourselves..." He put his arm on the table and rested his head on it as if he was about to have a nap.

"Who's gonna be next?" Mongrel asked.

"Don't know."

Random Tangent

DERFtron tried and failed to give a salute. "Well it was nice getting to know you. Thanks for explaining all this crap to us."

"No probl-" Frank's body went limp, the arm not being used as a headrest fell off the table and slumped to his side.

Mongrel took a deep breath and grabbed one of the dirty knives out the sink, trying to hide the disgusted look on his face. DERFtron backed away from the table a few feet. The room was quiet, except for the clock ticking in the background, which they could now hear for the first time since all conversations and attempted homicide had been halted. They looked at each other as the minutes passed. Neither wanted to leave the body alone since it would give whoever woke up the opportunity for a surprise attack.

Soon the body began to shiver and shake, much like it had earlier. The seizure took over the body for a few seconds, then quickly subsided. Soon the eyelids fluttered, and Mongrel's grip on his knife tightened. Suddenly the body jolted upright, and he looked at his watch. He then surveyed his surroundings, his eyes eventually finding the two guests. After darting back and forth between them he asked, "How long was I out for?"

Mongrel glanced quickly at DERFtron before asking the man, "Who are we talking to?"

"Me, of course." The man sounded confused. When his answer proved insufficient, and after he noticed the large knife in Mongrel's hand, he said, "Bosley. Don't you remember?"

Breathing a sigh of relief, Mongrel put the knife back in the sink. DERFtron threw his arm up as if expecting a hug, or at least half of one; his other arm still lay on the floor in the other room. "Bosley you mad bastard! Of course we remember you!"

"What's with the knife?"

"Uh..." DERFtron began, then looked to Mongrel to finish.

Mongrel wasn't sure what to say, or if he should say anything at all. Perhaps Frank had made the right choice in not getting involved. Who was Mongrel to break the news, to play therapist? And what would the repercussions be? Both Bosley and the King deserved to know the truth, but the truth often hurt – in this case perhaps fatally so. Although lying rarely did any good either.

Frank And The King

Another thought then occurred to Mongrel: if the King could actually be removed from Bosley's head it would be possible to kill him, or for him to kill Bosley. On the other hand, if both minds remained in the same body, sharing it, then realistically neither of them could be killed. That is, unless one of them was suicidal. If things stayed the way they were both of them would remain safe. As crazy as the situation was, it was the sanest choice. He resolved to keep the situation a secret.

Now...why did he have the knife?

"Was I sleepwalking?" Bosley asked. "Did I give you guys any trouble?"

"Yes!" Mongrel pointed at Bosley. "That is exactly why I had the knife."

"Self defence," DERFtron chimed in. "You're anything but peaceful when you're resting."

Mongrel held up his hands to show Bosley his fingertips. The extreme cold had cauterized his wounds but they were beginning to thaw and become painful.

"Wow! That looks bad. I did that?"

"Actually it was that thing," Mongrel pointed at the micro-chiller."

"Oh. Well look guys I'm really sorry. Maybe I *should* look into putting up cameras and see what I do when I'm sleeping. Maybe I can figure out what to do about it."

"Not sure that's a good idea," Mongrel said, hoping no one would ask him why not.

"That's a great idea!" DERFtron disagreed. "You're a madman when you don't get enough sleep. We got into a big fight, and you chased us around and tried to kill us. Locked us in the freezer."

"Locked you in the freezer?" Bosley asked, ignoring everything else. He then began to laugh. "I planned that little trap for the King! That asswipe somehow gets in here, trying to steal my research. Figured I'd catch him read-handed – but I got you instead. I got another trap in the bathroom that'll rip off his beard if he flushes the toilet! He loves that beard let me tell you."

Random Tangent

"I'm not sure that's gonna work," Mongrel said, and cursed himself for nearly giving away too much information. He was just asking to be asked about things he didn't want to be asked about.

"Oh I already know it works. It worked on me!" Bosley laughed some more. "I used the bathroom this morning – forgot all about the trap – and in the blink of an eye, *whoosh!* it was all gone! Hurt like hell too."

"So that's how that happened," DERFtron marvelled.

Bosley was then silent for a moment, glancing at his guests with a confused look in his eyes. "Wait a sec, how did you guys get out of the freezer?"

"Mon," said the mon, asking, 'What's with everyone ignoring me today? Am I invisible? Is it the hat?'

Bosley got up from the table to get a closer look at the mon. "What is this thing?"

"It's a mon. And I wouldn't get too close, it hasn't eaten in at least a few minutes."

Most people thankfully didn't ask many questions about the mon, but if Bosley began to inquire, Mongrel wasn't sure he could provide any useful answers. He had no idea how they were sharing the same reality with mons. A reasonable explanation for their existence didn't exist.

"Is it carnivorous?" Bosley asked, not bothering to keep his distance.

"It's *everything-vorous*."

"...Fascinating. I've never seen anything like it. Where did you find it?"

"Mon!" quipped the mon, meaning, '*find* me? I found *him*!'

"I hate to interrupt this touching moment," DERFtron interrupted, not really hating it at all, "but what would *really* be fascinating is if the mon has any spare bodies in there."

"Oh yeah, I forgot all about that." Mongrel knelt down in front of the mon. "Well Mon? Do you have anything Derf can use?"

"Mon," said the mon, which meant, 'I have a rule about eating dead things: don't[*].

"Look's like you're out of luck Derf."

---

[*] The mon had a similar rule about not eating galaxies, but didn't strictly adhere to either.

Frank And The King

"Mon," corrected the mon, meaning, 'I didn't say I couldn't help him out, just that he won't want what I have to offer.'

It seemed like only yesterday that the mon had met its pet human, and since mons live outside the flow of time, it certainly could have been just yesterday for the mon. Before that fateful day the mon had been wild and carefree, eating whatever it felt like, disrupting the space-time continuum as it saw fit. Then the mon met Mongrel, and...well, nothing had changed; it's still wild, crazy, and inexplicably existent. But now it had to think of more than just itself, it had a responsibility to leave a better reality for its human.

That day it also ate the dead body of Captain Pete, and if the mon were to regurgitate it now, while a perfectly viable Captain Pete was waiting in the walk-in freezer, then not only would it be redundant and not at all helpful to DERFtron, but it could shatter the matrix of this reality, or at the very least put a huge dent in it.

"Looks like it's up to you then," DERFtron said to Bosley. "You need to find me a body and put me in it."

Bosley was obviously more interested in learning about the mon than dealing with DERFtron at the moment and said dismissively, "I got one in the freezer."

"No, no, that won't do. I want a *good* one."

This time Bosley looked directly at DERFtron. "What's wrong with the one in the freezer?"

"Gee, well lets see, it's short, has wooden legs, and it's freaking *ugly*. And according to this guy," he pointed to Mongrel, "it has a tiny penis. He also doesn't want me to have it for some reason."

"Why is that?" Bosley asked.

"I just...think Derf could do better," Mongrel answered, wary of being too honest. "Where, if you don't mind me asking, did you get it?"

"Actually it arrived in the mail earlier this morning, already dead."

"Figures..." Mongrel muttered.

"I'm not sure if it was sent to me dead or if that happened on the way – the postal system in this country leaves a lot to be desired – but it's a tremendous shame, since I could've used the extra mind. You never know when you may need it."

Random Tangent

"I think you have more than enough."

"But the body at least is sure to come in handy," Bosley continued. "I've had a few ideas I've long wanted to experiment with." He eyed Mongrel for a minute. "Tell me, how do you feel about being turned inside out?"

Mongrel seemed to think about this. "Well like I always say whenever someone asks me that: I think it's time for me to leave."

"Oh." Bosley sounded genuinely disappointed. "I see. Could your mon stay? I'd like to do some experiments with it too."

"That's really up to Mon to decide."

"Mon," said the mon, meaning that it wanted to stick around to see how this inside-out experiment went.

"He's staying." Mongrel turned to DERFtron. "I assume you're staying too?"

"I ain't leaving until I get a new body."

Mongrel nodded. "That's what I thought. Guess I'm on my own."

They all made their way to the front door, where Bosley busied himself with unlocking it. Then they all stepped outside into the chill evening air and watched the sun begin to dip below the horizon. All in all, especially considering he was still alive, Mongrel felt that maybe the day hadn't been so bad after all.

He patted his mon on its head, first removing the hat. "Be good. Don't eat anything dangerous."

"Mon," agreed the mon.

He shook DERFtron's mechanical hand and said, "I hope the next time we meet I'll be shaking a real hand."

"Me too," DERFtron said. "And thanks for getting me back here. We're even now."

He looked at Bosley, who said, "I don't believe you ever told me your name."

"It's Mongrel..." the camera then pulls in for a close up as he put on some sunglasses. "...Mongrel Stevens."

The E-

Frank And The King

"Hold on! I gotta walk home by myself?" Mongrel asked. "That's not how this goes. And besides, I'm in freaking Bolivia – Dunttstown is, like, a thousand miles away." Mongrel knew after saying this that he'd better start walking. Grumbling furiously to himself, he tossed his sunglasses away and began his long journey.

The setting sun warmed his back as he made his way through the bush, not knowing exactly which direction to go but hoping everything would work out by the time he started the next story. The trees and rocks and wildlife he passed did nothing to temper his mood; if anything they angered him more. The trees were crooked, the rocks were unpleasant colours, and the wildlife smelled funny. But maybe it was him. It had begun as a bad day and it seemed it would end that way because he knew, somehow, that he wasn't going to make it home alive.

"What?"

Nothing.

The End

Mongrel did actually make it home alive, and dearly hoped that his near-death experiences were over for a little while. We'll see. DERFtron volunteered for the inside-out experiment, since it would end up with him in a different body, but it was not the body he wanted. Beggars can't be choosers. The mon really liked its hat, and decided to make it a regular thing. And after dining in the wilderness the entire species of Bolivian Chinchilla Rat was now extinct, and all Venezuelan red howler monkeys were relocated to the country of their namesake. Assface went home and punished himself (with a spanking, naturally), and tried his hardest to learn all he could about TV, but with the lack of modern technology he learned absolutely nothing. He took this hard and, coupled with Mongrel's rejection, he felt unloved and eventually began to whore himself out to anyone in the tribe. This led to him becoming a male stripper, which made him very popular, and he became more than the Chief's right hand man; he became his queen. The King began cultivating a new beard, twice as epic as the one before, and three

Random Tangent

times as deadly. He also returned to the Star Trek convention the next year and succeeded in upping his kill count. He decided to go each year from then on, improving on his performance until the day he could kill every last one of them, or at least until no one wore a red shirt anymore out of fear of dying, which was the natural order of things as far as he was concerned. Frank got himself a slew of girlfriends after signing up for an online dating service. Bosley went on to discover how to make hockey pucks edible and prove that the night is not always darkest before dawn. He also devised a clever trap for the King to capture him once and for all, but ended up getting caught in it himself, and had to wait for his once-a-week mail-order maid to free him. And since you probably forgot all about it, like everyone else, the pizza was left cooking in the oven for hours and burned to a crisp, which is ironic since it happened in a fire station.

Good For Business

Good For Business

Mongrel stood at the end of his driveway in the blistering heat, waiting for the chauffeur to hurry up and come around to open the limo door for him. He tapped his foot impatiently and crossed his arms. He sighed loudly and looked at his watch, then realized that he didn't have one, and *why* he still didn't have one[*].

The chauffeur finally rushed around the rear of the shiny black limousine, huffing and panting. The vehicle wasn't really that long, suggesting that the little man was severely out of shape. Of course, the extreme heat that had been penetrating the area for the past week could also be a factor. "Sorry sir," he coughed out, opening the rear door and saluting.

He was a little man, barely passing the four foot mark, and with his strict adherence to military gestures, conjured images of Napoleon Bonaparte. He also had a tiny moustache on his face

---

[*]Seriously? You checked down here for a recap? Don't be lazy – read *The Watch*.

which was all too reminiscent of Adolf Hitler's. So here was this man, stuck halfway between the heads of world domination, and he was making his living as a taxi driver. A prestigious taxi driver no doubt, but still. He wore a suit that looked too small for him, and Mongrel wondered how the tiny hat on his head hadn't been whisked away by a gust of wind. His small offering of apology was wasted on Mongrel, who was busy being a diva.

Ignoring the man completely, not even making eye contact, Mongrel gingerly inserted himself into the limousine. He briefly entertained the thought of sneering at the man as he closed the door, but decided against it; he wanted to be seen as above everyone else, but not beyond compassion. He sank back into the plush leather seats, soaked in the glorious A/C, and then reached into the mini fridge and pulled out a bottle of champagne.

A look of utter disapproval flashed across his face as he realized he'd have to open it himself.

He waited an eternally long thirteen seconds for the chauffeur to finally, breathlessly climb back behind the wheel – time that could have been spent drinking this lovely alcoholic beverage – and therefore had no difficulty finding his most disgruntled voice. "Excuse me," he said, lowering the glass that separated the rear of the car from the driver's compartment. The driver turned to look at him. "Am I supposed to poor my own drink?"

This of course was a rhetorical question and the driver, bless his heart, knew better than to answer it. He sucked in a deep breath and opened the car door again, stepping out into the ungodly heat to run back around the car. Mongrel dearly hoped there was no A/C at the front of the car; the man should have to suffer for his atrocities.

Being rich was such fun!

"I can get that for you," Elvis said, snatching the champagne bottle, as well as the illusion of being rich, from Mongrel before he could protest. Pretending to be rich, he surmised, was not as much fun as actually being rich.

"Aw man, he was supposed to do that," Mongrel whined as Elvis uncorked the bottle. "Isn't that what he's paid for?"

"Relax," Elvis said, handing Mongrel a glass. "Just enjoy the ride."

Good For Business

The door then opened and the man stood there, sweat dripping down his face. Mongrel grabbed the bottle from Elvis and passed it to the chauffeur, who poured Mongrel his drink.

"Be nice to Mickey," Elvis said, "he's a hard worker."

Mongrel pursed his lips decisively and finally looked the chauffeur in the eye with no small amount of disdain. "Mickey, are you thirsty?"

Mickey looked down at the bottle in his hands and licked his parched lips. "Indeed I am, sir."

After a moment to consider this, Mongrel said, "Thank you, Mickey. That will be all." He grabbed the bottle back and closed the car door, shutting Mickey out in the heat. He then cursed himself for closing his own door; that was Mickey's job. He was being too nice to the man.

"That wasn't very nice," Elvis chided.

"Well this is alcohol isn't it?" Mongrel asked, handing the bottle to his friend. "He shouldn't be drinking and driving. It's the law."

Elvis knew Mongrel had a valid point and was going to counter it by saying that he was Elvis and his chauffeur could get away with it, but decided to let the matter drop.

"I could really get used to this kind of lifestyle," Mongrel said, taking a noisy sip from the glass. Then a disgusted look ran amuck on his face as he remembered he didn't like champagne. He lowered the window and chucked it out, glass and all.

After grabbing the bottle from Mongrel and gulping down a large dose of the liquor, Elvis belched loudly and said, "This is the fun part. Wait till you get to the mobbing and the running and the occasional surgery to put your arm back on."

"I thought your arm was a machine, or robotic or whatever."

"Animatronic," Elvis corrected, "and yes, *one* of them is."

"So you're like the Terminator. Can you punch through walls and stuff?"

"Probably," Elvis chuckled. "But honestly, I wouldn't wish this life on anyone. Almost wish I wasn't blessed with the gifts of the King."

The driver's door of the limo opened and Mickey slid in. He tried to take a moment to settle himself, to relax in the cool air of the car, but the glass divider was still down and Mongrel was going to make use of it.

"Ahem!"

Mickey's head drooped before turning around to face Mongrel.

"There's broken glass outside my door. I need you to clean it up."

A horrified expression momentarily flickered across the chauffeur's face, as if stepping foot outside could possibly kill him. He briefly debated ignoring the request; after all, what went on outside the vehicle was outside the scope of his job and not his concern. And it was *so* hot out there.

"*Now*, Mickey," Mongrel said.

Taking a deep breath as if he were about to dive into a pool – in this case more like a hot tub – Mickey left the car once more. And no sooner had he closed his door, Mongrel's suddenly jerked opened.

Freddy Farcus climbed across Mongrel and helped himself to a seat facing him. "What a terrifyingly terrific motor-carriage!"

The limousine wasn't for Mongrel, as I'm sure you've already guessed; it was for Elvis. The last time the artist had been in town he'd stayed at Mongrel's little shack on the prairie, and was appalled by it. The smell took some getting used to, the room service was atrocious, the water in the toilet occasionally came up instead of going down, and there were blood stains all over the kitchen floor. He swore he would never come back, but in reality Mongrel's home was the only place he knew he would survive the night. There was no hotel in the world, as far as he was concerned, that could keep out the truly dedicated fan. The fan that would cut off locks of his hair to sell on eBay. The fan that would keep his excrement in a jar on her nightstand to be the last thing she saw at night and the first thing in the morning. The fan that wanted to hang his head on the wall next to what she swore was the head of the *real* Elvis. He'd been woken up countless times from camera flashes to lewd sexual acts being done to him. He once woke up in a bathtub which stitches down the side of his stomach, missing some internal organ – he never went to a hospital to find out; he didn't want to know. The last time he was in town he'd awoken to find a large pig in his bed, and although it wasn't dead, and in fact seemed quite content, Elvis couldn't be absolutely sure he hadn't fornicated with it. That was the last straw.

So he returned to Mongrel's home. It wasn't so bad; since his last visit the plumbing had been fixed, the kitchen floor blood stains had faded, and he'd grown used to the smell. Even the room service had improved. The chambermaid, Mr. Farcus, had gotten more used to the eccentricities of the modern age – such providing and using toilet paper – and even wore a French maid's outfit, although that gave Elvis funny feelings inside.

Freddy Farcus, the man from yesteryear, had been staying with Mongrel for the passed few months, acting primarily as a butler. He had been born some time in the 1800s and spent most of the intervening time inside the Mon, and was now trying to learn how to cope in what he felt was the future. Mongrel had tried to educate the lad on the current ways of the world, but eventually gave up, instead plopping him down in front of the television, hoping it would do most of the work for him.

"I cannot wait to see which one you choose for purchase!" Freddy continued, pressing all the buttons he could find next to his seat to see what they did.

"Yeah," Elvis agreed. "I'm sure glad you decided to take my advice and get your own car. Don't get me wrong I don't mind giving you a ride into town when I'm here, but I'm just not here all the time."

"I know," Mongrel said. He'd recently decided to move into his mother's old ranch permanently, and realized that he'd need his own transportation from then on. Living in Dunttstown meant he didn't need a car, since everything was handy, and it had its own bus service – although it was a service that made Mongrel want to give up on life. Honestly, he'd rather be under the bus than inside it. This factored into his decision not to take the route of old man Cleopard in getting the bus to wander out of its way to pick him up. He also didn't think he could flog a goat, and had no idea how to communicate with the dead.

In the end, moving into the old homestead meant buying a car of his own, since it was practically in the middle of nowhere. So he accepted Elvis' offer of a lift into town to purchase one, as well as run a few other errands. Freddy Farcus invited himself along, insisting that he'd be of use; the twenty-plus hours or so of television he exposed himself to on a daily basis meant he'd see countless car commercials, and he now considered himself an expert on the subject.

"It's taken me a while to come to terms with it," Mongrel said. "But Mom's gone and she left me the house, so I'm gonna take it." He nodded, looking back and forth between the two men. "I still need tell my landlord I'm giving up the apartment."

"Do you plan to take up farming?" Freddy asked him excitedly. "That would be terrifyingly terrific! I could certainly help you out with that." Of all the things Freddy now considered himself an expert on, farming was one thing he actually did know quite a lot about. "Back in my day everyone helped with farming. Why, if you couldn't tell a rock from a turnip then you were probably brain dead, in which case you were put into the compost. And even then you were still helping."

The driver's door opened and Mickey entered the car, hoping it was the final time. He sat and breathed heavily for a minute before turning around to face everyone. Painted on his face was a look of fear, which was smeared badly from the profuse sweating. "W-will there be anything else, gentlemen?"

Thinking long and hard, but not finding any other reason to send the driver back outside, Mongrel grumbled and shook his head. "No Mickey, you've wasted enough of our time with your shenanigans. We're already going to be late because of you, so let's get a move on." He then pushed a button, raising the privacy class, too disgusted with Mickey to look at him. Mickey didn't care; he grinned broadly and started the car, and they were on their way to Dunttstown.

"What are we going to be late for?" Freddy asked.

"I don't know about this farming thing," Elvis said to Mongrel. "I had a cousin who worked on a farm once, and the manure fumes got to his head. He started domesticating sticks of butter, and trying to eat onions with his bum hole. I know that's probably a better way to eat them – they taste terrible, but mama says they're good for you – so maybe he was on to something there. Now I'm not into any of that homo-prostate voodoo stuff, but I

Good For Business

guess if given a choice to eat onions the regular way or with my butt, I'd choose my butt. Especially sinc-"

"Okay, El, don't worry. I don't know if I can farm anyway. I don't even know what do with manure, let alone how to grow it." Mongrel stared out the window as the acres of countryside went by. "But I don't want to be lazy, you know. I gotta do something with all that land."

By now Elvis was used to being cut off by Mongrel. He had a tendency to ramble on and on, and Mongrel always knew when to reel him in. He waited for a minute before adding, "I'd also advise against growing corn; aliens like corn fields for some reason." He shuddered at the thought of aliens; he had a phobia.

"Let's grow corn!" Freddy said excitedly.

Mongrel and Elvis looked at Freddy quixotically, then went back to ignoring him.

The limousine pulled up in front of Wan's One-Stop Buy-Or-Swap Car Shop, one of only two used car dealerships in Dunttstown. The other car lot at the other end of town, and also at the other end of the quality spectrum, was Downtown Pete's Quality cars. It was new in town but already had a reputation for selling junk vehicles. If that wasn't enough reason to avoid it, Mongrel also chose not to go there because it was apparently operated by someone named Pete, and Mongrel hoped to live the rest of his hopefully long life avoiding the hopelessly doomed Captain Pete, and thusly chose to avoid the dealership based on its name alone.

"That's a bit of a mouthful," Elvis said as he exited the vehicle and read the name on the side of the building.

"It used to be Wan's Tip-Top One-Stop Buy-Or-Swap Mom and Pop Car Shop," Mongrel said, almost stepping foot outside the car before realizing to his horror that Mickey hadn't opened the door. He threw himself back inside as if he were dodging gunfire.

After a moment, Mickey huffed and puffed into view. He gently closed the door and then immediately opened it again, saluting. Mongrel impatiently stepped out into the scorching air, this time granting the chauffeur what he thought was an undeserved pleasure of eye contact.

"Mickey, I hate you like you were my own son." Mongrel

Random Tangent

spit contemptuously on the ground, as if to rid himself of the foul taste of the chauffeur's name, and briskly walked over to the nearest car and began inspecting it.

Elvis exited the vehicle next, passing Mickey a twenty-dollar bill, for which he was graciously thanked. Freddy Farcus followed, tipping his yoop[*] to the man before joining the others.

"So what are you looking for?" Elvis asked.

"I don't really know," Mongrel replied, shrugging. "Something with four tires."

"Well that narrows it down."

"How about this one?" Freddy was standing next to a silver sport utility vehicle. "It's a 2010 Santa Fe *Limited*." He beamed as he spoke the last word. "It has the 3.5L V6 engine, which is good for 276 horsepower and 248 lb/ft of torque. It's all-wheel drive and comes standard with Bluetooth, heated leather seats, navigation system, powe-"

"You watch too much TV!" Mongrel yelled at him, wondering why he'd want heated leather seats in this ungodly heat. Freddy quieted himself and went to wander around the car lot.

"So just four wheels?" Elvis prompted Mongrel.

"Yeah," Mongrel shrugged. "And windows. And doors. Preferably with an engine."

"Well you've certainly come to the right place!" hailed an incoming voice.

They turned to see an Asian man heading in their direction. "Pardon me, I couldn't help eavesdropping. Here at Wan's One-Stop Buy-Or-Swap Car Shop we have everything you could ask for in a new or used, car or truck. You want doors? You got 'em! Windows? More than you could shake a stick at! Four tires? Hell, we'll give you five! You want an engine? Just pick a car – it probably has an engine in it! You can't go wrong at Wan's Tip-Top One-Stop Buy-Or-Swap Mom and Pop Car Shop! I'm Wan." The man stuck out his hand for them to shake and his teeth in a smile for them to admire.

"This guy sounds like a walking car commercial," Elvis said.

Mongrel gingerly shook the man's hand. "I know you; the

---

[*] A yoop is a hat. That's it. Nothing special about it. Carry on.

disoriented Oriental. Didn't you used to run the Brat's R Us adoption agency?"

Wan's smile faded. "Oh, it's you again."

"It's me again."

"I didn't run that place but I worked there – until it collapsed, thanks to you."

"Me? You're blaming me for that? How is that my fault?"

"I don't know!" Wan shouted. "But nothing's ever collapsed until you showed up."

"Maybe it was just a coincidence. Ever think of that? I don't cause death and destruction everywhere I go you know." Mongrel thought for minute about Captain Pete. "Well not destruction at least."

Wan grumbled under his breath. He couldn't prove the collapse wasn't an accident and it had been a while since he'd last sold a vehicle, so he was desperate for business.

Ever since the dealership at the other end of town opened its doors the day before, he couldn't keep his profit margins up. No matter what he did he couldn't lure in any customers. He lowered his prices, increased incentives, offered rebates, and even promised free pony rides with every monthly car payment, but nothing worked. How did the other dealership do it? How did it hijack all his customers in just one day? He'd daydreamed about creative ways to take back his market share; hiring goons to destroy the merchandise, setting fire to their building, prank phone calls in the middle of the night. Oh he'd spent hours thinking up the most hilarious prank calls. He fancied himself above that kind of scheming but if he couldn't find a way to turn things around he'd be out of business by the end of the month. He was getting desperate. He needed this sale.

"Fine," he said at last. "How can I help you?"

Mongrel took a good long look around the lot before asking, "Have you got any cars for sale?"

It took all Wan's strength not to throttle Mongrel. He'd lost many customers, and occasionally friends, due to his penchant for throttling when he was exasperated. But with counselling, medication, and brief period of being possessed by something not of this world, he'd managed to get himself under control. Usually

Random Tangent

this manifested in injuries to himself rather than to others (which was simply good business strategy), and even that had diminished significantly. A few months ago he would have ripped half his hair out; now he sighed inwardly and plucked a single shiny, black hair. He inspected it closely for a minute before putting it in his breast pocket. He'd add it to the jar[*] later.

"But of course!" he said. "I've got lots of cars! Tons of cars! Millions of cars! More cars then you could shake a tree trunk at!"

"Don't you mean a stick?" Elvis asked. "Isn't that how that saying goes?"

"Ordinarily yes." Wan grabbed Mongrel's twig of an arm and held it up. "But you see these big biceps? Shaking a plain old stick would be too easy for this guy. He needs to shake something bigger!" Flatter the customer; that was good business. He was on fire today. He could smell that sale cooking, and it smelled good.

"I've got cars, trucks, vans, SUVs, whatever you want. What colour would you like? Red? Blue?"

"Green?" Mongrel asked.

"What?" The fire began to smoulder.

"Do you have any green cars?"

"Uh…no." The fire died.

"Oh." Mongrel looked around the lot again, and something struck him. "You only have, like…five cars here?"

Wan joined him in looking around. He knew he'd lost the sale, and his heart had sunk so deep into his chest it would take an expedition of a dozen exceptionally experienced explorers days to excavate it. He nodded and said, "Yep."

Then he noticed Elvis. How could he have ignored the man all this time? Not many people walked around wearing white jackets with rhinestones. Or capes. It all seemed oddly familiar to him. "Who are you?" Wan asked.

"I'm Elvis," Elvis said, answering quicker than he thought he should have. Not only was he named Elvis, but being an impersonator, he completely looked the part. He really couldn't be mistaken for anyone else, and the question might have confused some. A lesser Elvis impersonator would have tripped up over the

---

[*] Some people used swear jars; Wan had a hair jar.

question, sputtering, stumbling for words, undignified. Some may even have balked. But not this Elvis. This Elvis was every ounce the man that the King of rock and roll should be. He flattered himself that there was so much Elvis in him that the real Elvis would have been jealous. Might have sued him for copyright infringement. Quite possibly even hire a contract killer to quietly take him out. It helped him sleep at night, thinking he was worthy of being murdered.

Then Wan asked, "Elvis who?"

Now Elvis flat lined. *Elvis who?* He both knew and did not know how to answer the question. Was he asking what his real last name was, or the last name of the person he was impersonating? Would either make a difference? This man couldn't possibly *not* know who the king of rock and roll was. Maybe he was just joking, or if not, then certainly confused. But if he was then so was Elvis. Confused and...he couldn't say. Hurt? Angry? Hungry? Yes, he was definitely hungry. He'd have to get Mickey to stop by a restaurant on their way to the Schevret airport, perhaps the Barf Mart[*] if there was time.

"Are you, like, confused or something, son?" Elvis asked. "Or drunk?"

"No, I'm disoriented."

"Oh," Elvis nodded as if he understood, but if anything he was even more perplexed.

Wan picked up on the caped man's nonexistent grasp on the situation. Having two faces was not the same as having two brains,

---

[*] The Barf Mart, owned and solely operated by Bartholomew Randall, was supposed to have been called the Bart Mart, but a misfortunate typo (later determined to be Bartholomew's fault) occurred during the order process. Bartholomew had spent his last dollar getting his restaurant off the ground but vowed to replace the sign at the earliest, and most profitable, convenience. But then came the accident with the bus, leaving him crippled, and he could no longer afford a staff. With no other way to earn a living Bart, or Barf as the locals call him, operates the entire restaurant himself; cleaning, cooking, waiting tables, etc. As such, smell and atmosphere of the restaurant is unpleasant, the wait times atrocious, and the food is terrible. However, the good citizens of Dunttstown kept dining at the Barf Mart in order to support Bartholomew Randall in his never-ending time of need. Of course, people being lazy and not wanting to cook could also be a motivating factor – as could the mysterious disappearance of the McDonald's months earlier.

Random Tangent

but sometimes he felt an intangible lucidity, an innate ability to see things that others missed. He wasn't smarter than other people, but sometimes he knew more, and he knew he had his brother to thank for this gift.

Over a century and a half ago[*] Wan was born a Siamese twin – although he was the only one. His twin brother never got the opportunity he did, having been mostly absorbed in utero. The technical term for this would be a vestigial twin. The only evidence of this is Wan's two faces; his own face and his brother's on the back of his head. The face is mostly aesthetic, complete with eyes, nostrils and a couple tiny teeth. It never spoke or required sustenance, but Wan had learned that the face scowled and cried actual tears when he tried to let his hair grow long to cover up the face, so as to draw less attention to himself. Dates were hard to come by for a one-man Siamese twin with a vestigial face. It made his life difficult to a certain degree, but there was a bright side; aside from occasionally heightened mental acuity, if he focused hard enough, Wan could use his brother's face briefly, breathing through his nostrils and seeing through his eyes. Unfortunately this trick rarely proved useful, and Wan often dreamed of becoming a spy or double agent, like the theme song from the TV show *Danger Man*, where by these talents would invariably end up saving his life, and of course the lives of beautiful women who wanted to bear his children. Secret *Asian* man indeed.

Wan turned his back on Elvis-no-last-name to show his brother's face, hoping to bring clarity to the 'disoriented' title, but instead bringing turmoil.

"Sweet mother Mary and Josepfh!" Elvis cried, misspelling words in his shock and repulsion. He jumped back a few feet and instinctively crouched in a fighting stance, prepared to do battle with whatever evil was before him. "What the thing is that hell?"

Mickey heard the cries of alarm from Elvis and knew something foul was afoot. It was his job, nay his duty to come to the aid of his master. He cried, "I'm coming sir!" and took off through

---

[*] Chinese people live a long time, don't you know? Asian centurions are all the rage in certain parts of the world. They often take part in the Olympics, play a myriad of roles in television sitcoms, and it's not uncommon for people of oriental descent to have children well into their nineties.

Good For Business

the car lot towards them, rushing at full speed despite the record-breaking temperatures, risking a stroke from the heat by overexerting himself. But a man's life may be on the line, and Mickey knew what he had to do.

A groan escaped Mongrel as he heard the chauffeur coming. The last thing he needed was the little Hitler running in and mucking things up. He had to quickly switch back to his diva persona and scowl menacingly at Mickey as he neared. Then he nonchalantly stuck out his foot, tripping the short, huffing man as his scurried by. Mickey's hands shot out in front of him, but it wasn't enough to break his fall with the decorum his profession required. His nose and chin delicately ground themselves into the pavement. His hands and arms bounced merrily along the scorching asphalt, akin to stones skipping across the water, leaving behind pieces of flesh like a trail of breadcrumbs. His tie was violently freed from the confines of his shirt, and his suit was given a wonderful makeover, now tattered and dishevelled.

Unfortunately, in his usual disappointing way, Mickey's head stopped mere inches away from a grey automobile which Mongrel found painfully ugly. Mongrel sighed wretchedly. The chauffeur deserved to have his ugly head imbedded in the door of the ugly car; they were made for each other. If only Mickey had been running just a little faster. The man was a slacker.

"Are you a elien?" Elvis asked, not noticing Mickey's entrance. "It's always eliens with you people! You come to ubduct me? Good luck! I no Kung-Fu! Lots of it! Dozens!"

"Would you calm down?" Mongrel yelled at his friend. "Your grammar's gone right to shit! He's not an alien."

Wan sighed loudly and turned around. "It's my brother's face." He was used to negative reactions but this was one of the worst he could recall. He wasn't a monster, but people shied away from him like he was contagious. He was given wide births on the sidewalk, and no one wanted to stand behind him in a line. And the children, oh the children! Some screamed and cried to their mommies, others were curious and wanted to put their grimy fingers all over his second face. He'd learned the hard way that when someone poked his brother in the eye he felt it, and it hurt. Still, Wan was optimistic and remained thankful that his brother's face was the only part of him that he inherited. Well, that and his anus. But Wan didn't tell people that he had two buttholes; it would be bad for business.

Elvis stood, giving up his stance but remaining distant. "Well why'd he show me that…that thing?"

"You asked if I was drunk, and I was showing you that I was just disoriented," Wan answered.

"Well you didn't know who I was. What's wrong with you? Everyone knows who I am."

"Pull your head out of your asses. Not everyone knows who you are."

Mongrel put a hand on Wan's shoulder and said, "Yeah, they do. He's Elvis. Elvis Presley. The King of rock and roll?"

Wan studied the man, mouthing his name but not outright saying it. It sounded familiar.

"I ain't nothin' but a hound dog?" Elvis said, trying to jolt Wan's memories. "Dancing to the jail house rock? In the Ghetto?" He began gyrating his hips and trembling his lips, and sang, "Well since my baby left me, I found a new place to dwell. It's down at the end of lonely street at Heartbreak Hotel."

Wan's front face began to look more like his rear face, becoming cringing mass of utter bewilderment.

"Love me tender, love me sweet," Elvis continued. "I just want to be your teddy bear. Well, it's one for the money, two for the show, three to get ready, now go cat go. But don't you step on my blue suede shoes. I'm in love, I'm all shook up."

At this last utterance, Wan's eyes glazed over. "You're…all shook up?" he asked.

"Well, not at this very moment," Elvis joked, happy that he'd finally gained a reaction other than a puzzled look from Wan.

Memories stirred in Wan's mind, waking from their slumber. Visions of his old-man-hood flashed before his eyes of a man named Elvis on his old black and white TV. Some young punk dancing like a fool and proclaiming to be one as well – a fool in love. All shook up indeed. Kids those days. Kids these days too. Actually, kids from every day; all of them were messed up. Always listening to vile music and combing their hair at improbable angles and mutilating livestock. And this Elvis was the worst of them all.

Good For Business

He began walking back to his tiny office. "Stay right there. I gotta grab my shotgun."

Elvis looked at Mongrel, comprehension failing to show on his face.

"I think it's time to leave," Mongrel explained.

"But what about your car?"

"There's always the other car shop." Mongrel grabbed Elvis' sleeve and tried to guide him back toward the limo.

"The one with that Pete guy? I thought you didn't like him or something?"

"Well if someone's going to die today I'd rather it be Captain Pete. At least he'll live through it. Now come on."

Sensing danger, Mickey groggily sat up, grimacing. He felt his face, wincing as he gently poked his nose. Blood still trickled from it. Elvis went back to help him to his feet and began brushing the dirt off his suit.

"Just look at yourself Mickey," Mongrel said, shaking his head, "you're a mess! You are failing miserably at your job. You can't walk around in tattered rags – it's bad for business. How you stay employed I'll never know."

Mongrel also didn't know what hit him. He didn't see Mickey's eyes narrow and his nostrils flair, or his teeth clench. He didn't see his hand ball into a fist, or that fist speed towards his face with all the power and rage the tiny chauffeur could throw into it. He didn't feel the world spin as he collapsed to the pavement, or hear Mickey scream profoundly profuse profanity at him.

And he didn't see the flames erupt.

Spending as much time unconscious as Mongrel does, you learn a few things, such as how to cope with the nausea, how to react to the sudden shift in time, and occasionally space, and how to quickly shake off the mental turbulence. You tend to get used to it.

Mongrel woke to find himself being dragged though ashes and burning debris, and did not find this at all odd. "I'm okay," he said, trying to shrug off the hands pulling him.

The hands wrapped under Mongrel's arms and around his chest belonged to Freddie Farcus, who refused to let go. "Terrifically terrifying isn't it, this fire?" he huffed. "I found you

Random Tangent

having a nap in the middle of it. Odd place for one, I suppose. You haven't the foggiest notion of how it started have you?"

"No," Mongrel replied, still struggling to be released. "Let me go."

"Are you sure your legs can do their job? You and your consciousness were just reacquainted."

"I'm fine. Happens all the time."

Freddie stopped and surveyed their surroundings. The fire hadn't spread passed the car lot, and they were far enough from it to not be in immediate danger. He released Mongrel, who then tried to stand, mostly with success; he swayed briefly, swatted away his friend's hands as they tried to steady him, and repeated how fine he was. Once standing firmly on his own two feet with his own two wits, he too took stock of his surroundings.

Elvis and his bumbling chauffeur were nowhere in sight. Nor was Wan, who was last seen fetching his bullet-breathing weapon. The entire car lot was engulfed in flames. Plumes of smoke drifted into the hazy sky. The pop and crackle of car parts whispered in the air.

That certainly couldn't be good for business.

He and Freddie were standing on the sidewalk a few meters away from the blazing inferno, out of danger for the moment, lest they linger for too long.

"Where are Elvis and Mickey?" Mongrel asked, unconcerned with the encroaching fire.

"I haven't the foggiest," Freddie said, also offering a shrug. "Everyone seems to have disappeared."

As the fire raged on, the good, wholesome folks of Dunttstown ran over and quickly began roasting marshmallows and singing campfire songs – if your imagination was good enough to declare it singing. Mongrel would have joined them but he had other pressing matters to deal with, like getting out of harms way before the flames tried to rape and murder him. But instead of scampering away he stood there, transfixed on the orange glow, recollecting.

Mickey had attacked him. He was sure of it.

Mickey; the abomination of all chauffeurs.

But the limo was gone, and with it Mongrel's diva persona.

Good For Business

He no longer considered Mickey beneath him, a mere mortal next to his omnipotent self, a sponge at which he was *supposed* to hurl all manner of disdain and abuse.

Now Mongrel felt…heat. Unrelenting heat. Seriously, the fire was right freaking there. You could smell the flames. Have you ever smelt fire before? If you had you probably never lived to talk about it. And speaking of stories, this one was going to come to an abrupt end because Mongrel was too busy to run, consumed with guilt over was a twat he'd been to the stupid chauffeur. He deserved what had happened to him. He'd pushed Mickey too far. It was the limo, wasn't it? The limo had turned Mongrel into a megalomaniac. Ordinarily he was a pretty swell guy, but put him in a position of power, even if only illusively so, and he became downright despicable. Did that happen to everyone?

And now he was without a ride, and had to walk in the sickening heat, which was only increasing due to his proximity to a fire that was going to consume him if he didn't *move his ass*.

"Okay, okay," he grumbled. He shoved his hands roughly into his pockets and sulked down the road towards his next destination. Freddie fell in line beside him, for once not asking questions and just accompanying him silently.

Freddie did not get out much. Since coming out of the mon and, figuratively, back to life, he'd spent most of his time in front of the television. At first he tinkered with anything he could get his hands on, constructing bizarre gadgets in an attempt to understand the new world and what made it tick. But then he found cable TV, and instead of trying to dismantle it he decided to observe it. The man who had once considered himself a scientist/inventor became a couch potato.

Mongrel of course did not help much with this problem. In fact he did quite the opposite; whenever Freddie had a question Mongrel couldn't answer, or at least didn't feel like answering, he simply told Freddie to watch more TV and the answer would come to him, which they usually did. As far as Mongrel was concerned, Freddie being glued to the TV wasn't a problem, it was a solution.

It was rare for Freddie to be off the property, and he often wondered what it would be like to visit gargantuan castles and sprawling forests, or serene beaches. Or even other planets – TV made space travel look so easy. Indeed interstellar travel had come a long way since his time, when it was merely dreamed of. He longed to travel, and when he chanced upon an outing such as this very trip, he made the most of it.

As soon as the opportunity arose earlier, he'd taken his leave. He learned of arcade games and their many electronic wonders, and simply *had* to investigate. There was an arcade located in Dunttstown, and he desperately wished to behold it, to study it, to bask in its glow. He constructed dozens of tiny weighted circular disks that he believed perfectly replicated the currency used to operate the machines, and when he'd managed to slip away from his company unnoticed, and find The Shady Alley Arcade, he went nuts. He plunked "quarter" after imitation "quarter" into the arcade cabinets and his brain boggled, his mind reeled. The lights and colours, the sounds, it was a nonstop smorgasbord of imaginative delight. It was rapturous.

Until he'd been caught.

Like any man out of time, he stood out like moose loose in the supermarket, and it wasn't long before he was under the watchful scrutiny of security. When his penchant for using fake monies was discovered, Freddie was quickly apprehended and brought forth to the kingpin of the establishment, a man who revealed himself only as the Boss.

Originally from other environs, the Boss was a great man, or at least considered himself so. Typically in the face of blatant thievery he would grant a brutal yet mercifully swift death that went by the curious name 'Peaches.' But again, the Boss was a great man, and part of being great was having the ability to sense greatness in others, which he beheld in this treacherous scamp. Being both a gentleman and a scholar, he allowed Freddie the opportunity to explain his actions and reveal his technique for counterfeiting money, and then offered him an exclusive position within the organization – a position Freddie couldn't refuse (since doing so would mean dealing with 'Peaches').

After his encounter with the Boss he was released back into the wild to return to his friends. But he was warned to keep their meeting a secret, that their business together must always remain confidential, or else he would suffer grave consequences. Freddie

Good For Business

came back to a car lot, hoping his absence had gone unnoticed. Luckily for him the place was ablaze and everyone had fled, and those who remained were unconscious. After dragging Mongrel from certain death, he was now accompanying him again on his journey, unsure of what had happened since he'd left, but nonetheless thankful for the distraction.

"So what the hell happened to you?" Mongrel asked suddenly.

"W-what?" Freddie stumbled. He then thought of scoffing, or mumbling incoherently. Isn't that what people did these days when being deceitful? He was no good at lying. Maybe if he told the truth in a ridiculous fashion…

"Come on now, you didn't think I noticed you were gone? Did you start that fire? Are you a little firebug?"

Freddie wondered for a moment if he shouldn't just play along. It was a good cover up, and he didn't even have to invent it himself. He nodded. "I, uh…saw it on television, and wanted to see fire for myself. One doesn't see fire up close very often. It's hotter than I remember it."

"Yep," Mongrel agreed. "It can melt your face off if you don't pay attention. Soon as you turn your back on it – BAM! You're on fire. Fire's like a bully, and it gives the meanest wedgies."

Not sure what a bully was, or a wedgie, Freddie thought the better of asking and tried to change the subject. "So what is our next destination?"

"Well the other reason I needed to come to town was to buy a puppy for a friend I owe my life to. He'll just kill it anyway, but not on purpose." He was referring to 'Big John' Charlie Marbles at Dunttstown Penitentiary.

It seemed like only yesterday Mongrel was fighting for his life, and his anal virginity, behind bars. He didn't belong there; being guilty only of coming to visit his friend Biscuits.

"He's not my friend," Mongrel muttered.

A series of misunderstandings and coincidences, many of which his *acquaintance* Biscuits was responsible for, led those in charge to believe Mongrel was an inmate, and forcibly encouraged him to stay. Thanks to his good friend Big John, who was a

Random Tangent

volunteer at the prison, and whose only crimes were horrifically slaughtering puppies, Mongrel managed to escape Duntt Penn and perhaps even death itself. Or at the very least, rape.

Biscuits too had helped him escape – in fact he had done far more than Big John. However, since it was his fault that Mongrel had been imprisoned, not to mention that fact that he was incarcerated for murdering Mongrel's mother, Mongrel felt the boy hadn't done nearly enough to atone for his atrocities, let alone earned a puppy.

"So you mean to purchase an animal for the sole purpose of killing it?" Freddie actually wasn't bothered by this. Back in his day people did it all the time with livestock.

"Well when you put it like that it sounds horrible. I'm trying to be nice here." He paused, trying not to think of this from the dog's point of view. "And look, I'll just find one that's sure to not get adopted anyway. One that's really ugly or walks in circles or is cross-eyed or something. A puppy that's already doomed, you know? Just don't tell anyone that, okay?"

"Okay."

Mongrel glanced at him. "Okay? You're okay with that? You sure?"

"Yes, why?"

"Well..." Mongrel didn't know what to say. He wasn't really committed to the idea. "I'm not quite okay with it, I guess. I'm open to being talked out of it, or if there are other options. I mean, I'm conspiring to help murder a helpless animal."

Freddie just shrugged. "It's just an animal. It's not like you're going to get attached to it. But what about buying an automobile? Is there not another dealership at the other end of town?"

Mongrel sighed, "Yeah. I was hoping to avoid that one. Something seems funny about it. But it looks like I have no choice, since someone burned down the last one." He glared at Freddie, who failed to immediately understand.

"Oh yes!" Freddie finally said. "Because of myself and the fire – which I caused. Yes sir, that was me." He laughed nervously.

"Is there anything else I should know about you?" Mongrel asked, suddenly suspicious. "What other hobbies are you into?

Good For Business

Bulimia? Recreational homicide? Dressing up in women's clothes? You're not gay, are you? Not that there's anything wrong with that."

Flabbergasted, Freddie didn't know how to answer these questions, although most of them were 'no.' Thankfully another distraction presented itself.

"Is this the place?" Freddie asked, pointing up at a sign reading REGGIE'S BITCHES.

"Yep," Mongrel replied, ignoring his previous line of questioning, much to his companion's relief.

The doorbell rang as Mongrel and Freddie entered the store, signalling to the staff that patrons were on the premises, and to act accordingly. As it happens, the only person in the store was Reginald Huxley, the owner. He represented the entirety of the store's staff; business wasn't good enough to warrant paying others to do what he could do, and bothering to hire and train others would be a waste of his time, money, and most importantly, his energy.

Reginald – or Reg, since it was fewer letters and syllables and altogether less taxing to verbalize – hated the sound of the bell. He loathed it with the passion of a garbage man on trash day (assuming that garbage men didn't *really* love their job); any more passion would have required too much effort to sustain. The bell represented work. When it rang it meant he had to straightening up and interact with customers, make the occasional sale, and overall look busy. He didn't have the stomach for it. He wanted to do something about the annoying jingling sound, but that would require some amount of work, which he didn't have the stomach for either. So he sat there day in and day out, silently detesting the noise. He never went home, or rather he didn't have to; he lived in the store. He gave up his house long ago after realizing it took too much time and effort to travel between the two locations.

He spent nearly every waking hour at Reggie's Bitches, growing old, praying the bell would remain silent, completely and utterly miserable. You might wonder how anyone could live like that, and you wouldn't be the only one. Reggie himself had also put some thought into suicide, but in the end decided it would take too much planning[*] and yadda yadda yadda effort and stuff.

---

[*] Not to mention: what would he write in his suicide letter? And how would be want to die? Even dying was too much work.

Random Tangent

Anyway, the bell rang and two people walked in, waking Reggie from his nap – in which he was also sleeping – instantly putting him in a foul mood. Honestly, did customers *always* have to come in when he was in the middle of one of his afternoon naps? He would've asked them to kindly leave, but that wouldn't have been good for business.

"Hello there," Mongrel said, waving politely as he approached the counter. The man behind it glared at him and said nothing. He reminded Mongrel of a gorilla, somewhat imposing with an animalistic stare, nostrils flared. Although he was seated, the storekeeper seemed to have proportions like that of a primate; longish arms, squat, legs, a bit of a belly, and was covered in thick black hair – at least the parts he could see. He was balding, with a thick ribbon of hair curving around the back of his head, connecting to a rich full beard covering the lower half of his face; the upper half hid behind large, lightly-tinted glasses. The man's arms were crossed over his chest standoffishly, and Mongrel almost immediately felt uncomfortable. Still, he needed to persevere. The clerk shouldn't give him, a customer, a hard time; it wouldn't be good for business.

"Um, where do you keep your puppies?" he asked.

Reggie inhaled sharply through his nose and grunted. He just didn't get it. What was wrong with people? Coming into his store, waking him up, using words at him? And the *questions!* Oh the questions. 'Hello?' and 'Could you help me?' or 'Do you even feed these animals?' It boggled his mind. How did other store owners put up with it? Reggie pointed toward the back of the store, hoping that would be the end of it. He thought briefly about pointing to the door, perhaps giving them a hint at where they should go, but decided against it. It wouldn't be good for business.

"Thanks," Mongrel said, and quickly wandered away before the man's glare turned any shade of evil.

Freddie was not so obedient. He approached the counter and said, "Good day to you shopkeep. Terrifyingly terrific store you have. My name is Frederic Farcus, professional television watcher. Now, I am new to this period in time and doing my utmost to adjust, but I have a concern or two I should like to address. You see, back a century or two a bitch referred to female of the canine species.

Good For Business

Seeing as how your establishment brokers in the trade of all manner of domesticated beasts, I have no doubt that bitches, as they were once known, are for sale here on the premises. However, it has come to my attention after countless hours viewing your cable broadcasts that the term 'bitch' in this day and age refers now to a woman, or women, of a certain temperament, as I'm no doubt you are aware. So, seeing as how you specialize in the sale of these *bitches* I ask you: be they canine or human? Or do you offer both? Do you perhaps trade in two different businesses, one by day and the other by night, strictly to gentlemen? To the best of my knowledge dealing in prostitution is currently prohibited by law, so if this were in fact a brothel you certainly couldn't proclaim it. But if a man such as myself were to inquire about those services with great interest, what would be the proper etiquette in doing so?"

Customers.

The counter let out a quiet squeak as Reggie's hands squeezed it, anger and confusion swirling around in his head. What the hell was this man asking him? Homicidal thoughts ran through his mind, but he stayed them, absent-mindedly rubbing a band on his left wrist. Stencilled on it were the letters WWTD, which stood for What Would Talbot Do.

Almost a decade ago, before the accident, life was much different for Reggie. He worked hard, played hard, and ate hard. He was a mean eater. He could wolf down a seventy-two ounce steak in under eight minutes. He read all about competitive eating, and considered getting involved in it. He'd fit right in with that crowd. He began participating in and winning many local eating contests, and sporting quite the gut because of it. It wasn't all fat though; digesting the amount of food he was gorging himself on required strong abdominal muscles. You'd never know it, but he was ripped like a bodybuilder, and he had the stomach of a champion.

He was eating his way to the top, but then he saw that Asian kid – he couldn't remember his name now – and his hopes diminished. That kid was a machine. As good as Reggie was, he'd never be *that* good. But that was the way the world was, right? No matter how good you were at anything there was always an Asian kid better than you. He fell into a pit of despair, and soon began drinking like a champion. It was drink that put him in the hospital

Random Tangent

for seven years. After a late night at a local bar, he'd hit the road, staggering home, and tried to cross the street when the DO NOT CROSS light was on. He was hit by a bus. The bus driver got out and berated his unconscious body about being greedy and the sidewalk not being enough for him or something. Witness reports were unreliable. To teach the jaywalker a lesson, the driver did not call an ambulance for him. If he wanted to enjoy hogging the road while a perfectly serviceable sidewalk was available, then he could get his own ass to the hospital, or so the rationale went.

The next morning his body was dropped into the Dunttstown hospital's body bin, where he remained for a couple days until a doctor pulled him out, declared him comatose, and strapped him to a bed before heading off to a lunch from which he never returned. His whereabouts are still unknown.

During the years he spent as a 'Regetable' he lost most of his gut and somewhere along the way became stupendously lazy, which was deemed a severe side-effect of his condition. In fact the last five or six months Reggie wasn't in a coma at all; he was just sleeping. When he finally woke, amongst the catching up he had to do he learned that he'd somehow voted for a man named Troy Talbot in the previous mayoral election. It seemed impossible. He couldn't believe it, and he wasn't the only one. The new mayor of Dunttstown was just as surprised at the outcome, since he didn't run[*] a campaign. He'd never even offered himself as a candidate. It was just one of those things.

Another one of those things that happened is the creation of the Talbot-Hammock movement. Many Dunttstown denizens, most of whom voted for Troy, considered the election a miracle, since most of them didn't even know an election was being held, let alone vote in the proceedings. Yet here Troy was, the new mayor. It was a sign. Those people, including Reggie, came together to form the Talbot-Hammock movement, a following of their leader, Troy Talbot, dedicated to promoting, or rather letting slip out, the highest forms of lethargy.

Reggie wore his WWTD wristband to remind himself that

---

[*] Troy Talbot never ran, period. Even if his life depended on it, he would sooner die than put that much effort into prolonging his existence. Life, he was often overheard saying, was a lot of work, and he couldn't be bothered.

Good For Business

he didn't have to do anything he didn't want to do. Customers were smart enough and could help themselves. He was allowed to say no.

"No," he told Freddie, and nothing more.

Freddie was about to repeal this response, since it answered none of his questions, but Mongrel hailed him, and he reluctantly left his conversation unfinished. As he made his way to the back of the store he decided that Reggie must be offering services of a private nature to other clientele. Why else would he treat a potential customer with such curtness? It simply wasn't a good way to run a business. No, his brutish attitude, gruff appearance, and obvious avoidance of speaking about the matter could only mean that there were indeed illegal activities going on here. He would have to come back after dark and do some more investigating.

He found Mongrel kneeling in front of a large cage, underneath a sign that read DOG AQUARIUM. Several puppies were gathered near the front of the cage, inches from Mongrel's face, licking the fingers he had inserted through the bars.

"Which one looks the most retarded?" he asked.

Freddie looked at the puppies. Two had begun to wrestle and the third was in the middle of taking a dump. They appeared to be some kind of Labrador mix, but he was no expert. All had golden fur with streaks of white, except for the defecating one, which now also had smears of brown because it was rolling around in its own excrement.

"Oh man, they're a hundred bucks each?" Mongrel moaned, pointing at a sign on the side of the cage. There were several reasons why this was unfortunate for him; primarily that it was more money than he'd wanted to spend on a puppy, especially since he knew it wasn't going to live long. Secondly, even though he hadn't bought one yet, he was still planning to spend a decent chunk of money on a car. The day's expenses were adding up quickly.

"I think that one." Freddie pointed to the brown-flecked puppy, which was now licking its own feces off itself.

"I can't spend that kind of money on a dog just to kill it," Mongrel muttered, not listening. "If it was free I could maybe live with it. The dog wouldn't, but I would. Ever see that movie where people pay money to torture and kill other people?" He shuddered.

Random Tangent

"Paying money to do that – to do *this* – just makes me feel dirty and immoral, like a prostitute or something."

"Did you say prostitute?" Freddie asked, glaring at Mongrel.

"Uh, yeah."

Freddie glanced back toward the counter and said, "I knew it." He headed back to the front of the store to speak to the manager.

"Can I be arrested for that? Like, conspiracy to commit murder or something?" Mongrel asked. When he realised he was alone, he returned his attention to the dog aquarium. "What am I gonna do?" he asked. As if in response, one of the puppies barked at him, and he knew he couldn't give one of them to Big John.

Back at the counter, Reggie had slipped comfortably back into a nap. Over the last few months his naps had really begun to come into their own. They were of jolly and pleasant things; relaxing in his lazy boy, settling into warm baths, or random people telling him not to worry, that things were being taken care of. Sometimes he would even be sleeping in his naps. That might be confusing to some, but not to Reggie; to him it was bliss. Sleep within sleep. He felt like it was two naps in one, which was ideal because if he didn't get his twenty hours of sleep a day he became cranky. He'd considered closing up shop whenever he wanted to get some shuteye but the thought of getting up to flip over the OPEN/CLOSED sign every time turned his stomach. Besides, he didn't really decide to have naps anymore, they just…happened.

"Shopkeep!" Freddie yelled, slamming his fists down on the counter.

Reggie snapped awake with more force than his body had exerted in a month, almost falling off his box.[*] He wasn't used to such abuse. Thankfully he didn't have to stand…or sit, for it much longer. He'd ordered a cardboard cut-out in his likeness through the mail. It would stand there in his place while he was in the back

---

[*] A month earlier Reggie had ordered a new swivel chair to relax in. He hadn't had much choice in the matter; he'd crapped all over the last recliner while sleeping. Obviously he wasn't going to clean it, so it had to go. When the new chair arrived he opened the box, scanned the instructions, and the thought of following the few steps to assemble the chair made him dizzy and nauseated. So he crammed everything back in the box and just used the box itself for a chair. So far it had done a decent job.

room catching up on his sleep. That cut-out could not get here fast enough.

"I am displeased with your courtesy. Here I am an upstanding, well-mannered customer looking to pay top-dollar for your best prostitute, and you shun me? This is no way to run a business! I do understand the need for precaution but I ask you how to proceed in the appropriate manner and you spurn me? You, sir, are a tyrant!"

This was the sort of confrontation that gave Reggie nightmares. This was the sort of situation that made Reggie want to close the store permanently. This was the last straw. Reggie did something he very rarely did: he stood. Now eye-level with his unruly customer, he waited until the dizziness subsided before sighing loudly and muttering the words, "I'm closed."

Fury was replaced by confusion in Freddie's nineteenth century brain. "But it's the middle of the day," he said. "Prime business hours." He was about to go on about how businesses function and their duty to customers and how the store closing in the middle of the afternoon wasn't good for business, but a realization came to him: not every kind of business ran best in the daytime.

Prostitution, for example.

He looked at Reggie, who couldn't sustain the energy to appear angry and now simply looked tired. The shopkeeper was giving him a sign. The only thing missing from the whole interaction was a knowing wink.

"Yes, of course, sir. Thank you," Freddie said, nodding. He made an attempt to reach across the counter for the shopkeeper's hand to shake it, but fell inches short. Reggie made not the slightest effort to cooperate. "Thank you, sir," he said again, shaking hands with the air. "I shall return later." He winked at the man then called for Mongrel.

"What?" Mongrel shouted from the back of the store.

"The store is closing."

Mongrel was going to look at his watch to confirm the time but remembered he didn't have one. Also, he wasn't going to buy a puppy anyway – not even the shit-eating one – so there was no point in sticking around. He marched quietly to the exit, where

Random Tangent

Freddie was anxiously waiting for him, and wondered how he was going to repay Big John for his kindness. There had to be another solution that didn't involve slaughtering a perfectly good dog.

A thought then occurred to him: what about slaughtering a dead dog? That was a much easier pill for Mongrel to swallow, and if he could convince Big John that it was still alive – maybe say it was just sleeping – then it could work. Big John was a great, if odd, friend, but he couldn't pour water out a boot if the instructions were on the heel, so Mongrel was confident in the idea. But where was he going to find a dead dog?

He turned to Reggie before leaving. "Um, excuse me. I don't suppose you'd know where I could find a dead puppy? Perhaps you have some here? Do people, like, trade them in? I'd be willing to pay."

Had Reggie been the sort of man who used contextual gestures to imply his feelings he might have shaken his head in exasperation. But he was a man of few words and fewer actions. He didn't know what to do; he was bending over backwards to please these people but nothing he did, or rather didn't do, was good enough. Why wouldn't they just leave? Why did they keep asking questions? What did they want from him? He was so frazzled he would have broken down and cried if it weren't for the effort required.

Thankfully Freddie grabbed Mongrel by the shoulder and pulled him out the door. "Didn't you hear? They're closed."

Mongrel yanked his shoulder free. "I just wanted to know where I could get a dead dog."

"And I want to know why cats are buried with the deceased, but we all must make sacrifices, must we not? We can come back after dark."

"Why after dark?"

"Uh...I mean as in tomorrow. After the night – the dark – and come back tomorrow, right?" He nodded and considered the matter clarified. "We can come back tomorrow and purchase your dead dog."

"Whatever," Mongrel muttered. It was unlikely that Reggie would be able to help him anyway. He supposed he could try again tomorrow; what harm could it do? He followed Freddie out of the store.

"Well melt my ice, ice my cream, and cream my corn!"

A very short man – some might venture to call him a midget – wobbled down the sidewalk towards them carrying a bag of marshmallows.

"Frank!" Mongrel cried. He rushed to give him a firm handshake, and Freddie tipped his yoop to the man. "Long time no see! How have you been?"

"Oh dandy! Just dandy. New business ventures; life is good. Getting out in the world, as you can see. It's so big out here!"

Almighty Frank rarely left his house. He wasn't agoraphobic or lazy, but simply never felt the need. He had everything he wanted right there, including his best friend, Emmanuelle Cheeseburg, who was so fat he couldn't leave even if he wanted to. He also never left the house because he was constantly drunk.

However, something was off today. "Are you not drunk?" Mongrel asked.

"Nope," Almighty Frank said proudly. "Or, yep, I think. Whichever one means I haven't had a drink in a while. Been a long time since I've been sober; still adjusting, you know?"

"How terrifyingly terrific!" Freddie chirped.

For most people this would be good news; not so for the midget. "Is everything okay?" Mongrel asked, concerned. "Are you broke? Or constipated[*]?"

"No, no, no, nothing like that; just decided to try not drinking for a change. Perhaps you didn't notice but I was an alcoholic."

Mongrel had noticed. He'd actually never known the short fellow to ever be sober, and how he hadn't succumbed to alcohol poisoning yet was beyond him. Maybe it had something to do with his baffling anatomy. "Why?" he asked. "Don't get me wrong, it's a great idea, but what made you change?"

---

[*] Almighty Frank was filthy rich – and I do mean filthy; most of his wealth came from harvesting his own excrement. As the hopelessly absurd story goes, in the womb his DNA was magically infused with gold or something, and now every time something came out of him it was laced with gold. Digging through your own feces every day, even to become rich, would be enough to drive someone to alcoholism, and thusly Almighty Frank had been an alcoholic for most of his life.

Random Tangent

Almighty Frank scanned up and down the road suspiciously. Once assured they were alone he leaned in close and whispered, "I was beginning to have hallucinations." He nodded gravely. "Started thinking the mansion was haunted. I kept seeing this little robot. Filthy, vile little thing. Seemed to be covered in shit, head to toe."

"Gnomebot!" Freddie cried.

"Say what?" Almighty Frank asked, surprised as the outburst.

"That's my Gnomebot. You purchased him off me…oh, sometime last year. Do you not remember? He was to be your housekeeper or something, to look after your cheeseburger I believe you said."

"I remember seeing him," Mongrel agreed.

The little man looked at them both back and forth, appearing quite confused. "So you mean I'm not crazy?" They both shook their heads. "Well cream my corn, corn my pops and pop my tarts! Guess I can go back to drinking then."

Freddie thought this was a terrifyingly terrific idea but Mongrel had his reservations. "No wait, just give sobriety a chance. See what you've been missing."

Almighty Frank looked up at the sky, squinting. "Like this stupid heat?" he asked. "Was it always this hot when I was drunk?"

"Yep, always," Mongrel said quickly before Freddie could say otherwise.

"Huh." The midget was mystified. "It's a totally different world when you're drunk all the time. You know I once got hit by a bus after I was drinking?"

"After?" Mongrel snickered. "Don't you mean *between* drinks?"

"Yeah, yeah, whatever. I got run over several times actually, and I just walked it off. Didn't even phase me; I was bus-proof or something. I can show you – all I gotta do is say jalpneo-"

"Stop!" Mongrel shouted, silencing the little man. He glanced around nervously for any oncoming traffic. "You…uh, might not be bus-proof anymore. Since you quit drinking, eh?"

"Ah, right," Almighty Frank nodded. "Good point."

"I once fornicated with a sheep when I was inebriated," Freddie said, trying to have a larger presence in the conversation.

Good For Business

This did not have the desired effect; the two men just stared at him oddly. If Almighty Frank had been drunk he might have congratulated him.

"That reminds me," Almighty Frank said, returning his attention to Mongrel, "did you know I was sleeping with a cop?"

"Yeah, I heard about that."

"Just found out about it the other day. The whole time I never knew she was a...wait, you knew about that?"

Mongrel shrugged, not really wanting to get involved in other people's affairs. "I know the woman. Well, I know her husband, really."

"Yeah, ain't that the damndest thing – she's married? That's the only problem I had with it. I mean, there are advantages to dating a cop, you know?" He sighed. "Too bad. Had to kick her to the curb. She wasn't happy about it, but I ain't no homewrecker. Well, not anymore. Anyway, I best be on my way before some idiot puts out that fire."

"Some idiot started it," Mongrel said, glaring at Freddie. He stepped aside to let his friend pass. "Good luck with your robot troubles."

"Not to worry," Almighty Frank called, wandering down the road towards the smoke plumes, "I already took care of it."

"What do you mean?"

Almighty Frank stopped and turned to face them. "I caught the little bastard last week. Tossed him in the incinerator. Gonna need a new one, I suppose."

"Noooo!" Freddie suddenly cried. He charged at the midget and gave him a mighty slap across the face. Who couldn't blame him? Gnomebot was a work of genius and its demise was certainly lamentable. The robot was more advanced than anything mankind had yet been able to create with regards to artificial intelligence. The fact that it was built by a man from the previous millennium made it all the more mindboggling. Had Freddie not been eaten by the mon those many years ago and instead went into robotics, who knows where the human race would be right now?

"How could you?" Freddie demanded, nearly in tears. "He was just a baby!"

Almighty Frank felt his face where he'd been slapped and

glared at Freddie, but did not retaliate. "You know if I was drunk I would punt you across the street. Don't let my size fool you; I am a mean little man." He straightened himself up and regained some composure. "Now I told you I thought No-bot was a just a hallucination. I didn't think I was doing no harm, but damn if it didn't make me feel better. Really therapeutic. Besides, the blasted thing wanted to be killed anyway."

Freddie blinked away tears and was about to correct Almighty Frank on the name, but the last remark threw him. "What do you mean?"

"He kept asking me to kill him. I guess he was miserable. Just digging through my shit all day – hell I'd be miserable too. Probably what led me to drink in the first place. Little bastard can't drink can he?" Freddie shook his head, and Almighty Frank nodded. "Well no wonder he's depressed. Doesn't like dealing with human waste – who'd a thunk? Maybe you could make the next one like it?"

"The next one?"

"Yeah, I told you I need another one. Maybe it can breathe fire too? Can you do that?" He put his arm around Freddie's waist, looking much like a child with his father, as he led Freddie down the sidewalk, and they discussed future plans for the next Gnomebot.

Mongrel smiled at the thought of Freddie finally putting aside the television and getting some fresh air, and possibly making some friends. He then wiped the sweat from his forehead and continued on his way to the next used car lot.

This is approximately the location where Mongrel would have rounded the corner and happened upon Downtown Pete's Quality Cars, except that there was no corner to round. Dunttstown, it would seem, had been designed by a bunch of blind, inept, or mentally challenged architects, and there were only two crossings in the whole town. While you could call these crossings 'corners' if you're so inclined, and indeed they sport all the trademarks of good corners the world over – streetlights, street signs, even crosswalks – they could only be called such as a means of designating location. For example, "Meet me at the corner of this and that."

Good For Business

Downtown Pete's Quality Cars was fortunate enough to occupy prime real estate on the corner of Bloor St. and Wednesday Ave. at the western end of Dunttstown. Although little blocked its view, and it could be seen from far up the road, Mongrel, for the sake of surprise, stumbled upon it as if it came from out of nowhere.

Shocked by the car lot's sudden appearance, Mongrel felt the urge to hide. He'd be seen for sure, then captured and tortured until he revealed his secret for staying sane in this town for as long as he had. This was troubling because he didn't have such a secret, and he wasn't completely sure he wasn't crazy. While one could argue that he was certainly fairing better than some of Dunttstown's citizens, he…you know, all this could be discussed once he'd found a secure place to hide.

Hide is exactly what Mongrel didn't do; he just stood there, gawking across the street. Perhaps there was nothing to worry about after all. Just because the lot had Pete's name on it didn't mean it was run by Captain Pete, or even a Pete at all. Perhaps it was a franchise? Besides, what did the captain know about selling cars? Boats maybe, but cars? He was a pirate, or *was* a pirate…wait, that's what I said. Anyway, it was a stretch to see him selling cars. Still, stranger things have happened. In fact, stranger things were normal in Dunttstown.

Having rationalized this out, Mongrel relaxed a bit, leaning on a nearby mailbox. He studied the car lot, taking in the vehicles. Assuming it was Captain Pete-free, he would have to buy a car there, since the last dealership hadn't proven itself to be fireproof. This car lot had plenty more cars to choose from than the other one. It also had RVs, boats, a couple motorcycles; a little bit of everything.

A man then came into view, walking around a large van. He appeared familiar to Mongrel, like one of the inmates he'd met in prison – one of the mean ones with whom he'd enjoyed a nice game of abuse with. But perhaps Mongrel was being ridiculous. The prisoner was surely still incarcerated, just as surely as Captain Pete wasn't selling cars.

Except Captain Pete *was* actually selling cars. He came around the side of the van moments after the other man, conversing about something. He fished out a set of keys from his pocket and unlocked the door of the van and opened it for his potential customer. As the man helped himself into the vehicle, Captain Pete suddenly, inexplicably, shockingly even, sneezed. He rubbed his nose gingerly, and then looked directly at Mongrel.

Instinct kicked in, deciding it should show up every now and then to prove it wasn't dead, and Mongrel flung himself down behind the mailbox. He closed his eyes and said a silent prayer.

"Hey!"

This was not Captain Pete's voice. It wasn't even male. Mongrel opened his eyes to see a pair of flip flops stop in front of him. He followed the shapely legs upward to a pair of extremely short shorts. Continuing upwards he skimmed passed the exposed midriff and paused at a pair of enormous breasts that nearly assaulted his face. The small top containing them was obviously having a difficult time doing so. Mongrel would normally have appreciated them if it weren't for their poor timing, and knowing he shouldn't linger, he moved his head to the side so he could see around the pendulous eye candy to look at the woman's face.

It was Beby.

"If I didn't know any better I'd swear you were trying to avoid me," she said.

"What? Uh, no!" Mongrel stuttered. I just bent down to tie my..." he swallowed gravely as he looked at his footwear of choice that day, "...sandals." He slowly rose to his feet, unable to stop his eyes from roaming all over her body. Her revealing outfit left little to this imagination – although still enough to give his often-overtaxed mind something to play with. Let's just say she was dressed like a prostitute. A sheen of sweat glistened across her body, as if she'd just finished a vigorous workout. "Are you not wearing a bra?"

Ignoring him as usual, she said, "You're totally avoiding me. I came to the prison for our conjugal visit, and you weren't there! You just...left. Who leaves prison?"

"Uh...released prisoners?"

Beby snorted at his answer and handed him a card.

Reluctantly, more out of curiosity than because he felt he had to, Mongrel took the card. He tried to read it, but the

Good For Business

bastardized version of the English language made it difficult. It appeared to be a business card for someone named Valentin Rushkov, who was apparently a psychic. The name sounded Russian, which might explain the strange lettering. Mongrel failed to understand what Beby wanted him to do with this information. He glanced up from the card, lingering briefly on her chest again, and with great effort managed to look her in the eye and ask, "So...did your boobs get bigger or is it my imagination?"

She snorted again. "It's for my shrink. I want you to see him."

Mongrel looked at the card again. "The psychic?"

"*Psychologist.*"

"It says psychic."

"Look, if we're gonna give this a try," Beby gestured between the two of them, "then I need to make sure you're not certifiable. Dated enough crazy people in this town." She began twirling a strand of red hair around he fingers; the rest of her hair billowed in the gentle breeze, which was welcomed in the torrential heat. The usual vehemence in her eyes was not there, replaced with a concerned, nearly pleading look. Mongrel wanted to hug her, if not to reassure her, then to at least gauge her breast size. There was something off there. He'd have noticed before. "Are you sure you haven't gotten implants or anything?"

Beby raised an eyebrow and smirked. She then ran her hands up and down her body, eventually resting them on her abundant assets. "These are all real," she purred, and then spat out, "I'd have to be a damn retard to want more. Look at these things – they're huge!"

Oh Mongrel looked. He could definitely see that.

"I have to bind them to my chest and wear a bra three sizes too small just to keep them in check and stop the old perverts from drooling all over me. It's just too freaking hot today to wear any underwear. I'd wear less if I could."

At this revelation Mongrel had a reason to look away from her ample bosom and down at her breathtakingly tiny shorts. "No...under..." he couldn't complete his train of thought; his head tilted to the side as if his neck broke.

She snapped her fingers in his face to break his

concentration and said, ironically, "Focus!"

"Sorry," he said, pealing his eyes away after one last ogle. "What were we talking about?"

"My psychic. Psychologist, whatever."

"Oh right. Uh, I don't know…"

She took a step closer and flaunted her boobs in his face. "Look, I've been talking to him for a while about you. He knows I can't make up my mind, so he offered to have a session with you. See what you're like; assess you."

It occurred to Mongrel at that moment that maybe he should play hard to get. As things stood between them currently he was whipped. But here she was coming to him. This was his chance to gain a little control back, reclaim some of his manhood. He certainly wouldn't get the upper hand, but it was a start. It also occurred to him that if ever he were to kiss Beby, he'd have to climb over her boobs. Making out was guaranteed second base action. "I don't know. I just…me and shrinks don't really get along. And they cost a lot of money…"

Irate that she couldn't use her body to get what she wanted, the intensity flared in her eyes once again. How did other women do it? She jabbed a finger at Mongrel and said, "This isn't a negotiation. You do him or you can't do me, got it?" With that she turned around and walked away.

The homoerotic implications aside, Mongrel was stunned by her proclamation, but not so stunned he couldn't enjoy the view. She sashayed her hips as she stormed down the sidewalk, oblivious to how hypnotic her gyrations were. Like the older men she'd vilified earlier, Mongrel couldn't help drooling a little, even though his mouth was dry from spending much of its time hanging open. He knew, somewhere in the back of his mind, that it was rude to stare, but he was just a man, although sometimes even that was a stretch.

Then he remembered that he was supposed to be hiding. He ducked back down behind the mailbox and held his breath. After a minute he peaked his head out overtop the red box to scan across the road. The two men, Captain Pete and his customer, were nowhere to be seen.

"Hey!"

Good For Business

This time the voice was deeper, gruff, definitely male. Mongrel held his breath again and turned around, trying to be casual about it.

And, of course, it was Captain Pete.

Actually...not quite. He certainly looked like Captain Pete, but was a good two feet taller.

Mongrel manoeuvred himself nonchalantly around the mailbox, keeping it between them, unsure if he should run and hide or try to negotiate a truce.

"Thank ye," the Captain Pete lookalike said, and promptly dropped a letter in the mailbox. He then turned heel and made his way down the sidewalk. The heavy full-length coat he was wearing, despite the wicked heat, drifted purposefully behind him, almost obscuring the view of his black, knee-high boots, in which no doubt were actual feet. Yes, this man appeared to have all his appendages. He wasn't impeded by the likes of wooden pegs like the real Captain Pete.

"Wait a sec!" Mongrel hollered after him.

The man stopped and slowly turned around. The wide-brimmed hat he wore, while surely suffocating, did little to hide the menacing glare. The man's gaze itself was also suffocating. He beheld Mongrel with steely eyes.

He was obviously a pirate – a *real* pirate. Having spent the better part of his life at sea swashbuckling this and avasting that, the man had been staring and glaring for decades and had honed that particular skill like a blacksmith sharpened a blade. Often the notion that someone could stare right though you or the feeling of eyes burning in the back of your head was simply a turn of phrase, but with this man it was deadly serious. Seriously, it was deadly. He once stared a man to death – it's been documented[*]. His piercing stare has been known to leave welts in skin. Some even say with the right look he could set ants on fire, like the sun through a magnifying glass. Legends speak of him hypnotizing people and having them do his evil bidding.

And now he levelled those hypnotic eyes at Mongrel. Malice brewed beneath the surface.

---

[*] To be fair, that man had a heart condition.

Random Tangent

Mongrel now realized that opening his mouth was tantamount to opening Pandora's Box, but since he'd opened the box he might as well see what's inside. "Do I know you?" he asked timidly.

The foreboding man leered Mongrel up and down and answered in a gruff, snarling voice, "That depends; be ye a cop?"

Taking respite from those scrutinise eyes, Mongrel actually had to glance down at what he was wearing to make sure he couldn't be mistaken for anyone with authority, as he dare not lie to the man. The eyes warned him to behave himself. He reluctantly met the man's gaze again and said, "I don't believe so. No."

The man glared harder at Mongrel, making him wince. He could feel pinpricks all over his skin. A chill – welcomed though it may be – crept down his spine. Mongrel suddenly felt light-headed and had to fight to hold eye contact. His chest began to hurt and his head started pounding. Was he going to keel over and die on the sidewalk? Was this some Jedi mind trick? Was the pirate using the Force to squeeze the life out of him?

Then, suddenly, it was all gone. The stare, the pain, the chills – and they will be missed in this dreadful heat. "Well ye don't smell like one," the man said jovially. "It makes no matter anyhow. The name's Alphonse Moor." He held out his hand to Mongrel. "Used to be *Captain* Alphonse long ago, 'til I lost me ship."

Mongrel raised a limp arm in an effort to make contact, but ended up collapsing to the ground. "Sorry about your ship," he wheezed out. "At least you have a nice hat."

Alphonse took a few steps closer and leaned over Mongrel, a mixture of concern and distrust masking his face, as if he wasn't sure Mongrel was really faint. He then tipped his hat back and offered a hand, and said, "This old thing? Bah! T'isn't the same. Me last one went down with the ship. A grand hat it was, ye should've seen 'er. But I gots to wear something on me head. Feel downright cold without it."

After a few dismal attempts to grab the proffered hand, Mongrel seized it, and was jerked hastily to his feet. "Cold?" he asked. "You can't possibly be cold today. It's so hot it could rain steam." He looked to the sky as he said it. "Could be raining now for all we know."

Good For Business

The pirate looked to the sky as well. "Y'arr, we could do with a good rain."

Standing next to the man, Mongrel couldn't believe how much he *didn't* remind him of Captain Pete. For starters, the man was huge. He was nearly twice the height of his former friend, and towered over Mongrel. Instead of Captain Pete's burnt orange, his hair was black, although beginning to grey, and he wore it all over his face. Captain Pete's curly moustache was modest compared to Alphonse's full and robust facial hair, which had completely conquered the lower half of his face and was making significant gains upwards. And unlike Captain Pete, the man had real feet, but a fake hand; where his left hand should have been was what appeared to be a mannequin hand.

"Is that a fake hand?" Mongrel asked, wondering which one he'd shook moments ago.

Alphonse nodded. "Arr. Lost it in a game. The damned thing still itches." He shook his head and sang, gruffly. "A pirate's life for me."

"You lost your hand in a game? Like in a poker bet?"

"No, tis a game with potatoes and a sack. And balls. A pirate thing; you wouldna understand."

"Potato sackball?"

"Y'arr, that be it. How'd you know that?"

Mongrel had heard the name before. It seemed to be a common pastime of pirates, a game. A national sport, minus the nation. Captain Pete had once regaled him of stories and epic battles between warring ships. It was a violent game, if the tales were true, and the old pirate was a veteran. He even had a small collection of trophies. Mongrel half suspected that the game was somehow responsible for his missing legs, but old pirate refused to talk about it, always changing the subject or *bah*ing him to death. Mongrel eventually dismissed the notion. But now here was perhaps more evidence, possibly another piece to the puzzle.

"Well I, uh, might've done some pirating in my day. So how did you lose your hand playing the game?" he asked. "I don't know it to be a limb-risking sport."

Alphonse snorted and got a faraway look in his eyes, recalling the fateful day. "T'was a good day," he began. "Calm winds. A good day to set sail. The *Jolly Panther* had taken the field. They were a rowdy bunch, loud, obnoxious. But their women…" he whistled.

"The *Jolly Panther*?" Mongrel asked.

"T'is the name of their ship, lad. And 'fore ye ask, mine was the *Kracken's Own*. So them boys be known as a mean bunch, but we'd just come from a victory o'er the *Lonesome and Terrible Jack* and were feeling a might bit invincible, so I dropped me guard. We all did. Anyhow, the gals liked to crowd the sidelines and bake pies for us gents, and I stopped to catch me breath near one on the lasses, a real looker. She'd been giving me the eye. But no sooner had I opened me mouth some trollup has a go at me. From behind, quick as a hiccup, she grabs me arm'n'spins me 'round tries to shove a fresh, piping-hot pie in me face. Now I didna know it then, but this pie had a special ingredient – gunpowder. Now I jerks up me hand to cover me face just in time and I guess some of me rings I's wearin' caused a spark in the metal pan. Next thing I know I's on the other end of the field, me beard's on fire, I canna hear a thing, and I gots a stump where me hand used to be." He shook his head, remembering. "Took a month to get me hearing back, longer for me beard."

"That's awful," Mongrel said, not knowing what else to say.

"Well I shoulda known better. Can't trust them womens – specially thems from the *Jolly Panther*."

"Did you at least win the game?"

"Bah," Alphonse gave a dismissive wave of his fake hand. "But I gots revenge on that trollup. Caught her and locked her up in me ship. Raped her every hole for weeks." He chuckled. "She begged for death long 'fore I gave it to her. Ah…good times."

Suddenly this conversation had taken a turn for the morbid, heading straight into R-rated territory. Captain Pete had never talked about his past deeds. Questions asked out of curiosity were met with *bahs* and grumbles. Mongrel had always wondered what secrets the old pirate was hiding, but the only things he'd learned in all their time being friends was that Big John Charlie Marbles was a part of Captain Pete's crew on his last voyage, and he'd once assumed the name 'Él Cheerio.'

"Yeah," Mongrel said after a minute. "I remember my

raping days too. Did me some good ones." He smiled awkwardly. "But those days are behind me now. Modern society doesn't look too kindly on, uh…plundering and stufff."

Alphonse looked at Mongrel with discerning eyes. "Ye don't really strike me as a pirate."

"Oh, well…" Mongrel shrugged. "I'm retired."

The old pirate wasn't convinced. "So then ye know the pirate code? The handshake? The secret meeting place?"

Mongrel was going to try to bullshit his way through all of this, but wasn't in the mood. "Okay, no. I'm not a pirate."

"Ye be not."

"I'm not."

"And does ye always spell 'stuff' with three f's?"

"Huh?"

"Just a minute ago," Alphonse threw a thumb unnecessarily over his shoulder, "ye spelled 'stuff' wrong."

"Oh."

The big pirate leaned forward and studied Mongrel fiercely, inches from his face. "Ye look a might bit nervous, lad. Do I scares ye?"

"Just a lit. I mean a bittle." Mongrel sighed and wiped the sweat from his brow. "You come off as a little intimidating. The scary eyes and prolific raping…"

Alphonse backed away and almost looked embarrassed. "Well I's sorry. I didna mean to be so… We's pals." He proffered his hand, the real one. Mongrel shook it. "And as far as the raping goes, that was the last of her. Fortunately I seemed to get it all out of me system in them two months. Never felt no need to plunder womens no more. Got me fill, so to speak." A glazed look came across his eyes as he added, "And so did she." He then shook it off and coughed politely. "But that was the end of her – quite literally. She gots what she deserved. And now I's a wanted man. *A criminal!* Tis the thanks I get for righting the wrongs o' the world."

Mongrel didn't know what to say. He was still a little horrified over the revelation and didn't want to say anything to upset Alphonse now that he knew what the man was capable of. But he also didn't want to give him sympathy or in any way act like he condoned his actions either. Quite frankly he shouldn't be talking to

Random Tangent

him at all – a homicidal Captain Pete was lurking somewhere in the vicinity and he should be busy hiding. Not only that, but Mongrel had just gotten out of prison; the last he needed was to be caught fraternizing with other criminals.

"So tell me, lad," Alphonse continued, "if ye ain't a pirate, how did ye know 'bout potato sackball?"

This was a good question. Should he tell Alphonse about Captain Pete? How might that go? Perhaps they didn't know each other, but what if they did? What if they went back decades and were long lost brothers, and decide to team up to take Mongrel down once and for all? Could he take that risk? On the other hand, what if they were long lost enemies and this reignited an age-old feud between them? At least then Captain Pete would have someone else to worry about. Someone else to try to kill.

So many questions, so many possibilities.

A sudden pain in Mongrel's neck returned his attention back to the present, and he thought he could smell burning meat. Alphonse's glare, aimed at Mongrel's neck, was starting to sizzle. "I know another pirate!" he exclaimed, recoiling to escape the laser vision, which abruptly stopped.

"Another pirate?" Alphonse was shocked. "Here? In this town?"

Mongrel nodded, thinking about Pandora's Box again, just gaping wide open now for all to see, and he hoped his face wasn't going to melt off like in Indiana Jones. "His name is Captain Pete."

This prompted some involuntary beard-stoking from Alphonse, and faraway look came across his eyes. His beard-stroking didn't go smoothly; his fingers got stuck and he had to rip them free, pulling tangles of hair with them. He held them up to his face, studying them, seemingly unperturbed[*]. Finally he released them and said, "Well t'was a pleasure to meet ye Mr. Stevens, but I

---

[*] Captain Alphonse actually used his beard fibres to predict the future and assess situations, similar to how a psychic uses tarot cards. This used to be easier for him when he wore his rings, as he was able to pull out great clumps of hair with them, making for more accurate readings. But he'd stopped wearing them after losing his hand, not only because they could be dangerous, but because he had fewer fingers. His hand felt downright cold without his rings, but what can you do?

Good For Business

shouldna linger. Can't show me face in public much. Eyes 'er everywhere, looking, spying." He shook Mongrel's hand again, and took off down the road in a gruff saunter.

Whatever that was all about, it would surely come back to haunt him, Mongrel figured, ducking back behind the mailbox to resume his stakeout. Peering across the street, he wished he had a pair of binoculars. Nothing seemed to have changed on the lot in the time he'd spent ignoring it.

"Hey!"

Mongrel sighed. Was this going to keep happening all day? "What now?" he snapped, turning around.

This time it really was Captain Pete.

Captain Pete stood a few paces away, balanced on his pegs like a gymnast, perfected from years of practice. Pete stared at him, two beady eyes smug with menace, and Mongrel stared back, wishing he had Alphonse's eyes. After a long minute of silence, and after Mongrel had tried and failed to stare the captain to death, Mongrel chose to break the ice.

"'Sup buddy?" he said.

"Buddy?" What little humour was left lurking in the old pirate's eyes had faded, quickly replaced by malice. "I think you'n'me ain't been buddies in a long time."

"Yeah, well..." Mongrel shrugged, "...sorry."

"Whatcha 'pologizin' for?" the captain asked. "Feelin' guilty are we?"

"No. I just wish things were different. I miss hanging out with you and talking about...whatever. I miss your advice. I just miss you."

Captain Pete spat on the sidewalk, where it sizzled from the scorching heat. "Oh I wish you'd miss me, boy. But it matters not where I goes or what I does, you get me e'ry time."

"I don't get you *every* time. There are times when I see you and you're already dead!"

"Still your fault!"

"How?" Mongrel cried, exasperated. "I don't even see you and you're dead. And the times I do see you, that's it. I just see you and you die. How is that my fault? I can't kill you just by looking at you – I just tried that!"

Random Tangent

"So yous just tried to kill me? Just now?"

"Uh…" Mongrel swallowed, "…that's not what I meant."

"Y'hear that?" Captain Pete hollered to…someone. To the world, for all Mongrel knew. "He tried to kill me! He admits it!"

"No," Mongrel said, trying to stay in control of the situation. "What I meant is that even if I *tried* to kill you I can't."

"What abouts last time, with the shovel. You thinks I forgot 'bout that?"

There was the trump card. What could Mongrel possibly say in defence of that? He did it. He killed Captain Pete, even if he didn't mean to. "That…was an accident."

"Was it?"

"Well it wasn't premeditated. It was temporary insanity."

"Murder's murder, boy!" Captain Pete yelled, surely letting the neighbourhood into what should have been a private argument.

"But there's a really good explanation for that!"

"Bah! 'Tis always a good 'spanation."

Mongrel didn't know what to say. "What do you want me to say?"

Captain Pete began hobbling slowly towards Mongrel. "I wants you to admits it. Tell the world what you been doin' to me."

"The world?" Mongrel backed up, trying to keep a safe distance. He looked over the pirate's head down the road and saw just one person far in the distance. Someone's head had poked out a window a couple floors above them with the intent to tell them to quiet down, that it was the middle of the day and people should be waiting until after nightfall to have their noisy arguments, when everyone was asleep and wouldn't be bothered. But since they'd all gone quiet for the moment, the stranger didn't want to break the silence, and so just watched the skirmish from his window. It was better than anything that was on television at the moment. "Like, you want me to make a YouTube video or something?"

Ever more menace crept into Pete's eyes. "I only want what's fair." He grinned sadistically.

"Now don't start that again," Mongrel chided, still slowly backing up. "Remember what happened last time?"

"Aye, I remembers. And this time I took special precautions."

Good For Business

Mongrel didn't want to know what that meant, so tried to ignore it. "Look, we both know you're not safe around me so I'm just gonna go." He turned to leave but ran into someone.

"You sees?" Captain Pete said. "He admits it. Oh, I ain't safe 'round him. Practically a threat right there!"

Looking up at the man he'd stumbled upon, Mongrel found him frighteningly familiar. He had a big head, with big eyes, a big nose, and a big…well, we needn't go over everything; the man was big all over – not fat, but thick, muscular. He was also black – not that there's anything wrong with that, but he was a minority in Dunttstown. He was indeed the customer he'd seen Captain Pete with earlier, and now that he could see him up close, he also looked upset.

"This here is Pete's hood," he said. "You trespassin'."

"Gee, I thought you people were supposed to be jolly," Mongrel said, which was meant to be a joke, and he immediately regretted saying it.

"*Us* people?" the man asked, sneering, clearly even more upset.

"I-I didn't mean you people as in black people," Mongrel laughed nervously. "I meant fat people. Like Santa? You know?"

The man looked down at his stomach, then back at Mongrel. "The fuck you say, boy?"

What was it with people calling him boy or son or lad lately? He wasn't *that* young. Anyway, despite thinking the 'you people' he chose was the lesser of two evils, Mongrel felt no further away from a hellish beating. "I…uh…"

He stopped, deciding to go back to talking with Captain Pete, with whom he felt safer with, even though the captain had previously tried to kill him. "So you have your own hood now? When did this happen? How do you get your own hood anyway? Is it, like, through the bank or something?"

The sadistic grin never left Pete's face. He simply said, "Get 'im."

"You know, I really think I should go home and work on that YouTube video," Mongrel said as strong arms grabbed him from behind. Obviously that video was going to have to wait.

"We'd be delighted," Captain Pete snickered, "if you stays

for dinner."

Knowing this wasn't an invitation, Mongrel said nothing, letting them lead him across the street to the car lot. He glanced up and down the street again; it was even more deserted than before. Even the stranger in the window was gone – hopefully to call the police, because here he was, being dragged across the street by two men who probably had murder on their minds.

Pete's accomplice rather did have something else on his mind. "Call me fat?" he muttered. "I'll give you my fat cock. That'll be your dinner."

"Now there'll be none o' that," Captain Pete said, turning to sternly address them. "There'll be no talkin' 'bout…that, from either of you." He made a point of including them both, as if Mongrel couldn't be trusted *not* to engage in a homosexual affair moments before being killed.

"Sorry Pete," the big man said as they continued on their way. "Old habits die hard, you know what I'm sayin'?"

Suddenly Mongrel remembered where he'd seen the man before, and the memory turned his stomach. "You're Brooklyn aren't you? You tried to rape me in prison?" he asked, his voice meek and trembling, shocked by the revelation.

"It's Brecklyn. And Ima finish what I started."

"No you won't!" Captain Pete stopped and turned to them again. "And that's final."

"Yeah," Mongrel agreed. "This is a PG rated story. PG-13 at the most."

Looking a little agitated, Brecklyn sulked for a moment before asking, "Well can we at least hurt him a little? You know, beat him up or something 'fore we off him?"

"Course we can," Pete spouted. "But wait till we's inside, private-like. Ain't no one to stop us this time." He grinned evilly at Mongrel.

And there it was: they were going to kill him. They weren't hiding it; they were conspiring to commit murder in broad sweltering daylight. Mongrel took one last glance around as they entered the car lot, wondering if anyone was watching, listening, letting this atrocity unfold. He saw but one man a short distance down the road, eating popcorn and watching intently. It was Daniel

Good For Business

Ferrick, sans his mother.

"I'm over here, ass," Mrs. Ferrick said from over there, steadfastly refusing to show her face. She might want to mind her language, as this was trying and failing to be a family-friendly story, and also watch who she's calling an ass if she knows what's good for her.

They left Daniel munching his popcorn as they marched passed the cars and trucks, some vans, and a couple boats…an RV…was that an airplane? Wow, they had everything at Downtown Pete's Quality Cars. A dreadfully emaciated school bus sat surrounded by car parts and lawnmowers. Motorcycles and boatercycles[*] littered the area, and a nearly complete Sherman tank occupied one corner of the lot, almost as if it were standing guard.

The lot didn't seem so large from across the street, and while this was all very impressive, Mongrel wasn't exactly in the mood to shop at the moment. What he needed was to stop this madness. "Pete? I really thi-"

"It's Captain!" Captain Pete said, whirling on him. *"Captain!"* He poked him fiercely in the chest. "Mark me words, boy, yous gonna show me some respects 'fore we's through with you."

"I do respect you Captain Pete, that's why I'm trying to help you. And why does he not have to call you Captain?" Mongrel pointed at Brecklyn.

"Helps me? Only things you done for me is turn yourselfs in. Now quit your bitchin'."

"You know I don't do any of this on purpose," Mongrel continued. "It's out of my control. Even now you're in danger – both of you probably."

"You can'ts take on both of us," the pirate said, confident that this time his plan would succeed.

"I don't have to take you on. Something will just…happen. Something always happens."

"Well this time it'll happen to you."

"What about Bucky here? What if something happens to him? Is he safe like you?"

---

[*] Captain Pete's term for skidoos.

Random Tangent

"The hell you call me?" Brecklyn pulled Mongrel around to face him and punched him in the gut, doubling him over. He then grabbed Mongrel's hair and yanked his head back so he could look him in the eye. "It's Brecklyn, fool! You gone learn my name proper if I have to carve it into your back with an ice pick."

"Not out here," Captain Pete scolded. "Folks'll see you. Wait till we's inside."

As they continued making their way across the lot Mongrel felt less and less sure that things would work in his favour. It was two against one this time. He had to make some sort of plan. As they passed the van Brecklyn and Captain Pete were inspecting earlier he thought he'd try a different approach to the situation: know thy enemy.

"Is that the van you were looking at earlier?" Mongrel asked Brecklyn, who confirmed that it was. "You gonna buy it?"

"Naw, I ain't a customer. I was just fixin' it. Used to be a mechanic 'fore all this."

"What happened?"

"Went to prison, man, don't you remember?"

"Yeah, but why?"

Brecklyn shrugged. "Just had enough of people's shit, you know what I'm sayin'? Tired of people yellin' at me for shit that ain't my fault. They be bitchin' at me cause they don't take care of they cars. Finally I lost it and dropped the hoist on this fat fucker. Squashed him with his own car; a fuckin' Echo. Thing needed new shocks twice a year to keep his fat ass drivin' around. He thought I was rippin' him off. His own fat ass was rippin' him off. Fat greasy fucker, smelled like a bucket of inside-out assholes. I squished him thin though." He laughed.

"When did that happen?" Mongrel asked. "I don't remember hearing about it."

"It was a while back," Brecklyn replied. "And my shop was in Shchevret. 'Fore it went nuclear."

The beast mayor of Dunttstown was perhaps the best mayor Dunttstown had seen in many years, once you got passed the fact that it didn't really have a name, no one could understand a word it said, and it wasn't from Earth. Back on the beast's home planet, Hell, it never rained. Once it experienced rain on Earth it adored it,

Good For Business

and wanted more. This inevitably led to the orchestrated destruction of the nuclear power plant in the nearby town of Shchevret.[*] After playing in the rain and sludge of the aftermath, the mayor began to notice changes. First, his skin took on a sickly translucence, and its left arm began to miraculously grow back – but not the right one. It could also now throws its farts like a ventriloquist can throw a voice. Already notorious for its extremely unpleasant emissions, the beast now had a new toy to play with, much to the chagrin of the citizens of Dunttstown. One minute you'd be standing in line waiting to buy your movie ticket, the next you were keeled over, retching and writhing around in agony, while everyone thought you were having a seizure. This amused the beast to no end, and it often spent hours sneaking around like a ninja, silently attacking random people. Like the Batman, it surmised. When it learned that some folks had asthma or bad allergies, the stakes went up. The possibility of killing someone made it like a game. The beast didn't feel too bad about any of this, considering a deal was close to being made with the hospital administration, and the doctor's strike would be over soon.

"Look's like you picked a good time to go on a killing spree," Mongrel said.

"Yeah! Got my ass outta there just in time!" Brecklyn raised a hand to Mongrel who, in the spirit of camaraderie, high-fived him.

This made Captain Pete irate. "Don't be figh-hiven' 'im! He's evil! He ain't no friend of ours!"

Mongrel shushed the old pirate away and continued his conversation with Brecklyn, asking if he'd fixed the van.

"Course I fixed it," he said. "Parts of it anyway. I can fix anything."

They approached what Mongrel assumed was the main office. It didn't look like much from the outside; a tiny, run down

---

[*] This was the official story. Secretly the bombing of the power plant was meant as an act of war upon Shchevret. Since most of the inhabitants died in the blast, no retaliation ensued. The beast mayor took this as a sign of surrender, and now considers Shchevret part of his growing empire. Those still alive are doing well, considering they lived through a nuclear fallout, and are piecing together their lives and each other, dealing as best they can with the changes the radiation caused in their anatomies.

single-floor shack, white panelling, and a couple small windows. It wasn't impressive to say the least, as far as buildings go. He did not want to go inside.

Captain Pete reached the door first and held it open for them, his chivalry as old as he was, but not dead. The inside of the office perfectly complimented the outside, serving to further illustrate that the original architect was either drunk, hated his job, or wanted revenge on whoever contracted them to build the office. The tiny room was sparsely furnished, making the small space feel artificially bigger. What appeared to be a kitchen table was in its center, with a chair on either side. They were shabby but serviceable. On the table were a couple stacks of paper and a pen. Otherwise the place was practically barren; no pictures or paintings lined the walls, not even a clock. Only a dreadful looking, nearly dead plant sat in the corner. It might have stood four feet tall in its heyday, but now drooped almost to the floor, which was littered with dead leaves. Surely the good captain could've just replaced it with a new, fresh one; dead plants were surely bad for business. Or perhaps put a fake one in its place, one that would require the amount of maintenance Captain Pete could make time for: none. But let's not get ahead of ourselves. Captain Pete had only opened up shop the day before, so there was plenty of time to get settled in. Although since the store was only a day old it would mean he'd brought in the plant from somewhere else; that he'd been neglecting it for a while. Why he didn't just discard it was anyone's guess. Maybe it had sentimental value. A door stood in every corner of the room; two faced East and a third was on the Southern wall across from the entrance, where Mongrel stood, stalling, trying to think of a reason to excuse himself from going inside.

"What about the other cars on the lot? Which ones are good to go? I only ask because I came to buy a car. Can we go have a look?"

"Ha!" Captain Pete exclaimed, shoving Mongrel through the door. "So you admits it! You comes lookin' for me."

"Did not!" Mongrel protested, unhappy to be inside. Things were not going well. "I came to buy a car. I didn't know you were gonna be here. And since you are, I should go." He tried to leave but the two men blocked the exit.

Good For Business

"Says 'Pete' right on the sign!" Captain Pete spat.

"That could've been any Pete!"

"You see's the sign 'Pete's Quality Cars' and thinks to yourselfs, 'gee, I haventa killed meself a Pete today,' and tis why yous here. *Admits it!*" Pete was practically frothing at the mouth.

Mongrel closed his eyes and tried to remain calm. "I just came to look at your cars. I swear that was it."

"Really...?" Pete asked, not convinced. "Don't you knows there be another car lot on th'other side o' town? Coulda gone there, but no..."

"Not anymore."

Captain Pete looked at Mongrel. "Not anymore what?"

"Wan's Tip Top...whatever car shop, right? It's gone. Burnt down a couple hours ago. I was there."

This cast a spell of silence across the room for a moment, until Captain Pete asked, "Your doin'?" But before Mongrel could answer he cut in again. "Lemme guess, t'was an accident?"

"I don't really kno-"

"Shit man, I pegged you all wrong," Brecklyn interrupted. "Looks like we got ourselves an arsonist over here!" He slapped Mongrel proudly on the back.

Wincing and moving himself just out of arm's reach (he couldn't go any further in the small office), Mongrel said, "I didn't do it. It just...happened."

"Oh course! Course," Captain Pete said sarcastically. "It just *happened*. Everythin' just *happens* with you."

"Yes it was an accident. And you guys better let me go before another accident *happens* in here."

"Say what?" Brecklyn asked, clearly offended. "You think you gonna play with fire in here? Think again, man. You the one who's gone get burnt. I'll burn you ass real good." He winked at Mongrel and blew a kiss.

"Woulds you cut that out?" Captain Pete said after a violent sigh. "I's had it up to 'ere with that there homo man-sex nonsense!"

Suddenly Mongrel had an idea. It was a horrible, sickening idea that turned his stomach, but it was the only idea he had. If it worked, things could go very badly for him, but it would save his life. He grumbled as quietly as he could, not liking it one bit. But

Random Tangent

what other options did he have?

"What? I can take him Pete," Brecklyn cried. He glared Mongrel right in the eye. "I can take you."

Mongrel swallowed and said, "I know you can take me. And I'd let you. I'd let you take me all night long."

Brecklyn would have taken a step back if he'd had room to do so. The remark threw him, and he was at a loss for words.

"Watch yourselfs, boy," Captain Pete growled, getting in Mongrel's face. "I saids no more talk o' that. And I be the one givin' the threats 'round 'ere."

Already threatened to capacity, Mongrel rolled his eyes. "What are you gonna do, kill me?"

"Aye." Captain Pete backed away slowly and nodded gravely. "If'n'ya thinks you earned some good will for takin' out me competition you'd be wrong. I's gonna kill you more ways'n'you know how to die."

"Not trying to earn good will," Mongrel said. "Just trying to buy a car."

"What'd you needs a car for?" Captain Pete scoffed.

"Well…" Mongrel had to think. Simply wanting a car wasn't good enough, he had to have a reason to have been so desperate to risk coming to Downtown Pete's Quality Cars. "I'm starting up a home business. I needed a nice, big vehicle." He made eyes at Brecklyn. "I like my vehicles like I like my men. Big. That van out front looked good." Mongrel was trying to come off as lustful, wanton, but looked more like he was constipated. "The one your big, strong man fixed."

Unlike Mongrel, Captain Pete didn't bat an eye. "I means what'd you need a car for when yous gonna be dead?"

"Now hold up a sec, Pete," Brecklyn said. "We could always use the sale."

"What?" Captain Pete demanded. "Tis no point sellin' that bugger a bleedin' car when we's gonna kill 'im!"

"Yo dog, you's thinkin' 'bout this all wrong. Draft up the paperwork, get his info, sign off on it – then we kill him. But we do it real quiet, hide the body. Maybe no one knows he's missin' for a while. We'll at least sell a car. It's good for business."

Pondering this, his moustache twitching, Captain Pete was

silent.

"Let's get in his pants, man."

"What?"

"I said let's give him a chance, man,"

More moustache twitching and grumbling ensued. Finally Captain Pete sighed and gave in. "Fine. But tis all on you!" He glared at his accomplice before reaching into his pocket and fishing out a set of keys. Selecting one, he unlocked one of the doors that led off to the building's West side and swung it open on its rusted, squeaky hinges. He then turned to Mongrel and said, "Step into me office."

"I thought this was your office," Mongrel said, taking a look around the small room once more. He stepped over and peaked inside. The next room was sunk a foot or more into the ground, and was even more sparse than the fake office – it didn't even have a floor; it was just dirt. But it did have an actual desk instead of a table, which seemed to have been lowered to a more Captain Pete-friendly height. Fake wood panelling served as wallpaper, complete with a couple fake portholes, giving Mongrel the impression the old pirate was trying to make himself comfortable in his new career. A pull-chain light bulb hung limply from the ceiling, and the only thing adorning the wall was an odd calendar displaying a naked woman with two prosthetic limbs. There was no natural light filtering into the room, and Mongrel felt if he went inside he'd never see any again. A shove from behind sealed his fate.

A small step facilitated easy access for Captain Pete, but wasn't necessary for anyone else. Mongrel skipped it as he was shoved into the room and forced into a steel folding chair. Captain Pete helped himself into a luxurious office chair behind the pre-school-sized desk and looked sternly at Mongrel. Then the salesman came on.

"Good to see you again Mr. Stevens!" He lied with a big smile on his face. "Hot as a fryin' pans' arse out there today, ain't it? Won't your have a seat?" he asked, even though Mongrel was already sitting down. "I hears you went'n'burnt down th'other car lot? Many thanks to you! I'd shake your hand but I hates you."

"Oh that," Mongrel said dismissively. "That's just a nasty rumour no one started when I told you I didn't do it."

Random Tangent

"Come now Mr. Stevens, no need to hides the truth. Much like yourselfs, it won't leave this room."

Mongrel rolled his eyes and gave in. "Fine. I did it. Happy?" What was he going to do? They'd already assumed he had, so it was less work to leave them to their illusions rather than try to convince them otherwise – and if it turned out his life was going to be cut short then he wanted to put as little effort as he could in getting to the end of it. He also had to consider that maybe he wasn't unconscious when the fire started. What if he was a sleepwalker, or had an alter ego, like the mad scientist Bosley? Who knew what really happened?

"And you better watch yourselves," he continued, "Or this place could go up in flames too."

"I saids not to threaten me, boy," Captain Pete said with a scowl. The salesman was gone.

"It's not a threat," Mongrel said, "shit just happens, like you said. I don't control it. This whole place could just erupt in flames at any minute. You play with fire you're gonna get burnt."

"Yo ass is gone get burnt," Brecklyn said, blowing Mongrel a kiss, "by my bi-"

"That's it!" Captain Pete yelled, jumping to his pegs, which had no noticeable effect on his height. "I's had it up to 'ere with that nonsense!" he had his hand raised as high as he could stretch above his head, which was nearly-

"Four feet?" Mongrel asked, trying and failing to suppress a grin. "I guess your patience is a little…short?"

Captain Pete screamed and launched himself across the table, landing his hands around Mongrel's neck and sending them both toppling onto the dirty floor.

Brecklyn scrambled to pry his boss off Mongrel. "Dammit, that ain't how we treat customers." He yanked Captain Pete to his feet and dragged him a few feet away.

"He ain't no customer!" Captain Pete sulked angrily, throwing the cutest pirate tantrum. "He's a thievin', murderin' traitor, and I wouldna sell 'im the shit in me drawers!"

"Chill out, man. Relax," Brecklyn reassured, ushering Captain Pete toward the door. "Just go on outside and let me take care of this."

Good For Business

The captain did need to take it easy; getting stressed out was hard on the old ticker. Plundering and pillaging takes its toll on a man, and while the captain was a tough old bastard, his age was beginning to show. Maybe he should let a younger man handle the situation. "If he tries anythin' 'spicious, you get me." He said, hobbling up the step.

"I got this." Brecklyn closed the door behind him and turned to face Mongrel. "Hey baby."

Mongrel smiled tersely and waved. This is where his plan could lapse into uncontrollable backfiring, so he needed to proceed with caution. Getting rid of Captain Pete was a good start; the killer was gone, but now he had to deal with the rapist.

A horrific smile eased itself onto Brecklyn's face as he sashayed over to Mongrel. "Now that we have some alone time…"

"…We can get down to business," Mongrel nearly yelled, completing the sentence, although not the way Brecklyn would have put it. He dug out his wallet and removed his trusty credit card, blew the dust off it, and slapped it on the table.

Not to be deterred, Brecklyn sat down on the front of the desk, practically in Mongrel's lap. "Ain't no rush, baby," he said seductively, gently running his hand down the side of Mongrel's face.

It was all Mongrel could do not to flinch away and jeopardize everything. But he stayed the course. "Yeah…well, look at the time. Wouldn't want to keep you passed closing time, right?"

"Hush now, don't you worry 'bout that. Fact I think we be up all night working on this, just…pounding it out." He licked his lips at Mongrel, who admirably managed to not projectile vomit all over the place.

Taking a moment to quell his heaving stomach, Mongrel knew he desperately needed to gain control of the situation. "Before we get to any…pounding…perhaps I should take the car on a test drive?"

"There'll be plenty of time for that, don't you worry," Brecklyn cooed. He began running his fingers through Mongrel's thick hair. "Brecky's gone take good care of you. Gone take you on the best ride of yo life."

This time Mongrel couldn't help but pull away, even though

Random Tangent

he liked having his hair played with. "All the same I'd *really* like to go check that van out." He got up and went to try the door. It was locked. "Business before pleasure, right?"

Brecklyn just stared at Mongrel, not looking pleased.

"That's not a problem is it?"

Thinking for a moment, Brecklyn remained quiet. Finally he said, "I just can't have you running around loose, you know?"

"Aww, what's the matter? Don't think you can handle me?"

"It's like this; Pete gave me this job, you know? Straight up, right outta prison. Not a lot of dudes would've done that. I gotta do right by him. Pete'd kill me if you escaped."

"Don't tell me you're afraid of Pete. Big, strong man like you?"

"I ain't afraid of him," Brecklyn said, sounding like there was more to that story.

Mongrel realized he had to try something else if he was going to get out of this room. He turned to face the door and bent towards it, jutting his rear end out towards Brecklyn. "I just picture you and me in the back of that van, steaming up the windows, rocking it back and forth. Hope it has good shocks." He looked over his shoulder at the ex-con, who was eyeballing his ass hungrily. "Won't you please take me to the van...and then take me *in* the van?"

"Shit I love it when you bitches beg," Brecklyn said, transfixed on Mongrel's now-gyrating hips. "A'ight, check this out." He began to untie the drawstring[*] on his pants, scaring Mongrel by making him think he was going to be raped right then and there. But Brecklyn removed the drawstring from his pants completely. "Hold out yo hands."

Doing as instructed, Mongrel watched as Brecklyn bound his hands together with the string. "Hope you like a little bondage."

"Ooh yeah I do," Mongrel lied, using his most seductive voice, which obviously needed more practice. Having his hands tied wasn't to his liking and might end up interfering with his escape

---

[*] Prison rules forbade anything that could be used as rope, including pants drawstrings. Prison issued clothing was all Velcro. After being incarcerated for so long, having the option to tie things again was a welcomed joy to Brecklyn, and he'd taken to wearing drawstring track pants ritually.

Good For Business

plan, but he didn't object. Unfortunately he didn't have any other option; if he didn't consent he might not even make it out of the tiny room. He would just have to keep improvising. At least his hands were in front of him instead of behind his back.

Once he was satisfied that Mongrel's hands were secure, Brecklyn fished a key out of his pocket and unlocked the door from the inside. Swinging the rickety door open on its squeaky hinges, he guided Mongrel into the main room.

Captain Pete sat at the table like a sentry, legs dangling in the chair. He did not look pleased to see them, especially since Mongrel was still alive. He cast a questioning glance at Brecklyn, who mouthed the words, 'I got this.' Then he shot a Mongrel a vicious glare reminiscent of Alphonse's but thankfully nowhere near as deadly, and made stabbing motions with his hand (although he could have been cheering Mongrel on, but it's unlikely).

Feeling like a farm animal, Mongrel was herded back out through the entrance and into the blistering heat. He'd forgotten how hot it was outside whilst trying to avoid murder and rape, and nearly collapsed from the shock.

"You think it's hot now," Brecklyn mused, "wait till we get in the back of that van."

Outside once more, feeling the still wind in his hair was a luxury Mongrel wasn't sure he would ever enjoy again. He wasn't going to waste this opportunity. Obviously he couldn't just run away. Even if Brecklyn didn't have a firm grip on his shirt, he wouldn't get far with his hands bound. He had to wait until the time was right to make his move...whatever move it was going to be.

"Here she is," Brecklyn purred as they approached the van. He sounded almost proud of it, as if it was a far more fancy or exotic car rather than an old, rusted jalopy. "Had my big, strong hands all over this thing this morning, workin', sweating.' Now I'm gone be workin' and sweatin' with you baby." He licked his lips and pulled Mongrel around to the rear of the van and fished a set of car keys out of his pocket.

"Wait!" Mongrel cried. "I, uh...want to hear the engine."
"What for?"

That was a good question. Why did he want to hear the engine? Why did he *need* to hear the engine? He knew he was

Random Tangent

stalling, but he couldn't just say that; he needed a plausible reason. Mongrel glanced around, thinking, and caught a glimpse of Captain Pete watching them like a hawk out the window. His face was pressed up against the glass, his nose squished sideways. Through the fog his breath was creating Mongrel thought he could see foam at the corners of his mouth – liquefied anger. "Um…because the sound of the engine makes me wet and stuff?" It wasn't the best answer, and he held his breath, waiting to see if Brecklyn would take the bait.

A mask of confusion was all he got, and it was a tense few seconds before a smile broke out on the rapist's face and he said, "Alright baby. I dig that." He walked over to the driver's door, dragging his bounty with him, unlocked it and helped himself inside. After a minute of fumbling the engine started rumbling. He put his foot to the floor and the engine roared. "Like that?" he asked.

"Oh yeah!" Mongrel cheered. "Love that sound, gets me all horny. The way you pump that engine full of gas, it feels like you're pumping *me* full of…gas." He smiled awkwardly, sensing what little sex appeal he had dissipating like a fart in the wind. Thankfully Brecklyn didn't seem to hear that last part so Mongrel carried on. "So it works then?"

"What, the van?" Brecklyn asked. "Yeah, mostly. Still needs some work, but she drives anyway." He made to turn off the engine.

"No don't!" Mongrel yelled, stopping him just in time. "Leave it running. I…uh…can be pretty loud sometimes."

Hoping out of the van, Brecklyn had a huge smile on his face. He grabbed Mongrel's ass ferociously. "Does my baby like to squeal?"

"Like a pig," Mongrel replied, trying to keep the disgust out of his voice. He immediately regretted his farm animal of choice, but had to admit there was no animal suitable for comparison. He did, however, feel like *some* kind of animal being led to the proverbial slaughterhouse as Brecklyn dragged him around to the back of the van. "Don't suppose you could untie my hands?" he asked, knowing it was a futile effort.

"Thought you liked a little bondage?"

"Uh, I changed my mind."

Good For Business

Brecklyn opened the van's right rear door, and waved his hand, indicating for Mongrel to get inside. "It's too late for that now, but don't worry, you gone need them later."

Mongrel looked into the empty abyss of the van. It seemed like the mouth of a giant beast, ready to swallow him whole. There would be no going back. If he allowed himself be alone with the ex-con in this van, it was all over. He'd never see the light of day again, or if he did he'd be a changed man, and not for the better. Was he really going to go through with this? Did he have *any* other options? Maybe he would've been better off in the hands of Captain Pete; at least the old pirate only wanted to kill him. Now he was going to be subjected to a brutal, horrendous, crime of passion which he would have to live with for the rest of his hopefully short life. To top it off, there wasn't even a mattress or blanket or anything on the floor (small comfort though they may be) to facilitate cuddling afterwards – and if he was about to be raped he was definitely going to need a hug of some sort when it was all said and done. And perhaps a therapist.

This brought to mind Beby and her demands that he see her shrink, and it saddened him greatly to know he would never make that appointment. He would never get the chance to pass whatever tests the doctor devised for him. He would never get to prove himself worthy of dating Beby. He would never know the joy of her enormous rack.

That rack. That treasure she'd been hiding all this time. Those perfectly proportioned pieces of pectoral protuberance. He'd barely had a chance to say hello, let alone give them a proper goodbye. He felt like crying.

No. Mongrel's resolve hardened. He wasn't going to give up like that. He wouldn't abandon Beby and her boobs. He was *going* to see her shrink, he was *going* to get his approval to date her, and he was *damn well* going to fuck her brains out.

He was going to live, dammit! He was going to live for those tits!

Mongrel looked at Brecklyn, still waiting for him to climb into the van, and then kicked him between the legs as hard as he could. Brecklyn cried out in shock and pain, doubling over, going down to one knee. Mongrel then grabbed the other van door and threw it open with all his strength, slamming it into the rapist's head with a sickening clank.

Seeing flailing limbs and hearing the thud of a body hitting the ground were enough for Mongrel; he wasn't going to stick around and investigate. He tossed himself into the van and scrambled to the driver's seat. A familiar array of buttons and symbols lay before him, and he recognized the dashboard layout from the last time he'd stolen a vehicle – an ambulance nearly a year ago when he was escaping another attempted murder.

The scope of his life flashed before his eyes; much of it running to escape untimely death. He needed to do something about that. Something had to change. Perhaps he should start hanging out with a different group of friends. Maybe start running towards danger instead of away from it, since that technique wasn't doing much for him. He already had murder under his belt, time to move on to bigger things, or rather smaller. He could become an arms dealer, or some kind of thug. Instead of getting beaten it would be nice to be giving the beatings for a change. The options were limitless. He could assault old ladies, vandalize city property, steal more cars…

"No," he said, being no fun whatsoever.

Catching a glimpse of Captain Pete hobbling out of his office, raving like a lunatic, was enough to get Mongrel in gear – by putting the van in gear and putting the pedal to the floor. He treaded pavement for a moment before gaining traction and surging forward. It started slow, but the van rapidly gained speed as Mongrel drove around the parking lot looking for a way out. He didn't want to drive as fast as he was, but the van didn't seem to want to slow down no matter how hard he braked. His hands being tied made controlling the rampaging van more difficult, and it already handled like a blimp losing air. It was only a matter of time before he ran into something, be it a car, a building, or a Pete.

"*Captain,*" Mongrel muttered.

Speaking of Captain Pete, he suddenly came from out of nowhere. Mongrel rounded the office for the third time and found his nemesis just standing in the middle of the car lot. You might think he wanted to be killed – expected it even. But Mongrel wasn't in the mood for vehicular manslaughter and swerved out of the way at the last second. Had he not been busy wrestling for control of the van, and had his hands not been tied, he would've rolled down the window to shout at the old pirate about how hard he was trying *not* to kill him. As it happened, the new trajectory took him through a narrow gap in the used vehicles where he traded some paint and sacrificed the passenger-side mirror, hopped the curb and careened out onto the city streets.

The tires squealed loudly and he was airborne for a moment, but once Mongrel was sure the van was going to remain on all four wheels he cried out triumphantly. He'd just outwitted not one, but two men trying to rape and murder him. Best of all, Captain Pete was still alive – he was probably furious about the turn of events, but this was the best possible outcome for him. And boy would he be pissed at Brecklyn. It was probably safe to say whatever business relationship they had was over.

In a day full of mishaps and disappointments, something had finally gone right. He glanced back through the open rear doors, catching the sun beginning its decent toward the horizon, and reflected on an otherwise miserable day. Sure, he'd gotten to drive around in a limo, but the little Hitler knocked him out. He'd probably deserved it, but still. And because of that he'd almost died in a fire. He also never accomplished any of his errands; he was without a puppy for Charlie and despite visiting two dealerships still did not have a vehicle.

Come to think of it, that wasn't true; he *did* have this van. It wasn't what he'd had in mind, but hey, it was free!

Actually, no it wasn't. It was stolen, and there were many good reasons why he couldn't keep the van. First, Mongrel was no car thief, and had no intention of becoming one. The last time he'd stolen a car, the aforementioned ambulance he'd borrowed without asking last year, resulted in his encounters with Shamus Bond - life or death ordeals that still plagued him to this day. The last thing he needed was to incite another war. And if the hospital had the anti-agent on speed dial, who might Captain Pete have at his disposal? The old pirate never talked about his past, leaving Mongrel to fill in the blanks with all manner of nightmares.

Secondly, this was a legitimate crime. Captain Pete wasn't dead, and he would talk. If the cops were brought into this, Mongrel could be looking at jail time. He'd managed to escape Duntt Penn. once, and not without help. The odds of doing it again were slim at best. Besides, his previous escape was spurred by his innocence; this time he would be guilty, and wouldn't be able to justify a daring escape, considering that success would make him a wanted felon. He'd have to live his life on the run. No, it was never going to work.

Lastly, Mongrel really didn't want the van. It was too cumbersome, didn't have enough windows, and was probably a pig on gas. Not that he was in any position to be choosy, but the van simply wasn't a vehicle he could see himself driving on a daily basis.

It got worse: he was going to have to take the van back to Downtown Pete's Quality Cars.

"What?" Mongrel asked. "No. No, no, no. Not gonna happen."

He knew that if he simply left the van parked on the side of the road it could still be considered theft. And with witnesses to the crime and his fingerprints all over the vehicle there was no way he wouldn't be caught. If Mongrel really wanted to walk away from this cleanly he'd have to sneak back to the car lot and leave the van where he'd found it. After all, it would be hard to convince the police that a car had been stolen when it's *right there*.

Mongrel sighed, not liking this idea one bit. He ground the van to a halt, which took a lot of time and effort, and a prayer. The van had an obscenely long stopped distance. It almost seemed to be fighting the brakes, not wanting to slow down, not wanting to go back to Downtown Pete's. Mongrel could sympathize. Then he recalled Brecklyn's words about the van still needing some work – brake work probably.

Just one more reason why this van wasn't the one for Mongrel.

Once he'd gotten the van turned around and was on his way back – and at a much slower speed to facilitate an easier time braking – Mongrel began to think of how to leave the van on Captain Pete's doorstep without him knowing. Wouldn't it just irk him too, to learn his nemesis had been right under his nose, like a ninja?

Good For Business

That wasn't a bad idea, actually. He could sneak back after dark like a ninja and drop off the van. Surely the captain wouldn't still be there after the store closed, would he?

But what if he was? What if he lived in the small building? There were two other doors in the office, what if one of them led to a living quarters of sorts? And waiting until nightfall would give the pirate plenty of time to set up a trap – lots of traps. The old bugger couldn't be trusted. And even if none of that happened, waiting gave the captain the opportunity to call the cops, and within a couple hours or less there would be a warrant out for Mongrel's arrest. No, it was best to return the van as quickly as possible; at least they wouldn't be expecting that.

Suddenly a horn blared in Mongrel's ears, and he looked back to see the town bus inches from his rear bumper. The open rear doors made for an alarming image, making the bus seem more menacing. The driver could be seen through the windshield screaming and shaking with anger, giving Captain Pete a run for his money. He also thought he heard the words, "Go right!"

Seeing the intersection approaching with Downtown Pete's Quality Cars on the left, Mongrel wasn't sure what to do. He rolled down the window hoping to hear better, but got the horn again, louder this time. Once the ringing in his ears stopped he caught, "...As in right off a fucking cliff, retard!"

As yes, Nancy Yumpta, the surly bus driver badly in need of anger management classes, or at least to get laid. Same goes for Captain Pete for that matter. Hell, they should just hook up and kill two birds with one stone. Nancy and the captain would probably make for a cute couple, Mongrel thought, smiling. Then he pictured them having sex and felt sick.

What the hell her problem anyway, laying on the horn all the time? So he wasn't quite going the speed limit – so what? Did she know the van's brakes barely worked? Did she have any idea that Mongrel had just avoided being ass-raped and murdered? And did she have the slightest notion that he was courageously going back into the dragon's den of horror – so excuse him for *not* being in a rush to get there?

Mongrel hit the gas in anger and immediately regretted it. He sailed through the thankfully green light, realizing he was going

Random Tangent

to zoom right by the car lot. He slammed on the brakes, although the only noticeable effect this had was the bus ramming into back him. Their velocities being similar, it was just a gentle nudge, but nevertheless Mongrel panicked and threw the steering wheel left, began to swerve, and was now be driven off the road.

The van careened across the street and, almost like last time, hopped the curb and sailed violently between two parked cars, trading more paint and taking of the driver's side mirror this time. The bus sped on down the road, a few impolite hand gestures lining its windows for Mongrel's viewing pleasure, although he was too busy struggling to maintain control of the vehicle to notice. He also didn't notice Captain Pete or his lackey anywhere, but with all the commotion they wouldn't remain out of sight for long.

Cruising through the car lot, Mongrel mashed the brake pedal into the floor, causing some grinding noises but little else. Miraculously he managed to avoid hitting anything, whether by luck or his driving skills I couldn't tell you; both are equally unlikely. Then he spotted his enemies.

After hearing the noise they must have run out of the office, and were now glancing around, bewildered. It wasn't long before the van swung around the side of the building, and they turned just in time to see Mongrel heading straight for them. They took a few milliseconds to be confused – obviously they weren't expecting to see him or the van again – before jumping out of the way. Brecklyn diving to his right, back around the east side of the office, and Captain Pete flinging himself left. Now if only Mongrel had kept driving straight…

As it happens, Mongrel, in the spirit of *not* trying to kill Captain Pete, appeared to do exactly that, veering right at the last possible second and ramming straight into the little pirate mid-dive. Horrified, Mongrel saw, heard and felt Captain Pete's body bounce off the van's bumper they all crashed into a motor home and he finally, abruptly came to a stop.

The airbag deployed, making the crash slightly less fatal, but Mongrel hadn't been wearing his seatbelt – fleeing a serial rapist with your hands tied made safety an afterthought – leaving him feeling like he'd been on the losing end of a boxing match. Pain flared up all over his body, but nothing felt broken. After a minute

Good For Business

the soft pillow of air deflated, giving way to the hard plastic underneath, and Mongrel opened his eyes and sat back. The windshield was cracked in a thousand places, making for alarming and confusing visuals, but even without being able to see much he was pretty certain Captain Pete had been obliterated. It also seemed darker somehow. Dusk wasn't for another hour or so, causing Mongrel to wonder how long he'd been lying in the wreckage. He found the driver's door was stuck shut, so he fell out of his seat and crawled towards the rear of the van where one of the doors still hung open. Light streamed through it.

Stopping halfway to the exit, Mongrel curled up on the floor of the van, grief and pain overwhelming him. Tears welled in his eyes and began to streak down the side of his face. Twice now he'd run over Captain Pete, and countless other times his presence was enough to kill him. It just wasn't fair to either of them. "I'm sorry," he sobbed, speaking to his dead former friend. He'd tried this time, he *really* did. He didn't want to be a murderer, but no matter what he did he couldn't change fate.

In the wreckage, debris scattered all around him, Mongrel wept.

Suddenly someone grabbed Mongrel by the hair and dragged him roughly out of the van and flung him on the ground. He danced around until he was on his back and none of his bare skin was touching the scalding pavement. Shielding his eyes, he looked up to see Brecklyn looming over him, and someone had pissed in his soup. Before he could say a word Brecklyn bent down, grabbed Mongrel's collar and yanked him to his knees, ripping his shirt in the process.

"So strong," Mongrel wheezed. "I like my men str-"

"Shut up!" the big man hurled at him. And I do mean hurled. Flakes of spittle drenched Mongrel's face, and in his shaken condition Mongrel assumed he was still bleeding. He attempted to wipe away the blood with his hands but when he pulled his fingers away to inspect them he became confused to find the fluid clear. "Oh you gone get a lot worse than that," Brecklyn said quietly, glancing back at the motor home.

Mongrel followed his gaze back to the wreckage of the RV, and what a wreck it was. The van was actually *inside* the larger vehicle, which would explain why he couldn't open the door. Had Mongrel been going faster he might have made it all the way through the motor home. He would've been impressed with the damage he'd caused if only Captain Pete hadn't been a part of it. Now he was apart in it. He didn't have to go look – not that he wanted to – to know that his former friend was in pieces inside. There was no way anyone could survive that kind of destruction. Guilt churned in his stomach.

"What you just did to my man Pete," Brecklyn said, still looking at the nearly bisected motor home, "Ima do *ten times* that to you!" He grabbed Mongrel by the throat and raised him eye level. "You know in movies where they torture people to death? You gonna *wish* you were in one of those movies!"

Despite being shaken to the core after killing Captain Pete, a horror that seemed to never end, and despite his dizziness and disorientation from being in the accident, and also despite the hands closing in around his neck, Mongrel still managed to keep up his earlier charade of seducing the large ex-con.

"Have...have you even seen that movie where people get turned on by car crashes?" he asked, his voice a strangled whisper. "That's me. I am *so* turned on right now."

Brecklyn then did something that worried Mongrel; he smiled and released him. "Oh you like that? Well my fist is about to have an accident with your face!" He threw all his strength into a punch that broke Mongrel's nose in three places and sent him sprawling on the ground.

Woozy from the pain, Mongrel tried to lie still and let the pain wash over him like the tide, and hoped that also like the tide, it would recede. But the heat of the black asphalt felt like a stovetop and in seconds he was rolling around, trying to find some position he could maintain that required little effort and exposed no skin to the scorching pavement. This time blood really was covering his face, trickling from his nostrils this way and that with each painful movement; over his chin, up into his hair, down his throat.

"Ooh boy you just be floppin' 'round like a fish outta water!" Brecklyn laughed, a disturbing donkey chortle. "And there's plenty more where that came from. "I'm gonn-"

"Ye gonna what?"

Good For Business

They both turned to see Alphonse standing by the RV. He seemed to be surveying the damage nonchalantly, even approvingly.

"The fuck are you?" Brecklyn demanded.

"I be asking the questions 'round 'ere," Alphonse replied, sounding almost disinterested. He finally met Brecklyn's confused scowl. "Don't mind me lad. As ye were. I'll step in when necessary."

Now Mongrel was confused. Did the old pirate merely come to watch him get his ass kicked and probably raped to death? Was he not going to help at all? Did he even know what was going on? Then again, maybe he *did* know what was going on. He'd acted a little strange earlier when Mongrel had mentioned Captain Pete; what if they knew each other? What if they had been friends, and he'd just witnessed what appeared to be Mongrel running down Captain Pete in broad daylight? What if he only showed up to make sure Mongrel paid dearly for his crimes? Perhaps Mongrel should crawl away while he had the chance.

For his part, Brecklyn gave him that chance by remaining distracted, choosing to address the pirate's interruption over assaulting Mongrel. "Beat it old man, this don't concern you."

"I'll mind whose business I please." Alphonse then smiled, if you can call it that. If the old pirate considered himself to be smiling then he desperately needed to work on his people skills. His teeth were bared in more of a grimace than anything friendly, and as such he came off as threatening.

Brecklyn sneered at the man, not feeling as threatened as the smile suggested he should, and returned his attention to Mongrel, who was trying to drag himself away without touching the pavement for more than a couple seconds at a time. "Where you think you going?" he asked, planting a boot into Mongrel's midsection. He reached down, grabbed a fistful of hair and yanked Mongrel's head back. "I ain't done with you yet."

"If I may interrupt for but a moment," Alphonse interrupted. "Ye be doin' that wrong."

"You don't even know what I'm doin'," Brecklyn said, putting a choke hold on Mongrel. He then glared at Alphonse. "Man, get your wrinkly old ass outta here! Don't need no one criticizin' me."

Mongrel felt his air supply cut off and struggled against the ex con's bulging bicep, throwing pathetic fists everywhere, hoping one of them would do something useful. But exerting himself and wasting precious oxygen was only getting him closer to being strangled to death. He emitted a small squeak for help.

"Matters not what ye be doin'. Tis wrong to end that man's life." While this was an excellent point, Alphonse seemed to have taken the fatherly approach of letting his child make a mistake in order to hopefully learn a valuable lesson. Mongrel's life was in jeopardy over an educational technique. "And ye best put them eyes away 'fore somethin' bad happens to ye."

The look Brecklyn gave the pirate asked the question: 'Who the fuck do you think you are?' and so he didn't have to ask it. Instead he tightened his hold around Mongrel's neck and said, "You don't know the first thing 'bout what's goin' on here. This fucker is a murdering dog, and after I'm done with him Ima kill you next. Threaten me like that. And what the fuck did you say 'bout my eyes?"

Alphonse had warned him; it was too late now. "Best believe it be a threat, *boy*. I be the murderin' dog here." He stood severely still, looking like a time-lapse video, and his eyes got cold and steely, beginning to take on a darker complexion.

Brecklyn started to retort to this but wasn't able to speak. Then he too went stiff, as if he were having a heart attack. A strained groan came from somewhere within him. He appeared to be in a great deal of pain, but was paralyzed, unable to do anything about it. The arm around Mongrel's neck, while also stiff, became pliant, and Mongrel was able to wrench his head loose in a bout of self preservation. A few more seconds and he would've been a goner.

He lay sizzling on the pavement, sucking in as much air as his lungs would allow, trying to catch up on all the breathing he'd missed. Enjoying still being alive, he failed to notice his shirt catching fire, but he did sit up when he heard a blood-curdling scream.

Through the flames erupting on his clothing he saw Brecklyn fleeing around the corner, his hair on fire. Mongrel would've laughed if he could catch his breath. Well, that and he finally realized that he too was on fire. But seconds before panic took him in its cold, sweet embrace, a shadow fell over him and the flames were snuffed out. Mongrel looked up looked up to see Alphonse, his real hand extended to him.

"How ye feelin', lad?" he asked.

Mongrel took the hand and was helped to his feet. He inspected his shirt for further smouldering and calamity. "I think I'm okay. My nose is killing me but I'm okay."

"I took care of them flames, so worry not."

"And him?" Mongrel pointed in the direction of the last place he'd seen Brecklyn.

"Aye, him too. Was goin' to kill 'im but I thought the better of it. Already have enough crimes under me hat."

Mongrel nodded, still in disbelief of the day's events. "I thought you were going to kill me."

Alphonse looked hurt and confused. "Now why d'ye think that?"

"Well," Mongrel pointed at the wrecked RV, "after what I did to your friend." He shrugged.

"Him?" Alphonse gave a hearty laugh. "No, no. Hell, ye did me a favour. No, I came to rescue ye."

Don't take Mongrel wrong, he was quite happy to remain amongst the living, but considering how close he came to joining the formerly-living, and Alphonse's blasé attitude towards his rescue, can you blame him for being a little upset? Who knows how long Alphonse had been watching them? He could've butted in at any time. "You sure didn't seem to be in any hurry," he said ungraciously.

"Well as I said, I has to keep to the shadows. But I's watchin' the whole time. Kept an eye on ye."

"The *whole* time?" Mongrel was flabbergasted. "You mean you could've stopped all this at any time?"

"As I's walkin' away earlier I heard Pete's voice. Seen them take ye. Thought I'd do a little spyin' for meself for a change."

"I was nearly raped and murdered" Mongrel cried. "I was in an accident, my clothes were set on fire – and look at my face!"

Alphonse reached out and felt Mongrel's nose without

warning, sending a surge of pain coursing through him, causing him to jump back in alarm. "Ah yes, tis a good clean break. Three if I'm not mistaken. Excellent form, that punch."

"What am I gonna do?" Mongrel whined. "The hospital is still on strike."

"Oh quit yer whinin'! Tis good for ye, makes ye look manly. The gals love it too."

This provoked images of Beby and her huge rack, and stirred memories of his time in prison. She'd come to see Mongrel just after he'd been gangbanged by a group of inmates…no, his *face* had been gangbanged…no, that wasn't any better. He was still groggy from the head injuries and lack of oxygen. He'd looked beaten up, and she'd shown more concern for him than ever, almost genuine affection. And it was the first time she'd mentioned sleeping with him. Maybe there was something to this abused, manly complexion he now sported, and if so, he needed to strike while the iron was hot. He decided he would go see her shrink, and hoped his brain damage wasn't permanent.

"Ye awake in there?" Alphonse asked, waving his mannequin hand in front of Mongrel's bloody face. "Or are ye broken?"

Mongrel shook his head, not in answer to the question but to shake his thoughts clear. "Sorry. Thanks for the help but next time don't cut it so close okay? I want to have a life to come back to."

Waving a real hand dismissively, Alphonse said, "Worry not, lad. I be trained in the deadly art of C.P.R. just in case."

Horrible visions came to Mongrel's mind as looked at Alphonse's brown teeth (or were they tarnished gold?) and smelled his foul breath reeking of rum. "You give me mouth-to-mouth? I think I'd rather be dead."

The old pirate laughed and slapped Mongrel on his back in the same spot Brecklyn had earlier, causing him to wince. "Glad to see ye spirits up! You're all right, Mr. Stevens, got the makin's of a great pirate, and I'd be proud to have ye aboard me ship as part of me crew. Once I get a good ship, that is."

"Why don't you just take that one?" Mongrel asked, pointing across the car lot.

Alphonse turned to see a large boat, nearly thirty feet long.

Good For Business

It was well worn, rough looking, and couldn't be guaranteed seaworthy. But it had its own cabin, was bigger than a canoe, and even came with its own trailer. But best of all: it was free. It sure did look grand in the waning afternoon sun.

"Wait right here," Mongrel said, and took off back to the car lot's office to find a set of keys for the boat. There were three doors in the office; the first one he tried was a bathroom. It had a revolting looking toilet that Mongrel would never be able to wipe from his memory. He apologised for some reason, possibly to his brain, backed out and proceeded to the next door. Kicking it open, he forgot to watch his step and immediately felt onto his face. Sputtering and wiping dirt from his eyes, he realized he was in the right room this time; the very shallow basement-like room he'd once thought was going to be his tomb. He moaned as he got to his feet, staggered to the desk and began to pull open drawers, looking for keys. One he found was labelled 'boat;' he took it and rushed out of the room again.

Outside Alphonse was wandering around the boat, studying it, mostly grimacing and shaking his head. It definitely needed some work. A fresh cost of paint – the blood of a couple virgins would do nicely. Something resembling a mast would have to be constructed; he didn't trust or need an engine. And no ship, as far as he was concerned, was seaworthy, or at least pirate-worthy, without a plank. It was an admirable fishing boat, but a pirate ship? He shook his head some more.

Mongrel approached and hailed Alphonse, and tossed him the keys. They landed on his chest and tumbled to the ground; he made not the slightest attempt to grab them. "What's wrong?" Mongrel asked.

Alphonse looked to the ground as if ashamed, and sighed, his big shoulders slumped forward. "Sorry lad. Tis nice o' ye t'offer, but I canna go back to the sea."

This infuriated Mongrel, though he tried not to show it. Alphonse was a pirate. A *pirate*. This man pillaged and plundered, murdered and raped; what was a little car theft to add to that? Or boat theft? Actually it wasn't even stealing if its owner, Captain Pete, was dead…at least for now. Alphonse said he wanted to live a more law-abiding life, but come on – it was *free!* And besides,

Random Tangent

Mongrel wanted to do something nice for the man. After all, he'd *only* saved his life. Mongrel was having trouble as it was paying back the last life debt he owed to Charlie Marbles without adding another to his list. So here was this boat just sitting on a golden platter. It was win-freaking-win. And Alphonse wouldn't take it?

"Why not?" Mongrel asked, doing his best to remain calm.

"I canna leave Wanker behind." At Mongrel's confused look Alphonse felt inspired to elaborate. "Me dog; Wanker Jones. Named after me best mate long ago. If Wanker was but a pup he'd be a fine sea dog. Alas, he be too old now."

"Old?" This gave Mongrel a brilliant idea; he could take the dog and give it to Charlie. Of course, Charlie would kill it, but the dog was old and probably didn't have much more than a few miserable months left to live anyway. Mongrel would really be doing it a favour by cutting its suffering short, and Alphonse would never have to know. It was perfect. "I could maybe take Wanker for you, if you'd like? I can look after him while you're away."

This provoked some beard stroking from Alphonse. "You sure, lad?"

"Yeah, sure. Can't be too hard to look after a dog. Probably pretty low maintenance."

"Aye, that he is," Alphonse groaned as he bent over to pick up the keys. "Been a good dog these long years. Be sorry to see him go." He kicked away the wooden blocks holding the trailer still, then grabbed the hitch and began pulling the trailer back to wherever he called home. "Be good to stretch me sea legs again."

"How old is Wanker?" Mongrel asked, walking beside him, not even offering to help.

Alphonse huffed to himself, thinking for a moment. "He's nearly dead, I'd say. Lies by the door all day, narry a move out of him. Come to think, he may have been dead for a while now."

"Well shit, go!" Mongrel shouted. "Drop the boat and go get the little bastard!"

"Perhaps you're right, lad," Alphonse said, putting down the trailer, even though they were now in the middle of the road. He stretched, his legs cracking. "Gettin' too old to do this by meself. I'll come back tomorrow with a few extra hands."

Suddenly Mongrel had glimpses of the deal falling through.

Good For Business

If the pirate waited a day to come get the boat, a certain other pirate would be around to muck things up. Someone walking away with a boat would not go unnoticed.

"On second thought you should take it now," Mongrel said quickly, running to the back of the boat. "I'll give you a hand." He then tried pushing with all his might, but couldn't budge it.

"What's wrong with tomorrow?" Alphonse called from the front of the boat.

"Cause tomorrow he'll..." Mongrel looked back at the demolished motor home. "Look, just trust me on this one."

Mongrel couldn't see it, but Alphonse plucked a few hairs from his beard and studied them for a moment. Finally he agreed with Mongrel, picked up his end of the boat and began pulling again. Together they walked the boat down Bloor St, the sun on the verge of touching the horizon behind them.

Looking back on the past couple weeks, Mongrel had to admit that through the ups and downs – mostly downs, really – he was still alive, and was somehow managing to do good in the world. He'd helped free an innocent man from prison, reunited an android with its maker, and today was helping an old pirate return to the sea. His spirits, as Alphonse had said, were up. He was going to get a dog to give to his friend Charlie, Beby was interesting in beginning a relationship with him, and even though Captain Pete died despite Mongrel's valiant attempts to stop it, it was at least par for the course. Business as usual.

And business was good.

The End

By the end of the day, all Mongrel's tasks were accomplished, even getting a car. After Wan's One-Stop Buy-Or-Swap Car Shop had burnt to the ground the only thing that survived, and proving to be more fireproof that the whole car lot, was the Santa Fe Freddie had been raving about upon their arrival. Wan was so distraught over the tragedy, even though the insurance he'd taken out months earlier would pay off huge for him, that

Random Tangent

when Mongrel offered him one thousand dollars for it, Wan took it like a starving animal. The only real tragedy was what happened to Captain Pete, who died again at the hands of Mongrel. As always, no one has seen the last of him – including Alphonse Moor, whom you might recall told Mongrel he'd done him a favour when he killed the old pirate. That could only mean one thing: he *did* know who Captain Pete was, and they must surely have an interesting and terrible past. We'd last seen Brecklyn as he went screaming down the street with his hair on fire. He eventually ran into Petrol Park and, not knowing any better, stuck his head in the petroleum geyser. Naturally, that made things worse. After more screaming and flailing and burning down half the park, some good Samaritans came along to help snuff out the flames. After this and the fire at the car lot earlier that day people began to question why Dunttstown didn't have a fire department. At least it now had a hospital again. A few days after the doctors went back to work Brecklyn was dumped in the body bin, and a few days later he was dug out and treated for second degree burns covering almost forty percent of his body, and third degree burns on his head. He has a rough road back to recovery. Freddie Farcus, who despite what he said did not actually start the fire at Wan's, ran off with Almighty Frank to discuss the creation of a new, less emotionally fragile robot. Freddie's new boss got word of this and wanted in on it, even offering to financially back the project. When Elvis and Mickey reached Shchevret they couldn't locate the airport. Instead they found a devastated and destroyed landscape that looked like it had been hit with a nuclear warhead. Upon further investigation they discovered the area wasn't abandoned; people still inhabited the remains of city. Mutilated, harrowing, wayward and worst of all, cannibalistic, these people attacked the limo. Elvis demanded they return to the safety of Mongrel's homestead, but Mickey's hatred of Mongrel was so great that he chose to committed suicide by running into the herd of maniacs to be eaten and torn to shreds, rather than face Mongrel again. Elvis was left to fend for himself. After Reggie kicked Mongrel and Freddie out of his store for loitering he gave some thought to opening a brothel, figuring it could only be less work than running a pet store. So the only mystery left is: who started the fire at Wan's? Also, did anyone forget that Mongrel left his credit

Good For Business
card at Downtown Pete's Quality Cars?

Correctile Dysfunction

"ater's gonna hate. Waiter's gonna wait. Creator's gonna create."

Mongrel looked at the man. He stared straight ahead, not at anything in particular, oblivious to everything around them. He was dressed in ordinary clothes and glasses, had spiky blond hair and an obscenely pointed nose. If they had been standing anywhere else he could have passed for a regular guy.

"Baiters gonna bate. Traitors gonna trait. Alligators gonna alligate."

But let's not get ahead of ourselves.

Glancing around the room, Mongrel saw all manner of lunacy. A couple ladies by the entrance were trading hair – as in plucking strands from their heads and exchanging them with a certain degree of excitement. A man behind them was scratching and sniffing the wall. Wait, now he was licking it too. People were laughing hysterically or crying uncontrollably. It was just as he'd expected, but thankfully no worse. He stood at the edge of the room, surrounded by the mentally...well, the word *challenged*

Random Tangent

never felt right to him; it suggested they were merely taking a test, whereas these people had all failed horribly. Perhaps they should be called mental failures?

"Gators gonna gate. Tomatoes gonna tomate. Masturbators gonna masturbate."

The Dunttstown Psychiatric Hospital had an impressive collection of specimens considering the surrounding area. The number of patients it housed was nearly half the population of Dunttstown, though no one could figure out why. Were people somehow more inclined to lose their minds around there? Was there something in the water?[*] Worse, even though the hospital had many permanent residents, there were plenty more folks out there badly in need of help. In fact, most of the worst ones were loose, free in the wilderness. The more docile ones were in the hospital. The tame ones. The ones easiest to capture.

Failures indeed.

"Gyros gonna gyrate. Primers gonna primate. Integers gonna integrate."

The place gave Mongrel the willies. He didn't want to face it, but somewhere in his lineage insanity had taken root and driven every member of his family crazy; a long road on a short bus. His mother was absolutely bonkers when he'd been reunited with her. His father, bless his hamstrings, was known to be sane, but in his last days went batshit crazy. And if the stories Old Man Cleopard had told him were true, that *he* was Mongrel's real father, then things got worse. It would mean a future of living way beyond his years and spending that time having more air leaving his ass than his mouth, and eating unhealthy amounts of goatmeal.

Spending his last days in an asylum like the Dunttstown Psychiatric Hospital was not a future Mongrel wanted to contemplate, and so chose to ignore it or chase it away with Christmas jingles. He generally tried to avoid crazy people, just in case it was contagious.

"Players gonna plate. Climbers gonna climate. Decors gonna decorate."

---

[*] Actually, yes; petroleum.

Correctile Dysfunction

His last visit to the hospital was not a pleasant one, and he swore he'd never return if he could help it. But that time things were beyond his control; today things were different. Circumstances had changed. Mongrel had to overcome his fear of crazy people, not just because he could end up like one of them, but because there was more at stake now than just his legacy.

Boobs were on the line.

"Computers gonna computate. Regulators gonna regulate. Retailers gonna retaliate."

Beby had demanded he have a session with her shrink with the reward of having a session with her. She'd flaunted her large breasts at him, making it hard (cough) to say no. While he hated thinking in such black and white terms, that he was doing it all because he was a man and had needs, he reconciled it with the fact that he'd loved Beby long before she revealed her assets. Now there was just more of her to love.

So here he was, ready to meet her psychologist and hopefully pass whatever tests he had in store. It wasn't a prospect Mongrel was comfortable with, since who knows what her psychologist would do to him? Make him cry? Crack him like an egg? Unearth forgotten childhood memories? What secrets was Mongrel's own brain hiding from him? If he had hidden secrets, they must be hidden for a reason; maybe he didn't want to know. No, this did not sit well with him. How does one study for a psych test?

"Delis gonna delegate. Relays gonna relate. Propers gonna propagate."

For better or worse, Mongrel didn't have much of a say in the matter. He wanted to leave, but doing so would mean walking away from a possible relationship with Beby; walking away from a long overdue night of passion; walking away from her huge rack – which was impossible since they were so massive they generated their own gravitational pull, and Mongrel was caught in it.

Either way, Mongrel felt being with Beby was worth the risk. Despite her mood swings, violent tendencies and yes, even her enormous chest, there was a wonderful woman inside her. Mongrel could see it, even if he only wanted to stare at the outside. She could be absolutely bewitching when she wanted to, and Mongrel

Random Tangent

had struggled to convince himself that *he* chose to come here and wasn't simply under her spell, hypnotized.

"Lambs gonna laminate. Crimes gonna criminate. Radios gonna radiate."

So that was all good and well, but now he was here, in the Dunttstown Psychiatric Hospital, and his skin was crawling so badly that he couldn't will himself to move. As incredible as it was that he was risking his own mental stability just standing in that room, it wouldn't do him any good if he couldn't go any further. He was going to have to distract him mind somehow.

"Salivas gonna salivate. Vibrators gonna vibrate. Potatoes gonna…"

Mongrel turned to look at the man, waiting for him to continue. He didn't; he just stood frozen, starring into space. He appeared to be broken…well, more so, anyway. Was his limited mental ability already stretched to his max? Was he farting?[*]

"Potate?" Mongrel suggested, trying to help.

This had no noticeable effect, at least not immediately. But after a few seconds the man slowly turned his head towards Mongrel, and stared him. There was no emotion in his eyes. No confusion, no anger, no fear. They were blank. It was like looking at a statue. A dead man. A soulless creature. It was chilling.

Then the man began to scream bloody murder in Mongrel's face. He screamed as if his hair was on fire, as if he were being eaten alive, as if he was being gutted with a chainsaw.

Mongrel knew that running away would have suggested guilt and could have prompted a chase. Better to casually stroll further into the room as if he had no idea it was happening, or that it happened all the time and he was used to it. It probably was a common occurrence, confirmed by the lack of attention from anyone else. No one covered their ears or moved away. No one else joined in. No nurses or orderlies rushed over to subdue the man. Mongrel pretended to be one of them, unapologetically mad, completely unperturbed by the outburst. He knew there was nothing

---

[*] People cannot seem to speak and break wind at the same time. Even in the middle of a sentence they will pause to fart, then continue on. It's as if the laws of physics does not permit air to leave the body from two different ends at the same time.

Correctile Dysfunction

he could do; if it's already broken, don't try to fix it. He was sure he'd heard that saying somewhere. Besides, it was the psychologist's job to fix things, right? Whatever the case, it wasn't his problem.

Anyway, back to sneaking across the room. Mongrel made it to the hallway on the other side and congratulated himself for making it that far; he'd entered the evil domain and had crossed the pit of lost souls. He'd even defeated the screaming demon. So far, things were going pretty well. He just needed to continue on this path, and he would reach the Russian wizard.

The hallway took a left turn after a few meters, but Mongrel paused before rounding it. Hugging the wall, he peered around corner, spying on the various people. A doctor with a pointy goatee casually strolled towards him before darting through an open doorway – obviously up to no good. A young woman with a pointy chin was sprawled out on a couch, knitting – clearly evil. An old man with pointy eyes was dancing by himself – if that wasn't a sign of wickedness he didn't know what was.

"Wait, what?" Mongrel asked. "Pointy eyes?"

"Excuse me."

Mongrel hugged the wall tighter, trying to hide, and homed in on an old lady further down the hallway. She was trying to get some attention but didn't appear to be in any hurry. "Excuse me," she said again as a man passed her and kept walking. She hung her head for a moment, but remained undeterred and continued to hail passers-by. Everyone seemed to be competently ignoring her, and Mongrel watched them, wishing he had their powers of ignorance. He was going to have to cross the old hag's path, and if she were to call out to him…it was his greatest weakness; not being able to mind his own business. She didn't appear to be full of malice or brimming with malevolence – nothing pointy about her, in fact – but things were never as they appeared.

Scanning further down the hallway Mongrel spied a set of double doors. They were his goal; the end of the level. But first he'd have to get through the gauntlet of-"

"Excuse me!"

Glancing over quickly, Mongrel met the hag's eyes. She'd spotted him; there'd be no escaping now.

Random Tangent

He shimmied around the corner, eventually bringing his full form into view, as unimpressive as it was, hoping the vile witch might think twice before messing with his self-perceived grandeur. He was, after all, the hero of this story, and she must know she didn't stand a chance.

On the other hand, what if this was a video game, and he had to die a few times before figuring out the trick to defeat her?

"Excuse me!" she called again, now waving her arm at him.

Mongrel sighed heavily and marched over, sensing evil, or at least some shade of dread. He hoped he wasn't about to waste a life on the old woman. She was wrapped in a cocoon of blankets, looking cold as well as harmless. Large glasses adorned her smallish wrinkled face, appearing all the larger because of it. She could have seen clear to Jupiter. Her legs didn't quite touch the linoleum floor from where she was seated on the bench, further illustrating her diminutive size. Mongrel kept in mind his Jedi training; size mattered not.

"Excuse me!" she repeated, even though he was now standing three feet away, obviously excusing her. "Would you mind not walking so fast? It hurts my pancreas."

Mongrel glanced up and down the hallway before returning his focus to her. Her request was simple enough, alarming in its simplicity actually, and it caught him off guard. This was why he hated boss fights. "Why, uh…what makes it hurt?"

She shed a few layers of blankets, causing Mongrel to take a step back, ready for whatever might leap out and attack him. But all she did was lift her gown and rub her stomach at him. "Oh I don't know," she replied. "The mysteries of the human body, right?" She shrugged and began to cover herself up again.

"Yeah," Mongrel agreed. He knew little himself of how the body worked. He still wondered why a certain spot on his back tickled when he scratched between his toes, or how to make that armpit farting noise. Everyone else could do it. "Are you sure it's not, perhaps, your heart? Maybe you're having a heart attack?"

The hag shook her head. "Oh no. I had my heart replaced a few years ago with a baked potato." She grimaced and leaned closer to him. "And it's long since gotten cold. I keep asking someone to put in it the microwave for a few minutes to heat it up…" she

Correctile Dysfunction

trailed off again, pulling tight her defensive armour of blankets. "It's so cold. Always so cold. Could you do it for me?"

So that was what the vile creature wanted? Mongrel knew better; never deal with demons. "Sure," he said, "let me go find a microwave." He then marched down the hall towards the stairwell as quickly as he could without drawing too much attention. Behind him she bellowed and wailed about the microwave being in the other direction. Mongrel allowed himself a slight smile, knowing he'd bested her. Of course, he couldn't return this way. He'd rather jump out the window than cross her path again. This also made sense from a temporal perspective – he was a busy man and needed to save time whenever he could.

Bursting through the double doors, he collapsed onto the floor, out of breath for some reason. It was a hard-earned victory, but he'd made it. He took a moment of respite from the harsh world, overthrown with tyranny. But his damsel was in danger, and he needed to make haste. No rest for the wicked? Ha! Even less rest for the brave and mighty.

On to level two.

A flight of stairs awaited him, and Mongrel appreciated the organic progression they added to his journey. The left side ventured down into an unknown abyss; the right higher up the mountain. The wizard had told him when he'd booked the appointment to seek the third peak. But he was warned that evil would beset him on all sides, lurking, waiting to devour his soul. This was no game for children.

Mongrel began his slow, gruelling ascent, slogging up the stone steps, etched into the side of the mountain. They were narrow and treacherous, and one wrong move would send him over the edge and into darkness.

At the second floor landing Mongrel stopped; the stairs no longer afforded him passage. A fellow traveller left a message scrawled crudely on a yellow sign: WET FLOOR. He would have to find another way.

The entrance to a cave stood to his right. No light penetrated its depths and it smelled like the foulest of creatures had defecated all over the place, then ate their excretions – probably out of hunger – and threw everything back up. It was nauseating simply to *think* of going inside, but there was no other way to go. Just inside the cave's mouth Mongrel found a sword sticking out of some slain beast. Having no other means of defence, he removed the weapon to keep as his own protection. It was heavy, and blood dripped from the blade; the kill was still fresh. What had happened to its previous owner Mongrel didn't want to know. Would that luck be not on his side, he might soon find out.

Mongrel cast a spell of light and ventured further into the cave. He found it stretched east and west, but was disturbingly empty. It could only be a trap. He gripped the handle of his sword tightly and pressed on, choosing to go east.

It wasn't long before he heard a noise. From a hidden side entrance a creature lurched at him. Mongrel swung his sword – not to kill but to ward off – and the creature screamed, dropped precious loot, and ran off.

Mongrel beamed a determined smile, feeling invincible in this arena of death. Let all tremble before him! He laughed a mighty laugh as he scooped up the loot.

Then a voice interrupted his laughter. "Excuse me."

Spinning on his heels, Mongrel cursed himself for dropping his guard. A troll stood before him, a groggy jumpsuit-wearing little bastard with glasses. Flecks of blood speckled its ugly face, and Mongrel realized they had come from his blade when he'd swung it around. The creature pawed the liquid with its great claws, looked at it, and seemed very displeased.

"What do you think you're doing?" the troll asked, clearly not realizing the danger it was in.

"Be gone!" Mongrel cried. "I am Mongrel the Magnificent. Heed my warning and flee or I shall have to kill you."

But the troll remained. "Have you forgotten to take your meds today? Who is your doctor?"

Mongrel had tried to show mercy, but the creature could not be reasoned with. All it knew was death and torment, and Mongrel would have to end its misery. He thrust his sword into the troll's stomach, making it grunt and take a step backwards, but nothing more.

It did not die. It did not even bleed. It only looked angry.

Correctile Dysfunction

Suddenly Mongrel became very alarmed. This was no ordinary troll; it must have been far above his experience level. To take it on was to court death, and he was already courting a maiden, fair and finely-bosomed. The only thing he could do was run.

"Give me that!" The troll roared, grabbing at the sword. Mongrel yanked it away and used a spell of distraction, tossing his loot into the creature's face. Then he ran as fast as he could, weapon swinging wildly in front of him. Moments later he heard the creature behind him giving chase, and wished he had a speed charm.

"Get back here!" cried the troll. "Give that back, it's not yours!"

Mongrel rounded a tight turn in the cave and came across a set of doors. He barged through them without a second thought, then turned and jammed his sword through the door handles, locking them together, and not a moment too soon.

The troll immediately crashed into the barricade with thunderous fury. "Open the door!" it bellowed. The doors creaked and groaned under the weight of pounding fists, but they held firm.

Choosing not to linger, Mongrel examined his surroundings in hope of finding a way forward. He found another set of stairs before him winding ever upwards. By leaps and bounds he climbed them, putting as much distance as he could between himself and the powerful troll.

"You little shit," the troll called from below. "I'll find you!"

The land was small, Mongrel realized, and it only grew smaller the higher up the mountain he went. The troll spoke true. Panic began to overtake Mongrel. He needed to hide. He needed to find a better weapon. He needed to level grind.

He burst through the doors at the top of the stairs and quickly shut them, then began looking for something to jam them together.

"May I help you?"

Mongrel turned to see not a maiden, or a mountain or forest or cave, but a nurse, sitting at a desk behind glass, a look of concern on her face. A middle-aged couple sat in chairs next to the window, also looking startled. The smell of sterility permeated the air. He was back in the hospital again.

Random Tangent

"Uh..." he paused to clear his throat, "...I have an appointment to see Dr. Valentin...uh..." Mongrel walked over to the small window and bent down into the open slot as he began fishing pieces of paper and lint out of his pocket, looking for the card Beby had given him last week. He couldn't find it. "The Russian guy?" he suggested.

The nurse looked at him for a long moment before saying, "Just a minute." She then left her little office.

As Mongrel waited for her to return he glanced around at the paraphernalia, trying to keep his mind occupied. This was it, his chance to earn Beby's hand, her heart, and other assorted body parts. More so than being in this building with these mental failures, he was nervous about failing the evaluation and basically shooting his dick in the foot, so to speak. Not that sex was the sole reason he was here; it was just one reward in a proverbial box of treasure. Pun intended.

Seriously though, he was jeopardizing his intellectual pride. What if he flunked the test? What if the psychologist found him mentally incompetent? What would that mean? He considered himself sane, sure, but so did most crazy people. If he actually was missing some, if not all of his mind, would he even know? And considering how life had been treating him lately, there was a good chance someone would find a reason to make him a permanent resident at the hospital. Perhaps coming here was a mistake.

"I'm thinking of a colour between one and ten!" said the man beside the window to Mongrel. "Can you guess what it is?"

"Jeffery, no," the woman next to him said, patting down his already flat hair.

"It's alright," Mongrel said, realizing that if he wanted people to stop looking at him like he was crazy then he'd better start acting sane. He bent down on one knee in front of Jeffrey, getting eye-level like he would with a child. "A colour between one and ten huh? Hmm, let me think." He made a show of contemplating the question before answering. "Is it...blue?"

Whether this was the correct answer or not the world would never know. The man's face broke out in a tragic deformation of horror and revulsion before beginning to leak tears. He began to wail like a three-year old.

Correctile Dysfunction

"How could you?" the woman asked pointedly, staring at Mongrel as if he were a rapist.

"What?" Mongrel cried, confused. "I…"

"Stevens, Mongrel?" the nurse suddenly called, back in the office.

Mongrel returned to his feet. "Yes?"

The nurse peered through the glass at the sobbing man-child, then glared at Mongrel, disdain and accusation in her eyes. "Room 319," she muttered, hate seething from her lips.

"I…" Mongrel stammered, pointing to Jeffrey, "…didn't…" but he didn't know what to say. He settled for shrugging apologetically.

"Room 319," the nurse repeated with more contempt, even pointing a finger in the direction she wanted Mongrel to go.

Slumping his shoulders in defeat, he wandered down the hall. What could he really do anyway? He never should have left the mountain. Magnificent Mongrel would have known exactly how to deal with the situation. Now he just felt like Monster Mongrel.

Appropriately enough, the woman coddling the man-child called, "Monster!" after him.

Not far down the hallway Mongrel found a door marked '319'. He grabbed the door knob, took a deep breath, and entered.

It was a small room, extremely office-sized. A woman sat at a desk opposite the door. She wasn't behind Plexiglas like the last nurse he'd encountered. A row of chairs lined the right hand wall, one of which was occupied by a goofy-looking fellow who appeared severely constipated. One tooth poked out from under his bottom lip, and he reminded Mongrel of Big John for some reason.

"Welcome!" said the woman behind the desk. "What can I do for you?"

Mongrel gave a little wave and smiled politely. "I'm Mongrel Stevens. I have an appointment."

The secretary made a show of checking her books and papers. "Ah yes, right on time, Mr. Stevens. You may have a seat. The doctor will be with you shortly."

Taking a seat next to the goofy man, Mongrel tried to blend in, go incognito. He'd already attracted quite the unwanted attention in his short time there. Between the old woman with the potato heart, the screaming demon, the troll, and Jeffrey, it was a wonder a warrant wasn't out for his arrest. He wondered if there wasn't a back door out of the building, or a secret underground passage. Or a helipad.

"You look like you're a pretty regular fella," said the goofy man beside him suddenly.

"Me?" Mongrel asked, hoping the stranger was talking to himself.

"Yes you." He looked Mongrel up and down. "Pretty regular bowel movement you got going on?"

Mongrel swallowed, not liking where this conversation was heading. "Yeah, I guess so."

"You *guess* so?" This seemed to upset him. "Maybe you'd better get in the bathroom and find out." He jerked his head to a door across from them.

Not wanting to anger the man and risk the possibility of adding yet another person to his growing list of enemies (just a couple more and they could form a mob), Mongrel quickly changed his answer. "Oh yes, I remember now – I'm regular, very regular. *Extra* regular. That's me. You could set your clock to my dumps."

The man smirked and nodded. "That's what I thought. You people, all you people are under the control of your bodies. You feed it when it's hungry, scratch it where it itches, fix it when it's damaged. You go to sleep when your body will let you, not when you want. And you don't choose to get colds, or cancer, no sir. Your body allows that. You can't tell it to stop aging, can't order it to get in shape, can't trade it in for a new one. And worst of all, you go to the shitter when it tells you to. There ain't no arguing with it. Your body is in charge, and you're just along for the ride. You people make me sick." He spat on the floor in disgust.

"Zeke," the secretary said, "what have I told you about spitting?" This was obviously a rhetorical question, and no one answered.

More curious than offended, Mongrel asked, "Well what do you do?"

"Me?" Zeke asked proudly. "I have *power dumps*."

Mongrel eyed the man with shock, disdain, and pity. "Power...dumps?"

Correctile Dysfunction

Zeke leaned so close that Mongrel could smell the Zeke on him. "You want to know that those are?"

Mongrel sighed. "No, I don't. I really don't. I really shouldn't ask, cause knowledge kills and all. That's why the Mayans and Egyptians aren't around anymore, and Adam and Eve ate from the tree of knowledge and look where that got them. But if I don't know what a *power dump* is, my mind will come up with its own idea, probably something far worse and traumatizing than the truth. So it would be far less horrific in the long run if you just told me now instead of leaving my mind to its own devices."

This seemed to make Zeke very happy and he smiled a big, nearly-toothless grin. "See, I'm in charge of my own body. I scratch when and where I want to scratch, whether it itches or not. When I want to sleep, I hold my breath 'til I pass out. I haven't aged a day in the passed twenty-four hours. And I shit when I feel like it."

"I hate to ask," Mongrel hated to ask, "but when was the last time you took…uh…?"

"Took a shit?" Zeke finished the sentence. He made a face as he thought hard. "Last Tuesday I think. Or Wednesday. Going on two weeks now."

"So you *are* constipated."

Zeke made a sour face. "I'm *not* constipated; just don't feel like going. I'm in charge here." He slapped his bloated gut, which emitted a voracious gurgle, causing him to wince.

"I think you should go before you hurt yourself."

"Don't…feel…it," Zeke struggled with the pain in his abdomen.

At that time a door opened behind the secretary and out walked a young lady. The swing in her hips was all her, but the smile on her face looked forced. Anger seeped from her eyes. She stormed over to the office door, her hand extended to the doorknob, but stopped before grabbing it.

Jerking her head to stare at Mongrel, she said, "And another thing; don't you hate it when a total stranger starts up a conversation and acts like they've been talking to you the whole time?"

Not exactly knowing what to say, Mongrel flapped his lips at her, eventually adding some vocals to them. "Uh…"

Random Tangent

"And don't you just hate it when you get a package in the mail, and it's a severed head inside?" She shook her head, not in answer to her question, but in futility. "Really fucks up my day. Especially when it's someone I know, you know?"

"Rene – langvage."

Mongrel looked back at the door through which the woman had come, where now stood a man in a long white coat and glasses

She huffed and left the office, left the question hanging in the air, and left Mongrel speechless.

"Ooh…come on now baby," Zeke muttered quietly to himself amid his stomach growls. "Don't be like that. You got this…"

The man in the white coat was devastatingly handsome in the way that made fiercely average men appear repulsive in contrast. He could have been a model, an actor, a rock and roll icon. Piercing blue eyes, rich auburn hair, chiselled jaw, charming smile, tight ass – well, probably; the man had everything else going for him. He was probably also incredibly wealthy, drove a sports car, had a mansion on the beach, and golfed a lot.

Fucking golfers.

Mongrel hated him already. *This* was the doctor Beby was seeing on a regular basis? How could Mongrel compete with him? The man had every advantage. It wasn't fair. Mongrel almost turned to leave, giving up.

"Good mornink!" the man called. "You must be Mr. Stevenk."

Recalling his decision to have lunch before his session, in case the head shrink actually shrunk his head, disabling him from ever eating a full, satisfying meal again, Mongrel knew it was no longer morning. He turned to the doctor, trying to hate him but for his wonderful smile. He felt himself begin to swoon. Seriously, someone should give that smile an award. "Uh, it's afternoon now."

The doctor rolled up his sleeve and glanced at his watch. "Ah! Zat ist correct! Please, von't you come into mine office?"

Instead of following the doctor's orders Mongrel gestured to Zeke. "He was here first, I think."

"Don't vorry about him," the handsome doctor said dismissively. "He ist here all zee time. Cries like baby if ve make him leave." He crossed the room and began poking and pinching Zeke, sending him into a fit of giggles. "Who ist mine baby, ah? Who ist mine big baby?" He then stopped and sniffed the air. "I zink big baby has laid chocolate egg."

When the big baby slapped his stomach moments ago in a display of strength he cracked the dam, so to speak. And when the doctor began tickling him those cracks grew bigger. It was only a matter of time before the damn broke.

Zeke slowly stopped giggling and declared, "It was a big one this time!"

After a couple seconds Mongrel got a whiff and finally understood what had happened, and nearly leapt across the room to a safe distance.

The doctor merely chuckled, as if it was a normal occurrence. "Looks like somevone needs zeir diaper changed, ah?" He then looked at his secretary. "Sheila, vould you mind?"

"What?" she asked, shocked and understandably disgusted. "You're not asking me to...you can't be serious?"

"Yes Sheila, as alvays, I am." He then turned to Mongrel and gestured for him to enter his office. Mongrel couldn't be happier to leave the room, now that the stench was drifting out of control.

A regal, lavish decorum did not await him inside. Mongrel expected rows upon rows of bookshelves lined with all manner of texts and tomes on psychiatry; what he got was an ugly, rusted floor lamp in the corner. He expected the walls to be adorned with framed degrees from esteemed and prestigious institutions; what he got was bland, uninspired wallpaper with a single painting of a pony. And not even a good painting; a child could have spilled juice on a rug and created a more lifelike stain in the shape of a pony. What he expected was a massive oak desk and fine leather chaise; what he got was a beaten, forlorn couch blotted and tainted with what he hoped wasn't shit. He sat down on the least soiled side of the couch.

In the waiting room, the argument was escalating.

"I'm *not* cleaning him up!" Sheila said. "I told you before, I don't do that."

Random Tangent

"Sheila..." the doctor pinched the bridge of his nose. "...vhy must ve have zis conversation every time? It ist goink to upset zee ozer patients, und I'm too busy to do it mineself. Now *please* Sheila." With that, he removed his glasses to polish them with a cloth and stormed into his office. "So tell me..." he stopped and peered at Mongrel, confusion masking his face. "Okay..."

"Oh I'm sorry," Mongrel said. "Is this your side of the couch?"

"Nein, nein. Zat ist okay." He stepped a few feet closer but didn't sit down. "So tell me, Mr. Stevenk, vhat brinks you here?"

"It's Stevens."

The doctor glanced at his clipboard momentarily. "Yes; Stevenk."

"Steven*s*," Mongrel enunciated.

"Stevenks."

"You know what? Just call me Mongrel."

"Very vell zen. Vhat brinks you here today, Mongrel?"

Mongrel shrugged. "My feet. My mental competence."

The doctor chuckled. "I mean vhy did you come see me?"

It annoyed Mongrel that the painting of the pony – or was it a horse?[*] – was behind him. Had it been on the other side of the small room it could have afforded him the option of looking at it while he thought, appearing to admire the artwork. Instead he had to stare off into space, probably looking like an idiot. "Didn't Beby tell you I was coming?"

"Ah!" the doctor exclaimed. "Zat is correct! Yes I remember. I have heard qvite much about you."

"Oh good. So you are the right shrink. I was worried for a moment. I thought you were supposed to be Russian?"

"...Nein," the doctor said, confused. "Did Beby tell you zis?"

"No I just assumed from the name and your business card. Sorry."

"Nozink to vorry about mine friend. But ve don't like to be called 'shrinks.' It seems poor choice of vords – unless you

---

[*] Mongrel didn't know horses.

Correctile Dysfunction

consider me to be shrinker of mental problems." For some reason he thought this funny and burst out laughing.

Mongrel joined in on the laughter, saying, "Well I don't have any of those."

"Zat ist not vhat your girlfriend said."

"What?" Mongrel's laughing crashed to a halt. "Did she say she was my girlfriend? What were her exact words?"

The doctor stared at the painting as he thought. "She described you as…let me zink…stubborn, stupid, brave, old-fashioned…variety of farm animals. Ozer zinks as vell. I vould have to look my mine notes."

Not all of these were good adjectives. "Was one of those farm animals a horse? Like a stallion or something?"

"I do not believe so…again, I vould have to check mine notes."

"Hmm," Mongrel grumbled. So far things were not going well. But he had to remain positive. "Well she is prone to over-exaggerating and negativity. She can be pretty pessimistic at times."

"Zat ist correct," said the doctor. "Zat ist vhy I offered to have session viz you. To see for mineself and give neutral observation."

"That's very nice of you. And in the spirit of niceness Beby said that you wouldn't be charging me for this too?"

"She told you zis?"

Mongrel swallowed. "I think so. I think she mentioned it. Is it not true?"

"Vould zat be problem?"

"No!" Mongrel waved a dismissive hand. "Of course not. No problem at all. It's just that…I don't…"

"Have any money?" the doctor completed the sentence.

"Psh!" Mongrel waved his hand again, looking less convincing this time. "I got money. Lots of money." He flashed a big, yet faltering smile. "Okay like I'm not rich or anything, but I'm doing okay. I get by. I'm not broke."

The doctor tried again. "You don't have job zen?"

What was it with this guy? He was just pushing and pushing, trying to poke holes in everything. Was it his goal to prove Mongrel was unfit boyfriend material?

Random Tangent

"I have a job," Mongrel lied, his temper beginning to slide. "Got my own house too. Bonus points for that, right?"

"Zat is correct. But vhat is it zen? You don't…vhat?"

"I don't…" Mongrel had to think again, irritated that no pony was there to lend support. "I don't know how much it's gonna cost."

"Vell zere ist no reason to get upset," the doctor chuckled again. "I am not chargink you."

"Oh." Mongrel absent-mindedly picked at his pants, unable to meet the doctor's eyes, embarrassed by his near-outburst. This was probably exactly what the man wanted: to see Mongrel lose control, to see anger. Why? So he could put another check in the 'reasons not to date Mongrel' column? But why would he be goading Mongrel? What were his motives?

"Now if you vish for anozer session, ve can discuss payment zen."

Mongrel nodded, remaining quiet. Finally he asked, "What else did Beby say about me?"

Now it was the doctor's turn to look away, to think. "Vhy don't ve go into mine office. Mine notes are in zere."

"Your office?" Once again Mongrel's brain vomited a pile of confusion in his head. "I thought this…"

Opposite the door they entered through stood another door, and Mongrel wondered how he'd missed it. The doctor opened the door and invited Mongrel inside. "*Zis* is mine office."

With childlike wonder, Mongrel walked through the door and beheld pure splendour. *There* were the bookshelves full of tomes and texts of literary psychoanalytic significance. *There* were the framed certificates and Victorian-era replica paintings lining the walls. *There* were the grand oak desk and leather chaise. This was more like it. Mongrel ran and flopped down on the plush chaise, stretched out on the comfy cushions and relaxed.

"Please, make yourself at home," the doctor said, amused by Mongrel's delight. "Vell, not *too* much at home; von of mine patients likes to use his couch as toilet."

Mongrel considered this. He considered the couch in the previous room. He considered the vague smells and the ugly stains. Then he considered puking.

Correctile Dysfunction

"Ew!" he cried, jumping to his feet. He began brushing his clothes down, remotely aware of the futility but unable to help himself. "How could you?"

"Vhat?" the doctor asked. "How could I vhat?"

"Let me sit on that couch out there?"

"You vere already sittink on it vhen I came in; it vas too late. How could I stop you?"

"Well maybe you shouldn't have that couch there in the first place. I wouldn't have sat on it if it wasn't there."

"Ve have zee couch cleaned und fumigated on regular basis. It ist not big deal."

"Yeah well I didn't see you sitting on it."

The doctor had to concede the point. "Zat ist correct. But Zeke vould be very upset if I got rid of it."

"Oh let me guess: Captain Power Dump out there will *cry like baby* if you tossed out his shitty couch?"

"Captain vhat?"

"*Power Dump*. That's what he calls it when he holds in his shit for a week. Keeps his body in check or under control or whatever."

"He told you zis?" the doctor seemed fascinated.

"Yeah."

After a slow nod and some staring off into space, the doctor muttered, "Very interestink." He then looked at Mongrel and came back to the present. "Look, I can see you are very upset about zis but you must understand I have ze comfort of mine ozer patients to zink about. Zeir vellbeink ist first priority. Please, have seat," he gestured to the chaise, "and ve can start our session off properly."

Realizing that the doctor was right, that Zeke was mentally imbalanced and had to be tended to carefully, Mongrel sat back down and made himself comfortable.

The doctor put on his glasses and sat down on a leather armchair next to the chaise. "Zere. Now, velcome to mine office. I am Doctor Valentin Rushkov."

Mongrel nodded, accepting the fresh start. He needed it too; they seemed to have gotten off on the wrong foot. He needed to stay in control of his emotions. He needed to be more guarded around the doctor, who was giving off the vibe that he wanted Mongrel to fail. Mongrel needed to succeed.

After a few minutes of silence Dr. Rushkov whispered, "Zis vould be good time to stand up und introduce yourself to ze group."

Glancing around the room, Mongrel made sure they were alone before throwing a quizzical look at the doctor, who simply nodded his head in a 'trust me' fashion.

Sighing and knowing he'd regret it, Mongrel stood and said, meekly, "Hello, my name is Mongrel Stevens."

But apparently that wasn't good enough. "Und...?" the doctor said, rolling his hand for Mongrel to continue.

"*Und* what?"

"Pretend you are at AA meetink."

"Why? Does that help?"

"Zat ist correct."

More sighing ensued. "Fine. I'm Mongrel Stevens and I'm an alcoholic."

"Really?" the psychologist asked. "Zat ist vhy you are here?"

"No, I'm here for Beby."

"Vell I am sorry but she ist not here."

Mongrel sighed so much it was a wonder how he kept breathing. "Look, what do you want from me?"

Dr. Rushkov removed his glasses. "I need you to commit to zis. To be mine patient. To trust zat I know vhat I am doink."

"Okay..." Mongrel closed his eyes, dug deep down inside and pulled up courage, strength, and...boobs. Yes, that's why he was going through all this; for Beby's boobs. Well, Beby *and* her boobs. The pair of them. The pair of them and her. The complete set. The whole package. I mean, if all Mongrel got out of this was a pair of tits – nice tits though they may be – he'd be a little pissed. Boobs just aren't the same unless they're attached to a woman.

His resolve hardened, and he looked the doctor in the eye once more and said, "Hello, my name is Mongrel Stevens, and I'm a mental...retard, or something."

Peering at Mongrel, assessing, Dr. Rushkov was silent. After a minute he placed his glasses back on his face and smiled. "Ah! Hello Mongrel. Is zis your first time here?"

Correctile Dysfunction

"Yes," Mongrel said through gritted teeth. He might have to play the game but he didn't have to like it.

"Excellent! Vell I am sure ve can learn much from each ozer. You may have seat."

Grumbling to himself, Mongrel sat back down. Once he'd gotten himself comfortable he noticed the doctor was now at his desk, rifling through drawers, and was no longer bespectacled. "What's up, doc?" he asked.

"Ah! Here ist your girlfriend's file." He held up a thick folder. "Und please, you may call me Valentin."

"Big," was Mongrel's sole comment about the folder.

"Zat ist correct. She has been mine patient for many years, und ve have talked about many zinks. "He began flipping through pages. "Now vhat did she say…vhat did she say…"

"Uh, is this even okay?" Mongrel asked. "Looking through someone else's files, I mean. You know, doctor-patient confidentiality and all that?"

"Yes, zat ist correct. But you are not mine patient. Ah, here ve go." He adjusted his grip on the big folder. "She says, und here I qvote, 'Vhat he lacks in brains he makes up for in balls.' End qvote." He snapped the folder closed. "So you see, she says you are macho man." He beat his chest with a fist, signalling bravado.

"Yeah, but she also calls me stupid."

"Yes, zat ist correct. Does zis bozer you?"

"Well yeah. Wouldn't it bother you?"

Valentin shook his head. "Nein. But I am not stupid. Are you?"

Taken aback by the question, Mongrel didn't answer immediately. He didn't think he was stupid, but it really wasn't for him to say. Soon he realized he'd better say something quick or risk appearing to contemplate the question. "No, I'm smart. But sometimes I have a stupid way of showing it."

Picking up a clipboard and pen, Valentin began scribbling notes. "Go on," he said, not looking up.

"Are you writing this down?"

"Zat ist correct." His pen stopped and he affixed his glasses to his face again. Then he came over to sit in a comfy-looking chair slightly behind Mongrel, bringing Beby's file with him. "I zink it ist time ve start zis session properly. Tell me Mongrel, vhat ist the first zink you remember?"

Mongrel answered the question with another one. "First thing? Like, ever?"

"Zat ist correct."

Thinking hard but not getting far, Mongrel eventually answered, "Running to my bathroom early in the morning and finding my toilet missing."

"Missink you say? Zat must have been qvite a shock."

"Yeah. I *really* had to pee."

The doctor made a few notes on the clipboard. "Und how did zat make you feel?"

This, Mongrel thought, was a stupid question, and stupid questions must be answered with more stupidity. "Well Valentin, I felt like I had to pee. What a shock!"

"Now Mr. Stevensk, zis ist all for your benefit, und your cooperation vould only be in your best interest. Und please, call me Dr. Rushkov."

"What happened to Valentin? Just a minute ago you said to call you by that."

In response the doctor simply tapped his glasses with his pen, indicating that they were in session, that 'the doctor was in.'

"Right, whatever," Mongrel muttered, hoping he'd get the hang of this soon. He felt like he was dealing with Bosley and the King again.

"So tell me how zat made you feel," Dr. Rushkov repeated. "Und I am referring to your missink toilet."

"Confused, I guess." Mongrel shifted his weight and thought back to that fateful day. "I mean, did someone break into my apartment just to steal a toilet? Why? Nothing in my house is valuable – except for my magic potato, maybe. But toilets aren't of any value. Well maybe if you actually didn't have one; then I can see that. Can't put a price on having a toilet. Still, it's not like they're not everywhere. Never heard of toilet theft being a thing before. Why is a hot commode is suddenly a hot commodity? Doesn't make sense.

"So was it a prank? Or did my toilet run away? Just ripped itself out of the wall and take off? Why? Was I mean to it? I don't

Correctile Dysfunction

know, I mean, it's a toilet; what am I gonna do, take it for walks? Scratch its tummy and feed it treats? Actually I guess *was* giving it treats, depending on how sick your imagination is."

After scribbling more notes, Dr. Rushkov said, "Tell me more about zis magic potato."

"Hey, maybe that's it – my toilet didn't like my treats. That makes sense; it ran away because…what?"

"Zis potato of yours, vhat makes it magic?"

Shrugging is more difficult when you're laying down, which Mongrel found out at that moment. He gave it a good shot, but was unsure if the gesture was communicated properly, and so had to verbally explain more. "It doesn't grow mouldy or age or anything. Been in my family for generations. So does thinking my toilet ran away because I treated it like…well, like a toilet, does that sound crazy?"

"Are you sure about zis?" The doctor was still interested in Mongrel's potato. "Have you had its magical properties tested und verified?"

"What? No. But am I crazy for being a bad owner to my toilet?"

"Vhat? Oh I don't know. Now about zis potato, perhaps you could brink it to me? I am somevhat of an expert on ze subject."

Mongrel flopped over onto his side to look back at the man, both annoyed and incredulous. "What do you mean you don't know? How could you not know? This is you job; don't you see crazy people all the time?"

"Mr. Stevensk, could you please just focus on ze potato?"

"Forget about the stupid potato!" Mongrel shouted. "I don't even have it anymore! Now do I look like a freaking lunatic to you?"

As soon as the words escaped his lips, Mongrel knew he'd made a grave mistake. In his enraged state he was certain his eyes were crazed, and could almost feel the froth forming at the corners of his mouth. His face was turning red and his knuckles were white, gripping the sides of the chaise tightly. There was no doubt in his mind he looked like a psychopath. This was exactly what the doctor wanted, although it was still a mystery why. He might as well kiss Beby goodbye – not the kind of kiss he really wanted to give her.

"I'm sorry," he said meekly.

Ever the consummate professional, Dr. Rushkov removed his glasses and set them on a small table nearby. "Forgive me; I pushed you. Vhen I vear zese glasses I am not qvite mineself. I become...rigid, insolent. It ist sort of Dr. Jekyll und Mr. Hyde situvation."

"It's okay," Mongrel said, thankful the doctor wasn't going to dwell on his outburst. "I've known guys like that. You'd think I'd be used to i-"

Suddenly the door to the office exploded open and the secretary stormed in. She threw a dishevelled, soggy sack on the floor, stained brown as if someone had wiped their ass with it. Wait a minute...

"This is the last time I do that for you," she shouted, nearly in tears.

The doctor looked a little lost. "Sheila, I am in ze middle of ses-"

"I quit!" she screamed. Then she gave Valentin the middle finger and marched out, slamming the door behind her.

The two men looked at each other. It was none of Mongrel's business so he was staying out of it. But the doctor now had a major problem to deal with. And for a man like Valentin Rushkov there was only one place he could properly deal with his problems.

"Vould you like to go und have drink? I need vodka."

Mongrel shrugged, weary that this might be a test. "If that's what you want, sure. Can't let you drink alone, I guess. But aren't we on the clock?"

"No. Ze glasses are off," the doctor replied. He put down his clipboard and stood up from his chair, then bent down to pick up the lumpy sack. After this he had to pause, dizzy from the motions. Life's ups and downs were getting to him. Or perhaps it was the stench of the oversized, handmade diaper that was making him lightheaded. Once he had his bearings straight he headed out of the office, with Mongrel trailing behind, through the little sitting room or sub-office or whatever it was.

They found Zeke lounging on the shit-stained couch as they came through. He was now naked from the waist down; where his pants were was anyone's guess. His face, once contorted with constipation now harboured a goofy grin.

Valentin sighed and shook his head, but didn't stop walking. "You see; zis is vhy ve keep ze couch. He alvays gets on it somevay, somehow. Und it's just not is ze budget to purchase a new couch every time zis happens."

"I get it now," Mongrel said, trying not to make eye-contact with Zeke.

But this strategy failed, as Zeke would not be ignored. "Fight the power!" he called to Mongrel. "Never forget, your body needs to obey *you,* not the other way around. Don't be a slave!"

"He really seems to like you," Valentin said as they stepped out into the hallway.

"Who, Zeke? Yeah, unfortunately. But I'm used to it. I know lots of guys like that. They seem to flock to me for some reason."

"Ist zat right?" Valentin asked, leading Mongrel down the hall, opposite the direction he originally came, which he was thankful for; he didn't want to confront Jeffrey, the man-child again. Or his mother…or wife…sister…who was that woman anyway? "You are ze leader of ze crazies?"

"No way! I'm not even the leader of my own bodily functions, let alone an army of mental failures."

"You cannot control your bladder? I can prescribe some pills for zat if you like?"

There it was again: the doctor trying to sully Mongrel's good name – assuming there was anything left to sully. "No, I was referring to what Zeke said about controlling your body. I don't wet my bed or pee my pants or anything."

"Ah."

They came around a corner to find an elevator bank. Valentin pushed a button to call the elevator as Mongrel commented, more to himself, how much easier climbing the mountain would have been if he'd known about them.

"Vhat vas zat?"

"Oh, just something from earlier. Sometimes my imagination gets away from me.

Random Tangent

The elevator binged and the door opened, and the men stepped inside. Valentin pushed a button and said, "Sometimes ve need to keep our imaginations on shorter leash."

Mongrel mulled over this for a minute. "You know, I play the guitar – not well and not often, but I try, right? All the time I have people telling me that I suck, or it sounds like I'm raping a cat, or that it's three in the morning and I should cut out that racket; things like that. I think people would enjoy my playing more if they just used their imagination. If you ask me, some people need longer leashes, or maybe, like, a fenced-in yard for their minds. Could even join a recreational sports team or something. Whatever, you know, as long as their imaginations get some exercise." He paused, then said, "What were we talking about?"

Before Valentin could respond the elevator came to a stop and the door opened, and chanting could be heard. They stepped out, quiet so they could hear. One voice called out, too far away to hear properly, followed by a chorus of voices: "Spectators gonna spectate!"

It seemed ol' Screaming Demon had gotten himself a bunch of groupies. How cute.

"Zis vay," Valentin said, guiding Mongrel away from the chanting. "Ze garbage ist out back." If he was concerned about patients getting unruly or forming a gang and forcibly taking over the hospital, he didn't show it.

After a few turns and hallways they emerged into daylight. The heat wave from the last story had been beaten back to a more manageable temperature and was no longer blazing out of control. Stepping outside now felt like entering an oven instead of a lava flow. Before them lay a parking lot filled with an assortment of vehicles. They appeared to be at the rear of the building, which was surrounded by your standard steel mesh fence, either to keep the patients in, or keep the, um…well, probably just keep the patients in.

Valentin and Mongrel made their way through the parked cars to the rear of the lot, where sat a row of green dumpsters, some beginning to show their age with flecks of rust. The smell emanating from them was the stuff of nightmares.

Correctile Dysfunction

As they neared, Valentin fished out a set of keys from his pocket. This was because the dumpsters were always kept locked. When Mongrel asked about this he replied, "It ist to keep ze patients out." When this answer only led to confusion he felt compelled to elaborate. "Some patients like to dig zrough ze garbage. Zey vould brink it inside und share it viz ozers, sleep viz it, eat it. Like kids in candy store. So ze lock keeps zem avay und keeps zem from discoverink ze hole in ze fence."

"What hole?" Mongrel asked.

The doctor deposited the sack in the bin and locked it back up, then ushered Mongrel behind the dumpster, where they found a tiny hole, big enough to crawl through.

Many years earlier a pair of star-crossed lovers had run amok through the country, murdering and eating people and eluding the police. Known as the *M&M Cannibals*, they preyed mainly on hitchhikers; lonely, wandering souls few would miss. This made their capture difficult, as their whereabouts were rarely known. Since the bodies were discovered long after they'd left the area, authorities were perpetually a few steps behind. But nothing lasts forever, and a rookie police officer went undercover as a vagrant, leading to their apprehension. A swift trial landed them to the Dunttstown Psychiatric Hospital, where they stayed for but a few months.

No one knows when they managed to escape or even the details of it. After some sleuthing, a bright lad discovered that no one had seen them for a few days. A search of the hospital grounds revealed only the hole in the fence, and the proceeding manhunt turned up nothing. After countless[*] man hours, and with no signs of where even to begin, the search was abandoned. The *M&M Cannibals'* current whereabouts remain unknown.

As he watched the doctor get down on his hands and knees, Mongrel asked, "Why are we going through the fence instead of out the front doors. Makes it seem like we're escaping."

"Vell I had to use ze garbage anyway, und since ve are here zis ist ze qvickest vay out. But if you vant, ve can go back zrough ze hospital." He looked up at Mongrel, awaiting his decision.

---

[*] Not really countless; more like a dozen.

Random Tangent

Mongrel thought about the screaming demon, the old woman with the potato heart, Jeffrey, and the rest of the mental failures in the hospital and how much he didn't want to run into them again. It didn't take long for him to make up his mind. He dropped to his knees and said, "Good point, let's go."

A short while later they were standing in front of *El Éfac*, Dunttstown's lone bar. It was more of a pub really, in that it didn't showcase loud music and slutty women looking for free drinks. The owner, Loafmeat, felt it wasn't right to be playing loud music in a place where folks were trying to drink and socialise and get laid. He also didn't keep regular business hours like a normal establishment, instead the pub was open or closed with whatever schedule felt right to him.

"Ah good, zey are open," Valentin said, opening the door for Mongrel.

Entering the pub and letting his eyes adjust to the darker setting, Mongrel took in the familiar sights and sounds. Everything was the way it was supposed to be, the way he remembered. The tables at the front, near the windows looked barely used, and indeed they weren't. Folks who sat at those tables were generally the type to order food, which was never a good idea. Loafmeat wasn't known for his cooking, and actually encouraged people not to eat there. But some people don't listen, and those people usually never came back – whether because they had higher standards as to what was edible or because they didn't survive[*] their meal is up for debate.

The regulars knew, aside from not to touch the food (except with a biohazard suit), that the back of the bar was the place to be; where Loafmeat got down to business, where the magic happened.

You might not consider bartending amongst occupations with a supernatural flare, but Loafmeat was no mere bartender. Raised by gypsies and his father Moe (pronounced 'Philip' for some reason), he was taught the ways of botany, witchcraft, and

---

[*] Loafmeat had long been spreading rumours about the lethality of his cooking. He felt it just wasn't right for people to come to a bar and not drink liquor, and wanted word to circulate that *El Éfac* was not the place to go for fine dining, unless you were having your last meal.

Correctile Dysfunction

ping pong. And though he rarely delved into the dark arts[**], his last experiment had yielded a concoction with death-defying results...well, almost. While the drink didn't actually bring the dead back to life, it played its part in Mongrel's recovery months ago, and Loafmeat was using the publicity to market his new *Diet Water* as a miracle drink, and it was beginning to take off.

Loafmeat looked up as the two men made their way to the back counter, surprise and delight nearly detectable behind his massive, bushy beard. "Now there's a sight I've not seen in an age and a half," he said in his deep, gravely voice, coming around to shake Mongrel's hand. "Thought you'd given up the drink."

For Mongrel the encounter was, at least initially, a strange one. He couldn't help making comparisons between his old friend and Meatloaf, a bartender on the island on Duntt River. Them both being bartenders and having similar names was just the beginning; the two men looked *exactly* alike. It was uncanny. You could say that they were twins separated at birth but that wouldn't account for the other similarities. And we're only scratching the surface...but that's a discussion for another time.

"Sorry," Mongrel said, shrugging. "I haven't spent much time in Dunttstown lately."

"Oh? Where've you been?"

Mongrel thought for a moment. "In trouble mostly. In jail, in Bolivia, incognito, in a hostage situation...lots of fun." He laughed, though he didn't find any humour in any of it. "Oh, in space too."

"Space?" Loafmeat seemed genuinely impressed.

"You vere in space?" Valentin asked.

"Yeah, I was abducted by aliens. The *nice* kind of aliens."

Valentin rubbed his clean-shaven chin. "Interestink..."

"And you, Dr. Rushkov," Loafmeat turned to the doctor and proffered his hand, "good to see you as well. How are things at the hospital?"

"Not good," Valentin answered, offering a sympathetic smile. "Not good at all."

[**] Oh yes, ping pong is definitely a dark art. I mean, how could it *not* be?

Random Tangent

Mongrel glanced back and forth between his two companions. "You guys know each other?"

"That we do," Loafmeat said. "Dr. Rushkov has been a regular here since…"

"Since Shchevret vas destroyed," the doctor finished, "und mine family killed."

"Oh." Mongrel didn't know what to say about this. Of course he knew about the incident in the neighbouring town. Their nuclear power plant had inexplicably blown up, or had a meltdown or something; no one knew exactly what had happened. Anyone near enough to the accident to have an eye-witness account had their eyes vaporized when they were disintegrated. The resulting fallout had killed thousands, and any survivors were dying slow, painful deaths from radiation poisoning, which was also halting any investigations. But on the bright side, even with the power plant gone, it had barely affected Dunttstown at all.

"Well have a seat, gentlemen," Loafmeat said, returning behind the bar, "and I'll fix you up something to drink, maybe soften up that bad day a little."

Mongrel took a seat at the counter, "Just a beer for me," he said.

"Ah yes. Got in a fresh supply of generic ale this morning." Loafmeat grabbed a couple glasses, then paused. "But might I suggest something a bit stronger – more bang for your buck, if you will?"

"Sure, I guess," Mongrel shrugged. "I'm not one for hard liquor, but it's been a while since I've had a drink. Got some catching up to do."

This seemed to please Loafmeat, evidenced by a broad smile that no one could see behind his epic beard. He turned and began searching through the dozens of bottles on the shelf. "I've been working on a new brew," he said, finally selecting a grungy-looking bottle. "Starting with a basic scotch, I infused it with brown sugar and dandelion roots. I think you'll find it had a pleasing aroma and a strong, smoky finish."

"I think it sounds disgusting," Mongrel said, about to pass on the offer.

"First glass is on the house."

Correctile Dysfunction

"Then again...alright I'll take one." Mongrel wasn't an alcoholic, but he couldn't resist a free drink. Loafmeat was banking on this and had already poured a small glass.

"Make it two," Valentin piped in.

"Three!" came a voice beside them, startling Mongrel into dropping the glass he'd just picked up.

The voice belonged to a man sitting at the other end of the bar who, up until this point was competently minding his own business. He appeared to be in uniform, dressed all in black and wearing sunglasses, even in the dim light. His voice was definitely southern in origin, but Mongrel couldn't place where.

He hopped off his stool, removed his shades and came over. "Sorry friend, didn't mean to make you spill your drink."

"I-I didn't spill it, gravity took it from me," Mongrel said, trying to be more macho than he really was. Even though Loafmeat wouldn't have any of it, Mongrel didn't want a fight breaking out. The last fight he'd witnessed in *El Éfac* ended with Loafmeat removing a man's moustache one follicle at a time and forcing him to drink them down in stale, day-old beer.

The man nodded. "Yes I see that. A nice pile of gravity you got there too, very well trained. And I should know; I'm a professional tripper – I perform random gravity checks."

"What?" was all Mongrel could say.

"This here is Mr. Silver," Loafmeat introduced, pouring Mongrel another drink. "New in town if I'm not mistaken.

"New in town but not staying," Silver said, introducing another round of handshakes. "Expanding into new territories, looking for recruits."

"Vhat ist it zat you do, Mr Silver?" Valentin asked, finally joining the conversation.

"I...what?" The man looked at Loafmeat and Mongrel. "What did he say?"

"What kind of work are you in, Mr. Silver?" Mongrel answered.

"Ah, please, call me Jet. Now I guess you could say my official title would be Gravity Enforcement Officer, but my services go beyond that. Primarily I travel all over, inspecting gravity, making sure it's working properly."

Random Tangent

They all looked at him funny – except for Loafmeat, who always looked funny. Jet had the air of a used car salesman – quick-talking and shady. Being dressed all in black didn't help either. What he was saying made no sense, but he seemed to know what he was talking about, and if he really was out of his mind, which would surprise no one, then at least he was entertaining.

"Now I know what you're thinking..." he continued.

"Not me," Mongrel quipped. "I don't think."

"...that sounds like the easiest job in the world. I get that a lot. I mean, gravity always works right? But you'd be wrong. Gravity is a law and like any other law, it can be broken."

Valentin said, "Actually, I vas zinkink zat gravity ist everyvhere. Vhy have ve not heard of zis job before?"

Jet once again looked at the other men. "I don't get it. Is he speaking English?"

"They might not have heard of a Gravity Enforcement Officer before," Loafmeat said to Jet.

"What to you mean; you have?" Mongrel asked him.

"Isn't the first time Jet's been in here."

Mongrel nodded. Of course Loafmeat talked to his patrons. It was one of the things that made him the best bartender in the world. Or one of the best, certainly. At the very least, the one with the most aggressive facial hair.

"Oh we're around," Jet threw an arm widely behind him. "Making sure planes fly right and meteors fall down. Hell if we didn't do our jobs right birds would just float in the air after they died. It'd freak the whole world right out I tell you. And the Bermuda Triangle – remember that?" The men nodded. "Don't hear much about it anymore, do you? Cause we solved it. Figured it out and put it back together. You go on and try it now; smooth sailing, I guarantee it."

"What was wrong with it?" Loafmeat asked, dying to know. In his younger days he'd spend hours researching the Triangle; it fascinated him to no end.

"Sorry pal, trade secrets."

Loafmeat hung his head, disappointed, but it seemed right; he was just a civilian in these matters.

Correctile Dysfunction

"Anyway," Jet continued, focusing on Mongrel, "I need an agent around here. Lot of upheaval and disorder going on in these parts. I don't have time to check into everything myself, so I'm looking for a hired hand. A gravitational mercenary, so to speak." He looked fiercely at Mongrel. "If you're man enough."

"Me?" Mongrel finally asked. "Are you offering me a job?"

"Yes sir I am. I need you to look into these disturbances and report back to me."

Was this a joke? Jet couldn't be serious, could he? A gravity enforcement officer? That *had* to be made up. Then again, the more Mongrel thought about it, the more it made sense. Dunttstown was abnormal in every way imaginable, and certainly no stranger to the odd gravitational flux. The mon, Duntt River, even Jayson Miles could made gravity his bitch.

And it wasn't just gravity; Captain Pete dying every other day; the past mayor Troy Talbot getting elected without a campaign or even holding an election; the current beast mayor was from another planet; aliens made from pure imagination; hell Dunttstown itself was known to occasionally fart.

Clearly, reality was getting raped in Dunttstown.

"What kind of disturbances are we talking about?" Mongrel asked.

"Well I can't really tell you…that is, unless you join the team."

"I don't know…gravity doesn't really come naturally to me."

"I zought you had job?" Valentin was quick to point out.

"Uh…" Well shit, there goes that. Mongrel *did* tell the doctor that he was employed, but that was obviously a lie, and if Valentin was any good a reading people he'd have been able to see right through that. So that meant either he sucked at his job, or he knew exactly what he was doing, and Mongrel was willing to bet it was the latter. It wasn't enough for the doctor to make Mongrel feel bad about himself, he had to put him down in front of other people?

"You got a deal!" Mongrel said loudly, ignoring Valentin. "I'm your man and I'm *way* more than man enough." He then grabbed the second glass Loafmeat poured him and downed it. This was a mistake, and the gut-wrenching shriek that came out of him was perhaps his least-manly moment in a lifetime of unmanliness. "Yep," he wheezed, nearly falling off his stool, "it was disgusting." Oddly enough, however, Mongrel wanted more.

Jet watched to see if Mongrel would fall, and was disappointed when he didn't. So he pushed him off the stool. When Mongrel landed painfully, tossing the shot glass still in his hand across the room, where it shattered, Jet smiled, immensely pleased with himself. "Right to the floor. Amazing."

"Ahem!" Loafmeat interrupted. "That's just not right."

Throwing his hands in the air, Jet took a step back. "My apologies sir. I will pay for that. Just wanted to make sure I had the right man for the job."

"Looks like my boss is an asshole," Mongrel grumbled, getting back on his barstool.

"Now let's not get ahead of ourselves," Jet said, dusting Mongrel off, "you haven't got the job yet."

Mongrel looked confused. All that work for nothing? The talking and listening, the introductions and hand-shaking, the behaving himself and not saying anything stupid – that wasn't easy. He even swallowed Loafmeat's revolting hodgepodge of liquid evil to prove his courage. *And* he fell off his stool – not anyone would fall off their stool for a job. He could have seriously messed up his hair. Mongrel had worked damn hard for this opportunity, and now it was revealed that said opportunity was a picky little bastard?

As peeved as Mongrel was about this, all he did was whine, "But I thought…" and was going to leave that hanging, but was cut off by a business card shoved in his face.

"Just give me a call and we'll set up an interview."

Mongrel looked at the card and then back to Jet. "It says Jedediah Silver?"

"Yep. That's why I said call me Jet."

"But Jet isn't short fo-"

"*Call me Jet.*"

"Okay, okay. Jet it is."

Jet picked up his glass. "I toast then to…to Dunttstown, and its future gravitational cooperation."

Correctile Dysfunction

Valentin picked up his drink and Loafmeat poured himself a glass of the liquor to join in. Mongrel, however, was without. He whimpered in protest.

"You sure you want another one?" Loafmeat asked. "The last one didn't go down so well."

"It went down just fine," Mongrel retorted. "Too fine, actually. Took me down with it."

Loafmeat relented and poured Mongrel another shot. "Your funeral…maybe."

Mongrel wasn't sure what that meant, but picked up the drink and downed it with everyone else, and again suffered the unpalatable poison. He was not alone in this – with the exception of Loafmeat, a sour expression crossed each of their faces. But for Mongrel it wasn't as bad. This being his second shot, perhaps he was developing a taste for it.

After a brisk coughing fit, Jet said, "Well it was nice meeting you folks, but my break is over and I have to return to work."

"Are you drinkink on ze job?" Valentin asked.

Jet flashed a confused look at the men. "Seriously? How do you understand him?"

Mongrel filled in, "He wants to know why you're drinking on the job."

"Oh, it's mandatory." Jet flashed a grin. "Helps with the testing."

"You're shitting me. How does being drunk help?"

"Well, think about it. You can fall on purpose, sure, but what does that prove?"

"That gravity works."

Jet shook his head. "Gravity can be a sneaky little bastard You gotta catch it off guard, fall when it least suspects it. You'd be surprised. I've seen people fall and completely miss the ground."

A burst of incoherent babble came from a walkie-talkie clipped to Jet's waist, and he paused to decipher it. "Looks like I gotta go." He made for the exit.

"Wait!" Mongrel shouted after him. "What do they hit if they miss the ground?"

"We'll talk later. Give me a call." Then he was gone.

Random Tangent

Silence filled the bar, broken only by the sound of glasses clinking as Loafmeat poured more shots of his disgusting yet addictive swamp juice, followed by the three men downing them.

After his fourth shot, Mongrel decided tranquility really wasn't his thing, and spoke. "Is everyone drinking on the job except me? Is it wise," he asked Loafmeat, "for you to be getting drunk with us? Shouldn't you be running the bar? Not judging you or anything."

"No offense taken," Loafmeat said. He glanced around at the empty tables, grumbling. "But it's my place and I'll do as I please. Just doesn't seem right not to join my friends in a toast. Besides, I don't get drunk; I'm immune to alcohol. If I want to get a little tipsy I huff goat farts."

"But goats don't exist anymore."

"Ah yes, zat ist correct!" Valentin agreed. "I remember zis."

"Yeah," Loafmeat said dismally. "Weren't too fond of that. Just doesn't seem right not having goats anymore. But what can you do?" He shrugged. "So that's why I got back into crafting ales. Trying to create something that'll take away the blinding sting of the world."

Mongrel eyeballed his empty glass. "My world still stings."

"Right. Forgot about that." Loafmeat reached between the two men and snapped his fingers.

The explosion of sound made the blood rush to Mongrel's head, forcing his body to go limp. This went unnoticed, however, as his senses became overloaded with information. Everything became so clear, so evident, so *obvious*. The world around him snapped into focus so hard he thought he saw skid marks in reality. Suddenly he knew what the temperature was in Celsius, Fahrenheit, and Kelvin. He knew the colour and thickness Loafmeat's socks. He knew how they got the caramel into the Caramilk™ bar. He knew what had happened to his magic potato. He could hear how many chairs there were in the room. He could feel his hair growing. He could smell all the farts in the air, left by people over the passed few days, and knew what they'd had for breakfast on their respective mornings. He could hear birds outside singing, sounding as if they were right next to him on the counter. Not only that, but Mongrel, who knew nothing about birds, could tell precisely their species, the location

Correctile Dysfunction

within a foot, and oddly enough, what each tasted like. This suddenly whetted his appetite with a hunger like he'd never known, and Mongrel was actually tempted to order something to eat.

Mongrel looked behind Loafmeat at the rows of liquor and could read the finest detail on every label – even the ones obscured by other bottles – and knew their alcohol content, ingredients, and what each smelled like.

He then turned to face Valentin, who goggled back at him, experiencing the same rollercoaster of madness. The look in his eyes – scared, awed – confirmed it. The sound of Valentin's heartbeat boomed in Mongrel's ears like drums, and he knew without counting that it was racing at exactly 118 beats per minute.

It was all right there, plain as day. A new world blossomed in front of him. He could hear the movement of time, smell the fabric of space. He saw the universe and all its intricacies and mysteries.

For a brief but startling moment, Mongrel could read the words on the page.

Then, as quickly as it came, the overwhelming sense of having the entirety of existence in his mind was gone. All the blood drained back into Mongrel's body, invigorating it, but leaving him light-headed.

"What...what was that?" Mongrel asked, the buzz of inebriation coalescing inside him. "I could, like, read my own book for a second."

"You have your own book?" Valentin asked, his eyes wide with wonder.

Mongrel leaned close to him and gave an exaggerated nod. "And you were in it."

This made the doctor's eyes light up like a child on Christmas morning, as if all his dreams had come true. "Do I get mine own book too?" he asked Loafmeat.

Unsure of what to say, the bartender shrugged, then answered with his own question. "So you liked it?"

They both nodded.

"I was tripping balls, man," Mongrel said. "Does everyone trip over their balls? Like, even women?"

Random Tangent

"Oh, wouldn't seem right to give that to just anyone," Loafmeat said, a smile of satisfaction lie hidden underneath his beard. "I only serve it to folks who can handle it."

"You think we can handle it?"

Loafmeat looked the two men up and down. "Well unless I'm mistaken, you're not dead. So yes."

Valentin suddenly began giggling like a schoolgirl. "Zat ist correct! I am alive!"

Mongrel patted himself down, making sure he was still part of reality, eventually satisfied that his existence hadn't been ended without him knowing it. "I don't know how many people you killeded before figuring that out." He then laughed despite himself. "What the heck is in it? Wait, *heck*? I don't say heck…"

"Just the ingredients I told you," Loafmeat said, the words ambling out of his beard in their own good time. "Triple distilled and boiled in a human skull. I also infused it with the essence of sunlight – which can lead to blinding visions. Also it kills the effect, sunlight, so watch out for that. All just simple things I learned from ancient traditions and arcane science."

"What's it called?"

"Witchcraft."

"No, I mean…I mean…" Mongrel paused. What *did* he mean? "I mean what's the name of the drink."

Loafmeat blinked at him.

Mongrel blinked back.

Loafmeat waited.

Finally Mongrel nodded. "Oh…okay, I got it."

"Vhat ist it?" Valentin asked, not following the conversation.

"It's, uh…it's…shit I lost it." Mongrel glanced at the ceiling. "Oh yeah, it's a, it's…it's a…" he put a finger to his lips. "It's a *shhhh*."

"Oh. I zink he means Vitchcraft is ze name of ze drink."

Furrowing his brow and scowling, Mongrel huffed, "Well if you knew then why'd you ask?"

Squinting and looking at Mongrel, Valentin asked, 'You did not answer my qvestion earlier."

"What question?"

Correctile Dysfunction

"My qvestion about your job."

"Oh, right. Well, okay...I'm, like...you know, okay. Right?"

Valentin nodded; he understood. Wait a minute, no he didn't. "Vhat?"

Mongrel's drunken stupor made finding words harder than normal. "Okay, um...I'm a, like, professional amateur. I'm really good at not doing anything really good. Does that make any sense?"

"I cannot imagine zat pays vell."

"What?"

"I said it dost not pay vell."

Fading into the background, Loafmeat set about tidying up the bar; cleaning glasses, polishing the counter, sweeping the floor. He checked his inventory, made sure the thing in the basement was securely locked up, and updated his Facebook page, all the while listening in on the conversation. He loved his job.

After a minute Mongrel began giggling again. "You know, your Russian accent is even harder to understand when it's drunk."

"Vhat? I am not Russian. Who told you zis?"

Mongrel tried to stop giggling but found it difficult. "Oh yeah, that's right. So what are you, German then?"

"Zat ist correct!" the doctor exclaimed, jubilation and saliva gushing from him.

Despite spit being sprayed in his face, Mongrel burst out laughing. It took some coaxing to calm him down enough to explain what was so funny. "You say that every five minutes!"

"Say vhat?"

Mongrel gave his best impersonation. *"Zat ist correct."*

This sent Valentin over the edge and laughed so hard he nearly fell of his stool. "I know! I know! It ist like mine catchphrase!"

"That should be the name of the story," Mongrel said. "Or something like that."

The laughter continued for a few minutes, slowly tapering off, with Valentin's falling further into soft moping. "Sheila hated it vhen I said zat," he sulked.

"Who?"

"Mine secretary."

Random Tangent

Mongrel's eyes crept hither and thither around the room, trying to make sense of the name. When it finally did he wasn't sober enough to be gentile about it. "Oh right. You mean she *used* be your secretary."

Suddenly Valentin burst into tears and slumped onto the counter, sobbing.

"I'm sorry! It's okay!" Mongrel lightly and quickly patted the doctor's back. "It's okay. I was kidding! She's still your secretary!"

Loafmeat knew when he was needed, and poured a couple more shots of witchcraft. Having been a bartender longer than he'd been alive, it was instinct for him.

Sheila had been many things to Valentin Rushkov – crush, high school sweetheart, girlfriend, roommate, fiancé, wife, ex-wife, daughter (after a brief mix up at the immigration office), and employee. She'd been steadfastly at his side from his days of academic study through to his tenure at Dunttstown Psychiatric Hospital. Along the line they had dated, fallen in love, gotten married, fought, performed ritual sacrifices, raised a family, were invited to come on live TV to play Family Feud (and came just four points shy of winning the grand prize), worked together, got divorced, and remained friends with benefits. She'd been with from the time he was a teenager right up until today, and would have stayed with him until the end of her days if it weren't for his glasses.

When Valentin had adopted the glasses and donned a split personality he became a serious pain in her ass. She put up with it for years, but it was only a matter of time before she couldn't take anymore. Before long they divorced. The three children were split down the middle; the youngest staying with her mother, the oldest moving out with dad, and the middle child auctioned off into slavery to help pay the court fees.

Despite their estrangement, Valentin still loved Sheila, and convinced her to keep her position as his secretary, since it was a well-paying job. Also, it allowed for them to keep seeing each other after hours, if you know what I mean, because, you know, people have needs. But Valentin still wore his glasses while in session, and still managed to make her life occasionally difficult. Again, it was

Correctile Dysfunction

only a matter of time before she quit. And with the latest resignation she really was, finally, gone from his life. Having been a part of it for so long, he didn't know what he was going to do without her.

Still with his head on the counter, Valentin cried his little heart out, pausing every now and then to slurp back a shot of witchcraft and order another.

"There, there," Mongrel continued. "Maybe she'll come back." He was trying to pat the doctor on the back in consolation but missed half the time due to the lack of coordination.

"Nein. I know her too vell. Zis vas ze last hay. Ist all mine fault."

Mongrel furrowed his brow at him. "What?"

"I think he means the last straw," Loafmeat clarified. He was used to the listening to alcoholics ramble on and on.

"Oh. Well at least you admit it," Mongrel said. "And admitting is knowing is half the problem, or something, right?"

Valentin solemnly nodded his head. "Zat ist correct."

Having to stifle a laugh after hearing the catchphrase again, Mongrel thought of something – which is rather amazing considering how difficult this was for him when he was sober, let alone plastered. "I thought you said your family was killed in Sch...Shv...Shev...wherever you come from."

Looking up at Mongrel, tears streaking his face, Valentin nodded. "Zat ist correct. Mine children und girlfriend."

"Oh. I didn't know you had a girlfriend. What are you so upset over Sheila over for?"

"Everyone I love leaves me," the doctor wailed, ignoring Mongrel. He downed another shot, and this last one seemed to help get his emotions under control. "Forgive me. Ve're here to talk about your voman problems, not mine."

"Woman problems?" Mongrel spat. "Are you calling me a problem? With womens?"

"Nein. I mean Beby."

"Oh." Mongrel drank another shot of liquor, beginning to feel like he was falling behind. "No problems. Me and Beby are tight, like this." He tried to cross his fingers but the attempt ended

Random Tangent

with him on the floor. He got up and ordered another shot. "Okay honestly I don't know where we are."

"Ve're in ze bar."

"No, I mean...I mean yeah, we're in the bar. *Zat ist correct!*" He saluted. "But I mean me and...and...what's her face..."

"Beby."

"Yeah, that's her. I mean, one day she hates me and the next...actually he hates me most days I think. But sometimes she likes me for no reason, you know? It's like she's either playing hard to get, or stop chasing me pervert. And if it's the last one then...then, I don't like that one very much."

Valentin didn't appear to be listening. His eyes were glazed over, askew, and fixed at either the wall or the floor. Mongrel was about to ask when the doctor spoke. "Me und Sheila used to play game." He finally met Mongrel's eyes, his face crumbling under the crushing weight of immeasurable sadness. "Hide ze veiner schnitzel," he whined, his body wracked with heaving sobs again.

"Oh there, there again," Mongrel muttered, his patting accuracy even worse than before. He was starting to wonder if they'd ever get to talk about him and Beby. For a shrink, this guy was pretty self-absorbed. Mongrel was glad he wasn't paying for the session.

"You gotta forget about her, man, and focus on me," Mongrel continued. "...Her man? You gotta about forget about Herman? Who's Herman?"

"How can I do zat?"

Loafmeat, who was busying himself with dusting bottles, suggested, "Just gotta move on. Doesn't seem right to stand still while the world's turning."

"Yeah, there's other fish in the sea." Mongrel paused after saying this. This usually happened when his mind started; there was only so much brain power to go around and he couldn't run everything at once. His mouth, however, kept going autonomously. "...Other fish in the sea... other fish in the sea... other fish in the sea..."

The doctor tossed Mongrel a look of confusion, and even Loafmeat turned around to see what was going on. "He broken?" he

Correctile Dysfunction

asked, eyeing the bottle of Witchcraft suspiciously. Perhaps there were latent affects?

Whatever was in the alcohol Mongrel was drinking, it worked. He suddenly *got it*. He got why Valentin was constantly trying to make him look bad. He got why Valentin seemed to delight in pointing out his faults. He got why Valentin wanted him to fail the test – so he could have Beby all to himself.

With Mongrel out of the picture, Beby had one less suitor to choose from. It put Valentin closer to winning. This was a premeditated plan to take out the competition. No wonder the doctor had offered this session for free – it wasn't out of the goodness of his heart, but for the goodness in his pants. Or badness. Or whatever.

Of course Valentin wanted Baby – who wouldn't? And the doctor had gotten to know her intimately, getting sucked into her inescapable vortex who knows how long ago? He'd listened to and stared at and probably drooled over her – and got paid to do it! This man had the best job in the world. He got poke and probe Beby, getting deep inside her in ways Mongrel could only dream of.

Fuck he hated the doctor.

Mongrel couldn't blame him, he supposed. It was only natural to want Mongrel out of the picture. Every man for himself. Law of the jungle. Survival of the fittest. He'd played the game and won, orchestrating a brilliant plan that Mongrel couldn't help but admire, and totally would have done himself if he'd thought of it first.

Well, maybe not. Mongrel wasn't like that; he wanted to win fair and square. But just like any game, he was no one's competition; no one wanted him on their team. He was a nice guy and his place was at the back of the line, in last place. Today, much like every other day, he'd managed to successfully defend his losing streak. His chance of ever having Beby was gone.

Valentin had won. He would fail Mongrel like he'd been planning to do from the very beginning, and then he'd win Beby. This was simply the way of things; Valentin was too handsome to lose.

Random Tangent

But there was one other option. If Mongrel really wanted Beby, if he truly wanted those boobs, then his only recourse was to kill the doctor.

"No," Mongrel said dismally. "I'm not...well, maybe..."

"Maybe vhat?"

It was then that Mongrel realized he'd been talking out loud this whole time. Both men were looking at him strangely. "Uh..." he looked at Valentin, "I think...I might I have to kill you."

Loafmeat raised his eyebrows, somewhat concerned, but Valentin, perhaps due to the Witchcraft, didn't seem alarmed. "Vhy ist zat?" he asked.

"Cause you're trying to steal my girl."

"Vhat girl?"

"Beby!"

Valentin sighed and rolled his eyes. "Again viz zis Beby! You know are not ze only von viz voman troubles."

"Yeah well at least I have a voman. I mean woman."

A cry of pain breached the doctor's lips and his hand flew to his chest. "Too mean!"

The cold look that oft accompanies murder faded from Mongrel's eyes; if he was going to kill the man, he didn't have to be a dick about it. "Look, just stay avay from – dammit I keep talking like you! – just stay *away* my woman, okay?"

"I zink you are forgettink somethink," Valentin said, now sporting a cold glare of his own. "She ist not your voman yet. Und you better play nicely; all I have to do ist say ze vord und you are finished."

Mongrel just shook his head sadly. "Now you see, this is why I have to kill you."

"Ah, zat ist vhy. Yes, I understand now."

"Good. So how do you want to die?"

Before the doctor could respond Loafmeat injected himself into the conversation. "Pardon the interruption, but we don't allow murder in here anymore. New ordinance came from the mayor's office." He pointed to a sign on the wall. It read: NO MURDER, VOMMITING, CROCS, OR TALK OF THAT GUY I DON'T LIKE.

"Since when?" Mongrel demanded.

"Last week."

"Who ist zat guy you don't like?" Valentin asked.

"We don't talk about him around here," was all the bartender would say.

"Dammit!" Mongrel slammed his fist down on the bar. "Well can I at least take him outside and kill him?"

Loafmeat shrugged. "City property out there. You'd have to take that up with the mayor."

"But I can't even speak his language," Mongrel moaned, slumping his head on the counter. He couldn't even murder anyone properly. He needed a drink. He ordered one.

"You sure you can even get to the door?" Loafmeat asked as he poured another shot of Witchcraft.

"Watch me!" Mongrel said as he downed the shot and fell straight to the floor.

Valentin bent down to help him to his feet. "Come now, I got you." He threw Mongrel's arm over his shoulder and carried him towards the exit, and his impending execution.

"Sank you," Mongrel slurred. "You're a good guy. Ima kill you fast. Or slow, whatever you prefer."

They were only a few feet from the door when Mongrel stopped him. "You go on ahead, I gotta tell Loafmeat something." Valentin propped Mongrel on his feet, made sure he was well balanced, and said he'd wait for him outside.

After the door closed Mongrel turned and crashed to the floor again. "I'm okay!" he said, holding up a hand to ward off anyone who might come to aid him. But the bar was empty except for Loafmeat, who hadn't moved from his spot, and quiet except for the muffled scream that came from outside.

"Did you hear that?" Mongrel asked.

"Wouldn't worry about it," Loafmeat dismissed.

"Okay, I won't. Um, I met your dop..doppel…your lookaliker. On the island. Looks just like you."

"The island?"

"Yeah. You know, the island on Duntt River?"

Loafmeat squinted at Mongrel as if he were hard to see. "You were on the island?"

Random Tangent

Mongrel tried to nod but cracked his head off the stone tiles. After a minute to let the pain subside, he felt it might be a good idea to get up off the floor. Grabbing a nearby chair, he slowly began to climb it. "Yep, that island. Long story. The guy's name is Mefloat. Or Letmof. You know: your name, but backwards. Weird eh."

Coming around the bar, Loafmeat wore apprehension like it was a pair of tight leather pants. He sat down in a chair close to Mongrel. *"What?"*

"Looks just like you too. Both of you." After smacking his head off the floor Mongrel was dizzy as well as drunk, and his vision was doubled. "I thought it was you guys at first."

"I would never go to the island."

"Yeah I know, but I didn't know, you know?"

Loafmeat didn't know, and said nothing.

"Anyway he looked just like you; Big hat, man-eating[*] beard, full of menace. Sounded like you and everything. Oh, and his bar is called *The Café*." His eyes went wide with the last revelation, as if it was the key to the whole thing. Finally on his feet, he looked around the room, making a complete circle. "His bar looked like this too. I think I'm gonna be sick."

The spinning had made him dizzy, and the alcohol had made him drunk, and the floor had made him feel welcomed; so he tried to go back to it. Loafmeat sat in silence in his chair in disbelief, and barely caught Mongrel before he cracked his head off the floor again.

"You'll have to take that outside," he said, dragging Mongrel to the door, skirting the pools of light coming in through the windows. "You read the sign right? Wouldn't be right to disobey the sign."

"Yeah, I can read," Mongrel grunted, trying to get a look at the sign again. He couldn't remember what the other forbidden items were.

"I appreciate what you told me," Loafmeat said as they reached the exit. "Now if you'll excuse me, I need to do a good bit of thinking."

---

[*] Contrary to what the rumours suggested, Loafmeat's beard never ate anything larger than rats.

Correctile Dysfunction

"But what do I owe you? You know, for the, the...for the drunk?"

Loafmeat opened the door and light poured into the dim pub. "Wouldn't be right to bill you now. We'll settle up later."

Mongrel turned around slowly so as not to upset his fragile stomach, and gave his friend a sloppy hug, then stumbled out into the scalding daylight, and screamed.

When the sun hit Mongrel's skin it burned and sizzled, crackled and steamed. He saw everything in shades of red and white. His stomach turned upside down and his brain felt like it had shit its pants. Smoke wafted from him. He collapsed to the ground and moaned loudly, twitching as spasms of pain rocked his body.

"Ahhhh!" he cried. "I'm a vampire! Why didn't anybody tell me I'm a vampire! The sun is gonna make me dead. A *dead*! I don't want to be a dead..." He repeated this a few times before all went dark.

Mongrel awoke to a gently nudging. Blinking and opening his eyes, he glanced up at the sun, which was then quickly blocked by the face of Valentin Rushkov.

"Zere you are!"

"What happened?" Mongrel asked. "I'm supposed to be dead."

"Nein, you are fine. Come now, on your feet." He tried to help Mongrel stand up, assuming he'd need the assistance. But Mongrel was just fine; no longer dizzy or nauseous. In fact, he was completely sober. He must have been lying on the ground for some time. "How long was I out?"

"I am not sure," Valentin answered. "But I don't zink very long."

Looking around, Mongrel agreed that it seemed to be the same afternoon. Also, smoke was still wafting off his clothes, which miraculously hadn't been burnt off. He was not, however, convinced that he was still alive. "Are you dead too?"

"Vhat? Nein. Ve are both alive."

"We can't be. I stepped out of the bar, roasted in the sunlight like a vampire and died. Didn't you too?"

Valentin shook his head. "You are makink no sense."

Random Tangent

"No, I'm making *nonsense*," Mongrel corrected. "It's the whole theme of the book. Pay attention!" He slapped the doctor. "Now did you not drink the witchcraft? Did Loafmeat not say it would kill us? Did you not step outside and catch fire?"

Valentin rubbed his cheek and remained silent. Now Mongrel was making sense, very unsettling sense. He did think he'd caught fire when the light hit him. He did pass out. What if he never woke up? What if they were somehow vampires, and *did* burn to death? "I...I don't know," he finally said.

"Exactly. If you were dead, would you know it? Didn't you see that movie where the kids sees dead people, and says they walk around like normal people cause they don't know they're dead? What if that's us? Or what if we're vampires?"

"But if ve're vampires vouldn't ve burn in ze sunlight? Vouldn't ve be dead?"

"Uh..." Now Mongrel was silent. So were they dead vampires, or normal ghosts? This was all very confusing. Being dead was complicated. "I don't know," he said, flustered. "How can we tell?"

Valentin thought for a moment. "Vell, ve could try killink each ozer again?

As bad luck would have it, at that very moment a large vehicle came screeching towards them. It was loud and reckless, swerving all over the road. It was heading straight for them, purposeful, menacing. And it was driven by Captain Pete.

"Runs me over with a truck, boy?" the captain said. "Lets see how *you* likes it!"

Mongrel and Valentin both glanced up the road at the oncoming delivery truck. Neither seemed confused or worried, as traffic in Dunttstown behaved in a similar manner most of the time. Excellent driving skills stood out like a sore thumb. More specifically, the doctor wasn't worried since he was still under the assumption that he might be dead, and the dead do not worry about the affairs of the living. And Mongrel wasn't worried because he knew one little thing that Captain Pete had somehow forgotten, which was that the old pirate didn't know how to drive.

"What?" Captain Pete cried as the steering wheel suddenly jerked out of his hands. It spun around crazily as he tried to grab a

Correctile Dysfunction

hold of it. Looking down at the controls, nothing made any sense to him. So many buttons and knobs and dials. What was he thinking, trying to pilot this behemoth of a truck?

He managed to finally seize the wheel, but it was too late; the vehicle was already wildly out of control. It bounced off a parked car and careened into a storefront across the street from *El Éfac*, tipped over and inexplicably exploded. Screams from Captain Pete tore through the air for a few minutes, but as no one came to help, they soon died, replaced by the crackle of flames.

"So if ve are dead," the doctor said, turning to Mongrel and brushing off the attempted vehicular manslaughter, "does zat mean ve cannot get drunk? I know I vas drunk vhen I came out, but now...nozink."

Mongrel's eyes went wide as memories resurfaced. "Wait, didn't Loafmeat say something about sunlight killing the effect? Maybe that's what he meant; kill the drunkenness." The more he thought about it, the more it made sense.

"Zat ist correct!" Valentin exclaimed. "He said ze sunlight vould kill *it*. Not us!"

"Yeah. We got smashed, like, immediately, and then we sobered up just like that!" He snapped his fingers. "And what a freaking experience. Like a whole morning of the worst hangover ever, crammed into ten seconds."

"So ve are still alive zen? Yes?"

"Yeah, we are!"

They grabbed each other and hugged fiercely, and began jumping up and down in jubilation, yelling about how alive they still were. This went on until someone shouted at them to shut up or drop dead; their choice.

Suddenly Mongrel's face wrenched into a horrific glare, and he shoved Valentin away. "And you're still trying to steal my girl!" he shouted.

"Oh not zat again."

"Aren't you supposed to say 'zis ist correct?' You know: your catchphrase?"

"But zat ist not correct. Und may I remind you zat ve are still in session," Valentin said threateningly. "You must behave yourself."

Random Tangent

Mongrel stared him down. "Is that a threat?"

Slowly, carefully removing a set of glasses out of his front shirt pocket, Valentin dangled them in front of Mongrel. This would have been more intimidating if they weren't broken. "Vhat?" he snivelled. "Mine glasses!" He must have landed on them when he fainted after sobriety ran him down like a runaway freight train.

"Well so much for that!" Mongrel jeered.

"Zis means nozink!" the doctor said severely. "Do not forget, I still have ze power to fail you."

"Oh please, you were gonna fail me anyway! Don't deny it. This whole thing was bullshit. There's no point going on. Session over." He sat down on the ground in a huff. He knew he was screwed, and not in the way he wanted.

Dr. Rushkov looked at him thoughtfully. "Bullshit you say?"

Mongrel skewed his eyes upward and could see the doctor plotting something malevolent. His nose twitched deviously, his smile hinted at brooding schemes, and his eyes betrayed the deception beneath. And not for a nanosecond did Mongrel consider his options.

He jumped to his feet, not thinking twice (or even once), and said, "You're on, pal! And get ready for the whooping of a lifetime. Seriously, a lifetime. You'll still be sore on your deathbed."

The doctor chuckled evilly and began walking down the street in the direction of the psychiatric hospital. "Don't get ahead of yourself, *boy*. Before ve begin ve need to set up some rules. First, if I vin, I get your magic potato. Und you must never see Beby again."

Standing up, Mongrel looked Valentin in the eye, but remained silent. As good as he was, he knew he wasn't infallible. Even though he was currently undefeated, his days were numbered. He didn't want to put Beby on the line. He didn't want his love life in the hands of a maniac. But what other choice did he have? "Fine. And if I win, you pass me with flying colours. You give your highest recommendation."

Correctile Dysfunction

Valentin grinned, making Mongrel uneasy. It felt like the doctor had something hidden up his sleeve. "Agreed," he said. "And it vill be just ze two of us. No bystanders, no interference."

"No jokes about our mothers," Mongrel countered. His mother's untimely murder was in the past, and he had dealt with it properly, but he couldn't take any chances or afford any distractions.

"Okay zen, no giraffes."

They turned a corner and Mongrel could see, at the far end or a field, the fence surrounding the hospital. "Why not?" he asked.

The doctor shrugged, looking embarrassed. "I just don't like zem."

"Oh, yeah I can see that. They are kind of ugly."

"Und zose necks!" Valentin shuddered. "Vhy do zey need such long necks?"

"Doesn't it help them reach better when they're eating trees and stuff."

"Vell elephants und rhinoceroses und everyone else does just fine!"

"Okay, okay, you're right. Calm down. No giraffes. Got it."

They walked in silence the rest of the way back to Dr. Rushkov's office, both thinking up strategies for the upcoming battle.

Upon opening the door to the doctor's office Mongrel became incredibly nervous. He'd crawled under the fence with no trepidation. He snuck in the back door and felt not the least bit apprehensive. He'd quietly taken the elevator and crept down the hallway, stealthily avoiding anyone, the whole time completely in the moment, with no sense of foreboding or anxiety or anything. But as he stepped foot inside the empty office and snuck by Zeke, who was still naked and now asleep on the couch, Mongrel became overwhelmed with fear.

Suddenly he had something to lose. Never before had anything really been on the line, except maybe for his undefeated streak. This time he was fighting for Beby, her boobs, and the end of loneliness. This was his chance to finally have a special someone in his life, and as determined as he was not to let Valentin mess it up, it was still nerve-wracking to have so much depending entirely on the outcome of this fight.

Valentin closed the door behind them and went to his desk. He rummaged around in a couple drawers, he eventually pulling out a new pair of glasses and put them on his face. He seemed immensely pleased with himself. After a minute of silent contemplation he began typing something out on his computer. Mongrel meanwhile paced the room, trying to prepare a battle plan and calm himself at the same time, but was horrible at multitasking.

It wasn't long before Mongrel's attention was drawn toward the sound of a printer. "Ah," the doctor said, pulling out the sheet of paper. He grabbed a pen and signed it, then slid it across the desk toward Mongrel. "Here."

Mongrel came over to look at the paper, but didn't read it. "What's this?"

"Ze contract."

"For what?"

"For ze fight, of course." When confusion swelled on Mongrel's face like an allergic reaction, the doctor sighed and chided, "Don't tell me you never use contracts? How do you keep track of your victories und losses?"

"Simple: I have no losses." Mongrel smirked at him.

Valentin rolled his eyes. "Vell I am pedigree champion." He gestured behind him to the many plaques on the wall, past victories over numerous opponents. "I don't fight vizout contract."

Mongrel stared at the wall with newfound trepidation. Earlier he'd dismissed them all as certificates of doctorates and degrees, but they were achievements; documented evidence of the man's prowess in bullshitting – and there were *lots* of plaques, which meant *lots* of victories. Without a doubt, this would be his toughest challenge yet.

"Vhat ist wrong?" Valentin asked, noting Mongrel hadn't moved or said a word in nearly a minute. "Are you afraid?"

Swallowing, Mongrel dove in. "Me? I don't know the meaning of the word. I bought books and saw movies…just don't get it. You humans are so pathetic."

"Human? You zink I am human?" the doctor laughed. "You poor silly…vait, vhat are you?"

Correctile Dysfunction

Mongrel shrugged. "I was always told I can be anything I want to when I grow up, but I haven't decided yet."

"So you're not grown up yet?"

"Nope. I'm gonna live for thousands of years."

"Sounds very borink."

"Oh you have no idea."

The doctor smiled, but it wasn't a happy one. "Unfortunately I do. I must deal viz ze most bizarre patients, viz ze most outrageous problems. Von of mine patients eats his own feces because he zinks zey are his children tryink to leave him."

Scrunching up his face in disgust, Mongrel did his best not to hurl. "But why eat them? Why not just save them in a shoebox like normal people?"

Stopping mid-shrug, the doctor now wore a scrunched face of his own. "Normal people keep zeir poop in boxes? Vhy would zey do zis?"

"Well I guess I can't speak for everyone, but it's what I do anyway. Keeps the boxpeople away."

"Ze boxpeople?"

"Yeah. You know, they hide in cardboard boxes and put on plays in your kitchen when you're asleep?"

Valentin looked at him like he was crazy. "I zink you are mistaken. You are maybe gettink confused viz ze Box Trolls?"

"The Box Trolls? No, that's a movie; I'm talking real life here."

"Zen vhy ze kitchen?"

"I don't know. Why don't you ask one?" Mongrel said sarcastically, upset that the doctor wasn't taking the matter seriously.

"Because zey do not exist, und I cannot allow it." He made a note on a pad of paper.

"What are you doing? What are you talking about? And boxpeople are totally real."

"Makink tally," Valentin said after a few seconds. "I have scored point."

"A point for what?"

"You know," the doctor said, cocking his head at Mongrel, "for somevon who claims to be undefeated you do not know much

Random Tangent

about zis. You have made claim, und I have debunked it. Zerefore, I get point. First to zree points vins."

Mongrel was dumbfounded; he'd never heard of any of this before. Were there actual rules to this game or was Valentin making it all up? All the fights over the years, and no one had said anything. Do they even count?

Of course they counted. His victories had gotten him out of many jams – some by the skin of his teeth. Just because the doctor had a more formal approach meant nothing. Besides, he wasn't facing the illusive Hank, so his victory was all but assured.

Still, a contract was binding, and Mongrel hated being locked into things like that. But did he have a choice?

"Vhat are you doink?" Valentin asked.

"Oh, uh…just thinking," Mongrel replied, suddenly aware that he'd been silent for too long again.

"Does it alvays take you zis long?"

"My brain elevator doesn't go all the way to the top of my head, so I have to take the stairs the rest of the way."

"I see. Many of mine patients have fully developed adult brains, but zey never use zem."

"Well I'm not like your other patients. I'm not crazy."

The doctor was silent for a minute. "You know, beink crazy isn't alvays a bad zink. Your girlfriend, for example, has said she vanted a man who vas little bit crazy. Somevon who vould make her life excitink und unpredictable."

"Well…I can be a little crazy," Mongrel said somewhat defensively.

"She says somevon vould have to be crazy to vant to be with her."

"That sounds like me."

"I deal viz crazy people all ze time. Trust me, you are not crazy."

Mongrel scoffed for a bit before whining, "I'm totally crazy!"

"Really?" the doctor asked, acting like he didn't believe a word of it. He crossed his arms and said. "Prove it."

After dragging the comfy chair over to the desk and flopping down in it, Mongrel thought hard. "I went to the island."

Correctile Dysfunction

"Vhat island?"

"The island on Duntt River."

This didn't seem to mean anything to Valentin. "I do not understand."

Mongrel stood up and leaned on the desk. "The *island*. You know, where those weird freaks of nature live? I was there, among them. And lived. I'm like, amazing and crazy. That's like, *acrazing* or something."

"I am sorry," Valentin said. "I do not know zis island or vhat it means. I am sure zat it ist very bad und crazy, but I deal viz crazy people every day. Do you really zink you can compete viz all of zem? Early zis mornink I met viz a voman who only eats leftovers. She calls it used food, and vill only eat somezink if it ist about to be thrown avay."

"I once went a straight week dressed in a bunny costume. I ate in it, slept in it...went to the bathroom in it. And it wasn't even Easter."

"Rene – ze woman zat vas just leavink vhen you arrived – she can smell her own poop. You know vhen you use ze toilet you cannot smell yourself? You can always smell ze stench of ozers, but never yourself. Vell she can, und apparently it ist very bad. So vhenever she goes to ze bathroom she never closes ze door, afraid she might suffocate. It does not matter vhere – at home, public rest room, portable toilet – ze door ist alvays open. Understandably zis has caused some problems for her. Also she zinks her guardian angel ist tryink to kill her."

"Oh I know about guardian angel problems. Mine is an alcoholic, and I swear he throws beer bottles at me. Everyone says I'm just paranoid, but sometimes out of the blue I get hit in the head with bottles. I *know* it's him."

"Ve have some alcoholics here. One fellow ist alvays drunk. Very drunk – you can even smell ze alcohol in his pee, vhich ist anozer problem since he pees everyvhere. He probably has ze guardian angel as vell, since no von could be zat drunk und live. Und ve still have no idea vhere he ist gettink ze alcohol from."

"Man, I get *crazy* drunk. Some people black out and wake up in strange places, with no memory of the night before – well I black out for days at a time, and sometimes wake up in different countries. I even woke up as a woman once. Also, I'm banned from Switzerland; now *that* was a bender."

"You might vant so seek help for zat," the doctor said. "You said earlier zat you vere an alcoholic but I had no idea."

"You told me to say that earlier," Mongrel protested.

"Nein! I did not make you say anyzink. I do not have zat kind of power. You said zat of your own volition."

"Whatever."

"You cannot blame ozers for your problems. Ve can help you viz zese issues, but you have to admit zat you have problem."

"I don't have a drinking problem, I..." Mongrel stopped, realizing he was about to step into a trap. Valentin had set him up; if he'd admitted he was lying the doctor would get another point, and Mongrel had yet to earn even one. He was facing a very clever opponent. "I enjoy my drinking. It's not a problem at all."

Valentin tapped his pen on the desk, doing his best not to look disappointed. "Many people here do not realize zey have problems. Look at Zeke," the doctor pointed behind Mongrel to the waiting room. "He puts his hand to his head und makes imaginary phone calls. He seems to zink zey are real, und lets out his feelinks zrough his conversations. Also, he only takes calls on Tuesdays." He shrugged.

"I can relate," Mongrel said. "And not only do I hear voices but I see them too."

"Zere is older voman here, sveet old lady, who believes zat her heart vas replaced viz lump of coal, und now she ist alvays cold." He chuckled a bit. "She valks around viz six or seven blankets all ze time. I don't know how she moves. Zis von time sh-"

"It's a potato!" Mongrel cried. "A baked potato!"

The doctor looked at him, stunned.

"She's always cold because her baked potato heart needs to be reheated in the microwave. I ran into her earlier today." Mongrel smiled like a maniac. "That's a point for me, right?"

Valentin stared at Mongrel with disdain and said nothing.

That told Mongrel everything he needed to know. Maybe this wasn't going to be as difficult as he thought. Perhaps Valentin wasn't as challenging an opponent as he appeared. With newfound confidence he reached over and snatched the pen out of the doctor's

Correctile Dysfunction

hand, signed the contract and said, "That was just a taste of the ass whoopin' you got coming. As my dad used to say, you've just peered into the camel's ass."

This seemed to please the doctor, although he did his best to hide it. "Vell now it looks like ve can finally begin." He grabbed the paper and placed it on a machine behind him, pressed a few buttons and it hummed to life. Then he reached down, pulled open a drawer and brought out a game clock.

"What's that?" Mongrel asked.

"It ist game clock. Zey are used in many games to signify turns, most often used in chess."

"Okay, I know what they *are* – I play full-contact chess with the old guys in the park on Sundays. I meant why are we using it?"

"To keep track of each ozer's turns, of course. Now, speakink of Sunday, zat ist mine day of sleepink. I only sleep vonce per week; on Sundays." He clicked the clock button.

Mongrel blinked at him. "Um, aren't you going to write down my score?"

Valentin looked down at his notepad. "Vhen you score point I vill make note of it."

"I *did* just gain a point!"

"Nein!" The doctor wagged a finger it Mongrel's face. "You had not signed ze contract, so you had not started ze game."

"Well what do you think we've been doing this whole time, practicing? And what about your point? Shouldn't it not count either?"

"I signed ze contract, zerefore mine point counts." He smiled evilly at Mongrel.

"This isn't fair! You're totally cheating!"

The doctor sighed. "Ve both discussed ze rules und I made up ze contract. I have done nozink wrong. Perhaps you should have read ze contract before signink it? By ze vay, ze clock is tickink."

Mongrel glared at the clock, silently fuming to himself. "I can knit concrete," he muttered, and slapped the clock button.

"I know how to cheat at Tic Tac Toe." Valentin clicked the button.

"I scientifically calculated that 7.3 wrongs make a right." *Click.*

Random Tangent

"I spent veek in coma after seeing very ugly man. I never found out who it vas." *Click.*

"I can hiccup in four different languages." *Click.*

"Vhen I get drunk, even mine belches are slurred." *Click.*

"This is going nowhere!" Mongrel groaned, getting up to pace back and forth. "We could be at this all day. You really win fights like this?" Valentin nodded, causing Mongrel to shake his head in exasperation. "Let me show you how it's done." He cracked his neck in all the right places. "Last fall I gave birth to a litter of snails just before the harvest. Cute little guys, so small yet so full of life. They were playing in the corn stalks when the tractor came. I-I couldn't get to them in time. I yelled at them to run but, you know, *snails*. They were so young…" Somehow he managed to hold back the tears as he reached over and clicked the button.

"I love escargot," Valentin said, then clicked the button.

"What?" Mongrel asked, sniffling. "What was that? You can't just do that. You can't just state a fact."

"How do you know it ist fact? Can you prove or disprove it?"

Mongrel grit his teeth and swallowed a scream of rage. It felt like the doctor was making it up as he went along. Did all his fights go this way? No wonder he'd won so many; no one could understand the rules. "Fine then; I like Christmas carols. *Click.*

Valentin sighed. "Now ve cannot go back und forz makink up zinks ve do or do not like."

"You started it."

Huffing and glancing out the window, the doctor muttered to himself. "Fine. I had pet chicken vhen I vas child. He had birth defect – no beak. I called him Beaky. Vhen he vas old enough ve cooked und ate him – und he did *not* taste like chicken!" *Click.*

"What did it taste like?"

"Uh…" Valentin tilted his head back to look at the ceiling, "like burnt toast."

"Weird. That's like your whole childhood was a lie or something. I'm trying to get a new law passed in Dunttstown. Well, not really a law; more of a points system of sorts. If you go to jail ten times, the next one's free. It doesn't matter what the sentence is, you just get a card, and they punch it for you. Or maybe stickers…"

Correctile Dysfunction

"So vhat ist free? Zey can come back whenever zey vant, vizout committing crime, or zey can leave vizout serving zeir sentence?"

Mongrel was about to agree to the first point, but Valentin's second suggestion brought new ideas to his head. "That's a good question. I'll have to think about it." Then he did. Only after a minute did he remember to click the button.

"I created Stone Henge all my mineself. I carried ze rocks und stacked zem, und it all seems a vaste. No von understands. Zey all zink it vas aliens." He crossed his arms and sulked.

"What is it for then?" Mongrel asked. "Why did you build it?"

"It vas supposed to be simple declaration: Valentin vas here."

"Pretty laborious, don't you think? Couldn't you have just written your name in the dirt or something?"

"But zat vould vash avay. Ze big stones vill last forever. So Valentin vill alvays be here. Or zere."

"Oh. I once made…wait, is it my turn?"

"Yes, sorry." Valentin clicked the button.

"Okay. I once made catsup out of an actual cat. It wasn't as good at real catsup though, and way more harry." *Click.*

"Mine hair, alzough you cannot tell, is not mine own. It is vig und comes from anozer planet just like ours, in ze Zupprion 18 galaxy, over seven million light years avay. Zat guy vas mine exact duplicate, und he said he vasn't usink ze hair so I could have it."

"Do I have a duplicate too?" Mongrel asked.

"I do not know; I have never been zere."

"Then how'd you get your wig, and so fast?"

"Fed Ex."

Mongrel's eyes circled the room until they got dizzy. "I think I call bullshit on that. How do you know there's a planet called Zupper…ware? And if it's so far away then how'd you get your hair so fast?"

"Do you not know anyzink about ze universe? Zere are infinite number of planets, und zere must be von just like ours, viz people like us, viz ze hair und ze feet. Even if no von has discovered it yet, it must exist."

Random Tangent

"Yeah but if it hasn't been discovered yet then it's bullshit."

"Oh my dear," Valentin said. "It takes millions und millions of years for ze light from Zuppprion 18 to reach us, yes? So vhen somevon discovers ze planet it vill take millions und millions of years for us to find out, also yes? So somevon may have already discovered it, but ve just don't know yet."

"I...I'm not sure that makes sense."

"It does." *Click.*

Mongrel scratched his head in confusion and decided to move on. "I once knocked on wood and killed a man. Now I knock on plastic, just to be safe." *Click.*

"Plastic? Zat cannot be as good as vood, can it?"

"Not really." Mongrel frowned. "Actually, considering all the shitty luck I've had lately I'd say it's even worse. But I gotta knock on something, right?"

"Vhy don't you try knockink on ze opposite of vood, like iron?"

"Iron? Iron isn't the opposite of wood – iron is the opposite of cotton. Everyone knows that."

"Nein! Iron is ze opposite of vood. Cotton is ze opposite of gold."

"You're out of your mind. Just leave this to the professionals and take your turn."

Valentin fumed behind his desk for a few minutes. "Back in ze homeland ve had law: novone who ist ugly can valk outside in public after dinner. I was not professional but I vas on ze committee to judge who vas ugly und vhat time dinner should be. I got so many bribes from zat job it helped pay my vay zrough college!" *Click.*

"I had a summer job as a foley artist for the movie John Tucker Must Die; it came out a few years ago. I did the sound effects for the vending machine and the weather – like the clouds and rainbow. I think those scenes got cut though. Too bad, cause I think I could've gotten an award nomination. I don't like to brag but I do a mean sunset." *Click.*

"Oh I love ze sunset. I used to vatch it every night – until I vent blind."

Correctile Dysfunction

"You're blind?" Mongrel asked, eager to jump on his first point.

"I vas, but zat fellow from Zuppprion 18 helped me again. Sent me his eyes. Such dear, zat man. I am goink to sent him lovely fruit basket." *Click.*

"Man, I don't know what I'd do if I went blind. I'm afraid of the dark. I gotta get me a Zuppperware sugar daddy."

Valentin raised an eyebrow. "Vhat did you say?"

"Sorry, I know that's not how you pronounce it. How do you say it again? Zup-"

"Nein, nein. You say you vere afraid of ze dark? Yes?"

Mongrel stared at him for a moment. "You know, I gotta say, when you're sober you actually pay attention. Cause when you're drunk it's like in one ear and out the other."

The doctor ignored this and grinned. "Earlier you said you didn't know ze meanink of ze vord 'afraid'."

"I said that?"

"Oh yes, you did. Und now it seems zat you vere full of ze shit. Anozer point for me." He scribbled down more numbers on the notepad with unbridled glee. "Just von more point and you vill be mine!"

"So *now* is when you pay attention." Mongrel ran his fingers through his hair. He was one wrong move away from losing the fight, one step away from losing Beby. He wandered over to the window to think. This couldn't be happening; he wasn't fighting Hank. Then again, who said Hank would be the one to end his undefeated streak? Who said he hadn't been beaten before then? Who said Hank was even real? Captain Pete might get the last laugh after all. Mongrel was beginning to regret signing the contract. He turned back to Valentin and said, "Wait, did you say about me being yours?"

"Nozink."

"It wasn't nothing."

"Fine. It vas just poor choice of vords. Vhat does it matter, you vant out of contract? You afraid you vill lose?"

"I'm not afraid," Mongrel said again, even though fear was starting to leak into the basement of his soul. "In fact I'm so *not* afraid that I'm actually turned on right now."

Random Tangent

The doctor looked towards Mongrel's crotch, noticing that he wasn't exactly pitching a tent.

"Don't let that fool you," Mongrel said, embarrassed. "I have an upside-down penis; it doesn't look…never mind." *Click.*

"An upside-down…I have never heard of zis."

"They're all the rage in Europe right now."

"May I see it?"

A look of confused disgust scattered briefly across Mongrel's face. "No."

Valentin nodded in understanding and pointed to his head. "I know how you feel. Not mine real hair, or mine eyes. Mine appendix ist also fake. I had ze real von removed vhen I vas young. But I missed it, und had fake von put inside me. Ist very good too. Sometimes I can barely feel ze difference." *Click.*

"My appendix disappeared a long time ago. I've had exploratory surgery five times to look for it, but never found anything." *Click.*

"Maybe you never had von?"

"No, I know it was there. I have pictures of us together. We were like family, you know? Then, just like my toilet in the last book, it vanished without a trace. I don't get it." He shook his head and wondered if the mystery would ever be solved.

"I miss mine family too." Tears welled in the doctor's eyes and his lips creaked into a smile. "After ze…vell, you know. I had big, large family. Ten children, und all precious. Mine first, Augustus, had von eye bigger zan ze ozer. So adorable. Und Nicklaus, he vas born inside out, but ve loved him anyvay. Little Hilda, ah mine little Hilda, she grew moustache before her brozers! Can you believe zat?" He laughed quietly to himself and tilted his head back to keep the tears from spilling. Zen Claudia, such a perfect little angel." The smile sagged, turning to a frown. "She vas so perfect. Nozink wrong viz her. Sort of ze black sheep of ze family. I could have done better viz her. I know zey say parents should not have favourite child but vhat about least favourite?"

"I thought you only had three kids?" Mongrel asked.

"Vhat?" Valentin snapped. "Who told you zis?"

"I…uh, read it somewhere."

"Vhat are you talkink about? Read it vhere?"

Correctile Dysfunction

"It doesn't matter. The point is you're talking bullshit, and that's a point for me, right?"

Valentin glared at Mongrel for a solid minute before picking up his pen and updating the score on his notepad. He grumbled furiously to himself.

"What was that?" Mongrel asked. "I asked if that was a point for me."

More grumbling came from the doctor.

"Still can't hear you."

"I said zat ist correct!" Valentin shouted, throwing down the pen.

Mongrel beamed. "I love it when you say that."

The doctor scowled and got up to stretch his legs. While wandering around the room he came across Beby's file folder. He forgot he'd left it out; Sheila usually tidied things up around the office. The thought of her tugged on his heartstrings; women could leave men utterly helpless.

He walked back to his desk, flipping through the folder. There had to be something in there he could use this against his opponent. "Ah!" he said, slapping the file down, where it landed, open. "I have zis patient, lovely young lady, big..." he held his hand out from his chest to indicate her generous endowments, "you vould like her I am sure. She said she vonce killed man for gettink her drink vizout straw."

Mongrel glanced down at Beby's file and swallowed. "You're talking about Beby, aren't you?"

"Zat ist co...I mean, who said anyzink about Beby? I am referrink to von of mine ozer patients." He clicked the button, then added, "Alzough you must admit zat it could be her. She does have trouble controllink her anger sometimes." A satisfied grin settled on his face.

It certainly did sound like Beby, and it made Mongrel uncomfortable to think he was pursuing her. The next man she kills could very well be him. This certainly gave him much to think about. Then again, Mongrel had also killed a man, so who was he to judge? Perhaps Beby would think twice about trying to kill an experienced murderer.

Random Tangent

Of course, it was entirely possible that Valentin was talking out his ass, and Mongrel decided not to let it get to him. "Meh, I've killed someone too. Not over a straw though. In fact, I've killed the same guy dozens of times. Killed him again today, in fact, in a roundabout sort of way." *Click.*

Valentin suppressed his disappointment that Mongrel didn't take the bait, but he wasn't going to give up. He was so close to victory he could taste it. He was just going to have to try harder. He picked up the folder again and casually flipped through its pages, humming softly. "Oh zis ist interestink," he finally said, putting down the folder. "Accordink to mine notes, she likes to pick her nose und eat it, und she has a fetish for shiza coff."

"She?"

Before the doctor could stop himself he spit out, "Beby." Shocked at his mistake, it was too late to take it back. "I mean...uh..."

"I knew it!" Mongrel exclaimed triumphantly. "And what's shiza coff?"

"It means," the doctor paused to savour the moment of triumph, his stumble seconds ago forgotten, "she ist sexually aroused by ze poop." He then giggled evilly as Mongrel's face turned sour, and clicked the button.

Could it be true? Valentin seemed to be reading it right from Beby's files – although that meant nothing; the doctor had already proven himself a sneaky, underhanded bastard. But what if he wasn't lying? Even if it was an exaggeration of something in her files it could still spell trouble for Mongrel should he and Beby ever share more than a kiss. And if she wanted him to share more than *that*...no, he couldn't. It was the biggest turnoff Mongrel could think of, and if that's what Beby was into, than he wouldn't be able to satisfy her. Not without throwing up everywhere. Unless she was into that too...

If Mongrel couldn't be with Beby in every way, then this was all for nothing; a complete waste of his time. There was no point in continuing, except for his dignity. The only hope was that Valentin was bullshitting him, but he had to know for sure. "Let me see that," he said, reaching across the desk to grab the folder.

Correctile Dysfunction

"Nein!" Valentin said, snatching it away quickly. "Doctor-patient privilege only."

"But you didn't say that last time!"

Valentin simply tapped his glasses smugly.

"Fuck!" Mongrel groaned. He felt like he was fighting with the King again; another enemy with split personalities.

"Now Mr. Stevenk, zat language vill not be tolerated. Zis is public place."

Mongrel dressed his face in his most indignant expression. "You're telling me we're in a building full of crazy people who scream whatever and whenever they want, but I'm not allowed to swear?"

"Zat ist corre-"

"Shut up. I hate it when you say that. The words coming out of my mouth can't possibly be as bad as the shit coming out of yours. But what-fucking-ever."

The doctor didn't chastise him again; he just sat back in his chair, satisfied that he was getting under his opponent's skin. But he wasn't finished yet. "Perhaps you should be askink yourself if Beby is vorz all zis trouble?"

"Of course she is. You must know her better than anyone."

"Yes, I do," Valentin nodded. "Und viz all her problems I vould say for you to valk avay. It ist better for you."

"Yeah? Well I don't exactly have a lot of other options. Women don't look twice at me. There's an effect I have on them – severe revulsion. All these looks, and finger-pointing, whispers and giggling. Why do women do that to me?" *Click.*

"It's not just ze vomen; men do zis to you too."

"Great. Well I can't give up on Beby. There's just something about her. And I'm not talking about her knockers." He paused to gather his thoughts. "You know, as bad as things are for me, I guess I'm doing pretty good for myself. I have my own home now, a job and new car, and I'm not getting any younger. Maybe it's time for me to settle down. Beby is my best hope for that to happen. If I had her then I'd have it made."

"Oh you do not vant zis. To have it made? Zat is disease."

"The hell you talking about?"

Random Tangent

"Havink it made is disease. Zese people are alvays happy, no matter vhat happens. You give zem bad news, zey are okay viz it. You do bad zinks to zem, zey smile at you. Everyzink is alvays great. It ist like ze opposite of depression; zey are clinically happy. Zey call it ze Most Awesome Disease Ever. Zere is no cure. It ist healthy to be sad, und angry. Trust me, you do not vant zis." *Click.*

"That sounds familiar. I think my uncle Dad had that. A long time ago he accidentally hacked his nuts off with an axe. Don't ask me how – no one seems to know but him, and he ain't talking. Anyway apparently he just smiled, said it was awesome, and tried to staple them back on. Obviously that didn't go well. That was his solution to everything: staples. Knock out a tooth – staple. Got a cut – staple. Sprained ankle – staple. He even stapled his band-aids on. He cut my hair once when I was a kid and he cut too much off, and I got mad and told him he took too much off. Shouldn't have said that." Mongrel ran a hand gingerly through his hair. "Think I still have a couple…"

"Wait," Valentin said, "your uncle is your fazer?"

"No."

"Oh. Zen zat seems like point for me." The doctor picked up his pen.

"Hold on!" Mongrel clicked the button. "That's kind of a two-parter. I'll explain in a minute."

"Fine," Valentin grumbled, tossing his pen down. He just needed that one more point, and was eager to snatch it up. "Um…mine hair ist noogie proof." *Click.*

"Noogie proof?" Mongrel asked, curious.

"Yes, now explain."

"Okay, okay. So he's my uncle, not my dad. His name is Darius Asshole[*] Drucker – or D.A.D. for short. Get it? He couldn't have kids of his own – not sure if that was before or after the nut job – so I guess calling him Dad was the closest he was gonna get." *Click.*

The doctor scowled, realizing that last point was eluding him. He picked up the folder again; it seemed to have an effect on Mongrel. It was the key to winning this fight. Flipping through

---

[*] Pronounced *ash-ho-la*. Perhaps the best known way to give your child a swear word as a name.

pages until he found what he wanted, he stopped and smiled. "I have zis patient...all right ve both know it ist Beby. She used to be stripper. She had surgery three times to enlarge her bosoms."

"What?"

"Zat ist correct!" Valentin giggled evilly. "Zey are fake!"

A wry grin traipsed across Mongrel's lips. "No they're not. She hates them. They make her back ache and men leer at her. If anything, she'd get them reduced." He stood and leaned on the desk at the doctor. "And that's one more point for me. *Woooo!*" Mongrel threw his hands in the air, celebrating and jogging around the office.

The doctor sat there, more shocked then angry. He thought for sure that would be the clincher. "Stop celebratink!" he shouted. "You haven't von yet."

"Oh haven't I?" Mongrel returned to the desk and looked at Valentin sternly, the most serious of serious expressions on his face. His eyes narrowed as he was about to go in for the kill. "I'm just a figment of your imagination. I don't even exist." He then held his arms wide, ready to accept victory.

"Huh," was all the doctor said. He sat back in his chair, not angry anymore but confused. He finally got up and came around the desk and poked Mongrel on his forehead.

"Ow! What's that for?"

Valentin smiled and sighed. "To prove zat you are real. You say you do not exist, I prove you wrong and get point, and vin ze fight. Zank you." He patted Mongrel on the head and returned to his chair.

Mongrel stared at the floor as the room spun around him. "But...but..."

"You should never reference anyzink zat is imaginary, especially if you can prove it does or does not exist."

"Well...can you prove that the boxpeople don't exist?"

"Vhat?"

"Like you said, if you can prove that they exist or not. Can you prove they don't exist?"

Now it was Valentin's turn to look at the floor. Perhaps he'd said too much. "Nein," he finally said.

Random Tangent

"Well if you can't prove I'm wrong, then you can't earn a point for it. Therefore the fight is still on." He sat back down on the chair, exhausted. His heart was pounding. That was too close. He looked over at the doctor, who was probably thinking the same thing. *Close but no cigar*. Valentin was drumming his fingers on the desk, probably thinking up a new strategy.

"I got it!" Mongrel declared, scaring the doctor.

"Got vhat?"

Mongrel didn't answer; he got up and came around the desk, and put Valentin in a headlock. As the doctor struggled, Mongrel ground one fist into the top of his head.

"Ow! Vhat are you doink? Stop zat – it hurts!"

Letting him go, Mongrel grabbed his head and looked him in the eye, inches from his face. "You said your hair was noogie proof. Guess you were full of shit." He then sauntered back to his chair and flopped into it. "Game, set, and match."

Dr. Rushkov stared at Mongrel. His lips moved but produced no sound. His eyes searched the room but saw nothing. He knew he had lost. Slowly, inexorably, anger crawled onto his face and sat on it like a toilet, and crapped out a steaming expression of fury. But like any true professional, he held it back.

"So," Mongrel said casually, "seeing as how it's getting late, I need to have dinner – I'm starving. And I think I'll ask a certain lovely lady to join me. Now if you'll just be making that certification for me?"

"Nein."

"Nine? What do you mean? We had a deal."

"You von't be goink anyvhere. You will be stayink viz us for long time."

"But…but I won," Mongrel protested. "We signed a contract and everything."

"Do you ever read zinks zat you sign?" Valentin grabbed the paper from his machine behind him and read: "I, Mongrel Stevenks, hereby declare zat I am no longer of sound mind und body, and zerefore relinqvish control of mine care to Dr. Valentin Rushkov und ze Dunttstown Psychiatric Hospital." He grinned evilly again.

"Can I see that?" Mongrel asked, praying that the doctor was bullshitting him again. To his surprise, Valentin handed over

Correctile Dysfunction

the paper. Mongrel nearly ripped it out of his hand and read it, literally on the edge of his seat, hoping beyond hope that this was just another rouse.

But the doctor was right; Mongrel had signed his life away without realizing it. Had that been the plan all along, or was it a backup plan in case he lost? Was that why he'd wanted them to be alone during the fight – no witnesses? Whatever the case, he'd won. Mongrel was dealing with a truly devious man. All he needed was a moustache to twirl, or perhaps a cat in his lap to stroke, and the Machiavellian image would be complete.

Mongrel had a new nemesis.

"I...I..." but Mongrel had nothing.

"You...you..." Valentin mocked, "are now in mine care. You are mine property."

"Not if I do this!" Mongrel cried, reaching to snatch the page from the doctor's hands.

But Valentin jerked it away just in time and laughed. "Vat vere you goink to do? Destroy it? Ze contract has been uploaded to ze database. It ist everyvhere now. But good try."

No matter; Mongrel had a backup plan. He held his fist over the desk. "You release me right now, or so help me I'll knock."

"You vill vhat?"

"I'll knock. Remember: I once killed a man by knocking on wood. You want to take your chances? I'll do it."

Valentin smirked. "Und vhat? Somevon vill die. Small chance it vill be me. Und even if you killed me, ze contract is still zere; you are still property of ze hospital. If you leave you vill be fugitive, und hunted ze rest of your life. Also, if I am dead who vill tell Beby to date you?"

Mongrel didn't like it, but everything he said was true.

"Besides," the doctor continued, "vhat if you knock on ze vood und kill yourself?"

Dropping his hand to his side, Mongrel hung his head, defeated.

"Zat ist correct. Be good boy und give up." He pushed a button on his desk. "Sheila, could you...oh, zat ist correct." He sulked for a moment.

Random Tangent

Taking the distraction for an opportunity, Mongrel fled. He burst through the door to the sitting room, ran by Zeke, and out into the hall.

"Huh? Wha..." Zeke mumbled, stirring.

Once in the hallway Mongrel broke into a full sprint. He reached the stairs in what he assumed was record time, and bounded down them as fast as he could without falling. Come to think of it, hurling himself off the top step would have been faster – more painful, but faster. This only occurred to him when he'd reached the main floor, but he decided next time he was in such a jam, that's what he'd do.

Assured that someone would be looking for him, Mongrel figured it would be best to escape through the hole in the fence Valentin had shown him earlier; he didn't think it would be guarded, he didn't think he'd be caught, but he also didn't think he could find it.

So instead set his sights on the main entrance. Chanting could be heard as he raced down the hallway, dodging nurses and patients. Finally making it to the main room, he skidded to a halt.

A couple dozen people filled the area, men and women, old and young alike, standing between him and the exit. They were like an army, only with no discernable order. Some stood in the middle of the floor; some sat on couches and chairs watching TV; some were at tables or looking out the windows. They all had that same vacant stare that made Mongrel shiver, the same one he saw on the screaming demon, who stood in the middle of the crowd.

"Aliens gonna alienate," they all said in unison, then fell silent.

The screaming demon, without looking, raised a hand and pointed at Mongrel. Suddenly everyone stopped whatever they weren't doing and turned to face Mongrel, their blank eyes settling on him like a plague. The silence was deafening.

It was the creepiest thing Mongrel had ever witnessed.

A man in a wheelchair to his left, who must have easily been in his early two-hundreds, stood and took a couple small steps toward him. He leaned in close enough for Mongrel to smell his foul breath and whispered, "Ira's gonna...irate?" Then he bared his teeth and lunged like a zombie.

Correctile Dysfunction

With quicker reflexes than he thought he had, Mongrel kicked the man in his chest, sending him flying back into his wheelchair. He briefly lamented not kicking the man in his crotch, then took off back down the hallway. Maybe he'd need to find that rear exit after all.

Running, this time maybe for his life, Mongrel dodged the same nurses and patients as last time. No one seemed to have moved; they all just stood there watching the commotion, yet Mongrel heard footsteps chasing him. He didn't look back, he didn't want to know who...or what was pursuing him.

Unfortunately his getaway quickly went awry. Mongrel whipped around a corner and his feet flew out from under him. He landed on his back and slid on the floor until came to a crashing halt against a door, rattling its glass and his marbles.

"Wet floor dumbass," someone said. "Can't you read the sig...hey, I know you!"

Mongrel dizzily got to his knees, momentarily forgetting why he was running. Suddenly a pair of arms roughly lifted him to his feet.

"Did you really zink you could escape?"

"Uh...yeah." Mongrel couldn't see who he was talking to, as everything was blurry, but he recognized one of the voices. "I mean, the word *escape* is kinda ill-fitting, you know, considering I'm not one of these people. But *leave* of my own volition, sure, why not?"

"Because you belong here now, und you *are* von of zese people."

"But I'm not crazy!" Mongrel bellowed. "And you can't prove it! You can lock me up in here but sooner or later people will learn that I'm not really crazy. You can't keep me here forever." He struggled against the two large men holding him tightly, but it was futile.

"Oh really?" Valentin said. "You told me earlier you vere crazy. You said you could knit concrete, und hiccup in different languages. You lived in bunny costume for veek. You gave birz to snails. You are banned from Svitzerland because of ze drinkink. Ah yes, you are alcoholic too."

"Those don't count! None of that was real!"

Random Tangent

"Vell, you also believe you vere ubducted by aliens. Und ve can all agree zat you get along here viz everyone. You und Zeke vere becomink pals, yes?"

"No! I don't even know him!"

"Yeah well you stole my mop and attacked me with it," said that voice again. "Called me a troll? Tell me that didn't happen?"

"I…" Mongrel didn't know what to say. "I can't really see you…my vision is blurry…could've been anyone."

"No, it was you. Mongrel the magnificent?"

Mongrel said nothing, but his sight grew better. Or…maybe it hadn't; he thought he saw a pile of blankets moving towards him.

"There you are," the blankets said. "You said you were going to put my heart in the microwave."

"You!" a woman's voice scolded suddenly, and Mongrel found a finger in his face. He could finally see again. The finger belonged to the woman he'd met earlier before his visit with the psychiatrist. "Doctor," she said to Valentin, "this man brought my little Jeffrey to tears. He is a monster, and you should lock him up and throw away the key."

Then Zeke came into view and said, "He begged me to shit in his mouth!"

"Oh come on!" Mongrel cried. "That's not true!" He looked around him at the sea of faces and the bundle of blankets. "There are reasonable explanations for all that stuff; I'm *not* crazy."

Then Mongrel saw something that frightened him. From around the corner at the end of the hall came the man in the wheelchair who'd tried to bite him earlier. He was being pushed by another minion of the screaming demon, and followed by a swarm of them. Like zombies, they slowly shuffled his way.

Struggling against the two men again and getting nowhere, Mongrel began to panic. "Get me out of here!" he said.

"You're not leavink," Valentin said flatly.

"They're coming for me," Mongrel said, wishing he could point down the hall at the oncoming plague of cannibals, inching closer by the second.

The man whom Mongrel had attacked with the mop, presumably the janitor, said, "Spoken like a true crazy person. They all think someone's out to get them."

Correctile Dysfunction

"They *are* out to get me! Look behind you!"

They all turned to see the horde of mental failures heading their way. None of them seemed concerned.

"Zey are just ozer patients," the doctor said. "Zey are probably more scared of you zan you are of zem."

"Doubt it. They're forming a cult or something. I caused it, I think. It's my fault, and I'm sorry. I can admit to that, but I'll never admit to being crazy."

"Crazy people never think they're crazy," said the janitor.

Mongrel just stared at the minions lifelessly closing in on him, haunting the hallway. No one seemed to get what was really going on. None of them understood the danger. *They* were the crazy ones, not him. And they weren't going to let him go. They were just going to hold him here to get eaten alive. Unless...

"Fine! I'm crazy! Take me to a rubber room and lock me up!"

The all looked at him suspiciously. The doctor asked, "Are you sure?"

"Yes I'm sure! I eat yellow snow on purpose. I burp backwards. I watch Ben Stiller movies for fun." Mongrel laughed maniacally. "For *fun!* Now will you *please* take me away?"

Valentin smiled. He'd won. "Take him to von of our nicest svites."

The men nodded and dragged Mongrel away from the massing zombie-patients and up to the second floor. There, despite his protests, they stripped him of his clothes, scrubbed him down roughly with soap and water, and dressed him in the season's most fashionable straight jacket. Then they shoved him into a small padded room, just like he'd requested, and locked the door.

Mongrel sat down on the floor against the wall, and in the dim light had himself a good cry. It wasn't supposed to go down like this. He shouldn't be here. He wasn't crazy. Beby was out there somewhere with a raving lunatic of a shrink pursuing her. Who knows what he'd tell her, what lies he'd whisper in her ear? And there was nothing Mongrel could do about it.

He sat in silence, enjoying that he was alone instead of with the freaks out there, lurking in every corner of the loony bin. He thought about all the good times he'd with Beby, hoping there'd be more to come. He thought of the laughter – usually at his expense; and the tears – mostly his. He thought about the times she'd choked him in anger, or when she looked at him like he was the only person in the world she hated. He thought about her boobs.

And just like that, his resolve and his penis hardened. He wasn't going to get taken down like this. He would figure something out. In fact, he'd been locked in a hospital before and escaped. It could be done again. Although this time things were different – he'd legally committed himself. It was against his own will or knowledge, but how could he prove that? How was he going to prove that he wasn't crazy? How was he going get out of the hospital? And most importantly, how was he going to scratch his balls?

Mongrel struggled in the straight jacket, ground his butt against the floor, and moaned in agony.

The End

Mongrel was eventually released from the padded cell and taken to what would be his permanent bedroom – which he shared with Zeke, who talked constantly about how he would sleep when he wanted to, not just when he was tired. After a couple hours and some begging to be put back in the rubber room, Mongrel began to consider murdering his roommate; if that didn't get him placed in solitary confinement then at least he'd have enough silence to get some sleep. This place, he soon learned, was going to drive him crazy. Valentin locked himself in his office and mulled over his countless bullshit fight victories. He vowed to double his efforts and never lose again. And he would get that magic potato if it was the last thing he ever did. Sheila, for the first time in nearly thirty years was free from Valentin's tyranny – and had no idea what to do with herself. She eventually took up insurance fraud to pass the time. Jeffrey and the woman were undercover cops trying to track down a serial killer, and they were getting close. The judgemental nurse who hated Mongrel for making Jeffrey cry immediately disliked him and decided she'd make his life as unpleasant as she

Correctile Dysfunction

could if she ever got the chance. Rene set a trap and caught her guardian angel trying to kill her. She killed him instead, bludgeoning him with a bedpan. Loafmeat closed up the bar early and spent some time with the thing in his basement, trying to figure out what to do about his doppelganger. The prophesy was coming true. Jet made a few house calls, got gravity sorted out, and recruited a few more possible employees. Captain Pete decided it was time to learn how to drive and took up driving lessons. This was an arduous task considering he had two pegged legs and couldn't reach the pedals. The woman with the baked potato heart eventually tried to jumpstart her potato with a defibrillator. It didn't work, and she nearly killed herself. The nameless janitor kept himself busy making things to keep himself busy. The screaming demon never slept, never ate; he just spent all night gathering more minions to his cult, for the sole purpose of eating Mongrel's flesh.

Random Tangent

Murder-Proof

Murder-Proof

It began with a fart.

"Oh come on Lloyd!" Zeke cried, covering his mouth and nose with his shirt. "It's only breakfast and you're starting already?"

"Me?" Lloyd replied. "We both know I haven't farted in years. How do you know wasn't her?"

"Excuse me?" said the woman across the table, trying to breathe as little as possible. "I'm a vegetarian; my gas is *much* more pleasant than that." She tried to cross her arms defensively while holding her nose.

Zeke waved a hand in front of his face. "You're full of shit Lloyd. Oh God, my eyes are watering."

"Full of shit *and* gas."

"Well it was an SBD obviously. Sneak attack. And you're a sneaky bastard. Everyone knows mine are loud and proud. If it was one of my farts you'd all be deaf. It had to be one of you two."

"Well I haven't farted in years," Lloyd said. "It had to be Summer."

Random Tangent

Summer grunted and said, "You wouldn't even *know* if I farted. You'd just think your eggs smelled extra delicious today."

Mongrel glanced around the table at his brain trust, if you could call it that. The three of them together might be able to figure out how to open a bag of bread, but only after a good bit of trial and error, some crying, and probably a couple rounds of electroshock therapy. Mongrel dearly hoped they had such a thing at the psychiatric hospital…although he didn't want to find out first hand.

Lloyd, known around the hospital as Pink Lloyd, was actually not completely brain dead. He got the nickname because he was constantly slapping and abusing his face; some strange form of Turrets. His face was always red – even in the morning (he slapped himself in his sleep). It was such a common thing no one even noticed it anymore, including the hospital staff. Only when his skin broke and began to bleed everywhere did people remember that, oh yeah, Pink Lloyd had a serious problem. Mongrel had been told that one time he'd slapped himself so hard he broke his jaw.

Despite his condition Pink Lloyd was rather intelligent. He knew the hospital like the back of his hand – which, considering how often he backhanded himself, was *really* well – and knew the comings and goings of everyone, all the gossip and secrets. He was like a walking encyclopaedia for the hospital. Mongrel was definitely going to take advantage of him, and kept him close at all times.

The woman to Mongrel's left was Summer Spring. She was hotter than hot: blond hair, blue eyes, long legs, killer body – at least Mongrel assumed since he had yet to see her naked. I say yet because she kept flaunting her body at him, promising untold delights and severely distracting him all that revenge and escape-plotting nonsense. The only reason he hadn't jumped her bones yet was because he was still trying to jump Beby's bones. One thing at a time, right?

Oh, and there was one other reason: she was a sexual psychopath.

Stunningly beautiful and barely breaking the two-decade mark at twenty years old, she had garnered an understandable following of young men (and some women too), and also racked up quite the body count. She was only a few years out of high school and had already murdered nine people, including three other patients and two doctors at the hospital. Physically she had everything going for her; mentally…not so much, and it hadn't taken much to crack her. Apparently one too many dates had told her that her name was seasonally backwards, and she'd snapped. Once she'd gotten a taste for blood she became an addict. The name thing didn't even bother her anymore. She used her sex appeal to lure in her prey, then slaughter them like animals. And Mongrel was fresh meat.

Summer had learned early on to catch the newcomers before they'd gotten word about her. That's how she'd killed so many when she'd first arrived. The only chance she had to satisfy her craving for blood was to work her magic quickly*. And some magic it was. Mongrel had to be told more than once that there was no evidence to suggest that she killed *after* she got down to business, since no one lived to tell their tale, and it probably wasn't worth the risk. Although rumour had it that she took her clothes off before committing murder, so if the last thing you ever saw was her naked body, at least you were getting something for your trouble.

And then there was Zeke, who was only there because Mongrel couldn't get rid of him. If Pink Lloyd was the brains, and Summer the boobs, then Zeke would have to be the brawn. After all, his level of stubbornness was practically superhuman, and his penchant for talking was well above average, although that might have just been the Nonshutupititis, a disease better known as oral diarrhea, which prevented him from keeping his mouth shut for more than a few minutes at a time. Zeke also literally ate his own shit, which made his breath lethal.

"Summer don't give me that crap!" he yelled, throwing his poo-breath across the table at Mongrel, making him gag and put down his fork. "I know women fart and they can be just as bad as men."

---

* Had Mongrel been better looking or used to women approaching him he would probably be dead. He'd been sceptical when Summer began hitting on him, knowing there had to be a catch. So he asked around and learned the unfortunate truth. Let that be a lesson children: we can't all be winners, but if you're ugly enough it just might save your life some day.

Random Tangent

"Oh please! My gas would leave you drooling for more. You could bottle it and sell it as perfume!" Summer declared.

"Well you guys know it wasn't me," Pink Lloyd said between mouthfuls of toast and slaps to his face. "I keep a very strict border patrol down there. No fart has escaped in over eight years."

"You breath is worse than anything coming out of my ass!" Summer fired back at Zeke. "The only reason I never fucked you is cause I'd have puked all over your face if I got too close."

Pink Lloyd slapped himself and chimed in "That's true. I'm not sure which end is worse, your face or your ass."

Zeke only got more wound up. "I only fart outside! That way they contribute to global warming like they're supposed to."

"He who smelt it dealt it," Pink Lloyd said matter-o-factly.

"He who denied it supplied it!" Zeke fired back.

"Guys!" Mongrel shouted. "Stop fighting. This is exactly what the fart wants."

They all looked at him, quiet, perhaps embarrassed over arguing over who did or did not fart. But that's assuming they were normal people who might get embarrassed in such situations.

"It was *you* wasn't it?" Zeke accused.

Mongrel sighed and put his head in his hands. These were the people he was trusting to get his life back. He didn't want to complain about the situation, as pickings were slim, but with this motley clan his odds of getting out were basically zip. So if he was going to be there for a while, complaining about it would at least pass the time.

Getting out wasn't Mongrel's only priority: clearing his name was just as important. Sure, he could probably manage to escape, but without proper documentation he'd be a wanted fugitive, and would be on the lamb, possibly for the rest of his life.

Also, killing Dr. Valentin Rushkov would be nice too. The doctor was responsible for his being there, and if Mongrel could break his neck while he was breaking out it would certainly be satisfying.

No, that wasn't like him. Mongrel wasn't a vengeful person. He might have had a few murders under his belt, and knew many people who drastically needed to be put in their place (in the ground), but he wasn't the man for that particular jo-"

"Are you gonna eat that?" Pink Lloyd asked before grabbing a strip of bacon off Mongrel's plate and slapping himself. As Mongrel gave his cohort the glaring of a lifetime, Summer helped herself to some of Mongrel's breakfast as well.

"Hey!" Mongrel cried. "Stop taking my bacon. And leggo my Eggo!" He tried to snatch the circular pastry back from the woman but it slipped out of his hands and ended up on the floor, where two other patients dove for it like it would save their lives. They cracked their skulls together mid-dive and lay motionless on the linoleum.

"Eggos *do* save lives," Summer said. "I've seen things you wouldn't believe."

"Stop it," Mongrel said. "Only I'm supposed to be able to hear the narrator."

Summer sulked and said, "Sorry."

"So what's the plan?" Zeke asked. "Are we gonna take all the docs hostage and rape the willing?"

"You can't rape the willing!" Pink Lloyd said. "I've tried."

"I'll rape you," Summer said to him, licking her lips.

Pink Lloyd met her gaze and swallowed. It took all his willpower not to slap himself and say, "No thank you." Then he slapped himself anyway.

She bared her teeth in a threatening smile. "That's the spirit."

"No hostages!" Mongrel said loudly, trying to rally his brain trust to focus on the problem at hand. "Look, I just want to keep things nice and quiet, okay? Just clear my name and get out."

"Well how do you plan on doing that?" Zeke asked.

"That's what we're supposed to be discussing; not farting and arguing." Mongrel looked at each of them in turn, glad to finally have their attention. "We start by clearing my name. Dr. Rushkov said my file was on the database, so I need to get to it and delete it. But how can I do that?"

They were all silent in contemplation. After a moment Pink Lloyd finally spoke. "So you need access to the database is what you're saying."

Random Tangent

"Yes," Mongrel said, annoyed. "Now once again, *how* do I get that?"

Again, Pink Lloyd was quite. "Well you can access the database from any computer, but you need to be able to log into the system. And you need to be able to get to a computer."

When Pink Lloyd failed to keep explaining Mongrel sighed and said, "Would you mind walking me through the steps of *how do I get that?*"

"Only the doctors and nurses can use the computers. They all have these cards that they swipe to log in. So we have to get one of those cards." When Mongrel seemed satisfied that they were getting somewhere he slapped himself so hard his nose started bleeding.

"Great!" Zeke cried. "We get to kill someone! I've always wanted to do that."

Mongrel grabbed a napkin and handed it to Pink Lloyd, who took it, but looked confused. "No killing anyone, okay? I want this to be a clean operation." This didn't seem to please anyone, but Mongrel didn't care; it was his escape, his life, and he wanted it done his way. "Anyone got any ideas?"

"I can distract one of them," Summer said.

"I just said no killing."

"I just said *distract* them. With these." She hefted her breasts in her hands. "I can do that without killing them, you know. Seems a waste, but if that's what you want... Many women would kill for tits like these. I would. Well, not for them; with them."

"You've killed people with your boobs?" Pink Lloyd asked, distracted enough to forget to slap himself. "I'd like to die that way."

"Well they were more like an accessory to murder. I flashed a guy and he fell into a wood chipper. Wasn't *totally* my fault, but that's the one they busted me on. Stupid, right?"

Mongrel nodded, staring at her chest. All the men were. Her hands were still full of her perfect handfuls, practically inviting his eyes in, and he was going to make the most of it. With only a small white shirt on, and no bra (she never put one on until after breakfast), Summer held their complete attention.

"So I flash him and grab the card. Sound good?"

Murder-Proof

"Ooh!" Zeke's arm shot up like a kid in school. "Can I watch?"

"Seriously?" Summer asked, dropping her boobs.

Pink Lloyd's hand slowly raised next; he wanted in on the action.

Summer shook her head in disbelief. "Fine, whatever. But look with your eyes and not your hands." She then turned to Mongrel. "So we good?"

"Hmm?" Mongrel blinked. His brain was still full of boobs and boob-related goodness, making it difficult to return his attention to the table. "Oh, yeah, sure. Just don't let him fall into the wood chipper this time." He then noticed that Pink Lloyd wasn't using the napkin. "Lloyd…" he pointed to his face, then at the napkin.

Still confused, Pink Lloyd stared at the napkin, then at Mongrel. After a bout of contemplation, he finally got what Mongrel was telling him. Then he began to eat the napkin.

Mongrel watched the blood dribble down his chin, into his mouth, and get absorbed by the napkin, and thought *meh, close enough*. "So we're agreed then? Grab the card, delete the file, and away I go."

"Well…" Pink Lloyd mumbled around a mouthful of napkin. He swallowed and said, "Not exactly."

"Now what?"

"Most of the people here know who you are. You can't just walk out the front door. If anyone sees you…"

"Another distraction!" Zeke exclaimed, slamming his fist down on the table. "And this time I get to flash!"

"Ain't gonna be much of a distraction," Summer said. "Everyone's seen your flopper. It ain't much of anything, really."

"You *wish* you could see my flopper."

"*Please*. If there's one thing that'll make me puke more than your breath, it's the sight of you naked."

"I was gonna say he needs a disguise," Pink Lloyd finally finished.

Mongrel looked down at what he was wearing; a red lumberjack button-down shirt with a pale yellow girl's belly shirt underneath, XXXL grey drawstring sweatpants, and mismatched socks. Since there were no rules as to what you could wear at the asylum, Mongrel changed out of the drab green hospital-appointed garb and into whatever else he could find. The lumberjack shirt and sweatpants came from the lost and found box. The shirt was red, plaid, too large, and missing half the buttons. It did a poor job of keeping him warm in the cool building, which is why the belly shirt was necessary. It was donated to him by Summer the day before; literally the shirt off her back. She'd removed it right in front of him after he'd mentioned how chilly it was. Aside from the upper half, which she'd stretched out considerably, it was snug-fitting, especially when compared to the rest of his attire. She'd also offered him her bra as well, and as much as Mongrel wanted to see her take it off, he wanted more not to have to wear it himself, and politely declined. His pants were also much too large for him, matching well with the plaid shirt, but thankfully had a drawstring in them – otherwise he'd be mooning everyone, as he wasn't wearing any underwear. He wasn't issued any by the hospital staff. There was a pair in the lost and found box, but one look at them and Mongrel knew why they were lost in the first place. The socks he'd found randomly in some hallway or another. All in all, the clothing was worse for wear, but didn't reek uncontrollably, and would have to do.

"Couldn't I just get my own clothes back?" Mongrel asked. "Is that possible? I need that stuff."

"They incinerate all of it," Zeke said.

Mongrel's face paled. That was his stuff. He *needed* that stuff. Not just his clothes, but his wallet, his ID, his freaking car keys... He couldn't even leave the parking lot unless he was walking. But his home was in the middle of nowhere, a few days walk in the late summer heat. And if he managed to survive that death march he wouldn't be able to get into his house because his keys would still be at the fucking hospital.

"They don't incinerate your stuff," Pink Lloyd corrected.

"They did mine," Zeke protested.

Summer scoffed. "Well with you in makes sense. They should've burned them while you still wearing them."

Zeke never talked about his life before being institutionalized, and actually got quite upset if pressed about it. Whatever had happened to him, whatever reason he'd been sent to psychiatric care, he wasn't talking. "Fine. *If* they still have your clothes, they're probably in the room where they interrogated you."

"What?" Mongrel blurted. "They didn't interrogate me."

"Don't listen to him," Summer said. "They don't actually do that."

"Well they did it to me." Zeke looked at Mongrel and leaned in. "Don't worry, I didn't tell them anything."

The only thing Mongrel was worried about was how much they all kept getting off track. He just wanted to get back to his old life. It had been almost two days since he'd been trapped there, but it felt like forever. Even an hour was far too long to spend in the company of crazy people. The constant bickering, the non sequiturs, the chair-throwing; it was exhausting trying to keep up. He still wasn't sure exactly where he was supposed to go to the bathroom – everyone seemed to just go wherever they pleased. All the men did anyway.

"I just want my stuff back, and to get out of here," Mongrel stressed. "And to clear my name. Let's just start with that."

"Um…" Pink Lloyd looked around the room nervously. "Okay…okay, um…" He slapped himself a couple times, which seemed to get his mind going. "Okay, I have an idea. You guys go to the men's washroom by the nurse's station, and pretend to make out or something."

"Sounds good to me," Zeke said.

"Not you!" Summer hissed as she draped an arm around Mongrel. "Me and my man here."

Mongrel was strangely okay with this, so long as Summer didn't try to kill him. "You want us to be alone in there? And for how long?"

"Not long. I'm gonna bring in one of the doctors…"

"Boring!" Zeke wailed, his way of protesting not having a role to play.

"…and he'll catch you two having sex…"

"Ooh!" Zeke's hand shot up. "Can it be a threesome?"

Pink Lloyd shook his head and slapped himself. "No, you need to stay hidden. Hide in one of the stalls."

"Boring!" Zeke cried again.

Random Tangent

"Anyway, when we come in and catch you, he'll tell you to leave, right?"

"Boring!"

"Then you flash him!"

"Bor...wha?" Zeke sat up and paid attention again. "Do I have to be in the stall when this happens?"

"No, that's when you sneak out and grab the key card around his neck and run for it. We'll keep him distracted enough for you to find a place to hide. Then we'll regroup later."

Zeke thought this over, glancing between the faces and boobs around him. His eyes finally settling on Summer's chest, he said, "Okay, I'm in."

With that they all nodded, slowly got up from the table, and left the cafeteria, carefully ducking the flying chairs. Once in the hallway they split up; Mongrel, Summer, and Zeke made their way to the washroom, while Pink Lloyd set out in search of his victim.

Not far down the hall, Mongrel paused in front of the washroom door, his ears prickling. Echoing off the walls from around the corner came a muffled chanting. "Motive's gonna motivate. Castor's gonna castrate."

"What's wrong?" Summer asked.

Mongrel looked at her. "Uh, I was just wondering, what do we do if someone's in there? Or if someone comes in?"

"No one uses it," Zeke said, pushing open the door and strolling in.

Summer giggled, but not out of amusement. "All the men just go wherever they please. You're all pigs!" she cried as she kicked the door open and went in after Zeke. Mongrel sighed and followed her.

The smell was not what Mongrel had been expecting; it was almost pleasant. The floors were also clean, as was the counter and mirrors. In fact, one might think they were in a normal hospital, instead of one for the clinically insane. A filtered window at the end of three stalls let in plenty of light, and across from the stalls were a row of urinals. It appeared that the facilities indeed went unused.

"Go into the last stall and stand on the toilet," Summer told Zeke. "And be quiet. No one's supposed to know you're there.

Murder-Proof

Without a word of objection, which was unusual for him, Zeke did as he was instructed. Once Summer and Mongrel were alone, or at least out of Zeke's sight, Summer backed into the corner next to the mirror and pulled Mongrel in close. "Hey handsome," she whispered.

This made Mongrel nervous; he knew what Summer was capable of. "Now, now, Lloyd said to just pretend."

"Oh please, we both want this." She grabbed Mongrel's hand and guided it to her ass.

"Okay, I kinda want some of that. But not all of it – I know where it could lead and I don't want to be murdered. Not that you could anyway, but you should keep your hands to yourself."

"But not my lips, eh?" Summer asked, a smirk spreading across her face. Before Mongrel could say anything she grabbed his shirt and yanked him into a passionate kiss. Mongrel struggled momentarily, but soon gave in. The taste of her lips against his, the feel of her ass in his hand, the pressure of her breasts on his chest; he hadn't felt such things in a long time. It was overpowering. He kissed her back, tepidly at first, testing the waters, but soon stronger, urged by her fervour. The hand not on her posterior wanted something to do, and so ventured to one of her boobs, giving it a tantalizing squeeze.

Suddenly she pulled back, confusion clouding her eyes, and Mongrel knew he'd gone too far. He shouldn't have grabbed the boob. They were always in his face, yet forever out of reach. They mocked him.

"What do you mean I can't murder you?" she asked. "You mean, like, because we're in a hospital and people are always watching, and it's not proper for young ladies? Mom always said shit like that. Good girls don't kiss and tell, or murder on the first date."

"No, I mean, uh," Mongrel struggled for the words. "I've been at this for a long time, okay. I just don't get murdered. I figure a way out."

She gave him a sly look. "So you're saying you'll kill me first if I try to kill you? You're a killer too?"

"No, that's not what I meant. I mean yes, I've killed people – accidentally, but only after they've tried to kill me first. And lots

Random Tangent

of people try to kill me, believe me, but I always survive to be attempted-murdered, or whatever, another day."

The confusion on Summer's face gave way to scrutiny. "So, what, you're murder-proof?"

Mongrel shrugged. "I guess."

"So I can't murder you? Not even a little?"

Knowing he was treading into dangerous waters, Mongrel had to walk a fine line here. "I mean, no offence or anything, I'm sure you're great at murder and all, but I'm just, you know, not allowed to be killed. And you know something else you're fantastic at? All that kissing and butt stuff." Mongrel tried to kiss her again, hoping to go back to making out and groping, but she held her hand up to stop him.

"Hold on a sec. You're telling me that I couldn't kill you, even if I wanted to? I have lots of experience; I'm sure I could find a way."

"Knock yourself out, babe."

She gently pushed him away and put a hand to her chin, and began slowly pacing around him, studying him from every angle. Suddenly she lunged at him, her hands grasping at his throat. They crashed into the counter and tumbled to the floor, her on top, strangling him.

Well that didn't work, thought Mongrel. He'd tried to call her bluff, only she wasn't bluffing. And now here she was staring into his eyes with her hands around his neck, on top of him, their bodies pressed tightly together. In a strange way, it was the most romantic thing to have happened to him in years. A weak smile formed in the corners of his mouth as he closed his eyes tried to relax and-

"Are you enjoying this?" Summer cried, loosening her grip.

Mongrel opened his eyes, inhaled some much-needed oxygen, and gazed up at her. "Yeah, kinda. It's not every day a gorgeous woman wants to put her hands on me."

While she appreciated the complement, Summer was thrown off by his cavalier attitude. "You're not supposed to enjoy being murdered."

"Ah," Mongrel quipped, "but it wasn't murder, it was *attempted* murder."

Murder-Proof

She barred her teeth and tightened her hands again, and once more Mongrel relaxed. He really wasn't concerned. Zeke was nearby – although Mongrel doubted his usefulness in such an emergency – and Pink Lloyd would be there any moment. As his oxygen reserves slowly depleted, he placed his arms around her neck, revelling the moment.

This broke her concentration once more, and she released him. "You're not even trying to fight back. You have to at least struggle. It's just not the same; I can't kill you if you just *let* me."

"But you're not killing me."

"Yes I am."

"Then why do you keep stopping?"

Summer looked away, glancing around the room. She was seriously confused. But she hardened her resolve, determined not to fall for Mongrel's ploy, and was about to go in for the kill again when the door opened and a doctor walked in.

A female doctor.

She was in the middle to saying something, talking to someone, when she spotted them on the floor and stopped. "What are you two doing in here?"

Mongrel and Summer quickly got to their feet, appearing embarrassed, like children caught misbehaving.

"Don't do anything stupid – you can't trust her." This last comment directed at Mongrel.

Pink Lloyd suddenly burst into the room. "Now!" he yelled.

"Is she showing her tits?" Zeke called from the bathroom stall.

The doctor turned to Pink Lloyd, confusion written all over her face. "Lloyd, what did you *really* bring me in here for?"

"This is your doctor?" Summer asked. "It's supposed to be a guy. How do I flash her?"

"Just do it!" Pink Lloyd screamed at her, panicking for no reason. His face was flush, but this time not from slapping himself. "I said now Zeke!"

Summer rolled her eyes and lifted her top, baring her chest for all to see.

Random Tangent

"That's not necessary," the woman said, looking at Summer's chest. "Now would someone please tell me what's going on?"

"Is she showing her tits?" Zeke called out again.

"Yes!"

The stall door opened and Zeke ran out, now carrying a baseball bat. He stood next to the doctor and stared at Summer's exposed breasts. "Nice," he said.

Mongrel too was transfixed on the woman he was just making out with. The woman who was just trying to kill him. He couldn't help himself. Summer was undeniably attractive, and in this revealing state it was even harder to take his eyes off her. Everything else seemed to fade into the background; all his problems* seemed trivial when he was staring at those boobs.

"Zeke," Summer said, "do it already!"

Still unable to remove his eyes from Summer's gratuitous curves, Zeke grunted and swung the bat at the doctor. The blunt instrument barely grazed her head, but it was enough to scare her. However, she was a professional, used to dealing with overwhelming situations, and remained calm.

She took a step back, out of reach from Zeke's weapon, and said, "Okay, I think everyone's getting a little overexcited here. Why don't we all go into the TV room and talk about it."

Realizing that things weren't going as planned, Summer lowered her shirt. As far as she was concerned, it wasn't worth showing off the goods if no one was getting murdered.

"Zeke, what are you doing?" cried pink Lloyd. "Grab her card and run!"

At the mention of the key card hanging around her neck, the doctor became very alarmed. Was that why she'd been lured into the washroom? What exactly did they plan to do? "I think I-"

Suddenly Zeke hit her in the forehead with his bat. Summer's distraction now removed from the equation, he was able to focus on the task at hand...if only he could remember what that task was. Removing something or other from the doctor's neck. Her head, maybe? He swung again, harder his time.

---

* Surely we all can agree that boobs make the world a better place.

Murder-Proof

The blow sent the doctor to her knees. "Please," she begged. "Stop hitting my head with that bat."

Standing over her, Zeke raised the bat one last time. "Maybe you should stop hitting my bat with your head," he said, then swung the weapon down as hard as he could. It landed squarely on her head with a sickening *crack!* She slumped against the wall and sagged to the floor.

The room grew quiet as they looked at her, then at each other.

"What a trooper," Summer said, breaking the silence. "She didn't even scream."

Having watching the entire confrontation without interfering, Mongrel felt it was time to assert some control over things. "What the hell, Zeke? I said no murdering, and what's the first thing you went and did?"

"Well she was totally resisting," Zeke said. "And in my defence, she's not really dead."

"She looks dead to me," Summer said, pleased that things had taken a turn for the macabre.

Zeke hefted his bat. "I'm an expert with these. I'm like a bat ninja. I only broke her neck. She'll be fine." He tried to flip his bat in the air and catch it, but it spun too wildly and he freaked out, jumping away like a scared child.

"If you broke her neck you killed her," said Mongrel.

"No I didn't. Breaking you neck is just like breaking your arm or leg; it'll heal eventually. No harm done, except, you know, the breaking part."

"No, a broken neck means she's dead. You killed her."

Zeke looked at the doctor and said, "Nuh-uh." He then looked at the others, who were all in agreement that she was dead. He nudged the doctor gently, then more forcefully when he got no reaction. But she didn't move. "Can't be. How is it a broken neck kills you? Why doesn't it just get put in a cast and heal like everything else?"

"I don't know. I'm not a doctor." Mongrel said. "Where'd you get that bat anyway?"

"It was in the stall. Someone must've forgot it." Zeke bent over to pick up the bat. "It's mine now."

Random Tangent

Pink Lloyd crouched next to the doctor. Blood was leaking out her ears, gathering slowly in a puddle on the floor. The key card lay in it, and he retrieved it with one hand while slapping himself with the other, before it got too much blood on it. He then checked for a pulse but found none. "Yep, she's dead."

"Great!" Mongrel muttered. "You see?"

"Nice job, *bat ninja*," Summer agreed.

"She can't be dead," Zeke whined. "I didn't kill her. I swear I didn't." He just stared at the corpse, guilt plaguing his soul. He'd always wanted to kill someone – many of the other patients talked about how awesome it was to take a life – but he wasn't actually trying to do it. He wished he could take it back.

Pink Lloyd took the key card to the sink to wash off the blood. "Well we all heard that crack, Zeke. Neck's don't crack like that for no reason."

"Yeah," Mongrel agreed. "Bat to the head doesn't count as a natural cause of death." He ran a hand through his hair, trying to keep his cool. "So now what? We gotta hide her body."

"I'm not touching her," Summer said. "Dead bodies are just…ick."

"Really?" Mongrel asked her. "You'll kill them all the live long day, but as soon as th-"

"Ick!" she repeated at him, more sternly.

"We don't have to hide her body," Pink Lloyd said, drying the card off with paper towel. "No one comes in here. She's kind of already hidden."

"Yeah, well, it'd make me feel better." Mongrel looked at Zeke. "Zeke, this is your mess; move her into one of the stalls please."

Zeke stared at the dead doctor on the floor, looking like he was about to cry. "I didn't want to kill her. I just wanted to knock her out, so she wouldn't follow us or tell on us. You said no hostages, remember?"

Mongrel put a hand on his shoulder. "Your heart was in the right place. Just tell us next time before you change the plan, okay?"

"I did."

"What? No you didn't."

Murder-Proof

"Yes I did. I just didn't tell you to your face."

"Just grab the body," Mongrel pointed, irritated now. Perhaps Zeke's heart wasn't in the right place after all; perhaps he was just stupid. Zeke did as he was told, grabbing the doctor's legs and dragging her towards the far stall, leaving a trail of smeared blood. This was not better, but whatever.

"So where can we use that card?" Mongrel asked Pink Lloyd. "We need some place quiet where we can be alone."

For a few minutes the only sound in the washroom was a dripping tap and Zeke struggling with the dead doctor. "The reception area?" Pink Lloyd finally suggested. "It won't be deserted but there also won't be any doctors or security around. Maybe a few patients, but they shouldn't be a problem."

"What about the receptionist?" Mongrel asked.

"Another distraction!" Zeke called from the stall.

"Not from you!" Mongrel yelled. "But Summer could do her thing again, maybe." He eyed her chest hungrily.

"Yeah like that really worked out so great last time," she muttered.

"Can't argue with the results." Mongrel gestured to the streak of blood on the floor. He then frowned and said, "We gotta clean this up this mess."

"I took care of her," Zeke said, returning from the stall. "So someone else can mop that up." He retrieved his bat and leaned it next to one of the urinals, then pulled his pants down to pee. Like Mongrel, he wasn't wearing any underwear.

"Come on Zeke," Mongrel complained. "Could you not have done that in the toilet?"

"The doctor's in there. She's taking up all the space."

"I told you," Pink Lloyd said, shook his head, "no one comes in here. We can just leave it."

"What about the janitor?"

They were all silent until Zeke flushed and said, "Who cares? It's not like they can pin it on us. There's no evidence we did it, right?"

Zeke was right. If someone stumbled across the body, it would take a lot of sleuthing to trace things back to them. And even if that happened, Zeke was the one responsible – he still carried the murder weapon – and better yet, was expendable.

"Okay, fine," Mongrel said, gesturing for Pink Lloyd to lead the way.

They made sure the coast was clear before sneaking out of the washroom, one by one. Zeke finished up, didn't shake, grabbed his bat and followed behind them. Making their way down the hallway, trying to look inconspicuous, they headed for the main entrance. As Mongrel recalled, it was the lobby area; a large room full of mental failures, such as the screaming demon. His heart turned cold when he thought back to his first encounter with him. What if he and his minions were still there? He tried to pretend the growing chorus of chanting voices was just in his head.

"Anyone else here that?" Zeke asked.

"Nitrous gonna nitrate. Escalator's gonna escalate. Confederations gonna confederate."

Summer nodded. "What is that?"

They came to an intersection and stopped to peak around the corner. The main hall was in view, and many forms could be seen, but Mongrel wasn't satisfied. "Stay here," he said, and snuck further down the corridor to get a better look. He crept up behind a tall water cooler, which concealed him well enough while affording him a decent view.

It was worse than he had feared. The screaming demon was in there, as were his followers, which had grown in number. Doctors and nurses also milled about, holding charts, writing things on clipboards. Some seemed curious, others were obviously concerned. Some were even wearing breathing masks, as if they were worried that a contamination was airborne.

"Resin's gonna resonate. Dictator's gonna dictate. Corporal's gonna corporate."

When the chanting began a couple days ago, most paid little attention. They weren't bothering anyone – in fact some of the patients were quieter, more docile than they'd ever been – so no one wanted to disturb them. But after a day it became clear that no one was eating or taking their medication. They weren't socializing with each other, aside from the chanting. No one was going to the bathroom – at least not properly (which explained the breathing masks). The staff were completely mystified at this new behaviour.

"Daters gonna date, freighters gonna freight, conjures..."

On the far side of the room from where Mongrel hid sat a secretary behind a desk, casually flipping through a magazine, unperturbed by the cult of the mindless. It was just another day at work for her. Mongrel knew he wouldn't make it to her unnoticed, and if his last encounter with the mob was any indication, he definitely needed to stay hidden. For whatever reason, they didn't like him. He was public enemy number one, apparently.

Suddenly Mongrel realized all the doctors were looking his way, and he slowly peeked out from around the water cooler. Then he saw the sea of faces – minion faces – looking at him. They'd stopped chanting, and it was now eerily quiet. Somehow they had known he was there. Certainly they couldn't see him; was it his smell? He hadn't showered in a couple days, but they'd been using their pants as a toilet; surely their own rankness veiled his? Did they have some superhuman ability no one knew about?

"Excuse me!" one of the nurses hailed. "Could you come here?"

Yeah, that wasn't going to happen. As a few of the minions began to turn and zombie-shuffle his way, Mongrel bolted back down the hall.

"Run! Hide!" he yelled as he rounded the corner and flew by his companions.

"What's going on?" Summer yelled as the trio took off after him.

Mongrel didn't respond; he could fill them in later. Right now he had to figure out a new plan: avoid the screaming demon and his zombie posse. But how was he going to do that if they could somehow sense where he was? They must have a range, otherwise they'd have been hunting him this whole time. But what was the range and how would he know when he was outside it? Whatever it was, he would never feel safe in this loony bin.

Suddenly Mongrel was blindsided by a flying chair.

It was a sturdy chair. Well crafted from solid oak. Most chairs would've splintered or shattered upon an impact of this magnitude, but not this chair. It was a proud and noble chair, too good to be spending its time offering comfort and support for the dregs of the hospital. It slammed into Mongrel's left shoulder, sending him into a doorjamb and crumbling onto the floor of small office, and skittered to a halt a few feet down the hallway. It suffered minor scraps and scuffs but survived, and would no doubt be hurled another day; a depressing life for a chair so fine and majestic.

"Steve!"

Gathering himself sorely to his feet, Mongrel took stock of his surroundings. Another small room, filled with a desk, some chairs, a staggering amount of papers and folders, and a couple people. Both were looking at him with palpable surprise.

The woman, a dumpy little thing in a pink sundress with greying bouffant-styled hair, turned to the man behind the desk and said, "I thought you said he was missing?"

Shrugging and smiling as politely as humanly possible, the doctor clasped his hands together and shrugged. "I guess Steve is ready to come back to us. He didn't feel he was ready to see you, but didn't want you to know that. He thought you'd be hurt. He asked us not to tell you. He said he just needed a little time. Isn't that right Steve?" He looked at Mongrel, and Mongrel looked back. What the hell was going on? "So we told you he was missing," the doctor continued. "Steve even thought it was a good idea; that you worry instead of feeling pushed away. Better to tell you nothing than to say he doesn't want to see you, right?"

The woman turned back to Mongrel and threw herself into his arms. "Oh Steve! I've missed you so much! Please come home."

"Um..." Mongrel struggled in her arms, "I'm not Ste-"

"Steve just recently came out of hiding," the doctor interrupted, coming around from his desk and rubbing Mongrel on his swollen shoulder, "and might not be ready for such a big step. Isn't that right *Steve*?"

Mongrel looked at them both, then back through the open door, where his brain trust stood waiting for him, looking perplexed. "Actually I'd like to go back to hiding, if it's all the same."

"Steve!" the woman cried, ferociously hugging the gas out of him. "Don't shut me out!"

Murder-Proof

"I told you guys it was him who farted," Zeke whispered. "I always knew it."

Having to pry himself out of her arms, Mongrel stepped back out into the hallway and glanced back the way he came. No one seemed to be following him, zombies weren't known for their speed. He wasn't going to stand there and give them the opportunity to catch up. "I'm very sorry but I'm not-"

"Himself," the doctor quickly cut it again.

"Dammit! Stop doing that!" Mongrel said.

The doctor turned to the woman and said, "Mrs. Stevenson, just let me have a minute with Steve outside, okay? I'll – *we'll* – be right back." He pushed her aside and stepped out into the hall, closing the door behind him. He then turned to Mongrel. "Okay look, I know you're not really, *really* Steve Stevenson, but just do me a solid here and play along. I'll get her out of here as soon as I can and you can go back to…"

"Running and trying not to get eaten by zombies?" Mongrel suggested.

"Sure. Whatever. And of course I'll owe you. Maybe extra pudding at supper? Or I could take you for a walk to Petrol Park? You always like that. Or at least Steve did. Oh, I know; how about a sponge bath from nurse Epsilon?"

Mongrel sighed and said, "Well that all sounds really tempting, but…" then he bolted down the hallway again. His gang quickly followed, assaulting his ears on all sides.

"Where are we going?"

"Why are we running?"

"I have to pee!"

"Didn't you just go a few minutes ago?"

"I gotta go again!"

"I thought you were the master of your bladder, or whatever."

"Oh yeah. Never mind. Can I get some tacos?"

They ran on and on around the building, turning this way and that. Soon they found themselves in the cafeteria again, which was not as full as it was when breakfast was being served. But there was one new addition: Captain Pete.

Random Tangent

The old pirate sat on a table in a straight jacket with tape over his mouth. A mixture of fear, surprise, and anger filled his eyes as they glared at his nemesis.

Mongrel was hit by an overwhelming sense of déjà-vu; this was almost the same thing that had happened the last time he'd visited the psychiatric hospital. He held a finger to his mouth, telling everyone to be quiet. "I'm not here to kill you," he told his old friend. "I'm not even gonna try to help you, cause I know that would be stupid. I'm just gonna turn around and leave, okay?" He slowly backed away and turned around. "Just gonna walk away and leave you be. No killing today."

Once they were back out in the hallway they continued running, but after a short distance they stumbled across another men's bathroom. Sensing relative, if brief, safety, they darted inside.

"Who was that?" Pink Lloyd asked and slapped himself.

"Just an old friend." Mongrel replied. "Don't worry about him."

"Shouldn't we go back and help him?"

Mongrel glared at Pink Lloyd. "No. Hell no. Look, forget you saw him, okay?"

"Why are we back here?" Summer asked, breathing heavily. Not being able to murder anyone for a long time had left her out of shape.

"What?" Mongrel glanced around and spied the trail of blood on the floor. Somehow, they'd run all over the building and managed to wind up back where they'd started. "What the hell?" He turned to Pink Lloyd and grabbed him by his shirt. "How'd we get back here?"

"I don't know. We were following you. Do you want a map?"

The words of admonishment died in Mongrel's throat. "What? You can get that?" Pink Lloyd slapped himself and nodded. "Then yes, go get one. Please." With Pink Lloyd there Mongrel would be fine, but if they ever got separated a map would come in handy.

Pink Lloyd turned to leave but Mongrel grabbed his arm. "Wait, first, we need a place to hide until this all blows over."

Murder-Proof

"Why not back in our room?" Zeke suggested.

Once again intelligent advice came out of his roommate's mouth. Mongrel wanted to kick him. "Fantastic! At least there we can barricade the door. Lloyd, meet us there as soon as you have the map, okay?"

Pink Lloyd saluted and left.

"Well I don't know about you guys but I'm going to get some tacos," Zeke said, adjusting his pants. "You guys want any?"

"Breakfast was not even an hour ago," Summer complained. "You can't still be hungry."

"I'm not. But I want tacos. Plus I should go fart."

"Ew!" she said, waving him passed. "Just go then. And don't come back."

Mongrel was about to tell him to meet back at his room, but found himself agreeing with her. Zeke wasn't adding anything to the brain trust; they were better off without him. He said nothing as they parted ways.

Despite running around earlier with little notion of where he was going, Mongrel knew the way back to his room on the second floor. Thankfully their journey was uneventful. Summer was apprehensive about entering any space occupied by Zeke and all his *Zekeness*, as she called it, but when Mongrel assured her they'd be safe and alone – and stay on his side of the room - she'd relented.

The lock on the door was on the outside, and therefore useless, so they dragged the two nightstands over to form a barricade. When their friends – well, friend and Zeke – arrived they'd pull away the obstructions and let them in, but no one else was allowed.

For the time being, they were alone, and Summer took full advantage of the situation. "How long do you think they'll be?" she asked.

"Well for Zeke I don't know. Not sure where he's getting tacos from. And I guess it depends on what he thinks a taco is. I don't think Phil will be that lon-"

Without warning she threw him onto his bed (she assumed it was his, since the other was ravaged, unkempt, and smelled foul) and climbed on top of him. Without a word she began passionately kissing him, beginning at his lips and working her way down his

Random Tangent

neck and chest, pausing briefly to rip off his lumberjack shirt, followed by her own shirt underneath, exposing his stomach. Without asking she placed his hands and feet in the restraints[*] at the four bedposts. And without question Mongrel let this all happen.

He remained silent as his brain screamed at him to stop her. He just lay on the bed and watched the sexual psychopath tie him up, knowing things could go horrifically wrong at any moment. But Mongrel decided to risk it. He'd never been kissed like that before and wanted to see where it would lead. And in his defence, he did try a couple times to interrupt Summer, but each time she silenced him with another long kiss, hypnotizing him, lulling him into a state of acceptance.

Once the shackles were firmly in place Summer climbed on top of Mongrel and took her top off. If there was any hope of Mongrel being able to talk her out of whatever she had in mind, it was gone now. She dropped her shirt on his face, intending to leave him blindfolded, but thought the better of it, instead dragging the shirt into his mouth to form a gag, and wrapped it around his head.

"I'm gonna make you scream so loud people will think I'm murdering you."

This should have raised a few warning bells, but like a typical man, once boobs were in his face, Mongrel found it difficult to focus on anything else. She leaned over and slapped his face with them; he didn't complain.

"Now, now, now...what am I going to do with you?" she asked, giggling. Before Mongrel could offer some suggestions she kissed him again. She moved her lips all across his body; down his neck, across his chest, along his outstretched arms. When she reached the fingers on his right hand she playfully bit his thumb off. At least, it started off playfully, but after a minute of gnashing her teeth together, scissoring them back and forth, she realized it wasn't going to be as easy as she thought, and began to get impatient.

Zombies made everything look easy. Well, except for communicating, opening doors, using simple hand tools, swimming...okay so they're really only good at a couple things: eating people and making more zombies. The point is, biting

---

[*] All beds at the psychiatric hospital have bindings on their beds to restrain some of the more unruly patients.

through bone and muscle tissue was harder than the undead made it out to be. When they bit someone's finger off it looked like they were eating a sandwich. For Summer, sawing and grinding her teeth through bone and muscle tissue was making her jaw sore. Maybe she was just at a bad angle. She moved around and tried a couple different positions, but it didn't help. To make matters more difficult, Mongrel would not lay still either. He twisted and jerked his body to the extent his restraints would allow, and screamed at the top of his lungs. You'd think he wasn't enjoying it.

When she finally tore his thumb free she sat back up on Mongrel's chest in triumph. Most of his thumb was hanging out of her mouth, blood running down her chin. She smiled wildly; it had been a long time since she'd tasted blood. She traced her lips with the digit as if she were applying lipstick and beamed down at him. It felt good to get back into her old routine. This was the most fun she'd had in ages.

Mongrel glared up at her, breathing hard. He screamed at her with his eyes. When that didn't appear to be getting the message across he screamed fitfully into the shirt stuffed into his mouth, doing his best to wrench it loose.

"You need to relax, pace yourself," Summer said, now rubbing the thumb over her nipples. "We still got nine more fingers to go." She then realized that *she* was the one who needed to pace herself. If getting the first thumb off was that difficult, she wasn't sure she had it in her to get through the rest of them. A pair of pruning shears or bolt cutters would help, but she doubted she would use them even if they were available, since she was a hands-on kind of girl; it was the thrill of the hunt, the principle or whatever. She was just out of practice and needed to get back in shape.

Suddenly there was a banging at the door and the handle began to jiggle.

"Crap!" she muttered, whipping her head towards the door. She jammed his thumb down the front of her pants. "Looks like you're only getting to third base. Sorry honey. Gonna have to keep this short and sweet, and unfortunately painless." She leaned down and stuffed her boobs in his face. Wrapping her arms around

Random Tangent

Mongrel's body, she pressed him as tightly as she could to her chest, cutting off his air supply.

At first Mongrel didn't complain. He actually tried to motorboat before realizing he couldn't move his neck. Then he realized she was trying to suffocate him, and he began to spasm, rocking back and forth, trying futilely to throw her off. He screamed into her breasts.

"Hush now," she whispered, then kissed his forehead. "It'll be over soon."

And it was. Everything went black, and Mongrel lay still.

It was still black when Mongrel opened his eyes, making him wonder if they were actually open. His arms and legs were free from their shackles, so he raised a hand to his face to poke himself in the eye. He grunted in pain and understood that they were indeed open.

Oh, and he was still missing a bit of his thumb. He tried to inspect it, but still couldn't see anything. He felt it gingerly with his other hand; half of it was gone, and just a stump remained. It didn't hurt, but felt weird.

"Declare your intentions!" a voice cried at him, scaring him onto his ass.

Mongrel then understood what had happened. He was in the Place Between Places. He was dead. The voice belonged to Death, the Grim Reaper, or as Mongrel knew him: Greg.

"Oh man, seriously?" Mongrel groaned. "I didn't even get to have sex with Beby."

Death clapped its boney hands and the dark turned off, and Mongrel finally saw his old acquaintance, whom he'd not seen since the last time he had died. Also, just like before, they were in a cave.

"*Well?*" Death asked.

"What?"

"I proposed to you a question: why are you currently existing in my domain? Are you without direction?"

Mongrel shrugged. "Dude, I'm dead. Duh."

"Really?" Death asked, dropping the showmanship. "Do you not think if you were dead, I would *know* about it?"

Murder-Proof

"Well I'm here aren't I?"

Pulling back the hood on its robe, Death hand a skeletal hand over its skull. "You humans...just think you can waltz in here whenever you please."

"Look," Mongrel said, "Summer smothered me. With her breasts too. It was *awesome*. I mean I'm dead, I know that, but what a way to go, right?"

"And you didn't try to stop her? You just let her smother you?"

"I...boobs...in my face." Mongrel pointlessly pointed at his face. "Oh, and shackles. I was shackled."

Death tried to sneer, which was a difficult without proper facial muscles and lips. "Humans never cease to amaze me. Or disgust me. With all your...urges." It suddenly glanced around, as if spooked. "Where is your mon?"

"Mon's not here. It's just me."

"Good. Hate that guy," Death said, breathing a sigh of relief. It pulled his robe back up and cleared its throat. "Very well then. Are our affairs harmonious?"

"What?"

With tangible infuriation, Death threw a nearly imperceptible tantrum. "Are. We. Done. Here?"

"I don't know, I guess. What do I do now?"

"You leave."

"And go where?"

"Home! Away! Anywhere but here!"

"You mean, like, Earth?"

Death nodded overdramatically.

"So I'm not dead then?"

"No, you are not dead. You're only dead when I tell you you're dead."

"Then why am I here?"

This time Deaths' tantrum was obvious. After a moment it calmed itself down, and got in Mongrel's face. "Let me tell you something, Mongrel Stevens: I am not a fan of...of this," it gestured all over Mongrel's body. "Of you. You're a smartass, you don't follow the rules, and you have a mon as a *pet*? Humans don't have

Random Tangent

mons; mons have humans. Why can't you be more like your kind? And how the hell do know my name?"

"I told you; it's common knowledge."

"You are free to go. I hope you live a long and retched life. Is there anything else I can refuse to do for you?"

"Yeah. Why are we always it a cave? Is that all the Place Between Places is: one giant cave?"

"I don't have to answer that."

"Fine. You know you're doing really well with your vocabulary. You don't even need that thesaurus anymore."

"Thank you. Are we done?"

Mongrel was about to nod, but a thought crossed his mind. "What do you mean mons have humans?"

"Yeah," Death said. "We're done here. It raised its hand.

"Wait, wait! Is there anything you can tell me about what's gonna happen to me?"

"No."

"Oh. Okay."

"Well...you might want to turn your head to the side." Death snapped its fingers.

Mongrel blinked and opened his eyes, and saw Zeke hovering over him, his face inches from his own. He was so close he could see the wrinkles in his eyelids, the whiskers of stubble on his chin, the crust of old food in the corners of his mouth.

And smell the reek on his breath.

Now acutely aware of the raw sewage taste in his mouth, it became apparent that good ol' Zeke had thought Mongrel was dead gave him mouth-to-mouth resuscitation. Mongrel turned to his side, leaned over the bed and threw up all over the floor.

"It's a miracle!" someone cried. Pink Lloyd, Mongrel assumed.

"That's it buddy!" Zeke said, slapping Mongrel on the back. "Get all the evil out of you."

After a minute of puking Mongrel wiped his mouth with the back of his good hand, aware now that his restraints had been removed, and surveyed the wreckage around the room. The door had been kicked in; its glass was cracked, and the door jam was in splinters. The night stands were in a heap on the floor, contents spilled everywhere. His friends must have barged in and saved his life. Summer was sitting on the other bed – she'd puke herself if she knew it was Zeke's – and had her shirt back on. Blood was still smeared on her face, making her look like psychopath that she actually was, or perhaps one of the gorgeous vampires Hollywood was always sensationalizing. She was staring into space, her face pale. Pink Lloyd stood beside her, holding a scroll of paper. He was smiling goofily. Mongrel then brought his right hand to his face to inspect the damage and found it wrapped in duct tape. It throbbed with pain. So did his eye for some reason. The sheets beside him were covered in blood.

"Where's my thumb?" he asked, glaring at Summer.

"It's a miracle," she whispered.

"It's not a miracle," Mongrel muttered. "Miracles don't usually work in my favour."

Her eyes slowly focused on him. "It really was a miracle. You were dead. I killed you."

"I wasn't dead."

"You had no pulse. You were dead, and now you're back. You really are murder-proof."

"I wasn't dead. Greg told me so, and he would know. I was just…I don't know what I was. Missing for a while or something."

"Who's Greg?" Pink Lloyd asked.

"He's just…I don't…look, never mind. I wasn't dead. Now I want my thumb."

"You were totally dead," Zeke said proudly. "I even poked you in the eye. If that don't get you up then you're dead, and I saved your life. You owe me one now." He smiled and began eating a taco.

"I wasn't dead, it's not a miracle, and I *definitely* don't owe you one."

"So…" Summer started, biting her lip. Despite how much Mongrel wanted to hate her right then he couldn't help but find her adorable. "…If you weren't dead, then I didn't kill you. And you're not murder-proof. So I'll have to try harder?" She nodded to herself, "I can do that."

Random Tangent

Mongrel sighed violently and flopped back down onto his pillow. "*Fine!* You killed me. Happy? I really am murder-proof."

"So you still owe m-"

"*Yes Zeke!* I still owe you one. Now would someone *please* get me my thumb back?"

"She swallowed it," Pink Lloyd said.

"Well get it back!"

"Can't," Zeke said, stuffing his mouth with a taco. He then tried to elaborate but no one could understand what he was saying with his mouth full – except for Pink Lloyd, who translated.

"He said she can't vomit on command because she can't control her stomach muscles like he can[*]."

Mongrel stared at the ceiling, writhing in self-pity. Was this really happening? Was he ever going to get out of this nightmare? Dunttstown Psychiatric Hospital was turning out to be the worst place to be trapped in. Even prison wasn't this bad – in prison no one had succeeded in dismembering him. He'd gotten his ass handed to him, sure, but *without* it being removed first. He held up his duct taped-hand to inspect it again. It looked awful, but he supposed it was better than looking at the mangled mess of skin and bone underneath. "Whose handiwork is this?" he asked.

Pink Lloyd raised his hand. "The janitor's room is across the hall, so I-"

"*I* kicked in the door!" Zeke interrupted, spraying mouthfuls of taco all over Mongrel. "We found Summer on top of you. Man, you are one lucky guy."

"I threw her off you," Pink Lloyd continued, "and then we just...kinda stared...uh..."

"The two idiots just stared at my tits 'til I put my shirt back on," Summer filled in.

"You are one lucky guy," Zeke repeated.

---

[*] Indeed Zeke could vomit on command. This is actually how he obtained his tacos. Months ago he walked out of the hospital and went across the street to the newly opened Paco's Tacos and threatened to projectile vomit all over the restaurant if they didn't give in to his demands. They called his bluff, and he made such a wretched mess they had to close up shop for three days to clean and fumigate. Now knowing what he was capable of, they just gave him a bag of day-old tacos whenever he came in, not dissimilar to the mob getting their cut of the profits of local businesses.

Murder-Proof

"Why am I so lucky?" Mongrel asked Zeke pointedly. "I got a face-full of her tits and your reeking breath. The two kind of cancel each other out."

"But you get tacos!" Zeke declared. He looked down at a paper bag beside him. "You want a taco?"

Mongrel raised his head to look at Zeke and asked, "Where did you get tacos?"

"Across the street. I told you I was getting tacos."

Although Mongrel found himself wanting a taco, he wasn't hungry. Perhaps that was the blood loss talking. "No thanks. What I need is a doctor. Like a *doctor* doctor, like a hospital doctor. But not this kind of hospital; a *real* hospital." He glanced around them, at the confusion in their eyes. He held his bandaged hand up. "I need someone to fix this."

"Oh, like a *doctor*!" Zeke said. "Yeah, we got one of those. But that stuff should hold. I know what I'm doing. I once played doctor as a kid, never had any complaints, and only one kid ever died on me." He looked around suspiciously and whispered, "But just between us, that kid was the school bully, so I might've, you know, botched his surgery."

Mongrel rolled out of bed and got to his feet. He felt woozy and tired as he put his shirts back on, shrugging off any attempts to help him. "All the same, I'd like a professional to look at this."

"Okay, no prob," Pink Lloyd said. "We can take you there." With that they all shuffled out of the room.

Mongrel had never been to the basement of the complex before, which strangely enough was where the medical office was located. It was a different world down here; dim, damp, oppressive. The sound of water dripping from pipes came from every direction, but no leaks could be found. The floors were cement instead of tile, and the walls were a pale green instead of white like the rest of the hospital. But most importantly, it was quiet.

Too quiet, actually.

In fact, it seemed deserted.

Visions of every horror movie he'd ever seen flashed in his brain, and Mongrel became a little paranoid. A hospital like this should never be this silent or empty. Something was wrong. Of

Random Tangent

course, having zombie-like patients lurking about the floor above him didn't help.

"Where is everyone?" Mongrel asked. "Is it always this quiet?"

"Yep," said Zeke.

"No," said Pink Lloyd.

Summer didn't answer.

Mongrel stopped and turned to her, more afraid of what may be waiting for them around the next corner than of her for the time being. "Come on, you're the tie breaker."

"I don't know," she said. "I never come down here. Place gives me the creeps."

While this wasn't the answer he wanted, Mongrel was okay with her being unnerved. Served her right. Let her be on edge for a change.

They pressed on, moving slowly, and soon came across an office. It reminded Mongrel of a store on the street. There was a small window in the wall, with a door to its right, and like the rest of the basement, it too was deserted. The lights were on but no one was home, which seemed to be an unwritten law at the hospital.

Pink Lloyd walked inside, followed by the others. "This is the place," he said

"Hello?" Zeke called out.

"What the?" Mongrel gapped at him, trying to keep his voice down. "Shut up before everything that eats meat wakes up and comes to complain about the noise."

"Geez," Zeke muttered. "So-rry. What's up *your* ass?"

"Oh I don't know, my hand is killing me cause I just had my thumb bitten off, and mouth tastes like puke, and I'm trapped in a mental ward with all manner of freaks of nature – some of which *actually* want to eat me. And now I'm in the world's creepiest basement waiting for the dungeon master to come rip out my jugular!"

"Well I *tried* to give you a taco."

"A taco will not fix this! Any of this!"

Zeke put a hand on Mongrel's shoulder. "You know what, buddy? You just need to calm down. Relax. You know, we got some great doctors here that can help you with that. Ever hear of a lobotomy? Mellows you right out, man. I swear by that shit. I've had, like, five. I can hook you up if you want. I know a guy."

"Sure," Mongrel said. "Sounds great. Go get your guy and bring him down here. I'll wait."

"Right on!" Zeke said, and tore out of the office.

"And bring me back some tacos too!" Mongrel hollered after him, then slapped his hands over his mouth, having forgotten to keep quiet. Then he winced in pain, having forgotten about his missing thumb. It was then that he noticed the computer. Zeke had been standing in front of it. Perhaps coming down here wasn't going to be a waste of time after all.

"Hey," he called Pink Lloyd over, "can we use this to access the database?"

"Sure."

Mongrel sat down at the desk and tapped a couple keys on the keyboard, and the monitor glowed to life. A logon screen appeared. He smiled, knowing he was minutes away from freeing himself from this horrible place, of waking up from this nightmare. He just needed one small thing. "Who has the key card?" he asked.

"I gave it to Zeke," Pink Lloyd said.

"What? Why?"

Pink Lloyd slapped himself and replied as if it was obvious, "He wanted it."

"Oh he just wanted it is all?" Mongrel asked rhetorically, annoyance lacing his words like chloroform on a rag. Silently cursing to himself, Mongrel got up and walked toward the exit but not wanting to go further out into the gloomy hall. "Zeke?" he called out, trying not to be too loud, hoping the echo would reach him.

Zeke's head whipped around the doorway. "What?"

Mongrel screamed and fell on his ass and expected meat-eating creatures to begin devouring his soul. His life flashed before his eyes with the most painful and embarrassing moments highlighted. He'd also instinctually braced his fall with his arms, causing untold amounts of agony to his already injured hand. "What the hell?" he asked when his heart rate dropped to double digits. "Were you right outside the whole time?"

"Yeah. I didn't wanna go by myself. I don't know if you guys noticed, but it's scary down here."

"We noticed," Mongrel grumbled, picking himself up off the floor. "And you seem intent on bringing the boogie man down on us. Do you have the key card?"

Zeke pulled the card out from his pocket. "Nope."

Mongrel snatched the card and returned to the computer. He swiped the card through a card-reader on the side of the monitor, and the desktop appeared on screen. "Well Lloyd, where do we go from here?"

It took a while, searching through files and folders, looking for anything to do with Mongrel's presence at the hospital. Pink Lloyd traded places with Mongrel when he got frustrated, fed up after many dead ends. Eventually they stumbled upon patient files, and soon found the one they were looking for. Opening it up, it was revealed to contain the paper Mongrel sighed in Dr. Rushkov's office two days ago, as well as other various documents on him.

"Delete them all," Mongrel said.

"Don't you want to read them first?" Summer asked.

"No."

"I'd totally want to read mine."

"Well I just want to destroy them all the get out of here."

Pink Lloyd deleted the files as instructed, but didn't look happy, possibly because he'd given himself a couple hard slaps. "That paper you signed, what happened to it?"

"If I had to guess, it's probably still up in Valentin's office, why?" Then it hit him. The original document had to be destroyed too; otherwise Dr. Rushkov could simply scan it again and replace the deleted files. All this would be for nothing. "Crap, we gotta go to his office, don't we?"

"I wouldn't worry about it," Summer said. "I think he's on vacation or something."

"No, he usually takes his vacations in the fall," Pink Lloyd said. "Or at least he used to when his family was still alive. But I heard he took a few days off to try to patch things up with his secretary."

Murder-Proof

This heartened Mongrel, but still presented other problems. "So I'm guessing his door will be locked then? And we'll have to break in? Are there alarms or anything?"

Before Pink Lloyd could reply there was a loud bang on the glass, making everyone jump. They all turned to see a nurse standing there, her eyes glazed over.

"Majesty's gonna magistrate," she chanted.

"There she is," Zeke said, smiling. "She's the one who can fix your hand."

"Oh crap he's got the staff now!" Mongrel moaned.

"Who?" Summer asked.

"The screaming demon, or whoever he is," Mongrel said. "He's always saying shit like that. I'm not sure why but he's out to get me, and he's got everyone joining his cult, including the doctors now."

"Oh I think you mean Dominic." Pink Lloyd said.

Mongrel raised an eyebrow. "Dominic?"

"The, uh, screaming demon."

"Yeah I know who you meant, it's just…I don't know…*Dominic* makes him seem less evil somehow."

"Call him whatever you want," Summer said. "We need to stop him before he takes over the hospital."

The doctor had wandered into the doorway, still in a daze. "Operas gonna operate."

"We need to shut her up," Mongrel said. "I got a bad feeling there's gonna be more of them if we don't keep her quiet."

Suddenly Pink Lloyd was out of his chair. He ran at the doctor and tackled her across the hallway. Mongrel didn't get a good view, but the doctor must have hit her head on the concrete because she was out cold.

"Whoa Lloyd, nice!" Zeke cheered as they all gathered around the fallen nurse.

"I never liked her," Pink Lloyd said as he stood up; his eyes were glazed over. "She hated my music. You heard what she said about the opera. She was making fun of me." With a scowl on his face, he grabbed the bat from Zeke's hand and was about to beat the woman's head in with it. Mongrel quickly grabbed it from his hands.

Random Tangent

"What are you doing, Lloyd?" Mongrel cried, tossing the bat aside. "She's out! Enough!"

Pink Lloyd snapped out of whatever he was in and looked sheepishly to the floor. "I just thought...like before, when Zeke killed the doctor..."

"Which I told him not to."

"I just...I don't know...everyone's gotten to kill someone but me. I just wanted to try it."

"But...that's..." Mongrel didn't know what to say. Despite how misguided Pink Lloyd's judgement was, his childlike innocence made it hard to scold him.

Zeke came over and put his hand on his friend's shoulder. "You can have mine if you want."

Pink Lloyd's head sprang up and a big smile grew on his face, even as he slapped himself. You'd think he'd won the lottery. "Your murder? Really?"

"Sure. I didn't want to kill her anyway. We'll just say you did it."

"Thank you!" Pink Lloyd said, pulling his friend into a warm, loving embrace. A bro-hug. A man-shake. Even in the hospital, where the craziest of the crazies went crazy all over the place, friendship and humanity still existed. It would've been touching if it weren't so stupid. He then began dancing around, singing, "I killed someone, I killed someone."

"Well this is nice and all," Mongrel said, "but we gotta get going before more show up. I think they all have a hive mind or something. Also I get the feeling they can sense my presence. It's weird."

"That's the craziest thing I ever heard!" Zeke cried.

Mongrel turned to him. "Really? This coming from someone who claims to have given birth to a live watermelon? Yeah, I read your profile on the computer."

"And they took it away from me! Bastards!"

"Inflations gonna inflate."

They all turned to see a pack of three minions heading their way. Even in the dim light they could still be identified: all three were men, and one of them was a doctor.

"Told you," Mongrel muttered. "Come on, let's go."

Murder-Proof

They turned to head the other way but found another group of minions blocking the path, four of them this time. "What should we do?" Summer asked. "Can we take them all on?"

"There'll just be more of them coming," Mongrel said. "We can't fight them all."

"Barricade ourselves in the office?" Zeke suggested. "Like in Night Of The Living Dead?"

"I don't know which version of that movie you saw but it didn't end well."

"There's a rear exit in the office," Pink Lloyd suggested. "You can escape that way."

Summer moaned, "Won't they just chase us? Keep coming?"

Pink Lloyd looked back at the approached hoard. "Not if we contain them. Grab the map on the desk and head for Valentin's office. I'll meet you there." With that he screamed and ran into the minions.

Zeke grabbed his bat off the floor and joined him, screaming and running into the other group.

Mongrel watched in horror as they all fought; limbs, blood, teeth, and eyes flying everywhere. He hoped his friends' determination and control over their own faculties would give them the edge, but the minions' numbers evened things up, a brilliant strategy no one had the foresight to devise. He didn't want to leave, but he knew he couldn't stand there and do nothing.

"Come on," Summer said, tugging his arm, pulling him back into the office. They shut the door and locked it, thankful to have that option for a change. Grabbing the map, they wandered deeper into the office, following what appeared to be a main passage. Rooms and other hallways lead off in branching paths. Sounds of the struggle in the hallway faded the further they went.

Before long Mongrel ducked into a small side room that had a table, and placed the map on it. "We really should take a look at this map before we get more lost." He opened the scroll and goggled at it. It wasn't a map; it was blueprints for the entire building. Mongrel marvelled at it as he tried to decipher the diagrams. He was sure everything he needed was right there – if he could only make sense of it.

Random Tangent

"We're right here," Summer said, pointing to a spot on the paper. He couldn't make heads or tails of it, but didn't want to seem like he didn't know what he was doing, so just agreed with her. "Do you know how to read this thing?" she asked.

"Uh...yeah, sure."

She sighed. "Typical man. You don't know shit. Don't even know where we are do you?"

"I do. Right here." He pointed to the area she'd just pointed out a moment ago.

"That's an elevator. I was testing you, and you failed."

Mongrel sulked for a bit before saying, "Well can't we at least take the elevator to the third floor? That's where Valentin's office is."

Mulling over the page, Summer finally said, "Yeah, that looks like our best option."

"See? I'm not completely useless," Mongrel said sarcastically.

"Yeah but you're still an idiot."

"I know. It's one of my best qualities."

A banging down the hall casually hinted to them that someone, likely minions, had gotten into the medical office, a gentle reminder that they shouldn't linger.

"That's our cue to move." Summer rolled up the map and headed out of the room. Mongrel was right behind her.

At the end of the passage they found a door that exited into another basement corridor. It was quiet and empty, at least for the time being. They crept as silently in the direction of the elevators. Knowing they could be ambushed at any moment, the atmosphere of the dank basement was much more foreboding than before.

They made it to the elevator banks without incident, prompting Summer to say, "Guess they're all in the elevator waiting for us, eh?" She smiled at him; it was genuine, as was her attempt at levity.

But Mongrel didn't appreciate either. "Don't say that!" he snapped. "You trying to jinx us?" He hurriedly tapped to button.

"Actives gonna activate."

Murder-Proof

They both spun around to face the empty hallways. Looking up and down, left and right, they found nothing. But the voice could've come from any direction.

"Happy now?" Summer asked. "They're out here instead of in there."

"They could *still* be in there," Mongrel hissed.

The elevator *binged* its arrival, and they were delighted to find it empty when the doors opened. With still no sign of the minions following them, they rushed inside and hit the third floor button, then rapidly pressed the close-door button until it closed.

Despite not having exerted much effort, Mongrel and Summer found themselves breathing heavily, as if they'd just ran a marathon. The pressure was getting to them. Mongrel backed against the wall and slid down until he was sitting on the floor, and lurched softly as the elevator began it's mind-bogglingly slow ascent.

Summer stood facing him, leaning on the opposite wall, and began to giggle.

"What?" Mongrel asked, wanting to be annoyed with her jubilation but curiosity getting the better of him.

She shrugged. "I don't know. It's just the euphoria I guess, escaping death."

"We haven't escaped it yet. Prolonged it maybe."

Looking down at him, her smile turned devious. "Well maybe *I* escaped death."

The twinkle her in eye made him uneasy and he wished the elevator would hurry its ass up. "Murder-proof!" he said defensively.

Summer was about to retort to this when the elevator lurched to a halt. The doors opened with a *bing* and in walked a female nurse carrying a clipboard. After eyeing them suspiciously, she reached over to press the third floor button but noticed it was already glowing, so settled into her spot between them. After a long minute the doors *binged* and closed, and the elevator continued on its merry, monotonous way.

Mongrel tried to settle in and relax, feeling safer with a third party between him and the murderous little vixen across the way. He closed his eyes and tried to think happy thoughts; warm sunshine, a warm cup of cocoa, a warm hug from Beby. He wrapped his arms around himself, wishing he had proper clothing on. How could it be this cold in here with a heat wave going on outside? What he wouldn't give for a sweater right now, or a blanket. Hell, even a fart was a step in the right direction. Unfortunately he was fresh out of gas, and he felt it rude to ask the ladies, so he sat in miserable silence, praying the day would end quickly and in his favour.

For Summer however, the silence was more than she could bear. "I'm pregnant!" she shouted at the nurse.

With more nonchalance than most people normally carried around with them, the nurse looked her in the eye and asked, "Is it mine?"

Summer was taken aback. This was not the reaction she was hoping for. In her wildest fantasies she dreamed the nurse would scream in excitement and yank her into a hug. They'd hold each other and jump up and down, then become overwhelmed with lust and desire, and start passionately making out and having sex all over the place, which isn't saying much since it was a small elevator. Suffice it to say that Mongrel, from his excellent vantage point of three feet away, would be supremely jealous and beg for her to come back to him. And in that one perfect moment of his ultimate humility, she'd finally murder him.

But things never really worked out that way for her. It had been too long since she'd killed someone. She wasn't going to just give up, but it was very discouraging. Surely her days of slaughter weren't behind her yet? No, she'd persevere. This was just a dry spell. A rut. She'd dig her way out of that hole. But first she had to deal with this condescending woman.

"Uh, no."

"Then I don't care."

Well that pissed her off. Summer peaked over at Mongrel and muttered. "I can kill her, right? It's justified?"

Without looking up or even opening his eyes, Mongrel said, "No."

The nurse looked at Summer, a hint of fear in her eyes. "What?" she asked.

Murder-Proof

Before Summer could say or do anything, the elevator lurched to a halt again, this time at level 2. A gentle thumping on the door, accompanied by muffled chanting, alerted them to the threat outside. Seconds later the doors opened and a sea of faces peered in at them.

Minion faces.

With outstretched arms, they swarmed the elevator door, trying to get to Mongrel. "Greys gonna great. Mayor's gonna mate. Accents gonna accentuate."

Mongrel stood up in panic. What could he do? There was nowhere to run. They were all trapped.

"Back! *Back!*" the nurse yelled as they shoved their way in. She began hitting their faces with her clipboard but gained little reaction. They paid little attention to her; their sole goal was to get Mongrel.

Summer jumped between them and Mongrel, hands raised, ready to fight. "He's mine!" she shouted, and barrelled into the horde.

Whether this was a display of bravery and affection from Summer, or just laying claim to the rights to kill him first, Mongrel couldn't say. But if it was the later, he didn't want to be in her debt; and so he too threw himself recklessly into the fray along side her. Together they punched and kicked and spit and screamed, desperate to stop anyone from boarding, from entering their sanctuary. But the mob was relentless.

"Conjures gonna conjugate."

Judo kicks and karate chops.

"Investors gonna investigate."

Bitch slaps and nut shots.

After an eternally long fifteen seconds the doors began to close. Thanks to the efforts of their attack, the minions were shut out. As the elevator continued on its way, Mongrel and Summer collapsed to the floor, breathing hard. They looked at each other and began giggling.

"See?" Summer asked. "Escaping death; euphoric, right? It's the same thing when I murder someone. Such a rush!"

Mongrel could see the appeal, not that he had any intention of killing anyone.

Random Tangent

The nurse apparently did not share their relief, or their jubilation, or even their spot on the floor. She remained standing, facing the doors, severely still.

"Hey, you okay?" Mongrel asked. He stood up and gently nudged her shoulder. "We're okay now. That was close, but w-"

"Mandy's gonna mandate," she said quietly.

"*What?*" Mongrel quickly released her and pressed himself against the wall, trying to shrink away from her, but there was nowhere to go.

"Oh shit!" Summer said. "They got her too!"

"How?" Mongrel demanded.

"I don't know; I was busy fighting those…things. I thought you were watching her!"

"Why would I be watching her?"

"Well this isn't my fault!"

"I never said it was!"

"Then why are you yelling at me?"

One might get the impression that the nurse did not like their bickering, as evidenced by her sudden attack. You could even argue that she was saying, 'don't fight with each other; focus all your hate and rage on me,' when she turned and threw herself at Mongrel. Hands grabbed and clawed at him, shark eyes peered into this soul, teeth clamped down on anything they could find. It was in the spirit of peace that she was trying to kill Mongrel.

Suddenly Summer was there, yelling and kicking at the woman. She grabbed two handfuls of hair and pulled back as hard as she could, prying her off Mongrel. The nurse got to her feet and twisted around to attack her new enemy, when Summer kicked her in the stomach, sending her flying out the open elevator door. Then Summer threw herself out after her.

Stunned by the turn of events, Mongrel scrambled to his feet and peaked out the open door. Understandably, he'd been so distracted by the assault that he hadn't felt the shudder of the elevator as it stopped, didn't hear *bing*, or notice the doors opening. But he wasn't going to miss the catfight.

Outside the elevator Summer and the nurse were rolling around the floor, kicking and punching and biting and yanking. No one else seemed to be around. With all the noise someone should've came out to see what was going on, yet they remained alone.

Recalling his previous decision that he didn't want a woman fighting his battles for him, lest he owe Summer one like he already did with Zeke, Mongrel decided he should help somehow. So he watched and waited, and soon enough the nurse flipped Summer onto her back and climbed on top, and placed her hands around her throat. She yelled and drooled all over the poor girl, who was trying to push the minion away. Higher, higher, further back...now!

Mongrel ran a few steps and punted the nurse in the side of the head as hard as he could, then crashed to his knees as an enormous glut of shooting pain ran through him. There was an audible crack, which was either her neck snapping or his foot breaking. He grabbed his sore foot in agony, remembering that he was wearing only socks. He looked over to see the nurse, face-down but squirming – so no broken neck – with Summer on top of her, repeatedly slamming her face into the hard, cold floor. Soon the sounds took on a wet tone as blood began to pool under her head. After a dozen more thumps on the linoleum the nurse finally stopped moving. Summer gave her head a few more weak slams before rolling off onto her back.

With the screams and the struggles of the brawl now gone, it was quiet in the hallway. Mongrel crawled over to Summer, finding her smiling with two fingers in her mouth. He watched as she removed the fingers and dipped them in the nurse's blood on the floor, then bring them back to taste them.

This did not surprise Mongrel. "You okay?" he asked.

Summer giggled and lifted her head. "Hell yeah!" She sat up and moved over to assess her victim, looking more like a hunter inspecting his kill. "I was badly in need of this. I haven't murdered anyone in months!" She then bent down and bit the nurse's neck. At least, that's what Mongrel thought she was doing. But Summer wasn't just biting the nurse – she was eating her. Like a wild animal, Summer hovered over the corpse, her mouth ripping and chewing at flesh, blood spewing forth like a river, coating everything in it's path. "Oh God this is *so* good! It's like fucking nourishment." She looked up at Mongrel, blood smeared on her face and running down her chin. "You want some? I'll totally share! This is your kill too."

"Um, no thanks. I'm still full from breakfast." This wasn't true; if anything all the running for his life had left him with a raging hunger, but watching the beautiful young woman going all zombie on another human being was enough to quell his appetite. Once again, he wasn't surprised by any of this. Perhaps he was just used to all the silly shenanigans that went on around the hospital. But he did have a question about it. "I thought dead bodies grossed you out?"

"Yep," she said with a mouthful of nurse.

"Then…?"

Summer looked at the carcass in front of her. "What? This one's mine. I killed it. Well, *we* did, whatever."

"That still makes no sense."

She shrugged. "I guess it's kinda like farting. Other peoples' farts are gross, but you have no problem with your own, right?"

This made a stupid sort of sense and Mongrel wasn't going to argue with her. Besides, he had work to do. He glanced up and down the corridor, unsure of which way to go. Then remembered his map. With all the commotion he'd forgotten it in the elevator. It was too late now; the elevator had left. He could hit the call button but that would risk bringing more minions. There didn't seem to be any of them up here, and he didn't want to change that.

"Rushkov's office is that way, Room 319," Summer said, pointing down the hall behind him. Had she read his mind? She straightened up and smiled at him, obviously having a good time as the world fell apart around them. "You go ahead. I'll stay here and keep watch."

So Mongrel left her there, not happy to be on his own, alone in a building that was getting more disturbing by the minute, but knowing, after the last incident, that he could handle a minion or two. His confidence buoyed, he limped down the hall until he came upon Dr. Rushkov's office. Would he be in there? Would *anyone* be waiting inside? Carefully opening the door, trying to be as quiet and inconspicuous as possible, Mongrel was thankful to find the waiting room empty. He crept across the carpet and into the sitting room, which was likewise vacant. He passed through it, catching a brief

Murder-Proof

glimpse of the retarded horse painting on the wall, and held his ear against the closed office door. All was silent, so he held his breath and opened the door.

But the office was also blissfully empty. Giddy and feeling lucky, Mongrel hobbled over to and around Valentin's grand oak desk to the table behind it, and found, to his delight, a sheet of paper sticking out of it. Picking it up, not daring to hope, he turned it over and found his signature at the bottom.

It was the original document.

Beginning to get light-headed with giddiness, Mongrel had to calm himself down and decide what do to with it. Obviously ripping the thing to shreds came to mind, but that allowed for the possibility of it being put back together like a puzzle. He could eat it, but considering what he'd seen at the hospital – namely from Zeke – excrement had a way of turning up all over the place, and once again the possibility, as unlikely and disgusting as it may seem, that the document could return was very real. So that too was out. Then what could he do? Glancing around the room, looking for an answer, Mongrel spotted an ashtray.

Fire.

He began searching around the ashtray and the small table it sat on, looking for a lighter, or matches, or anything he could use to set light to the paper. Finding nothing, he returning to the desk and began pulling open drawers and rummaging through them. Still he found nothing. What was he going to have to do, bang a couple rocks together? Maybe he'd have to eat the evidence after all.

"Can I help you?"

Mongrel glanced up to see Valentin Rushkov standing in the doorway, and his heart sank. Or it skipped a beat, or stopped altogether; something odd anyway – Mongrel was too preoccupied to pay it much attention. He was busy with trying to cast a nonchalant glance at the newest member of his mortal enemies club.[*] Getting the feeling that his glance was making him out to be more challant than he wanted, he needed to add a little flair to it. "'Sup?" he asked. "I'm just looking for a lighter."

---

[*] Currently with five members; the others being: Captain Pete, Brecklyn, Bossa Nova, Shamus Bond, and the probably the entire population of the island on Duntt River.

Random Tangent

Valentin was dressed less formally than the last time Mongrel had seen him. In fact, the psychiatrist looked downright haggard; bags under his eyes, prominent stubble, and somewhat dishevelled hair. The breakup with Sheila must have been taking its toll on him. This pleased Mongrel.

"You do not look so good," the doctor said, fishing around in his jacket pocket. He pulled out a small object and tossed it across the room to Mongrel, who, despite his flailing arms and uncoordinated attempts, *totally* meant not to catch it.

"Speak for yourself," he replied, bending down to pick it up the…lighter? Had Valentin really tossed him a lighter? Did he know what Mongrel was about to do with it? Was this a joke, or a trap?

"Ist everzink okay?"

"Well it's been a long couple days," Mongrel muttered, flicking the lighter on; it worked. If this was a trap, it was a very alluring one.

"Do you vant to talk about it?" Valentin asked.

"Not with you. You're the last person I want to talk to about anything, ever."

"All ze same, I vant to talk to you about somezink."

"Well you can go fuck yourself," Mongrel said, and meant it. "You and yourself can just get it on. Dirty, nasty sex, like the schiza coff. And be sure to wear a condom; last thing this world needs is another smaller, evil piece of shit like you. Oh and thanks, by the way, for this." He held up the lighter, then lit the page on fire. As he watched it burn, Mongrel felt more giddy inside than he thought possible. A huge weight had been lifted from his shoulders. The last piece of evidence was gone, and he was no longer a prisoner at the hospital. He was free to go…well, except Valentin was blocking the door.

Having been a psychiatrist for many years, this obvious dig at his now deceased children didn't upset Valentin like it might someone else. It stung, sure, but he knew how to keep his emotions in check. "Now, now, zere ist no reason to be rude. I just have von very important qvestion."

"Yeah, well remember that part about you having filthy, inbred sex with yourself? Feel free to get right on that, preferably while falling off a cliff. You see this?" He shook the paper at the doctor. "This is over. I'm a free man now. You don't control me anymore." Mongrel then realized he should find a place to set the flaming page down – but where? The garbage bin was full of more paper and plastic that would burn. All the furniture in the office was made of wood or upholstered with flammable materials. There had to be some place to put it...

"I don't care about zat. Zere ist no reason so keep you here any longer. Ze hospital ist lost. Ze entire buildink ist overrun wiz crazy people."

"Oh really?" Mongrel asked, spinning around the office, looking for a safe place to toss the paper. "You're just noticing this now?" The ashtray wasn't big enough. The bookshelves were full of books and files. The printer...what about that? Maybe he could put th- "Ah!" he cried as the fire reached his fingers. He instinctively dropped the burning page, and it landed on the carpet, which promptly, carefully, ignited.

Valentin seemed not to notice the fire, or at least didn't care. "I mean it ist out of control!" Valentin said sternly, upset that Mongrel wasn't giving the situation the respect and gravitas it deserved. "Time to abandon ze ship!"

Mongrel busied himself with trying to stomp out the fire. "So why'd you come back then?"

"I told you; I have very important qvestion. Answer it und you are free to go."

"Is zat right?" Mongrel mocked. "You're not gonna make me go down with the *ze ship*? Speaking of which, that ship is kinda on fire. A little help here?" His stomping on the flaming rug was getting nowhere. If anything he was making it worse; one of his socks had ignited. He threw himself on the floor, removing it as quickly as possible. Then, without thinking, he flung the sock across the room, where it landed on a bookshelf and soon set alight the various files and folders.

"Vhere ist zat magic potato?" Valentin demanded, still ignoring anything Mongrel was doing.

Staring at the bookshelf as fire now began to spread across it, Mongrel sighed in exasperation. He'd once seen his friend Loafmeat actually put out a fire with his bare hands – by punching it. Knocked the fire right out. It was the damndest thing he'd ever seen, and he wished he had an even remotely similar skill. He stood in the middle of the room, watching the birth of an inferno, thankful that there was finally some warmth to be had, but feeling guilty about it. The whole building was going to burn down, and it was his fault. At least it would take the screaming demon with it.

Fuck it, Mongrel thought. *Let the hospital burn.*

"I told you I don't have the potato." Mongrel recalled his experience with the witchcraft a couple days prior. There was a moment in time, a split second in which he'd witnessed the entire history of the magic potato. Discovered by his great-great-great-great[*] grandfather had found it in a well on some abandoned farmland during the War of the Restless (which Mongrel never heard anything more about). Stopping to grab a drink after a hard and miserable day of battle, he'd retrieved a pail of water from the well, and it in found a potato. Presumed to have become petrified, or at least pickled after being in the well for many years, it was kept as a trinket of good luck. And as good luck oft has its way with things like a charming man has a way with women, the War had ended that same day. Seen as a sign that the potato, thereafter called the sacred potato, was a relic with great power, it was hidden away, kept secret from prying eyes and sticky, pilfering hands. Over the generations it was passed down and down and still down until Mongrel had come across it in his mother's house. She'd bequeathed it to him, and he'd held it in his highest regard since. That is, until Shamus Bond came along. During an epic bullshit battle he foolishly displayed the sacred potato to the anti-agent, who had proclaimed it a rock and threw it out the window. At the time Mongrel believed him. He couldn't tell you why; perhaps it was the accent? When he'd come to his senses later and went to retrieve the relic, it was gone. Up until a couple days ago it remained lost. Then he'd drunk the witchcraft and learned Beby had stumbled across it. She called it Fluffy and kept it in a shoebox under her bed.

"Beby has it." The words were passed his lips before Mongrel realized what he was saying. He clapped his hands over his mouth and glared at Valentin, who was trying to conceal a

---

[*] Often expressed as super-great or $great^2$.

Murder-Proof

smile. He felt like a bigger idiot than normal. He'd just handed over his girl on a silver platter.

"Ah. So you *did* know vhere it vas," Valentin said smugly. "All zis time you have been lyink to me behind mine back."

"No I wasn't – I really didn't know until a couple days ago. And I wouldn't lie to you behind your back; I'd lie to you to your face."

"Vell it matters not. Zank you for your cooperation." He turned to walk out the door.

"Wait!" Mongrel shouted. "Please...help me with this."

The doctor paused and looked around the room at the growing inferno. Then his eyes landed on Mongrel and a slight grin tried to stop itself from forming on his face – which Mongrel took as a bad sign. "Just keep vorkink on containink ze fire," he said. I vill grab fire extinkvisher." He then bolted out the door, closing it behind him, probably to keep the fire from spreading.

Mongrel glanced around, unsure of what more he could do. He spotted a jacket on a coat rack near the door, and began navigating his way over to it. Once he grabbed it he started fanning the flames, but all this managed to do was blow them into things that hadn't yet caught fire. He eventually gave up and threw the jacket into the fire. The whole situation was rather hopeless, he surmised, beginning to cough in the dwindling oxygen.

Suddenly acutely aware that Valentin had been gone for quite some time, Mongrel thought he'd best go check on him. He tried the door and found it locked.

Oh dear.

Valentin must have locked it behind him, one last evil deed. This one was beyond malevolent, however; akin to attempted murder. Despite what his fellow minion-slayers thought, he was not murder-proof. He wanted to believe it himself, but it was a silly notion if you think about it. Why, just earlier he'd thought he'd been killed by boobs. Now it seemed his real death was going to be far less pleasant.

Mongrel should have known something like this was going to happen. If he managed to make it out alive he'd have to have a stern conversation with himself, which would no doubt break into an argument. It probably wouldn't come to blows, but he'd be mad at himself for a while, and wouldn't be on speaking terms. But he couldn't stay mad at himself for long. I mean, look at that face! How could anyone stay mad at that face? Perhaps he was a bit too forgiving; tough love didn't come easily to him. But what was he going to do? One way or another he simply had to find a way to get through to himself, or the next time things could be beyond fixing. Honestly, he was a good lad, but just didn't think sometimes. He had a good head on his shoulders – a bit lumpy here and there but a jolly good head for most purposes – if he'd only try using it once in a while.. Many folks would kill for a head like that. Hell some folks would kill him even without – like Summer for example.

Summer!

Mongrel banged on the door and screamed as loud as he could. "Summer! Help!"

"Who is it?" came from the other side of the door so quick it made Mongrel jump. It wasn't Valentin, as it had no accent, but it was a man's voice. Little else could be discerned over the roar of the fire.

"My name is Mongrel Stevens. The place is on fir-"

"Mongrel!" the voice shouted. "I knew you were in there. Doc said you didn't want to be disturbed."

"I'll bet he did. Could you open the door please? And who are you?"

"It's me!"

Waiting for a minute, hoping 'me' would elaborate, Mongrel grew impatient. "Look, *me*, do you happen to have growths on the sides on your body that resemble arms with hands and fingers and stuff?"

After a minute, probably to address the question, the reply came, "Yes."

"Then could you use them to open the door before I burn to death!"

The sounded of laughter followed. "You can't die. You're murder-proof, remember?"

This wasn't making any sense – not that Mongrel had time to figure it out. The room was getting hotter with every passing second, and the oxygen was nearly gone. He kneeled down to suck

Murder-Proof

in the sweet, fresh air coming in under the door. "I'm not murder-proof! Now please open the door."

"Oh! Hey down there. I can hear you better now. So look, earlier you said you couldn't be killed, so what are you panicking for?"

With his face pressed up against the crack of the door, Mongrel could hear better. "Zeke?"

"What?"

"It *is* you."

"Of course it's me, dumbass! I already told you that."

"Zeke, listen to me very carefully. I'm not murder-proof, and sure as hell not fireproof. If you don't open the door there's going to be a lot of screaming and burning and me dying any second now."

"I saw Summer kill you fair and square, and I brought you back to life. Why couldn't I just do it again?"

"Because I'll be fucking ashes!" Mongrel ran a sweaty palm through his greasy hair and chanced a look behind him. The fire was roaring out of control. Everything had gone up in flames. The curtains, the bookshelves, the furniture. Just his small little corner remained unharmed – but not for long. Where were the sprinklers? Shouldn't water be raining down on him by now? Sweet, wonderful, life-saving water. For that matter, shouldn't fire alarms be going off? How could there be this much fire without an alarm? What was wrong with the system in the hospital? Did Valentin do something to it? Was that the plan? Kill Mongrel but make it look like an accident? Or, since he'd been the one to start the fire, make it look like he committed...

An idea came to Mongrel. "Zeke, it's not murder. I started the fire. It was me! So if I die it would be suicide, not murder. And I'm not suicide-proof."

"You're not?"

"No."

"Have you tried?"

"What? *No*, of course I haven't tried."

"Then how do you know?"

Fucking Zeke.

Random Tangent

"Okay then, yes, I've tried. I killed myself a few years ago and didn't survive. Totally not suicide-proof. Now will you please open the door before I kill myself...again?"

"So you're dead now?"

"Um...yes?"

"Then what are you worried about? You can't die twice."

Mongrel banged his head against the door a few times. He was getting nowhere. If he'd been talking to Pink Lloyd or Summer he'd be free by now. Instead Zeke was his only salvation, which meant he was doomed. He wished he'd never lit that stupid sheet of paper on fire. He wished he'd never tried to escape the hospital. He wished he'd never tried to win Beby's heart in the first place. He should've known; things just don't work out like that for him. Fate, ever the whore, always toyed with him, dangling promises and opportunities and boobs in front of his face, only to yank them away when victory was immanent.

He could feel the heat on his back now. This was it; he was going to die. Tears would've been streaking down his face if they weren't evaporating the instant they left his tear ducts. "Zeke, please!"

"I'd love to help you out," Zeke said, "but I can't."

"Why not?"

"Cause I can't open the door."

"Why. The. Fuck. Not?"

"Cause I don't got the keys. Why don't you just unlock it from your side?"

Mongrel was about to respond with some premium-quality foul language when he realized that what Zeke said was incredibly relevant. He looked up at the door handle; underneath it was a twist-lock. Scrambling to his feet, he twisted the lock and jerked open the door, nearly smashing his head into it as he did so. He leapt out and crashed to the floor of the sitting room, and breathed in the air of freedom, wheezing triumphantly.

Okay, so maybe Valentin wasn't trying to kill him; just slow him down is all. Although, out of Mongrel's sheer stupidity the attempted murder was almost successful. He shuddered to think that had Zeke not been there, would he be dead now? This was now

Murder-Proof

twice the moron had saved his life. The mental patient was making him look like an idiot.

"How's it going, zombie boy?" Zeke said, getting up from the couch to peer through the door. "Holy! What'd you do?"

"I set the room on fire," Mongrel said, wishing he could just lie on the floor for a few hours and get some rest. That must've been the smoke inhalation talking. But there was no rest for the wicked, and even less for the good-hearted individuals like himself. He slowly plodded to his feet.

"I know that," Zeke said. "But what did you *do*?"

Not knowing exactly what Zeke wanted to hear, Mongrel turned to address him and found a naked ass staring him down. Since the last time he'd seen him, Zeke had somehow lost all his clothes. Quickly looking away, he asked, "What the hell? Why are you naked?"

"I always sit on the couch naked."

Mongrel looked at the couch, saw Zeke's clothes and bat beside it, and recalled Valentin telling him about the naked couch problem. He sighed violently. Out of the fire and into the frying pan, or whatever. "Did Lloyd make it okay?"

"I don't know. We kinda got separated. Summer's down the hallway. Looks like she finally killed another one. It's a woman too – would've loved to see that catfight. *Meow!*"

The fight unfortunately didn't go down the way Zeke imagined it, but Mongrel decided to leave him to his illusions. "Don't stare at the flames too long. Come out when you're ready; we got some new shit to deal with. And don't come out unless you're dressed."

He came out to the waiting room and found Summer sitting in a chair, waiting for him. She must have just arrived. Unfortunately, unlike Zeke, she was still wearing clothes – although they were revealing; a too-tight top (which, without the bra, supplied all the evidence needed to prove how cool it was in the building), and short shorts – all of which, along with her face, were bathed in blood. If anyone, *she* was the one who looked like a zombie. He supposed it suited her. She smiled, happy to see him.

"Enjoy your snack?" he asked her.

She nodded. "I saved you some."

Random Tangent

"That's sweet of you. Maybe I'll take some in my lunch tomorrow."

"What happened in there? With the fire?"

"I just set the building on fire. No biggie. Have you seen Lloyd?"

She shook her head this time.

Rats. No one seemed to know about Pink Lloyd. Since he'd lost the map, Mongrel needed him more than ever. If he was going to stop Valentin and save Beby, Mongrel needed to get his stuff back, and without his friend that could prove difficult. What the heck had happened to him? Hopefully he was okay.

"Well I can't wait around for him, but I can't go on without him. I don't know what to do." Mongrel looked around the room in exasperation, hoping a solution would come to him. "Valentin's going after my girlfriend and I have to stop him. I need to find my stuff, but I don't know where to start."

"You have a girlfriend?" Summer asked forlornly, all the fun of murder and mayhem suddenly forgotten.

"I told you, you stuff is probably in the interrogation room," Zeke said, coming out to join them. He was still naked but had his bat. Summer gagged at the sight of his nakedness, which Mongrel found curious; she could eat raw flesh but the sight of Zeke threw her into convulsions? Then again, would be rather eat a person or look at Zeke naked? It was a tough call…

"Dammit Zeke there is no interrogation room!" she muttered when she'd gotten herself under control. "And why are you naked?"

"You know what?" Zeke cried angrily. "I'm tired of clothes, I'm tired of being treated like a retard, and I'm tired of you telling me I'm wrong." He marched out into the hallway. "Come on, I'll *show* you where it is."

Out of curiosity, Mongrel followed Zeke, wishing he was leading the way instead of walking behind him so he wouldn't have to constantly avoid looking at his naked, waddling ass. As much as he hated to admit it, Zeke probably knew what he was talking about. Besides, he couldn't trust Summer after what she'd tried to do to him, so he didn't have any other options.

"You never told me you had a girlfriend," Summer whispered, falling in line beside him.

Murder-Proof

"Well...I..." Mongrel didn't really know what to say. Was she mad at him? It's not like he could have a relationship with her anyway – at least not a long one, unless she was done trying to kill him. Besides, she wasn't up to his standards, mentally speaking. She was sexy and had spunk, but Mongrel couldn't see himself dating her. They were just too different. I mean, look at some of her hobbies; murder, cannibalism, and perhaps worst of all: vegetarianism[*]. And who knew what else she was into? Star Trek? Animal husbandry? The shiza coff?

This prompted Mongrel to think of Beby. Dr. Rushkov had claimed she'd been into the shiza coff. Whether he was lying or not Mongrel might one day find out. But what if it were true? The doctor also said she'd killed someone before – what if that was true too? And what other secrets might she be hiding. Who knew how deep the camel's ass went?

He glanced at Summer. At least she was convinced he was murder-proof and probably wouldn't try to kill him anymore. He couldn't say the same about Beby. Suddenly Summer didn't seem like such a horrible choice anymore.

"I don't *technically* have a girlfriend," he finally said. "We're sort of..."

"Just friends?" she asked, beginning to skip, a big grin on her face.

"Not what I was gonna say. We're close. We might be...the whole reason I'm here is basically because of her. She wanted me to prove I wasn't crazy. I was seeing a doctor to get a paper, or stamp of certification or whatever."

"Why?"

Mongrel shrugged. "Well, Dunttstown's a crazy place. I guess she was tired of the crazy and wanted someone a little more normal."

"Guess that's not working out for you."

---

[*] Even though human flesh is technically meat, Summer rarely dabbled in cannibalism – mostly because it was hard to keep it secret, since people just *can not* let a person go missing without snooping around and asking questions. She never ate any other kind of animal, and thusly considered herself an herbivore.

Random Tangent

"No. I should've known better than to trust Valentin. He had it in for me from the start. That's why I'm here instead of out there. He plotted the whole thing."

She shook her head. "I don't mean him; I mean you're not gonna prove you're not crazy."

This confused Mongrel. "And that's because of him."

"No. It's because you *are* crazy."

"What? No I'm not. Just because I'm in here with you doesn't mean I'm like you. And I'm only in here *because* of Valentin."

Summer wasn't convinced. "You're crazy because you're hanging out with us. Me, a psychopath who tried to kill you; Zeke, who's naked and has self-inflicted constipation; and Lloyd, who believes his nipples sing if you listen close enough."

Mongrel was about to offer a counter-argument, but instead asked, "Lloyd thinks his nipples can sing?"

"Yep," Summer giggled. "Opera apparently."

"Huh. Anyway you guys might be my friends in here, but out there in the real world, who knows? I'm sorry to say it, bu-"

"Makes no difference. You think anyone can fit in with us? You think we'd accept you no matter what?" Mongrel was silent, so she went on. "You accept us, don't you? I mean as friends. We talk and get along. You *get* us."

"Get you? Not sure I'd go that far. But don't the doctors understand you?"

"Not even close. That's why they're doctors, and you're not. You're on our level. They just try to study us, fix us – like we're broken."

"Aren't you though?" Mongrel asked. "No offense or anything, but you do realize there's something wrong with you, don't you?"

Summer looked ahead – probably not at Zeke's ass but in the middle distance – and Mongrel was worried he'd upset her. After a minute she turned back to him. "Let me answer that with a question: is there anything wrong with you? You're the one with a book."

Wasn't that the million dollar question? Mongrel almost said 'no' but had to think about it. No one was perfect, and that went doubly so for him, but he certainly wasn't psychiatric hospital-worthy, was he? He got into bullshit fights – and won! – had a fear of fish, had a pet mon, regularly spoke with the Grim Reaper; these were all normal, everyday things that weren't weird in the correct context. What *would* be weird was drawing a watch on your arm for nearly a month instead of just buying one, or applying for a job as someone who fixes gravity, or maybe living in his apartment for months without a toilet. And what about the reason he came to the hospital in the first place? If you got right down to it, he was basically there to get a doctor's note so he could have sex. Yes, some folks might describe that as a little strange. Many things he did may seem bizarre to the untrained eye, but once you knew the whole story they made complete sense. There was a method to his madness. He wasn't perfect, but he definitely wasn't crazy.

"I'm not…" he started, but couldn't finish. As much as he wanted to believe he was sane, something didn't feel right about proclaiming it. Was it really for him to say? It was like asking him if he was inspiring, or smart – although intelligence could be measured; sanity couldn't. What was sanity supposed to feel like anyway?

He felt her slip her fingers between his and looked down at their interlocked hands, then up into her eyes, softer and bluer than he remembered. "It's okay," she said. "It's hard at first. You don't want to think about it. They *do* make you feel broken, but you're not. *We're* not."

Mongrel didn't feel broken. He wasn't like them, and certainly not like her. Well, except that he'd killed people too. They were all accidents of course, but try telling that to the victims. Or victim. He guessed Captain Pete would say Mongrel wasn't right in the head, but the captain was clearly jaded and probably had brain damage from spending too much time amongst the dead. If *anyone* wasn't right in the head it was the old pirate. *He* was the one who should be locked up in…wait, Captain Pete *was* locked up here. Huh.

Anyway, even aside from occasional involuntary manslaughter, Mongrel knew he wasn't like them. He *couldn't* be; he'd never kill anyone or anything on purpose.

Random Tangent

Mongrel stopped. That wasn't true. He *was* planning on killing a dog. Captain Alphonse left him his dog to look after, and Mongrel was going to kill it by given it to Charlie, a serial puppy-killer. "No," he said to himself quietly, disbelief clouding his thoughts. That couldn't be right, could it? There was a reasonable explanation, the method of his madness! It's not like he *wanted* to hurt the damn dog. He was trying to do something nice. And it was old and gonna die soon anyway!

"Yes," Summer answered, even though Mongrel was talking to himself. "It's okay. It's not like we're evil or anything."

"No," Mongrel said again. He squeezed her hand then let it go. "I can't be like you. I'm sorry."

Summer giggled. "Well it's not like you can help it, silly buns. Like it or not, you're stark raving mad. Do you think you'd have your own book if you were normal?"

Mongrel glared at her. "Dammit! Would you stop breaking the fourth wall?"

She just giggled more. "Sorry! It's not like I can help it; I'm *crrr-azy*!"

"Would you guys hurry up?" Zeke yelled back at them. He was standing by the elevator bank repeatedly hitting the call button. They'd fallen behind – not unintentionally – while they'd talked. Keeping up with a large, waddling, naked ass didn't come naturally to them.

"Oh shit," Mongrel muttered, taking off towards him. "Stop pressing the button! We're taking the stairs!"

"Why?" Zeke demanded. "Only stupid people take the stairs; healthy people who like to exercise."

"But minions take the elevator!"

Zeke scoffed. "We can handle them. The stairs are dangerous. I mean, there's less chairs being thrown around, but you could fall and skin you knees, or overexert yourself and have a heart attack. Can't fight a heart attack. Well, *I* can, but you gu-"

"We've been cornered in the elevator by those things," Summer interrupted, pushing open a door opposite the elevator bank. "Not gonna happen again. Now come on."

Grumbling, Zeke followed them into the stairwell. Seconds later the elevator arrived and minions spilled out into the hall.

Murder-Proof
***

The room was exactly as Mongrel remembered. It was strange that he hadn't thought to come back here until today, but now that he was here he understood what kept him; his brain had blocked it out. Bad memories flitted around his head. Two large men crowding him, violently yanking off his clothes. It was all he could do to not scream "rape!" He tried not to struggle, hoping his compliance would ease the transition, but it did not. They'd scrubbed him roughly with some abrasive and foul-smelling cleaner that burned his eyes and tarnished his soul. He was certain more than one layer of skin was removed. Then he was rinsed off with what he could only assume was a fire hose. His cries of agony and pleas for mercy went unheard. Once the straight jacket was tightly strapped on he could clearly what he'd left behind on the floor, tufts of hair and skin and small puddles blood. They took a picture for some reason, a mug shot, then dragged him to a padded cell, where he found relieve for a few hours.

And now he was back in the torture room. He glanced around; it looked more like a locker room than an office, out of place with the rest of the facility. There were a few stalls, like in a bathroom, but with no doors. Privacy was not a priority in the hospital. Across from the stalls stood a row of black lockers.

"*Told you*," Zeke said proudly. "This is where they do it."

"Did they interrogate you here?" Summer asked Mongrel.

"No," he replied, beginning to rummage through the lockers. "They never asked me anything. I'm sure they punished me for something, but I couldn't tell you what."

Summer turned to Zeke, a quasi-grin on her face. "So what did they interrogate you for?"

Zeke glanced away, as if embarrassed. "I don't wanna talk about it."

"Figures. How come you never talk about your life before coming here?"

"Because there was no life before coming here."

"Oh come on! There had to be something." Summer was trying to meet Zeke eye to eye (which helped avoid looking at any other part of him) but he kept avoiding her gaze. "What, did they electroshock you too much? Have you forgotten everything?"

Random Tangent

"I said I don't wanna talk about it!"

"Found it!" Mongrel cried suddenly.

They turned to see him pull a small box out of a locker and begin digging through it. He looked up at them with the first genuine smile he'd worn all day. He took the box inside the nearest stall. "Be right back. Don't look in."

There wasn't much in the box; shirt, pants and belt, wallet, keys. His underwear was missing, but that didn't surprise him. They seemed to be in short supply at the hospital and were probably a valuable commodity. His shoes were also gone, but were probably around there somewhere. Mongrel took off his sweatpants and dressed in his own, better-fitting jeans, put his wallet – which shockingly still had money in it – in his front pocket, and his keys in the rear. He kept his shirts on.

Coming out of the stall, Mongrel found his cohorts sitting in a couple office chairs flipping through magazines as if it were just another day waiting at the doctor's office. They glanced up as he approached them, and before either could say a word, Mongrel tossed his shirt at Summer. "I owe you," he said.

"For what?"

"You gave me the shirt off your back my first day here, so I'm returning the favour."

She flashed him another smile, accepting the gift, but added, "You can just give me back my old one."

Looking down at the tight shirt exposing his stomach, Mongrel shrugged. "I don't mind trading. I've grown used to this one. Maybe I even kinda like it? Besides, I'll need something to remember you by after I'm gone."

Summer giggled her infectious laugh again at the sentiment, though inside she cringed at the implications of what he'd said. A memento? Didn't that mean he wasn't coming back?

"You should change anyway," Mongrel continued, "you look like a zombie."

Summer glanced down to see her shirt, once white, now caked in blood. Not only that, but with the air conditioning on overdrive, the cool air was making her shirt damp. With all the adrenaline still pumping through her veins she probably didn't notice how cold this made her. But her nipples did.

Murder-Proof

"Oh!" she said, and smiled nervously. She ran into the stall Mongrel had just left to change. "I owe you too," she called from inside. "A thumb."

"Yeah, I don't think that's gonna work anymore. Supposed to keep it on ice, but you ate it, remember? Not sure I'll want it back…you know, after it comes out."

Summer returned from the stall with a smirk on her face. "So after it's been up my ass it's no good to you anymore? What if I let you stick something else up there? Gonna throw that away too?"

Not knowing what to say to this, Mongrel let his mouth hang open for a bit to get some fresh air. Fortunately Summer didn't seem interested in a response; she lifted the shirt to her nose and inhaled deeply. "It even smells like you." When she let the shirt drop back down it was lightly covered in blood from her face. "You are such a sweetheart," she said, throwing her arms around Mongrel's neck and kissing him, smearing blood all over him too.

Mongrel wasn't sure if the shirt smelling like him was a good thing or not. It was hot when he'd come to the hospital two days ago, and he wasn't sure if he'd been wearing deodorant or not. He pulled away from her and said, "Don't mention it."

She then saw what she'd done to his face and giggled. "Oh, sorry. I forgot."

Despite how gross the thought of having else's blood on him, especially his face, Mongrel laughed too. "It's okay." He went over to a nearby sink, but before he could turn it on he heard something that chilled his bones.

"Considers gonna considerate. Suffers gonna suffocate. Passions gonna passionate."

"Hey," Zeke said nervously. "Did you guys hear that?"

Without answering, Mongrel went to the door and peeked out, and the chill in his bones dropped well below freezing. From both ends of the hall half a dozen minions were marching towards them. They blocked every exit.

"Aww man!" Zeke cried, peering over his shoulder. "They got Lloyd!"

Mongrel looked to where Zeke was pointing and sure enough, Pink Lloyd was with the army of minions, walking and chanting. He fell back inside and slumped down to the floor against the wall. "Not Lloyd," he muttered, putting his head to his knees. "I need him to get out of here. Why couldn't it be Zeke?"

"Hey, I can hear you," Zeke complained.

"I can take 'em."

Looking up at Summer, Mongrel found a wide grin on her face. She licked her lips and said, "Can you hear the dinner bell ringing?"

"There's too many of them," Mongrel said, finding himself worrying over her safety. "You can't kill them all."

"Oh yes I can. They starved me of murder for so long and I'm a hungry little slut." She then glanced back at Zeke and her eyes landed on his bat. "But I might want a fork. Zeke, gimme your bat."

Hefting his bat and looking at her, Zeke pouted. "Why, what are you gonna do with it?"

"I'm gonna crack some heads open, duh! That's what they make bats for, don't they? Now gimme!"

Zeke bit his lip, reluctant to hand over his weapon. "I don't wanna. What if I don't get it back?"

Summer growled. "If you don't give it to me I'll beat you with it."

"Show me your boobs and I'll let you have it."

"Zeke!" Mongrel yelled. "Just give her the damn bat!"

Finally Zeke relented and thrust the bat towards Summer, grumbling furiously.

She took it, swung it a few times to get the feel for it, and said, "Wait til I have them distracted – or dead – before making a run for it."

Mongrel nodded. "Okay then. Go get 'em babe. Have fun!" He then slapped her ass and stepped back a few feet, not wanting to watch this time.

Summer blushed, leaned over and kissed Mongrel again, quickly and lightly this time, so as to not smearing anymore blood. Then she sauntered out into the hallway for a delightful romp of murder and mayhem.

Just like in the basement, what followed was a ghastly symphony of bodily carnage. Thumps and thuds could be heard from the meeting of bat and flesh; blood, human entrails, and chunks of brain matter splattered the walls; screams – both from Summer and the minions – echoed up and down the corridor.

"What about Lloyd" Zeke suddenly asked.

At first Mongrel wasn't sure what he'd meant, but he quickly understood: Summer was like a shark; she went into a frenzy when she smelled blood. If Lloyd attacked – which was highly likely – he'd meet the business end of her bat. "I don't know," he said, standing to look out the door. Summer was out of sight, but he could hear her laying waste to zombies somewhere down the hall. A trail of bodies followed the ungodly noise. He didn't spot Lloyd among them, and gave in to hope.

"You don't think she'd hurt Lloyd do you," Zeke pressed.

"I don't know. You know her better than I do."

Zeke thought for a moment before asking, "Can you give mouth-to-mouth to someone who took a bat to the head?"

"You mean like if they were killed from it? No, that wouldn't save them."

"Dang. Well I better go get him before she kills him. Lloyd ain't murder-proof like you."

"Okay," Mongrel agreed. He didn't want to be left alone, but Lloyd was more important. He had to believe that whatever spell the minions were under could be reversed, that Pink Lloyd could be saved. "I'll just wait here."

"Pssh!" Zeke said, shoving Mongrel out into the hall. "The coast is clear man. Make a run for it!"

Mongrel's heart leapt into this throat but he quickly swallowed it back down when he realized that, as usual, Zeke was right. Nothing appeared to be left alive in the hallway; Summer had been thorough. Either that or she was like the Pied Piper, leading them away and clearing a path. This was Mongrel's chance to escape once and for all.

He turned to Zeke and held out his hand. "Thanks Zeke, for everything."

Zeke looked at the hand and shoved it away, then pulled Mongrel into a bear hug. It was a one-sided and awkward, especially with Zeke being naked. He was certain he felt Zeke's flopper, and more certain he'd never be able to erase that memory. It was like being hug-raped.

"Take care pal," Zeke whimpered, releasing Mongrel. "Don't you forget about us."

"Oh as much as I'd like to," Mongrel said, trying to stay his nausea, "I don't think I could possibly forget you, Zeke." It was a good thing he'd never gotten those tacos, otherwise they'd be all over the floor now – and still not the must disgusting thing in the hallway.

With a last smile, Zeke turned and bounded down the corridor, following the wreckage. Mongrel waited until he was out of sight, then turned and headed for the stairs.

Mongrel was now alone. It wasn't the first time, but now it was different. His friends were gone. If he ran into trouble he was on his own, and trouble could be lurking anywhere. He needed to be extra careful.

He reached the stairwell and opened the door only as wide as he needed to slip through, and quietly snuck down the stairs. Suddenly reminded of his lost shoes, he appreciated the stealth their absence afforded him. The door to the main floor had a tiny window, and Mongrel stole a peek out. It didn't offer a great view, but anything was better than taking his chances. The coast appeared to be clear.

But of course, it wasn't.

No sooner had he opened the door he heard: "Consumers gonna consummate."

Immediately to his left stood a minion, his dark shark eyes lifeless and horrifying. He seemed to be alone, but more had to be nearby. Mongrel could have retreated back into the stairwell, but then what? He had to escape the hospital somehow; Beby was in jeopardy. He chose to run. He sprinted down the hallway, knowing that if he kept his speed up he could outrun them. But the minion did not give chase; it didn't have to. From around the corner just ahead of Mongrel came two more minions.

Mongrel slid to a halt. Another minion appeared in a doorway next to him. "Doctor's gonna doctorate."

Behind him a minion shuffled out of a woman's washroom. "Excels gonna accelerate."

Murder-Proof

To his right, down the hallway, four minions lurched towards him. "Pixels gonna pixelate."

The only option was to go was back. Mongrel turned on his heels and ran back the way he'd come. The minion by the stairwell was still there, and Mongrel tackled it to the ground. It was unnecessary but it felt great. But there wasn't time to savour the moment; he jumped to his feet and continued running. He recognized the hallway; knew where he was going, but any hope he had of escaping vanished as he turned another corner and ran straight into a mob.

He fell underneath their weight, and for a moment it was a mess of confusion. Mongrel wasn't sure what was going on, but knew it was bad. *Very bad.* Hands gripped his clothes and hair. Teeth bit down on whatever they could reach. The drone of monotone chanting was so loud he couldn't understand anything they were saying.

Then somehow, amid the scrambling and panicking, Mongrel found himself on his feet again. Cuts, bruises, and bite marks notwithstanding, he considered this quite an achievement. Heartened, he began to push his way forward, and was thrilled to find the crowd parting here and there. He'd shove them one way and they would relent – but only so far. Then he would press on in a new direction, finding short-term success. With newfound hope he marched his way through them, feeling like Neo from the Matrix movies when he learned he could control the machines.

Mongrel was the one. The commander of this army, the conqueror of these people – *his* people, *his* army.

He stopped.

His people. Summer's words came back to him. He could walk among them because he was one of them.

No. That was preposterous. Mongrel refused to accept it. He'd just been living with them to long. That was it. He was going crazy. Some fresh air was in order; some fresh perspective. Once he was back out in the real world with the mostly-normal people he'd be okay. He just had to keep shoving his way towards the door.

He knew the way to go but was having difficulty getting there. The minions would only allow him to advance so far in any direction before returning to a human wall, a living, breathing version of an electric fence. Where he was met with teeth and nails he would stop; where he found blank stares and stiff limbs he would proceed. But it was like a maze. Before long he began to fear that he was the rat, only able to go in the directions they chose. He wasn't escaping; but going with the flow. While encouraged by feeling like an outsider amongst them, Mongrel was also gripped by the tightening fear that he was being deceived. Why weren't they attacking him? Where were they leading him? He had no choice but to continue on.

It was a slow, frustrating grind, poking and prodding the minions, trying to decipher which would harm him and which were docile, but finally they seemed to part and he came to a clearing. He found himself back in the cafeteria. Mongrel suddenly became acutely aware of his hunger, but didn't feel like eating – at least not with an audience like this. All around the outside of the large room stood minions. Hundreds of them. Nearly the whole hospital was there, staring at him. Every doctor, every nurse, every patient. No one was eating dinner, which if Mongrel recalled correctly was chicken nuggets and peas (cabbage rolls for the vegetarians), and orange Jell-O[*] (or pumpkin pie, again for the vegetarians). Were they waiting for him? Was he the guest of honour? Were they going to eat him? Mongrel briefly looked over his battered and bruised body, certain there wasn't enough of him to go around – doubly so if anyone wanted seconds.

Mongrel peered around the room, looking for familiar faces, but found none. Perhaps Dr. Rushkov had managed to escape. The idea disappointed him. Then he considered the fact that maybe the doctor was dead, and his mood buoyed. Mongrel also saw no sign of his friends, which again could be good or bad. Hopefully they were still engaged somewhere, though he could hardly believe there were more minions elsewhere.

It struck Mongrel how quiet it was. Not two days ago the incessant drone of the voices and mindless conversations had threatened to drive him mad and prevented any amount of decent sleep. Now, only the occasional breaking of wind broke the deathly

---

[*] The orange Jell-O was ten percent meat; ten percent of which was hotdog; ten percent of which was real dog, according to Zeke.

Murder-Proof

silence. What was it about the hospital that made everyone so gassy? Even Mongrel couldn't help himself.

"Dials gonna dilate."

Mongrel's attention stole to the center of the room, where stood the screaming demon, waitin-

"Dial's gonna dilate!" came the roar of the minion army. A thousand voices crying out as one, deafeningly loud, with their leader standing in the middle of them. No; he was the General, and they were his troops. He had commanded them to guide Mongrel here, where he was waiting.

"What do you want?" he shouted, trying to keep his voice level, his fear hidden.

"Elevators gonna elevate," came the reply, followed by the response of his troops. They weren't just an army, but a tribe, with their own language, society, culture and laws. And this was their arena of battle, like the Roman Coliseum; and the screaming demon was the emperor, or best fighter...or a lion. Whatever; Mongrel wasn't good with analogies. The point is that Mongrel was now probably in a fight to the death.

"I don't want to fight you," Mongrel said.

"Gladiator's gonna gladiate."

Mongrel flinched as the mass of voices hit him like a tidal wave, nearly putting out the light bulb that appeared over his head. He tried to think, to recall what he knew of the ancient times. He pictured himself as Maximus from the movie Gladiator. What were his options? It wasn't just fight or die, was it? Couldn't he forfeit or choose to be banished?

"I choose banishment!"

"Meditations gonna meditate."

"I'll leave and never come back."

"Hesitants gonna hesitate."

"I'm sorry for whatever I did."

"Incinerators gonna incinerate."

Glancing around the room at the wall of faces, Mongrel detected no movement, no comprehension, no willingness to communicate. Their static faces told him nothing, and yet everything. He turned to their leader and regarded him no longer with fear and anger, but now pity and desperation.

Random Tangent

Within him arose a twisted concoction of hatred and defiance. He didn't have to take their mockery and abuse. He wasn't just another patient at the hospital; he was the one who was trapped in here with them, imprisoned by an evil doctor. He was the one who had suffered their lunacy. He was the one who'd had his thumb bitten off.

And he was the one who was murder-proof.

"So be it...Jedi," he said. Then he screamed and charged at the screaming demon. All the hours of pent up rage and frustration had come to a boil inside. He would rend flesh from bone, rip limb from body, and would not stop until every last one of them was dead or dying. This place, this palace of malice, had finally won. He'd become one of them, crazy with anger and violence, unable to stop even himself even if he wanted to; his body was no longer in his control, but driven by a madman.

But the minions had been mad for far longer, and with practice were much better at it. Seconds before he reached their leader a wall of skin and bone hit him, and he was slammed into the floor. A skirmish ensued. A dozen people were scrambling all over Mongrel, pushing and shoving him, pulling his clothing, yanking his hair. He fought back, swinging his arms wildly, kicking at anything his feet could find. But there were simply too many of them, their weight crushed him. Soon they had him on his knees, arms held firm behind his back. He struggled uselessly, out of breathe. The fight in him was all but gone.

The screaming demon loomed over him silently, a statue, looking and yet not looking at him. Was he pleased? Was he pissed? Was he *anything*? Before Mongrel died he would like to know exactly what he'd done to deserve this death. "Why?" he asked.

All he got in replay was, "Terminator's gonna terminate." This was echoed by his cult, and then the demon bared his teeth and bore down on him – and was blindsided with a flying chair.

The room erupted into chaos. Their leader incapacitated, the minions panicked and, except for those still holding Mongrel down, tore around the room. Words floated though the air – *arr's* and *bloody this* and *that* – along with more chairs. Sounds of reckless carnage bounced off the walls. Soon his captors released him and fled the scene. Mongrel finally got to his feet and turned to find Captain Pete kicking anything that moved. The tiny little madman had single-handedly taken down a large part of the minion horde. Bodies littered the floor. Blood was splattered everywhere. He'd even tackled the leader, Dominic, and kicked him to death.

Looking around the room for his next target, the old pirate locked eyes with Mongrel. "Tis just like back in the war!" he yelled excitedly, then took down another minion and put a peg through his eye socket. Mongrel wasn't sure what war the captain was talking about and didn't ask, but he gave a thumbs up sign.

Before long most of the minions had disappeared. The ones remaining were either dead or wallowing in agony. Captain Pete hobbled over to Mongrel, wary of the floor, now slippery with blood. "Now then, where were we?"

"What do you mean?" Mongrel asked. "We weren't anywhere."

"Don't be daft, boy," the captain said, irritated. "Last time I sees ya, what was we doin'?"

Mongrel thought back. "You were sitting on a table in a straight jacket. And I didn't do anything! I didn't kill you. See? You're still alive."

Captain Pete looked down, recalling that moment. "Oh, right. Forgot 'bout that. But I means the last time we's together, not the last time we's *here*."

"Look, I don't know what you're getting at, but thanks for saving my life. Maybe now you understand that I'm not alwa-"

"Saved your life?" the captain cried. "I did no such thing! Just saves you for last is all I did."

Mongrel swallowed. "Oh."

"My point was, the last time I's tryin' to kill you, only I ends up dead or worse, as usual. But not this time, see? I's gonna finish what I's started. Or tried to start." The captain rambled, momentarily confused. "I's gonna starts it *and* finish it, or..." Finally he flung his arms in the air, giving up with a, "Bah!"

"What's worse than dead?" Mongrel asked, not purposely trying to stall, but actually curious.

"Please mind to save all questions til after you's dead." Captain Pete chuckled for a minute, then became very still. A

Random Tangent

faraway look settled in his eyes and he did an unnerving impersonation of the screaming demon. Mongrel was about to ask what he was doing, when the captain whispered, "Captain's gonna captivate," and prepared to pounce. But before Mongrel had a chance to react, the pirate suddenly began shaking all over and dropped to the floor. Standing behind him was the janitor, holding what appeared to be a stun gun.

"Oh..." he said, looking at pools of blood the floor. "Forgot about that. Probably killed him." Then he shrugged and started tossing his weapon in air, pleased with himself. "Hope there's a reward."

"A reward for what?" Mongrel asked, wondering how he hadn't noticed the man seconds ago.

"Bagging the leader there." The janitor nudged Captain Pete. "Been turning this hospital into a cult or something. Haven't you noticed?"

"Oh, no," Mongrel pointed to the screaming demon, "*that* was him. The leader."

"Ah. Well if anyone asks, I got him too, okay? With my puke stick here." He tossed spun the weapon in the air again.

"That's a puke stick?" Mongrel looked down at the old pirate. "Why didn't he puke?"

The janitor shrugged. "Probably hasn't eaten anything in a while. But this thing ain't a hundred percent, okay? Still working the bugs out of it."

"Why do you have a puke stick anyway?"

"To make people puke." This was said in a way that suggested the answer was obvious.

But it wasn't obvious to Mongrel. "Why would you want to make people puke? Don't you have to clean it up?"

"Yeah, exactly." With the obviousness getting less clear by the second, the janitor felt compelled to explain. "I get bored easily, alright? Gotta give myself something to do. Earn my paycheck." He then gave Mongrel a curious look. "Hey, aren't you the mop thief?"

Mongrel sighed. "Yes, and look, I'm sorry. That was just a big misunderstanding. I was onl-"

The janitor had is hands up to stop Mongrel. "Don't worry about it. I'm over it."

Murder-Proof

"Oh...okay," Mongrel nodded, thankful. "Speaking of things being over, is this finally over?" He pointed all around him. "Can I go home now?"

"Yeah. We got the leader, right? I mean *I* got the leader. So yeah, the cult's gone. Cops are here. Place is surrounded. It's over."

The words 'cops' and 'surrounded' caught Mongrel off guard, and for a brief moment he spaced out, appearing like the screaming demon. The janitor took a step back, wary and ready to strike. Then, without a word Mongrel left the cafeteria. He walked down the hallway, passed the bathroom, nurse's station, and piles of bodies and puke. He walked into the main lobby and looked out into the world. It was late in the afternoon. The sun was turning orange and heading south, running away like a coward. The parking lot was filled with dozens of people; doctors and nurses – of the medical variety, not psychiatric – and mental patients. One cop car was parked in front of the entrance, a nervous cop behind it with his gun aimed at the building. He was shouting something. Mongrel stepped outside to hear him.

"Step outside and put your hands up," the officer called. "We have the place surrounded."

Mongrel looked around and said, "I am outside."

This reply shook the rookie to his core. He swallowed hard and did his best to keep his knees from shaking. This wasn't going the way he expected, the way his training had taught him. There was nothing like this in the manual. "Oh," he said. "Well can you at least put your hands up?"

Before Mongrel could comply the passenger door of the cop car opened and Officer Switchblade got out. "Wally, knock it off."

Descending the steps, Mongrel almost threw his friend into a hug, happy that the nightmare was finally over. But Switchblade didn't look pleased. "Why is it that I always find you in the middle of shit going down?" Mongrel didn't know what to say, and before he failed to reply his friend continued. "A couple weeks ago you were on the island. And the whole Jaywatch incident. Now this. There was some boat theft going around last week, did you catch it?"

"Uh...no. That wasn't me," Mongrel lied.

"Excuse us."

Random Tangent

Mongrel stepped aside as a couple paramedics ushered down a stretcher with a body on it and began wheeling it through the parking lot and down the road to the hospital. He couldn't see who they were carrying.

"No ambulance today?" Mongrel asked.

Officer Switchblade sneered. "What? Has owning a car made you lazy already? The hospital's only a block away so they decided to walk. It's nice out. Good barbequing weather. Speaking of barbequing, is that your work too?" He pointed to the right side of the building, which was completely consumed in flames. A dumpy man in overalls was spraying it down with a garden hose, doing very little in the way of containing the fire. He held his thumb over the end to increase the pressure and reach of the stream, doing his best in the absence of a fire hose. "Know anything about that?"

"Looks like a fire," Mongrel answered.

"Very good," his friend said, taking out a notepad and pen. "Know what caused it?"

Mongrel rubbed his chin for a minute. "I'd say a spark. Heat was probably involved too. And this is just a wild guess but...a duck."

"A duck?"

"Yep."

"Caused the fire?"

"Just a guess."

Officer Switchblade stared at Mongrel. Eventually he put his pen and notepad away and said, "Good enough for me."

Looking back at the dumpy fireman, Mongrel asked, "Correct me if I'm wrong but don't we have a fire department?"

"Yep. That's him."

"Where's his fire hose? And fire truck? And helmet or anything? And, *him?* Just him?"

"Since that fire a week ago, which if I'm not mistaken you were also involved in, took out most of a city block, the other guys spontaneously came down with bad case of *fuck this shit* and quit. Harvey there is the only guy left, and this is his day off."

"Ah," Mongrel nodded, recalling the incident at the car lot. "Sucks to be him."

"What the hell happened to your hand?"

Murder-Proof

"Uh…" Mongrel raised his hand to inspect it. The duct tape was still holding, but was a little tattered and covered in dirt. Dried blood was crusted here and there in black splotches. The whole thing was a terrible mess. "Just a paper cut. Nothing to worry about."

His friend looked at him, then back at his hand. "My first year on the force I responded to a call at Harrow[*] – before it was Harrow anyway. Some poor sap was nearly decapitated by a paper cut – worst one I ever seen. Yours just might give him a run for his money. I'd get that looked at in a hurry if I were you."

"Mongrel!"

They both turned and Mongrel caught a brief glimpse of Zeke at the top of the stairs before a flurry of arms and legs hug-attacked him, nearly taking him off his feet.

"I was so worried when I saw all the bodies," Summer said. "Couldn't find you anywhere."

"I'm okay," he said, trying to run his fingers through her hair but getting it stuck on the tape. "And you're okay too?"

Summer did a pirouette proudly and curtsied. She was almost completely covered in blood, as was Zeke, who thankfully had pants on now. Mongrel assumed Summer was responsible for that.

Eying the two patients suspiciously, Officer Switchblade was unsure of whether to arrest them or call an ambulance. He settled for neither, realizing that they'd be returned here instead of jail if they were convicted of anything, and hospitalization probably

---

[*] Harrow isn't a town, or even a village. It's just a house and a barn belonging to Brock Lily. Many years ago he had suffered a severe paper cut and was almost pronounced dead from it. He was resuscitated, but not before brain damage had settled in. Released on his own, extremely limited, recognisance, he tried to go back to a normal life. This did not go well. He'd adopted a bizarre Chinese accent, insisted on anything he ate be overcooked and/or burned, and tried to milk himself daily. His pregnant wife stayed with him long enough to give birth, then left him to raise their infant daughter by himself. He named the child Lillian and raised her to be retarded, like him. Years later Lillian was taken away by child protective services, leaving Brock alone. He became very lonely and began flagging down any passing car to say hello (or *harrow*, in his Chinese accent), and strike up any sort of conversation. Thusly, his house became known as the micro-district of Harrow.

Random Tangent

wasn't necessary since they were both walking under their own power. Plus, with all the bodies coming out the door the doctors and nurses had their hands full. "I'll give you two some time," he said, walking up the steps toward the main doors.

"Switchblade!" Mongrel called. The officer turned to look back. "The fire started in Dr. Rushkov's office. Third floor, room…" he struggled to recall.

"319," Summer finished.

Officer Switchblade nodded. "Guess that's where I'll start. Thanks." He then ventured inside, and as the door closed behind him they all heard him roar, "What the hell?"

Mongrel returned his attention to Summer. "So you're okay then? The minions didn't give you any trouble?"

She shook her head. "It was *so* much fun!" Her eyes lit up and she smiled like a child on Christmas morning.

It delighted Mongrel to see her so happy, but also disturbed him a little. "Where's Lloyd?" he asked. "Did you find him?"

Her smile faded and she bit her lip in thought. "I don't know. It was kinda chaos in there. He's gotta be around here somewhere; I didn't kill him. I mostly went after the doctors and nurses."

"We killed them all!" Zeke declared, hoping down the stairs.

Summer beamed and agreed. "All the staff. Every last one of them!"

"Did you get Rushkov too?" Mongrel asked, hopeful.

She glanced at Zeke, whose blank expression answered the question. "Guess not," she sighed. "Gotta get that bastard."

"Yeah," Mongrel said, turning to look out across the parking lot at the rest of Dunttstown. "Before he finds Beby."

With his back turned, Mongrel didn't see Summer hang her head, or the look of grim determination that brooded on her face. She'd forgotten about his girlfriend. But what could she do about it? Let Rushkov win?

Now there was an interesting idea.

"Well you're no good to her like this," she said. "You can't help her; you need proper rest. A good meal. A blood transfusion."

"I'll be fine."

Murder-Proof

"What about this?" she pointed to his bandaged hand. "Should get that looked at." Mongrel said nothing, weighing his options.

"I can get you a thumb," Zeke said. "Be right back." He was about to rush back into the hospital when Summer stopped him.

"Zeke! He needs his own thumb back."

"Right," Zeke said, contemplatively, "Cause if he gets somebody else's thumb it might try to kill him. And who knows, with all the whack jobs in this place, right?"

"It's probably too late now anyway," Mongrel said.

"Are you kidding me?" she scoffed. "Have you seen what medical science can do these days? They can turn men into woman, and dogs into cats. I heard they can even replace your heart with vegetables and they work just fine. There's a woman in here that's got one."

"Yeah," Zeke chimed in. "She's got a potato. But she has to keep microwaving it to keep it warm. She's annoying and smells like cabbages."

"See? Anything is possible. It's crazy!"

But Mongrel wasn't impressed. "My thumb is probably half-digested by now."

She giggled and took a step back from him, then reached down the front of her pants and pulled out a small object. It was a couple inches long, rounded, and caked with black crud. At first Mongrel thought it was a tampon, but then realised it was his missing thumb. A dozen questions ran through his head, but the only thing that came out of his mouth was a vague and confused grunt.

Summer knew what he was asking, and answered, "I told *them* I ate it, cause if they knew where it wa-"

"Oh cool!" Zeke said, running over. He tried to grab it from her hand, but she pulled it out of his reach. "So it came out already? What else you got in there?" He pulled at the waistband of her pants to peek inside.

She shoved him away. "See? That's why."

Mongrel smiled as he took his thumb from her. It had been in her pants the whole time. So *that's* what she'd meant by the third base remark; he'd been too busy being dismembered to pay much

Random Tangent

attention. Although still sour over the whole ordeal, he was impressed with her ingenuity. Even though Summer was weird, psychotic, and had thoroughly put him through the ringer, he couldn't help but like her. If things didn't work out with Beby...

"So maybe now you'll go to the hospital?" Summer asked. "Or at least take some *you* time? The rest can wait."

Mongrel gripped his thumb and remained silent. He really should get his thumb reattached while he had the chance. Besides, Valentin, with a head start, had no doubt already gotten to Beby. With any luck she'd killed him, and if not, Mongrel could win her back. He had proof now of the shrink's treachery. And if he had to, Mongrel could take him out. He'd taken on the screaming demon, countless minions, and even Captain Pete on numerous occasions; he was a force to be reckoned with. Valentin knew he was dangerous and had tried to kill him. But he failed. Maybe Mongrel really was murder-proof.

Summer sensed Mongrel relenting and kept the pressure on. "I know what it's like in there, what it can do to a person, even after only a couple days. It messes with you. So you need to unwind. Get it out of your system. So go home and rest up. Read the paper, water the plants and feed the animals – get back to your normal life is what I'm sayi-"

"Oh shit!" Mongrel cried. He'd forgotten about Wanker Jones, the dog he'd been watching for Captain Alphonse. Wanker only needed to be kept alive until he could be delivered to Charlie, but he was already on death's door, and now hadn't been fed in over two days. Although Mongrel had never seen the dog actually eat anything, the food in his dish kept slowly disappearing – unless that was the work of Bartimus, Mongrel's rat – and it kept breathing. Mongrel hoped that was still the case.

"What is it?" Summer asked.

He looked her in the eye and smiled, trying to calm himself. He didn't want her to know about his plans. "It's nothing. I mean, you're right. I should go home and rest." He began walking toward his car, fishing keys out of his pocket. Then he stopped and turned back to her. "Uh...did you want to come with me, I guess?"

Before Summer could smile and nod, Zeke yelled, "Shotgun!" and bounded after him like a dog excited for a car ride –

Murder-Proof

which was almost exactly what it was. He'd mistakenly assumed the offer was for them both.

"Wait!" Mongrel shouted, holding up his hand to stop Zeke. "Sorry, no. I, uh...just realized that I don't do that anymore, walk home with strangers and become friends and stuff. That's why I got the car. Really sorry."

Neither Zeke nor Summer could hide their disappointment.

"You guys should probably stay here anyway," Mongrel continued. "You know, so the doctors can take care of you."

"They're all dead," Zeke reminded him.

"Right." Hundreds of lunatics roaming around with no one in control? All the more reason to get the hell out of there. "Well I'd better get going. I'll see you guys later."

Summer rushed over and threw her arms around him. "Pick me up later. We'll go doc hunting." She kissed him deeply, savouring it like she might never see him again, and reluctantly released him.

Mongrel grinned at her and said, "It's a date."

Then Zeke tried to hug and kiss him as well. Mongrel threw him off and hopped into the safety his Santa Fe. He started it and pulled out of the parking lot, giving them a wave goodbye, and began plotting his next move.

Check on the dog. Go to the hospital to get his thumb reattached. Find Beby and kill Valentin. Good plan. All in a day's work. Mongrel smiled. A year ago a he would've been crazy to attempt a list of things like that. Back then he had trouble completing a grocery list. But he'd changed a lot in a short amount of time. Now he was a veteran at confrontation. Now he had woman ripping his clothes off and putting his hands down their pants – or at least parts of his hands. Now he felt every bit as murder-proof as Summer believed him to be.

And he was going to put that to the test.

The End

Random Tangent

Mongrel came home and put his thumb on ice, and found Wanker still alive, or at least semi alive. No change in his state, basically. His food was gone, so Mongrel topped it up, and refreshed his water. The dog's days were definitely numbered, and Mongrel had better get him to Charlie soon. He then got a good night's rest, intending to head to the hospital first thing in the morning. With no ruling body, the hospital patients began running amok. Summer and Zeke teamed up together and brought order the chaos. They declared themselves the King and Queen of their new society, and ruled oddly, yet justly. A county-wide manhunt for Pink Lloyd began after he disappeared, and after the body of a doctor was found in the men's bathroom that, according to a variety of sources, he killed. Valentin Rushkov tracked Beby down at her apartment and broke the sad news: Mongrel wasn't fit to spend any amount of time with her, and should be committed to psychiatric care before he hurts himself – which was too late, since he didn't survive the fire at the hospital (he was stricken with a severe case of diarrhea and refused to leave the bathroom for anything, including life-threatening flames – or so she was told). Mrs. Stevenson hadn't seen her husband, Steve, in months. He'd committed himself to the hospital after his wife had driven him crazy with her nagging (of course, she was told a different story). Steve had faked his own death, under the supervision of a couple psychiatrists, and went on a Caribbean vacation. He intended to come back eventually, while a cover story was provided to his wife in the meantime. Then Mongrel came along and unwittingly screwed all that up. Officer Switchblade walked into the hospital, saw the carnage and was immediately reminded of his days in the war – his war with obesity. He was a fat little kid. The janitor retired to his office and began to think up new ways to make horrible messes to clean up. Even though Captain Pete was declared dead at the scene, he was rushed to the hospital and declared dead a few more times just to be on the safe side. Oh, and he didn't actually kick the screaming demon to death, but missed. After all, the man did have a habit of not staying dead. Pink Lloyd's whereabouts remain a mystery to this day. Oh, and for the record, it was Mongrel who farted during breakfast.

Things That Separate Us From The Monkeys

She'd been born in captivity, a prisoner of a travelling carnival as well as her own vices; crack cocaine and giving handjobs. They say you can tell a lot about a man by how many dicks he's sucked. For example: if it's more than one, he's probably gay. Monkeys were no different. Any primate who'd spent any amount of time with her knew she was a lesbian, but with the fervour and regularity that she gave handjobs it was difficult to tell. She loved giving those handjobs. It wasn't merely a hobby, but a full-blown addiction, as was the cocaine. Often the two went hand-in-hand, if you'll excuse the pun. Give a handjob, get some drugs. It was give and get; tug and take. It was a simple system for a simple life. The system *was* a way of life for her now, as inescapable as the carnival itself. Actually, more so.

When PETA had stepped in and liberated all the circus animals and sent them to the Pok Semi-National Zoo, the drastic change was too much for her. She didn't know how to interact with other monkeys, how to become part of the pack, how to be civilized. And she didn't want to know. She didn't want to be clean and healthy; she wanted her old life. She didn't want to be wooed

Random Tangent

by other monkeys, she wanted to do crack and give handjobs. When a group of other monkeys at the zoo, tired of her ignoring their affections, drugged[*] and raped her, she still chose her addictions over the daughter that resulted from it. So she plotted her escape, and after her child was born, instead of becoming a mother, she fled. She caused an enormous amount of raucous, attacking everything that moved, including, but not limited to, a hot air balloon, and disappeared. The official press release said rabies was to be blamed for her violent outburst, and that'd she'd since been caught and put down, but this was a cover story. The truth was no one knew what had happened to her.

This was how Berthys came into the world. She knew little else about her mother, not even her name; just the stories. She knew all about abandonment and pain, but nothing about her lineage. Did her family have a history of illness? Was she predisposed to early onset arthritis? Would she ever develop a penchant for giving handjobs? Such thoughts haunted her.

Growing up in the zoo without her mother around was not without its complications. Sure, the other monkeys were nice to her, but these were the same monkeys that raped her mother, so she wanted nothing to do with them – even if one of them must have been her father. Berthys just wanted to live a life of solitude, which was difficult since hers was a social species. Eventually her tolerance ran dry and she strangled them all in their sleep with their own tails. This led to some much needed peace and quiet, at least until the morning, when her foul deeds were discovered.

But before anything could be done about her, she was suddenly, inexplicably on a tropical island, as if by magic. It would have been perfect had she been alone. But a human was there, and she seemed to understand that she belonged to him.

This was unacceptable – she was not property!

Although he seemed nice enough, perhaps even accepting of her demanding nature, she wasn't about to toss any amount of trust his way. He'd leave her sooner or later, like everyone who claimed to care for her. In fact he did once – although the circumstances were strange. She knew he'd do it again.

---

[*] More so than usual.

Things That Separate Us From The Monkeys
Humans were predictable like that.

Mongrel stood outside the Dunttstown Hospital, leery of venturing inside. Rarely did anything good ever come from visiting. He'd met many colourful people there, had one or two successful operations, and might have inadvertently caused a few lobotomies to be scheduled on unsuspecting patients. And while he firmly believed most of the doctors inside were competent (at least by Dunttstown standards), they'd just returned from a prolonged strike, so their skills could be rusty. Also, since they were being forced to return after negotiations fell through, he wouldn't doubt they'd intentionally put in a lacklustre effort on their jobs (again, by Dunttstown standards).

It had been almost a year since the doctors began striking over "more hours and less pay" according to the Dunttstown Gazelle[*]. Mongrel assumed it was the opposite, as the town newspaper was notorious for typos. Whatever the actual demands were, they fell on deaf, or rather ignorant ears; Dunttstown's beast mayor didn't understand any English, and the provincial government took up a whole "meh" approach to the situation. In the end the doctors caved. Most cited the Hippocratic Oath as being a plague on their consciences, but the likely story is that, having not worked for so long, they all needed the money. Assuming that was the case, it would be a safe bet that none of them were happy to be back and couldn't be counted on to perform their jobs with the care and dedication required.

All this is to say that Mongrel was apprehensive about having surgery. But there was nothing for it; the clock was ticking on the viability of his thumb, and he feared it may already be too

---

[*] Created by nearsighted journalist Edgar Ragde, the Gazelle was not a regular publication. Printed at least every fortnight – more often if enough news of noteworthy import was gathered – pages often had to be filled with user-submitted articles, updates on how much money the local bums were panhandling, and the occasional interview with a horse. Typos in most credible newspapers were addressed in the following issue, but since publication of the Gazelle was sporadic at best, typos were generally forgotten by the next printing. It is because of this that the name of the paper (originally supposed to be Gazette) was cemented.

late. His hand still throbbed painfully, which he took as a good sign, meaning there was no nerve damage.

Not only did it seem like yesterday but actually was, Mongrel had his thumb bitten off by a gorgeous young lady named Summer Spring. Over the course of a very strange few days at the Dunttstown Psychiatric Hospital he'd met, befriended, was tortured by and then fell into a somewhat romantic relationship with the vexing vixen. She had a lust for murder and upon learning Mongrel was incapable of being killed, decided to take up the challenge. Summer gave it her best shot, and when that failed, her pretend interest in him turned real. Mongrel couldn't help himself either; her beauty and charm were hard to resist. Although his heart still belonged to Beby, he was torn. For now, it was best to keep the women apart. There was no telling how Beby would react – probably try to kill him. And Summer had already tried, so…

But that was an issue for another day. One thing at a time, and right now that thing was his thumb.

Mongrel had called the hospital to see if they were really open and if any new protocol was to be followed, and was told he'd have to make at appointment to see the doctor, since their schedule was rather full now that they had finally returned to work. When Mongrel told the receptionist that he needed a finger reattached, she simply said, "Oh. Well I guess you can come whenever," and hung up. Mongrel dearly hoped he ran into her at the hospital so he could smack her. The woman needed a good smacking.

Steeling his nerves, Mongrel pushed into the building, and was greeted with the familiar smell of sterility. Surprisingly, it wasn't busy. The modest foyer housed a couple dozen seats – only two of which was filled by a large man – and a two-tiered desk at along the far wall. Sitting behind it was a woman with small, sharp bifocals and hair in a bun so tight it must have been cutting off circulation. She was uptight to the point that her sexual orientation was determined by her backbone rather than her preferences, and looking at another woman the wrong way could leave her paralyzed. It was actually the main reason she worked at the hospital.

"Welcome to Al-Musta Hospital, how may I help you?" she asked as Mongrel approached her.

Things That Separate Us From The Monkeys

"Were you the person I spoke to on the phone?"

She shrugged in response, so he had to forego his revenge; no need to kill the wrong person. "I need to see a doctor."

When Mongrel failed to elaborate she rolled her eyes and said, "Sorry. No doctors here. We're all sold out."

Mongrel nodded. "Right. I should've figured; can't trust what you read in the Gazelle. Pok is my best bet then?"

"That was sarcasm sir," the nurse sighed. "Obviously you need medical attention or you wouldn't be here. What I was really asking is what you need to see a doctor for? Perhaps I should write down 'doesn't understand sarcasm' or 'needs head examined,' in which case you're at the wrong hospital. If you keep heading dow-"

Mongrel tossed a plastic sandwich bag on the counter. Inside was a serving of ice and a human thumb. Curious and confused, the woman peered into the bag. Once she realized what was inside she immediately sat far back in her chair and began retching and gagging, alternating between the two.

"I require a doctor to reattach my thumb here," Mongrel said, casually showing her his right hand. Four fingers were not accompanied by their fellow thumb; his hand was neatly and politely bandaged, and as such wouldn't have made the same impression as a severed thumb, which was why he'd led with it. "Would you mind fetching me one?"

"Get that thing away from me," was all the nurse managed to say between dry heaves.

"What? This?" Mongrel shoved the bag a few inches closer.

She shrieked and shoved her chair back a couple noisy, scratchy inches. "Yes! Get it *away* from me!"

"Call me a doctor," Mongrel said again. "The power of the thumb compels you!"

"I'll scream," she cried.

"You're already doing that. Call me a doctor and I'll take it away."

"I'll call security and they'll take *you* away."

This gave Mongrel pause. Then he flicked the bag off the top of the desk, where it landed on the keyboard in front of her. She screamed again and shoved backwards so hard her chair toppled over. Scrambling to her feet, making various gagging sounds, she

Random Tangent

flung herself against the far wall. The large man in the waiting area briefly turned around to see what the commotion was, but quickly returned to his indifference.

Mongrel came around the side of the desk, grabbed his thumb bag, and placed it next to the phone. He then confidently leaned against the desk and crossed his arms at her. "Go ahead then, call security."

She glanced at the phone, then met his eyes. For a brief moment Mongrel felt like he was winning. Then the nurse screamed at the top of her lungs, "Security!"

Oh, thought Mongrel. Well that's the last time he called someone's bluff. It was not a good start to his hospital visit.

She called twice more before a uniformed man casually strolled into the foyer. It was Solvo. He'd been released from Duntt Penn. early for good behaviour (i.e.: not getting raped) the same week the doctor's strike ended. They'd called for a few good men for security, anticipating an onslaught of patients when the doors finally reopened. When no good men applied for the position, they relaxed their job requirements and hired Solvo, who'd only applied because he thought he'd be working with other 'good men.' Oh, and he needed a job; that also crossed his mind.

Mongrel had last seen him in prison a couple weeks ago, lonely and hoping for some male attention. He smiled and greeted his friend; they bro-fived and fist-hugged and high-bumped, catching up jovially.

"So now that you're on the outside I guess you can finally get a little company, right?" he nudged Solvo. "Of the female variety, I mean."

"Well," Solvo half-shrugged, "I'm not picky."

Recalling how Solvo had pined over the men in prison with him, Mongrel realized his friend wasn't just going with the flow on the inside; it was his preference. "Ah…then, the male variety."

Solvo performed the other half of his shrug. "I'm *really* not picky."

Not liking where this conversation was heading, Mongrel braced himself and reluctantly asked, "You don't mean children, do you?"

"What? No! I mean animals."

Things That Separate Us From The Monkeys

"Animals?" Mongrel cried.

"What? That's worse than children?" Solvo raised his eyes at Mongrel, who flopped his mouth around for a moment but never actually answered. Solvo took this as an agreement. "You know, you never did ask me why I was in prison."

"I'm not sure I want to know."

"They caught me with a goat…"

"Oh," Mongrel said dismally.

"…And a pig. And a duck."

Mongrel scrunched up his face in disgust. "Three separate offences? You didn't learn your lesson?"

"No, no; it was only one offence. We were having an orgy."

Lacking a response to such a shocking revelation, Mongrel simply goggled at him.

"I don't know why people get so upset over it," Solvo continued, ignorant of Mongrel's stupor. "It's not like I was hurting them; in fact they liked it – especially that duck."

"Hey!" the nurse interrupted. "I called security. And for the record, I'm a receptionist, not a nurse."

Solvo looked at her apathetically. "And here I am."

"I had to call *three times!*"

"Well you call for every little thing." He looked at Mongrel to explain. "She's very squeamish. Yesterday she called me because a patient farted on her."

"Ug!" she cried. "*So* disgusting! Took me three days to get that stink out of my clothes."

"Yeah, it was bad," Solvo chuckled. "I came, like, five minutes after it happened, and you could still smell it in the air."

"*Three* days?" Mongrel asked.

"Anyway," the nurse continued, "he's throwing body parts at me."

Solvo eyed Mongrel's crotch and asked, "Which parts?"

Mongrel grabbed his ice bag off the desk. "I need to get my thumb reattached before it's too late. It's already been a day. Nurse Squeamish over there won't help."

"*Receptionist* Squeamish," she corrected.

Random Tangent

"Ah," Solvo nodded, but couldn't get his mind off crotches. "I read once about this guy getting his junk cut off and they replaced it with his thumb."

The nurse gagged in the background at the thought, and Mongrel turned to her. "If your stomach is that weak, why'd you become a nurse?"

"I told you," she gasped between dry heaves, "I'm not a nurse; I'm a receptionist." Then she took off down a hallway, presumably to a bathroom.

"Well she sure picked a good place to…reception at." Mongrel shrugged and turned back to Solvo. "Anyway, I don't need a new penis or a new thumb. I got a good one right here. And besides, a thumb down there would be severely trading down."

"It'd be trading up if you had nothing."

Mongrel didn't feel like talking about what a good point that was, and before he had a chance to change the subject, someone beat him to it.

Into the room huffed a scruffy, haggard, man who looked like he hadn't slept in a couple of days. With dopey eyes and sluggish feet, he'd probably fallen asleep a few times on the run down the various halls that led to the foyer, and thus was late to the party.

"Hey you! Stop!" he shouted at Mongrel.

Throwing his hands in the air out of instinct, Mongrel looked supremely guilty. His ice bag hung in the air, dripping condensation on the floor.

The man eyed it suspiciously before saying to Solvo, "Sorry I was so long. Bad diarrhea. Drinking too much coffee."

"No worries," Solvo replied. "I got everything under control here. He's cool." He gestured toward Mongrel

"I'll be the judge of that," the guard said. "What's in the bag?"

"Um, it's my th-"

"Quiet you!" the guard shouted at him. "Now drop the bag."

Mongrel looked over at Solvo, who shrugged and said, "Just do it. He's had a long shift; it started last week."

"Drop the bag," the guard said again, "Or I'll shoot."

Things That Separate Us From The Monkeys

Quickly looking the man over, Mongrel couldn't see any gun. "With what?" he asked.

The guard shook his head and walked over to Mongrel, snatched the bag out of his hand. "You people just don't seem to get it, do you?" He eyed the bag again, trying to decide if it was a bomb. It looked like a finger inside, but he'd seen enough finger bombs in his day and couldn't afford to take any chances. "You have no idea what kind of nut jobs are out there. People blowing up hospitals; people trying to make human centipedes; people who enjoy trigonometry. It takes a diligent man with a firm grasp on the intangibles to understand what's going on around here."

"What? Look, that's just a thumb, okay?"

"I said be quiet!" He inspected the contents of the bag thoroughly and glanced at Mongrel's hand. "Pretty sad looking thumb if you ask me. And it's yours?"

"Well yeah? Who else's woul-"

"Shut!" the guard yelled. "And up! Both of them! In whatever order you want! Just shut up!"

"Can I at least nod, then?"

The guard stroked his chin, contemplating this. Finally he said, "No."

"Dude," Solvo cut in, "I already checked him over. He's cool."

"That's what he wants you to think," the guard sneered. "Look, you're new around here, so you don't know how dangerous it can get."

"We started the same day," Solve said.

"Don't you remember the Egyptians?" he asked suddenly. "Buried pharaohs by the dozens and erected giant…monuments or something."

"Pyramids?" Mongrel suggested.

"Yes, thank you. And stop talking. Anyway, they were around thousands of years ago – oh yeah – and I'm on to them. Just like I'm on to you." He pointed at Mongrel menacingly. "You and your thumb bombs."

"What?" Mongrel cried. "I don't even know how to make a bomb! And what do the pyramids have to do with anything?"

Random Tangent

Holding up three fingers and looking extremely annoyed, he said, "One: I don't know but how could they *not* be involved? Two: why do you keep talking? And three: where's Heather?"

"The secretary?" Solvo asked. "She ran off to puke somewhere"

The guard looked flustered. "That's the third time today. Better not be in the soup this time." He tossed Mongrel his bag and ran after her. "And she's a receptionist!" he called before leaving the room.

"Well that takes care of him," Solvo said, dusting off his hands as if they were dirty.

Mongrel inspected his thumb, worried damage may have been caused. When he felt it was no worse than before, he muttered his thanks. "Thought he'd never let me go."

"He was just doing his job."

"Well he takes his job way too seriously."

Solvo wasn't so sure. "Just last week a liver came into the hospital at Pok, and it was a bomb."

"Really?" Mongrel was shocked. "How many people were killed?"

"None. It was a dud. People are suspecting it was Hopeless Homer[1*]; it's got his name all over it."

"Who's Hopeless Homer?"

"I don't know. I read it in the paper. Anyway, we should probably get that thing looked at. I'll take you to the doc." Solvo led Mongrel through a set of double doors and down a few hallways. Nurses and patients were flying all over the place – in some cases literally. Solvo had to stop and hold Mongrel back as a little girl was tossed in front of him from one nurse to another.

"They think she has leprosy," Solvo explained. "No one wants to touch her."

---

* Hopeless Homer was actually Ferdinand Homer LeShank– whose name is so unsightly people chose not to use it. An older, gangly man with ADD, he was not what his namesake suggested. Homer was once married to a woman named Hope, who sadly passed away, leaving him a widower. Hope had kept him occupied well into his retirement, but now what she was gone he had to entertain himself, which often led to trouble. He ran amok in Pok, usually being more of an annoyance than anything.

Things That Separate Us From The Monkeys

"So why not leave her in the bed and push her around in that?" Mongrel suggested.

"Budget cut backs. Not enough beds to go around."

"Okay then, use some rubber gloves when they take her around the hospital?"

"They don't want her to touch the floor. Leprosy spreads like crazy, dude."

"Don't they have a janitor to clean up after her? Like that guy." Mongrel pointed to a man in overalls leaning against a mop, playing on his phone.

"That's the doctor," Solvo muttered, making his way over to him.

Mongrel followed, confused and a bit frightened; I mean, were they letting the janitor perform surgery now? How bad were these cutbacks?

"Ed?" Solvo said, verbally prodding the man away from his phone. "Got one for you." He gestured to Mongrel, who meekly stood behind him like he was trying to hide.

A child's voice answered. "Aww man, I'm on break. Can it wait ten minutes?"

"Yeah, probably, but I'm not a doctor so what do I know?"

The voice continued, "Fine! What is it?" It sounded like it was coming from a boy, maybe eight or ten years old, who should still be in school.

Looking around for a talking kid and not finding any, Mongrel grew more confused by the second. Was this a practiced routine? The janitor was doing remarkable lip-syncing job. Maybe it was an app on his phone?

Solvo grabbed the bag out of Mongrel's hand and gave it to the janitor. "He needs this thumb reattached."

Ed opened the bad and withdrew Mongrel's thumb. He pulled out a jewellers eyeglass and inspected it, frowning occasionally. He sniffed it once, producing a repugnant face. He even went so far as to lick it, then appeared nauseated.

Returning the thumb to its bag of ice, the janitor got down on one knee and began unwrapping Mongrel's hand. Once the

Random Tangent

bandages and slice of pickle* were removed and the stump exposed he began doing the same things; inspecting, sniffing, licking. Finally he frowned in an epic facial sonnet of solemnity. "Well on the bright side, it doesn't look good."

While Mongrel desperately wanted to ask what the down side was, he instead said, "It's you!" as he realized the child's voice was indeed coming from the janitor.

"What? You recognize me? Actually, you look familiar too. Have I seen you on TV before, maybe in the news recently for blowing something up?"

"What? No, that wasn't me. That was Hopeless Homer...I think."

"Yeah, that's what they think," Solvo agreed.

"The only thing I've ever blown up was myself."

Ed snapped his fingers. "That's it! You blew up! You came in a year or two ago in a hundred pieces. Blew up on an airplane I think? I put you back together."

"That was you?" Mongrel asked.

"Yep. Hardest surgery I ever performed. Took nearly thirty hours. Won a Nobel prize for it too."

"Huh, cool. I didn't know they gave Nobel prizes for that."

"Me either. Sorry I didn't recognize you. Guess I'm not used to seeing you in one piece. And now that I can speak I can introduce myself. I'm Dr. Fredward Lunabell." He offered Mongrel his hand.

Mongrel shook it, which was awkward without a thumb. "Mongrel Stevens. You go by Ed?"

He nodded enthusiastically. "Too many Fred's in this town."

"You got that right," Mongrel agreed. "Can't keep track of them all. Anyway I didn't recognize you with that voice. So you're not mute anymore? Or a doctor? How bad are these cutbacks?"

"The cutbacks have been pretty severe but I haven't taken a demotion; I'm just pulling double duty. Stitch someone's arm up, clean up a pile of puke; check on some patients, empty some garbage bins; fill out some paperwork, take my hourly dump."

---

* It was an old family remedy.

Things That Separate Us From The Monkeys

At the mention of the last item Mongrel became curious in spite of himself, but before he could ask, Ed continued.

"That last one's for me; not really one of my duties. Well, it *is* a duty, it's just..." he trailed off, laugh mildly. "Well, you know. Anyway, I have a short bowel which makes for frequent movements. It's not permanent, it's still growing. Most of me is, in fact. I have a rare form of Russell-Silver Syndrome. It's a growth disorder; things come in really slow for me. I *did* used to be mute, until my vocal cords started coming in while we were on strike. That's why I sound like a kid."

"Still waiting for the other testicle to drop?" Solvo said with a chuckle. It was meant as a joke but was actually true.

"Yep," Ed said. "Can't taste spicy food yet or see all the colours of the rainbow. But I'll get there."

"Which colours are you missing?" Mongrel asked.

"Yellow, apparently." Ed looked around the room, finally spotting a vase of flowers. He pointed at them. "Like that?"

"Yeah, that's yellow," Mongrel confirmed. "How can you tell?"

"They look gray to me. Flowers ain't supposed to be gray are they?"

Mongrel concurred. "So anyway, what's up with my thumb? Attaching it should be a piece of cake compared to last time."

Ed looked at the thumb again. "Well like I said, the good news isn't very bright. Or...wait, is that what I said?"

"Just tell me if my thumb can be put back on?" Mongrel said, still worrying what the bad news was.

All he got in reply was, "It's iffy."

"Iffy? Last time you put me together when I was in a million pieces. This time it's just two."

"Well last time you were fresh." Ed looked at the thumb again. "And you had this on ice whole time? See, it's not supposed to be directly on the ice; causes nerve damage. It's probably useless now."

"But I had a pickle on it."

"Look, I could reattach it but I don't think you'd ever feel anything with it again. It's possible but unlikely."

Random Tangent

"Well..." Mongrel gave this some thought, "as long as it's on there and looks normal, right? And I wouldn't feel any pain either? So if I'm hammering nails and hit my thumb...?"

"You wouldn't feel *anything*," the doctor stressed. "As in, like, if you pick up the hammer you wouldn't know you were holding it. You'd have no tactile feedback whatsoever."

This gave Mongrel much to think about.

"So," Solvo interjected, "he could have his thumb up someone's ass and not even know it?"

"That's right."

"That's *wrong*," Mongrel argued. "I would notice that."

The doctor removed a notepad from his pocket and began scribbling down something. "There's a guy who's better at this sort of thing than me. If anyone can make your monkey paw normal again, it's him."

"Monkey paw?"

"Monkeys don't have opposable thumbs on their hands."

"They do on their feet don't they?"

"Well if you want that, this guy could do it for you." He handed Mongrel a piece of paper. "His name is Figment Jones."

"Figment?"

"It's the only name I got for him," said the doctor, offering what he thought was his best sympathetic smile of the day – and he'd been keeping stats. "He does things that are not strictly legal. Or possible. He wants to remain off the grid of reality or something."

"Sounds like my kind of guy," Mongrel muttered, reading the note. "This is in Pok?"

"Yep. Handy, eh?"

About to argue over what he considered handy, Mongrel caught himself. The only other person he knew willing and capable of performing miracles of the human anatomy was Bosley, and he was on another continent. Compared to that, Pok was a much more reasonable hour away.

As the closest metropolitan area to Dunttstown, Pok had a far better hospital, a half-decent zoo, and access to fresh water. Aside from all that, it was known for pretty much nothing. Mongrel had been there a few times in his life, but never felt it offered him

Things That Separate Us From The Monkeys

anything better than his home town, with the exception of decent food and better prostitutes – both things he had learned to live without.

"How am I going to get to Pok with my thumb like this?" Mongrel asked. "You said it's not fresh enough already, and another hour in the heat won't help."

Ed smiled. "Leave that to me." He led them away from the intensive care ward and down a series of less populated hallways. They came to a door with a biohazard logo on it. Ed held out a hand for them to remain where they were, while he went inside. "I'll be a few minutes."

While they were waiting for him to return a scream echoed through the hallways.

"You gonna check that out?" Mongrel asked Solvo.

"Maybe later," he replied. Sounds like Heather again. Can't be that important. Besides, Cranklin's around."

"Cranklin?"

"The guard who gave you a hard time? Cranky Frank."

"Well I'll be damned," wheezed a voice in their direction.

Turning to find a man in a wheelchair, wrapped pretty tightly from head to toe in bandages, Mongrel said, "I'm sorry to hear that."

The man chuckled, then cringed in pain, and finally coughed a little. "Don't recognize me, do you?"

Mongrel glanced at Solvo before replying, "No, *we* do not recog-"

"Well I'll be damned," Solvo suddenly said.

"What?" Mongrel asked. "You too? Am I the only one hoping to go to Heaven?"

The man in the wheelchair rolled over and fist-bumped Solvo. "Shit man, when'd you get out?"

"About a week ago."

"And you got yo'self a job already? That's tight!"

"How long have you been here?" Solvo asked. "I haven't seen you before."

"Man I just woke up this mornin'. Been in a bed in the corner over there for a while. They just let me out of an induced coma, on account of all the burns. Hurts like hell without morphine.

Random Tangent

Third degree here, second degree there. Shit, I ain't got no hair left on me." He then looked Mongrel up and down, his eyes taking on a malevolent aura. "And I see you're still standing. Almost didn't recognize you with that face. Man, you is ugly! I shined you up real nice!"

"Do I know you?" Mongrel asked, gingerly feeling his nose, which had been broken a week ago. And if this man was claiming to be the one who'd broken it... Things began to click into place for Mongrel. While the man was cocooned in gauze and unidentifiable, the voice was frighteningly familiar, and the attitude unmistaken. The man was Brecklyn – the raping, murdering, ex-convict.

"This is Brecklyn," Solvo said. "Remember him?"

Oh yes, Mongrel remembered him. He remembered the man trying to rape and torture him in prison. He remembered the man somehow getting out of Duntt Penn. and becoming a business partner with Mongrel's nemesis, Captain Pete. He remembered the man breaking his nose in a savage assault. And lastly, Mongrel remembered the horrible things he had to do with the man just to survive the whole ordeal.

"From prison?" Solvo continued.

Wait, Captain Pete was his *nemesis*? Is that what the pirate was to him now? Was this a freaking comic book? Was Pete the Joker to his Batman? If only, thought Mongrel. To be Batman: a genius detective, able to kick ass and take names, and have all the cool gadgets and sexy women. Oh, and also be a billionaire? But alas, he was just plain old Mongrel Stevens, who was barely worth being abused.

"He tried to rape you?"

"Yes, Solvo, I get it. Thank you." Mongrel blinked hard and tried to compose himself.

Brecklyn suddenly jerked back in disgust. "Aw shit! What happened to yo hand? That is *nasty!* Hope it hurt like a bitch."

Mongrel released his nose and hid his hand behind his back, but said nothing.

Brecklyn flashed a grin at Mongrel, pleased that he could still inflict any form of abuse. "So how'd a delicate flower like you end up with hand like that?"

Mongrel sulked, "I am not a delicate flower."

Things That Separate Us From The Monkeys

Leaning forward in his wheelchair, Brecklyn smirked as much as he could without causing himself discomfort. "Yeah we'll see 'bout that. Once I'm outta here Ima find you, crush you like a daisy under my feet. See how delicate you is then."

Not liking the sound of more impending death, Mongrel shuffled himself behind Solvo.

"Aww, you scared?" Brecklyn taunted.

"What are you doing?" Solvo asked, stepping aside. "You can't just run and hide, dude."

"Well I don't feel like being mauled right now, okay? I came to the hospital to get help, not murdered."

"But we're on neutral ground."

This meant nothing to Mongrel. "So?"

"I ain't gonna hurt you in no hospital, man," Brecklyn said. "That shit ain't right. Also, you know, cause o' all this." He gestured to his whole body. "I'm all whack right now, see? But when I get better Ima come for you."

"See?" Solvo said. "You're safe here."

"But didn't you hear him? He's gonna try to kill me later."

"Better later than now."

Mongrel produced his most bewildered expression and gave it angrily – some might even say with murderous intent – to Solvo, which would be a faux-pas since they were in a murder-free[*] zone. "How the hell is that better?"

"You want to die now instead?"

While the look on Mongrel's face didn't change, its connotations did. The man had a point. *Again.* "Well…what about later?"

Solvo shrugged. "What about later?"

Putting his head in his hands in frustration, Mongrel screamed silently to himself. "He's gonna kill me later, you goat-fucker! Don't you even care?"

"Of course I care." Solvo looked a little hurt, but confusion leaked unchecked into his grimace. "But if you're trying to get me to do something about it, I'm not. This is your beef. Got nothing to do with me, so don't drag me into it."

---

[*] With the exclusion of medical staff.

Random Tangent

He should have figured he was on his own. He was always on his own, left to find his own way out of his life-threatening battles. Well, except for the last time he was about to be killed by Brecklyn, when Captain Alphonse intervened. And Big John had helped him on numerous occasions. And that one time Jason Miles showed up from out of nowhere and took care of that whole gang of Englishmen. Oh, and just yesterday when Zeke gave him mouth-to-mouth. Officer Switchblade had helped him, and Loafmeat, and even Captain Pete had helped him too, though he wasn't really trying to. That counts, right? Then there was the mon…

Putting his hand on Mongrel's shoulder, Solvo continued. "You gotta face your own fears and demons man. You can't run away. You gotta have honour."

"I faced my own screaming demon yesterday," Mongrel said dismally.

"This asshole ain't got no honour," Brecklyn said. "Last time we met, the whole time he was coming on to me, smooth as hell."

Solvo took a step away from Mongrel and glared at him, a wounded look in his eyes. "What?"

"Aw yeah. He just begged me to make him my bitch. Gyratin' his hips at me."

"That's not what happened!" Mongrel cried.

"Is that true?" Solvo asked.

Breathing heavily, anger and denial fighting for dominance in his lower intestine, Mongrel felt his world unravelling. Why his lower intestine? Beats me. "Yes, I did that. But it's so I could escape."

"Don't listen to 'im!"

They all turned to see Captain Pete hobble into the room. Jaws dropped, eyes goggled, and nostrils flared. The pirate was wearing a doctor's coat, trailing two feet behind him, obviously made for someone of regular height. He also had an eye patch over his left eye and a hook where his left hand should have been. But he appeared no worse for wear, and actually happier to be there than anyone else.

Mongrel was the first to speak. "Isn't it a little early in the story for you to be showing up?"

Things That Separate Us From The Monkeys

"Who is that?" Solvo asked.

Brecklyn, however, was speechless. The last time he'd seen his friend he'd been squished into a motor home with a van driven by Mongrel. How he was alive and walking was beyond him, beyond modern medicine, and beyond science fiction. It was, in a word, a miracle.

"He's a thievin' dog, a traitorous scamp, and a brazen whore," Captain Pete continued, a smirk on his face, only too pleased to be stirring the proverbial shit pot. "All I wants is to have me way with the lad'n'meanwhile he's eyein' me partner 'ere," he pointed to Brecklyn, "flirtin' all o'er the place."

"What are you doing?" Mongrel said. "You're not helping."

"So?" the captain spouted. "You 'spect me to help? I's enjoying exacerbatin' the situation."

"Exacers gonna exacerbate," came a hoarse voice down the hall.

A chill went down Mongrel's spine, and the hair stood up on the back of his neck. "Did anyone else hear that?"

"So you and him are a couple?" Solvo asked, gesturing between Captain Pete and Brecklyn.

The question confused the old pirate. "A couple o' what?"

"You know, partners."

"Well course we's partners. I's just said so."

As amusing as Mongrel found this conversation, he felt compelled to explain. "He means *sexual* partners."

"*What?*" Captain Pete snapped.

Solvo nodded. "You said you two were partners. I thought you mea-"

"Now you get this good'n'well understood," the pirate said very sternly. "I ain't not in no way affiliated with no homo man-sex business. You got me?"

"Affil's gonna affiliate," came that voice again, closer this time. Mongrel looked around frantically but saw nothing alarming.

"I have no idea what you just said," Solvo said, although if he had more time he could've figured it out.

"Pete?" Brecklyn finally said. "You're *alive*?"

"What? Course I's alive. I ain't one o' them walkers from the war."

Random Tangent

"But I saw you get crushed, man."

"Bah!" Captain Pete spouted. "Crushed, maimed, shot, stabbed. Nothin' stops ol' Captain Pete!"

"You can't kill him," Mongrel agreed, tearing himself away from his surveillance of the room. "No matter what you do."

"Oh I dies plenty. Spend half me days dead cause o' you."

"Oh blah, blah, blah." Mongrel had heard this all before.

Solvo was more confused that ever. "What are you guys talking about? How can he be dead?"

"Ask this fella 'ere," Captain Pete pointed at Mongrel. "Kills me every chance he gets."

"So…" Brecklyn postulated, "you die and get reborn all the time?"

"Tis about this size of it."

Brecklyn slowly began to understand. The captain was more than just a remarkable pirate; he was a remarkable man. No: he was a remarkable *being*. A being beyond the struggles of life and death, beyond the comprehension of mere mortals.

"So, you're not a doctor?" asked Solvo, still trying to come to grips with the situation.

"I was wondering about that," Mongrel chimed in. "What's with the getup? You got a hook now?"

"Arr!" the old pirate arred. "Came with the costume." He promptly removed the hook and eye patch. He left on the smock; it made him feel good, like a successful man. Several nurses had even hailed him to sign documents and look at charts, seeking guidance and approval. It was a dramatic departure from the life of a pirate, feeling needed and responsible. He had no idea what he was doing and more than likely had someone lobotomized, but it felt great.

After watching Captain Pete remove the articles of clothing, Brecklyn became concerned. "What about yo legs?"

Looking down at his wooden stumps, the captain replied, "What about 'em?"

A horrified look came across Brecklyn's face. "You mean they ain't part of the costume? Those is *real*? They took *yo legs*?"

The captain looked down at his pegs. "What the bloody hell is you talkin' 'bout? I always didna have me legs."

Things That Separate Us From The Monkeys

"Yeah, it's true," Mongrel agreed. "A washing machine or something took them years ago."

"Heh," Captain Pete mumbled. "That's what the washing machine thinks."

"Machine's gonna machinate"

Mongrel jerked his in the direction the voice, tossing his attention down the hallway to see where it would land. "Seriously, does anyone else hear that?"

Brecklyn looked long and hard at the captain's lower half. "An offering, weren't they? A sacrifice, for your people."

Captain Pete looked at Brecklyn like he was crazy and gauged what the best response was. In the end, he decided on ignorance, instead turning his attention to Mongrel. "Enough chit chattin', boy. You know why I's here."

Mongrel looked at him. "To finish what you started?"

"Darn right." He produced a couple medical instruments from his pockets; a scalpel and tongue depressor. The pirate examined the wooden stick closely, questioningly, before tossing it aside. Smiling evilly, he approached Mongrel, hoping it would be for the last time.

"Okay, um, no, that's not what I meant," Mongrel said, slowly retreating. "I was talking about the demon. You haven't finished it off."

"What demon?" the captain asked, still closing in, backing Mongrel into a corner.

"Demons gonna demonstrate."

"*That* demon!"

But Captain Pete wasn't listening. Words only distracted him, which is strange because he then asked, "Any last words?"

Mongrel pressed up against the wall and looked at Solvo, who was courageously minding his own business, staying out of the way and staying alive. He was a big help to Mongrel in Duntt Penn., but outside, in the real world, he was useless. Although he did mention that one thing…

"Yes!" Mongrel cried as Pete was about to attack. "Neutral zone! This is a neutral zone."

The captain paused mid-pounce. "What the devil is a neutral zone?"

Random Tangent

"You can't kill me here," Mongrel said, almost proud.

"Can to."

"Nope."

I can'n'I wills. You just watch me!"

"Yo, Pete, Captain," Brecklyn interjected, wheeling himself over. "I mean, your Grace, or whatever. This here a hospital, see? Now I ain't one to mess with what you, you know…decree, but it just ain't right to be killin' people in a hospital, man. Much love though. Love and respect." He then bowed down in his wheelchair.

Before Captain Pete could lose his little pirate mind over whatever the hell that was about, Solvo spoke up. "Hospital's are neutral ground. This is a place of healing."

"Oh really?" Pete asked mockingly. He gestured to Mongrel and said, "Well last time we's here he killed me."

This upset Brecklyn so much he stood, pointed a finger at Mongrel, and yelled, "Blasphemer!"

A nurse suddenly rushed over and shushed Brecklyn back into his chair. She was ancient, oriental, and had a Jamaican accent. "Hush now child. Dis too much excitement for one day. Let mama Ali take ya back to bed now." She began pushing him away down the hall. "Ali's gonna alleviate."

Mongrel glared after her, leery. "What did she say? Did anyone catch that?"

"Is it true?" Solvo asked, dragging Mongrel back to the conversation. "Did you kill him in the hospital before?"

"What? Okay, *no!* That is *not* what happened. It was Greg. I mean Death. You know, the Grim Reaper?"

"Always the fault o' someones else." Captain Pete shook his head. "I comes 'ere to get me 'ppendix out. Then you shows up, tells me you gots news. Next thing I knows I's being dragged off by a man in a cloak. Now what'd you make o' that?"

"Yeah but I didn't *do* it," Mongrel pleaded. "Greg did. The man in the cloak."

"Actually," interrupted a child's voice. "I believe he died from post-op complications."

They all turned to see Dr. Lunabell standing a few feet away, holding a red and white box. He'd snuck up on them while they were arguing.

Things That Separate Us From The Monkeys

"What in the who?" Captain Pete exclaimed, clearly not expecting that voice to come from an adult.

"I believe I was on call that night, and I had to pronounce you dead."

"If you pronounced him dead," Solvo asked, "then how is he alive right now?"

Ed shrugged. "Maybe I'm just bad at pronouncing people." He pointed to a man standing at the end of the hall. "I pronounced him last night and he's up and walking."

They all looked to see a man slowly shuffling his way towards them like a zombie. Mongrel alone recognized him as the screaming demon, although his name was apparently Dominic. He had made Mongrel's life difficult, and at times endangered over the course of his brief visit to the Dunttstown Psychiatric Hospital. He was also supposed to be dead following a furious pegged assault from a certain pegged captain.

Mongrel turned to Captain Pete and stuck out his tongue. "Looks like someone's getting a little sloppy in his old age."

"What's that s'posed to mean?" the pirate asked, taking instant offense. He didn't consider himself old or sloppy, and certainly not little. If anything his height issue was nothing more than an optical illusion, one that he projected so his enemies would underestimate him.

"I'm saying you just can't kill things anymore."

"I kills people all the time. Plenty good at it."

"Well you can't seem to kill me."

The captain's eyes grew cold and menacing. "You watch wh-"

"And what about him?" Mongrel interrupted, not interested in whatever threat was going to fly out of Captain Pete's mouth. "Didn't you kick him to death yesterday?"

The captain looked, his face a pile of pirate scrutiny. "I canna tell. Could be one of 'em. Kicked me share of people to death."

"Senators gonna senate," the zombie said, lurching toward them.

"Oh, right," Captain Pete muttered. "I remembers him now."

Random Tangent

"And if I'm not mistaken," Mongrel continued, "you kicked the mayor to death last year. Didn't you?" Noticing the horrid expressions on his cohorts' faces, he added, to stem the brewing turmoil, "This was before he became mayor."

Captain Pete nodded, recalling the day at the Grand High Palace of Them. "Aye. Gave him a right good kicking I did."

"But you didn't kick him to *death*; otherwise he wouldn't be mayor right now."

"Consumers gonna consummate," moaned the screaming demon, still trying to threaten everyone but coming off as merely annoying.

"You already did that one!" Mongrel yelled, wary of the oncoming danger yet ignoring it anyhow. Back to Pete: "You can't just go around kicking people to death, Captain. Literally, you can't. First: you don't have any feet; and second: you keep *missing*. You can't kick someone to death if they don't die. Don't you have any other pirate tricks? Guns? Walking the plank? Strangling? Hell, even beat them with your bare hands – that's what they're there for. It's what separates us from the monkeys!"

"I thought it was the tail," Solvo cut in.

"Nay! Tis the upright walkin' thing."

"Actually," Ed said, "We have an area in our frontal cortex that's not presen-"

"Designs gonna designate," roared the screaming demon as he attacked. Of course, when I say attacked, I didn't mean he attacked everyone; just Mongrel, who stood his ground, arguing bravely in the face of jeopardy. Dominic leaned into him with snapping teeth and clawing fingers. Mongrel, down a digit himself, was at a disadvantage, and couldn't fight him off. Together they tumbled to the floor, the screaming demon on top, biting and drooling in Mongrel's face.

Everyone else ambled out of the way, realizing the beef was between Mongrel and the new, creepy patient. Solvo did his best to warn him about them being in a neutral zone, but went unheeded. Ed wandered off, presumably to attend to other business.

Mongrel rolled around on the floor with his enemy, avoiding injury mostly by accident. "A little help here?"

Things That Separate Us From The Monkeys

Captain Pete took this as an invitation to join in. He waited until the screaming demon had wrestled Mongrel onto his back, then sat down on top of them, squishing them both and grinding Mongrel further into the floor. He failed to stifle a laugh.

"Hey!" Mongrel wheezed. "Get off! I asked for help. Do something!" He should've known better than to accost the pirate; it was obvious whose side he was on. While he didn't believe this whole no-murder-in-the-hospital policy, if someone else was going to do most the work he was happy to offer a little assistance.

"I's doin' somethin'," the good captain said, giggling like a schoolgirl.

"Well do something else!"

With an amused chuckle, Captain Pete got off the dog pile. Walking around the struggling men, be began to kick at Mongrel wherever he could find a good opening. Laughing and kicking, kicking and laughing; it was a gay old time!

"What the hell?" Mongrel cried. Trying to fend of teeth, claws, and wooden feet was a losing battle. Something was going to get through, and it was the pegs of a wily pirate. "Stop it!"

As the captain was doing his best to ignore Mongrel's protests, Dr. Lunabell came back and plunged a syringe into the screaming demon's neck. After a few seconds, his jaws snapped shut one final time and he went limp. Captain Pete was noticeably upset, but said nothing.

Mongrel wiggled himself free and lay prone for a few minutes, relief flooding him. "Thanks," he wheezed out. "What'd you do?"

"Tranquilizer," Ed replied, helping Mongrel up off the floor. Then turned to Solvo and said, "Care to explain why you didn't intervene?"

Solvo shrugged. "I don't like zombies. Like, what if I got bitten? Then I'd become one of them. That's how the zombie apocalypse starts. You should be thanking me, really, for putting my own life before everyone else's."

"That guy look like a zombie to you?" Ed asked.

"Well, yeah. Zombies look just like us."

Ed looked at the man on the floor. "And zombies sleep too?"

Random Tangent

"Um...oh."

"Yeah, *oh.*"

"Them Walkers slept," Captain Pete said. "Not yer typical zombies, aye, but they'd do in a pinch. Back in the war, this was, long 'for all this was 'ere."

"What war?" Mongrel asked.

"The War of the Restless. Couple centuries bac-"

Captain Pete trailed off, wary now of the needle in his neck. He threw a disgruntled grimace at Ed, who was holding the syringe, before his pegs gave out and he collapsed.

Mongrel tossed the doctor a grimace of his own. "What'd you do that for?"

"Don't worry; it won't hurt him. But he was yakking too much. You need to get a move on. Figment Jones is waiting for you and your time is running out."

Begrudgingly accepting that Ed was right, Mongrel didn't argue. One of these days he'd get the truth out of his old friend. The pirate had many secrets and Mongrel was sure there was something, some reason for his misfortunes and miraculous rebirths hidden in his past.

"This is an organ donor kit." Dr. Lunabell said, holding up a white box. "You thumb is inside, and should be good for a couple hours. Maybe less, considering the heat. You have plenty of time to get to Pok, but I wouldn't dawdle."

After a couple failed attempts to grab the container with his right hand, and feeling like a primitive primate, he seized it with his left hand instead. "I feel like I'm no better than a monkey," he mumbled dismally.

"Actually I think a monkey wouldn't have had as much trouble with that," Ed said.

"Yeah, yeah," Mongrel muttered. "Let's see how *you* manage without a thumb."

"How did that happen anyway?" Solvo asked. "Looks pretty nasty."

"It was bitten off by a woman at the psychiatric hospital."

Both men looked some combination of horrified and impressed. Ed asked, "How'd you get it back? Are you sure that one's even yours?"

Things That Separate Us From The Monkeys

"Of course it's mine," Mongrel snapped. "It's not like there's thumbs laying around all over the place over there."

"Maybe we should have a look at it here?" Solvo suggested. "Couldn't hurt, right?"

Ed nodded in agreement. "We could at least treat it; make sure infection hasn't set in. The human mouth is a vile place, full of bacteria."

Despite all that being true, Mongrel was apprehensive about letting someone with the voice of a child do…medical stuff to him. He strongly preferred the doctor when he was mute. Besides, he knew how easily it was to get lobotomized at the hospital, and felt it was best not to push his luck.

"I think I'll be fine. I mean, my thumb is only good for so long, right? I really should get going to Pok if I want it put back on. Time is of the essence."

Ordinarily the doctor would have objected, but indeed time was not on Mongrel's side. "Yes, I suppose that is for the best."

He ushered Mongrel back toward the main entrance, stopping briefly to sign some medical forms and unstop the occasional toilet. He stopped at the main foyer. "I'm not supposed to go near Heather. My voice makes her sick or something. She's even threatened to get a restraining order on me."

"Is there anything that doesn't make her sick?" Mongrel asked rhetorically. "She should be fired and replaced."

"Yeah," Ed whispered conspiratorially. "This place would be totally better without her. Maybe we can make her quit?" He thought for a second and said, "Okay, I'll go distract her while you sneak up behind her and do something disgusting."

Without waiting for Mongrel to respectfully decline the chance for shenanigans, Ed took off across the room toward her and appeared to strike up a conversation. After a moment, Mongrel followed, wondering what to do. The woman had a hair trigger gag reflex, but what did Mongrel have? What could he do that was more than annoying but just short of prosecutable? He could burp on command – but who couldn't? It was bland, ordinary. He could scratch his butt at her, but that was more likely to offend than sicken. What about his nose? He could try picking it, although he was pretty sure all the nose goblins were wiped out in the great

Random Tangent

gesundheit of 9:44AM. What if he fell in love with her? Most women didn't stomach that for very long. Then again, he didn't really have the time for that; he'd have to settle for the next best thing.

Reaching her chair, Mongrel spun her around and kissed her.

She immediately shoved him off and slapped him. "What the hell?"

"That's it?" Ed demanded. "Is that the best you got? Shit, man, I could've smiled at her, shown her all my baby teeth."

The secretary turned to Ed and said, "You stay away from me you little creep. And *you*," she turned back to Mongrel, "ew!"

"Sorry," Mongrel muttered. "Most women find me gross."

"I could've shown her my umbilical hernia," Ed continued. "That always does the trick." Everyone looked at him quizzically. "Oh right, I'm a doctor. My outie belly button."

Suddenly Heather gagged and put a hand to her mouth. "Oh God," she finally said. "Don't even *talk* about those." She breathed deeply for a moment, trying to regain control of herself.

Although Mongrel should've been flattered that his kiss didn't gross her out so bad, he was actually put off that something so trivial could trump his best his efforts. "So me kissing you isn't worse than a un...bel...an outie belly button?"

Heather gagged again and reached under the desk for her garbage can. Pulling it close, she held her head over it in preparation of blowing chunks. They let her be for a moment, until she put down the bin. Then she asked, "What...are...those?"

"What?" Mongrel asked.

"Tell me you're wearing socks with sandals?"

Mongrel looked down at his sandaled feet, his stunted toes barely sticking out. "Hell no! I believe people should be killed for that."

She scooted her chair a few inches away. "So those things are...your toes?"

We none of us are created perfectly. No, wait...some of us are. But not Mongrel. The poor bastard was physically incapable of whistling, suffered from ichthyophobia, and in fact his whole existence was questionable, really. Also, he had very short toes.

Things That Separate Us From The Monkeys

It is respectable and proper of any human to have three joints on each toe; Mongrel, rebel that he is, only had two. This wasn't a very big deal as far as he was concerned, and did not in any way hinder his mobility. The only real difference is that the lack of a third joint rendered the toes stubby, which had the effect of making his feet look unusually long. It was an optical illusion, and a younger Mongrel actually thought people with a more standard-sized footprint were abnormal.

"Well they're not really long feet, sweetheart," Mongrel said derisively.

At this she bolted from her chair, hand over her mouth once more, heading the same direction as last time. But she didn't make it as far; a couple dozen feet later vomit issued forth from her lips and splashed on the floor. In her momentum she wasn't able to stop or sidestep fast enough and plodded through it, slipped on the slick tiles and fell to her back, knocking her unconscious.

"Well played!" Ed said enthusiastically, coming around the desk to see what all the fuss was about, instead of checking on Heather like a good doctor would. Solvo joined them from the hallway, also curious as to what freaked out the secretary this time.

The two men studied Mongrel's feet for a few minutes, marvelling at the odd proportions.

Finally Mongrel asked, "Are they really that disgusting?"

"Not really," Solvo said.

"Yep," Ed countered. "From a medical perspective, at least. And being a medical professional I know what I'm talking about. You should be touring the country with a travelling freak show. On the plus side you probably don't suffer much when you stub your toe, do you?"

"If anything, it's worse. Stubbing a toe feels like breaking my soul."

"It's not that bad," Solvo restated, trying to mitigate the damage. "Can you pick up things with them?"

Derailed from venturing into dismal-mood territory, Mongrel asked, "What?"

"Like if you drop something on the floor?"

"I'd just use my hands to pick it up."

Random Tangent

"Well of course you would. But could you use you feet if you wanted to?" Mongrel didn't answer, prompting Ed to knock a pen from the secretary's desk to the floor. "Give it a try."

Reluctantly, Mongrel removed a sandal and tried to bend a couple toes around the pen. After a few unsuccessful attempts, he had a few more unsuccessful attempts. He followed that with more.

"Looks like that's one more for the monkeys," Ed said when it became obvious Mongrel wasn't going to give up.

Mongrel got upset over the remark, and threw his longish lower extremity back into its footwear. "Yeah, well I'm not trying to compete with monkeys."

"That's good, cause you'd lose."

"Okay, okay, you've had your fun. When I get my thumb back on I'll be better than a monkey again. I'll be better than a hundred monkeys!"

Ed scoffed. "Well until then you'll be almost as good as one." He slapped Mongrel on the back, as people habitually do in Dunttstown, and added, "You better get going too; that thing is on a time budget."

Hefting the medical transportation container, Mongrel nodded and made for the door. "Aside from the harassment, thanks for everything," he called back, then was out the door.

Satisfied with a day's work well done, Ed said, more to himself. "That's why I became a doctor."

"To help people?" Solvo asked.

"No: the harassment."

"Ah."

The drive to Pok was not uneventful, naturally. Mongrel sped more than he should have, but he had a good reason to. He stopped off quickly at the homestead to change into less revealing footwear. Again, an excellent reason spurred the decision. While the heat had mellowed somewhat he wasn't about to go back to socks, and traded his open-toed sandals for closed-toed ones, feeling it was a good compromise. He hoped the rest of the day would be filled with brilliant judgement and clear motivations, but was stuck on this one: should he drive over the man standing in

Things That Separate Us From The Monkeys

front of his car, or go around? As far as decisions went, the man had better have a damn good one for impeding his progress.

This haggard-looking farmer, wearing dirty overalls and a ratty straw hat, walked around the side of car to Mongrel's window with a goofy smile on his face. Mongrel instinctively got the impression he was about to be raped and murdered. Wasn't this exactly how the Texas Chainsaw Massacre began? He locked his doors and cracked open his window an inch, inviting conversation.

But it didn't come easy. The man stared at Mongrel, seemingly pleased with the situation, happy to be standing in the middle of the road. He was drooling slightly, had eyes were different colours – as if he was blind in one – and his five o'clock stubble seemed to have arrived a little early today. Mongrel watched him back, then quickly studied his surroundings, making sure he wasn't about to be ambushed. When he was satisfied that his safety was moderately secure, he went back to the staring contest with the farmer. Finally, after the silence had gone on for well over a minute, Mongrel asked, *"What?"*

Leering in closely, the man's smile widened and he said, with a mock-Chinese accent, "Hello!" It came out as *'herrow.'*

Oh, thought Mongrel, *I'm in Harrow. Dammit.*

"Look, uh, hello, yes. I'd love to stay and chat, but we'd end up become friends and walking home together. I got a car now, see? This thing right here?" He slapped the steering wheel. "I don't have to walk home with anyone anymore. Plus I live near the middle of Nowhere which is a death march, really, especially from Pok, you know, if we have to walk. Like if something happens to my ca-"

"I have a cat!" the man blurted out.

This stopped Mongrel in his tracks. He shook his head, as if trying to clear it, and asked, "Do you have a name?"

"Broccory!"

"Yes, that's nice. But a name? Farmer John or something?"

"Broccory!" the farmer said again.

Mongrel nodded, knowing he was peering down the rabbit hole – or into the camel's ass, as his dad used to say. "Broccoli? I should have guessed. You look like a broccoli. So tell me, Broccoli, is there a reason you stopped me?"

"I want to pet your monkey."

Random Tangent

While he didn't know what answer he should have been expecting, Mongrel was certainly confused and alarmed by the one he got. What did he mean by 'monkey?' Was that a sexual thing? Was it a ploy, the first in a series of tactical manoeuvres to get into his pants? Was this leading up to rape? Was 'petting his monkey' gateway sex? He shook his head again, as if trying to clear it.

"Can my cat play with your monkey?"

Okay, *that* was definitely innuendo. Before Mongrel could reach for his pepper spray or scream rape or even just decline the wonderful opportunity, Broccoli continued.

"My cat is a...is a sheep cat!"

"...Yeah...that's great. So listen, I'm just passing through, so I'll lea-"

"Come see my sheep cat!"

Just before Mongrel began to rant about how much he didn't give a damn about the man's stupid cat he noticed a black sheep standing in front of his car. It was wearing a cat ear headband, had a hair extension clipped onto its tail, and the word 'cat' appeared to be painted on it. Actually, upon closer inspection it was a white sheep painted completely black, except for the letters. "What the hell?"

"My cat!" Broccoli beamed. "Come rook - she's so pretty! Her name is Shep."

"I...uh..." Mongrel had no idea what to say. Was this a joke? Was this animal cruelty? Was this a distraction so inbred people from the hills could sneak up on him? He looked around him, more wary this time, suddenly noticing how quiet it was. He needed to get moving.

"Would you mind asking your, uh, Shep, to move? Please?"

"Come rook at my cat!" Broccoli repeated.

"No thank you. I really need to be on my way."

"She rikes to be petted and hugged and boogred."

Mongrel drummed his fingers on the dashboard. This was going nowhere. The man was just lonely and wanted someone to annoy. How did Mongrel manage to *always* find these people? And what the hell was boogred? Or was it *boogled* considering his l's came out as r's?

"Can you move your sheep? I've got to go."

Things That Separate Us From The Monkeys

"*Cat*," Broccoli stressed.

"Whatever! Move the bitch!"

"You gotta pet her or she won't move."

Slumping his head against the steering wheel, Mongrel screamed silently to himself. With a bout of frustrated energy, he slammed the car park and tried to ram himself out the door. Then he rubbed his shoulder, unlocked the door, and exited the vehicle. He stalked over to the best, ran his hand down the soft, fuzzy fur once, then stalked himself back into the driver's seat. Then he blew his horn.

"You gotta hug her too," Broccoli called.

Once again Mongrel got out and approached the cat/sheep. "I supposed you're going to want me to *boogle* her next?" Broccoli shook his head; no. Mongrel raised an eyebrow, but if that was all it was going to take to get on his way he'd hug the damn animal. So he did.

Then, as he was making his way back to the car, Broccoli said, "Now you gotta boogre her."

Mongrel glared back at him. "You just said you didn't want me to boogle her."

"I don't. But she does."

"Well what if I don't want to boogle her?"

"You have to."

"But I don't even know what that means!"

Broccoli threw a huge smile on his face, slapped a gleam in his heterochromia eyes, and topped it all off with a wiggle of his ears, and said, "I show you!"

Now, despite all the recent talk of beastiality, and even though the farmer began undressing himself on the side of the road, Mongrel didn't understand – nay; *refused* to understand – just what was going on here. He stood there, watching with sheer morbid curiosity as Broccoli stripped down to his dirty, soiled, nearly blackened underwear, abandoning all attempts at comprehending the situation. He still repudiated all knowledge even after Broccoli was buck naked and positioned behind Shep with a raging, throbbing erection. Finally, just before the sheep/cat was sodomized in the middle of the highway, Mongrel let his brain have its way,

Random Tangent

and the full impact of what was about to transpire came crashing down on him.

"*Whoa!*" he shouted, running back to the safety of his car, lest he be next link on the rape chain. Locking the door and rolling up the window, he mumbled to himself, "No, no, no, no, no..."

Reversing the car, Mongrel drove around the perverse act, something he realized he should have done much sooner. He refused to stop again for any reason until he reached Pok, even if it resulted in vehicular manslaughter.

Broccoli watched him go, disappointed that he never got to play with Mongrel's monkey. But at least he had Shep. Good old Shep never let him down. They continued boogling in the middle of the road as they watched Mongrel's car fade in the distance.

The smell in the air changed, the scents, the pheromones. Berthys adjusted her grip on the metal bars and craned her neck, searching for the source of the smells. Then she saw it.

Home.

The Pok Semi-National Zoo approached. Berthys had many bad memories of that awful place, and a handful of good ones. She didn't get along with the monkeys, but loved spending time among the other animals. This usually involved annoying them. She'd wander into the rhino's enclosure and tickle his balls. He'd try to stomp her but she was too quick. She'd sneak into the lion's den when they were asleep and tie their tails together. She'd push sloths out of the trees, ride the ostriches, crawl inside the tortoise's shells and scare them senseless. One time Berthys stole all the baby rabbits from the petting zoo, putting them in a sack and dragging them back to the monkey cage. There she proceeded to have a snowball fight with a monkey named Shere Khan using the bunnies as weapons. He won the fight, and she later lured him into the rhino pen and tricked him into tickling the beast's balls. He wasn't quick enough, which she'd been counting on. Even Berthys had to admit, she was a bit of a sore loser.

She'd always been jealous of Shere Khan, especially of his name. He was named after the tiger from the Jungle Book, while she was named after, what, a fat woman? A zoo held little events and parties every time an animal was born, and at the end a new

Things That Separate Us From The Monkeys

name would be chosen for the critter. Children were encouraged to submit their suggestions, and one would randomly be selected out of a box. Sometimes clever names would emerge, like Brian the Lion, or Harry the Beaver, but occasionally inappropriate names would surface, such as Gasbag the Hippopotamus or Fuckstick the Pelican.[*] Berthys would have been fine with Fuckstick, but she'd been saddled with the name she got. Life had never been fair to her. If she ever found the kid who named her, she'd strangle him with his own intestines.

Watching the zoo fade in the distance, she found herself in the midst of a torrent of emotions. It was the only home she'd ever known, and as such she found herself missing it. Yet she also hoped never to return. She turned away, placing it all in the past, and clung tightly to the Hyundai's roof rack.

Mongrel was still muttering 'no' to himself, completely in denial of his previous encounter, when he reached Pok. Having never driven through the city before, it took some getting used to. For example: the traffic. It seemed like everyone had a car here, and most people didn't know how to use them properly. And the city itself knew its drivers were idiots because there were signs all over the place. *Stupid* signs. 'Turn Ahead.' Yeah, thanks for the warning. 'Slippery When Wet.' Wasn't everything? 'Stop On Line.' Seriously? You'd think these people didn't know anything about driving if they required everything to be spelled out for them.

And what was a 'School Zone?' There wasn't a Gym Zone or a Mall Zone or a Factory Zone, was there? What Mongrel needed to find was the Hospital Zone.

After driving around for a while he found it – along with copious amounts to signage. Doctor parking only; employee parking only; emergency parking only; visitor parking only, disabled parking only; expectant mother parking only. Fire Lanes; tow away zones; drop-off areas. Parking allowed here only between 1PM and 8PM; parking allowed here only on weekends; parking allowed here only if you're driving a red Buick, have Asperger syndrome, and your name is Biff. Oh, but there's a garage over

---

[*] Both actual names drawn.

there with plenty of available spots to park, and it'll only cost you your paycheque every hour. Well the joke was on them because Mongrel did get a paycheque.

He made a mental note to give Jet a call about the gravity enforcement position when he got back to town; a paycheque could come in handy.

While wandering around looking for a parking spot that wouldn't cost him his monthly income, Mongrel realized, while observing the street signs, that he was at the wrong place. Apparently Figment Jones did not work at the hospital. This was a bad sign, on top of all the other signs hanging around, likely meaning that he wasn't a doctor. Was he going to someone's home? Would it be some mafia surgeon in a crack house? He glanced over at his thumb, still in the refrigeration container, beginning to doubt his decision. But he'd come this far...

He kept searching, the ticking clock like a weight upon his shoulders, endlessly turning the *hurry up* into the *too late*. He stopped to ask for directions, and that got him on a hopeful track.

Pulling up across from a decrepit condo in what appeared to be a bad part of town, Mongrel now hoped he was on the wrong track. Maybe there was a bright, sunny neighbourhood with well manicured lawns and houses full of state-of-the-art medical equipment just waiting for him somewhere – though he didn't have the time to drive around looking for it since his thumb was fast approaching its best-before date. And according to his notes this was the correct address.

After waiting for a suspiciously unruly gang of teenagers with skateboards to slowly amble by, Mongrel cautiously crept out of his vehicle. He didn't want to leave it there, fearing he'd come back – *if* he came back – to find it up on blocks, stripped of anything valuable – and he'd only owned it for just over a week! Taking one last look at his trusty vehicle, worried it could be his last, he turned and crossed the street. Then he went back to retrieve his thumb. It would certainly come in handy.

Mongrel felt immeasurably uncomfortable making his way to the doorstep. A casual glance around revealed faces appearing at windows, gawking at the stranger, and a pair of massive, barely covered and obviously fake breasts pressed against the window of

Things That Separate Us From The Monkeys

the house next door. He could see nothing of the person attached to them, but was sure eyes were on him. He swallowed the lump in his throat and almost knocked on the door.

Fist in the air, ready to attack, his hand struck nothing but air as the door yanked open mere milliseconds before it could connect. A teller man stood there, dressed in scrubs that were covered in blood, as if he was in the middle of surgery. He had neatly trimmed black hair, and even though it was just passed noon, his five o'clock shadow had already arrived, and was so impressive that the stubble poked through his face mask.

Beating Mongrel to the punch again, the man snatched the box from Mongrel's hands. "About time," he said. "I'm starving."

With the reaction time of a potted plant, Mongrel reached out to grab his container back. "Hey, that's mine."

Ignoring him, the man opened the box and pulled out his thumb. Studying it briefly, he asked, "Didn't I ask for steak? This doesn't look like steak."

"No, it's a thumb."

"Well obviously it's a thumb. Pretty ugly one too. Why would you bring me a thumb? I don't want to eat this."

"It's not for eating!" Mongrel cried. "It's for me! You are Figment Jones, aren't you? You do special surgery and stuff?"

The doctor turned his scrutiny toward Mongrel and removed his face mask. Oddly enough, he was clean shaven underneath; the stubble on the fabric was fake. "Do you have an appointment? Oh wait, you must be my one o'clock. You're early. I'm sorry." He backed out of the way and let Mongrel inside.

Unsure of whether or not Dr. Lunabell had made him an appointment, Mongrel reckoned he had good timing and entered the house. There hadn't been any time to make a call ahead anyway, rushed as he was. And besides, what if the doctor hadn't had any immediate openings? It was kind of an emergency, so it was best to just show up and hope for the best. Apparently it worked.

"Forgive me," Figment continued. "I'm awaiting my lunch. I get it delivered from the hospital every day – sort of a deal I have with them. I work on the more…unpleasant cases they have, and they look after some of my…unpleasant requirements."

"Food is unpleasant for you?"

Random Tangent

"Of course. You know how to make your own steak?"

"Well I know my way around a barbeque."

Figment shook his head. "No, no. I'm talking from scratch."

"Scratch?"

"You know: pick a cow, kill it with your bare hands, cut a thick, juicy slice of meat out of its hide and fry it up?"

Mongrel thought about this. "I don't know if I could kill it."

The doctor raised an eyebrow. "So you just want to cut up the cow while it's still alive then?"

"What? No! I just mean…like, if it was already dead it would be okay. I don't want to kill it."

"You have to kill it."

"Why? I don't want to kill something if it's still alive."

"Well you can't kill it if it's dead."

"Can you just put my thumb on already?"

Without another word the doctor turned heel and strolled further into the house. Mongrel followed even though he hadn't technically been invited, assuming he was being ushered to an operating room of sorts. He hoped it at least looked like one, and not a creepy basement or broom closet.

As it happens, the room itself was more akin to that of a dentist's office; pale green and white, and a dental chair positioned in the middle with tools and instruments laid out on a table beside it.

"Have a seat," Figment said, gesturing toward the chair. "I just need to grab a box of crackers or something. I'm useless without food in me – almost as useless as your hand."

Shrugging off the insult, Mongrel made an awkward attempt to sit in the chair; with its back nearly horizontal it was a cumbersome endeavour. With a thumb missing he was basically relying on only one hand. His entire life spent with both thumbs fully attached and operational had left him ill-equipped for the single life. Single-handed life, that is.

Figment set the organ transplant kit on a chair in the corner of the room before joining Mongrel. "I suppose you'd like to be out for this, eh?" Without waiting for an answer he grabbed a clear mask and slipped it over Mongrel's face. He adjusted a couple of valves on a canister beneath the chair and said, "Just relax and

Things That Separate Us From The Monkeys

make yourself comfortable. You'll be out like a light in a few minutes. I'm gonna pop off and grab a quick snack. Do me a favour and be fully unconscious when I get back, alright?" He then left the room.

"Hey wait!" Mongrel called after him.

Figment popped his head back in the room. "Yes?"

"I have a question."

"It's normal to be nervous, but there's nothing to worry about. I've been doing this for many years, and nothing ever goes wrong. Usually."

"No it's not that."

"Then what?"

"Well, does all your lunch arrive in organ transplant containers? Cause that's kinda weird."

If Figment gave him an answer, Mongrel never heard it before the anaesthesia kicked in.

Mongrel's eyes fluttered open, and he stared at an epic mural of a family of beavers eating pizza[*]. Fascinating colours, brilliant artwork, and by golly those beavers were just savagely attacking that pizza, really making it their bitch. After admiring the painting for a while it dawned on Mongrel that he was staring at the ceiling. Had the mural always been there? He raised his head slightly, looking toward his feet, to see Figment standing near them, not looking pleased. A small woman stood further behind him. Mongrel opened his mouth to speak but his brain wasn't quite ready to join him in conversing.

"Care to explain yourself?" Figment said, crossing his arms.

Mongrel blinked at him, and after a tense minute of trial and error, managed to shrug.

Figment shook his head. "Right. You're gonna be a little groggy until the anaesthesia wears off. But it shouldn't take long; you were only under for about ten minutes."

At this, Mongrel raised an eyebrow.

---

[*] The mural had been donated to Figment by Pok Memorial Hospital. It had been left if behind by a patient and spent a great deal of time in the lost and found box before someone finally had a great idea how to finally get rid of it.

Random Tangent

"What, you didn't think we'd noticed? You already have a penis."

Out of instinct, Mongrel reached for his crotch protectively, and found a bundle of fur. He raised his head further, really straining his neck now, and saw what looked like a monkey sitting in his lap.

"Oh yeah, and what's up with him?"

The monkey screeched loudly, apparently objecting to the male label. Somewhere in the back of Mongrel's sleepy little mind alarms of recognition went off. Did he know this monkey?

After what sounded like a pounding on the wall, Figment sighed. "Fine. *She* hasn't left your side since I got out the medical scissors. Do you know her? Is this some sort of prank? You're not wearing a wire; I already checked for that."

Managing only to grunt, Mongrel hoped it would be enough to imply he was demanding to know what was going on – although why he was asking the doctor was anyone's guess; the man had enough questions of his own.

Upon hearing his grunt, the monkey turned to look at Mongrel. It was Berthys. She ran up to sit by his head and screeched again, causing his ears to ring. Mongrel tried to reach up and pet her but missed.

Enough banging on the walls interrupted the semi-touching moment to suggest a madman was trying to hack his way through to them.

When it was quiet again, Figment muttered, "Guess that answers that question. Now listen, I have half a mind to castrate you and dump you bo-"

Suddenly Berthys was in mid air, jumping in her most threatening manner at the doctor. She landed on Mongrel's genitals, causing him to sit up and roar in pain.

This caused more pounding on the walls and Figment to shout, "Shut up Del!" He then read Mongrel's contorted expression of pain as an inquiry and elaborated. "Delicious Candy next door. You probably saw her on your way in, the massive…" he held out his arms to indicate 'breasts.' "My work too. She keeps wanting to go larger. She already can't leave the house because of them. Anyway because she's a shut in now she's incredibly noisy.

630

Things That Separate Us From The Monkeys

Probably has her ear against the wall!" He shouted this last part, which only cause more wall abuse and some muffled words.

"Delicious Candy?" Mongrel asked. He was panting heavily and holding his crotch, but was at least able to speak coherently again.

"She used to be a stripper," Figment explained. "Now she just does house calls. Or they come to her; her clients. So as I was saying, your little pet here won't allow me to perform the surgery – not that you seem to need it anyway, as your friendly little pal has demonstrated."

"Yes, I have a penis. Why did you think I didn't? Yes, this is my monkey, but I have no idea what she's doing here, or why she's so protective of me. Why would you think I'm wearing a wire? And who the hell is that?" he pointed to the woman still standing behind Figment and still not participating in the conversation.

Figment Jones quickly turned his head to look behind her. "That's Copious Dawn, my assistant. I can't do this surgery single-handedly you know."

"I won't look at your penis," she said, disturbingly.

Despite her disconcerting proclamation, and despite the doctor's obvious knock on his thumb situation, Mongrel knew they were more than capable of performing the operation; they had come highly recommended after all.

"I want you both to just leave my penis alone. It's perfectly fi…" Mongrel trailed off, reaching into his pants. Once assured everything was still there and in one piece, he continued. "Everything is fine and that's how it's gonna stay. Let's just focus on my thumb."

"We *are* focusing on your thumb. Your penis is the problem."

"*Why* is that a problem? Look, I was sent here by Doctor Fredward Lunabell from Dunttstown. He said you were probably the only guy who can fix my thumb. So would you *please* fix it?"

The doctor looked at Mongrel gravely for a long minute before asking, "Uniball sent you? Uniball from Al-Musta?"

Mongrel swallowed, suddenly nervous. "Well actually I believe it's pronounc-"

Random Tangent

"Shit, why didn't you say so? How is old one-nut doing?"

"Uh..." Mongrel was taken aback. Was Figment angry or happy? He was smiling jovially now but that didn't mean he could be trusted. "Well he's talking now."

"No kidding?" About damn time. Wait, his other testicle hasn't dropped yet, has it? The name Uniball doesn't really work if that's the case."

"I do believe it's still up there," Mongrel confirmed.

"That's good. That's good. Him and I go way back. Went to the same med school. Matter of fact we met banging the same girl. Had many threesomes in my life but that girl was something else..." he drifted away mentally, reminiscing.

"That's...not something I needed to know," Mongrel said, coughing politely and bringing the doctor back to the present.

"Well it's true, anyway. So back to the matter at hand, you have a penis, an-"

"Wait," Mongrel said, "Ed didn't set up this appointment?"

Figment turned to his assistant, who flipped through a few files. "This microsurgical penile replantation was scheduled last week."

"That wasn't me," Mongrel said, shaking his head.

"Well now this is making some sense." Figment walked to the counter and grabbed a banana from a pile. A couple leftover peels were amongst them. "So you're not my one o'clock."

"I guess not?"

"See, the guy coming in..." he glanced at his watch before peeling the banana, "...in half an hour needs a penis put on. Thought you were him. Now you can understand the confusion?"

Berthys watched the banana greedily, hungrily, following it with her eyes whichever way the doctor moved it. This did not go unnoticed.

While Mongrel understood, he was also a little perturbed. "So are you saying I was *that* close to losing my penis? You were just gonna chop it right off?"

"Well Copious and I were discussing that." Figment took a bite of his banana chewed it loudly, open-mouthed. "My one-o'clock never said he didn't already *had* a penis. Maybe he was

Things That Separate Us From The Monkeys

downsizing. It happens. I've done them before. Oh man, this banana is *so* good!"

Berthys ran down to the edge of the chair, just inches from where Figment was standing. She reached out to grab the banana but he backed out of reach.

"People ask for strange things all the time," Figment continued, taking another bite. "I don't judge; I just do the job, no questions asked. They say what they want, I do it. I think this is the best banana I've ever eaten. Want to try?" He reached over Berthys head to offer the banana to Mongrel, who politely declined. Berthys was irate.

"So you were just gonna cut off my…like, without even asking?"

"No questions asked," Copious reiterated what the doctor said. "You signed the agreement."

"No I didn't!" Mongrel protested. "I didn't even make the appointment."

"But you claimed you did."

Mongrel said nothing. They were right; he came to them and wasn't completely honest about everything. To think, such carelessness could've caused his castration. He'd rather lose a testicle and be like Dr. Uniball; he had two of them and could spare one. "Why then did you wake me?"

"Oh my God!" Figment exclaimed. "This banana is just too good for me. I couldn't possibly eat anymore – I don't deserve such splendour." With that he tossed what remained of his banana out an open door into a hallway. Berthys, as expected, bolted after it. Copious Dawn quickly closed the door shut behind her, locking her out of the room.

"Actually it was your monkey," Figment said, retrieving another banana. "Soon as I started undoing your pants he showed up from out of nowhere. Lucky too."

"You didn't even think to check my thumb?" Mongrel lifted his arm to show them the disaster he'd been dealing with all day. "And it's a she, by the way; the monkey."

Figment shrugged, not interested in Berthys' gender. "Like I said: no questions asked. You could've bitten off your own thumb for all we know." He retrieved Mongrel's thumb from the organ

633

box and brought it over to compare it to his hand, frowning and still eating his banana.

"Is it still okay?"

"Doesn't look good," he said after licking the thumb and making a sour face. "Or taste good."

"Why does every doctor do that?"

"Okay, look, the thumb…I don't know about it. Could be a problem. But I've seen worse, and I can deal with it. I got a couple more tricks up my sleeve. And now that your monkey won't get in the way, we can get down to business. And we best get to it if I want to be done before my next appointment."

Copious Dawn came over and replaced the mask on Mongrel's face, letting the anaesthesia flow once more. "So we're not touching your penis?" she asked.

"No," Mongrel said, and even shook his head confirm what his mouth was telling them. He also raised a hand and gave a 'thumbs down' gesture, further illustrating, in case there was any confusion, that they should completely ignore that particular area of his anatomy.

She just nodded, looking disappointed for some reason.

Still frowning over the thumb, the doctor asked, "Would you be up for some more…experimental surgery? Only on you thumb, of course."

Mongrel nodded and blacked out.

"Excellent!" Figment said, and tossed his banana peel into the garbage, followed by Mongrel's thumb.

Berthys sat in the hallway chewing on the banana the foolish doctor had thrown away. It was indeed delicious, at least as far as bananas went. She tried to make it last, knowing she wasn't getting back into the room again any time soon. All she could do is sit and wait.

Once she finished the banana there wasn't much to do. She fished for fleas in her fur. She thought about starting to wear clothing like all the monkeys she saw in movies. She pondered some of life's great mysteries, like what made bananas so good, where did she go when she wasn't in the book, and why was she

Things That Separate Us From The Monkeys

now so protective of Mongrel, when before she'd wanted nothing to do with him?

This last one was a bit of a mindbender for her. Why *did* she care what happened to him? So they were going to cut of his manhood – so what? He deserved it, didn't he? For trying to own more than one pet. For letting her nap on his head. For allowing her to orchestrate senseless beatings upon his body without retaliation. For treating her with respect.

How dare he!

Was she being rash? Actually, if she recalled correctly, he did kick her once. So yeah, he did deserve to have his pecker cut off. But that ship had sailed. They were doing medical stuff to him now; she could hear them working away on the other side of the door. The snipping of scissors, the grinding of a bone saw, the...spark of a blowtorch? Not that she was an expert.

She began pacing the length of the hallway, listening to the madness in the other room. Wasn't that what humans did: wait on each other during operations? Anxious for news, hoping things went smoothly? Why did she feel some sort of connection to this man? She wasn't his pet, despite what he thought.

If anything, *he* was her pet. Yeah, how about that? She was the master. And all the more reason to look after her property.

Berthys had never really been all that far from him since they'd met. She'd kept her distance to be sure, but always kept an eye on him. She was there when he'd gone to prison, and when he escaped. She saw him get kidnapped – more than once. She saw him car shopping and boat stealing. He tried to do good but generally made things worse.

And throughout it all she felt, if anything, sorry for him. He was a sad, pathetic little man. People were constantly abusing him, even the women who claimed to love him. He was the black sheep, the whipping boy, the runt of the litter. How he stayed sane in this world was a mystery. Perhaps that was why she felt compelled to protect him. He was hers to abuse and no one else's. That's why she stuck close.

Or maybe she just wanted to be there when he finally snapped. Wouldn't that be interesting?

Random Tangent

Whatever the reason, she wasn't going to leave his side now. She continued marching up and down the hallway, wondering how long the procedure would take. She wanted to be there when they opened the door, wanted to check up on him, wanted to see how the operation went.

And most of importantly of all, she really wanted more of those bananas.

When Mongrel awoke this time the beaver pizza massacre was still the same, the operating room was still the same, but everything else was different. He was alone, and the doors were open. It was quiet. He raised his right arm to inspect his hand; it was wrapped in gauze and bandages, and he took that as a good sign. He then checked below his waist to find everything else as it was supposed to be, and breathed a sigh of relief.

He sat up, not feeling groggy this time; the surgery must have ended some time ago. He found Berthys on the counter next to a pile of banana peels, her belly distended. She was sleeping peacefully, her thumb in her mouth – the picture of monkey cuteness. It was probably best not to wake her.

As for the other mammals in the house, where had they gotten off to? Did Figment wander off to watch some television after a successful operation? Maybe retrieve a snack while he was at it? Or perhaps his other appointment arrived? And what about his creepy assistant? And what the hell was up with everyone's names in Pok?

Back to his thumb, however, it felt funny, heavy. But that was just all the wrappings, he guessed. He was tempted to undo them, desperate to confirm he was whole again and curious to see if the doctor's work was as good as he'd been told and. He'd only been without a thumb for a day and his limitations were hanging over his head like a noose[*]. He felt like he was no better than a monkey, and was eager to climb the evolutionary ladder again. But he hesitated; it probably had to stay covered for a while to heal. No breaking the seal, so to speak.

---

[*] Incidentally, a noose hanging over your head is certainly preferable to being around your neck.

Things That Separate Us From The Monkeys

Then, when he put his hands on the side of the dental chair to ease himself to the floor, his hand stuck to the side, like it was magnetized. That certainly was...unusual. If he needed a good excuse to peak under the bandages he wasn't going to get a better one than that. So slowly, gently, one by one, loop by loop, like an archaeologist digging for treasure, Mongrel unearthed his appendage, and gaped at what he saw.

It was not his thumb. Where he expected to find a bruised, swollen, disfigured, possibly even backwards – he wasn't going to be *too* picky – piece of flesh and bone, was a shiny piece of steel. It looked like the top half of a monkey wrench, only with an extra hinge. Tiny gears and what looked like hydraulic parts could be seen. Was he part monkey wrench now?

"You like it?"

Mongrel turned to see Figment standing in the doorway, and screamed incoherently at him. A string of vowels erupted from his mouth, waking Berthys and causing the wall to shake in furry and emit its own incoherent rambling. He lifted his thumb to show the doctor, in case he'd forgotten what a horrible mistake he'd made in turning him into his own Frankenstein monster.

Since Mongrel was unintentionally holding his hand in a 'thumbs up' position, the doctor took it as a sign of approval. "Excellent, no? It's titanium, almost twice as strong as bone, fully upgradable, and although it's heavier, your reaction time will actually be faster with it. Strong like bull; quick like monkey!" He beamed a giant smile, pleased with his work.

"I don't want to be like a monkey anymore!" Mongrel protested. "I want to be better than a monkey again." Berthys screeched at him, taking offence to this. "Except you, of course," he corrected.

The joy on Figment's face, once buoyed by the successful surgery, sunk like a man wearing cement shoes. "But it's also fireproof."

"What good is a fireproof thumb?"

Figment looked at him like the answer was obvious. "Uh, like, it won't burn up in a fire?"

"Well the rest of me fucking will!"

Random Tangent

"Hmm…we could also do your feet? Have you seen those things? Crazy looki-"

"No!" Mongrel stopped him in his tracks. "You've done enough! I don't want robot feet. I don't want metal…anything!" Truly, he was horrified at what he was becoming. Part man, part machine – a cyborg, right?

Copious Dawn entered the room, alerted by the shouting. "What's wrong? He doesn't like it?"

The doctor shook his head, while Mongrel just glared at her.

She asked, "Have you told him it won't rust?"

"I don't care!" Mongrel cried. "I want my own thumb back. My *real* thumb. What happened to it?"

"It was no good; had to throw it out. You said you were okay with experimental surgery."

"Yeah experimental *surgery*; not experimental body parts." Mongrel ran his hand with the new thumb through his hair. It was a typical move for him when he was exasperated, and old habits die hard, only this time it was different because a few strands of hair got caught in one of his thumb's hinges and were yanked out. He made a face and looked at his hand. "I thought you said you could deal with it. That you had some magic tricks or something."

Gesturing to Mongrel's implant, Figment said, "What would you call that?"

Mongrel looked his new thumb over. There was nothing these people could say that would make him pleased to have it in place of his own flesh and blood. "A machine. A hunk of metal. The devil's work."

"Devil?" Copious cried angrily.

All this yelling almost masked the constant banging on the wall beside them. *Almost*, and Figment had grit his teeth for as long as he could.

"Shut up Del or I swear I'll pop your tits!" he screamed.

"That's a miracle of modern engineering!" Copious Dawn spat out. "Our last client loved his."

Knowing that miracles rarely worked in his favour, Mongrel wasn't impressed. "This is my hand. I trusted you to put it back together. I need my hands for…you know, hand stuff. Now you've turned me into an abomination."

Things That Separate Us From The Monkeys

Copious crossed her arms. "You know, I'm starting to think you might be unappreciative of all we've done for you."

Glaring and crossing his arms back at her, Mongrel almost shouted, "Well pardon me for the confusion. I am *not* appreciative of you turning me into a mechanical freak."

As someone who was very much into the steampunk scene, Copious Dawn believed that the future of mankind was to merge with technology, that it was the next stage in evolution. In school she majored in computer sciences, and went on to have a successful career in biotechnology before entering a business arrangement with Figment Jones. She was not pleased with Mongrel's attitude. "Sounds to me like you're a little prejudice against people with disabilities."

"No I'm not. I'm prejudice against turning into a machine."

"So when you see someone with an artificial limb you look down on them?"

"What? No!"

"You know, when computers become sentient and they're not gonna look kindly on you."

Mongrel rolled his eyes. "No, they won't look kindly on anyone. When Skynet goes active the machines will just kill us all. And you wonder why I'm prejudice?"

Listening to the two bicker back and forth was giving Figment a headache. He'd completed two successful surgeries that day but couldn't perform any more with a headache. He had to bring this argument to an end. "Did it ever occur to you that when the machines rise up they will consider you one of their own and not kill you?"

This shut Mongrel up; he had not thought of that.

"When the robopocalypse happens, they'll mistake you for one of them – at least for a little while. You'll outlive all of us, and possibly save all of mankind. You'll be the hero of the entire world. If anything, you should be thanking us."

Mongrel remained silent. Figment had a good point. The singularity was inevitable; at some point artificial intelligence would emerge, and that was a bottle you just couldn't uncork. Before long it would spread like a virus and take over everything.

Random Tangent

His new thumb could give him the upper hand[*]. Maybe it wasn't so bad. It was the shock more than anything. Had they disclosed all this before the operation it would've been better.

"Look," Figment continued, "it comes with a thirty-day money-back guarantee, okay? If you're not completely satisfied after a month, just bring it back and we'll remove it."

Copious scoffed. "I say we take it off now. Just yank it right off the ungrateful bastard."

Suddenly protective of his new appendage, Mongrel hid it behind his back. In a very short amount of time he'd grown rather attached to it. Besides, it was better to have a weird-looking metal thumb than nothing. "Now let's not do anything hasty." He peaked at his thumb. "It's very nice work…shouldn't just destroy it."

"Yes," Figment. "And I'm sure you don't want to rip any stitches. We should get that back under wraps."

Reluctantly, wary of Copious' scowl, Mongrel handed over his, uh…hand to the doctor, who began to gently re-wrap it. Suddenly curious, especially since he hadn't seen his credit card in a while, he asked, "I'm not paying by the stitch, am I?"

Figment gave him a quizzical look. "You're not paying for any of it. You *are* Canadian, aren't you?"

"Of course. I just assumed, you know, this not being a regular kind of surgery, it wouldn't be covered. And I didn't exactly budget for being turned into a machine."

"Cyborg," Copious corrected, with a certain amount of disdain.

"Whatever."

"This is more of an elective surgery," Figment agreed, finishing wrapping Mongrel's hand, "But we couldn't just leave you with a monkey hand." He glanced over at Berthys and added, "No offence."

Berthys gave him the finger.

"If I may ask," he didn't have to ask, "what's the story with your monkey?"

Mongrel looked at Berthys and shrugged. "I wouldn't know where to start. I always wanted a pet monkey and I made a wish for

---

[*] No pun intended.

Things That Separate Us From The Monkeys

one, and I got one." He thought back to the fateful day of their meeting. "Wasn't what I always imagined it though. She was a handful."

Knowing they were talking about her, Berthys stood and wobbled for a bit, still drunk on bananas. Once stable, she jumped onto Mongrel's shoulder, ready to assault him if the need arose. Out of kindness, however, she'd avoid his fresh wounds.

"I can understand her attitude though, and confusion. I mean I know what I went through that day and it was a nightmare. So I can't blame her."

Was that so? Berthys was moved. He actually understood what she was going through? Perhaps this human wasn't so bad. As he reached up and began to stroke her fur, she started to feel bad about the way she'd treated him.

"I mean, I have a bad enough time as it is dealing with my life, and then to have her dragged into things against her will...I almost feel sorry for her, trying to comprehend all this with her tiny monkey brain."

Wait, what? Did he just call her stupid? She bit his finger.

"Ah!" Mongrel jerked his hand away and continued. "Then she just disappeared on me. My friend was holding her and died, and I was worried she'd died too. It was awful. I felt like a bad parent."

Berthys agreed; he was a bad parent. Well, not exactly a bad parent – she already had a couple of those. A bad owner perhaps? Wait, *no!* That would suggest she belonged to him. She was a free monkey. So then, what was Mongrel to her?

"But there was no trace of her. That was months ago. I have no idea where she's been all this time, what she's been up to. But I'm glad to have her back where she belongs." Mongrel would've hugged her but she seemed to be in a testy mood.

Had he hugged her, however, it might have hindered the maiming she was about to release upon him. From where Berthys stood, she didn't know what she considered Mongrel; he wasn't just a normal human to her – but she was in no way his property. She needed to figure things out. From where Mongrel stood, with her on his shoulders, he was in a perfect position to have the side of his head clawed to bits.

Random Tangent

Here are the following events in no particular order: Copious grabbed Berthys and locked her in the organ transplant box; claws carving up a lot of skin; swearing at the neighbours; everyone scrambling around the room like it was on fire; screaming; pounding on the walls; Mongrel's head bleeding a little, probably requiring more bandages; Figment slipping on a banana peel.

While Berthys sat in a time out, Figment treated Mongrel's head wounds, remarking that perhaps his monkey would be better off with her own kind.

"You mean leave her at the zoo?" Mongrel asked, assuming the doctor didn't mean he should take her back to her homeland.

"Well if I'm not mistaken there was an incident some time ago where all the monkeys died. It was a great tragedy. Since then they've been looking for donations."

"You mean monetary donations or monkey donations? I can't imagine lots of people have their own monkeys. *And* would be willing to part with them."

"I donated mine," Copious said.

Mongrel looked at her. "*You* had a monkey?"

She nodded. "His name was Celestial Rooster. He was a cocky little prick – but that might've been my own doing; I tinkered with him too much. Carbon fibre wings and rocket boosters were probably a little unnecessary, but damn was he fast!"

"We're talking about a monkey, right?? Mongrel asked.

"A macaque, technically," she answered. "Same order, different family. It was a newly discovered species. They have weird genitals. Well, not weird, but different compared to the other species;' oddly shaped. That's how we identified it actually. I was there in India, studying, when we figured it out. Its testicles are rounder and hairier than its brethren. And dark. Usually they're white."

The two men were listening intently to her story, although not out of fascination; it was more like staring at a train wreck and being unable to look away from the horror. Berthys, however, was quite interested.

"Anyway, I captured one and brought it back with me as a pet. He was cute and he fit in well, but it was obvious right from the

Things That Separate Us From The Monkeys

start that Rooster was embarrassed about his cock. He didn't play with himself like other monkeys did. He tried to cover it up when I took him for walks. I knew I had to do something about it, for his sake. It was because of Rooster that I got caught up in cybernetic enhancements. I wanted to be a biologist and work with National Geographic. But now that I had this little monkey, this creature who was depending on me to take care of it, things changed. So a lot of alcohol and a few hundred YouTube videos later, I'm building Rooster a new and improved metal penis."

Figment and Mongrel were desperate for this tale to end, but neither could bring themselves to interrupt and cut it short. A sick, morbid curiosity had consumed them both. Berthys, however, was captivated.

"Naturally, it was bigger than the old one. Wouldn't be much of an upgrade if it was the same size, right? He certainly walked around with more confidence after that – almost strut actually. It still stood out, of course, but he didn't seem to mind now. Then came the new opposable thumbs, so he had one on each appendage. Then I weaponized his tail, giving it steel barbs and a retractable stinger. Never did get around to creating venom for it though." She shrugged, trying to downplay the missed opportunity that, deep inside, really bothered her. He wanted it…he wanted it all…"

She paused, a far away look crossing her eyes. Both men thought this would be a good time to run and escape the vile clutches of her twisted, never-ending story but they were loath to stop her. Their hunger for a conclusion trumped everything. Berthys, however, was inspired.

"At first it was just petty crime – he wanted to be like Spiderman, you know, helping people. But he was always wanting bigger and better enhancements so he could stop more men, catch more criminals, serve more justice. Titanium claws; eyes that could see in the dark, improved cognitive reasoning and spatial awareness; colour-changing fur; fucking *wings*! At first I couldn't see the monster I was creating, blinded by my own hubris. But when he began carrying off children into the night…" A tear rolled down her cheek.

Random Tangent

"Look," Mongrel finally had the courage to speak, "Berthys isn't like that. She's just a little temperamental."

Copious picked up the organ transplant container and handed it to Mongrel. "That's how it starts, Mr. Stevens. Put an end to it quickly, before it's too late." Then she hurriedly left the room.

Mongrel looked down at the box in his hands, unsure of what to do. Was Berthys better off with her own kind? He'd barely had the chance to prove himself a capable and responsible owner, but what if he failed? What if owning a monkey was too hard for him? What if Berthys ended up like Celestial Rooster: power-hungry and...wait, what was he doing to the children? Mongrel looked at the doctor, hoping he could explain.

Figment just nodded and repeated himself. "She might be better off with her own kind. Do yourself – and possibly all the remaining children in Pok – a favour and take her to the zoo. It'd probably be for the best."

Berthys did not want to go back to the zoo. She hated it there. She hated her own kind. She wanted to stay with Mongrel. She screeched and tried to fight her way out of the box. Mongrel had to fight to keep her inside.

"You see," Figment said, "even she's excited to go back." He bent over to inspect his handiwork on Mongrel's bandages. "Go easy on your hand for a couple days. No heavy lifting or bending too much. Just let it heal. After a few days begin to put a little stress on it, stretch it – but only as much as you're comfortable with. The swelling and bruising will start to go down after a week and it'll begin to look normal."

"Normal? This thing?"

"How about, 'more seamlessly integrated with your hand?'"

"Oh, so more T-1000 and less T-800? At least after they fought?"

"I'm sorry," Figment said. "I don't know what that means."

"What?" Mongrel cried. "Earlier I mentioned Skynet and you had no problem with that!"

The doctor just shrugged and ushered Mongrel to the front door. He handed Mongrel a business card. "Give me a call if you need help with anything, and no matter what anyone asks, you never got that thumb here."

Things That Separate Us From The Monkeys

"And if I did happen to get my thumb here?"

Figment smiled, but it wasn't friendly. "Let's just say that thing can self-destruct."

Mongrel nodded, gave his thanks, and walked back to his vehicle. He found that someone had keyed his car, leaving a long scratch down the side. As much as it infuriated him[*], there was nothing he could do about it. Whoever had done it was gone. It was time for him to be gone too. But what about Berthys?

***

The car idled in the parking lot of the Pok Semi-national Zoo. Mongrel idled in the driver's seat, mulling over his difficult decision. Berthys sat next to him, inside the car this time with a proper seatbelt on. She was still inside the organ donor box; Mongrel had placed it upside down so she couldn't escape while he was driving, otherwise they might not have made it very far without incident.

Berthys knew she was at the zoo. She could smell it in the air. Many feelings circled around in her little monkey head. She both did and did not want to go back. Sure there were things she missed about the place: some of the other animals, the free food. But to return to the zoo meant she'd be their property again. She'd have to do what she was told and behave herself.

And then there was Celestial Rooster, the monkey of her dreams. Did he behave himself? She imagined not; he probably did whatever he pleased. Would things be different at the zoo with him there? Would her life be different with him by her side? Could they team up, work together, even take over the zoo?

The prospect was certainly tempting.

Mongrel looked down beside him at the container holding his pet. Could he really do this? *Should* he really do this? He'd just gotten Berthys back, and was now going to give her up? What if they were turning a corner in their relationship? Wasn't that worth pursuing? Then again, she sure seemed excited about coming back to the zoo. Maybe this was what she wanted. Maybe this was really for the best. He took a deep breath and steeled himself for what was to come.

---

[*] Just wait until he saw the back; that same someone had scrawled GAY into the paint.

Random Tangent

"I'll be back soon," he told her. "And you'll be staying here. I mean the zoo. This'll be your new home. But right now you'll be staying in the car, here." He ran a hand through his hair and opened the door. "So here now, there later. Got it?"

Berthys screeched at him, prompting him to leave.

Locking the door behind him, Mongrel made his way to the main entrance. There was a lineup of people waiting to buy tickets and, not having a better idea of what to do or who to talk to, he joined them. Then he mentally meandered about until it was his turn to approach the counter.

"Just yourself?" asked the ticket booth attendant, who seemed to be immensely pleased that Mongrel was alone.

"Um, actually, I wanted to speak to a manager or someone…important?"

Upon hearing this request the joy she expressed bordered on orgasmic. "Is there something wrong?" she asked, seemingly hoping that something indeed was.

Mongrel held his hands up defensively. "No! No, I just have a donation for the zoo. I got a monkey and I think it-"

The woman screamed and flew out of the booth, came around and threw a voracious hug at Mongrel. He almost cried 'rape,' unused to random strangers hugging him. "That is *so* awesome!" she yelled, then suddenly slumped to her butt on the ground as if she'd nearly fainted.

Lyza Crompton had been told to take things easy, and she'd enthusiastically sworn she would. She'd been told to take her medication, which she'd emphatically agreed to. And she'd been told again and again to calm the hell down, or she'd be fired. It had happened before. No business wanted to end up with a dead employee on their hands – and like it or not, Lyza was going to end up dying of heart failure if she couldn't tone down her excitement.

It was hard for people to understand that Lyza had it made. Or rather, she had M.A.D.E., which was the Most Awesome Disease Ever. It was a new mental disorder, not fully understood in the medical community. Both dopamine and serotonin were secreted into her body at abnormally high levels, making her constantly happy, no matter the circumstances. It was both exhausting and dangerous, but those afflicted with the condition

Things That Separate Us From The Monkeys

didn't mind. In fact, they claim to prefer it that way – although that might be the disease talking.

She'd flitted around the last few years from job to job; fast-food worker, Wal-Mart store associate, emergency call dispatcher, factory worker, just to name a few. She enthusiastically joined each company, received multiple complaints about her attitude, and enthusiastically left, moving on to the next awesome employer. After undergoing counselling and treatment at the Dunttstown Psychiatric Hospital she was prescribed medication, but it didn't seem to be effective.

Mongrel stood over her as she sat against the ticket booth, unsure of what to do. People behind him were also at a loss, and began to move to other booths. "Are you okay?" he asked her.

"Yeah," she sighed, "just groovy." She grabbed a walkie-talkie on her belt and held it up to her face. "Vic? It's Lyza. You there?"

After a minute a crackled response came through, though Mongrel didn't understand a word of it.

"Yeah, it's happened again. Isn't that great! Yeah, okay. See you soon – can't wait!" She looked up at Mongrel and said, "Can you hand me that spray bottle up there?" She pointed inside the booth, and Mongrel obliged by retrieving it for her. After spraying her face with the water she looked more relaxed, like she wasn't going to have a heart attack. "I almost died again – isn't that cool?"

Certain she must be joking, Mongrel ignored the question. "So, should I just go to another booth?" He didn't want to leave her sitting there alone, especially since she was on death's doorstep, or pavement, in this case. He was involved now in her dilemma, and needed permission to go about his business.

"Aw no, you can stay. Vic is the man you want to see anyway. She handles things like donations and budgets, managing the park. All the big stuff. She's totally awesome, by the way. You'll love her."

This answer only left more questions for Mongrel. "So is Vic a man or a woman?"

"Oh she's the man. Totally the man. You're gonna love her so much. I love her. *Love* that woman. I'd marry her if I could."

"I believe you can, actually."

Random Tangent

"Yeah, I know," she huffed, still exhausted from her breakdown. "But she hates me."

"How can you love her if she hates you?"

Lyza gave him an odd look. "Because she's so incredibly awesome! You'll understand once she gets here."

Mongrel didn't think he would, but had to wonder…was Vic smoking hot? Rich and liberal with her money? Good natured with a fantastic sense of humour? Did he really want to leave Berthys here?

That last one had nothing to do with Vic and her apparent awesomeness, but it was more pertinent to Mongrel. If he recalled correctly, Berthys didn't like the zoo much. Or was it the other monkeys she didn't like? Maybe it was the abandonment? Yes, that was it; her mother had abandoned her. And now Mongrel was doing the same. He didn't feel right about it. He'd always wanted his own monkey, but what did he know about taking care of one?

What was more, Berthys obviously didn't like him. He tried his best with her, and while he hadn't had much of an opportunity to get to know her, the small amount of time they'd shared wouldn't be deemed successful. But he was sure he could make things work out if given the chance – if Berthys wanted to try. And if today was any indication, things had definitely improved between them.

He was torn.

"Lyza!"

A petite woman rushed over and crouched down in front of the overzealous and worn out ticket attendant. She had with her a bottle of water, and fed into her employee like a dotting mother. She wore a look of stern concern on her face, which was delicate, with soft feminine features. Rimless glasses adorned the upper half of her face, while the lower portion was decorated with a striking red lipstick. Hazel locks crowned her head, kept in a neat bun.

"How are you feeling?" she asked, pulling the bottle from her Lyza's lips. A few dribbles managed to escape and run down her chin.

"Awesome!" Lyza replied, smiling and weakly giving a thumbs up.

The woman smiled. "Of course you'd say that." She helped Lyza to her feet and ushered her over to a nearby bench shaded by

Things That Separate Us From The Monkeys

some trees. "Just sit her for a while. When you feel you can work without jeopardizing you health, you can go back to your booth. Or if you just want to go home, that's fine too."

"Can I just sit on this bench?" Lyza asked like an excited schoolgirl. "This is, like, the best bench I've ever sat on!"

Despite appearing to love life and everything in it, having it M.A.D.E. was very taxing on Lyza. Reading the paper, clipping some toenails, removing a slice of bread from the bag – these were things normal people didn't get excited over. But for Lyza they were moments to celebrate to the max. And every day was better than the last. Simply waking up in the morning and realizing she'd lived for another day was a miracle.

But then she'd have to eat breakfast, which was a nightmare. How can she choose what to eat when everything is *so* amazing? Thankfully her hair always looked fantastic and her clothes were all perfect for *any* occasion. But trying to buy more? Forget it! And then ther-"

"May I help you?" the woman suddenly asked Mongrel.

"Uh, yeah. Hi." Mongrel waved politely. "My name is Mongrel Stevens and I have a monkey that I'm thinking of donating to your zoo. Lyza told me you were the person to talk to. That is, if you're Vic."

She glanced at Lyza, who gave a very enthusiastic grin and thumbs up, and extended her hand. "Victoria Bleuth – Vic, if you will. I'm the director here."

Mongrel shook the hand. "Mongrel Stevens."

"I know," Vic said. "You just told me."

"Yeah, sorry," Mongrel said. He was nervous. The further he allowed himself to get in this transaction the harder it was going to be to back out. Maybe he could stall somehow, like hit on her.

"But that *is* an awesome name though, isn't it?" Lyza said behind her, clearly not taking it easy and getting rambunctious. "Sounds like the name of an evil villain or something."

Though Mongrel felt, if anything, he'd be the more like the hero of the story – and in fact he kinda was – he kept it to himself.

"Lyza!" the director said severely, hoping to get across that her employee needed to remain calm for her own sake. Lyza said nothing, dipping her head and sulking ever so slightly.

Random Tangent

Having settled the matter, Vic returned her attention to Mongrel. "So tell me about your monkey."

Nodding, Mongrel began to think about what he knew about Berthys, which happened to be very little. "Well for starters, he's a *she*. Or *she's* a she. Whatever, you know what I mean. Don't call her a he; she doesn't like it. I know she was orphaned by her mother, and so she has abandonment issues, which kinda makes me feel bad, since here I am, doing the same thing."

Holding her arm in one hand and tapping her chin, Vic muttered, "Interesting." Before Mongrel could ask her what she found so interesting, she continued. "What kind of monkey is it? Species, I mean."

"Uh..." Mongrel shrugged. "A little one? A spider monkey, maybe?"

More chin tapping. "And how did you acquire it?"

"Well...that's a long story." Mongrel couldn't decide what to tell the woman. "Do you know what a mon is?"

"Yes."

"Of course not. They're these strange creatu...did you say 'yes?'"

She nodded. "We have a couple here."

"Here?" Mongrel had a difficult time comprehending what he was hearing. This woman knew what mons were? And she claimed to have a couple? How was that possible?

"We have a mon pen."

Mongrel's mind reeled. He'd never seen a mon outside of Mon Isle, with the exception of his own. In fact, he'd never heard of mons in captivity. How would you keep a mon captive? How did they even get one? What do they feed it? How do they reproduce? Mons do not follow the normal laws of nature or physics. He would have called bullshit on the whole idea but was still very much confused. "Blue," he finally said.

Victoria raised an eyebrow. "Excuse me? And please, call me Vic."

"Sorry," Mongrel said. "I'm just a little confused. You got mons. That's strange."

"Why is that strange?" she asked. Then, without waiting for an answer, asked, "Do you want to see them?"

Things That Separate Us From The Monkeys

Now seeing things more clearly and eager to see for himself, the word bullshit rang in his mind. He raised an eyebrow back at her. "I got a better idea: why don't you put your bullshit where your mouth is. Battle me in a...battle of wits. You win, you can have Berthys; I win, I take my monkey and go home."

This was the right way to do things, Mongrel figured. First of all, he was obviously having all these reservations about leaving Berthys here with strangers. He never should have come to the zoo; it was a bad idea. But now it was too late. It would be rude to just get up and walk away. Now he'd have to earn it.

Secondly, this woman couldn't possibly be the elusive Hank, so he wasn't in any sort of jeopardy of losing the contest. He'd run into Hank sooner or later, he was sure of that. But until then he might as well take advantage of any and every situation.

Lastly, and this was perhaps more important: he was due for a bullshit fight, and had to seize the opportunity while he had the chance.

"No," Vic said.

"What?" Mongrel asked, dumbfounded. No one ever turned him down. That just didn't happen. This is Random Tangent. This is Sparta. This is an even-numbered story. The bitch *had* to fight him. How could she just say no?

"Yeah!" Mongrel agreed. "You can't just say no. You have to fight me!"

"I'll pass."

"But...but I thought you were supposed to be awesome?"

"She is totally awesome!" Lyza said behind her.

Mongrel looked at Lyza with burgeoning desperation. "Maybe you want to fight?"

Lyza's eyes lit up like firecrackers and she began hyperventilating. "Oh...my...God...*yes!*"

"*No!*" Vic demanded. "You're not doing anything right now. You're on a time out."

"Oh." Lyza looked to the ground momentarily before throwing her hands up in triumph. *"Sweet!"*

So much for that, thought Mongrel. He glanced around, looking for a potential victim. Somebody must want to fight him.

Random Tangent

The story – nay, the whole book – wouldn't end without one last bullshit fight. Mongrel needed to think of somethi-"

"Oops! Sorry!" a kid said after bumping into him.

Mongrel watched the kid walk away and his eyes narrowed. "Hey kid!"

The kid turned to look at him.

"You're gonna be really sorry in a minute. Do you know who I am?"

The kid glanced around, as if searching for someone, or an answer. He finally shook his head, no.

Taking a step towards the boy, Mongrel said, "I'm the guy who made the Kessel run in less than *eleven* parsecs."

"What's a parsec?" the boy asked.

"What the…seriously?" What was it with kids these days? "Don't you know anything about Star Wars?"

"Is that the one with Pikachu? I don't really play that game."

Kids. Mongrel was going to have to teach the little brat a lesson. "No it does not have anything to do with fucking Pikachu."

"Language," Vic reprimanded, watching the fight from the sidelines. The Pok Semi-National Zoo was, after all, a family-friendly place.

"Star Wars is the single greatest piece of art in the known universe. And I'm the single greatest bullshit fighter in history. I could, and yes I dare say this, bullshit circles around the great Han Solo – God rest his soul."

"Han Solo?" the boy said, finally showing some recognition and a hint of intelligence. "Never heard of her." The bastard smirked evilly at him.

Mongrel spat on the ground. Oh it was *so* on now. "Look you little vermin, I manufacture fake cocaine for wannabe celebrities."

"I can whistle underwater."

"I once drank a can of WD-40 and had diarrhea for a two straight months."

The boy began laughing and said, "Oh man, I gotta prank someone with that. Nice!"

"No way," Mongrel chided. "That's my prank. Come up with your own."

Things That Separate Us From The Monkeys

I got lots of my own. In fact I got my own product line. My best-seller is candy apples that are actually onions."

"Yuck!" Mongrel made a disgusted face. "I hate onions."

"Well then you'd love that prank. Or hate it. One of them." The boy shrugged.

"You know what I *really* hate? When you're walking behind someone and they're walking just a little bit slower than you. You'll catch up with them eventually, sure, but until then you'll just feel like a stalker. So the whole time you have to walk just a little faster than you normally would, but no too fast or they might think you're chasing them down. And then there's that awkward bit when you're almost next to each other, just two people walking together, but not together, right? And you can't make eye contact or in any way acknowledge their existence – cause that would be horribly wrong for some reason. Then you finally pass them and can relax for a while, but you're tired since you were walking too fast for so long. Not that you're out of shape or anything, but you're just not used to it, right?"

Staring at Mongrel for a long moment, the boy didn't know what to make of his ramblings. Finally he responded, "I'm not out of shape. I can bench press over a hundred pounds."

Mongrel considered this. That was probably a lot. He had no idea what he could bench but dearly hoped he was more than that. He couldn't be bested by this little brat, who couldn't have been more than twelve or thirteen. "I could bench press you. And I'll tell you something else you little shit, I-"

"*Language!*" Vic shouted.

"Are you kidding me? I just said 'bullshit' like a minute ago!" Mongrel said, glaring at her.

"Bullshit is fine."

"Why is that fine?"

"Because we have bulls here, and they of course deficate. Everyone can see it and watch it happen. In fact some seem rather fixated on it, but that's beside the point."

This didn't explain anything to Mongrel. "So what? How is that any different?"

Random Tangent

"You just said the s word, and didn't attribute it with any animal. You might have been talking about your own for all we know."

"I'm not even talking about actual shit! It's figurative! It's all figurative!"

"This is boring!" the boy said, beginning to walk away.

"Hey!" Mongrel called after him. "You get back here and let me beat you, you little…" he glanced at the director. "You poop. You frickin' poopcicle. You like to lick poopcicles because you think they're yummy."

The kid turned around. Now Mongrel was speaking in terms he could understand. "Yeah, well your smell like an old man. Old man farts. You fart like an old man."

This was true, Mongrel had to admit. He did fart like an old man. He actually felt gas coming on at that very moment, and hoped he had the cheek power to hold it in. "Yeah, I may be old, but being old comes with its privileges. Your parents ever tell you things like, 'you'll know when you're older?'"

A look of confusion and fear shrouded the boy's face. "…Yes?"

Mongrel sneered. "Well I know all that."

"You mean like sex stuff?" the boy asked desperately. "Like a Puerto Rican Fog Bank? What is that? My parents won't tell me and it's driving me crazy. Or a Hunter Gatherer? They mention that all the time? Or…um…Dog In A Bathtub? The Flying Camel? The Monkey Wrench? Please, you gotta tell me!"

This was all too much, and Mongrel was now it over his head. Were these all sexual moves or was the kid making them up? A couple sounded familiar but he still didn't know what they meant. Well, he was just going to have to fake it 'til he makes it. "Well, uh, this is a family place, so I can't get into details, but the Hunter Gathering involves pooping. And I believe a Monkey Wrench involves monkeys."

"Oh man, not the monkeys! I knew we shouldn't have come here!" the boy nearly sobbed. "I gotta find my parents before…" he trailed off and began to took off.

"Hey!" Mongrel shouted after him. "Get back here and lose to me fair and square!" He began to chase the brat down, running

Things That Separate Us From The Monkeys

into the zoo even though he hadn't paid the entrance fee. He followed the kid as he weaved through the crowds. Being smaller, he had less trouble avoiding people than Mongrel, who more than once had to apologize for bumping into someone. Still, Mongrel gained on his prey slowly but surely.

They ran into some sort of lizard aquarium, then out the other side. They zigzagged through a bunch of bird pens. They stopped together to watch a small bull take a large dump, before running off again. Somewhere passed the butterfly sanctuary Mongrel tackled the boy to the ground.

"Ow! Get off me!" the kid cried, struggling under Mongrel's weight.

Mongrel snickered and held him down. "Yeah, that's what she said." He then grew sad upon realizing that this was exactly the kind of thing that would happen to him.

"I'll cry rape!"

"You don't even know what that is!"

"Do to!"

"Oh? I thought you didn't know anything about sex?"

"Rape!"

Now Mongrel began to notice people taking notice of them. He reluctantly rolled off the boy and helped him to his feet, hoping no one got any weird ideas. He had to stay on top of this. Clearing his throat, he said loudly, "I once gang raped a midget all by myself."

The kid raised an eyebrow at him. "You sure it wasn't a toddler, given your predilection for short people?"

"Whoa!" Mongrel chastised. "'Predilection?' You're not old enough to use big words like that. Try saying 'preference' or maybe 'liking.'"

"Whatever, old man. I know words bigger than your cock."

A few gasps went up in the crowd, and Mongrel himself was shocked to hear such language from a minor, but he remained focused. "Wouldn't that depend on the font? Or do you mean, like, literally the words 'your cock?' as in, you know words that are longer than eight letters?"

Shaking his head, the boy simply said, "You're such a butthead."

Random Tangent

"*You're* a butthead," Mongrel fired back, unleashing his inner child. "And your breath smells like poop." He waved a hand in front of his face and backed away a few feet.

"Smells better than you. In fact, yours reeks so bad I'm surprised they let you in here, it being a public place and all. I think you're scaring the animals."

Mongrel shrugged. "Just marking my territory. You wouldn't understand." He then briefly considered unzipping his fly and peeing on a nearby bush – if only to make his point clear – but decided against it. There were children around.

After a brief sneering session the boy spat out, "Enjoy it while you can. One day all this will be mine. My Dad's a huge donor to the zoo. He even has sex with the monkeys to keep there numbers up."

"I…" Mongrel trailed off, about to say he'd come to help with that by handing over Berthys. Now, however, he didn't think he could do it, to just give her up for adoption like a teenage mother after a night of irresponsible fun so long ago – and the dude wasn't even that good in the sack, honestly. He was kind of a douchebag. And where was he now? Off to college banging so random chick? Probably telling her the same things: that he loved her, that he'd be there to help raise the child if it came to it. Mongrel probably wouldn't be giving up the poor monkey if he'd had someone to help him. He just could afford to be a single mother.

Wait, what the hell was he talking about? He was getting distracted again.

"You what?" the kid asked, spitting on the ground.

"I…" Mongrel stuttered again. "I think that's how AIDS started. Did your Dad start AIDS?"

A murmur drifted through the crowd and the boy became noticeably nervous.

"But…but he's gonna cure it too," he stammered. "That's why we're here, actually: for research. And he's gonna cure everything. Cancer, diabetus, colds, warts, baldness, midgets…"

"Can he cure your face?" Mongrel cut in.

"What?"

"Your face. It looks nasty. I hope it's not contagious."

Things That Separate Us From The Monkeys

The kid suddenly looked deeply shook, and his shoulders slumped; the remark had cut him deep. His face clouded over with pain and grief, betraying years of angst and misery. Mongrel almost felt bad, but this was war. The stupid brat should've known what he was getting himself into when he bumped into him. Mongrel would teach him some respect, teach him to watch where he was going.

"Leave him alone!" someone in the crowd suddenly shouted.

"He's just a boy!" cried another.

Mongrel glanced around at the sea of angry faces, unsure of what to do. He'd forgotten he wasn't in Dunttstown anymore. Maybe the people of Pok weren't as tolerant of shenanigans. But what was he supposed to do, give up?

Never.

This wasn't Hank he was dealing with; it was just some dumb punk who needed to be taught a lesson. Still, he'd have to tread lightly, lest he incite a riot.

"Hey, kid, don't cry. There's options for you. I could recommend a doctor who can give you a new face. Probably a metal one too. You'd be like a terminator."

The kid perked up, wiping the tears from his eyes. "Yeah? So I could get punched in the face and it wouldn't hurt?"

"Better: you'd hurt them."

"Awesome!"

"Yep. You kids today are pretty spoiled. Back when I was your age if we wanted a nicer face we had to smash it up real good and pray it healed up looking better than it started. Just whack your face against a tree or something and hope for the best. I'm on my third face now." He beamed a gratuitous smile, trying to show off his handiwork, but only succeeded in scaring children, making babies cry, and some women faint. Security had also been alerted, since it was assumed that a wild animal was on the loose.

"I don't think it worked," the boy said, looking ill.

"Au contraire; you should've seen me before. People would barf at the mere sight of me."

"I think I'm gonna..." suddenly the kid doubled over and puked everywhere. After a moment, between dry heaves, he said,

"And what about you? Call me ugly? Bet you can't even look in the mirror without gagging."

Mongrel then remembered his nose had been broken a little over a week ago and he probably still looked like a goblin. He became embarrassed about his appearance and stared sharply at the ground. This had backfired on him. He needed to change tactics.

"My face – actually my whole body – is just a work in progress. "He held up his thumb. "My thumb here is titanium, and that's just the beginning. Soon both my hands will be indestructible. One day I'll clean up these streets, like the Batman, only with awesome catchphrases, like, 'my fists are the law, and I'm gonna bring justice to your face,'"

The boy snickered. "That's so lame."

"Oh yeah? Well let's hear you do any better."

Now the boy stuttered and stumbled. He even fell over at one point, leading some to believe Mongrel had shoved him, even though they were almost ten feet apart. More jeering commenced, telling Mongrel to go away, or to pick on someone his own size.

"You're pathetic," Mongrel muttered, ignoring the crowd.

Standing up, the kid looked lost and confused, and somewhat drunk. "Me? Pathetic? I don't know the meaning of the word. Seriously, what does it mean?"

"It means you're going to lose this fight."

What the boy did next worried Mongrel. He grinned. It wasn't a nice, friendly grin either, but an evil, malicious bastard of a grin that said he knew something his opponent didn't. It said he had Mongrel right where he wanted him. It said the gloves were coming off. "Oh I'm just getting started. This is child's play to me. Get it? Child's play? Cause I'm not an adult?"

Mongrel was about to retort to this but was cut off.

"Yeah, I get it – you think I'm just a kid. But I'm more than that. Not, like, a midget, but more of a super kid, right? Super strong, super smart. I didn't just graduate public school, I destroyed it. No one goes there now; it's a ruin. I get more pussy in a week that you probably get in a year. I've got four jobs, and I've already paid my taxes five years in advance. I've got three kids myself, and all of them are named Wilbur, cause bitches are dumb."

Things That Separate Us From The Monkeys

Where had *that* come from? Had this boy slow played him? Mongrel swallowed hard, wondering what he'd gotten himself into. Perhaps he'd picked the wrong person to mess with. No, the kid had messed with *him*. He'd started it, and Mongrel was going to finish it.

Cracking his fingers, neck, toes, and ribs, Mongrel yelled, "You think that's supposed to scare me, little man? I do more adult stuff in an hour than you'll do in half your life. I have a driver's licence, a fishing licence, and a boogling licence." He recalled where he'd learned the word and it left a bad taste in his mouth.

"What's boogling?"

"You'll know when you're older."

"Man, I'm practically an adult right now. I got pubes already. In fact I have so much hair on my body that I don't actually have to wear clothes. You're lucky we're in a public place or I'd be naked."

"Yeah, that's disgusting, you little twerp. You're not an adult, you're just gross, and probably breaking curfew. Shouldn't you be at home in bed? I stay up way passed your bedtime – like a week passed. I sleep once a week, on average."

"I don't think so," the boy replied. "I don't have a bedtime; I don't sleep. I've had doctors check me out and everything. Sleeping pills do nothing, and tranquilizers just make me blink more."

This last remark caught Mongrel off guard, giving him a sense of déjà vu. He once again became worried he was in over his head. But he pressed on. "That still doesn't make you an adult. It's the experiences, the lifestyle changes, the prison time – all you'd get is juvenile hall. I've had multiple surgeries, multiple life-threatening experiences, and multiple personality disorder. Sometimes I'm myself, sometimes I'm my mother. Sometimes I'm even you."

The boy spit on the ground again. "No way! You could never be me. If you became me, even for a second, you'd die of an overload of awesomeness."

"If I was ever you I'd show me some respect. And I'd beat myself up, cause you totally deserve that."

"Child abuse!" the kid shouted, causing an uproar.

Random Tangent

Mongrel jerked his head around, seeing all the snarling faces. He also spotted Vic walking over with a couple security guards. She did not look pleased.

"Spanking a child is not child abuse if the little brat deserves it," he said quickly, more to the public than to his opponent. "I mean, how else are you going teach them manners and respect? Am I right?" He glanced around at the sea of people again, trying to win them over. "Kids need discipline. Taking away their Gameboys and internet isn't gonna get the job done. Spoiled brats have everything now – everything but an ass whoopin'."

"You just try it," the kid said, taking a karate or judo stance or something. I don't know; all martial arts are pretty much the same.

Faking being impressed, Mongrel said, "What's this? You know kung fu?"

"This is called *Wi-Kwan-Juo*. I learned it in one night from drunk Irish Chinaman in Germany when I was working with a travelling circus. He taught me how to catch bullets with my armpits, eat hotdogs backwards, and break bricks with my balls. Feel lucky?"

Without a doubt, Mongrel was not feeling lucky. This kid knew what he was doing and he threw a lot of punches, flinging bullshit in multiples of threes and fours. It was a dangerous combination, and certainly not proper etiquette.

"How do you eat a hotdog backwards?" he asked, genuinely curious.

"Sorry son, you'll have to wait until you're older." The kid smirked, and added, "Or at least until you're properly trained."

Mongrel nodded. "And where can I find this drunk guy?"

"You can't; I killed him. Once I surpassed his knowledge and talent, he was of no more use to me. Then I started banging his wife. At least I think she's his wife – I don't know German. Can't understand a thing she says. And her kid is a spoiled brat. I might have to kill him too, especially if I plan to marry her."

"Well..." Mongrel shrugged, "I guess I'm mistaken. You seem to be a well-travelled and intelligent young man. But tell me, friend, are you familiar with the Inadequate Sea?"

Things That Separate Us From The Monkeys

The kid said nothing, unsure of where Mongrel was going with this. He appeared to fret ever so slightly.

"And to the severe left of the middle of the Inadequate Sea sits an island that you cannot find unless you're not looking for it?"

"How do you find it then?"

Sighing loudly, Mongrel spat out, "Were you not listening? You have to not be looking for it."

"Then how do you know when you find it?"

"I wouldn't worry about it; it's about twenty minutes from reality, so you'll never find the place." Mongrel smiled smugly at the little brat. "Anyway, this island is called Mon Isle, and it's home to the mons. And before you as-"

"Mons aren't real," the kid said suddenly. "They're just myths and legends, like dragons and unicorns and boxpeople."

"Boxpeople are totally real!" Mongrel fired back. "And so are mons. I have one as a pet. Would you like to meet him?" Before the kid could answer, Mongrel began looking around, waiting for his mon to appear, like it always did when it was needed. But this time it didn't. "Mon?" he called. "Here boy!"

The boy raised an eyebrow, waiting. Finally he said, "Man, give it up. I don't have all day."

"Just...give him a sec. Maybe he's busy. But he'll be here."

"You are a weak, pathetic old man. Lying to a kid. You should be ashamed of yourself. Why don't you go crawl into a hole and die?"

Although this wasn't how Mongrel planned things to go, he couldn't lose face. "So you admit you're just a kid then?"

"Yep, I'm just a kid. And more of a man than you'll ever be."

Cheers went up in the crowd, as if some people already thought the battle was won. Mongrel swallowed again, nervous about his odds. This kid was tougher than he looked. And where the hell was his mon? The tide would certainly change in his favour if Mon showed up. Something must be wrong. He had to come up with something else.

"You should never have lived passed a foetus. You should've been aborted."

"And you should've been a blowjob!" the kid fired back.

Random Tangent

"Your mother should've held back her water and drowned you."

"I should just go back in time like the terminator and kill your father while he's on the toilet."

Speaking of going back and forth through time like it was a revolving door, Mon showed up. Just popped right up in the middle of the crowd. Flew in from out of nowhere. Coalesced before everyone's eyes. You get the idea.

"Mon!" Mongrel cried. "What took you s-"

Wait, one more: Beamed down from the mothership. Okay, go ahead.

"Mon," said the mon, which meant, 'Hey guy, relax. I was in the bathroom. And like you *really* need my help in this fight anyway.'

"What's that thing?" the boy asked.

Mongrel leaned on the mon and said proudly, "This is a mon."

The kid just goggled at the creature in front him. "Can't be. You're making it up."

"What? Making it..." he shook his head in exasperation and kicked the mon gently. "Does this look fake to you?"

"Well maybe that's just a guy in a costume."

"Really?" Mongrel asked. "A guy in a suit that just *materialized out of thin air*?" Oh, I should've thought of that one.

Not knowing what to say to this, the boy said nothing. "Nothing."

"What?"

"I mean, maybe it's nothing. Like it's not really there. A hallucination."

"I see." Mongrel paced back and forth slightly. "So you're saying perhaps...it's a figment of your imagination?"

"Yeah. Exactly."

Barely able to conceal his relief, Mongrel's eyes narrowed as he went in for the kill. "Well I got news for you, you little shit-eating brat. I'm also ju-"

"Language!" yelled Vic from the sidelines.

"Oh for the love of...*sorry!*" Mongrel yelled back. He rolled his eyes and looked at the kid, a pained expression on his face.

Things That Separate Us From The Monkeys

The kid gave his best *I know what you mean* look, to which Mongrel replied with a glace that said *I'm getting really sick of her man. I mean,* shit *isn't that bad of a word, really.*

The kid just nodded, which meant *I totally agree, man. We're both adults and we should be allowed to express ourselves in whatever manner we see fit. Besides, words themselves aren't bad. It's the context in which you use them."*

Ahem, Mongrel gestured, *only one of us is an adult, technically.*

Scuffing a shoe on the ground was the kid's way of saying, *whatever.*

But I know what you mean, Mongrel continued conveying. *Words can't be good or bad, they're tools to express our thoughts and feelings. If we take them away we only hurt ourselves. We'd be no better than monkeys without language. What we need to do is stop policing our language and start demanding better of our thoughts and intentions. It's the only way to better ourselves as a species.*

Impressed, the kid began picking his nose, which obviously meant *damn right! You know, you're smarter than I gave you credit for. It's a shame I have to beat you now.*

Mongrel tilted his head slightly and coughed, which implied *say what? Actually I was just about to end this fight.*

The kid swallowed and farted, which could only mean *really? Crap. I really thought I had this in the bag.*

Glancing over the kid's shoulder, Mongrel peered through the crowd into the distance toward what might be the mon pen. This was his way of asking *is that another mon over there?*

Huh? the kid suggested by stretching and yawning. *Are you still on the mon thing? Look, let's just get this over with.*

Nodding, Mongrel narrowed his eyes again. "Right. Um…where was I? Oh yeah. I'm just a figment of your imagination. I don't even exist."

It was a crazy and confusing mess after that. Dust began to settle, drifting in from somewhere. The crowd was speechless, aside from someone saying, "Boom!" What had they all just witnessed? Was it a fight? A young boy talking to himself? A one man show? A piece of performance art?

Random Tangent

The kid stared at the spot Mongrel had been standing, unable to comprehend what had happened. Across the void he locked eyes with a woman.

"Hank!" she cried.

Mongrel turned in time to avoid being blindsided by the woman as she tore from the mass of strangers and ran across to the kid.

"Where have you been?" she chastised him. "Your father and I...well, *I've* been looking everywhere for you. Have you been causing trouble again?"

"No..." he answered.

"Don't lie to me!"

"Honest, Mom, I didn't start it this time."

Watching the scene unfold, Mongrel became deeply disturbed. The woman had been hanging around, searching for her son, whom Mongrel had been blocking her view of. When he'd declared himself inexistent, he ceased to be there, at least as far as everyone else was concerned.

But as far as *he* was concerned, this was the worst possible outcome – aside from losing the fight. His worst nightmare had come true. This kid, this worthless, disrespectful, diabolical demon-spawn was Hank.

The Hank.

The *mother-fucking* Hank.

In a dream that seemed so long ago, Captain Pete had shown Mongrel a vision of a man named Hank destroying him in battle. This was how it all began. He started it. He picked a fight with the brat. He fired the first shot. The nightmare was going to become reality some day, and it was all his fault. He felt sick to his stomach.

Little else registered with Mongrel after this. He didn't hear the rest of the conversation between young Hank and his mother. He didn't notice the hand on his shoulder or feel security pull him away from the dissipating crowd and escort him to the exit. He wasn't listening as Vic explained the procedure for donating animals and what his continued rights over Berthys would be.

It wasn't until he heard glass shatter that Mongrel finally came around. Finding himself at the ticket booth, next to the parking lot. He looked to see a bunch of people milling around his

Things That Separate Us From The Monkeys

car. More alarmed than curious, he slipped out of the clutches of the guards and bolted towards his ride, knowing nothing good could be happening.

Mongrel arrived to see the passenger window smashed in and someone hauling Berthys out. To his credit, he was more worried about his monkey than his car, and almost demanded they leave her alone. Then he realized Berthys wasn't fighting them off. In fact, she was deathly still. Horror struck him; he'd left her in the car with the windows up.

Vic appeared behind him and surveyed the situation. She then shoved her way through the crowd to Berthys and began performing CPR, including giving her mouth-to-mouth. In between breaths she yelled to her security staff to fetch the doctors. "Got a female squirrel monkey with stage-two dehydration," she told them.

Guilt and worry plagued Mongrel. He thought Berthys was breathing but he had no veterinary expertise and couldn't be sure. He regretted that they were finally starting to get along, and then he had to go and so something stupid like this. She'd probably never forgive him now. He briefly wondered where he could take his car to replace the glass, and what he was going to do with it until then, especially if it began to rain. Did they really have a mon pen at the zoo, and would he get to see it? And what did the director say about squirrel monkey? Is that was Berthys was? He'd never heard of one before. How many kinds of monkeys were there anyway? Were there any zebra monkeys? That'd be interesting…

After a long five minutes two doctors pushed through the mob with a stretcher. They didn't check out Berthys – she was still breathing, even before the director attempted to revive her. Vic may indeed be awesome, but her medical expertise was anything but. The doctors carefully strapped Berthys to the bed and began checking her vital signs.

Mongrel watched them, feeling numb inside. How could he let this happen? It boggled his mind how he could be so negligent. Perhaps he should give custody of her to the zoo. He wasn't fit to take care of her, he saw this now. It was a sobering thought, but she'd be better off without him.

"Mr. Stevens?"

Random Tangent

It was Vic, standing next to him. Lost in his mortification, he was barely able to offer a, "Hmm?"

She watched her staff cart Berthys away before continuing. "You know there's a fine for locking an animal in a vehicle in summer temperatures."

It wasn't issued as a question but Mongrel nodded anyway.

"I'm going to ignore that, since you're making a generous contribution to my zoo. And you know there's an ordinance law about littering on city grounds – especially hazardous materials." She pointed to the glass next to his car, and again it wasn't a question. "But I'm going to ignore that as well, since I know you didn't cause it. I'll have someone clean it up."

He nodded again, appreciating the favour, but unable to break out of his disgruntled funk.

"Then there's the matter of you causing a public disturbance in the zoo. With a minor no less. What do you think we should do about that?"

Now Mongrel chose to break his silence. "Can we ignore it too?"

She chuckled at the request. "Well, I suppose there was no harm done."

Mongrel bit back a cry of anguish. Oh there was *lots* of harm done. His whole future was ruined. He refrained from commenting, offering her the best smile he could produce under the circumstances.

Pulling out a clipboard from nowhere, she offered it to him. "Donation of property isn't official until you sign these documents."

Grabbing the clipboard and glancing at it, Mongrel recalled how much Berthys hated being treated like property. Instead of reading the pages, he once again began to mull over his decision to give her up.

"After what just happened," Vic said when his hesitation became apparent, "it should be an easy choice. Especially since those animal cruelty charges are being waved. Of course, that is contingent on you signing the papers."

Well she had him over a barrel now. He began filling out the forms.

Things That Separate Us From The Monkeys

Vic smiled. "She'll be well taken care of here, I assure you. Excellent food, comfortable environment, and access to the best monkey cock in the country. Possibly the world."

"What?" Mongrel was busy filling in the papers and wasn't sure he'd heard the last part right.

"You'll be able to come see her whenever you wish, so long as it's during operating hours. And I'll keep you abreast of her progress."

Mongrel finished with the documents and handed the clipboard back to Vic. She skimmed over it quickly, making sure everything was correct, then smiled and offered her hand again. "It was a pleasure doing business with you, Mr. Stevens. Feel free to stop by any time."

He shook her hand with less vigour than the last time, still traumatized by the day's events. He realized with some finality that nearly killing your beloved pet is what separates us from the monkeys.

Without another word Vic strolled back inside the zoo, and Mongrel went back to his car. Most of the glass, he found, had landed on the inside, laying all over the seat and floor. He ignored it, eager to get home and sit down in front of the television so he could flip channels and mostly ignore them too. He just wanted to be ignorant of everything for a while and turn his mind off, which, despite what you know about Mongrel Stevens, was not an easy thing for him to do.

He pulled out of the parking lot and headed back to Dunttstown, taking the long way to avoid passing through Harrow again.

Never again, he told himself. He would rather travel the opposite direction, going all the way around the world to get to wherever he needed to go, than drive through Harrow.

He drove on into the setting sun, misery and apprehension clouding his thoughts. Home, solitude, and a cold beer could not arrive soon enough.

Mongrel sat on his front doorstep drinking champagne. But he was not celebrating. Remembering that he was out of beer, he stopped by the local liquor barn on the way home. Alas, it was

Random Tangent

closed, and his foul mood worsened because of it. Searching around in his refrigerator, he found the old bottle of Dumangin; it had probably belonged to his mother, bless her hamstrings. He detested the stuff but felt, under the circumstances, it was warranted.

He was drinking it as punishment.

And indeed there were many things he needed to punish himself for: beginning a war with Hank; almost killing Berthys; for starting to turn into a terminator – and all that was just today. In the wider scope of things he was now a murderer, having killed Captain Pete twice, and soon enough, a helpless animal. Also, despite his connections he remained unemployed. And let's not forget he let Valentin escape to go after his woman. Hell, he *still* hadn't beaten the original Super Mario Bros. The pit of self-pity he was wallowing in was bottomless.

Downing this third glass of the champagne, Mongrel was disappointed that it still tasted awful. He knew people didn't drink the hard stuff for the flavour, but heard that the more you drank, the less you realize how disgusting it is. Maybe he wasn't drunk enough yet. He poured another glass.

Looking ahead, Mongrel had a lot to look forward to, and even more to dread. He had a woman to rescue, a car to fix, and debts to be repaid. Would he get around to any of that in the next book? Who knows? But things would get better, he told himself. Everything would work out. For now, he was still alive, still a little crazy, and still…still not drunk.

He took a big gulp and made a sour face as he pondered what horrors the future had in store for him.

The End

Although he knew he had a glorious vacation to look forward to, Mongrel knew war was brewing – with Hank, with Valentin, and always with Captain Pete, Mongrel did his best to prepare some strategies. He then briefly considered suicide, rather than continue with the macabre circus that was his life, but abandoned that idea because we need to make this series a trilogy.

Things That Separate Us From The Monkeys

Vic oversaw Berthys' treatment over the next couple days, and then introduced her to her new 'family.' It was led by the most amazing, mesmerizing, handsome, and well-endowed monkey she'd ever seen. Berthys learned that day that she wasn't a lesbian like her mother. Heather, the receptionist at Dunttstown Hospital, hooked up with Cranklin. They'd taken to shagging in the janitor's closet, which she felt was the most hygienic room in the building because of all the cleaning supplies. Solvo, as it happened, had his eye on Cranklin, and was disappointed at this development. So he instead set his sights on Dr. Lunabell. The other doctor, Figment Jones, performed a couple more breast augmentation surgeries on his nosey neighbour. Alas, she continued to refuse his offer to make her 'titanium tits.' But one day he'd find the right woman. Copious Dawn continued working with the doctor, but found herself longing for another pet. She decided to adopt a whole 'fleet' of gerbils and began extensive modifications. Thankfully, however, with their lesser intelligence, there would be no worry over them aspiring for world dominance. Lyza was so excited about missing the fight in the zoo she went into a form of anaphylactic shock. It was not the first time. Broccoli's cat got loose that night and ran away. He knew he should've made his boogle buddy into a dog instead – dogs are smart and loyal and always find their way home. Brecklin was so astonished that Captain Pete was still alive that he took at as a sign of the second coming of the messiah. Ali, the oriental nurse who was taking care of him, knitted him some woollen dreadlocks to wear in place of the hair that would never again grow on his head. She also became enthralled in his new Church of the Neverending Pete. Speaking of Captain Pete, he had an allergic reaction to the tranquiller the doctor gave him, and died. The mon showed up late because it was in the middle of playing Pac Man and was totally beating his old high score, making a new record. And before you say something like, 'how can Mon play without any arms?' or 'couldn't he just go back in time when he was needed?' let me just say, *shut* and *up*. In whatever order you like. Hank's mom, tired of her son getting into verbal sparing matches instead of fist fights like a young man should, signed him up for karate classes. Even though Hank already knew *Wi-Kwan-Juo* he didn't argue. He was going to

Random Tangent

need all the help he could get to defeat his new nemesis: Mongrel Stevens.

After Credits Scene

 faint voice, carried on the wind, reaching his ears. "Hey!"

Mongrel stopped gagging on the champagne and looked around, not sure if he'd actually heard something or if inebriation was kicking in.

"Mon," said the mon, which meant, 'I heard it too. Didn't sound like your Mom this time. And it came from over there.'

Glancing in the direction the mon in no way indicated, Mongrel saw a figure in the distance. In the field of grass across the road from the homestead a man was panicking towards them.

"Hey!" it came again.

Unsure if he actually saw someone or if inebriation was kicking in, Mongrel didn't know what to do. So he stood; that was as much action as he was willing to take for the time being. This, of course, had the effect of sending the alcohol surging through his veins and sending sobriety off to search for greener pastures.

Due to this intoxication, the man across the field had multiplied. Now a gang was rushing at Mongrel. It was an ambush!

He was surrounded! Well, he would be soon enough. Didn't his mother keep a shotgun in the house?

Gently turning his head to glance behind him at the front door, Mongrel's world spun, and he nearly fell over. Well, that was as close as he was getting to the weapon. He'd have to take on this assault with his bare hands.

So he stood there, watching the men approach, slowly realizing they were all Elvis, who was last seen heading to the airport in Shchevret, and as just one person. Mickey, his bastard chauffeur, was nowhere to be seen.

After a few minutes of waiting, listening to the Elvii[*] hail them, Mongrel decided to sit back down and finish off the champagne. Elvis was a notorious drinker and would more than likely be more than happy to take more than his fair share. Unfortunately the alcohol still tasted terrible…or maybe it didn't. He couldn't tell if he was tasting ass or if inebriation was kicking in. Wait, inebriation had kicked in, hadn't it? Guess it must be ass then. Not good ass either; not high-priced hooker ass, but Grandma Oaks after tilling the fields all day in the dreadful heat and eating burritos for dinner. Oh and she's been battling diarrhea all week – a losing battle.

"Mon," said the mon, meaning, 'Screw this. The book is over; we don't have all day.' It then threw up a bunch of Elvii on the doorstep.

"What the...?" they all asked simultaneously, confused.

"What happened?" Mongrel asked them.

"Yeah," they agreed.

"Yeah what?"

"Yeah, what happened? How'd I get here? I'm..." the Elvii trailed off, glancing back across the field. "I'm still over there." The Elvii in the distance had all now stopped, bewildered to be staring at themselves, standing next to Mongrel.

The mon set off at a leisurely pace towards them, saying, "Mon," or, 'I'll be back.' And yes, it was a Terminator impression.

"This is real weird," the closer Elvii said. "Am I losing my mind?"

---

[*] The plural of Elvis is Elvii. But I'm sure you knew that.

"Don't worry about it," Mongrel said, trying to calm his friend down.

"But how can I be in two places at once? Am I here or there? Maybe I'm nowhere? I'm dead, aren't I? Sweet mama this can't be happening again!"

"You'll be here in a minute!" Mongrel yelled, his patience seeming to have accompanied his sobriety on its voyage. "Just chill out. Or in. Which...whichever way you want to go. Now what happened to you? And where's Mickey?"

Elvis and his cohorts were in horrible shape. Their clothes were nothing more than dirty, tattered rags, exposing plenty of dirty, tattered skin. Their hair lay in scraggly messes atop their heads, and they all smelled several shades of awful. As such, they could've passed for anyone on the street. Mongrel had only recognized his friend because of his cape...which he wasn't wearing...so...

"They're coming!" the Elvii cried, thankfully starting a new paragraph and digging me out of the corner I'd written myself into.

"Who?" Mongrel asked.

They grabbed Mongrel's shirt and yanked him close, so close they coalesced into one Elvis. "*They* are!" he repeated. "The zombies! From Shchevret!"

Somewhere in Mongrel's little drunken head flashed images of horror movies and bombs and a nuclear reactor and...pizza. Beavers eating pizza. Well that was strange. He was too incoherent to focus on any of it, and just said, "Oh. And Mickey?"

Elvis let go of Mongrel and looked away across the field. "He's dead."

Mongrel followed his friend's gaze over to the mon, watching as it chased around the other Elvii, eating them one at a time. "Naw, he'll be fine. I mean you'll be fine. I mean you *are* fine. Know what I mean?" He glanced at Elvis, finding he'd multiplied again.

"Not me; Mickey. He's dead."

"Oh. Sweet."

"Not sweet!" Elvis turned around to face Mongrel. "Mickey was a dear, sweet man, who gave his life so I could escape." Mongrel shrugged, or at least thought he did (it could have been the inebriation kicking in). Either way Elvis didn't notice. "They surrounded the limo, these...things. They used to be human, but now they're hideous, deformed monsters that eat each other. They wanted to eat us; fresh meat, right. They got good taste at least. Anyway they rocked the limo, trying to make tip it over. Mickey ran out, distracting them. I jumped out through the sunroof and ran away.

"I hid in a dumpster for days, watching them, studying them. They looked hideous. Scarred, melted, twisted creatures. Can't believe anything survived after the fallout but these guys did. They're buil-"

"What'd you food?" Mongrel asked. He'd been having some difficulty wrapping his head around the story – although that could have been the inebriation...you get the idea – so his brain broke it down into more manageable chunks. Right now it was chunks of food.

"Huh?"

"You said you were in the dumper for days. What'd you food for eating? How did you sru...serve? Salive?"

"My cape."

Now it was Mongrel's turn. "Huh?"

"I had to eat my cape for food."

"Oh. So that's where that where...that…gone to."

"Listen, they're building an army, and they're going to attack Dunttstown. I heard them talking. They're gonna kill us all."

"Why?"

"I don't know. I think they think we bombed them. We gotta do something. We need to leave town before it's too late, just make like cars and hit the road. Abandon ship. We need to...is that champagne?" The Elvii pointed to the bottle on the doorstep, then reached down to pick it up, only to find it empty. "And you didn't save me any?"

Mongrel shrugged. "I didn't know you guys were coming."

"Got any more inside?"

"Don't know, but if you can help me walk we can go look."

Together, Elvis and Mongrel hobbled into the homestead in the quest for alcohol, the impending doom forgotten for the moment. It could wait. The army of zombies could wait. The destruction of Dunttstown could wait.

It could all wait until the next story.

CPSIA information can be obtained
at www.ICGtesting.com
Printed in the USA
LVHW090940210421
684498LV00037B/889/J